Harivamsha

PRAISE FOR THE MAHABHARATA

'The modernization of language is visible, it's easier on the mind, through expressions that are somewhat familiar. The detailing of the story is intact, the varying tempo maintained, with no deviations from the original. The short introduction reflects a brilliant mind. For those who passionately love the Mahabharata and want to explore it to its depths, Debroy's translation offers great promise in the first volume.'

—*Hindustan Times*

'[Debroy] has really carved out a niche for himself in crafting and presenting a translation of the Mahabharata . . . The book takes us on a great journey with admirable ease.'

—*The Indian Express*

'The first thing that appeals to one is the simplicity with which Debroy has been able to express himself and infuse the right kind of meanings . . . Considering that Sanskrit is not the simplest of languages to translate a text from, Debroy exhibits his deep understanding and appreciation of the medium.'

—*The Hindu*

'Overwhelmingly impressive . . . Bibek is a truly eclectic scholar.'

—*Business Line*

'Debroy's lucid and nuanced retelling of the original makes the masterpiece even more enjoyably accessible.'

—*Open*

'The quality of translation is excellent. The lucid language makes it a pleasure to read the various stories, digressions and parables.'

—*The Tribune*

'Extremely well-organized, and has a substantial and helpful Introduction, plot summaries and notes. The volume is a beautiful example of a well thought-out layout which makes for much easier reading.'

—*The Book Review*

'The dispassionate vision [Debroy] brings to this endeavour will surely earn him merit in the three worlds.'

—*Mail Today*

'This [second] volume, as voluminous as the first one, is expectedly as scholarly . . . Like the earlier volume, the whole book is an easy read.'

—*The Hindu*

'Debroy's is not the only English translation available in the market, but where he scores and others fail is that his is the closest rendering of the original text in modern English without unduly complicating the readers' understanding of the epic.'

—*Business Standard*

'The brilliance of Ved Vysya comes through [in Volume 3], ably translated by Bibek Debroy.'

—*Hindustan Times*

Harivamsha

Translated by
BIBEK DEBROY

PENGUIN BOOKS
An imprint of Penguin Random House

PENGUIN BOOKS

USA | Canada | UK | Ireland | Australia
New Zealand | India | South Africa | China

Penguin Books is part of the Penguin Random House group of companies
whose addresses can be found at global.penguinrandomhouse.com

Published by Penguin Random House India Pvt. Ltd
7th Floor, Infinity Tower C, DLF Cyber City,
Gurgaon 122 002, Haryana, India

First published in Penguin Books by Penguin Random House India 2016

Translation copyright © Bibek Debroy 2016

10 9 8 7 6 5 4 3 2

ISBN 9780143425984

Typeset in Sabon by Manipal Digital Systems, Manipal
Printed at Repro Knowledgecast Limited, Navi Mumbai

www.penguin.co.in

MIX
Paper from
responsible sources
FSC
www.fsc.org   FSC® C047271

For Prakash Javadekar

Contents

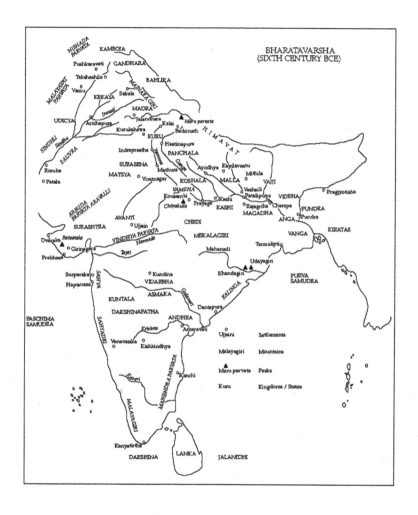

BHARATAVARSHA
(SIXTH CENTURY BCE)

NISHADA PARVATA
KAMBOJA
Pushkaravati
GANDHARA
Takshashila
BAHLIKA
MALAYAVAT PARVATA
Vanu
MAINAKA GIRI
Sakala
KEKAYA
MADRA
Iravati
UDICYA
Arichapura
Jalandhara
Kalai
Meru parvata
KURU
Badrinath
Kurukshetra
H I M A V A T
SINDHU
Sindhu
SALVYA
Indraprastha
Hastinapura
KURU
Roruka
SURASENA
PANCHALA
Patala
MATSYA
Mathura
Ayodhya
Kapilavastu
Viratnagar
KOSHALA
Mithila
VAMSHA
MALLA
VAJJI
Kousambi
Prayaga
Kashi
Vaishali
VIDEHA
Pragjyotisha
Chitrakuta
KASHI
Patalipura
ARBUDA PARVATA ARAVALLI
AVANTI
CHEDI
Rajagriha
Champa
PUNDRA
Ujjain
MAGADHA
ANGA
Pundra
SURASHTRA
VINDHYA PARVATA
MEKALAGIRI
VANGA
KIRATAS
Dvaraka
Raivataka
Narmada
Dvaraka
Giridnagara
Tapi
Mahanadi
Tamraliptio
Prabhasa
Udayagiri
Surparaka
SAHYA
Kundina
Khandagiri
PURVA SAMUDRA
Haptanasa
VIDARBHA
ASMAKA
KALINGA
KUNTALA
Godavari
Dantapura
PASCHIMA SAMUDRA
DAKSHINAPATHA
ANDHRA
SAHYADRI
Krishna
Amaravati
Vanavasika
Kishkindhya
Ujjaini   Settlements
Kaveri
Malayagiri   Mountains
MALAYA GIRI
MAHENDRA PARVATA
Kanchi
Meru parvata   Peaks
Kuru   Kingdoms / States
Kanyatirtha
DAKSHINA
LANKA
JALANIDHI

Acknowledgements

The Bhandarkar Oriental Research Institute (BORI) in Pune was formally established in July 1917. But that's the formal establishment. I think of it as 1916, because that's when the Mahabharata Project, identified with BORI, was conceived. After consulting 1,259 manuscripts, a Critical Edition was published, the work lasting from 1919 to 1966. The *Harivamsha* followed, between 1966 and 1969. The Mahabharata Project work continues, with a cultural index and a bibliography.

For me, the time spent in Pune at the Gokhale Institute of Politics and Economics was also an opportunity to familiarize myself with BORI and the Critical Edition. I treasure the time spent in the BORI Library. My personal Mahabharata Project took off much later. An unabridged translation in English, based on BORI's Critical Edition, was published by Penguin (India) between 2010 and 2014 in ten volumes, later brought out in a boxed set in 2015. The *Harivamsha* is a supplement/appendix to the Mahabharata and the *Harivamsha* translation was also planned as part of my Mahabharata Project. As mentioned, BORI's Critical Edition had incorporated the *Harivamsha*. But though a supplement/appendix, the *Harivamsha* is also somewhat different from the Mahabharata. Therefore, it was decided not to bring it out as part of the Mahabharata translation, but as an independent volume. This is the result.

That result was driven by Meru Gokhale and Ambar Sahil Chatterjee at Penguin. Paloma Dutta was the able editor for the Mahabharata translation. Therefore, she continued as the editor for the *Harivamsha* and that made life a whole lot easier. My wife,

Suparna Banerjee (Debroy) was a constant source of support, as she was for the Mahabharata. Those who wrote kind reviews of the Mahabharata volumes were a source of encouragement too.

I have known Prakash Javadekar for many years. If I remember right, I first got to know him in connection with my work on the States. He is from Pune and I owe a lot to that city for kindling my interest in this kind of work. Earlier this year, the ministry of human resource development, Government of India, presented sets of the ten-volume Mahabharata translation to UNESCO. Prakash Javadekar is now the minister for human resource development. This gives me an opportunity to embarrass a friend from Pune by dedicating this volume to him. He has written on loans (IMF, farmers), unemployment and inflation, in Marathi. Perhaps he will now write on other things, including those that Pune is famous for, in Marathi and in English.

Introduction

The *Harivamsha* is not a Purana, though it is often loosely referred to as a Purana. The word Purana means ancient and, as texts, the Puranas are ancient accounts. There are many texts that are referred to as Puranas. To be classified as a proper Purana, a text needs to cover five topics: (1) *sarga*, the original creation; (2) *pratisarga*, the periodic cycles of secondary creation and destruction; (3) *vamsha*, the genealogies of the gods and the *rishis*;[1] (4) *manvantara*, the eras, each presided over by a Manu; and (5) the solar and lunar dynasties. In lists of the Puranas, there are the great Puranas, the Mahapuranas, and the minor Puranas, the Upapuranas. There is no consensus on what counts as Upapurana and what does not. Lists vary from one part of the country to another. However, there is consensus on the list of Mahapuranas. There are eighteen of these and their names are; (1) *Agni Purana*; (2) *Bhagavata Purana*; (3) *Brahma Purana*; (4) *Brahmanda Purana*; (5) *Brahmavaivarta Purana*; (6) *Garuda Purana*; (7) *Kurma Purana*; (8) *Linga Purana*; (9) *Markandeya Purana*; (10) *Matsya Purana*; (11) *Narada Purana*; (12) *Padma Purana*; (13) *Shiva Purana*; (14) *Skanda Purana*; (15) *Vamana Purana*; (16) *Varaha Purana*; (17) *Vayu Purana*; and (18) *Vishnu Purana*. In some cases, the *Bhavishya Purana* is included in the list of eighteen. When that is done, either the *Shiva Purana* or the *Vayu Purana* is included in the list, but not both. In greater or lesser degree, all the Mahapuranas satisfy those five characteristics, the *Vishnu Purana* more than the others.

---

[1] Sages.

The Mahabharata was composed by the sage Krishna Dvaipayana Vedavyasa. There were many regional versions of this Sanskrit text. Between 1919 and 1966, the Bhandarkar Oriental Research Institute in Pune sifted through these various versions and brought out a Critical Edition of this Sanskrit text. Since unabridged translations of the Mahabharata in English are rare, a translation was published by Penguin Books India between 2010 and 2014 and a boxed set has been brought out in 2015.[2] The *Harivamsha* needs to be read in conjunction with the Mahabharata, and not independently. This translation should also be read in conjunction with the Mahabharata translation and not independently. It is a continuation and incidents and characters will not necessarily be clear without that continuity. After the Critical Edition of the Mahabharata was published, the Bhandarkar Oriental Research Institute also published a Critical Edition of the *Harivamsha* (1969–71), as a *khila* (meaning supplement or appendix) to the Mahabharata text. The Mahabharata composed by Vedavyasa includes the *Harivamsha*. This translation is based on the Critical Edition of the *Harivamsha*, as was the case with the Mahabharata translation. Two points need to be made about this Critical text. First, at the risk of some subjectivity, the quality of editing in the Critical version of the *Harivamsha* is not as good as that of the main Mahabharata. In some instances, we have had the temerity to point this out. Second, there are versions of the *Harivamsha* floating around, in Sanskrit, with translations in vernacular languages. Compared to those, the Critical text has done some ruthless slashing. We will return to this point later. Therefore, many incidents one associates with the *Harivamsha* are missing from the Critical text and will also be missed in this translation. To the best of my knowledge, there are only two unabridged translations of the *Harivamsha* in English. The first was done by Manmatha Nath Dutt in 1897, after he had

---

[2] Translated by Bibek Debroy in ten volumes, http://www.penguinbooksindia.com/en/content/mahabharata-box-set%3Frate=KEqyZxcJhQcwgT6_S3CAIxdXiAcmWtKpn7lEYOgR620.html

completed his translation of the Mahabharata. The second is an
ongoing online translation.[3]

The pattern followed in this *Harivamsha* translation also
follows that of the Mahabharata translation. The intention is to
make the translation as close to the original Sanskrit text as is
possible. In the process, the English is not always as smooth as
might have been the case had one taken more liberties. If a reader
has the Sanskrit in front, there will be an exact correspondence
between the Sanskrit and the English. This cannot be achieved
with a verse translation, though the *Harivamsha* is in verse. Hence,
the translation is in prose. Some words cannot satisfactorily be
translated, *dharma* being a case in point. Therefore, such words
are not translated. This is a translation, it isn't an interpretation.
However, a straightforward translation may not make everything
clear to the reader. This explanation is done through footnotes and
should be sufficient to explain the text. Because this translation is
meant to be accessible to the ordinary reader, there was a conscious
decision to avoid diacritical marks. Names, proper names and
geographical names, are therefore rendered as close phonetically as
is possible. The absence of diacritical marks sometimes can cause
confusion, such as between Vasudeva (Krishna) and Vasudeva
(Krishna's father). When there is a danger of confusion, not obvious
from the context, this has been avoided by rendering Krishna as
Vaasudeva and Krishna's father as Vasudeva.

What is the *Harivamsha* about? In a general sense, it is about
Krishna's life. When we first encounter Krishna in the Mahabharata,
he is already an adult. Where was he born? What were his childhood
and other exploits, those not recounted in the Mahabharata?
The *Harivamsha* answers such questions. But such questions are
also answered in the Puranas, at least some of them. The belief
is that after composing the Mahabharata, Vedavyasa composed
the Puranas. The Mahabharata is believed to have had 100,000
shlokas or couplets. The Critical Edition of the Mahabharata has
a little short of 75,000. Even that, in the ten-volume translation,
converts into something like 2.25 million words. Together, the

---

[3] http://www.mahabharata-resources.org/harivamsa/

eighteen Mahapuranas amount to another 400,000 shlokas. The Mahapuranas differ greatly in length, from around 10,000 shlokas in the *Brahma Purana* to more than 80,000 shlokas in the *Skanda Purana*. Nor were they necessarily composed at one point in time, with a range of anything between second century CE to tenth century CE. In all probability, Vedavyasa composed an original Purana that is now lost and all the present Puranas are additions and embellishments on that lost original. The Puranas are classified in different ways. For instance, some emphasize creation and are therefore identified with Brahma. Some are identified with Vishnu and some are identified with Shiva. But these are not neat silos and all of them traverse similar ground, with minor variations in the stories too. Among the ones identified with Vishnu and known as *Vaishnava Purana*s are the *Vishnu Purana* and the *Bhagavata Purana*. Most of what is found in the *Harivamsha* will be found in these two texts. In the Mahabharata, Krishna may have been elevated to the status of a divinity in some parts. But in other parts, he does display human attributes. Purely in those relative terms, in these two Puranas and in the *Harivamsha*, Krishna's divine status is primary and the human traits are secondary.

Once he composed the Mahabharata, the *Harivamsha* and the Puranas, Vedavyasa taught these to his disciple, Vaishampayana. Janamejaya was the son of Parikshit, Abhimanyu's son. On the occasion of King Janamejaya's snake sacrifice, Vaishampayana recounted all three texts to Janamejaya and the assembled sages. On a subsequent occasion, Ugrashrava Souti recounted the same story to sages who had assembled for a sacrifice in the Naimisha forest. It is by no means essential that the *Harivamsha*, as we have it today, was necessarily composed at a single point in time. The earlier parts, and it is impossible to disentangle the earlier from the later, probably go back to the first or second century CE.

Standard texts of the *Harivamsha* are divided into three sections or *parvas*—'Harivamsha Parva', 'Vishnu Parva' and 'Bhavishya Parva'. In general, 'Harivamsha Parva' has stories that precede Krishna. There are stories about the Vrishni lineage, but not about Krishna. 'Vishnu Parva' is about Krishna's exploits and 'Bhavishya Parva' is about the future, about *kali yuga*. Compared

to non-Critical versions that float around, the Critical text of the
Harivamsha has seen merciless slashing across all three sections.
What remains is 118 chapters: forty-five chapters in 'Harivamsha
Parva', sixty-eight chapters in 'Vishnu Parva' and five chapters in
'Bhavishya Parva'. There are 2,392 shlokas in 'Harivamsha Parva',
3,368 shlokas in 'Vishnu Parva' and 205 shlokas in 'Bhavishya
Parva'. There are thus 5,965 shlokas in all of *Harivamsha*. Non-
Critical versions will often have double this number, reflective of
the slashing. Instead of numbering the chapters within the three
sections separately, we have used a continuous numbering, one that
the Sanskrit text also uses.

Harivamsha Parva

Chapter 1

Shounaka[1] said, 'O Souti! You have recounted the extremely great account of those born from the Bharata lineage, all the kings, the gods, the *danava*s, the serpents, the *rakshasa*s, the *daitya*s, the *siddha*s, the *guhyaka*s, their extraordinary acts of valour, the supreme and wonderful accounts of their births and the determinations of dharma.[2] In gentle words, you have spoken about these sacred and ancient accounts. Our minds and ears have become happy and delighted and are full of *amrita*.[3] O Lomaharshana's son! You have also spoken to us about the birth of those from the Kuru lineage. However, you have not spoken about the Vrishnis and the Andhakas.[4] Tell us about them.'

Suta replied, 'Janamejaya asked Vyasa's intelligent disciple about this.[5] Following this, I will tell you the truth about the

[1] A group of sages, headed by Shounaka, gathered in the Naimisha forest for a sacrifice. Ugrashrava Souti, the son of Lomaharshana (or Romaharshana) told them the story of the Mahabharata there. Souti means the son of a *suta*, sutas being bards or raconteurs. Ugrashrava also recounted *Harivamsha* to the sages.

[2] This is a reference to the Mahabharata. Broadly, danavas and daityas are demons. However, danavas are the offspring of the sage Kashyapa and Danu, while daityas are the offspring of the sage Kashyapa and Diti. *Gandharva*s are semi-divine species, skilled in singing and dancing and companions of Kubera, the lord of wealth. Siddhas and guhyakas are also semi-divine species. *Uraga*s, synonymous with *naga*s, have been translated as serpents. They aren't quite snakes, since they have semi-divine qualities and dwell in a separate nether region. Rakshasas are a different species from daityas or danavas. They can be loosely described as demons, but are also sometimes described as companions of Kubera. Dharma has many meanings—religion, duty, law, rules. Therefore, it is best to leave it untranslated.

[3] Divine ambrosia or nectar.

[4] The Vrishni and Andhaka lineages were part of the Yadava lineage. The Kurus refer to both the Pandavas and the Kouravas, descended from a common ancestor named Kuru.

[5] King Janamejaya was the son of Parikshit, descended from the Pandavas. Vyasa means Vedavyasa or Vyasadeva, his complete name being Krishna Dvaipayana Vedavyasa. Vedavyasa classified the Vedas

lineage of the Vrishnis, from the beginning. After having heard the entire history about the Bharata lineage, the immensely wise Bharata Janamejaya[6] spoke to Vaishampayana. "The account of the Mahabharata has many meanings and is extensive in its compass. O *brahmana*![7] You have told me about it in detail and I have heard it. You have spoken about many brave ones, bulls among men, and the names and deeds of the *maharatha* Vrishnis and Andhakas.[8] O supreme among brahmanas! You have also spoken about their deeds. O lord! However, you have only spoken about this briefly and not in detail. I am not satisfied with what you have already recounted. It is my view that the Vrishnis and the Pandavas were related. You know about their lineages and were a direct witness. O store of austerities! Speak about their lineage in detail. I wish to know about who was born in whose lineage. What is the wonderful story of their being created earlier, by Prajapati?"[9] The great-souled and great ascetic was honoured well and asked in this fashion. He thus recounted the story in detail, following the due order.'

Vaishampayana said, 'O king! Listen to the sacred and divine account, one that is destructive of all sins. I will tell you about these wonderful and diverse accounts, honoured in the sacred texts. O son![10] If a person sustains this and ceaselessly listens to it, he manages to uphold his own lineage and obtains greatness in the

---

(hence the name Vedavyasa) and composed the Mahabharata, which he taught his disciple Vaishampayana. On the occasion of a snake sacrifice, Vaishampayana recounted the story of the Mahabharata to King Janamejaya, a story that was subsequently retold by Ugrashrava to the sages in the Naimisha forest.

[6] From a common ancestor known as Bharata, the Kuru lineage was also known as the Bharata lineage and Janamejaya also belonged to that line.

[7] The first of the four *varna*s. Their tasks were studying, teaching, performing sacrifices and officiating at the sacrifices of others.

[8] A maharatha was a great warrior, who could fight with all kinds of weapons and take on 10,000 enemy soldiers at once.

[9] Prajapati literally means lord of the subjects (offspring). Here, it means the creator, Brahma.

[10] The word used is *tata*. While this means son, it is affectionately used for anyone who is younger or junior.

world of heaven. The eternal and unmanifest cause has existence
and non-existence in his soul. He is Pradhana or Purusha. Though
he is without a sense of ownership, he is the lord of the universe
and everything flows from him. O great king! Know him to be
the infinitely energetic Brahma. He is the creator of all beings and
he seeks refuge with Narayana. Mahat[11] resulted from him and
Ahamkara from Mahat. From this, all beings were created. The
diverse gross elements were created from the subtle elements and
this is the eternal nature of creation. Depending on my wisdom
and based on what I have heard, I will now describe this in detail.
This recounting will enhance the deeds of the ancestors. Listen. All
of them were firm in their tasks and sacred in their deeds. This
recounting leads to the enhancement of riches, fame and lifespans,
slays enemies and leads to heaven. You are purest among those
who are pure. I am capable of telling and you can comprehend.
Therefore, I will tell you about the supreme story of the creation
of beings, including the lineage of the Vrishnis. The illustrious
Vishnu Svayambhu[12] wished to create different kinds of beings. He
first created water and then released his energy into it. We have
earlier heard that water is known by the name of Nara. Since he
lay down on it earlier, he is known by the name of Narayana.[13]
While he lay down on the water, a golden egg was generated and
Svayambhu Brahma was himself born from this. This is what we
have heard. The illustrious Hiranyagarbha[14] resided inside it for an
entire year and thereafter divided the egg into two, thus creating
heaven and earth. Between the two halves that were in the water,
the lord created the sky. The earth was flooded with water and he
created the ten directions.[15] Desiring to create, Prajapati created the

[11] Literally, great. This is the manifest form. Ahamkara is ego or
consciousness.
[12] *Svayambhu* means someone who created himself. This is a term used
for Brahma, but also for Vishnu and Shiva.
[13] *Nara* (that is, *naara*) means water and *ayana* means place of refuge.
One whose place of refuge is the water is Narayana.
[14] Brahma, the one with a golden origin.
[15] North, north-east, east, south-east, south, south-west, west, north-
west, above and below.

forms of time, thoughts, words, desire, anger and attachment. From his mind, he created the seven greatly energetic ones—Marichi, Atri, Angiras, Pulastya, Pulaha, Kratu and Vasishtha.[16] It has been determined that these are the seven ancient brahmanas. These seven were born from Brahma and have Narayana in their soul. Having created them, Brahma again created Rudra from his wrath. He also created Sanatkumara and the other rishis, who were the ancestors of the ancestors.[17] O descendant of the Bharata lineage! Rudra, and those seven, began to create offspring. However, Skanda and Sanatkumara restrained their seed.[18] Those seven[19] created divine and great lineages and large numbers of gods are also included in them, as are many *maharshis*.[20] They performed rites and had offspring. He also created lightning, thunder, clouds, the rainbow,[21] aquatic creatures and rain. For the success of sacrifices, he fashioned hymns of the Rig Veda, the Yajur Veda and the Sama Veda. We have heard that the gods known as Sadhyas are always engaged in performing sacrifices. He created the superior and the inferior creatures from his own body. Prajapati thus created large numbers of beings that dwelt in the water. He then divided his body into two, and one half of the body became Purusha.[22] The other half became female and gave birth to many kinds of creatures. In this way, they[23] pervade heaven and earth in their greatness. Vishnu created a great and radiant being. Know that being as Manu and manvantara is

[16] The seven great sages or *saptarshis*. The names do vary sometimes.

[17] Four sages who were created through Brahma's mental powers—Sanatkumara, Sanaka, Sanatana and Sanandana.

[18] That is, they did not have any offspring. This is a reference to Sanatkumara, Sanaka, Sanatana and Sanandana. There has been no mention of Skanda (Kartikeya) yet. However, Skanda is sometimes equated with Sanatkumara.

[19] The saptarshis.

[20] Great rishis.

[21] The text uses two words for rainbow, that is, two types of rainbows were created—*rohita* and *indradhanu*. Indradhanu means Indra's bow and is the ordinary rainbow. Rohita means straight and is a special kind of rainbow that cannot be seen by humans.

[22] Male.

[23] The male and female principles.

named after this.[24] There is a second creation that is said to have
occurred after the mental one. This is known as Vairaja creation
and was done by the lord.[25] The first cycle of creation was not born
from wombs and was a creation that resulted from Narayana. If a
man knows about this original creation, he obtains a long life and
has fame, riches and offspring. He obtains the destination that he
desires.'

Chapter 2

Vaishampayana said, 'After having completed the mental
creation, Prajapati became Purusha. As his wife, he obtained
Shatarupa, who was not born from a womb.[26] O great king.
Shatarupa was created in accordance with dharma and in her
greatness, she pervaded heaven. For ten thousand years, she
tormented herself through extremely difficult austerities. Because
of those blazing austerities, she obtained Purusha as her husband.
O son! This Purusha is spoken of as Svayambhuva Manu. Seventy-
one yugas are said to constitute one manvantara.[27] Through Vairaja

[24] Each manvantara (era) is presided over by a sovereign known as
Manu. It is because humans are descended from Manu that they are known
as *manava*. There are fourteen manvantaras and fourteen Manus to preside
over them. The present manvantara is the seventh and the Manu who
presides over this is known as Vaivasvata, because he was born from the
sun (Vivasvat). At the end of any manvantara, there is a minor destruction
of sorts and Manu's task is to recreate. This is a minor destruction and
creation, not the major one.

[25] Vairaja is a name used for the Manus. This is a creation undertaken
by the Manus.

[26] Shatarupa means one with one hundred forms.

[27] *Satya (krita) yuga* consists of 4,000 divine years, *treta yuga* of 3,000
divine years, *dvapara yuga* of 2,000 divine years and kali yuga of 1,000
divine years. Between these yugas, at the end of one and the beginning
of the next, there are respective intervening periods of 400 years, 300
years, 200 years and 100 years. Thus each cycle of satya–treta–dvapara–
kali, known as a *mahayuga*, consists of 12,000 divine years. Seventy-one

Purusha, Shatarupa had a son named Vira. Through Vira, Kamya[28] had sons named Priyavrata and Uttanapada. O mighty-armed one! Kamya was the daughter of Kardama Prajapati.[29] Kamya had four sons named Samrat, Kukshi, Virat and Prabhu. Atri Prajapati accepted Uttanapada as his son. Through Sunrita,[30] Uttanapada had four sons. Sunrita possessed excellent hips and was famous. She was Dharma's daughter. Following dharma, the auspicious one became Dhruva's mother. Through Sunrita, Uttanapada Prajapati had sons named Dhruva, Kirtimat, Apyayasmat and Ayaspati. O descendant of the Bharata lineage! O great king! Dhruva desired extremely great fame and tormented himself through austerities for three thousand divine years. Delighted, the lord Brahma granted him a spot that is like his own. The Prajapati does not move and is stationed in front of the saptarshis.[31] On seeing his pride, prosperity and greatness, Ushanas, the preceptor of the gods and the *asuras*,[32] composed a shloka. "Wonderful are his austerities and valour. Wonderful is his learning. Wonderful are his vows." That is why Dhruva is stationed ahead of the saptarshis. Dhruva's wife, Shambhu, gave birth to sons named Shlishti and Manya. Shlishti's wife, Succhaya, gave birth to five unblemished sons— Ripu, Ripunjaya, Vipra, Vrikala and Vrikatejasa. Ripu's wife, Brihati, gave birth to Chakshusha and he possessed every kind of energy. Through Pushkarini, Virana's daughter, Chakshusha had a son named Chakshusha Manu. This great-souled Prajapati was thus descended from Virana's lineage. O foremost among the Bharata lineage! Through Nangala, who was the daughter of

---

mahayugas constitute one manvantara, the lifespan of a Manu and fourteen manvantaras are one *kalpa* (one of Brahma's days).

[28] Vira's wife.

[29] As stated, this is somewhat confusing. This Kamya seems to be different from the one who was Vira's wife.

[30] Uttanapada's wife.

[31] The saptarshis are the constellation Ursa Major (Great Bear) and Dhruva is the Pole Star.

[32] The asuras are demons, the word being used as an antithesis of the *suras* or gods. Ushanas or Shukracharya is actually the preceptor of the demons. The preceptor of the gods is Brihaspati.

Vairaja Prajapati, this Manu had ten immensely energetic sons—
Uru, Puru, Shatadyumna, Tapasvi, Satyavit, Kavi, Agnishtut,
Atiratra, Sudyumna as the ninth and Abhimanyu as the tenth.
These were Nangala's immensely energetic sons. Through Agni's
daughter, Uru had six extremely radiant sons—Anga, Sumanasa,
Khyati, Kratu, Angiras and Shiva. Through Sunitha, Anga had a
single son named Vena. Vena enraged all the great beings because
of his oppressions. For the sake of offspring, the rishis kneaded
his right arm.[33] When the rishis kneaded his right arm, a great son
was born. On seeing him, the sages exclaimed, "This immensely
energetic one will delight the subjects. He will obtain great fame."
When he was born, he wielded a bow and was clad in armour.
He was full of energy and seemed to burn everything down.
Vena's son, Prithu,[34] protected everything and was the first of the
*kshatriya*s. This lord of the earth consecrated himself for a royal
sacrifice.[35] Accomplished bards and minstrels were generated from
this sacrifice. O great king! O descendant of the Bharata lineage!
Desiring to ensure subsistence for the subjects, with the gods and
the large numbers of rishis, he milked the earth to obtain crops.[36]
Using their own respective vessels, the ancestors, the danavas, the
gandharvas, large numbers of *apsara*s, the snakes, other sacred
creatures, the herbs and the mountains also milked the earth.
Having obtained their desired milk, they were able to sustain their
lives. Prithu had two sons named Antardhi and Palina and they
were knowledgeable about dharma. Through Antardhi, his wife,
Shikhandini, had a son named Havirdhana. Agni's daughter was
Dhishna. Through Havirdhana, she had six sons—Prachinabarhi,
Shukra, Gaya, Krishna, Vraja and Ajina. The illustrious
Prachinabarhi was a great Prajapati. O great king! He made the
subjects prosper, just as Havirdhana had. O Janamejaya! As long

---

[33] Vena had been killed by the sages, without having had any sons.

[34] Prithu means large or wide and was so named because Vena's arm
was large.

[35] A *rajasuya* sacrifice, which establishes a king as an emperor of the
earth.

[36] Prithu did the milking. Thus, the earth is known as *prithvi* or *prithivi*.

as Prachinabarhi remained on earth, *prachinagra kusha* covered the surface of the earth.[37] After performing great austerities, the lord and king obtained the ocean's daughter, Savarna, as a wife. Through Savarna, the ocean's daughter, Prachinabarhi obtained ten sons. All of them were known as Prachetas and they were accomplished in *dhanurveda*.[38] All of them tormented themselves through great austerities and observed the same kind of dharma, immersed in the water of the ocean for ten thousand years. When the Prachetas were engaged in these austerities, the earth was no longer protected and became covered with trees. Consequently, the subjects were destroyed. The trees rose up into the sky and the wind was incapable of blowing. For ten thousand years, the subjects found it impossible to move. Realizing this, all the Prachetas resorted to their austerities and released wind and fire from their mouths. That wind uprooted and dried the trees. The terrible fire burnt them down. In this way, the trees were destroyed. On discerning that the trees were destroyed, but some branches were still left, the powerful king Soma[39] approached and said, "O kings! O all of you who are descended from Prachinabarhi! Restrain your anger. You have made the earth bereft of trees. Pacify the fire and the wind now. This beautiful maiden is the daughter of the trees and is a source of riches. O sons![40] Knowing what the future holds, I have borne her in my womb. This maiden is named Marisha and she has been fashioned from the trees. O immensely fortunate ones! She will be your wife and will extend Soma's lineage. Using half of your energy and half of my energy, she will give birth to a learned son named Daksha Prajapati. Through your energy and my energy, he will be like a fire generated from a fire and will again populate what has been burnt down with subjects." The Prachetas agreed to Soma's words. They withdrew their rage from

[37] An auspicious sign. Kusha is sacred grass and prachinagra is that kind of grass that always has its tips pointed towards the east. Alternatively, Prachinabarhi performed so many sacrifices that the earth was covered.

[38] *Dhanu* means bow and *veda* means knowledge. But dhanurveda means the science of war.

[39] Soma is the lord of trees and herbs. Soma is the moon god.

[40] The word used is tata.

the trees and following dharma, accepted Marisha as a wife. O
descendant of the Bharata lineage! Through part of Soma and the
ten Prachetas, Marisha gave birth to the greatly energetic Prajapati
Daksha. To extend Soma's lineage, he had sons and created mobile
and immobile objects, bipeds and quadrupeds. After this, through
his mental powers, Daksha created women. He bestowed ten of
these daughters on Soma and thirteen on Kashyapa. The lord
bestowed the remainder, known as *nakshatra*s, on King Soma. The
gods, birds, cattle, serpents, daityas, danavas, gandharvas, apsaras
and all the other species were born from these.[41] O Indra among
kings! Since then, offspring have resulted from sexual intercourse.
The earlier creation is said to be one that resulted from resolution,
sight and touch.'[42]

Janamejaya asked, 'You have earlier spoken about the
creation of the gods, the danavas, the gandharvas, the serpents, the
rakshasas and the great-souled Daksha. O unblemished one! You
have said that Daksha was born from Brahma's toe.[43] How could
the great ascetic again have been born as a son of the Prachetas?
O brahmana! I have a doubt about this and you should explain it
to me. He was Soma's grandson.[44] How did he become his father-
in-law?'

Vaishampayana replied, 'O descendant of the Bharata
lineage! For all creatures, birth and destruction are perennial.
Rishis and learned people are not confused on this account. O
king! Daksha and all the others are born in every yuga and again
die in every yuga. The learned are not confused on this account.
O lord of men! Who was elder and who was younger was not
determined by who was born first. Austerities were supreme
and power was the determining factor. A person who knows
about Daksha's creation of mobile and immobile objects obtains
offspring, traverses everything and attains greatness in the world
of heaven.'

---

[41] From the daughters who were Kashyapa's wives.
[42] Through mental powers and without intercourse.
[43] This has not actually been said earlier.
[44] Daksha was the son of Marisha, who was Soma's daughter.

Chapter 3

Janamejaya said, 'O Vaishampayana! Tell me in detail about the creation of gods, danavas, gandharvas, serpents and rakshasas.'

Vaishampayana replied, 'O lord of the earth! Svayambhu first instructed Daksha that he should create subjects and he then created beings. Listen. The lord initially created rishis, gods, gandharvas, asuras and rakshasas through his mental powers. However, despite his efforts, the subjects did not proliferate. Prajapati again thought about the creation of subjects. He decided to create diverse kinds of subjects by resorting to the dharma of sexual intercourse. He thus accepted Prajapati Virana's daughter, Asikni, as his wife. She was full of extremely great austerities and was capable of sustaining the worlds. Thus, five thousand valiant sons were born through Daksha Prajapati and Virana's daughter, Asikni. On seeing those extremely fortunate offspring prosper, *devarshi* Narada, agreeable in speech, spoke to them. This was like a curse on their own selves and they were destroyed.[45] Through Daksha's daughter, the supreme lord[46] had earlier been born as one of Kashyapa's foremost sons. But the sage was now scared that Daksha would curse him. The great lord, Narada, had already been born earlier. However, the supreme devarshi was again born through Asikni, Virana's daughter. The bull among sages was born again and he was just like his father.[47] Daksha had sons who were famous as Haryashva.[48] There is no doubt that they became detached in every kind of way and were destroyed. The infinitely valorous Daksha prepared to destroy him.[49] With the maharshis leading the way, the great lord[50] restrained him. The great lord brought about a pact with Daksha

---

[45] Narada's words of wisdom made them lose interest in material objects, the senses, the world and procreation. Subsequently, a more mundane explanation is given.

[46] Narada.

[47] Daksha.

[48] The five thousand sons. The recital goes back a bit.

[49] Narada.

[50] Virana.

and said, "Through my daughter, Narada will become your son."
The supreme lord bestowed his beloved daughter on Daksha and
because of the fear of a curse, the rishi Narada was born through
her.'

Janamejaya asked, 'How were Prajapati's sons destroyed by
maharshi Narada? O foremost among brahmanas! I wish to hear
the truth about this.'

Vaishampayana replied, 'Daksha's sons, the Haryashvas, were
immensely valorous and were about to create offspring. Narada
appeared before them and said, "You are foolish. You do not know
the inside of the earth and what is above it and below it. How can
you create subjects?" On hearing these words, they left in all the
directions. They have still not returned, like rivers that head to the
ocean. When the Haryashvas were destroyed, the lord Daksha, the
son of Prachetas, again had one thousand sons through Virana's
daughter. They were the Shabalashvas and they too wished to have
offspring. O son! However, Narada urged them with the words
that he had spoken earlier. All of them spoke to each other. "The
great rishi has spoken appropriately. There is no doubt that we
must follow in the footsteps of our brothers. Once we know the
measurements of the earth, we can happily create subjects." They
also departed along those paths, in all the directions. They have still
not returned, like rivers that head to the ocean. O king! O lord!
Since then, whenever a brother sets out to search for a brother, he is
destroyed. There is no need to reflect on this. Daksha Prajapati got to
know that his sons had been destroyed. Through Virana's daughter,
Daksha again had sixty daughters. This is what we have heard. He
gave ten to Dharma, thirteen to Kashyapa, twenty-seven to Soma,
four to Arishtanemi, two to Bahuputra, two to Angiras and two
to the learned Bhrishashva.[51] O descendant of the Bharata lineage!
Arundhati, Vasu, Jami, Lamba, Bhanu, Marutvati, Samkalpa,
Muhurta, Sadhya and Vishva—these are the ten who were the wives
of Dharma. Listen to the names of their offspring. It is said that
the Vishvadevas were born from Vishva, the Sadhyas from Sadhya,
the Marutvans from Marutvati and the Vasus from Vasu. O son!

[51] Ten remain unaccounted for.

The Bhanus were born from Bhanu and Muhurta and others from Muhurta. The Ghoshas were born from Lamba and Nagavithi from Jami. Every object on earth was born from Arundhati. All of these beings were born through mental resolution alone.

'O king! The wives of Soma were also bestowed on him by Daksha, the son of Prachetas. All these stellar bodies are known by the names of nakshatras.[52] Within the category of divinities, there are other gods who are foremost among radiant ones. I will tell you in detail about the eight who are famous as Vasus. Apa, Dhruva, Soma, Dhara, Anila, Anala, Pratyusha and Prabhasa—these are said to be the names of the Vasus. Apa's sons were Vaitandya, Shrama, Shanta and Muni. Dhruva's son was the illustrious Kala, who controls the worlds. Soma's son was the illustrious Varcha and all rays originate with him. Dhara's sons were Dravina and Hutahavyavaha. Through Manohara,[53] he had sons named Shishira, Prana and Ramana. Anila's wife was Shiva and through her, Anila had two sons named Purojava and Avijnatagati. Agni's[54] son was Kumara, who prospered through rearing in a clump of reeds.[55] Shakha, Vishakha and Naigamesha followed him.[56] Since he was the offspring of the Krittikas, he is known as Kartikeya. Pratyusha's son is known to be the rishi named Devala. Devala had two learned and forgiving sons. Brihaspati's sister was a beautiful lady who practised *brahmacharya*. She became successful through *yoga* and roamed around the entire universe, bereft of attachment. She became the wife of the eighth Vasu, Prabhasa. The immensely fortunate Prajapati Vishvakarma was born from her. He was the creator of thousands of works of artisanship and was the architect of the gods. He was supreme among artisans and created all their

[52] There are twenty-seven lunar mansions or nakshatras. Since some nakshatras are constellations, *nakshatra* should not really be translated as star.

[53] Dhara's wife.

[54] Anala is another name for Agni.

[55] Kumara is Skanda or Kartikeya. There are various stories about Kartikeya's birth. For example, he was found in a clump of reeds and reared by the Krittikas (the Pleiades).

[56] This is a literal translation. It can be interpreted to mean that these three were also Agni's sons, younger to Kartikeya.

ornaments. He also constructed all the *vimanas*[57] for the gods. Men who earn a living through artisanship follow that great-souled one. There were Ajaikapada, Ahibudhnya, Tvashta and the valiant Rudra.[58] Tvashta had an immensely illustrious and handsome son named Vishvarupa. Hara, Bahurupa, Tryambaka, Aparajita, Vrishakapi, Shambhu, Kapardi and Raivata—these are said to be the eleven Rudras and they are the lords of the three worlds.[59] Hundreds of infinitely energetic Rudras have been named.

'O lord of the worlds! Hear the names of the offspring of Aditi, Diti, Danu, Arishta, Surasa, Surabhi, Vinata, Tamra, Krodhavasha, Ira, Kadru and Muni.[60] In an earlier manvantara, there were twelve excellent and supreme gods and they were named the Tushitas. When that immensely illustrious and former *chakshusha manvantara* was over and they realized that *vaivasvata manvantara* was about to present itself, for the welfare of all the worlds, they met and spoke to each other. "Come. Let us swiftly enter the goddess Aditi. It will be best if we are born in the next manvantara." At the end of chakshusha manvantara, all of them mentally spoke to each other in this way. They were born through Marichi's son, Kashyapa, and Daksha's daughter, Aditi. In this way, Vishnu, Shakra, Aryama, Dhata, Tvashta, Pusha, Vivasvat, Savita, Mitra, Varuna, Amsha and the infinitely energetic Bhaga were born again. These are known as the twelve Adityas. In the former chakshusha manvantara, the gods were the Tushitas. In vaivasvata manvantara, they are known as the twelve Adityas. Soma's twenty-seven wives have been spoken about and they were good in their vows. They had blazing and infinitely energetic offspring. Through his wives, Arishtanemi had six sons. The learned Bahuputra had four sons known as Vidyut.

[57] Celestial vehicles.
[58] This is left dangling. There is a shloka that has been excised from the Critical Edition. In that shloka, Surabhi obtained Mahadeva's favours and obtained these sons through Kashyapa.
[59] We only have eight names. The Critical Edition again excises a shloka and that has the missing three names, Mrigavyadha, Sarpa and Kapali.
[60] These are the thirteen of Daksha's daughters who were married to Kashyapa. Yet again, there is a problem with the Critical Edition, since the listing has twelve names. The missing name is Khasha.

The best hymns of the Rig Veda, honoured by *brahmarshi*s, were generated from Angiras. The sons of devarshi Bhrishashva were the weapons of the gods. O son! In this way, because of their wishes, after thousands of yugas, the thirty-three gods are born again.[61] O Indra among kings! This is said to be the nature of their creation and destruction. O Kouravya! Just as the sun rises and sets, from one yuga to another yuga, the gods are also destroyed and created. O descendant of the Bharata lineage! In addition to Aditi, we have heard that through Diti, Kashyapa had two sons, Hiranyakashipu and Hiranyaksha. There was also a daughter named Simhika and she married Viprachitti. Hiranyakashipu had four renowned and energetic sons—Anuhlada, Hlada, the valiant Prahlada and Samhlada as the fourth. Hlada's son was Hlada.[62] Hlada had Ayu, Shiva and Kala as sons. Prahlada had a son named Virochana and Bali was born through Virochana. O lord of men! Bali had one hundred sons. Of these, Bana was the eldest. The others were Dhritarashtra, Surya, Chandrama, Chandratapana, Kumbhanama, Gardabhaksha, Kukshi and others. The eldest Bana, was extremely strong and was devoted to Pashupati.[63] In an earlier era, Bana gratified the lord who is Uma's consort. He desired the boon that he might always find pleasure by his[64] side. Hiranyaksha had five learned and extremely strong sons—Jharjhara, Shakuni, Bhutasamtapana, the valiant Mahanabha and Kalanabha. Danu had one hundred brave and fierce sons. They were devoted to austerities and extremely valorous. Hear the names of the foremost—Dvimurdha, Shakuni, Shankushira, Vibhu, Ayomukha, Shambara, Kapila, Vamana, Marichi, Maghavan, Ida, Gargashira, Vikshobhana, Ketu, Ketuvirya, Shatahrada, Indrajit, Sarvajit, Vajranabha, the mighty-armed Ekachakra, the immensely strong Taraka, Vaishvanara, Puloma, Vidravana, Mahashira, Svarbhanu, Vrishaparva and the valiant Viprachitti. All of these were Danu's

---

[61] The number of gods is often described as thirty-three—twelve Adityas, eleven Rudras, eight Vasus and two Ashvins.

[62] The father is Hlaada and the son is Hlada.

[63] Shiva. Shiva's wife is Uma.

[64] Shiva's.

sons and they were born through Kashyapa. The immensely strong
Viprachitti was the foremost among the danavas.[65] Svarbhanu had
a daughter named Prabha and Puloma a daughter named Shachi.
Upadanavi, Hayashira and Sharmishtha were the daughters of
Vrishaparva. Both Puloma[66] and Kalaka were the daughters of
Vaishvanara. Those great-spirited ones[67] were married to Marichi's
son[68] and they had many offspring. Through them, Marichi's son,
the great ascetic, had sixty thousand supreme danavas as sons. The
danavas known as the Poulamas and Kalakeyas were immensely
strong. They resided in Hiranyapura and because of the favours of
the grandfather, could not be slain by the gods. They were killed
by Savyasachi.[69] Other than this, through Simhika, Viprachitti had
immensely brave and extremely fierce danavas as his sons. They
were fierce in their valour and were born through a union between
a daitya and a danava.[70] Thirteen greatly strong ones are known
as Saimhikeyas[71]—Vyanga, the powerful Shalya, Bala, Mahabala,
Vatapi, Namuchi, Ilvala, Khasrima, Anjika, Naraka, Kalanabha,
Saramana and the valiant Sharakalpa. These best among danavas
extended Danu's lineage. They had hundreds and thousands of sons
and grandsons. The daityas known as the Nivatakavachas were
born in Samhlada's lineage. They cleansed their souls and were
extremely great in their austerities.

'The extremely great-spirited Tamra is said to have had six
daughters—Kaki, Shyeni, Bhasi, Sugrivi, Shuchi and Gridhrika.
Kaki gave birth to owls and crows, Shyeni to hawks, Bhasi to
predatory birds and Gridhrika to vultures. O scorcher of enemies!
Shuchi gave birth to large numbers of birds that dwell in water.
Through Sugrivi, horses, camels and donkeys are said to have been

[65] Danava means Danu's son. Daitya means Diti's son.
[66] Pulomaa.
[67] Puloma and Kalaka.
[68] Kashyapa.
[69] Hiranyapura means golden city. The grandfather (Brahma) gave
them a boon. Savyasachi means Arjuna and this story of Arjuna destroying
them has been described in the Mahabharata.
[70] Simhika was a daitya, Viprachitti was a danava.
[71] Sons of Simhika.

born in Tamra's lineage. Vinata had two sons, Aruna and Garuda. Of these, because of his own deeds, Suparna[72] was fierce and the best among birds. Surasa had one thousand infinitely energetic snakes as sons. O son! Those great-souled ones possessed many heads and roamed around in the sky. Kadru also had one thousand strong and infinitely energetic sons.[73] They also possessed many heads and were known as those who were under Suparna's control. The foremost among them have always been Shesha, Vasuki, Takshaka, Airavata, Mahapadma, Kambala, Ashvatara, Elapatra, Shankha, Karkotaka, Dhananjaya, Mahanila, Mahakarna, Dhritarashtra, Balahaka, Kuhara, Pushpadamshtra, Durmukha, Sumukha, Shankha,[74] Shankhapala, Kapila, Vamana, Nahusha, Shankharoma, Mani and others. Know that all the categories that are descended from Krodhavasha are fanged. The birds on land and in the water are said to be the offspring of Dhara. Surabhi gave birth to cows and buffaloes. Ira gave birth to all kinds of trees, plants, creepers and grass. Khasa gave birth to yakshas[75] and rakshasas and Muni to the apsaras. The great-spirited Arishta gave birth to the infinitely energetic gandharvas.

'These mobile and immobile objects are mentioned as the descendants of Kashyapa. They had hundreds and thousands of sons and grandsons. O son! In this manvantara, heaven is known as Svarochisha. In vaivasvata manvantara, a great sacrifice was performed for Varuna. It is said that for the sake of generating offspring, Brahma himself offered oblations. Earlier, he had created seven brahmarshis through his mental powers. The grandfather himself generated them as his sons now. O descendant of the Bharata lineage! After this, there was a conflict between the gods and the danavas.[76] When Diti's sons were destroyed, she went and pleased Kashyapa. Worshipped properly by her, Kashyapa was

[72] Garuda.

[73] These were also snakes.

[74] Shankha is named twice.

[75] Yakshas are semi-divine species and companions of Kubera, the god of treasure.

[76] Though asuras, daityas and danavas have different meanings, they are often used synonymously and interchangeably as words for demons.

gratified. He offered to grant her a boon and requested her to ask
for a boon. She said, "I desire an infinitely energetic son who is
capable of killing Indra." The immensely ascetic one granted her
the boon that she desired. However, after having granted the boon,
Marichi's son said, "If you desire a son who will kill Indra, you
must carefully nurture the embryo for one hundred autumns. You
must be pure and resort to supreme vows. If you sustain the embryo
in that fashion, you will have that kind of son." O lord of the earth!
The goddess told her husband, the great ascetic, that she would act
in that way. Accordingly, Kashyapa found pleasure in impregnating
Diti, so that an infinitely energetic offspring would result, who would
be superior to all the categories of the gods. He permeated her with
his energy, something that was impossible for even the immortals to
withstand. Having done this, the one who was devoted to his vows
retired to the mountains to practise austerities. The undecaying
chastiser of Paka[77] continued to search for a deviation in her and
discerned one before the one hundred years were over. Without
washing her feet, Diti lay down to sleep. While she was sleeping, the
wielder of the *vajra* penetrated through her side and shattered the
embryo into seven fragments. When the embryo was thus split by
the vajra, it began to weep and Shakra repeatedly told it, "Do not
cry." Indra, the afflicter of enemies, was enraged. Using the vajra,
he sliced each of those seven fragments into seven fragments. O bull
among the Bharata lineage! The gods known as the Maruts were
created in this way.[78] They came to be known as Maruts because
of what Maghavan[79] had said. Those forty-nine gods are the aides
of the wielder of the vajra. O Janamejaya! Different kinds of beings
began to prosper in this way. For each such class, Hari appointed
a Prajapati. O descendant of the Bharata lineage! He gave the first
kingdom to Prithu to rule and other kingdoms followed in due

[77] Indra killed a demon named Paka.
[78] The Maruts are sometimes identified with the Rudras. They are also
wind gods and companions of Indra. The number of Maruts varies and is
sometimes given as seven or forty-nine. The etymology given here is based
on *ma* (do not) and *rud* (cry).
[79] Indra.

course. Hari is Purusha, Vira, Krishna, Jishnu, Prajapati, Parjanya and Tapana.[80] He is everything that is manifest in the universe. O bull among the Bharata lineage! If a person knows this account about the creation of beings properly, he suffers no fear about being unable to find a means of subsistence. How can he entertain any fear about the world hereafter?'

Chapter 4

Vaishampayana said, 'The grandfather made Prithu, Vena's son, sovereign over the kingdom. In due course, he divided up the dominions further. Birds, herbs, nakshatras, planets, sacrifices and austerities were earmarked as Soma's kingdom. Varuna's kingdom was the water and Vaishravana[81] became the lord of kings. Vishnu became lord of the Adityas and Pavaka[82] of the Vasus. Daksha became lord of the Prajapatis, Vasava[83] of the Maruts and the infinitely energetic Prahlada of the daityas and the danavas. Vaivasvata Yama[84] was instated in the kingdom of the ancestors and also over the yakshas, rakshasas and kings.[85] Girisha, the wielder of the trident, became the lord of all the *bhutas* and *pishachas*.[86] The Himalayas became the lord of the mountains and the ocean of the rivers. The lord Chitraratha[87]

---

[80] Purusha means the Being. Vira is the brave one. Jishnu is the victorious one. Prajapati is protector of beings. Parjanya is the god of rain and Tapana is the sun.

[81] Vishrava's son, meaning Kubera.

[82] Agni.

[83] Indra.

[84] Yama is the son of Vivasvat (the sun).

[85] There is an inconsistency. For yakshas, rakshasas and kings, it should be Kubera.

[86] Girisha is Shiva. Bhutas are ghosts, demons and spirits, Shiva's followers. Pishachas are also demons, but the term is usually applied to those that feed on human flesh.

[87] King of the gandharvas.

became the lord of the gandharvas. Vasuki became lord over nagas and Takshaka over *sarpas*.[88] Airavata was instructed to be the king of the elephants.[89] Uchchaishrava became lord of the horses and Garuda of the birds. The tiger became the king of animals and the bull of cows. Plaksha[90] was indicated as the king of trees. In this way, in due order, the grandfather divided the dominions. O descendant of the Bharata lineage! He also established the guardians of the directions. He consecrated King Sudhanva, the son of Vairaja Prajapati, as the guardian of the eastern direction. He consecrated King Shankhapada, the son of the great-souled Kardama Prajapati, as the guardian of the southern direction. He consecrated the great-souled King Ketumanta, the son of the undecaying Rajasa, as the guardian of the western direction. He consecrated the invincible King Hiranyaloma, the son of Parjanya Prajapati, as the guardian of the northern direction. They ruled the entire earth, with its seven *dvipas*, habitations and the subregions, in accordance with dharma.[91] These lords of men followed the rites prescribed in the Vedas. They observed a royal sacrifice and made Prithu the emperor over all the kings in the various dominions. This is what happened when the manvantara associated with the infinitely energetic Chakshusha was over. When the manvantara associated with Vaivasvata commenced, the earth was divided into dominions in this fashion. O Indra among kings! O unblemished one! If you are favourably inclined towards hearing it, I will describe vaivasvata manvantara in detail.'

[88] Henceforth, we will translate nagas as serpents and sarpas as snakes. Though the two words are often used synonymously, there is usually a difference between nagas and sarpas. Nagas are semi-divine and have powers, including the ability to assume any form at will. Unlike sarpas, nagas also have a world of their own, in the nether regions.

[89] Airavata arose from the churning of the ocean and became Indra's elephant. Uchchaishrava also arose in similar fashion and became Indra's horse.

[90] The holy fig tree.

[91] Dvipa means a continent or region of the earth. The earth was commonly believed to be divided into seven continents.

Janamejaya replied, 'O Vaishampayana! Tell me about Prithu's birth in detail. How did the great-souled one milk the earth? How did the ancestors, the gods, the rishis, the daityas, the nagas, the yakshas and the trees perform the milking? O Vaishampayana! In particular, tell me about the vessels that they used. In due order, especially tell me everything about the calves and the milk. What was the reason why Vena's arm was kneaded in those ancient times? O father![92] Tell me the reason why the maharshis were enraged.'

Vaishampayana said, 'I will tell you about how Prithu was born from Vena. O Janamejaya! Listen devotedly and with single-minded attention. O king! I do not recount this to those who are impure, inferior in mind, ungrateful and injurious, or to those who are without disciples and vows. This is blessed and is honoured in the Vedas. It leads to heaven, fame and a long life. O king! Listen properly to the mystery spoken about by the rishis. If a person bows down before brahmanas and always recites the account of how Prithu originated from Vena, he does not sorrow, on account of what he has done and what he has not done.'

Chapter 5

Vaishampayana said, 'Earlier, there was a lord who was Atri's equal and he was the protector of dharma. He was born in Atri's lineage and this Prajapati's name was Anga. His son was Vena, who did not know about the purport of dharma. This Prajapati was born through Sunitha, Mrityu's daughter.[93] Since he was the son of Kala's daughter, Vena suffered from the taints of his maternal grandfather.[94] He turned his back on his own dharma and frequented the world of desire. This king established

[92] The word used is tata. This means father, but is used for anyone who is senior and superior.

[93] Vena's mother was Sunitha.

[94] Mrityu and Kala are both being used as words for Death.

ordinances that were contrary to dharma. He transgressed the
dharma of the Vedas and was always devoted to *adharma*. At
the time of that Prajapati, there were no sounds of *svadha* and
vashatkara at sacrifices performed by the subjects.[95] Therefore, the
gods no longer drank the soma offered at these. O extender of
the Kuru lineage! Since the time for that Prajapati's destruction
had arrived, the cruel one promulgated a rule that there should
be no sacrifices and no oblations. "I am the one who should be
worshipped through sacrifices. I am the sacrifice and the one who
sacrifices. The oblations offered at sacrifices are meant for me."
He transgressed all the ordinances and appropriated everything
for himself. All the maharshis, with Marichi at the forefront, said,
"We will consecrate ourselves in a sacrifice that will last for many
years. O Vena! Do not observe adharma. It is not the view of the
virtuous that this constitutes dharma. Though there is no doubt
that you have been born as a Prajapati, it is for your destruction. At
that time, you took a vow that you would protect the subjects." All
the assembled maharshis spoke to him in this way. However, Vena
was evil in his intelligence and thought what was inferior to be
superior. He laughed at them. "Who other than me is the creator
of dharma? Who other than me should be listened to? There is no
doubt that you do not know of my superiority because of your
folly. If I desire, I can burn the earth down, or flood it with water.
Without even thinking about it, I can slow down the progress of the
firmament and this earth." The maharshis sought to persuade King
Vena, who was overcome with insolence and strength. When they
didn't succeed, they became angry. In their rage, those great-souled
ones seized the one who was swollen because of his strength. They
kneaded his left thigh. When they kneaded the king's left thigh,
a man manifested himself. He was extremely short and dark. O
Janamejaya! Frightened, that man joined his hands in salutation
and stood there. On seeing that he was supremely anxious, they
asked him to sit. O supreme among eloquent ones! He was the

[95] Vashatkara is the exclamation 'vashat' made at the time of offering
an oblation. Svadha is said at the time of offering oblations to the ancestors
and *svaha* is said at the time of offering oblations to the gods.

progenitor of the lineage of *nishadas*.[96] The fishermen were also created from the sin in Vena. O son! There were others, the Tumuras and the Tumburas, who reside in the Vindhya mountains and are addicted to adharma. Know that they were also created from the sin in Vena. In their anger, the great-souled maharshis then again kneaded Vena's right hand, as if it was a piece of wood used to kindle a fire. Prithu arose from this. His form blazed like the flames of a fire, and he was like a dazzling fire. From the time of his birth, he held the bow known as Ajagava,[97] which makes a loud roar, and divine arrows. For his protection, he was clad in immensely radiant armour. When he was born, all the beings were delighted. O great king! They assembled before him and Vena went to heaven. O Kouravya! Having given birth to a virtuous son, the great-souled tiger among men was thus saved from the hell named *put*.[98]

'To consecrate him, all the oceans and the rivers presented themselves and brought their water and all kinds of jewels. With the gods and the descendants of Angiras, and with all the mobile and immobile objects, the illustrious grandfather himself arrived to consecrate Vena's son and the immensely radiant protector of the subjects as the king in that great kingdom. Following the prescribed rites, those who knew about dharma consecrated the greatly energetic and powerful Prithu, Vena's son, as king and sovereign. The subjects were not delighted with his father, but were delighted with him. Because of this, he came to be known as king.[99] When he proceeded,[100] the water in the oceans was stupefied and the mountains offered him a path. That is the reason his standard never got attached to either. At that time, through the mere thought, the earth yielded grain, even when it had not been tilled. The milk of

[96] Nishadas were mountain-dwelling tribes who were outside the caste system. The word nishad means an instruction to sit.

[97] This is also the name of Shiva's bow.

[98] One goes to the hell named put if one does not have a son. Since a son saves (*trayate*) from the hell named put, a son is known as putra.

[99] *Rajan* means king and this is being etymologically linked to delighting (*ranjana*).

[100] On his chariot, along the water and along the sky.

the cows yielded every object of desire and there was honey in every hand.[101] At this time, on a day, when an auspicious sacrifice was performed in honour of the grandfather, an immensely intelligent suta, who gave rise to the suta class, was generated as offspring.[102] It was at this great sacrifice that the wise magadhas were also born. To praise Prithu, the maharshis summoned them there. All the rishis said, "Praise the king. This lord of men is a right recipient of praise and your task is to do that. At this, the sutas and the magadhas told all the rishis, "We will please the gods and the rishis through our own deeds. O brahmanas! However, we know nothing about this energetic king's deeds or manifestations of fame. How can we compose hymns of praise?" Engaged by the rishis, they began to praise the deeds that the immensely strong Prithu would perform later. O Janamejaya! In the three worlds, since that time, the practice of using sutas, magadhas and bandis for praise and benedictions has been adopted. Prithu, the lord of subjects, was extremely delighted at the praise and gave sutas the land of Anupa and magadhas the land of Magadha.[103] On seeing this, the maharshis were extremely happy and told the subjects, "This lord of men will grant you means of subsistence." At this, all the subjects approached the great king who was Vena's son and said, "Following the words of the maharshis, identify means of subsistence for us." When all the subjects approached in this way, wishing to do what would ensure welfare for the subjects, the powerful one grasped his bow and arrow and rushed towards the earth. Terrified of Vena's son, the earth assumed the form of a cow and fled. Prithu seized his bow and rushed after the fleeing one. Out of fear for Vena's son, she went to Brahma's world and all the other worlds. However, wherever she

[101] The text uses the word *putaka*. This means the hands, held together in the form of a cup. But it also means leaves arranged in the form of a cup. Therefore, one could also have said, there was honey in every flower.

[102] The sutas were charioteers, as well as raconteurs of tales. *Magadha*s were minstrels and bards. So were *bandi*s. But magadhas seem to have also composed, while bandis sung the compositions of others.

[103] The land of Anupa was in Vidarbha, in Maharashtra now. Magadha is mostly in Bihar, with some parts of Bengal, Odisha and eastern Uttar Pradesh.

went, she saw Vena's fierce son, with the bow and arrow. Resorting
to great yoga, the great-souled one was invincible, even before the
immortals. She could thus find no escape from Vena's son. Finally,
the one who is always worshipped in the three worlds joined her
hands in salutation and told Vena's son, "You should not see any
dharma in killing a woman. O king! Without me, how will you be
able to sustain the subjects? O king! I am the one in whom all these
worlds are established. I am the one who holds up the universe. O
king! You should know that for my sake, you should not destroy
the subjects. You should not kill me. There is no benefit in it and
you should not desire it. O lord of the earth! For the sake of the
subjects, listen to my words. All tasks become successful if they are
started in the appropriate way. O king! Search for a means so that
the subjects can be sustained. O king! If you kill me, you will not
be able to sustain the subjects. O immensely radiant one! If your
anger is pacified, I will become full of grain. It is said that women
must not be killed, especially those who are of inferior species.[104] O
lord of the earth! Be established in that spirit and do not abandon
dharma." The great-minded king heard many words of this kind.
The one with dharma in his soul controlled his rage and spoke these
words to the earth.'

Chapter 6

'Prithu said, "In this world, if a person kills many beings for the
sake of a single entity, whether that single entity is he himself
or someone else, he commits a sin. O auspicious one! O fortunate
one! However, for the happiness of many, if a single entity is killed,
then one does not commit a major sin or a minor one. O earth!
Therefore, unless you act in accordance with my words and ensure
benefit to the universe, for the sake of the subjects, I am going to kill
you. You are reluctant to come under my subjugation. I will now
slay you with my arrow. I will establish myself in your place and

---

[104] In the sense of subhuman.

myself sustain the subjects. O supreme among those who uphold
dharma! You are capable of imparting life to all the subjects and
sustaining them. Therefore, accept my rule. If you become my
daughter, I will withdraw this arrow, terrible to see, that I have
raised to kill you."

'Vasundhara[105] replied, "O brave one! There is no doubt that
I will arrange all this. Search out a calf for me, so that, driven by
maternal affection, I can yield milk. O supreme among those who
uphold dharma! Make my surface smooth and flat everywhere, so
that the milk I yield does not flow away to uneven terrain."'

Vaishampayana continued, 'Using the ends of his bow, Vena's
son removed hundreds and thousands of mountains and made other
mountains rise. The surface of the earth was no longer as uneven
as it had been during the earlier creation. At that time, cities and
villages could not be constructed. The growing of crops, tending
to cattle and agriculture couldn't happen. Nor were there routes
for traders. O Indra among kings! Because of what Vena's son
had done, all these became possible. O unblemished one! In all
the places that had become plain, all the subjects found pleasure
in residing. We have heard that food for the subjects consisted of
fruits and roots and that this led to great hardship. O tiger among
men! Therefore, he[106] thought of the lord Svayambhu Manu as a
calf and used his own hands to milk the earth. That is how Prithu,
Vena's powerful son, created all the crops. O son! It is on the basis
of that food that the subjects always survived. It has been heard
that the rishis milked the earth again. Soma was the calf and the
immensely energetic Brihaspati, the son of Angiras, did the milking.
O descendant of the Bharata lineage! At that time, the hymns were
the vessels. The eternal and unmatched *brahman*,[107] the essence of
austerities, was manifested in the form of milk. It has been heard that
using golden vessels, the large number of gods, with Purandara[108]

---

[105] Vasundhara is a name for the earth. One explanation for the word
vasundhara is that the earth holds and sustains (*dhara*) riches (*vasu*).

[106] Prithu.

[107] Brahman or *paramatman* is the supreme soul or being.

[108] Indra.

at the forefront, again milked the earth. Maghavan was the calf
and the lord Savita did the milking. The gods sustain themselves
on that energetic milk.[109] It has been heard that the ancestors, who
are infinitely valorous in their abodes, used silver vessels to milk
the earth again. The powerful Vaivasvata Yama was the calf then.
Kala, the one who brings an end and who destroys all beings, was
the one who did the milking. It has been heard that the nagas also
did a milking, using Takshaka as a calf. O supreme among men!
They used a gourd as a vessel and the milk was poison. O best
among the Bharata lineage! O lord of the earth! Airavata did the
milking for the nagas and the powerful Dhritarashtra did it for
the sarpas.[110] Those fierce ones are giant in form and immense in
strength, sustaining themselves on that[111] for obtaining food, their
conduct, their valour and their austerities. It has been heard that the
asuras milked the earth again. They used an iron vessel and obtained
the *maya*[112] that destroys all enemies. Virochana's son, Prahlada,
was the calf. The immensely powerful Madhu, who possessed two
heads, was the officiating priest and the one who did the milking
for the daityas. Since then, all the asuras know about maya and base
themselves on maya. Their immense wisdom and infinite strength
is also based on that. O king! It has been heard that the yakshas
milked the earth again. O great king! They used a vessel that had
not been baked and obtained the undecaying *antardhana*.[113] The
auspicious yakshas made Vaishravana[114] the calf. The supreme rishi
has said that they sustain themselves on that.[115] O bull among men!
The rakshasas and pishachas milked the earth again. They used the
skulls of corpses as vessels and their offspring sustained themselves
on that. O extender of the Kuru lineage! Rajatanabha was the one

---

[109] Meaning amrita.

[110] Airavata and Dhritarashtra are also the names of nagas.

[111] The poison.

[112] The powers of illusion.

[113] Antardhana means disappearance. Here, it means the knowledge of
being able to disappear (and appear) at will.

[114] Kubera.

[115] The rishi who has said this is Vedavyasa. The yakshas sustain
themselves on antardhana.

who did the milking. O Kouravya! Sumali was the calf and the milk was blood. The rakshasas, the yakshas, who are the equals of the immortals, the pishachas and the large number of bhutas subsist on that. The large number of gandharvas and apsaras milked again, using a lotus leaf as a vessel. O supreme among men! They made Chitraratha the calf and obtained pure fragrances. O supreme among the Bharata lineage! At that time, the extremely strong and great-souled king of the gandharvas, Suruchi, whose complexion was like that of the sun, was the one who did the milking. It has been heard that the mountains milked the goddess earth again and the personified forms of herbs and many kinds of jewels manifested themselves. The Himalayas were the calf and the giant mountain of Meru did the milking. The mountains were the vessels and the mountains sustain themselves on what was obtained. It has been heard that the trees and plants also milked the earth. They used *palasha*[116] as a vessel and obtained the power of regenerating, even when severed or burnt down. A blossoming *sala* tree did the milking and Plaksha was the calf.

'The sacred earth is the one who generates and sustains. She is the origin and the foundation for everything, mobile and immobile. She is like a cow that can be milked to yield every object of desire. She is the one who germinates every kind of crop. This earth, which extends up to the frontiers of the ocean, is also famous as Medini. Every part of her was flooded by the fat from Madhu and Kaitabha.[117] O descendant of the Bharata lineage! Since she followed the instructions of King Prithu, Vena's son, and became his daughter, the goddess is also spoken of as Prithvi.[118] Prithu divided the earth and cleansed her. He made her prosperous and the yielder of crops, with cities and habitations. O supreme among kings! This was the power of the king who was Vena's son. There is no doubt that the large number of creatures should bow down before him and worship him. The immensely fortunate brahmanas,

[116] A tree, the flame of the forest.
[117] Madhu and Kaitabha were two demons killed by Vishnu. Their fat (*meda*) created the earth and led to the name Medini.
[118] Or Prithivi, named after Prithu.

accomplished in the Vedas and the Vedangas,[119] should also worship Prithu, because he gave them their eternal means of subsistence. So should immensely fortunate kings who desire to remain kings. The powerful Prithu, Vena's son, was the first king and deserves to be worshipped. Brave warriors who desire to obtain victory in a battle should also worship that first king. That king was the first warrior. If a warrior chants the name of King Prithu and advances into battle, even if that encounter is extremely terrible in form, he surpasses it with ease and obtains fame. There may be prosperous *vaishya*s who are engaged in the livelihood of vaishyas. If they bow down before Prithu, who provided a means of subsistence, they will obtain great fame. There may be pure *shudra*s who are engaged in serving the other three varnas. If they desire supreme benefit, they should also worship Prithu. I have specifically spoken to you about the calves, the ones who did the milking, the milk and the vessels. What will I describe to you next?'

Chapter 7

Janamejaya said, 'O Vaishampayana! O one who is rich in austerities! Please describe in detail all the manvantaras, how they were created and how they were destroyed. O brahmana! I wish to hear about the Manus and their durations. I wish to hear the true account of the manvantaras.'

Vaishampayana replied, 'O son! I am incapable of describing it in detail, even if I were to speak for one hundred years. O Kouravya! I will tell you about the manvantaras in brief. Listen. O son! Earlier, there were Svayambhu Manu, Svarochisha Manu, Outtama, Tamasa, Raivata and Chakshusha. O Kouravya! The present Manu is said to be Vaivasvata. O son! It is said that the

[119] Vedanga means a branch of the Vedas and these were six kinds of learning that were essential to understand the Vedas—*shiksha* (phonetics), *kalpa* (rituals), *vyakarana* (grammar), *nirukta* (etymology), *chhanda* (metre) and *jyotisha* (astronomy).

four Manus who will come are Savarni Manu, Bhoutya, Rouchya and Merusavarni. O son! These are the past, present and future Manus. I have recounted them to you, as I have heard them. I will now tell you about the rishis, their sons and the large number of gods. Marichi, Atri, the illustrious Angiras, Pulaha, Kratu, Pulastya and Vasishtha—these are Brahma's seven sons. O king! They are established as the saptarshis[120] in the northern direction. At the time of Svayambhu Manu, the gods were the Yamas. Agnidhra, Agnibahu, Medha, Medhatithi, Vasu, Jyotishmat, Dyutimat, Havya, Savana and Putra—these were the ten immensely energetic sons of Svayambhu Manu. O king! I have thus spoken to you about the first manvantara. At the time of Svarochisha Manu, Vasishtha's son, Ourva, Stamba, Kashyapa, Prana, Brihaspati, Datta and Atrishchyavana—these were the maharshis, great in their vows. Vayu[121] has spoken about them. At that time, it has been said that the gods were known as the Tushitas. O son! The great-souled Svarochisha Manu's sons were Havirdhra, Sukriti, Jyoti, Apa, Murti, Ayasmaya, Prathita, Nabhashya, Nabha and Surya. O protector of the earth! They were extremely energetic and valorous and I have spoken about them. I have thus spoken to you about the second manvantara. O lord of men! I will now tell you about the third. Listen. Hiranyagarbha gave birth to extremely energetic sons known as the Urjas. These seven became famous as Vasishtha's sons and were known as the sons of Vasishtha.[122] I have spoken about the rishis. O great king! I will now recount the ten handsome sons of Outtama Manu. Listen. They were Isha, Urja, Tanupa, Madhu, Madhava, Shuchi, Shukra, Saha, Nabhasya and Nabha. The gods of that manvantara are said to be the Bhanus. I will now tell you about the fourth manvantara. Listen. O descendant of the Bharata lineage! O king! Kavya, Prithu, Agni, Jahnu, Dhata, Kapivat and Akapivat were the saptarshis. O son! O descendant of the Bharata lineage! Their sons and grandsons have been mentioned

---

[120] The seven rishis, the constellation of Ursa Major.

[121] The wind god.

[122] They were reborn as Vasishtha's sons during the third manvantara and became the saptarshis of that manvantara.

in the Puranas. During the manvantara of Tamasa Manu, the gods were the Satyas. Dyuti, Tapasya, Sutapa, Tapomula, Tapodhana, Taporati, Kalmasha, Tanvi, Dhanvi and Parantapa—these were the ten extremely strong sons of Tamasa Manu. O great king! Vayu has spoken about what happened after the fourth manvantara. Vedabahu, Yadudhra, the sage Vedashira, Hiranyaloma, Parjanya, Urdhvabahu, the son of Soma, and Satyanetra, the son of Atri, were the saptarshis thereafter.[123] During this manvantara, the gods are said to have been the Abhutarajas, Prakritis, Pariplavas and Raibhyas. Listen to me. I will tell you about his sons. Dhritimat, Avyaya, Yukta, Tatvadarshi, Nirutsaka, Aranya, Prakasha, Nirmoha, Satyavak and Kriti—these were the sons of Raivata Manu. O lord of men! After the fifth manvantara, I will tell you about the sixth. Listen. Bhrigu, Nabha, Vivasvat, Sudhama, Viraja, Atinama and Sahishnu—these were the seven saptarshis. O son! Hear the names of the gods during the manvantara of Chakshusha Manu. O Indra among kings! The names of the five categories of gods is said to be Adya, Prabhuta, Ribhu, Prithuka and Lekha. These were the residents of heaven. All these great-souled and immensely energetic ones were the sons of the rishi Angiras. O great king! O king! Through Nangla, it is said that there were ten famous sons, Uru and others.[124] During the current period of Vaivasvata Manu, the saptarshis are Atri, the illustrious Vasishtha, the great rishi Kashyapa, Goutama, Bharadvaja, Vishvamitra and Jamadagni, the son of the illustrious and great-souled Richika, as the seventh. They are now in heaven. During vaivasvata manvantara, the gods are said to be Sadhyas, Rudras, Vishvadevas, Vasus, Maruts, Adityas and Ashvins. During the current manvantara, Vaivasvata Manu had ten great-souled sons. Of these, Ikshvaku was the foremost. O king! O descendant of the Bharata lineage! The deeds, sons and grandsons of these extremely energetic maharshis exist in all the directions. In every manvantara, the forty-nine[125] are established in the sub-directions, to ensure the observance of dharma and the

---

[123] During the fifth manvantara of Raivata.
[124] These were the sons of Chakshusha Manu and his wife was Nangla.
[125] Maruts.

protection of the worlds. When each manvantara is over, twenty-eight of these winds go to heaven, having completed their tasks. They go to Brahma's world, where there is no disease. Others, who are full of austerities, take their places. O descendant of the Bharata lineage! O Kouravya! Including the current one, I have thus spoken to you about seven manvantaras. O descendant of the Bharata lineage! Now listen to all the manvantaras that will come. O son! Listen to me. There are actually five Savarni Manus. Of these, one is the son of Vivasvat and four are the sons of Prajapati Parameshthi. O king! They are the maternal grandsons of Daksha and the sons of Priya. These extremely energetic ones performed great austerities on the slopes of Mount Meru and became Merusavarnis. The son of Ruchi Prajapati is said to be Rouchya Manu. Ruchi had sons through the goddess Bhuti[126] and they are known as Bhoutyas. In this world, these are said to be the seven manvantaras that are yet to come. Savarni manvantara will arrive soon and the seven maharshis for this future one are said to be in heaven. Listen. Rama, Vyasa, the extremely learned Diptimanta, Atri's son, the extremely radiant Ashvatthama, descended from Bharadvaja and Drona's son, Sharadvat Goutama,[127] descended from Goutama, Galava, descended from Koushika, and Ruru, descended from Kashyapa—in future, these seven great-souled ones will become the supreme sages. O descendant of the Bharata lineage! Savarni Manu will have ten sons—Varivat, Avarivat, Sammata, Dhritimat, Vasu, Charishnu, Adhya, Dhrishnu, Vaji and Sumati. Arising at the right time, if a man always recites the names of the past and future maharshis, he obtains happiness. O son! For a full one thousand yugas, the earth, with its oceans and habitations, are ruled by kings. Thereafter, the subjects and their austerities are always destroyed.

'I will now tell you that a little more than seventy yugas, divided into krita, treta and the others, is said to be a manvantara. The recital of the names of the fourteen Manus leads to an extension of fame. O king! The Vedas and all the Puranas speak of the powers of these Vishnus and their subjects and offspring. This

---

[126] Ruchi's wife.
[127] Meaning Kripacharya.

recital is blessed. There is destruction at the end of a manvantara. There is creation at the end of a period of destruction. Even if I speak for one hundred years, I am incapable of describing this. O descendant of the Bharata lineage! O bull among the Bharata lineage! In every manvantara, we have heard about the creation of subjects and their destruction. However, some gods and brahmana rishis are not destroyed, but remain. They are full of austerities, brahmacharya and learning. It is said that when one thousand yugas have been completed, a kalpa is over. All the creatures are then burnt down by the rays of the sun. O lord! Placing Brahma at the forefront, the large number of Adityas merge into the lord Hari Narayana, the best of the gods. At the end of a kalpa, he is the one who repeatedly creates all beings. He is the eternal and unmanifest god. This entire universe belongs to him. O best among the Bharata lineage! O immensely radiant one! It is the time of Vaivasvata Manu now and the time for creation has presented itself. I will speak to you about the ancient Vrishni lineage. The lord and great-souled Hari was born there, in the Vrishni lineage.'

Chapter 8

Vaishampayana said, 'O scorcher of enemies! Vivasvat[128] was born through Kashyapa and Daksha's daughter. Vivasvat's wife was the goddess Samja, the daughter of Tvashtri. The beautiful one is famous in the three worlds by the name of Surenu. The illustrious one was the wife of the great-souled Martanda. Though she was named Samja[129] and possessed youth, beauty and the radiance of her own austerities, she was not content with her husband's form. The sun god Martanda blazed in his own energy. This burnt her body and she didn't wish to approach near. Because she had done it innocently, Kashyapa had pronounced,

[128] The sun god. Martanda is another one of his names.
[129] Meaning harmony or consciousness.

"This egg will certainly not be dead."[130] That is the reason he is spoken of as Martanda. O son! Vivasvat always possessed a surfeit of energy. Because of this, Kashyapa's son scorched the three worlds excessively. O Kouravya! Aditya, supreme among those who scorch, had three children through Samja. One was a daughter and two were Prajapatis. The first was Vaivasvata Manu and Prajapati Shraddhadeva[131] came next. Yama had a twin sister named Yamuna. Samja was unable to countenance Vivasvat's dark complexion. She constructed a form that was just like her, with the same complexion, and this was known as Chhaya.[132] O lord of men! Using her powers of maya, Samja created Chhaya, who arose. Chhaya joined her hands in salutation and bowed down before Samja. "O one with the beautiful smiles. Tell me. What is my task? Instruct me. I am standing here, awaiting your instructions. O one with the beautiful complexion! Command me." Samja replied, "O fortunate one! I am leaving for my father's abode. Without any fear, you dwell in my residence. I possess two sons and this daughter, slender at the waist. Take care of them and do not reveal to the illustrious one what has happened." Savarna said, "O goddess! Depart cheerfully. O queen! Unless my hair is seized, or unless I am cursed, I will not divulge what has transpired." Having instructed Savarna and hearing her reply, the spirited one bashfully went to Tvashtri.

'When she reached her father, her father reprimanded the auspicious one. He repeatedly directed her to return to her husband. However, the one with the unblemished form did not return. She assumed the form of a mare, went to the Uttara Kuru region, and began to roam around amidst the grass there. Taking the second Samja to be the real Samja, Aditya had a son through her and he was

[130] Kashyapa was married to Aditi and Aditi conceived Surya. At that time, Budha arrived, asking for alms. Since she was pregnant, and not because of a deliberate insult, Aditi was late in serving Budha. Budha cursed her that the egg/embryo (*anda*) would be dead (*mrita*). Kashyapa nullified the curse, using his energy. Hence, Surya is known as Martanda.

[131] Yama, the god of *shraddha*s (funeral ceremonies).

[132] Chhaya means shadow or reflection. Savarna means with an identical complexion, and Chhaya is also known as Savarna.

just like him in form. O son! The lord was just like the preceding Manu and because of this, he came to be known as Savarni Manu.[133] O son! Samja[134] was ordinary. Therefore, she was more affectionate towards her own son and not towards the elder children. Manu pardoned this. But Yama was incapable of tolerating it. In childish anger and with force, Vaivasvata Yama showed the beautiful one his foot and censured her. His mother was extremely miserable. In rage, Savarna cursed him. "Your foot will fall down." Yama went to his father, joined his hands in salutation, and told him everything. He was anxious because of the severe curse and agitated because of Samja's words. He asked his father to withdraw the curse and said, "A mother should be affectionate towards all her sons. However, she neglects us and displays more affection towards the youngest. I raised my foot towards her, but it did not touch her body. Even if I have done that in childish folly, you should pardon me. O lord of the worlds! O supreme among those who scorch! I have been cursed by my mother. O lord of the earth! Through your favours, let my foot not fall down." Vivasvat replied, "O son! You know about dharma and you are truthful in speech. There is no doubt that there must have been a grave reason for anger to have entered you. I am incapable of rendering your mother's words false. Worms will seize flesh from your foot and roam around on the surface of the earth. In that way, your mother's words will come true and you will also be freed from your curse." Aditya asked Samja, "All the sons are equal. Nevertheless, why do you display greater affection towards one?" Despite being repeatedly asked by Vivasvat, she did not reply. O descendant of the Kuru lineage! At this, the illustrious one desired to curse and destroy her. She then told Vivasvat everything truthfully.[135]

---

[133] The preceding Manu was Vivasvat Manu. Savarna has been explained earlier. Hence, because he was like Vivasvat Manu, he was known as Savarni. However, he could have also been known as Savarni because Chhaya's name was Savarna.

[134] The second Samja.

[135] The Critical Edition excises a shloka where Vivasvat seized her by the hair, preparatory to cursing her.

'Hearing this, Vivasvat was enraged and went to Tvashtri. Following the proper rites, Tvashtri worshipped Vibhavasu.[136] He comforted the one who wished to burn everything down in his wrath. Tvashtri said, "You do not deserve this excessive energy in your form. Unable to tolerate it, Samja is wandering around, amidst the grass in the forest. O lord of the earth! You will now see your praiseworthy wife, the performer of auspicious deeds. She possesses the strength of yoga and has resorted to that yoga.[137] O god! O scorcher of enemies! If this appeals to you, it is my view that I should now reduce your form and make it handsome." O descendant of the Bharata lineage! Tvashtri approached Martanda Vivasvat, raised him on a wheel and began to slice off his energy. When the energy was sliced away, his form became resplendent. He became more and more handsome and seemed to be even more beautiful. By resorting to yoga, he saw his own wife in the form of a mare. Thanks to her energy and her vows, she was incapable of being assaulted by any creature. Adopting the form of a horse, the illustrious one arrived in front of her. However, taking him to be someone else's husband, she refused to have intercourse with him and ejected Vivasvat's semen through her nose. The gods who are supreme physicians, the Ashvins, were generated from this.[138] The two Ashvins are known by the names of Nasatya and Dasra. They were the sons of Martanda, the eighth Prajapati. O Janamejaya! The sun god then showed himself to her in his beautiful form and on seeing her husband, she was satisfied.

'Meanwhile, because of what he had done, Yama suffered from great mental affliction. Therefore, in the form of Dharmaraja, he followed dharma and delighted the subjects. Because of his auspicious deeds, the greatly resplendent one obtained lordship over the ancestors and became a guardian of the worlds. Savarni Manu, rich in austerities, became a Prajapati. He will be the Manu in the future *savarni manvantara*. Since then, he has incessantly been observing austerities on the slopes of Meru. His brother obtained

[136] Surya.
[137] Thereby assuming the form of a mare.
[138] *Ashva* means horse.

the status of the planet Saturn.[139] Desiring to bring an end to the danavas, through the excess energy that was shaved off, Tvashtri fashioned Vishnu's *chakra* and it was impossible to withstand in battle. The illustrious daughter Yami was the youngest.[140] Yamuna became the best among rivers, the sustainer of the worlds. In the worlds, Manu is also referred to as Savarna. The second son is known as Shanaishchara. This is the birth of the gods. A person who hears it and nurtures it is freed from all difficulties and obtains great fame.'

Chapter 9

Vaishampayana said, 'O bull among men! Vaivasvata Manu had nine sons who were his equals—Ikshvaku, Nabhaga, Dhrishnu, Sharyati, Narishyanta, Pramshu, Nabhanedishtha as the seventh, Karusha, and Prishadhna as the ninth. O son! O lord of the earth! Before that, in a desire to obtain sons, Prajapati Manu had offered a sacrifice to Mitra and Varuna. O descendant of the Bharata lineage! These nine sons were generated because of that. O supreme among the Bharata lineage! While that sacrifice was going on, Manu summoned Mitra and Varuna and offered oblations to them. It has been heard that Ida[141] was born from this. She was divine in form. She was clad in celestial garments and adorned in divine ornaments. Manu, the wielder of the staff, told Ida, "O fortunate one! Come to me." However, Ida replied, "O supreme among eloquent ones! I have been born from a part of Mitra and Varuna. I will go to them. I cannot destroy dharma, nor be destroyed by it." Having said this to the god Manu, Ida, the one with the beautiful hips, went near Mitra

---

[139] Saturn is known as Shani, or Shanaishchara, the one who moves slowly. We haven't been told anything about Shani yet. He was the son of Surya and the shadow Samja and a brother to Savarni Manu.

[140] Of the children born through Surya and the real Samja. Yami is another name for Yamuna.

[141] Alternatively, Ila.

and Varuna. She joined her hands in salutation and spoke these words to them. "O gods! I have been born from your parts. What can I do for you?" The virtuous Ida, devoted to dharma, spoke in this way. Listen to what Mitra and Varuna told her. "O one with the beautiful thighs! O one who is beautiful in form! We are delighted at your truth, your dharma, your faith and your self-control. O immensely fortunate one! You will obtain fame as our daughter. You will also become a son who will extend Manu's lineage. O beautiful one! You will be famous in the three worlds by the name of Sudyumna. You will be devoted to dharma and will be loved in the universe. You will extend Manu's lineage." Having heard this, she withdrew and returned to her father.[142] Budha[143] desired to have intercourse with her. O king! Through Soma's son, Budha, she gave birth to Pururava. As soon as he was born, Ida became Sudyumna. O descendant of the Bharata lineage! Sudyumna had three sons who were extremely devoted to dharma. They were Utkala, Gaya and Vinata. O king! O best among the Bharata lineage! Utkala obtained the north, Vinata the west and Gaya the eastern region known by the name of Gaya.

'O son! O scorcher of enemies! When Manu entered into the sun, his sons divided the earth into ten regions. Ikshvaku, the eldest son, obtained the country in the middle. Because Sudyumna had been a woman, he did not possess the qualities required. O extender of the Kuru lineage! However, because of the words of Vasishtha, the great-souled Dharmaraja[144] gave him the status. O great king! The illustrious one, who possessed the signs of being both a man and a woman, handed over the kingdom he had obtained to Pururava, Manu's son. O bull among kings and supreme king! Narishyanta had one hundred sons. O descendant of the Bharata lineage! Nabhaga had a son named Ambarisha. Dhrishnu had a kshatriya son named Dharshnika, who was firm in battle. Sharyati had twin children. The son was famous as Anarta and the daughter was Sukanya, Chyavana's wife. Anarta's son was the immensely

---

[142] Manu.
[143] Mercury.
[144] This seems to be a reference to Vaivasvata Manu.

radiant Reva. In the kingdom of Anarta, there was a city named Kushasthali.[145] Reva's son was Raivata. He was devoted to dharma and Kakudmi was also his name. He was the eldest among one hundred sons and obtained the kingdom of Kushasthali. With his daughter, he had once gone to Brahma's world to listen to the gandharvas. O lord! Though this was a short duration for the gods, it happened to be many yugas on earth. He returned as a young man to his city, which was surrounded by Yadavas. The beautiful city of Dvaravati had been created,[146] with many gates. It was protected by the Bhojas, the Vrishnis and the Andhakas, with Vasudeva at the forefront. O scorcher of enemies! On learning the truth about what had happened, Raivata bestowed his daughter Revati, excellent in her vows, on Baladeva. Having done this, he retired to Mount Meru and resorted to austerities there. Rama,[147] with dharma in his soul, sported happily with Revati.'

Janamejaya asked, 'O bull among brahmanas! The duration that had passed was of many yugas. How was it that Raivata Kakudmi and Revati did not have to face old age? Sharyati's descendant[148] went to Meru. How are his children still on earth then? I wish to hear the truth about this.'

Vaishampayana replied, 'O bull among the Bharata lineage! O unblemished one! In Brahma's world, there never is any old age, hunger, thirst, death, or the cycle of the seasons. Kakudmi Raivata went to that world. O son! At that time, the rakshasas slew the good people in Kushasthali. He had one hundred great-souled brothers who were devoted to dharma. They were not killed by the rakshasas, but fled in different directions. O lord of the earth! O great king! Their extremely great lineage came to be known as the Sharyatis. O best among the Bharata lineage! O extender of the Kuru lineage! In all the directions, these kshatriyas, with dharma in their souls, hid themselves in many kinds of secret places. Nabhaga had two

---

[145] Identified as Dvaravati/Dvaraka. After Anarta, the kingdom was also known as Anarta.

[146] In Raivata's absence.

[147] Balarama.

[148] Raivata.

vaishya sons, who later became brahmanas. Karusha's sons were
the kshatriyas known as Karushas and they were indomitable in
battle. O Janamejaya! Because they killed their preceptor's cow, the
Prishadnas were cursed that they would become shudras. I have thus
spoken about all nine sons. O son! When Manu sneezed, Ikshvaku
was born as a son.[149] Ikshvaku had one hundred sons and they gave
away copious quantities of donations. Of these, Vikukshi was the
eldest. Since he possessed a broad chest,[150] he couldn't be worsted
in battle. He was extremely devoted to dharma and the lord became
the king of Ayodhya. It is said that he[151] had fifty sons, of which,
Shakuni was the foremost. O lord of the earth! They protected the
country of Uttarapatha.[152] O lord of the earth! Another forty-eight
of his sons, with Vasati as the foremost, protected the southern
direction. Shashada[153] went on a hunt and there was a hare that
had been earmarked for a funeral ceremony. Without offering it
at the funeral ceremony, he ate it. On Vasishtha's words, the lord
Ikshvaku abandoned him. O son! However, when Ikshvaku died,
Shashada returned and began to dwell there again. The one who
did not fight[154] had a valiant son named Kakutstha. Kakutstha's son
was Anena and Anena's son was said to be Prithu. Prithu had a son
named Vishtara and Vishtara had a son named Ardra. Ardra's son
was Yuvanashva and Yuvanashva's son was Shrava. The king who
was known as Shrava built Shravasti.[155] Shravasta's[156] son was King
Brihadashva. His son was King Kuvalashva, extremely devoted to
dharma. Having killed Dhundu, this king came to be known as
Dhundumara.'

Janamejaya said, 'O brahmana! I wish to hear the truth about
the slaying of Dhundu, because of which Kuvalashva came to be
known as Dhundumara.'

[149] *Kshut* means to sneeze. Hence the name.
[150] *Vikukshi* means one with a broad chest or belly.
[151] Ikshvaku, not Vikukshi.
[152] Literally, the northern road. The northern part of Jambudvipa.
[153] The last of Ikshvaku's sons.
[154] Shashada, because he had been banished.
[155] In Uttar Pradesh, the capital of the Kosala kingdom.
[156] The same as Shrava.

Vaishampayana replied, 'Brihadashva had one hundred sons who were archers. But the father instated Kuvalashva in the kingdom. Having instated his son in the kingdom, the king departed for the forest. However, the brahmana rishi, Utanka, restrained him from leaving.

'Utanka said, "Your task is to protect and you should act accordingly. O king! I am incapable of performing my austerities without any anxiety. The plain of the desert is near my hermitage. This is an ocean that is full of sand and is known by the name of Ujjanaka. There is an extremely terrible rakshasa by the name of Dhundu and he is the son of Madhu. He is gigantic in size and immensely strong. He cannot be slain by the gods. He hides himself inside the earth, in the vast territory that is covered with sand. To destroy the worlds, he lies down there and practices terrible austerities. O son! He exhales his breath after an entire year and at those times, the earth and all its groves tremble. A great dust arises from the wind created by his breath. The path of the sun is obstructed and the earth trembles for an entire week. There are sparks from the coal and there is an extremely terrible smoke. O son! Because of this, I am incapable of remaining in that hermitage. For the welfare of the worlds, restrain the one who is gigantic in form. When he is killed by you now, the worlds will be comforted. O lord of the earth! You alone are capable of slaying him. O unblemished one! Vishnu had granted me a boon earlier. Thanks to that, Vishnu's energy will permeate your energy. O lord of the earth! A little bit of energy is incapable of withstanding Dhundu's great energy, even if he tries for a long period of one hundred yugas. He will only be burnt down. His valour is so great that even the gods are incapable of withstanding him."'

Vaishampayana continued, 'The great-souled Utanka spoke in this way to the *rajarshi*.[157] For Dhundu's destruction, he offered him his son, Kuvalashva. Brihadashva said, "O illustrious one! O best among brahmanas! I have laid down my weapons. But there is no doubt that this son of mine will become Dhundumara." Having instructed his son that he should attack Dhundu, the rajarshi left

[157] Royal sage.

for the mountains and, firm in his vows, resorted to austerities. To kill Dhundu, with his one hundred sons, King Kuvalashva left with Utanka. On Utanka's invocation and for the welfare of the worlds, the illustrious lord Vishnu's energy pervaded him. As the invincible one advanced, a loud voice was heard from the firmament. "This handsome prince will become Dhundumara." The gods covered all the directions with celestial garlands. O bull among the Bharata lineage! Divine drums were sounded. The valiant one, best among victorious ones, advanced with his sons. Having reached, he began to dig the extensive ocean of sand. O Kouravya! He was pervaded by Narayana's energy. Therefore, the immensely energetic one had his strength reinforced. O king! His sons dug and discovered Dhundu hidden inside the sand, enveloping the western direction. Flames issued from his mouth and he seemed to whirl the worlds around in his rage. A torrential flow of water issued, as if from the great ocean. O best of the Bharata lineage! It was as if large waves of water had been stirred by the moon. Leaving aside three, the rakshasa burnt down the one hundred sons. O Kouravya! At this, wishing to destroy Dhundu, the immensely strong and greatly energetic king approached the rakshasa Dhundu. The king, who was a *yogi*, resorted to yoga. He stemmed the force of the water and used fire to pacify the water. He slew the gigantic rakshasa, whose strength was in the water. The king then showed Utanka what he had done. Utanka granted a boon to the great-souled king. "You will possess inexhaustible riches and be unvanquished by enemies. You will always be addicted to dharma and have eternal residence in heaven. Your sons, who have been killed by the rakshasa, will obtain undecaying worlds in heaven." Of the three sons who survived, Dridhashva is said to have been the eldest. Dandashva and Kapilashva were the two younger princes.

'Dhundumara's son, Dridhashva, had a son named Haryashva. Haryashva's son was Nikumbha, always devoted to the dharma of kshatriyas. O king! Nikumbha's son, Samhatashva, was accomplished in battle and Akrishashva and Krishashva were Samhatashva's sons. Their mother was Dhrishadvati.[158] She was

---

[158] She was Samhatashva's wife.

the daughter of the Himalayas and she also had a son named Prasenjit. Prasenjit obtained a wife named Gouri, devoted to her husband. Cursed by her husband, she became the river Bahuda. Her son was the great king, Yuvanashva. Yuvanashva's son was King Mandhata, who conquered the three worlds. His wife was Bindumati, Chitraratha's daughter, and her son was Shashabindu. She was virtuous and her beauty was unsurpassed on earth. She was devoted to her husband and she had ten thousand younger brothers. O king! Through her, Mandhata had two sons—Purukutsa, who knew about dharma, and King Muchukunda. Purukutsa had a son named Trasadasyu. Through Narmada, he[159] had a son named Sambhuta. Sambhuta had a son named Sudhanva, who was the afflicter of enemies. Sudhanva's son was King Tridhanva. The lord, King Tridhanva, had a learned son named Trayyaruna and he had an extremely strong son named Satyavrata. However, he was evil-minded and abducted and married a lady who had already been married to someone else, thus violating the mantras of marriage. He was driven by childishness, desire, delusion, delight and fickleness. In his desire, he abducted a maiden who belonged to someone else in the city. Scared of adharma, Trayyaruna abandoned him and full of rage, spoke many words of censure. Thus addressed and abandoned by his father, he repeatedly asked, "Where will I go?" His father told him, "Dwell with *shvapakas*.[160] O worst of the lineage! I no longer desire descendants through a son like you." Thus addressed, he followed his father's words and left the city and the illustrious rishi Vasishtha did not restrain him. O son! Abandoned by his father, the brave Satyavrata began to dwell near shvapakas. His father left for the forest. O Indra among kings! Because of that adharma,[161] for twelve years, the chastiser of Paka did not rain down in that kingdom. At that time, the great ascetic, Vishvamitra, had left his wife in that kingdom and had gone to the shores of the

---

[159] Trasadasyu.

[160] Shvapakas are sometimes equated with *chandalas*. *Shva* means dog and *paka* means to cook. Thus, shvapaka means someone who cooks dogs (eats dogs) or cooks for dogs (lives with dogs).

[161] Because there was no king in the kingdom.

ocean to perform great austerities. To sustain her youngest son, his
wife tied a noose around the neck of the son in the middle, offering
to sell him in exchange for one hundred cows. O descendant of the
Bharata lineage! The prince,[162] with dharma in his soul, saw that the
maharshi's son was being offered for sale, with a noose round his
neck, and freed him. To satisfy Vishvamitra and out of compassion,
the mighty armed Satyavrata sustained them. O son! Because he
had been bound at the neck, maharshi Koushika's son became the
great ascetic Galava and he was freed by that brave one.'[163]

Chapter 10

Vaishampayana said, 'Because of his devotion, compassion and
pledge, Satyavrata humbly sustained Vishvamitra's wife. He
slew deer, boar and buffaloes that roamed around in the forest and
tied their flesh near Vishvamitra's hermitage. Because of his father's
instructions, the king had left for the forest and for twelve years,
consecrated himself in a vow that he should not be detected by
anyone. Since he was the officiating priest and the preceptor, the sage
Vasishtha protected the kingdom of Ayodhya and the inner quarters.
However, Satyavrata was driven by his childish sentiments and his
strength. Therefore, he always bore a great deal of rage towards
Vasishtha. When his father had cast away his beloved son from the
kingdom, the sage Vasishtha had not restrained him. This was the
reason. The mantras of marriage are completed when seven steps
have been taken together. But Satyavrata did not believe in these
seven steps. O descendant of the Bharata lineage! "Vasishtha knows
dharma. However, he did not save me." These were the thoughts
and rage Satyavrata harboured towards Vasishtha. To determine
his action, the illustrious Vashishtha had used his intelligence to
evaluate the qualities. But Satyavrata did not understand this secret

[162] Satyavrata.
[163] Vishvamitra was descended from Kusha and is therefore Koushika.
Gala means throat or neck and Galava's name was derived from that.

reason. Because he was dissatisfied with what his great-souled father had done,[164] the chastiser of Paka did not shower down for twelve years. O son! "This earth finds it difficult to sustain anything. If he is able to follow this great vow, he will save his lineage. I will thereafter instate his son in the kingdom."[165] This was the view of the sage and that was the reason why the illustrious Vasishtha did not restrain his father from abandoning him. The powerful one observed that great vow for twelve years.

'There was a time when flesh could not be obtained and the prince saw the great-souled Vasishtha's cow, which was capable of yielding milk to satisfy every object of desire. O Janamejaya! Overcome by anger, delusion, exhaustion, hunger and adharma, the king slew it. He ate the flesh himself and fed it to Vishvamitra's son. On hearing this, Vasishtha was enraged. Vasishtha said, "Had you not committed two more sins again, I would have brought you down because of this cruel sin. Failing to satisfy your father, slaying a cow that belongs to your preceptor and eating meat that is not permitted—these are the three sins you have committed." Because of the three sins he had witnessed, the great ascetic addressed him as Trishanku and he came to be known as Trishanku.[166] When Vishvamitra returned, he saw that his wife had been sustained. Delighted with Trishanku, the sage granted him a boon. The prince told his preceptor about the boon he desired.[167] The fear resulting from twelve years of drought was over. While the gods and Vasishtha looked on, the sage Koushika[168] performed a sacrifice and instated him in the kingdom. His wife was named Satyaratha and she was born in the Kekaya lineage. She gave birth to an unsullied son, Harishchandra. King Harishchandra was known as Traishanka.[169] He performed a royal sacrifice and was renowned

[164] Trayyaruna, abandoning a kingdom without a king.

[165] Vasishtha was putting Satyavrata through a test.

[166] Tri means three. Shanku means cone, being used here in the sense of sin.

[167] The Critical Edition excises a shloka where Trishanku desires the boon that he might be able to go to heaven in his own physical body.

[168] Vishvamitra.

[169] Trishanku's son.

as an emperor. Harishchandra's son was the famous Rohita. Rohita's son was Vrika and Vrika gave birth to Bahu. O son! Though he[170] was born in a yuga of dharma, he was not excessively devoted to dharma. Therefore, this king was driven away by the Haihayas and the Talajanghas. Bahu had a son named Sagara and he was born with poison. He resorted to Ourva's hermitage and was protected by Bhargava.[171] King Sagara obtained the *agneya* weapon[172] from Bhargava and having slain the Talajanghas and the Haihayas, conquered the earth. O best among the Kuru lineage! The undecaying one knew about dharma and restrained the dharma followed by Shakas, Pahlavas, Paradas and other kshatriyas.'[173]

Janamejaya asked, 'Why was the undecaying Sagara born with poison? How did the immensely energetic one, the angry and undecaying king, destroy the dharma followed in the lineage of the Shakas and other kshatriyas? O store of austerities! Tell me everything about this in detail.'

Vaishampayana replied, 'O son! O lord of the earth! Bahu confronted a hardship and his kingdom was seized by the Haihayas and the Talajanghas, accompanied by the Shakas. Yavanas, Paradas, Kambojas, Pahlavas and Khashas—these five categories contributed their valour for the sake of the Haihayas. With his kingdom having been seized, King Bahu left for the forest. He gave up his life in the forest. His miserable wives followed him there. One of these was born in the Yadava lineage. Though she was expecting, she followed him. Her co-wife had given her some poison earlier. Having prepared her husband's funeral pyre in the forest, she[174] got ready to ascend it. O son! However, overcome by compassion, Bhargava Ourva restrained her. With the undecaying one, she went

---

[170] Bahu.

[171] Bahu was defeated by the Haihayas and Talajanghas and fled to the forest with his two wives. One of the wives was expecting and the other wife fed her poison (*gara*). The son was born with the poison (the meaning of the word Sagara). The sage Ourva, born in the Bhargava lineage, saved the mother and the child.

[172] Divine weapon named after Agni, the fire god.

[173] The dharma followed by them wasn't proper dharma.

[174] Sagara's mother.

to his hermitage, with the embryo and the poison. Thus, mighty-armed King Sagara was born. The great-souled Ourva performed his birth and other rites. He taught him the Vedas and the science of weapons and gave him weapons. The immensely fortunate one gave him the agneya weapon, difficult for even the immortals to withstand. Because of the strength of these weapons, he became powerful. He swiftly slew the Haihayas, like an enraged Rudra among the animals. The supreme among renowned ones spread his fame throughout the world. The king decided that he would annihilate the Shakas, the Yavanas, the Kambojas, the Paradas and the Pahlavas. Slaughtered by the great-souled and brave Sagara, they sought refuge with the learned Vasishtha and bowed down before him. On seeing them, the immensely radiant Vasishtha subjected them to a pledge. He granted them freedom from fear and restrained Sagara. Sagara followed his preceptor's words and the pledge he himself made. Having destroyed their dharma, he altered their attire. He shaved half of the heads of the Shakas and released them. He shaved the entire heads of the Yavanas and did the same for the Kambojas. He made the Paradas wear their hair loose and made the Pahlavas sport beards. The great-souled one robbed them of studies and vashatkara. O lord of the earth! O son! The Shakas, the Yavanas, the Kambojas, the Paradas, the Kolisarpas, the Mahishakas, the Darvas, the Cholas and the Keralas—all these were kshatriyas. But because of the great-souled Vasishtha's words, Sagara took their dharma away from them. The king conquered the earth through dharma. Consecrating himself in a horse sacrifice, he made the horse wander around. While the horse was wandering around along the south-eastern shores of the ocean, it was stolen and penetrated the earth. The king's sons began to dig in that region. As they dug in that spot, along the great ocean, they approached the original being, the god Hari Krishna Prajapati Vishnu, sleeping in the human form of Kapila. O great king! As he awoke, the energy from his eyes burnt down all the sons, barring four. O king! These were Barhaketu, Suketu, King Barhadratha and the brave Panchajana, the extender of the lineage. The illustrious Hari Narayana granted them the boon that the fame of the lineage of Ikshvaku would be without decay and would never fade, that the ocean would be known as the lord's[175] son and that he would dwell in heaven for eternity. The ocean accepted the offering and worshipped the king, thus obtaining the name of Sagara[176] because of his deeds. From the ocean, he also obtained the horse meant for the horse sacrifice. We have heard that the extremely illustrious one performed one hundred horse sacrifices and had sixty thousand sons.'

Janamejaya asked, 'O brahmana! Through what destiny did Sagara have sixty thousand brave, extremely powerful and valorous sons?'

Vaishampayana replied, 'O lord of men! Listen to this. Sagara had two wives and they destroyed their sins through austerities. Ourva granted them boons. One of those spirited ones accepted the boon of sixty thousand sons, the other said that the boon of a single son who would extend the lineage would be sufficient. One of them desired the boon of many brave sons, the other of a single one who would extend the lineage. The sage agreed. One gave birth to the extremely strong King Panchajana. It is in the sacred texts that the other gave birth to a bottle gourd that was full of seeds. Like sesamum, there were sixty thousand in that fetus and these cheerfully began to grow, waiting for the right time. O king! Each of these[177] was immersed in a pot that was full of *ghee* and a maid was earmarked to take care of each of these. In the course of time, ten months passed and at the right time, sons who extended Sagara's delight were born. O king! In this way, the lord of the earth had sixty thousand sons who were born from the seeds of the gourd. Through Narayana's energy having penetrated, there was also a great-souled son, King Panchajana. Panchajana's son was the valiant Amshuman. His son was Dilipa, famous as Khatvanga. O unblemished one! He went to heaven. But in a short while, he came back to life again.[178] Through his intelligence, he comprehended the truth of the three

---

[175] Sagara. Hence, the ocean is known as Saagara.

[176] That is, Saagara.

[177] The sixty thousand.

[178] King Dilipa went to heaven to visit Indra and there is a story about how he slighted the divine cow there. Here, the sense seems to be that he didn't go to heaven after death. He went on a short visit, and thus came back to life.

worlds. Dilipa's son was the great king Bhagiratha. He is the lord
who made Ganga, the best among rivers, descend and advance
towards the ocean, which is why she is thought of as his daughter.[179]
Bhagiratha's son is famous as King Shruta. Shruta had a son named
Nabhaga, who was extremely devoted to dharma. Nabhaga's son
was Ambarisha, the father of Sindhudvipa. Sindhudvipa's son was
the valiant Ayutajit. Ayutajit's son was the extremely illustrious
Rituparna. He was powerful and knew the divine art of playing
with dice. He was also King Nala's friend. Rituparna's son was
Artaparni, the lord of the earth. He also became known by the
names of Kalmashapada and Mitrasaha. Kalmashapada's son was
the famous Sarvakarma. Sarvakarma's son was known by the name
of Anaranya. Anaranya's son was Nighna. Nighna had two sons,
Anamitra and Raghu. They were supreme and bulls among kings.
Anamitra had a learned son named Duliduha, who had dharma in
his soul. Dilipa, Rama's great grandfather, was his son. The long-
armed Dilipa had a son named Raghu. Raghu's son was Aja and
Aja's son was Dasharatha. Dasharatha's son was Rama. He was
immensely illustrious and found solace in dharma. Rama had a
famous son named Kusha. Kusha's son was Atithi and Atithi's son
was Nishadha. Nishadha's son was Nala and Nala's son was Nabha.
Nabha's son was Pundarika and Pundarika's son was known as
Kshemadhanva. Kshemadhanva's son was the powerful Devanika.
Devanika's son was the lord known as Ahinagu. Ahinagu's son
was the king named Sahasva. O bull among the Bharata lineage!
In the ancient accounts, there are two famous Nalas. The first was
the son of Virasena and the other was an extender of the Ikshvaku
lineage.[180] There were extremely energetic kings in Vivasvat's
lineage, the lineage of Ikshvaku, and the foremost ones have been
recounted.[181] Vivasvat is the god who ensures the sustenance of

---

[179] This was to save Sagara's sixty thousand sons. Ganga is known as
Bhagirathi, Bhagiratha's daughter.

[180] That is, Nishadha's son.

[181] Vivasvat is the sun god and this is the solar dynasty. Ikshvaku
was Vivasvat's grandson, so Vivasvat's lineage and Ikshvaku's lineage are
synonymous.

subjects. He is the god who presides over funeral ceremonies.[182] A person who properly reads about the sun god's creation obtains offspring and proximity with the sun god.

Chapter 11

Janamejaya said, 'O foremost among brahmanas! How did Aditya Vivasvat become Shraddhadeva? I wish to hear about the supreme rites of funeral ceremonies and about the original creation of the ancestors. Who are known as the ancestors? We have heard the brahmanas say that the ancestors who are in heaven are gods among the gods. The ones who know about the Vedas also say this. I wish to know about this. What is said to constitute their categories and their supreme strength? Which of our deeds at funeral ceremonies please the ancestors? When the ancestors are pleased, what are the supreme benefits we are united with? I wish to hear about this and about the supreme categories of the ancestors.'

Vaishampayana replied, 'I will tell you about the supreme categories of the ancestors. When asked by Bhishma, Markandeya recounted them. In earlier times, when he was lying down on the bed of arrows, Dharmaraja had asked him the questions that you have asked me.[183] I will progressively tell you what Bhishma had said. Asked by Markandeya, this is what Sanatkumara had chanted.

'Yudhishthira asked, "O one who knows about dharma! If one desires nourishment, how can one obtain nourishment? I wish to hear this recounted. What should one do to avoid sorrow?"

'Bhishma replied, "If one desires all the fruits, one should please the ancestors through funeral ceremonies. One obtains this through

---

[182] The text uses the word Shraddhadeva, the god of funeral ceremonies. Here, it is being used for the sun god. However, Shraddhadeva is also Yama, Vivasvat's son.

[183] Dharmaraja is Yudhishthira. Yudhishthira asked Bhishma, when he was lying down on the bed of arrows, and Bhishma repeated what he had heard from Markandeya.

a funeral ceremony and thereafter, after death, one obtains delight. O Yudhishthira! Through the ancestors, one advances towards the desire for dharma, the desire for offspring and the desire for nourishment."

'Yudhishthira said, "Whose ancestors remain in heaven and whose descend into hell? It is said that subjects must always reap the fruits of their deeds. There is no doubt that funeral ceremonies are performed with a desire for the fruits. Three funeral cakes are always offered. How do they reach the father, the grandfather and the great-grandfather? How do the offerings at funeral ceremonies reach the ancestors? How are we capable of rendering offerings to the ancestors who are in hell? We have heard that offerings are rendered to the gods and ancestors who are in heaven. O immensely radiant one! I wish to hear about this in detail. O infinitely intelligent one! Tell me about this in detail. How are offerings given to ancestors thought to lead to salvation?"

'Bhishma replied, "O destroyer of enemies! I will tell you the truth about what happens. My father, who has gone to another world, had spoken about this earlier. At the time of a funeral ceremony, I was about to offer a funeral cake to my father. However, my father's hand arose out of the ground and seized it. That hand was adorned with ornaments and bracelets. The fingers and palm were red. This is what I witnessed in earlier times. I decided that these were not the rites laid down in the rituals. Therefore, without reflection, I laid down the funeral cake on kusha grass. At this, my father was extremely delighted and spoke to me in a sweet voice. He said, 'O best among the Bharata lineage! O unblemished one! I am pleased with you. Since you are my son, I have obtained success in this world and in the next. O one who knows about dharma! You are a virtuous and learned son. O one who is firm in vows! O unblemished one! To establish dharma in the worlds, I wished to test you. Whatever a king establishes as the yardstick of dharma is what is always held up by subjects as a measure of conduct and is followed. O best among the Bharata lineage! You have acted in accordance with the eternal dharma of the Vedas. You have my eternal and unabated affection. Therefore, I am extremely pleased with you. Out of my affection, I will bestow a boon on you, one

that is extremely rare in the three worlds. Accept it. As long as
you wish to remain alive, death will not be able to influence you.
In truth, death will only be able to exert its power after obtaining
your permission.[184] What other supreme boon do you desire? What
will I grant you? O best among the Bharata lineage! Tell me what
is in your mind.' Having been thus addressed, I joined my hands in
salutation and honoured him. I said, 'O excellent one! If you are
pleased with me, I have obtained success. O immensely radiant one!
If you wish to show me your favours, you should yourself give me
the answer to a question I will ask you.' The one with dharma in
his soul responded, 'O Bhishma! Tell me what you wish. O son!
O descendant of the Bharata lineage! I will dispel the doubt that is
there in your question.' My father was invisible and had gone to the
worlds earmarked for the virtuous. I asked him about the curiosity
that had been generated in me. 'O father! It has been heard that the
ancestors are gods among the gods. Are the ancestors the same as
the gods or are they different? Whom should we offer sacrifices to?
What offerings should be rendered at funeral ceremonies so that
the ancestors are gratified? O father! For those who have gone to
another world, what fruits are obtained from funeral ceremonies?
I have a grave doubt and great curiosity about this. O one who
knows about dharma! Tell me about this. It is my view that you
know everything.'

   "'Shantanu replied, 'O descendant of the Bharata lineage! I will
briefly tell you what you have asked. O unblemished one! Listen
to everything with an attentive mind, about the reason offerings
are given to ancestors at funeral ceremonies and the resultant fruits
and about the origins of the ancestors. O son! Together with the
gods, the ancestors are the original gods in heaven. In this world,
that is the reason gods, humans, danavas, yakshas, rakshasas,
gandharvas, kinnaras and giant serpents perform sacrifices for
them. When they are satisfied at funeral ceremonies, the universe,
with the gods and the gandharvas, is satisfied. That is Brahma's
injunction. O immensely fortunate one! Without any distraction,

---

[184] The standard story in the Mahabharata is of Bhishma obtaining this
boon after he took a vow of celibacy.

perform sacrificial ceremonies for them. That will bring you benefit and all the fruits that you desire. When you worship them, recite your name and your *gotra*.[185] O descendant of the Bharata lineage! Even if they are in heaven, they will be content and will satisfy us. Markandeya will tell you everything else that remains to be said. That descendant of the Bhargava lineage is devoted to his father and knows everything. To show his favours to me, he has come here now, to this funeral ceremony. O immensely fortunate one! Ask him.'"

'Bhishma continued, "Having said this, he vanished."'

Chapter 12

'Bhishma said, "At this, I followed his words, controlled myself and approached Markandeya. I asked him the question that I had earlier asked my father. The greatly ascetic Markandeya, with dharma in his soul, spoke to me. 'O Bhishma! O unblemished one! I will tell you the truth. Listen attentively. O lord! It is through the favours of my father that I have obtained this long life. It is because of devotion to my father than I have obtained supreme fame in this world. I ascended Mount Meru and tormented myself through extremely difficult austerities for many thousand years, until an entire yuga had come to an end. On one occasion during that time, I saw the firmament blazing in energy, as a gigantic vimana advanced from the northern mountain. On a couch on that vimana, I saw a being who was the size of a thumb. He blazed like the sun and looked like a fire inside another fire. I lowered my head in obeisance and bowed down before the lord who was in that vimana. I worshipped him with *padya* and *arghya*.[186] I asked the invincible one, 'O lord! It is my view that you are a god among the gods. Whom do I know you as?' O unblemished one! The one with dharma in his soul smiled and

[185] Family name, denoting common lineage.
[186] Padya is water for washing the feet, offered to a guest. Arghya is a gift that is given to a guest.

replied, 'A person who does not comprehend me has not undertaken excellent austerities.' In a short instant, he assumed another supreme form. Earlier, I have not seen such a form in any man."

"'Sanatkumara said, 'O lord! Know me as Brahma's eldest son, born through his mental powers. I have been generated with austerities and energy and have Narayana's qualities within myself. O Bhargava! You may have heard of Sanatkumara in the ancient accounts of the Vedas. I am he. May you be fortunate. What can I do for you? Brahma's other sons are younger than me. The lineages of those seven invincible brothers have been established—Kratu, Vasishtha, Pulaha, Pulastya, Atri and Angiras.[187] They hold up the three worlds and are worshipped by the gods and the danavas. We[188] resorted to the dharma of mendicants and immersed ourselves in our atmans. O great sage! We did not engage in desire and the dharma of generating offspring. Know me to be the child that I was born as. That is the reason I have come to be established by the name of Sanatkumara.[189] With a desire to see me, you have devotedly shrivelled yourself through austerities. Now that you have seen me, what can I do for you?'"

'Markandeya continued,[190] "Thus addressed, I replied to the eternal one. O descendant of the Bharata lineage! When the illustrious one was pleased and gave me permission, I asked him. O unblemished one! I asked the eternal one the truth about the creation of the ancestors and the fruits of funeral ceremonies. O Bhishma! The lord of the gods dispelled my doubts. Pleased in his soul, he spoke to me for many years. He said, 'O brahmana rishi! I am delighted with you. Listen to everything in detail. O Bhargava! Brahma created the gods and wanted them to be active towards him.[191] However, having been created, desiring the fruits, they

---

[187] The seven great sages, saptarshis. Marichi's name has not been mentioned explicitly.

[188] Sanatkumara, Sanaka, Sanatana and Sanandana.

[189] *Kumara* means boy or child and *sanat* means forever. He was known as Sanatkumara because he remained a child perpetually.

[190] The text does not say that it is Markandeya speaking. We have added it for comprehension, though it is obvious.

[191] Active in worshipping Brahma.

started to worship themselves. The foolish ones were cursed by Brahma. They became senseless and lost their consciousness. The worlds comprehended nothing and were also confounded. Everyone went to the grandfather and bowed down before him. To show his favour to the worlds, the lord said, "Since you have committed a transgression, you will have to perform atonement. For the sake of obtaining knowledge, go and ask your sons." Afflicted, and for the sake of performing atonement, they asked their sons. Controlling themselves, they were thus instructed by their sons, who knew about dharma, were always accomplished and possessed the insight of the truth. They were instructed about atonement for transgressions in words, thoughts and deeds. Having ascertained the truth about atonement, the residents of heaven regained their senses. Their sons told them, "O sons! You may go now."[192] Because of the words of their sons, it was as if the gods had been cursed once more. For dispelling their doubts, they went to the grandfather.[193] The god told them, "You know about the brahman. The way you have been addressed is correct and there has been no violation in this. O gods! You are the ones who generated their bodies. However, since they have granted you knowledge, there is no doubt that they are your fathers. Understand that you are like fathers to each other, the gods and the ancestors. O residents of heaven! Comprehend this." The residents of heaven returned to their sons and said, "Let us be affectionate towards each other. Brahma has dispelled our doubts. Since you have brought understanding to us, you are like our fathers. O ones who know about dharma! What is your desire? What boon can we grant you? What you have spoken is correct and there is nothing wrong in it. Therefore, because of what you have said, we have become like your sons. That is the reason you have become ancestors and there is no doubt about this. If a person observes rites, without faithfully performing funeral ceremonies for the ancestors, the fruits are obtained by rakshasas, danavas and serpents. O ancestors! When you are worshipped through

---

[192] Since they had been instructed as students, the gods had become like the sons of their sons.

[193] How could fathers become sons?

funeral ceremonies, the undecaying Soma is always worshipped
and prospers. When Soma is satisfied through funeral ceremonies,
he satisfies the world, covered with oceans, mountains and forests
and enveloped with mobile and immobile objects. If men desire
nourishment and perform funeral ceremonies, the ancestors
always grant them nourishment and offspring. The fathers and
grandfathers are always present. If a person renders offerings and
the three funeral cakes to them at funeral ceremonies and worships
them, reciting his name and his gotra, they always think of him.
O sons of the residents of heaven! Let these words be true. Let us
be fathers and sons towards each other."'" In this way, the gods
are the ancestors and the ancestors are the gods. The gods and the
ancestors are each other's fathers.'

Chapter 13

'Markandeya said, "The resplendent and illustrious god of the
gods spoke to me in this way. I again asked Sanatkumara,
the god without decay, the illustrious one who is the foremost
among the immortals, about my doubts. O scorcher of enemies! O
Gangeya![194] Listen to everything, right from the beginning. 'What
are the categories of ancestors and what are the types of worlds they
are established in?[195] Where are those gods, the extenders of Soma,
the foremost among the gods?'

"'Sanatkumara replied, 'In heaven, there are said to be seven
categories of ancestors and they are supreme among those who
meditate. Of these, four are embodied and three are without
form.[196] O one rich in austerities! I will tell you about their worlds,
their creation, their powers and their greatness. Listen. There are
three supreme categories that are the embodied forms of dharma.

[194] Ganga's son, that is, Bhishma.
[195] This is Markandeya, asking Sanatkumara.
[196] The four embodied ones are Sukala, Angiras, Susvadha and Somapa.
The three without form are Vairaja, Agnishvat and Barhishad.

I will recount their names and their worlds. Listen. There are resplendent worlds known as Sanatana.[197] These disembodied sons of Prajapati dwell there. O best among brahmanas! As sons of Viraja, they are known as Vairaja. The diverse gods follow the indicated rites and worship them. They are knowledgeable about the brahman and obtain the eternal worlds. However, because they deviate from yoga, they are reborn after one thousand yugas. But when they regain their memory, they obtain supreme *sankhya* and yoga.[198] They are successful and obtain the destination of yoga, from which, return[199] is extremely rare. O son![200] These ancestors are yogis and the extenders of yoga. Earlier, through the strength of their yoga, they invoked Soma. O supreme among brahmanas! Therefore, at funeral ceremonies, offerings must be rendered to these yogis. They represent the supreme and first creation and are named Somapas. Their daughter, born through mental powers, is the great mountain named Mena. She is the supreme wife of the Himalayas and her son is said to be Mainaka. Mainaka's son is the handsome and giant mountain named Krouncha. It is sparkling and the best among mountains, encrusted with many gems. The king of the mountains[201] had three daughters through Mena: Aparna, Ekaparna and Ekapatala as the third. These three performed austerities that were extremely difficult even for the gods and the danavas. They thus tormented the worlds, with their mobile and immobile objects. Ekaparna had only a single leaf for food. Ekapatala only ate a single *patala* flower.[202] One of them ate nothing

---

[197] We have taken this as a proper name. It can also be an adjective, meaning eternal.

[198] The six schools of philosophy (*darshana*) are sankhya, yoga, *nyaya*, *vaisheshika*, *mimamsa* and *vedanta*. The text doesn't make it clear whether sankhya and yoga are treated as separate entities here (the way we have translated it), or whether the word sankhya is merely being used as a qualifier for yoga.

[199] In the sense of rebirth.

[200] The word used is tata.

[201] Himalayas.

[202] *Eka* means one and *parna* means leaf. Hence, Ekaparna means 'one leaf' and Aparna means 'no leaf', or 'not even a leaf'. Patala is a pale red flower.

at all. Miserable and driven by maternal affection, her mother said, "Uma" and tried to restrain her.[203] The goddess, the performer of extremely difficult austerities, was thus addressed by her mother. In the three worlds, the beautiful one came to be known as Uma. All three possessed the powers of yoga and their bodies were full of austerities. All of them knew about the brahman and all of them held up their seed.[204] The beautiful Uma was the eldest and best among them. She possessed great powers of yoga and was devoted to Mahadeva.[205] The great-souled and intelligent Asita-Devala was a great brahmana and a preceptor of yoga.[206] Ekaparna was given to him as a wife. Know that, in a similar way, Ekapatala was bestowed on Jaigishavya. These two immensely fortunate ones were presented to two preceptors of yoga. The sons of Marichi are in the world known as Somapada. These are the ancestors in heaven and the gods worship them. They are renowned as the Agnishvats and all of them are infinitely energetic. Their daughter, born through mental powers, was Achchhoda, who proceeded downwards and became a river. The celestial lake, known as Achchhoda, arose from her. She saw Ayu's illustrious son, famous as Vasu, in the firmament and addressed Vasu as her father.[207] Acting wilfully, she committed this transgression in her mind. Since she desired someone else as her father, she deviated from yoga and fell down. As she was dislodged from heaven and fell down, she saw three vimanas. In these, she saw minute ancestors.[208] They were extremely subtle and indistinct and were like fires inside a fire. Distressed as she was falling down, she shrieked at them, "Save me." Addressed by her, they replied, "Do not be frightened" and stationed her in the

[203] 'U' is an exclamation and can't really be translated, unless one renders it as 'Oh'. 'Ma' means don't.

[204] They practised celibacy. Holding up the seed is normally an expression used for males. This usage is rare.

[205] She married Mahadeva.

[206] Asita-Devala are sometimes spoken of as two different sages (Asita and Devala) and sometimes a single sage.

[207] She didn't know who her real father was.

[208] The word used is *trasarenu*. This means minute. Trasarenu is the small and mobile speck of dust that is seen to move inside a sunbeam.

sky. Through their favours, the ancestors comforted her in tones of assurance. The ancestors saw that the maiden had been dislodged from her prosperity because of a transgression. They said, "O one with the beautiful smiles! Through your own fault, you have been dislodged from prosperity and are falling down. Whatever be the deeds performed by the gods in heaven, the gods receive the fruits of those deeds in exactly the same bodies. For gods, the fruits of deeds are instantaneous. For humans, they occur after death. O daughter! Therefore, you will obtain the fruits of your austerities after death." Having been addressed by the ancestors in this way, she gratified the ancestors. Driven by compassion, all of them thought of ways to show her favours. Having ascertained the truth about what was certain to occur, they told her, "O maiden! When Vasu is born as a king, you will be born as his child. Having been born as a daughter in this way, you will again obtain the worlds that are extremely difficult to get. Through the brahmana Parashara, you will give birth to a son.[209] That brahmana rishi will classify the single Vedas into four parts. Mahabhisha's sons will extend Shantanu's lineage. They will be Vichitravirya, who will know about dharma, and the lord Chitrangada. Having given birth to sons in this way, you will regain this world. Because you have committed a transgression towards your ancestors, you will have to go through this inferior birth. In the twenty-eight dvapara yuga, you will be born as the son of the king and Adrika, as the daughter of a fish."[210] Thus addressed, Satyavati was born as the daughter of a fisherman. The

---

[209] This identifies Achchhoda as Satyavati, who gave birth to Krishna Dvaipayana Vedavyasa, as Parashara's son. Shantanu married Ganga and had Devavrata (Bhishma) as a son. Subsequently, Shantanu married Satyavati and had Vichitravirya and Chitrangada as sons. In an earlier life, Shantanu was Mahabhisha.

[210] Twenty-eighth dvapara means the twenty-eight mahayuga. She was born as the daughter of King Vasu, more specifically, Uparichara Vasu. Satyavati's mother was an apsara named Adrika. Cursed, Adrika was born as a fish. Adrika wasn't Uparichara Vasu's wife. Uparichara Vasu's semen was swallowed by Adrika, in the form of a fish. Eventually, this fish gave birth to Satyavati, also known as Kali or Matsyagandha. Though the child was presented to Uparichara Vasu, he gave the daughter to a fisherman to rear.

beautiful one was born from a fish, as the daughter of King Vasu.
There is a beautiful world named Vaibhraja in heaven. The famous
ancestors known as the Barhishads reside in heaven there. Those
infinitely energetic ones are worshipped by all the diverse categories
of danavas, yakshas, gandharvas, rakshasas, nagas, sarpas and
suparnas. They are the sons of the great-souled Pulastya Prajapati.
Those great-souled and immensely fortunate ones are ascetics and
are full of energy. Through their mental powers, they had a famous
daughter named Pivari. She herself practised yoga. She was the wife
of a yogi. She was the mother of a yogi. That supreme among the
upholders of dharma will be born when dvapara yuga nears. There
will be a great ascetic named Shuka, born in Parashara's lineage.
That great yogi, a bull among brahmanas, will be born in that yuga.
Like a blazing fire without smoke, he will be generated through
the two kindling sticks that are Vyasa.[211] Through Pivari, daughter
of the ancestors, he[212] will have a daughter. He will also have four
extremely strong sons who will be the preceptors of yoga: Krishna,
Goura, Prabhu and Shambhu. The daughter will be Kritvi. She will
be Anuha's queen and Brahmadatta's mother. Having had these
offspring, the one with dharma in his soul,[213] the preceptor of yoga,
will resort to great vows. The great yogi will go to the destination
from which there is no return.[214] O sage! The ancestors without
bodies have the forms of dharma. The account about the lineages of
the Vrishnis, the Andhakas and the others begins from here.

"'I have spoken about the three.[215] O foremost among
brahmanas! Listen. I will now tell you about the other four, the
ones who are said to be embodied. Kavi's daughter was Svadha
and through her, Kavi's daughter, Agni had sons. The ancestors
named Sukala are Vasishtha Prajapati's sons. O Bhargava! They are
always radiant in the world of the gods. Brahmanas worship them

---

[211] *Arani* is a stick used to kindle fire, two being used to create the
friction. Shuka was Vedavyasa's son.

[212] Shuka.

[213] Shuka.

[214] In the sense of rebirth.

[215] The ones without form.

to obtain all the objects of desire. Through their mental powers, they have a daughter. She is famous in heaven by the name of Gou. O brahmana! In your lineage, she was bestowed on Shuka[216] as his queen. She is also known as Ekashringa and has extended the deeds of the Sadhyas. She pervades the worlds that owe their origin to the sun god. O son! In ancient times, the Sadhyas reared the sons of Angiras. To accomplish the desired fruits, the categories of kshatriyas revere them.[217] Through their mental powers, they had a famous daughter named Yashoda. She was Vishvamahat's wife and the daughter-in-law of Vriddhasharma. O son! She was the mother of the great-souled rajarshi, Dilipa. O son! In that yuga of the gods, in ancient times, the maharshis were delighted at his great horse sacrifice and sung a chant. "In performing this sacrifice, the great-souled Dilipa has been extremely controlled. Not only will he go to heaven. But he will also be a truthful and great-souled man who has witnessed it and has heard about the birth of Agni, Shandilya's descendant."[218] The ancestors known as the Susvadhas are the forefathers of Kardama Prajapati. Those bulls among brahmanas are the sons of the great-souled Pulaha. They are in the celestial world and can roam around as they will, like birds. O son! For the sake of obtaining the intended fruits, the categories of vaishyas revere them. Through their mental powers, they had a daughter, famous as Viraja. O brahmana! She was Yayati's mother and Nahusha's queen. I have spoken about three categories so far.[219] Hear from me about the fourth. Through Svadha, the Somapas were born as Kavi's sons. They are revered by the shudras, who are the sons of Hiranyagarbha. They exist in the celestial world known by the name of Manasa. Through their mental powers, they had a daughter named Narmada, supreme among rivers. She nourishes the subjects, flowing in a southward

---

[216] There may be a typo here, Shukra being intended instead.

[217] The sons of Angiras.

[218] There were two famous sages named Shandilya. One was the son of Asita and the other was Vasishtha's son. This is probably the one who was Asita's son, since this Shandilya had a disciple named Agnivesa.

[219] Sukala, Angiras and Susvadha.

direction. She is Purukutsa's wife and Trasadasyu's mother. O son! From one yuga to another yuga, when the dharma of performing funeral ceremonies goes into a decline, Prajapati Manu revives it again. O supreme among brahmanas! This was the original creation of all the ancestors, who follow their own respective dharmas. They are also collectively known as Shraddhadeva. Having first uttered "svadha",[220] when offerings are rendered to all the ancestors at funeral ceremonies, using vessels made of silver or embellished with silver, they are pleased. Soma, Agni and Vaivasvata[221] must be worshipped through oblations into a fire. If there is no fire, the water can be used.[222] If a man is devoted in pleasing the ancestors, the ancestors are delighted with him. The ancestors grant him nourishment, large numbers of offspring, heaven, freedom from disease and everything else that is desired. O sage! Rites performed to ancestors are superior to rites performed to gods. It has been said that the ancestors must be worshipped before the gods. They are swiftly pleased and are devoid of rage. They confer supreme prosperity on the worlds. Their favours are never fickle. O Bhargava! Therefore, bow down before them. O brahmana rishi! You are devoted to your father and there is no doubt that your devotion is true. I have instructed you about what is best. However, experience it directly yourself. O unblemished one! I am granting you divine eyesight and the knowledge. O Markandeya! Without any anxiety and without any distraction, see their movements. You have been successful in observing the rites. But with eyes that are made of flesh, even a person like you is incapable of seeing the yoga-based movements of the gods or the supreme movements of the ancestors.'"

'Markandeya continued, "The lord of the gods was stationed before me and spoke to me in this way. He gave me the eyesight and knowledge, extremely difficult for even the gods to obtain. Blazing like a second fire, he then went away to wherever he desired. O best

---

[220] Svadha is uttered when offerings are rendered to the ancestors. When offering are rendered to the gods, the invocation used is svaha.

[221] Yama.

[222] The ritual is symbolically performed in water.

among the Kurus! Without any anxiety, listen to what occurred and what I saw through the favours of that god. For men on earth, this is extremely difficult to comprehend.'"

Chapter 14

'Markandeya said, "O son! In an earlier yuga, there were some brahmanas who were the sons of Bharadvaja.[223] They followed the dharma of yoga, but deviated because of the wickedness of their conduct. Having acted against the dharma of yoga, they were dislodged. Bereft of consciousness and submerged in great darkness, they fell down on the shores of Manasa.[224] They were confounded. Meditating on the meaning of yoga, they never attained it and all of them were destroyed, following the dharma of time. O bull among men! Having been with the gods for a long period of time, they deviated from yoga. They were born in Kurukshetra as the sons of Koushika. In the name of performing the dharma of funeral rites for the ancestors, they will commit violence. Thus deviating again, they will be reborn in an inferior lineage. However, because of their father's favours and because of the good deeds they had committed in their earlier lives, they will remember what had occurred in their earlier lives. Controlled, they will eventually always follow dharma. Because of their own deeds, they obtained the status of being brahmanas again. Because of what they had done in their earlier lives, they regained yoga. They obtained success again and the eternal abodes. In this way, if your intelligence repeatedly turns towards dharma and you are devoted to the dharma of yoga, you will obtain supreme success. O one who knows about dharma! There is no dharma that is superior to the dharma of yoga. O Bhargava! It is the best among all kinds of dharma. Therefore, follow it. Eat in limited quantities and control your senses. If you are controlled and devoted, in the course of time,

---

[223] This is Markandeya repeating Sanatkumara's words.
[224] Lake Manasa.

you will attain the dharma of yoga. The illustrious god said this
and vanished instantly. It seemed to me that eighteen years was
like a single day.[225] I worshipped that lord of the gods for eighteen
years. Through the favours of that god, I did not suffer from any
exhaustion. O unblemished one! I did not suffer from hunger or
thirst. I did not realize the passage of time. It is only later that my
disciples told me how much time had passed."'

Chapter 15

'Markandeya said, "After speaking these words, the lord
disappeared. O unblemished one! Because of his favours,
divine sight and knowledge manifested themselves before me.
Thus, I saw the brahmanas who were the sons of Koushika. As
the lord had told me, these were the ones who had been born in
Kurukshetra. The seventh of those brahmanas was famous by the
name of Pitrivarti. He possessed goodness of conduct and was
reborn as King Brahmadatta. This king was the son of Kritvi,
Shuka's daughter. He was born in Kampilya, supreme among cities,
and his father was Anuha, best among kings."

'Yudhishthira asked,[226] "Whose son was Anuha and what was
the period during which he existed? His son[227] was the immensely
illustrious king who was foremost among the upholders of
dharma. What was the nature of King Brahmadatta's valour?
How did the seventh one become a lord of men?[228] The illustrious
Shuka is revered in the worlds. He is the soul of yoga. The
lord cannot have bestowed his daughter Kritvi, the performer
of famous deeds, on someone with little valour. O immensely
radiant one! I wish to hear about this in detail. You should speak

[225] Sanatkumara spoke for eighteen years, but it seemed like a single
day to Markandeya.
[226] Bhishma is recounting the story to Yudhishthira.
[227] That is, Brahmadatta.
[228] From among the seven brahmanas.

to me about Brahmadatta's character. How did those brahmanas conduct themselves in this world? You should tell me everything that Markandeya said."

'Bhishma replied, "O king! I have heard that this lord of men was a contemporary of the royal sage, Pratipa, my grandfather. Brahmadatta was a great king and yogi, a supreme among royal sages. He was devoted to all beings and engaged in the welfare of all beings. His friend was the immensely illustrious Galava, the preceptor of yoga, who used the power of his austerities to progressively elaborate the principles of shiksha.[229] Kandarika, with yoga in his soul, was his[230] adviser. Those infinitely energetic seven continued to be born in seven kinds of species for seven times in each, but remained each other's aides.[231] That is what the immensely energetic and great ascetic Markandeya recounted. O king! I will recount the lineage of the great-souled and ancient Pourava Brahmadatta to you. Listen. O king! Purumitra's son was King Brihadishu. Brihadishu's son was the immensely illustrious Brihatdhanu and his son was the famous king Brihaddharma, who was extremely devoted to dharma. His son was Satyajit, whose son was Vishvajit. Vishvajit's son was Senajit, lord of the earth. Senajit had four sons who were revered in the worlds—Ruchira, Shvetakashya, Mahimnara and Vatsa. This Vatsa or Vatsaka was the king of Avanti. Ruchira's son was the immensely illustrious Prithushena. Prithushena's son was Para and Para's son was Nipa. O son! Nipa had one hundred infinitely energetic sons. O Indra among kings! They were brave maharathas with possessed strength in their arms. All these kings were known as the descendants of Nipa. In that lineage descended from Nipa, there was a king who extended his fame through his deeds. He ruled in Kampilya. His name was Samara and he endeavoured to fight.[232] Samara had three

---

[229] We have interpreted shiksha as one of the six Vedangas. However, since Galava's name is associated more with a treatise on vyakarana, shiksha may well mean instruction in general.

[230] Brahmadatta's.

[231] This is probably a reference to the brahmana Galava and the kshatriya Brahmadatta.

[232] The word *samara* means fight or battle.

sons who were extremely knowledgeable about dharma—Para, Paara[233] and Sadashva. Para's son was Prithu. Prithu had a son named Sukrita, who was the performer of good deeds.[234] He had a son named Vibhraja,[235] who possessed all the qualities. Vibhraja's son was the king named Anuha. He was immensely illustrious. He was Shuka's son-in-law and Kritvi's husband. Anuha's son was the lord and royal sage Brahmadatta, with yoga in his soul. His son was Vishvaksena, the scorcher of enemies. It has been heard that because of his good deeds, Vibhraja was born again as Vishvaksena, Brahmadatta's son. Vishvaksena's son was King Dandasena and his son was Bhallata, whom Radheya[236] slew in earlier times. Dandasena's son[237] was brave and great in soul, the extender of his lineage. O Janamejaya![238] However, Bhallata's son was extremely evil in his intelligence. He became king and was the king who brought an end to the Nipas. It was because of him that Ugrayudha destroyed all the Nipas. Ugrayudha was insolent and was addicted to pride. He was always devoted to what was unlawful. When he engaged against me in battle, I slew him."

'Yudhishthira asked, "Whose son was Ugrayudha and which lineage was he born in? Why was he killed by you? Tell me that."

'Bhishma replied, "Ajamidha's son was the learned King Yavinara. His son was Dhritiman and Dhritiman's son was Satyadhriti. The powerful Dridhanemi was Satyadhriti's son. Dridhanemi's son was King Sudharma. Sudharma's son was Sarvabhouma, the lord of men. He was known as Sarvabhouma because he brought the entire earth under a single king.[239] In this lineage of Pourava, there was a great king named Mahati. He gave birth to the valiant King Sannati, who obtained his name because

---

[233] Written in this way to distinguish from Para.

[234] Sukrita means the performer of good deeds.

[235] The text says Bibhraja. But since this is subsequently written as Vibhraja, we have changed it here.

[236] Radha's son, Karna.

[237] Bhallata.

[238] Because Bhishma is speaking to Yudhishthira, this should really be addressed to Yudhishthira, though everything is being retold to Janamejaya.

[239] The word *sarvabhouma* means the entire earth.

of his righteousness.[240] Sannati's son was the extremely powerful
Karta. The great king Nipa was the lord of Panchala and was
Prishata's grandfather.[241] He was slain by his valour.[242] O son!
Ugrayudha was evil in his intelligence and was always engaged in
enmity.[243] He obtained a blazing chakra and became powerful, thus
causing the end of the Nipas. Having killed the Nipas and other
kings, he became intoxicated with pride. At that time, my father had
died and was lying down on the ground, surrounded by me and my
advisers.[244] O Indra among kings! Ugrayudha sent a messenger to me
and through him, made me hear impure words. 'O Bhishma! O bull
among the Kuru lineage! Your illustrious mother, Gandhakali,[245] is
a jewel among women. As a wife, bestow her on me now. There is
no doubt that this kingdom is prosperous with armies and all the
jewels that the earth possesses. I will give you whatever you wish
for. If you desire the kingdom, your life or your lineage, obey my
instructions. Otherwise, you will not find any peace.' At that time, I
was lying down, on a bed of grass.[246] While I was thus lying down,
he struck me with the messenger's words and they were like the
flames of a fire. O unblemished one! I thus discerned the evil-minded
one's intentions. I instructed all the commanders of my soldiers
to get ready for battle. 'O descendant of the Bharata lineage! My
blazing chakra cannot be pacified and is invincible. As soon as my
enemies see it, they run away.'[247] Vichitravirya was a child and was
dependent on me. On seeing that his[248] soul was full of rage, I made

[240] *Sannati* means righteousness or virtue.
[241] Prishata is a named used for both Drupada and Dhrishtadyumna.
Here, it is not clear who is meant by Prishata. Moreover, grandfather is
used in a loose sense and could mean any ancestor. Subsequently, Prishata
is referred to as Drupada's father.
[242] That is, Nipa was slain through Karta's valour.
[243] The Critical Edition excises some shlokas and there is a break in
continuity. With those shlokas added, Ugrayudha was descended from
Karta and it was Ugrayudha who killed Prishata's grandfather, not Karta.
[244] Bhishma was performing the funeral rites for Shantanu.
[245] Satyavati.
[246] As part of the funeral rites.
[247] These are Ugrayudha's words and should have come earlier.
[248] Ugrayudha's.

up my mind to fight. O bull among men! However, my advisers,
those who were skilled in counsels, officiating priests, those who
knew about the rites of the gods, and well-wishers restrained me.
Knowing about the sacred texts, with gentle words, they asked me
to refrain from battle. O unblemished one! At that time, they made
me listen to words that were full of reason.

'"The ministers said, 'O lord! The wicked one's chakra may
be whirling, but you are observing a period of purification. This
should never be regarded as the prime time for waging war. We
should first resort to conciliation, donations and dissension.[249] By
then, you will be purified and can engage, after having worshipped
the gods. You will make brahmanas offer beneficial offerings into
the fire. You will make brahmanas recite words of benediction.
Having then obtained the permission of the brahmanas, you can
depart for victory. At this time, one should not use weapons
and one should not enter into a battle. Since this is a time of
purification, that is what the instructions of the elders are. One
should first attempt conciliation, donations and dissension. After
that, you can slay him through your valour, just as Maghavan
killed Shambara.'"[250]

'Bhishma continued, "O lord of men! At that time, hearing the
words of the wise ones, especially the elders, I restrained myself. O
best among the Kuru lineage! At that time, I progressively followed[251]
the supreme course of action indicated by those who knew about
the sacred texts. I entreated the evil-minded one with sama and
the other techniques that the sacred texts had thought about, but
was incapable of persuading him. O son! Since he was addicted to
the adharma of desiring another person's wife, he would not be
restrained. However, because of his own deeds, censured by the
virtuous, his supreme chakra had already been controlled, though
I did not know this. Having completed the rites of purification, I

---

[249] Respectively, *sama, dana* and *bheda* (sowing dissension in the
enemy's ranks). The fourth method of handling an enemy is *danda*
(chastisement).

[250] Maghavan is Indra and Shambara was a demon killed by Indra.

[251] Sama, dana, and bheda.

left the city on a chariot, with a bow and arrows. The brahmanas pronounced words of benediction and I proceeded to fight with the enemy. Approaching him, I began to fight with my strength and the strength of my weapons. It was like an encounter between the gods and the asuras and lasted for three days. Because of the power of my weapons, he was burnt down in the forefront of the battle. O scorcher of enemies! In front of me, the brave one gave up his life and fell down. O son! During this time, when King Ugrayudha, the lord of Nipa was slain, Prishata advanced against Kampilya. O king! With my permission, the greatly radiant one obtained his own ancestral kingdom of Ahichhatra back.[252] Arjuna swiftly defeated Drupada is battle and offered Ahichhatra and Kampilya to Drona.[253] Drona, supreme among victorious ones, accepted them both. But as is known to you, he returned Kampilya to Drupada. This entire story about the lineages of Drupada, Brahmadatta and the brave Ugrayudha has thus been narrated. This is the ancient history of what transpired. When asked by Markandeya, Sanatkumara also chanted to him the fruits of funeral ceremonies, performed in a self-controlled way and that of good deeds. O great king! O descendant of the Bharata lineage! You will hear about the conduct and the seven lives of Galava, Kandarika and Brahmadatta as the third. They were yogis who followed the brahman."'

Chapter 16

'Markandeya said, "I will tell you about the supreme fruits of funeral ceremonies. O descendant of the Bharata lineage!

---

[252] Ahichhatra was the capital of North Panchala and is now in the Bareilly district of Uttar Pradesh. Since Kampilya is separately mentioned, Panchala was divided into North Panchala and South Panchala, with Kampilya as the capital of South Panchala. Kampilya is today's Aligarh.

[253] This incident has been described in the Mahabharata. There was enmity between Drupada and Drona. As Drona's student, Arjuna performed this task.

This is what Brahmadatta obtained for seven lives.[254] O unblemished one! On performing funeral ceremonies, their minds quickly turned towards dharma, even though they had oppressed dharma earlier. I will tell you about those seven brahmanas, who performed an act of adharma when they observed rites for their ancestors in Kurukshetra. Sanatkumara saw them and instructed them. Their names were like their deeds and they were Vagdushta, Krodhana, Himsra, Pishuna, Kavi, Khasrima and Pitrivarti.[255] O son! O descendant of the Bharata lineage! They were the sons of Koushika.[256] But having been cursed by their father, all of them became Gargya's disciples and started to observe vows. On the instructions of their preceptor, all of them acted properly and took his milk-yielding *kapila* cow[257] and her calf to graze. O descendant of the Bharata lineage! However, along the route, they were hungry and overcome by childish delusion. With their minds overcome by cruelty, they wanted to kill the cow. Kavi and Khasrima tried to restrain them from doing this. But they were incapable of restraining the other brahmanas. There was a brahmana named Pitrivarti among them. He always performed funeral ceremonies and ablutions. He adhered to dharma and angrily spoke to all his brothers. 'If we must do this, let all of us control ourselves and do it properly together. If we do this, there is no doubt that this cow will also achieve dharma. If we follow dharma in worshipping our ancestors, we will also not be tainted by adharma.' O descendant of the Bharata lineage! Thus addressed,

---

[254] These seven lives were as Bharadvaja (sons of Bharadvaja), Koushika (sons of Koushika or Vishvamitra), Vyadha (as hunters), Mriga (as animals), Chakravaka (as birds), Hamsa (as swans) and Shrotriya (as learned brahmanas).

[255] Vagdushta means someone who is evil in speech and is a term also applied to a brahmana who doesn't have a sacred thread. Krodhana is someone who is prone to anger. Himsra is someone who is violent. Pishuna is someone who is wicked, in the sense of indulging in calumny. Kavi is someone who is wise. Khasrima is someone who roams around in the sky, metaphorically meaning someone who is interested in the life hereafter. Pitrivarti is someone who is devoted to his father.

[256] Meaning Vishvamitra.

[257] Kapila is a brown cow and is also a term generally used for an auspicious cow.

all of them consecrated the cow, worshipped the ancestors by using it as an offering and thus used the cow.[258] They seized the calf, went to the brahmana[259] and uttered a lie. 'A tiger has killed the cow. Accept the calf.' He accepted it. Those brahmanas acted wrongly against their preceptor and resorted to falsehood. In due course of time, their lifespans were exhausted and they died. They were cruel and acted violently towards their preceptor, like those who were not *aryas*. The seven brothers were reborn as those who were fierce, conducting themselves violently.[260] O son! They were spirited and powerful and became the sons of a hunter. However, they had consecrated the cow and following dharma, had worshipped the ancestors with it. Therefore, though they were reborn as a different category of being, they retained memories of what had occurred. Those seven were born in the land of Dasharna as hunters who were accomplished in dharma.[261] All of them were devoted to their own dharma and were devoid of avarice and falsehood. They only did that much as was necessary for sustaining life.[262] For the rest of the time, they devoted themselves to dharma and reflected on their own deeds.[263] O lord of men! The names of those revered hunters, who were supremely devoted to dharma, were—Nirvaira, Nirvrita, Kshanta, Nirmanyu, Kriti, Vaidhasa and Matrivarti. O son! In the forest, though they were immersed in a dharma that required violence, they dwelt in this way, satisfying and worshipping their aged mother and father. Following the dharma of time, their mother and father eventually died. They then discarded their bows and gave up their lives in the forest. Because of their auspicious deeds, they were reborn as animals[264] that remembered their past

[258] We have translated this extremely literally. They sacrificed the cow and ate it.

[259] Their preceptor, Gargya.

[260] They were reborn as hunters, the third birth.

[261] There is a typo in the Critical Edition, which says *jama*. This makes them daughters of a hunter, which is contradictory. The word must be *jata* (born).

[262] They did not kill excessively.

[263] In the former lives.

[264] Specifically, wild animals. This is the fourth birth.

lives. As a result of the fright and the force, they were anxious and dwelt on beautiful Mount Kalanjara.[265] The names of those animals were Unmukha, Nitya-vitrasta, Stabdha-karna, Vilochana, Pandita, Ghasmara and Nadi. Since they remembered their earlier lives, they reflected on the purpose of everything. They were controlled and roamed around in that forest. They were without attachments.[266] They were devoid of opposite pairs of sentiments.[267] All of them roamed around in that forest. They followed the dharma of behaving equally towards everyone and were auspicious in their deeds. They followed asceticism. They sustained their lives on a little bit of food and avoided drinking water. O descendant of the Bharata lineage! O unblemished one! The footprints of those virtuous ones, who avoided drinking water, can still be seen on Mount Kalanjara. O son! Thus, their deeds were beyond what is good and bad. They were therefore reborn as *chakravaka* birds, moving from an inauspicious birth to a superior one.[268] As aquatic birds, those seven dwelt in an auspicious spot, on an island in a river. They were like sages who followed dharma and abandoned the dharma of looking for a mate. The names of those birds are said to be Sumana, Muni, Suvaka, Shuddha, Chhidradarshana as the fifth, Sunetra and Svatantra. Among the seven who were born, the fifth one was also known as Panchika. The sixth was reborn as Kandarika and the seventh as Brahmadatta. They performed asceticism in their seven lives. They followed the yoga of detachment and retained the wonderful knowledge of their earlier lives, what they had learnt in the household of their preceptor, about the knowledge of the brahman. Therefore, though they roamed around in this cycle of life, they were established in the brahman. All those birds followed brahmacharya and could roam around as they willed. They wandered around there, reflecting on the dharma of yoga.

[265] They were anxious because they would be hunted by predators. As hunters, they had used force and caused fright in their former lives.

[266] Such as to female deer.

[267] Happiness and unhappiness, heat and cold, enmity and friendliness and so on.

[268] This is the fifth birth.

'"While the birds were wandering around there, King Vibhraja, the lord of Nipa and descended from the Pourava lineage, arrived there, accompanied by his wives. His body was radiant and he was powerful. The handsome one was surrounded by the women from the inner quarters and entered that forest. On witnessing this kind of royal prosperity, the chakravaka bird known as Svatantra desired that he too might attain this state. 'I have performed good deeds, observed austerities and controlled myself. I have emaciated myself through fasting and asceticism. But all those have been rendered fruitless.'"'[269]

Chapter 17

'Markandeya said, "Two companions of that chakravaka bird said, 'We have always sought to bring you pleasure. We will become your advisers.'[270] Thus addressed, he[271] turned his atman and intelligence towards yoga. At this time, Suvaka addressed him. 'You are abandoning the dharma of yoga and think that the satisfaction of desire is more important. You desire an objective that is inferior. Therefore, listen to me. O son![272] You will become the king in the supreme city of Kampilya and these two friends of yours will become your advisers.' The other four birds cursed and abandoned the three who had strayed by desiring a kingdom. Those three[273] had lost their senses and had deviated from yoga. But cursed in this way, they sought refuge with their four companions. Those four were merciful and showed them their favours, Sumana speaking on their behalf. 'There is no doubt that this curse will come to an end. When that happens, you will become humans and will resort to yoga. Because of our father's favours and because

---

[269] The bird is thinking this. Otherwise, he would have been reborn as a king.

[270] If you become a king.

[271] Svatantra.

[272] The word used is tata.

[273] Reborn as Panchika, Kandarika and Brahmadatta.

of good deeds, this Svatantra will understand the language of all creatures. Earlier, while observing dharma for the ancestors, it was he who had protected the cow, thereby imparting knowledge to all of us and facilitating recourse to yoga. There is a shloka whose words will be full of meaning. In that human life, when a person makes you hear it, you will resort to yoga again.'"'[274]

Chapter 18

'Markandeya said, "Those seven dwelt in Manasa. They were devoted to the dharma of yoga. They always subsisted only on air and water and dried up their bodies. King Vibhraja, with the handsome body, went to that forest. He was surrounded by the women of his inner quarters, like Maghavan in Nandana. On seeing that the birds were resorting to the dharma of yoga, while he himself behaved like an ignorant person, the king was distressed. He went to his city and reflected about this. He had a son named Anuha, who was supremely devoted to dharma. Since he always minutely scrutinized the dharma of everything, he obtained such a name.[275] Shuka bestowed his daughter Kriti, who possessed all the revered and auspicious marks, on him. She possessed the good qualities of virtue and conduct and was always devoted to the dharma of yoga. O Bhishma! I have already told you what Sanatkumara instructed me, about that spirited and beautiful one being a daughter of the ancestors. She is supreme among those who uphold the true dharma, one that is impossible for those with uncleansed souls to comprehend. She is the embodiment of yoga. She is the wife of yoga. She is the mother of yoga. When I spoke to you about the creation of the ancestors, I told you about her earlier. Vibhraja, the lord of men, summoned the citizens and the brahmanas who pronounced benedictions. Pleased in his mind, he instated Anuha in the kingdom. With his wives, he left for the lake, so as to perform

---

[274] The shloka occurs in Chapter 19.
[275] *Anu* means a minute particle.

austerities. On the shores of that lake, he abandoned desire and tormented himself through austerities. The great ascetic gave up food and survived on air. O descendant of the Bharata lineage! His resolution was that he would unite himself with yoga and be born as a son of one of those.[276] With this resolution, he engaged himself in great austerities. Vibhraja, the great ascetic, was as radiant as the one with the rays.[277] O best among the Kuru lineage! Because of his radiance, that forest is known as Vaibhraja. The lake is also known as Vaibhraja. O king! The four birds who followed the dharma of yoga and the three who had deviated from yoga gave up their lives.

'"With Brahmadatta at the forefront, all those great-souled ones, cleansed of sin, were born in the city of Kampilya. Those four remembered their earlier births, but the other three were confused. Svatantra was born as Anuha's son, known as the immensely illustrious Brahmadatta. As a bird, he is the one who had earlier desired that he should attain this state. Chhidradarshi[278] and Sunetra were born as Vabhravya and Vatsa, as the sons of learned brahmanas, and were accomplished in the Vedas and the Vedangas. They were companions from that earlier life and became Brahmadatta's friends. The fifth was also known as Panchala[279] and the sixth as Kandarika. Panchala was accomplished in the Rig Veda and became the preceptor. Kandarika was accomplished in the chants of the Sama Veda and became the adhvaryu. Thus, they were skilled in two Vedas.[280] King Anuha's son could understand the languages of all creatures and he became acquainted with Panchala and Kandarika. They were under the subjugation of desire and addicted to sexual pleasures. However, because of what they had done in their earlier lives, they knew the truth about dharma,

---

[276] One of those birds.

[277] The sun.

[278] The same as Chhidradarshana.

[279] Alternatively, Panchika.

[280] There were four classes of priests, though the classification varied over time. The *hotri* is the chief priest and is accomplished in the Rig Veda. The adhvaryu is the assistant priest and is accomplished in the Yajur Veda, though later, the *udgatri* came to be identified with the Sama Veda. In addition, there was the brahmana or *purohita*.

kama and artha. Anuha, supreme among kings, consecrated the unblemished Brahmadatta in the kingdom and attained the supreme destination. O descendant of the Bharata lineage! Asita-Devala's daughter was unassailable in her yoga. Her name was Sannati and she was Brahmadatta's wife. Sannati was virtuous in her intelligence and conduct, devoted to the dharma of yoga. He[281] obtained the supreme maiden from Brahmadatta.

'"The four remaining chakravakas were born as companions and brothers in Kampilya, as the sons of a learned brahmana who was extremely poor. Their names were Dhriti, Mahamana, Vidvan and Tattvadarshi. Those four studied the Vedas and there were no gaps in their knowledge. They remembered what had transpired in their earlier lives. Devoted to yoga, all those accomplished ones wished to leave[282] and sought their father's permission. The father replied, 'O sons! If you abandon me in this way, that will be adharma. You have not taken care of my poverty. Nor have you obtained the merit of generating sons. How can it be proper for you to depart without tending to me?' All those brahmanas then spoke to their father again. 'We will devise a means so that you can sustain yourself. Go and approach the unblemished Brahmadatta and his ministers. Make him hear this shloka, which is deep in meaning. With a happy mind, he will give you all the villages and other objects of desire that you seek. O father! You will be able to depart cheerfully.' Having said this, all of them worshipped their senior. Resorting to the dharma of yoga, they advanced towards supreme withdrawal."'

Chapter 19

'Markandeya said, "Vibhraja[283] possessed yoga in his atman. He was united with austerities and was known as

---

[281] Brahmadatta.

[282] For the forest.

[283] The Critical Edition says Vaibhraja. Though Vaibhraja (Vibhraja's son) also makes sense, we have corrected it to Vibhraja, as that seems more likely.

Vishvaksena. On one occasion, with his wife, Brahmadatta was cheerfully roaming in the forest, like Shatakratu with Shachi.[284] The lord of men heard the voice of a male ant. Overcome by desire, it was shrieking piteously and seeking the favours of a female ant. The small female ant was angry and the male one was trying to pacify it. On hearing this, Brahmadatta suddenly burst out in great laughter. O afflicter of enemies! At this, Sannati was miserable, distressed and ashamed.[285] She spent many days without any food. When her husband tried to restrain her, the one with the beautiful smiles replied, 'O king! Since you have laughed at me, I am not interested in remaining alive.' At this, he told her the reason, but she did not believe him. O king! She angrily told him, 'This cannot be true. How can a man understand the language of an ant? That is only possible through the favours or the gods, or as a result of good deeds performed in an earlier life, or through the fruits of austerities. O king! O lord of men! It cannot be known otherwise. If you really do know it, then prove it to me. O king! Otherwise, I take a pledge that I will give up my life.' O lord! The king heard the queen's harsh words and, extremely distressed, devotedly sought refuge with the supreme among gods, the lord Narayana, the lord of all beings. The god Narayana Hari, the illustrious one who is compassionate towards all creatures, showed himself before the king and said, 'O Brahmadatta! Your welfare will be ensured in the morning.' Having said this, the illustrious god disappeared.[286]

'"The four brahmanas had given a shloka to their father. Having studied the shloka obtained from his sons, he thought that he had become successful. He wished to approach the unblemished king when he was with his ministers and on seeing him, he desired to make him hear the shloka. Having obtained the boon from Narayana, the king happily bathed his head and proceeded to enter the city on a golden chariot. Kandarika, bull among brahmanas, grasped the reins. Vabhravya was engaged in fanning with a

[284] Shachi is Indra's (Shatakratu's) wife.
[285] She thought Brahmadatta had laughed at her.
[286] Narayana appeared before Brahmadatta during the night, presumably in a dream.

whisk. The brahmana decided that this was the best time to make
the king and his advisers listen to the shloka. 'There were seven
hunters in Dasharna and they became animals on Mount Kalanjara.
There were chakravaka birds in an island in a river and we are
headed there.' O unblemished one! O descendant of the Bharata
lineage! On hearing this, Brahmadatta and his advisers, Panchala
and Kandarika, were confounded. While the citizens saw them in
this dishevelled state, the reins, the goad and the whisk fell down.
O scorcher of enemies! For an instant, the two of them and the
king remained stationed on the chariot in this way. They then
regained their senses and returned.[287] They remembered the lake
and the yoga. He[288] gave the brahmana a large quantity of riches
and objects of pleasure. He instated Vishvaksena, the scorcher of
enemies, in his own kingdom. With his wife, Brahmadatta left for
the forest. The patient Sannati, Devala's daughter, was extremely
delighted and spoke to the king, who had gone to the forest to
pursue yoga. 'O great king! I knew that you knew about the speech
of ants. However, since you were addicted to desire, I feigned to
be angry, so as to goad you. From here, we will now head towards
the supreme and beneficial destination. Yoga had vanished from
you, but I have made you remember it again.' On hearing his wife's
words, the king was extremely delighted. He regained yoga in the
forest and obtained the destination that is so very difficult to get.
With yoga in his soul, Kandarika became successful and through his
deeds, obtained the pure destination of yoga, the supreme samkhya
yoga. In due course, he composed the absolute text that is known
as Panchala.[289] The great ascetic obtained the best of fame and the
status of being a preceptor of yoga. O one without decay! This is an
ancient account that I myself witnessed. O Gangeya! If you sustain
this, you will also be united with what is beneficial. If others sustain
such supreme conduct, they will never be born as inferior species.

[287] To the city.
[288] Brahmadatta.
[289] Samkhya is one of the six schools of darshana (philosophy),
identified with Kapila. The text known as Panchala is probably the same as
the one taught by the samkhya teacher Panchashikha.

If one hears about this account, which is deep in its meaning, one obtains the great destination. O descendant of the Bharata lineage! The dharma of yoga always circles around in his heart. Amidst all these bonds, such a person always finds peace. Such people become successful and their minds turn towards the objective that is extremely difficult to obtain on earth."'

Vaishampayana said, 'In ancient times, this was chanted by the intelligent Markandeya. This is the instruction about the fruits of funeral ceremonies and the invocation of Soma. Soma is the illustrious god whose invocation brings supreme benefit to this world. In connection with the lineage of the Vrishnis, listen to the story of his lineage.'[290]

Chapter 20

Vaishampayana said, 'O king! The illustrious rishi Atri was Soma's father and was born. In deeds, thoughts and words, and through the control he engaged in, Atri ensured the welfare of all the worlds. He had dharma in his soul, was rigid in his vows and showed non-violence towards all creatures. The immensely radiant one stood with his hands raised upwards and was like a piece of wood that had become petrified. In ancient times, he tormented himself through such austerities and this asceticism is known as Anuttoma.[291] We have heard that he did this for three thousand divine years. He did not blink and stood there, holding his seed up. O descendant of the Bharata lineage! A great intelligence manifested itself in his body and that was the essence of Soma. With his soul cleansed, Soma's essence rose upwards in his body and exuded from his eyes in the form of water that issued in the ten directions and radiated them. On seeing the ten embryos, ten goddesses[292] rushed forward to nurture them, but were incapable of

[290] Soma's lineage.
[291] Meaning unsurpassed.
[292] The ten goddesses of the ten directions.

doing so. The powerful embryos violently fell down from these ten goddesses and gave rise to the one with the cool rays, the one who nourishes everything and illuminates the worlds. The directions were incapable of holding onto the embryos. Suddenly, the embryos fell down on the earth. Brahma, the grandfather of the worlds, saw that Soma had fallen down. Desiring to ensure the welfare of the worlds, he established him on a chariot. O son! He[293] was full of the Vedas, immersed in truth and possessed dharma in his soul. We have heard that the chariot was yoked to one thousand white horses. The god who was the great-souled Atri's son fell down. At this, Brahma's seven mental sons began to praise him, invoking the sacred texts. Angiras was there and Bhrigu's sons. They chanted from the Rig Veda, the Yajur Veda, the Sama Veda and the Atharva Veda, associated with Angiras. Soma's radiant energy was praised in this fashion and illuminated the three worlds, in every direction. In that foremost of chariots, he circumambulated the earth, right up to the frontiers of the ocean, twenty-one times. Some of his energy fell down on earth and from that blazing energy, the herbs were created. It is through this that the illustrious Soma, the lord of the universe, nourishes the four kinds of subjects that are there in the worlds and the universe.[294] O immensely fortunate one! Through the praise and through his own deeds, the illustrious one obtained more energy. For one thousand *padma*[295] years, he tormented himself through austerities. There are golden-complexioned goddesses who sustain the universe. The god Soma became their treasure and became famous because of his own deeds. O Janamejaya! Brahma, supreme among those who know about the brahman, granted him dominion over seeds, herbs, brahmanas and water.

'The immensely energetic one, king of kings, was thus instated as king over dominions. Through his own radiance, the supreme among radiant ones began to illuminate the three worlds. Daksha, the son of Prachetas, bestowed his twenty-seven daughters, who

[293] Soma.
[294] Those born from eggs, those born from wombs, those born from sweat (worms and insects) and trees and plants.
[295] Padma is an indeterminate, but very high number.

were great in vows and known as Dakshayanis, on Indu.[296] These
are known as the nakshatras. Soma, supreme among the Somas,[297]
obtained that great kingdom. He prepared for a royal sacrifice at
which one hundred thousand different kinds of *dakshina* would be
paid. The illustrious Atri was the hotri and the illustrious Bhrigu
was the adhvaryu. Hiranyagarbha was the udgatri and Brahma
functioned as the brahmana.[298] The illustrious lord, Hari Narayana,
was the assistant priest. They were surrounded by the brahmana
rishis, with Sanatkumara at the forefront. O descendant of the
Bharata lineage! We have heard that, as dakshina, he gave away
the three worlds to the foremost among brahmana rishis who were
assistant priests. Sinivali, Kuhu, Dyuti, Pushti, Prabha, Vasu, Kirti,
Dhriti and Lakshmi—these nine goddesses were in attendance. O
Indra among kings! He was thus worshipped by all the gods and
the rishis. He performed the bath after the sacrifice and was radiant,
illuminating the ten directions.

'He obtained prosperity that was extremely difficult to
obtain and was revered by the sages. O son! His intelligence was
confounded and his humility was destroyed. Brihaspati had an
illustrious wife named Tara. Ignoring all of Angiras's sons,[299] he
swiftly abducted her. The gods, accompanied by the celestial rishis,
entreated him. However, he would not release Tara to Angiras's
son. The immensely energetic Ushanas had earlier been a disciple
of Angiras, Brihaspati's father, and he took his side.[300] Because of
his affection, the illustrious god, Rudra, took Brihaspati's side and
seized his *ajagava* bow.[301] The great-souled one affixed the supreme
weapon known as *brahmashira* and released it at the daityas,[302]

---

[296] Indu is another name for Soma, the moon god.

[297] The Somas are also a class of ancestors.

[298] Hiranyagarbha is Brahma's name. Since Brahma cannot have been
both priests, in this case, Hiranyagarbha probably means Surya, the sun god.

[299] Brihaspati and the other sages.

[300] Ushanas is Shukra and he took Soma's side. Shukra is the preceptor
of the demons and Brihaspati of the gods, so there was always rivalry
between Shukra and Brihaspati.

[301] The name of Shiva's bow, made of horn.

[302] The text says released it at the gods, which is a clear typo.

thereby destroying their fame. The famous battle known as
Tarakamaya then waged between the gods and the danavas and it
led to great destruction in the worlds.[303] O descendant of the Bharata
lineage! The gods who survived, the Tushitas, went to Brahma, the
grandfather and original god, and sought refuge with him. Brahma
himself restrained both Ushanas and Rudra Shankara and handed
over Tara to the son of Angiras. The brahmana Brihaspati saw
that Tara was expecting and said, "This womb belongs to me and
someone else's seed shoud never be nurtured there." The foetus
blazed like the fire and she aborted it on a bed of grass. This child
became the slayer of bandits. As soon as he was born, the illustrious
one's beauty surpassed that of the gods. In their suspicion, the gods
asked Tara, "Tell us truthfully. Is this Soma's son or Brihaspati's
son?" Despite being asked by the gods, she did not say anything
in reply, good or bad. At this, the child who would be the slayer
of bandits, started to curse her. However, Brahma restrained him
and asked Tara to clarify the doubt. "Tell me the truth. O Tara!
Whose son is this?" She joined her hands in salutation and spoke
to the lord Brahma, the granter of boons. "This great-souled child,
the slayer of enemies, is Soma's son." Prajapati Soma, the one who
nurtures, inhaled the fragrance of the child's head. This intelligent
son is known by the name of Budha. In the firmament, when Budha
ascends, it causes disturbances.[304] O great king! Through him, the
princess obtained a son, Pururava, Ila's son.[305] Through Urvashi,
he had seven great-souled sons. Meanwhile, Soma was afflicted by
tuberculosis.[306] Afflicted by tuberculosis, he was helpless and his
disc started to fade. He sought refuge with his father, Atri. The

[303] Though daityas and danavas are used as synonymous terms, daityas
are the sons of Diti and danavas are the sons of Danu. They are thus cousins.
The word asura is also used as a synonym and this means the antithesis of
suras or gods.
[304] In astrology, Soma and Budha are regarded as enemies. This
probably means that Budha causes a disturbance to Soma.
[305] The princess is Ila, Vairaja Manu's daughter. Pururava was the son
of Budha and Ila. Pururava married Urvashi.
[306] Soma was cursed by Daksha, because he loved Rohini more than
the other co-wives.

immensely illustrious Atri arranged for the sin to be cleansed. Once he was freed from tuberculosis, in every direction, his prosperity began to dazzle. O great king! I have recounted Soma's birth and the deeds that extended his fame. I will now recount the names in his lineage. Listen. This account is sacred and blessed, it ensures a long life and freedom from illness. It ensures the success of all resolutions. If one listens to the account of Soma's birth, one is freed from all sins.'

Chapter 21

Vaishampayana said, 'O great king! Budha's son was the learned Pururava. He was energetic and generous and performed sacrifices with copious quantities of dakshina. He was valorous and knew about the brahman. In a battle, the enemies found it difficult to defeat him. On earth, he performed the celestial *agnihotra* sacrifice. He was truthful and his intelligence was auspicious. He was restrained in the indulgence of sexual desire. In the three worlds, his fame was always unmatched. He was knowledgeable about the brahman, forgiving, learned about dharma and truthful in speech. Abandoning her pride, the illustrious Urvashi accepted him.[307] O descendant of the Bharata lineage! For ten years, the king dwelt with her in the beautiful Chaitraratha forest, for five years along the banks of the Mandakini, for five years in Alaka,[308] for six years in Vishala,[309] for seven years in Nandana, supreme among forests, for eight years in Uttarakuru, which possesses trees that yield all the fruits one desires, for ten years at the feet of Gandhamadana and thereafter, for eight years on the summit of Meru. Extremely happy, the king found delight with Urvashi, in these best of groves, treasured even by the gods. The lord of the earth ruled over his kingdom from Prayaga, in the most sacred of

---

[307] Urvashi was a celestial apsara and Pururava was a mere man.
[308] Kubera's capital.
[309] Another name for Badarikashrama.

countries, that was revered even by the maharshis. He had six sons
who were like Indra in their energy. Those great-souled ones were
born in heaven and their names were Ayu, Dhiman, Amavasu,
Dridhayu, Vanayu and Shatayu. They were Urvashi's sons. Ayu
had five sons and all of them were brave maharathas. Nahusha
was the first to be born and Vriddhasharma, Dambha, Raji and
Anena were born after that. They were famous in the three worlds.
Raji had five hundred sons who were famous as the Rajeyas. They
were famous kshatriyas and they caused fear in Indra himself.
There was an extremely terrible battle between the gods and the
asuras. At that time, both the gods and the asuras went to Brahma
and asked, "O illustrious one! Who amongst us will be victorious
in the battle? O lord of all creatures! Tell us. We wish to listen to
your words."

'Brahma replied, "On whichever side the lord Raji fights,
wielding his weapons, there is no doubt in the three worlds
about that side being victorious in the battle. Perseverance exists
wherever Raji is. Prosperity exists wherever perseverance is.
Wherever there is perseverance, prosperity and dharma, victory
exists there."'

Vaishampayana continued, 'When the gods and the danavas
heard the god speak about Raji's role in the victory, they were
delighted. O bull among the Bharata lineage! Desiring their own
victories, they approached him. The extremely energetic king was
an extender of Soma's lineage. He was Svarbhanu's grandson and
Prabha's son.[310] Cheerful in their minds, all the daityas and the
danavas went to Raji and desiring victory, sought the boon that he
should take up his bow on their behalf.

'Raji said, "When I am victorious, if all the large number of
gods, with Shakra at the forefront, follow dharma and make me the
Indra, only then will I fight in the battle."[311]

---

[310] Svarbhanu is Rahu. Prabha was Rahu's daughter and Raji's mother,
Ayu being the father.

[311] There is an inconsistency in the Critical Edition, which doesn't exist
in non-Critical versions. The daityas and danavas have requested Raji, but
he is responding to the gods. In other versions, both sides request him.

'The danavas replied, "Our Indra is Prahlada and it is for his sake that we are trying for victory. O king! That being the case, adhere to the agreement that you contract with the gods."'

Vaishampayana continued, 'The gods told the king that if they were victorious, he would be the Indra. Thus addressed, he slew all the danavas, who deserved to be killed by the one who holds the vajra in his hand. The lord Raji destroyed the supreme prosperity of the danavas and brought their prosperity under his subjugation. He destroyed and killed all the danavas. With the gods, Shatakratu declared himself to be the son of the immensely valiant Raji. He spoke these words to Raji. "O father! There is no doubt that you are the Indra of all subjects. This is because of your deeds and because I, Indra, will be famous as your son." He heard Shakra's words and was deceived by the maya. The king was delighted with Shatakratu and signified his assent. The lord of the earth obtained a heaven that rivalled that of the gods. He had one hundred sons and they attacked Shatakratu's place in the world of heaven, known as Trivishtapa, several times. After several days had passed, the immensely strong Shakra was deprived of his kingdom. He was deprived of his fortune and told Brihaspati, "O brahmana rishi! All the cakes that were offered to me at sacrifices have been destroyed. Can you at least arrange for a jujube,[312] so that I am always capable of sustaining my energy? O brahmana! I am emaciated. I am distracted. I have lost my kingdom. I have lost my seat. I have lost my energy. I am weak. I am senseless. O lord! Raji's sons have done this to me." Brihaspati replied, "O Shakra! If this is truly what has happened, you should have told me about it earlier. O unblemished one! There is nothing that I will not do to ensure your pleasure. O Indra of the gods! There is no doubt that I will try to ensure your delight. You will soon obtain your share and your kingdom back. O son! I will act to ensure this. Let there be no lassitude in your mind." He then acted so that Indra's energy might be enhanced. The supreme among rishis acted so that their[313] minds might be overcome with confusion. They became deluded

---

[312] *Badari.*
[313] Raji's sons'.

and intoxicated with anger. They turned against dharma. They
acted against brahmanas and lost their energy and valour. Indra
regained the prosperity of the gods and the supreme state. All Raji's
sons, addicted to desire and anger, were killed. A person who listens
to this account of Shatakratu losing and regaining his state, and
sustains it, never suffers from any calamities.'

Chapter 22

Vaishampayana said, 'Nahusha had six sons who were like
Indra in their energy—Yati, Yayati, Samyati, Ayati and Aryati.
Yati was the eldest and Yayati was born after him. As a wife, Yati
obtained Kakutstha's daughter, named Gam. He resorted to the path
of salvation and became a sage who was immersed in the brahman.
Among the other five, Yayati conquered the earth and had two
wives, Devayani, the daughter of Ushanas,[314] and Sharmishtha, the
daughter of the asura Vrishaparva. Devayani gave birth to Yadu
and Turvasu. Sharmishtha, Vrishaparva's daughter, gave birth to
Druhyu, Anu and Puru. Pleased, Shukra gave him[315] an extremely
radiant chariot. It was divine and made out of celestial gold, drawn
by divine and supreme horses that were as swift as thought. He
conveyed his wife on that resplendent chariot. Yayati was invincible
in battle, even against the gods, with Vasava.[316] On that best of
chariots, he conquered the earth in six days. O Janamejaya! Right
down to you, all the Pouravas,[317] those named Pouravas, have
enjoyed that chariot. It remained in the kingdom of the descendants
of Kuru till the time of Parikshit's son.[318] After that, because of
the intelligent Garga's curse, the chariot departed. Garga had a
young son. By causing violence to him through cruel words, King

[314] Shukracharya.
[315] Yayati.
[316] Indra.
[317] Those descended from Puru.
[318] Parikshit's son means Janamejaya.

Janamejaya became guilty of the sin of killing a brahmana. The royal sage's body began to smell of iron[319] and he roamed around, here and there. Though he avoided cities and the countryside, he could not obtain peace anywhere. He was tormented by grief and bereft of his senses. The king sought refuge with Indrota, Shounaka's son. O Janamejaya![320] For the sake of cleansing the king, Indrota, Shounaka's son and supreme among brahmanas, performed a horse sacrifice for him. When he bathed after the sacrifice, the smell of iron left him. O king! Delighted, Shukra gave that divine chariot to Vasu, the lord of Chedi, and Brihadratha[321] obtained it from him. O descendant of the Kourava lineage! Having slain Jarasandha, Bhima cheerfully handed over that supreme chariot to Vasudeva.

'Yayati conquered the earth and its seven continents, right up to the frontiers of the ocean. The king who was Nahusha's son divided it among his five sons. The intelligent king gave Turvasu the south-eastern direction. Nahusha's son gave Druhyu the west and Anu the north. He instated Yadu, the eldest, in the north-east. The king who was Nahusha's son instated Puru in the middle. The entire earth and its habitations are divided into seven continents. All those regions are protected in accordance with dharma. O supreme among kings! I will next tell you about the offspring who resulted. The king cast aside his bow and arrows and gave the burden to his five sons. The unvanquished King Yayati, the lord of the earth, having cast aside his weapons, looked at the way the earth was ruled and was delighted. Having thus divided the earth, Yayati told Yadu, "O son! There is something else to be done.[322] Accept my old age. In the form of a youth, I wish to roam around the earth. When that is done, I will take back the old age from you." Yadu replied, "O king! I have promised a brahmana alms and he has not yet told me what he wants. Until that task is done, I cannot

[319] Implying that he became an outcast.

[320] Therefore, the Janamejaya who was cursed must have been different from the Janamejaya who was Parikshit's son.

[321] Vasu's (also known as Uparichara Vasu) son. Jarasandha was Brihadratha's son.

[322] Yayati was still addicted to pleasures.

accept your old age. There are many taints associated with old age.
One cannot eat and drink as one wills. O king! Therefore, I am not
interested in accepting your old age. O king! You have other sons
and you love them more than me. O one who knows about dharma!
Ask this boon of acceptance from one of the other sons." Having
been thus addressed by Yadu, the king became full of anger. Yayati,
supreme among eloquent ones, censured his son and said, "Under
dharma, has any refuge other than you been indicated for me? O
extremely stupid one! I am your preceptor and you have slighted
me." O son! Saying this, he angrily cursed Yadu. "O foolish one!
O lord of men! From now on, your offspring will never enjoy a
kingdom." O bull among the Bharata lineage! Having been rebuffed
by Turvasu, Druhyu and Anu, the king also cursed them in a similar
way. O supreme among royal sages! As I had told you earlier, the
unvanquished Yayati wrathfully cursed them. O descendant of
the Bharata lineage! Having cursed the four elder sons, the king
repeated his words to Puru. "In the form of a youth, I wish to roam
around this earth. O Puru! If you think it proper, please accept my
old age." The powerful Puru accepted his father's old age. In Puru's
form, Yayati roamed around the earth. O supreme among the
Bharata lineage! With Vishvachi,[323] the lord roamed around in the
grove of Chaitraratha, treading the path of desire and searching for
its end. When the lord of the earth saw that his desire was no longer
increasing, he went to Puru and took back his old age. O great
king! In this connection, listen to a chant that was recited by Yayati.
Through this, all desire is withdrawn, like the limbs of a tortoise.
"Through enjoying pleasure, the birth of desire is never pacified.
Instead, it increases, like ghee offered into a blazing fire. It is my
view that one cannot tread the path of contentment with all the
paddy, barley, gold, animals and women that are available on earth.
If one does not harbour injurious sentiments towards all creatures,
in deeds, thoughts and words, one obtains the brahman. Such a
person does not frighten others, nor is he frightened by them. If one
does not desire or hate, one obtains the brahman." Having said this,
with his wife, the royal sage entered the forest. For a long period

[323] The name of an apsara.

of time, he performed great austerities. He performed austerities on Bhrigutunga. At the end of those austerities, the immensely famous one gave up his body and, with his wife, obtained heaven. O great king! There were five supreme and royal sages in his lineage. They pervaded the entire earth, like the sun with its rays. O royal sage! Yadu's lineage is revered by the royal sages. Listen to it. Hari Narayana, the extender of the Vrishni lineage, was born in it. O lord of men! A man who always listens to Yayati's character obtains good health, offspring, a long life and fame.'

Chapter 23

Janamejaya said, 'O brahmana! I wish to hear the truth about Puru's lineage and also about Druhyu, Anu, Yadu and Turvasu. O supreme among brahmanas! You should progressively tell me everything.'

Vaishampayana replied, 'In connection with the lineage of the Vrishnis, first listen to your own lineage. O great king! First hear about the great-souled Puru's lineage, where you have been born. O king! I will first tell you about that in detail. O scorcher of enemies! I will certainly tell you about Puru's supreme lineage and about Druhyu, Anu, Yadu and Turvasu. Puru's son was Pravira and his son was Manasyu. Manasyu's son was the king named Abhayada. Abhayada's son was the king named Sudhanva. Sudhanva's son was Subahu and his son was Roudra. Roudra had sons named Dasharneyu, Krikaneyu, Kaksheyu, Sthandileyu, Sannateyu, Richeyu, Jaleyu, the immensely strong Sthaleyu, Vananitya and Vaneyu. O Indra among kings! He also had ten daughters, who were *putrikas*[324]—Rudra, Shudra, Bhadra, Malada, Malaha, Khala, Bala, Talada, Suratha and Gopabala. These ten were gems among women. A rishi named Prabhakara was born in Atri's lineage and became their husband. Through Rudra, he had a son named Soma. Svarbhanu struck Surya

---

[324] A putrika is a daughter who is brought up as a son, in the sense that the daughter's son becomes a heir.

and made him fall down from the firmament to earth. When the
world was enveloped in darkness, he[325] displayed his powers. As the
sun was falling down, the brahmana rishi spoke words of assurance
and Surya did not fall down from the firmament to earth. The
famous and great ascetic thus established the superiority of Atri's
gotra. In sacrifices, the gods accordingly decreed that riches should
be earmarked for Atri's lineage. The great-souled one was always
addicted to fierce austerities. Through the putrikas, he had ten sons
whose names were based on those of their mothers. O king! Those
rishis were accomplished in the Vedas and established their own
gotras. Though they were deprived of Atri's riches,[326] they came to
be known as Svastyatreyas.

'Kaksheyu had three sons who were maharathas—Sabhanara,
Chakshusha and Paramekshu. Sabhanara's son was the learned King
Kalanala. Kalanala had a son named Srinjaya who was learned about
dharma. Srinjaya's son was the brave King Puranjaya. O great king!
Puranjaya's son was Janamejaya.[327] The royal sage, Janamejaya, had
a son named Mahasala. His fame was so well established that even
the gods knew about him. Mahasala had a son named Mahamana
who was devoted to dharma. When the brave Mahamana was
born, large numbers of gods worshipped him. O descendant of
the Bharata lineage! Mahamana had two sons, Ushinara, who was
knowledgable about dharma, and the immensely strong Titikshu.
Ushinara had five wives who were born in the families of royal
sages—Nriga, Krimi, Nava, Darva and Dhrishadvati as the fifth.
Ushinara had five sons who were the extenders of the lineage. He
obtained these sons when he was old, after he had performed great
austerities. Nriga had a son named Nriga.[328] Krimi had one named
Krimi. Nava had a son named Nava.[329] Darva had one named
Suvrata. O king! Through Dhrishadvati, Ushinara had a son named
Shibi. O son! Shibi's descendants are known as Shivayas and Nriga's

---

[325] Prabhakara.
[326] Because they were the sons of putrikas.
[327] Obviously a different Janamejaya.
[328] The mother is Nrigaa and the son is Nriga.
[329] The mother is Navaa and the son is Nava.

as Youdheyas. Nava's city is Navarashtra and Krimi's is Krimila. Suvrata's is known as Ambashtha. Hear about Titikshu's offspring. O descendant of the Bharata lineage! Titikshu became the king in the eastern direction. His son was the mighty-armed Ushadratha, whose son was Phena. Phena's son was Sutapa and Sutapa's son was Bali. Though this king was born in a human womb, he used golden arrows. In ancient times, this king used to be the great yogi, Bali.[330] He had five sons who extended the lineage on earth. Anga was born first and Vanga and Suhma came after that. Next there were Pundra and Kalinga. These are said to be the Baleya[331] kshatriyas. Baleya brahmanas also extended their lineages on earth. O descendant of the Bharata lineage! Delighted, Brahma granted boons to Bali. These ensured that he would be a great yogi and would have a lifespan that would endure for one kalpa. He would also control and establish four varnas on earth. Having been thus addressed by the lord, Bali obtained supreme peace. O king! After a long period of time, he obtained that state. Hear about the five regions of Vanga, Anga, Suhma, Kalinga and Pundra and the offspring of Anga. Anga's son was the great Dadhivahana, Indra among kings. Dadhivahana's son was King Diviratha. Diviratha's son was like Shakra in his valour. He was learned and his name was Dharmaratha. His son was Chitraratha. The great-souled Dharmaratha performed a sacrifice on Mount Vishnupada and drank soma with Shakra there. Chitraratha's son was Dasharatha. He was famous as Lomapada and his daughter was Shanta. Dasharatha's son was the brave and immensely famous Chaturanga. This extender of the lineage was born through Rishyashringa's powers.[332] Chaturanga's son is famous as Prithulaksha. Prithulaksha's son was the immensely famous king, Champa. Champa's city was Champa,[333] which was earlier known as Malini. Through the favours of Purnabhadra,[334]

---

[330] In an earlier life, this Bali was the Bali of the *vamana* (dwarf) incarnation.

[331] Named after Bali.

[332] The sage Rishyashringa performed a sacrifice so that Chaturanga might be born.

[333] Champaa.

[334] A sage.

Champa had a son named Haryanga. For him, Vibhandaka used mantras and brought down the supreme mount, the elephant that could repulse enemies, down to earth.[335] Haryanga's son was Karna and his son was Vikarna. Vikarna had one hundred sons who extended Anga's lineage. All the kings in Anga's lineage have thus been recounted by me. They were great-souled and devoted to the truth. They were maharathas who had offspring.

'O great king! Now hear about the lineage of Richeyu, Roudrashva's son. O king! This is the lineage in which you have been born. O king! Richeyu's son was King Matinara. Matinara had three sons who were extremely devoted to dharma. They were Tamsurodha, Pratiratha and Subahu. All of them were devoted to dharma. They bathed themselves in the vows of the Vedas, were truthful in speech and were devoted to the brahman. O Janamejaya! There was a maiden named Ila who studied and knew about the brahman. She was bestowed on Tamsu. The royal sage Tamsu Surodha had an immensely illustrious son named Dharmanetra.[336] He was brave and devoted to the brahman. His wife was Upadanavi. Upadanavi had four sons who extended Surodha's lineage—Duhshanta, Suhshanta, Pravira and Anagha. Duhshanta's heir was the valiant Bharata. He was also known as the great Sarvadamana and he possessed the strength of one thousand elephants. Through Shakuntala, the immensely famous Duhshanta had this son, who would become an emperor. It is after Bharata that all the Bharatas have been named. O lord of the earth! O son! Bharata's sons were destroyed because of their mothers' rage. I have told you about it then.[337] O king! The great

[335] The sage Vibhandaka was Rishyashringa's father. The mount in question is Airavata, Indra's elephant. For Haryanga, Vibhandaka brought Airavata to earth.

[336] There is some inconsistency. Tamsurodha seems to have been a single name earlier. Now it seems that Tamsu had a son named Surodha and Surodha had a son named Dharmanetra.

[337] This is a reference to Adi Parva of the Mahabharata, but the story of the curse is not recounted there. Bharata had three wives. But these sons were not fit to be emperors and were cursed by their mothers. A son was born through a sacrifice, accepted by Bharata as a son, and ruled after him.

sage Brihaspati was the son of Angiras. This lord[338] had a son
named Bharadvaja, who performed a great sacrifice. Earlier, all the
sacrifices[339] performed for the sake of a son had been unsuccessful.
Therefore, when a son was born through the sacrifice performed
by Bharadvaja, he was named Vitatha.[340] Vitatha had five sons—
Suhotra, Sutahotara, Gaya, Garga and the great-souled Kapila.
Sutahotara had two sons—the great-spirited Kashika and the
lord Gritsamati. Gritsamati's sons were brahmanas, kshatriyas
and vaishyas. O king! Kashika's son was Dirghatama and his
descendants are known as the Kasheyas. Dirghatama had a
learned son named Dhanvantari. Dhanvantari's son is famous as
Ketuman. Ketuman's son is said to be the brave Bhimaratha. He
is also famous as Divodasa, the destroyer of all the rakshasas.
O king! At that time, the city of Varanasi had been depopulated
by a rakshasa named Kshemaka. O bull among men! It had thus
been cursed by the intelligent and great-souled Nikumbha.[341] The
city was uninhabited for one thousand years. When this curse was
pronounced, Divodasa, the lord of men, built a new and beautiful
city beyond the boundaries of his kingdom, on the banks of the
Gomati. Bhadrashrenya had one hundred sons who were supreme
archers. Having slain them, Divodasa, the lord of men, made the
city inhabited. Divodasa's son was the brave King Pratardana.
Pratardana had two sons, Vatsa and Bhargava. The prince
Alarka[342] was known in this world as King Sannati. The lord of
the earth destroyed the descendants of the Haihayas.[343] The great-
souled Durdama was one of Bhadrashrenya's sons. However,
because he was a child, Divodasa had shunned and spared him.
He[344] forcefully seized his ancestral kingdom back from Divodasa.

[338] Brihaspati.

[339] Performed by Bharata.

[340] Vitatha means failure.

[341] One of Shiva's attendants. There are various versions of this curse,
all involving Divodasa.

[342] Presumably Vatsa's son.

[343] Bhadrashrenya belonged to the Haihaya dynasty. Divodasa initially
killed Bhadrashrenya's one hundred sons, but spared the young Durdama.

[344] Durdama, when he grew up.

King Bhimaratha's[345] son was Ashtaratha.[346] O descendant of the Bharata lineage! O great king! Following the norms followed by kshatriyas, his young sons were killed and this brought an end to the enmity. Alarka[347] became the king of Kashi. He was devoted to the truth and to brahmanas. He ruled for six thousand and six hundred years. He was youthful in form and extended the lineage of the Kashis. Through the favours of Lopamudra,[348] he obtained an extremely long life. When the period of the curse was over, the mighty-armed one slew the rakshasa Kshemaka. The king built the beautiful city of Varanasi and reinhabited it. Alarka's son was the immensely illustrious Kshema. Kshema's son was Ketuman and his son was Varshaketu. Varshaketu's son was named Vibhu, the lord of men. Anarta was Vibhu's son and his son was Sukumara. Sukumara's son was maharatha Satyaketu. He had an immensely energetic son who became a king who was extremely devoted to dharma. His name was Vatsa and the region is therefore called Vatsabhumi. This is a region that the Bhargavas travel on. These are the sons of Angiras who were born in the Bhargava lineage. O bull among the Bharata lineage! There were brahmanas, kshatriyas, vaishyas and shudras among them.

'Suhotra had a son named Brihat. Brihat had three sons— Ajamidha, Dvimidha and the valiant Purumidha. Ajamidha had three illustrious women as wives—Nili, Keshini and the beautiful Dhumini. Through Keshini, Ajamidha has a powerful son named Jahnu, who performed the great sacrifice that is known as the immense *sarvamedha* sacrifice. While this was going on, Ganga desired to have him as her husband and advanced towards him. When he did not desire this, Ganga started to flood the sacrificial ground. O supreme among the Bharata lineage! On seeing that the sacrificial ground was being flooded in all directions, Suhotra's descendant angrily told Ganga, "I will drink up the water that you are flooding the three worlds with. O Ganga! You will instantly

---

[345] Divodasa's.
[346] Another name for Pratardana.
[347] Pratardana's grandson.
[348] Agastya's wife.

reap the consequences of your pride." The maharshis saw that
the great-souled one began to drink up the Ganga. They entreated
the immensely fortunate one and she came be known as Jahnavi,
his daughter. Jahnu married Kaveri, the daughter of Yuvanashva.
Because of Ganga's curse, half of her body later became a river.[349]
Jahnu had a beloved and valiant son named Ajaka. Ajaka's son was
Balakashva, lord of the earth. Kushika, who was extremely attached
to hunting, was his son. This king was reared with Pahlavas and
other forest dwellers. The lord Kushika tormented himself through
austerities, so that he might have a son who was Indra's equal.
Frightened that this might happen, Shakra took birth as his son.
Maghavan himself was born as Kushika's son, King Gadhi. Gadhi's
sons were Vishvamitra, King Vishvaratha, Vishvajit and Vishvakrit.
O king! His daughter was Satyavati. Through Satyavati, Richika
had Jamadagni as a son. Vishvamitra's sons are famous as Devarata
and the others. They are renowned in the three worlds. Listen to
their names. There were Devashrava and Kati—the Katyayanas are
said to be descended from them. Hiranyaksha was descended from
Shalapati and the Renuyas from Renuka. O king! The Samkritya,
Galava and Moudgalya gotras are famous. They are reknowned
as the great-souled Koushikas. Among them are said to be Panini,
Vabhrava, Dhananjaya, King Devarata, Salankayana, Soushrava,
Lohitya, Yamaduta and Karishaya. O king! There are other
Koushikas who are famous as Saindhavayanas. It has been said
that many Koushika rishis intermarried among themselves. O great
king! Because of these alliances between the brahmana rishis, the
Koushikas, and the Pouravas, many famous lineages of brahmanas
and kshatriyas emerged. Among Vishvamitra's sons, Shunahshepa
is said to be the eldest. This Bhargava, supreme among sages,
obtained the status of becoming a Koushika.[350] Vishvamitra had
seven other sons, Shabara and the others. Through Dhrishadvati,
Vishvamitra had a son named Ashtaka. Ashtaka's son was Louhi.

---

[349] There are several versions of the story, most centring around
jealousy between Ganga and Kaveri.

[350] This seems to be a reference to Vishvamitra becoming a brahmana
from the original status of a kshatriya.

'I have so far recounted those who were descended from Jahnu.
O bull among the Bharata lineage! Now hear about Ajamidha's
other line. Through Nili, Ajamidha had a son named Sushanti.
Purujati was Sushanti's son and Purujati's son was Bahyashva.
Bahyashva had five sons who were the equals of the immortals.
They were Mudgala, Srinjaya, King Brihadisha, the brave Yavinara
and Krimilashva as the fifth. These five protected a famous region.
Know that the prosperous region protected by these five, populated
by virtuous people, is Panchala.[351] "This is enough to protect this
spot." Mudgala's sons were the extremely illustrious Moudgalyas.
Through Indrasena, Vadyasvha was born.[352] The great-souled
Srinjaya had a son named Panchavana and Panchavana's son was
King Somadatta. Somadatta's son was the immensely illustrious
Sahadeva. Sahadeva's son was King Somaka. Somaka's son was
Jantu, who had one hundred sons. The youngest of these was
Prishata, the lord who was Drupada's father.

'Dhumini, Ajamidha's third queen, desired sons. O lord of the
earth! Your forefathers are descended from her. Desiring sons, the
queen immersed herself in observing vows. Desiring sons, the queen
resorted to the vow of brahmacharya. She tormented herself through
austerities for one hundred years, a feat that is extremely difficult
for women to observe. She ate auspicious food in limited quantities.
Following the ordinances, she poured oblations into the fire. O
Janamejaya! She observed agnihotra and slept on a mat of kusha
grass. When the queen was thus engaged, Ajamidha united with her.
She gave birth to Riksha, who was handsome, with a complexion like
that of smoke. Samvarana was Riksha's son and Samvarana's son
was Kuru, who abandoned Prayaga and set up Kurukshetra. This
was a beautiful and sacred spot, frequented by auspicious ones. His
lineage is extremely vast and you Kouravas are named after him. Kuru
had four sons—Sudhanva, Sudhanu, the mighty-armed Parikshit
and Pravara—whom the enemies could not vanquish. Parikshit's

---

[351] *Pancha* means five. Bahyashva felt that five sons were enough to
protect the region and no more were necessary.

[352] The Critical Editon excises a shloka that tells us that Indrasena was
the eldest of the Moudgalyas.

son is Janamejaya, who is extremely devoted to dharma.[353] The names of the other sons were Shrutasena, Ugrasena and Bhimasena. Janamejaya had two sons named Suratha and Mahimat. Suratha had a valiant son named Viduratha. Viduratha's son was the maharatha Riksha. This is the second king who possessed that name. O king! In your lineage, there have been two Rikshas, two Parikshits, three Bhimasenas and two Janamejayas. The second Riksha's son was Bhimasena. Pratipa was Bhimasena's son and Pratipa's sons were the three maharathas Shantanu, Devapi and Bahlika. O king! You have been born in a lineage that comes from Shantanu's offspring. O lord of the earth! Bahlika's kingdom was known as Saptabahvya. Bahlika's son was the extremely illustrious Somadatta. Somadatta had sons named Bhuri, Bhurishrava and Shala. Devapi became a sage who was a teacher for the gods. The great-souled Chyavana happily accepted him as an adopted son. Shantanu accepted the burden and became the king of the Kouravas.[354] O descendant of the Bharata lineage! Through Kali,[355] he had a son named Vichitravirya. This was Shantanu's beloved and unblemished son, with dharma in his soul. In Vichitravirya's field, Krishna Dvaipayana had sons named Dhritarashtra, Pandu and Vidura.[356] Pandu's son was Dhananjaya and Dhananjaya's son was Soubhadra.[357] O lord of men! Abhimanyu's son, Parikshit, was your father. O king! This is the Pourava lineage, into which, you have been born.

'I will tell you about the lineages of Turvasu, Druhya, Anu and Yadu. Turvasu's sons were Vahni, Vahne and Gobhanu. Gobhanu's son was the undefeated king, Trishanu. Trishanu's son

---

[353] Janamejaya does not need to be told this and some non-Critical versions do not have these shlokas.

[354] Devapi became a hermit. Although Bahlika was older than Shantanu, Bahlika preferred to rule over his own kingdom, rather than rule in Hastinapura.

[355] Satyavati's name.

[356] Vichitravirya died without having sons. His wives were Ambika and Ambalika and Vichitravirya's field means these wives. Krishna Dvaipayana had intercourse with Ambika, Ambalika and a servant maid. Dhritarashtra, Pandu and Vidura were respectively born.

[357] Abhimanyu, known as Soubhadra after his mother, Subhadra.

was Karandhama and his son was Marutta. I have earlier told you
about another King Marutta, who was Avikshit's son. Since this
king was without a son, he undertook sacrifices and gave away
copious quantities of dakshina. The lord of the earth had a daughter
named Sammata. As dakshina, he gave her away to the great-souled
Samvarta and obtained an unblemished son in the form of Pourava
Duhshanta.[358] O supreme among kings! In this way, like the onset of
old age, Yayati's curse penetrated the lineage of Pourava Turvasu.[359]
Duhshanta's son was Sharutthama, the lord of men. Sharutthama's
son was Akrida and Akrida had four sons—Pandya, Kerala, Kola and
King Chola. The prosperous countries of Pandya, Chola and Kerala
were named after them. O king! Druhya's son was King Babhrusena.
His son was Angarasetu, who was also known as the lord of the
wind gods. In a battle, after an extremely great encounter that lasted
for fourteen months, Yuvanashva's son killed the powerful one.[360]
Angara's son was King Gandhara. It is after him that the great
kingdom of Gandhara has been named. The horses from the land of
Gandhara are supreme among horses. Anu's son was Dharma and his
son was Dhrita. Dhrita had a son named Duduha and Pracheta was
his son. Pracheta's son was Sucheta. I have recounted Anu's lineage.

'Yadu had five sons who were like the sons of the gods—
Sahasrada, Payoda, Kroshtu, Nila and Anjika. O king! Sahasrada
had three sons who were extremely devoted to dharma—Haihaya,
Haya and Venuhaya. It has been said that Haihaya had a son named
Dharmanetra. Dharmanetra's son was Kanta and Kanta had four
sons—Kritavirya, Kritouja, Kritadhanva and Kritagni. It was from
the fourth son, Kritavirya, that Arjuna was born.[361] He possessed one
thousand arms and became the lord of the seven continents. On a chariot
that was as resplendent as the sun, he single-handedly conquered the
entire earth. For one hundred years, he performed extremely difficult

---

[358] Samvarta passed Sammata on to Duhshanta's father. But following
the putrika tradition, Duhshanta was regarded as Marutta's son.

[359] Hence Marutta didn't have any sons.

[360] Yuvanashva's son is Mandhata and he killed Angarasetu.
Angarasetu is also referred to as Angara.

[361] This Arjuna is not to be confused with the Pandava Arjuna.

austerities and tormented himself. Kartavirya worshipped Datta, who had been born from Atri's lineage.[362] The greatly energetic Datta granted him four boons. As his first supreme boon, he desired that he might possess one thousand arms. As the second, he desired that if he turned towards adharma, a virtuous person should restrain him. As the third, he desired that he should be able to conquer the earth through his ferocity, while being devoted to dharma. As the fourth, he desired that he would defeat many in battle and kill thousands of enemies, but while being engaged in an encounter, would be slain by someone who was superior in fighting. He was a lord of yoga. O descendant of the Bharata lineage! Through his yoga and his maya, when he fought in a battle, the one thousand arms indeed manifested themselves.[363] Following the proper norms and using his ferocity, he conquered the entire earth, with its continents and habitations, with its cities and its oceans. Following the decreed ordinances, he performed seven hundred sacrifices in those seven continents. O Janamejaya! This is what we have heard. In all the sacrifices, the mighty-armed one gave away copious quantities of dakshina. All the sacrificial stakes and all the sacrificial altars were made out of gold. O great king! All the gods, stationed on their ornamented celestial vehicles, and the gandharvas and the apsaras, always attended these sacrifices.

'There was a learned gandharva named Narada,[364] the son of Varidasa. He was astounded at the grandeur of all this and recited a chant. "Indeed, no other king can follow the path Kartavirya has taken and match him in sacrifices, donations, austerities, valour and learning. Even when he used his chariot to advance into the seven continents with a sword, a shield and bow and arrows, men saw that a yogi was traversing those seven continents."[365] As alms, the valiant one offered the seven continents to the fire god.[366] At this, the lord

---

[362] Datta means the sage Dattatreya.

[363] When he was not fighting, there were only two arms.

[364] Not to be confused with the celestial sage.

[365] The text does not indicate where the chant ends. This seems to be a likely place.

[366] Agni was hungry. As alms, Kartavirya offered the seven continents to Agni and Agni burnt them down. Vasishtha's hermitage wasn't spared either. Apava is Vasishtha's name.

Apava angrily cursed Arjuna. "O Haihaya! You have not spared that part of the forest which belongs to me. Therefore, though you have been successful in accomplishing extremely difficult deeds, those will be surpassed by Pandava Kouravya Arjuna, dear to Kunti. The powerful and ascetic brahmana, Bhargava,[367] will swiftly crush you, sever your one thousand arms and kill you." O afflicter of enemies! That lord of men followed dharma and used his power to protect his subjects, so that their possessions were not destroyed. Because of the great sage's curse, Rama delivered death to him. O Kouravya! This is a boon that he had himself asked for earlier. The great-souled one had one hundred sons. All of them were accomplished in the use of weapons, powerful, brave, illustrious and had dharma in their souls. But out of these, only five were left—Shurasena, Shura, Dhrishtokta, Krishna and Jayadhvaja. Of these, Jayadhvaja was Avanti's great king. Kartavirya's sons were brave maharathas. Jayadhvaja's son was the immensely strong Talajangha. It has been heard that his one hundred sons are known as the Talajanghas. O great king! Vitihotra, Sujata, Bhoja, Avanti and Toundikera—these are famous as Talajanghas and are from the lineage of the great-souled Haihayas. The names of many noble ones born in the lineage of the Bharatas are recounted. O king! Among the Yadavas, there are many performers of auspicious deeds, Vrisha and others. Vrisha's son was Madhu and Madhu had one hundred sons. These descendants of Vrisha were known as Vrishanas or Vrishnis. Since they are all descended from Madhu, they are also said to be the Madhavas. Those descended from Yadu are known as the Yadavas, though they formerly used to be called the Haihayas. If a person always recounts the story of Kartavirya's birth, his riches are never destroyed. Instead, what has been lost is regained. O lord of the earth! These are the five lineages of the sons of Yayati. O great king! Just as the five elements nurture all mobile and immobile objects, these brave ones are praised in the worlds and hold up the worlds. A king who knows about dharma and *artha* listens to the creation of these five lineages and such a lord also has his own five offspring[368]

---

[367] Parashurama.
[368] A metaphor for the five objectives mentioned later.

under subjugation. He obtains five boons that are extremely difficult to obtain in this world. These are a long life, fame, riches, sons and prosperity. O descendant of the Bharata lineage. The account of the creation of these five lineages must be heard and retained. O Indra among kings. Now hear about the lineage of that excellent man, Kroshtu. He was descended from Yadu, organized sacrifices and performed auspicious deeds. If a person hears about Kroshtu's lineage, he is freed from all sins. It is in his lineage that Vishnu Hari, the lord who extended the Vrishni lineage, was born.'

Chapter 24

Vaishampayana said, 'Kroshtu had two wives, Gandhari and Madri. Gandhari gave birth to the extremely strong Anamitra. Madri's two sons were Yudhajit and Devamidusha. From these three sources, their descendants extended the Vrishni lineage. Madri's sons had two sons, Vrishni and Andhaka.[369] Vrishni had two sons, Shvaphalka and Chitraka. O great king! Shvaphalka had dharma in his soul. Therefore, wherever he happened to be, there was no disease. Nor was there fear or drought. O supreme among the Bharata lineage! On one occasion, the lord who is the chastiser of Paka[370] did not rain down in the kingdom of the king of Kashi for three years. He[371] made the extremely revered Shvaphalka reside in his kingdom and Harivahana[372] showered down. In return, the king of Kashi bestowed his daughter on Shvaphalka as a wife. Every day, she used to give a cow to a brahmana. So she was known as Gamdini.[373] Shvaphalka's son was Akrura. He was generous and persevering and performed sacrifices. He was learned and devoted

---

[369] Vrishni and Andhaka were actually the sons of Yudhajit, but the text has 'sons' in the plural.

[370] Indra. Indra killed a demon named Paka.

[371] The king of Kashi.

[372] The one with the tawny horses, Indra's name.

[373] Meaning, giver of a cow.

to guests. He gave away large quantities of dakshina. There were also Upamadgu, Madgu, Mridura, Arimejaya, Arikshepa, Upeksha, Shatrughna, Arimardana, Charmavrit, Yudhivarma, Gridhra, Bhoja, Antaka, Avaha and Prativaha.[374] There was a beautiful daughter named Sundari. O descendant of the Kuru lineage! Through the beautiful-limbed Ugrasena,[375] Akrura had two sons named Prasena and Upadeva, who were as radiant as the gods. Chitraka had sons named Prithu, Viprithu, Ashvagriva, Ashvabahu, Suparshvaka, Gaveshana, Arishtanemi, Ashva, Sudharma, Dharmabhrit, Subahu and Bahubahu. He had two daughters named Shravishtha and Shravana.

'Through Ashmaki, Devamidhusha had a son named Shura. Shura had ten sons through his queen, Bhojya. The eldest was Vasudeva, also known as Anakadundubhi.[376] When he was born, drums were sounded in the firmament. A great sound of drums arose in heaven and a large shower of flowers rained down on Shura's house. In the entire world of men on earth, there was no one equal to Vasudeva in beauty. He was best among men and his beauty was like that of the full moon. After this were born Devabhaga, Devashrava, Anadhrishti, Kanavaka, Vatsavan, Grinjima, Shyama, Shamika and Gandusha. There were also five beautiful daughters— Prithukirti, Pritha, Shrutadevi, Shrutashrava and Rajadhidevi. Each of these was a mother of brave sons. Kunta married Shrutadevi. The king of Chedi married Shrutashrava and their son was the immensely strong Shishupala. In an earlier life, he was Hiranyakashipu, the king of the daityas. Vriddhasharma married Prithukirti. Their son was the immensely strong Dantavaktra, the lord of Karusha. Pritha was adoped as a daughter[377] and the Kounteyas were born, carrying forward Pandu's line. King Yudhishthira, who knew about dharma, was born from her and Dharma. Bhimasena was born from the wind god. Dhananjaya was born from Indra and became a brave *atiratha*,[378] Shakra's equal in valour.

[374] The names of Akrura's brothers.

[375] Ugrasenaa.

[376] Krishna's father. *Anaka* means a drum (or thunder cloud), *dundubhi* also means a drum.

[377] By Kuntibhoja.

[378] An unmatched warrior, superior to a maharatha.

'Anamitra's son was Shini, the youngest of those in the Vrishni lineage. Shini's son was Satyaka and Satyaka's son was Yuyudhana Satyaki. Devabhaga had an immensely fortunate son named Uddhava. He was said to be supremely learned, like Devashrava. Through Ashmaki, the illustrious Anadhrishti had a son named Nikritashatru. Shrutadeva[379] had a son named Shatrughna. It has been heard that Shrutadeva had another son who was brought up by the ignoble Nishadas. O great king! He was reared by the Nishadas and his name was Ekalavya. Vatsavan had no sons. Therefore, the powerful Vasudeva, Shura's son, gave him his own son Koushika. Gandusha was also without sons, until Vishvaksena[380] gave him four sons—Charudeshna, Sucharu, Panchala and Kritalakshana. O bull among the Bharata lineage! Rukmini's mighty-armed and brave son is the youngest of them all and never retreats from battle.[381] Whenever Charudeshna advanced, thousands of crows followed him at the rear, wishing to feed on the ones that Charudeshna would slay. Tantrija and Tantripala were Kanavaka's sons. Grinjima had two brave sons named Vira and Ashvahanu. Shyama's son was Sumitra. Shamika obtained a kingdom. His son was Ajatashatru, the destroyer of enemies. I will now recount the names of Vasudeva's sons. Listen. Originating from three sources, the Vrishnis had many extremely energetic branches. A person who nurtures this account never suffers from a calamity.'

Chapter 25

Vaishampayana said, 'O king! Bahlika's daughter was Rohini, descended from the Puru lineage. O great king! She was Anakadundubhi's favourite and eldest wife. Through her, he obtained his eldest son, Rama.[382] The other sons were Sarana,

---

[379] Identical to Devashrava.

[380] Vishnu.

[381] This doesn't belong. Rukmini married Krishna and their son was Pradyumna. But Krishna hasn't been born yet.

[382] Balarama.

Shatha, Durdama, Damana, Shvabhra, Pindaraka and Kushinara.
O descendant of the Kuru lineage. Rohini also had a daughter
named Chitra, who was given the new name of Subhadra and
was known by it. Through Devaki, Vasudeva had the immensely
illustrious Shouri[383] as a son. Through Revati, Rama had a beloved
son named Nishatha. Through Subhadra, Partha had the charioteer
Abhimanyu as a son. Through the princess of Kashi, Akrura had
Satyaketu as a son.[384] Vasudeva had seven immensely fortunate
wives. Listen to the names of the brave sons that he had. Bhoja
and Vijaya were sons through Shantidevi. Vrikadeva and Gada
were sons through Sunama. The great-souled Agavaha was a son
through Vrikadevi, who was the daughter of the king of Trigarta,
whose priest was Shishirayana. He had a question about virility
and to test the manliness, placed his hand on the testicles.[385] Having
been falsely accused, Gargya was overcome by rage and for twelve
years, his complexion assumed the hue of black iron. To prove the
accusation wrong, he proceeded to have intercourse with a cowherd
girl. However, the cowherd girl was actually an apsara who had
assumed the attire of a cowherd girl. Though the unblemished
Gargya's seed was extremely difficult to hold, she nurtured the
embryo. It was on the instructions of the wielder of the trident[386]
that she had assumed human form and became Gargya's wife. She
thus gave birth to the immensely strong king known as Kalayavana.
In a battle, the front half of his body looked like that of a bull, while
the rear half looked like that of a horse. The king of the *yavanas*
was without a son and reared the child in the interior quarters of his
palace.[387] O great king! That is the reason he came to be known as
Kalayavana. When he became a king, desiring to fight, he asked the

[383] Shura's descendant, meaning Krishna.

[384] This sentence doesn't belong here.

[385] This requires explanation. Gargya was the priest of the Yadavas and
was Shishirayana's brother-in-law. Doubting Gargya's virility and taking
him to be a eunuch, Shishirayana placed a hand on Gargya's testicles.

[386] Shiva. Gargya was devoted to Shiva.

[387] This requires explanation again. Having given birth to the child, the
apsara vanished and Gargya handed the child over to a king of the yavanas.
The yavanas are Ionians or Greeks.

best among the brahmanas about whom he should fight with. The lord Narada told him about the Vrishni and Andhaka lineages. He attacked Mathura with an *akshouhini* of soldiers.[388] Once there, he sent a messenger to the houses of the Vrishnis and the Andhakas. With the immensely intelligent Krishna at the forefront, scared as they were of Jarasandha, the Vrishnis and the Andhakas consulted among themselves.[389] Though this is not what they desired, all of them resolved to flee. Showing their respect for the wielder of the *pinaka*,[390] they abandoned the beautiful city of Mathura. They desired to set up their homes in Kushasthali Dvaravati. If a person is pure and is controlled in his senses, and if he listens to the account of Krishna's birth on auspicious occasions, he becomes happy and learned and does not suffer from any debts.'

Chapter 26

Vaishampayana said, 'Kroshtu had an immensely illustrious son named Vrinjivan. Vrinjivan's son was Svahi, supreme among those who offered oblations to the gods. Svahi's son was King Rushadgu, supreme among eloquent ones. Rushadgu performed a great sacrifice at which many kinds of dakshina were offered, so that he might have one hundred sons. The foremost among them was the colourful Chitraratha, with many kinds of deeds. Chitraratha's son was the brave Shashabindu. He was a supreme royal sage who undertook sacrifices at which large quantities of dakshina were offered. King Prithushrava, extensive in fame, was Shashabindu's son. He was praised as someone who knew about the Puranas. Prithushrava's son was Antara. Antara's son was Suyajna. Suyajna's son was Ushata, who performed all the

---

[388] An akshouhini is an army and consists of 21,870 chariots, 21,870 elephants, 65,610 horses and 109,350 infantry men.

[389] Jarasandha attacked Mathura eighteen times and made the Yadavas flee to Dvaraka. In some accounts, Kalayavana was Jarasandha's general.

[390] Shiva, Kalayavana having been born through Shiva's favours.

sacrifices. Ushata was supreme among those who uphold their own dharma. Shineyu, the tormentor of enemies, was Ushata's son. Marutta, the king who was a royal sage, was his son. Marutta's eldest son was Kambalabarhisha. Thinking about the world hereafter, he performed supreme dharma. Kambalabarhisha desired one hundred sons. After those one hundred sons, he obtained Rukmakavacha as a son. In a battle, Rukmakavacha killed one hundred armoured archers, shooting sharp arrows from his bow. He then attained the supreme end.[391] Rukmakavacha's son was Parajita, the slayer of enemy heroes. Parajita had five immensely valiant sons named Rukmeshu, Prithurukma, Jyamagha, Palita and Hari. Their father gave away Palita and Hari to the king of Videha. Rukmeshu became the king and Prithurukma supported him. The two of them banished Jyamagha from the kingdom and he started to dwell in a hermitage. He found peace in the forest, until he was goaded by some brahmanas. He then mounted a chariot and hoisting a standard, headed for another country. He dwelt alone on the banks of the Narmada, in a city named Mrittikavati, which was on the Narmada. Having conquered Mount Rikshavanta, he next began to dwell in Shuktimati. Jyamagha's wife was Chaitra and she was aged and virtuous. Though the king was without a son, he did not take another wife. Having been victorious in a battle, he obtained a maiden. Scared, the lord of men went to his wife and said, "This is a daughter-in-law." On hearing this, she asked, "Whose daughter-in-law is she?" He replied, "She will be the wife of the son you give birth to." The maiden then resorted to fierce austerities. Because of that immensely fortunate maiden, the virtuous and aged Chaitra had a son named Vidarbha. Through the learned princess who became a daughter-in-law, Vidarbha later had two brave sons, Kratha and Koushika. They were accomplished in fighting. Vidarbha had another son named Bhima and Bhima's son was Kunti. Kunti had a son named Dhrishta, who was powerful and irresistible in battle. Dhrishta had three brave sons who were extremely devoted to dharma. Their names were Avanta, Dasharha and the powerful Vishnuhara. Dasharha's son was Vyoma and his

---

[391] Died in battle.

son was Jimuta. Jimuta's son was Vrikati and Bhimaratha was his son. Bhimaratha had a son named Navaratha. Navaratha had a son named Dasharatha and Shakuni was his son. Shakuni's son was Karambha and Karambha's son was King Devarata. Devakshatra was his son. Devakshatra's son was the great-souled Daivakshatri. Devakshatra's beloved son seemed to have been born in the womb of the gods. Since his speech was sweet, he was known as Madhu[392] and his lineage is known as that of King Madhu. O extender of the Kuru lineage! Through a princess of Vidarbha, Madhu had a son named Purutvan, who was supreme among men. His mother was a princess of Vidarbha named Bhadravati. His[393] wife belonged to the Ikshvaku lineage. With her as a mother, he had a son named Sattvata. He possessed spirit and all the qualities and extended his fame. A person who knows about the offspring of the great-souled Jyamagha obtains supreme delight and is blessed with offspring.'

Chapter 27

Vaishampayana said, 'Sattvata was spirited. Through Koushalya, he had sons—Bhajina, Bhajamana, Divya, King Devavridha, the mighty-armed Andhaka and Vrishni, the delight of the Yadu lineage. Hear in detail about the offspring of four of these. Bhajamana's two wives were the daughters of Srinjaya—Bahyaka and Upabahyaka. Through them, he had many sons. Through Bahyaka, Srinjaya's daughter, Bhajamana's sons were Nimi, Kramana, Vishnu, Shura and Puranjaya. Through Upabahyaka, Srinjaya's daughter, Bhajamana's sons were Ayutajit, Sahasrajit, Shatajit and Dashaka. King Devavridha performed great austerities, having made up his mind that he desired a son who would possess all the qualities. He controlled his soul and touched the waters of the river Parnasha. Because he constantly touched the water, the river was kindly disposed towards him. The supreme of rivers thought in this way.

---

[392] Madhu means sweet.
[393] Purutvan's.

"This lord of men has turned his mind towards the beneficial. However, he has not yet approached a woman who can bear him such a son. Therefore, I should myself approach him and take part in his vow." The river assumed the form of a supremely beautiful maiden. The lord, the king, accepted her. After ten months, the supreme among rivers delivered King Devavridha's son, Babhru, the possessor of all the qualities. Those who know about the Puranas chant the qualities of the great-souled Devavridha and about how he made his pledged lineage come true. "Babhru is best among men and Devavridha is the equal of the gods. We have not heard about a person like him[394] earlier. Nor have we seen such a person, at close quarters, or from a distance." Babhru, Devavridha's son, despatched seven thousand and sixty-six men to heaven. He was generous and performed sacrifices. He was intelligent and devoted to brahmanas. He was firm in wielding weapons. He had an extremely great lineage, those known as Martikavata Bhojas. Through the daughter of Kashi, Andhaka had four sons—Kukura, Bhajamana, Shami and Kambalabarhisha. Kukura's son was Dhrishnu and Dhrishnu's son was Kapotaroma. Kapotaroma's son was Taittiri and his son was Punarvasu. Punarvasu's son was Abhijit. Abhijit had twins, Ahuka and Ahuki. They are famous and supreme among those who are renowned. This chant about Ahuka is cited. "He was surrounded by white horses. He was great and young in form. With eighty shields, Ahuka advanced in front of the army." Among those who followed this infinitely energetic Bhoja, there was no one who did not have one hundred sons, did not possess one thousand and one hundred weapons, was not the performer of auspicious deeds and was not the observer of sacrifices. With the Bhoja's permission, there would be ten thousand elephants in the eastern direction, with silver and gold harnesses. There would be another one thousand in the northern direction. The Bhoja Ahuka brought the lords of the earth under his subjugation, on a chariot that tinkled with bells. The Andhakas bestowed Ahuka's sister on the lord of Avanti. Through the daughter of Kashi, Ahuka had two sons—Devaka and Ugrasena. They were like those born from the wombs of the gods. Devaka had four sons

---

[394] Devavridha.

who were like the residents of heaven—Devavan, Upadeva, Sudeva and Devarakshita. He had seven daughters that he bestowed on Vasudeva—Devaki, Shantideva, Sudeva, Devarakshita, Vrikadevi, Upadevi and Sunamni as the seventh.[395] Ugrasena had nine sons and Kamsa was the eldest. The others were Nyagrodha, Sunamna, Kankashanku, Subhumaya, Rashtrapala, Sutanu, Anadhrishti and Pushtiman. They had five sisters—Kamsa,[396] Kamsavati, Sutanu,[397] Rashtrapali and the beautiful Kamka. Ugrasena and his offspring are those who were generated in the Kukura lineage. A man who sustains the account of the infinitely energetic Kukura lineage in his soul, obtains a lineage with a large number of sons.'

Chapter 28

Vaishampayana said, 'Bhajamana's son was Viduratha, foremost among charioteers.[398] Viduratha's son was the brave Rajadhideva. Rajadhideva then had brave sons—Datta, Atidatta, the powerful Shonashva, Shvetavahana, Shami, Dandasharma, Dattashatru and Shatrujit. Their sisters were Shravana and Shravishtha. Shami's son was Pratikshatra and Pratikshatra's son was Svayambhoja. Svayambhoja's son was Hridika. All of Hridika's sons were terrible in valour. Kritavarma was the eldest and Shatadhanva was in the middle. There were also Devanta, Naranta, Bhishaka, Vaitarana, Sudanta, Adhidanta, Kinasha, Dama and Dambhaka. Devanta had a learned son, Kambalabarhisha. His other sons were the brave Asamouja and Nasamouja. Since Asamouja possessed no sons, it is said that Andhaka bestowed his sons, Sudamshtra, Sucharu and Krishna, on him.

---

[395] To distinguish with the sons, Shantidevaa, Sudevaa and Devarakshitaa.

[396] Kamsaa.

[397] Brother and sister possessed the same name.

[398] In the list of Bhajamana's sons, this name has not been mentioned earlier.

'Kroshtu had two wives, Gandhari and Madri. Gandhari gave
birth to Sumitra, who brought delight to his friends.[399] Madri's
sons were Yudhajit and Devamidusha. Anamitra was victorious
and extremely strong. There was no one who was not his friend.
Anamitra had a son named Nighna[400] and Nighna's two sons were
Prasena and Satrajit, who were the conquerors of enemy soldiers.
While he dwelt in Dvaravati, from the ocean, Prasena obtained a
divine and extremely large gem named Syamantaka. Placed in the
abode of the Vrishnis and the Andhakas, this gem produced gold.
The rain-god showered down at the right time and there was no fear
of disease. From Prasena, Govinda desired this gem, Syamantaka.[401]
However, though he was capable of doing so, he did not seize it. On
one occasion, wearing the gem, Prasena went out on a hunt. While
he was roaming around in the forest, for the sake of the gem, a lion
killed him. The immensely strong king of the bears chased after the
lion and killed it. Seizing the gem, it entered its cave. Knowing that
Krishna had desired the gem, all the Vrishnis and the Andhakas
were scared that Krishna had killed Prasena for the gem. Knowing
of their suspicions, the one with dharma in his soul didn't tell them
that he had not done the deed. Instead, he resolved to go to the
forest and bring the gem back. Krishna and the men who wished
him well[402] followed Prasena's footsteps and searched the supreme
Mount Rikshavanta and the excellent Mount Vindhya. After he
was tired out from searching, the great-minded one saw the dead
bodies of Prasena and his horse. However, he did not find the gem.
Not very far from Prasena's body, he then saw the lion's dead body.
Because of the footprints of the bear, he deduced that it had been
killed by a bear. Following those footprints, Madhava entered the
cave. In the huge den of the bear, he heard a female voice. O king!
This was the nurse speaking to Jambavat's[403] young son, using the

---

[399] There is repetition with what has been stated earlier and some
inconsistencies.
[400] Inconsistencies again.
[401] Krishna decided that he was more suitable to possess it.
[402] There were friends who followed Krishna.
[403] The name of the king of the bears.

Syamantaka gem to play with him. The nurse said, "Do not cry. The
lion killed Prasena and Jambavat killed the lion. O excellent child!
Do not weep. Here is Syamantaka." These words swiftly emerged
from inside the den. The wielder of the Sharnga bow[404] entered the
hole and saw Jambavat. Inside the den, Vasudeva[405] fought with
Jambavat. Govinda used his fists and fought for twenty-one days.
When Krishna entered the hole and did not emerge, the others, with
Vasudeva[406] at the forefront, returned to Dvaravati and reported
that Krishna had been killed. Meanwhile, Krishna defeated the
immensely strong Jambavat. The king of the bears honoured him and
bestowed his daughter, Jambavati, on him. Because of the entreaties
of the king of the bears, which were pure, he also accepted the gem
Syamantaka and emerged from the hole. Having accepted the gem,
Achyuta,[407] the one with a cleansed soul, gave it to Satrajit, in an
assembly of all the Satvatas. Thus, Krishna, the slayer of enemies,
freed himself of the false accusation. By obtaining the Syamantaka
back, he cleansed himself of the presumed sin that had tainted him.

'Satrajit had ten wives and one hundred sons through them.
Three of them are famous and Bhangakara was the eldest. The
brave Vatapati and Upasvavan were the others. O lord of men! He
also had three daughters who were famous in all the directions—
Satyabhama, supreme among women, Vratini, firm in her vows
and Padmavati. As wives, he gave them to Krishna. Bhangakara
had two sons, Samaksha and Nareyu, both supreme among men.
They possessed all the qualities and were famous because of these
qualities. Madhu[408] had two sons, Prishni and Yudhajit. Prishni
had two sons named Shvaphalka and Chitraka. Shvaphalka
obtained the princess of Kashi as a wife. Her name was Gamdini,
because she used to donate a cow every day. O descendant of the
Bharata lineage! She gave birth to the brave and learned Akrura.

---

[404] The name of Vishnu and Krishna's bow, made of horn.
[405] Krishna.
[406] Krishna's father. Krishna is Vaasudeva.
[407] Krishna's name, the one without decay.
[408] It is not clear which Madhu this is. From the names of the sons, it
seems that Madhu is a name being used for Vrishni and there is repetition.

He was immensely fortunate and performed sacrifices at which copious quantities of dakshina were distributed. The other sons were Upasanga, Madgu, Mridu, Arimardana, Girikshipa, Upeksha, Shatruha, Arimejaya, Charmabhrit, Arivarma, Gridhrabhoja, Nara, Avaha and Prativaha. There was a beautiful daughter named Varangana. She was Samba's famous queen and her daughter was Vasundhara, who possessed beauty and youth and charmed all creatures. O descendant of the Kuru lineage! Through Ugrasena's beautiful-bodied daughter, Akrura had two sons named Sudeva and Upadeva. They were as radiant as the gods. Chitraka had sons named Prithu, Viprithu, Ashvasena, Ashvabahu, Suparshvaka, Gaveshana, Arishtanemi, Sutadharma, Dharmabhrit, Subahu and Bahubahu. The daughters were Shravishtha and Shravana. Thus is recited the great account of the false accusation against Krishna. If a person knows about it, a false accusation never touches him.'

Chapter 29

Vaishampayana said, 'In his heart, for a long time, Akrura had desired the gem Syamantaka and he had also desired the unblemished Satyabhama. A similar desire had been harboured by Shatadhanva, descended from Babhru Bhoja. Krishna handed over the gem Syamantaka to Satrajit. In the middle of the night, the immensely strong Shatadhanva killed Satrajit. Seizing the gem, he gave it to Akrura. O bull among the Bharata lineage! Having formed a pact, Akrura accepted the gem. "Let us have a pact and do not tell Achyuta that the gem is with me. We are both going to be attacked by Krishna. There is no doubt that all of Dvaraka will be under my subjugation now." When her father was slain, the illustrious Satyabhama was afflicted with grief. She ascended a chariot and left for the city of Varanavata.[409] She reached her husband's side and shedding tears, miserably told him about what

---

[409] This concerns an incident from the Mahabharata. Duryodhana plotted to burn down the Pandavas in a house of lac in Varanavata. The

Bhoja Shatadhanva had done. With the Pandavas having been burnt, Hari was offering oblations of water to them. For the sake of the lineage of his cousins,[410] he handed over this task to Satyaki.

'Madhusudana swiftly arrived in Dvaraka. The handsome one spoke these words to his elder brother, the wielder of the plough.[411] "O lord! The lion killed Prasena and Satrajit has been slain by Shatadhanva. It seems to me that Syamantaka is headed towards me and that I will be its owner. Let us quickly ascend a chariot and go and kill that immensely strong Bhoja. O mighty-armed one! Syamantaka will belong to us." There was a tumultuous encounter between the Bhojas and Krishna. Attacked from all directions, Shatadhanva looked for help towards Akrura. Deciding that Bhoja deserved to be killed by Janardana, Akrura did not help Hridika's son,[412] though he was capable. He resorted to deceit. Afflicted and afraid, Bhoja's thoughts turned towards running away. Using a foremost horse, he fled for one hundred *yojanas*.[413] O king! Bhoja possessed a famous horse named Hridaya and it could dash for one hundred yojanas. However, wishing to fight with him, Krishna pursued him. After one hundred yojanas, Hridaya tired and slowed down. On seeing the chariot pursuing him, Shatadhanva's mind was afflicted with grief. O descendant of the Bharata lineage! He abandoned the dead horse, which had fallen down on the ground, because of fatigue and exertion. As he fled on foot, on the chariot, Krishna told Rama, "O mighty-armed one! You remain here. My horses are also tired. I will pursue him on foot and seize the gem Syamantaka." Achyuta pursued Shatadhanva on foot. O king! The one who knew about supreme weapons slew him near the boundaries of Mithila. But though he killed the immensely strong Bhoja, he did not see Syamantaka. When Krishna returned, the wielder of the plough told him, "Give me the gem." Krishna replied, "I don't

---

Pandavas were presumed dead and Krishna went to Varanavata for the funeral rites.

[410] Kunti (Pritha) was Krishna's aunt.

[411] Balarama.

[412] Shatadhanva.

[413] A *yojana* is a measure of distance, between 8 and 9 miles.

have it." Rama became full of anger and told Janardana. "Shame
on you. You have dishonoured me earlier too. I have tolerated it
because you are my brother. May you be fortunate. I am departing.
I have nothing more to do with you, or with Dvaraka, or with the
Vrishnis." Rama, the destroyer of enemies, entered Mithila. The
lord of Mithila honoured him and gave him all the objects of desire.

'During this time, the supremely intelligent one of the Babhru
lineage collected all the diverse kinds of materials required and
incessantly performed sacrifices.[414] The gem was like a talisman
and he consecrated himself for the sacrifices to protect it. Gadhi's
wise and immensely illustrious descendant did this for the sake
of Syamantaka. There were many kinds of objects and the best
of riches and jewels. The one with dharma in his soul performed
sacrifices for sixty years. The great-souled one's sacrifice has come
to be known as Akrura *yajna*. All the many kinds of dakshina and
all the diverse objects of pleasure were offered. King Duryodhana
went to the lord who was in Mithila.[415] From the powerful
Balabhadra,[416] he learnt the divine art of fighting with the mace.
Later, with the Vrishni and Andhaka maharathas, the great-souled
Krishna sought Rama's favours and brought him back to Dvaraka.
O bull among the Bharata lineage! With Satrajit and his relatives
having been killed in an encounter, Akrura and the Andhakas
became extremely strong. There was a fearful clash within the kin
and Krishna remained an indifferent spectator. Akrura and his side
was defeated and the chastiser of Paka ceased to shower down.[417]
When it did not rain down, the kingdom faced many kinds of
difficulties. The Kukuras and Andhakas pacified Akrura. When
the lord of generosity returned to Dvaravati again, the one with
the thousand eyes[418] showered down and there were waterbodies
in Kachchha.[419] O descendant of the Kuru lineage! To please

[414] The person is Akrura. The idea is that the possession of Syamantaka
enabled him to collect these materials.
[415] Balarama.
[416] Balarama.
[417] Because Akrura had left Dvaraka, with his fortunate Syamantaka.
[418] Indra.
[419] A marshy area, Kutch in Gujarat.

Vasudeva,[420] the intelligent Akrura showed him proper honour and bestowed his sister on him. Through his yoga, Krishna deciphered that the jewel was with the descendant of the Babhru lineage. In the midst of an assembly, Janardana told Akrura, "O lord! You have the gem, supreme among jewels, in your possession. O one who deserves respect! Give it to me. Otherwise, do not show me false honours. For sixty years, you have committed many injuries against me. After this great period of time has elapsed, you must show me proper respect." Thus addressed by Krishna in the assembly of all the Satvatas, with difficulty, the immensely intelligent one from the Babhru lineage yielded the gem. The scorcher of enemies received it from Babhru's hands. However, cheerfully, the noble Krishna again returned the gem to Babhru. Having obtained the gem Syamantaka from Krishna's hands, Gamdini's son no longer concealed it. He was as radiant as the one with the rays.'[421]

Chapter 30

Janamejaya asked, 'I wish to hear in detail about the deeds of this slayer of enemies. I wish to hear about the intelligent Hari Krishna, without anything being left out. Tell me progressively about the lord's incarnations and deeds. You should explain to me his nature in the brahman. The lord Vishnu is the lord of the gods and is the destroyer of enemies. How did the intelligent one become Vasudeva, born in Vasudeva's lineage?[422] He is auspicious and is surrounded by the immortals, adorned by the performers of virtuous deeds. Having abandoned the world of the gods, how did he arrive in the world of mortals? The lord's powers pervade heaven and earth and he is the origin of gods and men. He is one with a celestial soul. How did he come to be associated with men? He is the one

---

[420] Krishna.

[421] The sun.

[422] The former is Vaasudeva (the son), while the latter is Vasudeva (the father).

who whirls the cycle, yet he was born amongst inferior men. He is
the supreme one who wields the chakra. How did his intelligence
turn towards becoming human? He is the one who protects the
cycle of the universe and all the worlds. How did the lord Vishnu,
the protector, descend on earth? He is the creator and the soul of
the great elements. He is the one who sustains and nurtures them.
He is the womb of prosperity. How could he have been born in
the womb of a woman on earth? He is the one who conquered the
worlds and divided them into three, with a part earmarked for the
thirty gods. His powers divided the universe into three worlds and
the three classes of paths.[423] When the time for destruction arrives,
he drinks up the entire universe and creates a form that is full of
water. In ancient times, the one with an ancient soul assumed the
form of a boar. The destroyer of enemies brought up the earth on
the points of his tusks.[424] In ancient times, for Puruhuta's[425] sake,
the supreme among gods conquered the undecaying three worlds
and gave them and the earth to the gods. In ancient times, having
assumed the form of a lion, he tore the immensely valorous daitya
Hiranyakashipu's body into two parts and killed him.[426] In ancient
times, the lord assumed the form of the subterranean fire known as
Samvartaka.[427] In the nether regions beneath the ocean, he drinks
oblations offered in the form of water. He is the brahman, with one
thousand feet, one thousand rays and one thousand forms. From
one yuga to another yuga, he has been invoked as the god with one
thousand heads. The grandfather's[428] abode arose from his navel
when the entire universe was like a single ocean. A lotus rubbed

[423] The three worlds are heaven, earth and the nether regions. The
three paths are presumably dharma, artha and *kama*.

[424] This is Vishnu's boar (*varaha*) incarnation. The earth was dragged
down into the waters by the demon Hiranyaksha and Vishnu rescued the
submerged earth.

[425] Indra's name.

[426] Vishnu's man–lion (*narasimha*) incarnation.

[427] Madhu and Kaitabha had stolen the Vedas and taken them to the
nether regions. Vishnu assumed the form of a horsehead and rescued the
Vedas. But the horsehead form remained in the ocean.

[428] Brahma's.

against another lotus was like the kindling. He killed the daityas in
the *tarakamaya* battle.[429] He assumed a form that was of all the gods,
wielding all the various weapons. With Garuda holding him aloft, he
brought down Kalanemi.[430] He obtained amrita from the northern
shores of the ocean. When there is great darkness, he lies down in
eternal yoga. In ancient times, resorting to divine austerities, he gave
birth to the gods through Aditi.[431] After they were born, he saved
Shakra from difficulties, when he was assailed by large numbers of
daityas. He covered the worlds through his steps and banished the
daityas to a residence in the oceans.[432] He ensured heaven for the
gods and made Puruhuta the lord of the gods in heaven. He devised
the rites for *garhapatya* and the *anvaharya* ordinances.[433] He devised
techniques for the *ahavaniya* fire,[434] the sacrificial altar, the kusha
grass and the sacrificial ladle. He also did this for pots and other
sacrificial vessels and the bath at the end of the sacrifice. He created
the three spokes of a sacrifice and the offering of *havya* and *kavya*.[435]
Havya is earmarked for the gods and kavya for the ancestors. He
decreed the rites for determining shares at sacrifices and the rituals
of a sacrifice. He is the one who knows yoga. He is the one who
determined sacrificial altars, kindling, soma, strainers for the soma,
the wooden frame around the fire, the objects required at a sacrifice
and the choice of the place for the fire. For the best of sacrifices,
he framed the rules for assisting priests, performers of sacrifices
and sacrificial animals. Through his own deeds, the supreme lord
classified this in ancient times. Depending on the yuga, he assumes

[429] The encounter over Tara.

[430] Demon killed by Vishnu.

[431] The gods, the Adityas, are the descendants of Kashyapa and Aditi.

[432] A reference to Vishnu's dwarf (vamana) incarnation and the incident
concerning Bali, the king of the daityas.

[433] Garhapatya is the fire that burns in households. Anvaharya has
various meanings, the simplest being the monthly sacrificial rites offered to
the ancestors on the day of the new moon.

[434] The eastern fire at a sacrifice.

[435] Havya is oblations offered to the gods, kavya is oblations offered
to the ancestors, the third spoke is these two categories being earmarked as
respective recipients.

a corresponding form and roams around the worlds. He created *kshana, nimesha, kashtha, kala,* past, present, future, *muhurta,* lunar day, month, solar day, year, season and the different kinds of measurements of time prevalent among men.[436] He laid down the principles for the development of lifespans and the signs associated with bodily beauty. He is responsible for the three varnas,[437] the three worlds, the three kinds of knowledge,[438] the three kinds of fire,[439] the three kinds of time,[440] the three kinds of deeds,[441] the three kinds of techniques[442] and the three kinds of qualities.[443] Through his infinite deeds, the eternal one created the three worlds. He is the creator of all creatures and qualities. His soul pervades all creatures and qualities. He is the one who finds delight in yoga. He is the lord of what is past and what is in the future. Therefore, he is the lord of destiny. But men only seek to comprehend him through their senses. He is the refuge for those who observe dharma. He takes away the refuge of those who perform evil deeds. He created the four varnas and he is the one who protects these four varnas. He is the one who knows about the four kinds of knowledge.[444] He is the one who resorts to the four ashramas.[445] He is the one who is in the firmament, beyond the directions. He is the one who separates the wind from that which is not the wind. He is the light of both the sun and the moon. He is the lord of yoga. He is the one who dispels the form of

[436] Kshana is a measurement of time, with differing interpretations. A second or an instant is accurate enough. Muhurta is forty-eight minutes. Nimesha is the twinkling of an eye, a minute. Kala is a small measure of time, but that measure is not consistently defined. In terms of astronomy, kala is one-sixtieth of a degree, that is, a minute. A kashtha is one-thirtieth of a kala.

[437] Shudras are not mentioned.

[438] Probably the Rig Veda, Sama Veda and Yajur Veda.

[439] Ahavaniya, garhapatya and *dakshinatya* (the fire that burns in a southern direction).

[440] Past, present and future.

[441] This probably means *nitya karma* (daily rites), *naimittika karma* (occasional rites) and *kamya karma* (rites performed for a specific objective).

[442] Superior, average and inferior.

[443] *Sattva, rajas* and *tamas.*

[444] The four Vedas.

[445] Brahmacharya, *garhasthya, vanaprastha* and *sannyasa.*

darkness. He is said to be supreme radiance. He is said to be supreme
austerities. He is said to be supreme among the supreme. He is the
supreme paramatman. He is the origin of the celestial Adityas. He is
the lord who is the destruction of the daityas. He is the destruction
that comes at the end of a yuga. He is the destruction that brings
an end to the worlds. He is the bridge that acts like a bridge to the
worlds. He is the sacrifice and the rituals of the sacrifice. He is what
is known by those who know about the Vedas. He is the lord with
power in his soul. His form is in Soma. His form is in the fire that is
in all creatures. He is as radiant as the fire. His form is in the minds
of all humans. He is in all ascetics in the form of austerities. He is
humility in those who follow good policy. He is energy in those who
are energetic. For the sake of the supreme welfare of the worlds, he
is the creator of everything that is created. He is the image for those
who want to revere the image. He is mobility amidst those who are
mobile. The wind was created from space. The fire, the breath of
life, was created from the wind. Fire is the breath of life for the gods.
Madhusudana is the breath of life for the fire.

'Blood results from succulent juices.[446] It is said that flesh
results from blood. Fat is born from blood and bones are said to
result from fat. Marrow results from bones and semen is born from
marrow. Semen penetrates the womb. Thus, succulent juices are the
foundation of all action. Therefore, water possesses a primary role in
the first creation that results from Soma. Know that what happens in
the womb is the second creation. Semen is the essence of Soma. The
menstrual blood has fire as its essence. Creation results from these
juices and semen, that is, a combination of the moon and fire. Semen
results from phlegm and blood results from bile.[447] The heart is the
place for phlegm and the navel is the place for bile. In the middle
of the body, the heart is said to be the place for the mind. The fire
god resides between the navel and the throat. Know that the mind
is Prajapati. Soma should be thought of as phlegm. Bile is said to
be the fire. Therefore, the entire universe is a combination of fire
and Soma. Just as clouds are created, the wind and the paramatman

---

[446] The juices are in food.
[447] *Kapha* and *pitta* respectively.

enter through a process of intercourse. Inside the body, it grows
and is again divided into five types—*prana, apana, samana, udana*
and *vyana*.[448] Prana occupies the first position. It circles around and
ensures growth. Apana is towards the bottom of the body and udana
is towards the top of the body. Vyana distributes it and samana
withdraws it. The creature is pervaded by these and the senses come
into being. Earth, wind, space, water and energy as the fifth—using
their own respective combinations, these lead to the manifestation
of the senses. The body is a manifestation of earth. Prana is a
manifestation of wind. The gaps inside the body are a manifestation
of space. The juices flowing out of the body are a manifestation of
water. The light in the eyes is a manifestation of energy. The mind
is said to be that which controls everything. This includes carnal
pleasures. Semen originates because of this. This is how the supreme
being created all the eternal worlds. How did the imperishable
Vishnu come to arrive in the human world? O brahmana! I have
a doubt about this and I am struck with great wonder. How did
the one who is the supreme among destinations come to assume a
human form? I have heard about the origin of my lineage and about
my ancestors. I now wish to progressively hear about Vishnu and the
Vrishnis. The gods and the daityas have said that Vishnu is a great
wonder. O great sage! Tell me about the extraordinary incident of
Vishnu's origin.[449] Tell me about this marvelous account, one that
will bring happiness. The infinitely energetic Vishnu is famous for
his strength and his valour. Vishnu's deeds on earth have made the
creatures marvel. Tell me the truth about these.'

Chapter 31

Vaishampayana said, 'The questions you have asked about the
wielder of the Sharnga bow are great in import. I will tell you

[448] Prana is the breath of life or the life force. Prana draws breath
into the body, apana exhales it. Vyana distributes it through the body and
samana assimilates it. Udana gives rise to sound.
[449] On earth.

to the best of my capacity. Hear about the Vaishnava fame. It is good fortune that your mind has turned towards hearing about Vishnu's powers. I will tell you everything about Vishnu. Hear about his divine conduct. He is described as one with one thousand faces, one thousand eyes, one thousand feet and one thousand heads. He is the undecaying god who acts in one thousand ways. He is radiant and possesses one thousand tongues. He is the lord with one thousand eyebrows. He has one thousand forms and one thousand beginnings. He is the undecaying one with one thousand arms. He is the time for offering an oblation. He is the act of offering oblations. He represents the oblations. He is the one who offers the oblations. He represents the sacred vessels, the sacrificial altar, the consecration, the plate and the pestle. He is the ladle, soma, the sacrificial basket, the sacrificial rod and the sacrificial strainer. He is the dakshina and the offerings. He is the adhvaryu, the chanter of Sama, the brahmana, the assistant priest, the sacrificial seat and the act of pressing out the soma juice. He is the sacrificial post, the kindling, the sacrificial spoon, the sacrificial vessel, the sacrificial ladle and the sacrificial mortar.[450] He is the front of the sacrificial arena. He is the hotri and represents the bricks used in the altar. He represents rites of atonement and arghya. He is the grain and the kusha grass. He is the mantra that conveys the sacrifice. He is the fire, the different shares at the sacrifice and the one who conveys these shares.[451] He is the first receiver of the offerings. He is the one who accepts the soma. He is the oblations offered into the flames. He is the water used in the sacrifice. Brahmanas who know about the Vedas speak about sacrifices and the eternal lord in this way. Vishnu is the lord of the gods. He is the intelligent one who wears the *srivatsa* mark on his chest.[452] He has manifested himself in one thousand ways on diverse occasions. The grandfather has said that he will again manifest himself in many ways in the future. O great king! You have asked me about that sacred, pure and divine account. Why did the illustrious Vishnu take birth in Vasudeva's

---

[450] Multiple synonymous words are used for the same object.
[451] The fire.
[452] Vishnu bears the srivatsa mark (or curl) on his chest. This is the place where Lakshmi resides.

family? I will tell you about it. Listen to the complete account. Hear about the greatness of Vasudeva[453] and the immensely radiant one's conduct. For the welfare of the gods and the mortals and for the prosperity of the worlds, the one who is in the souls of all creatures manifests himself through his deeds. I will tell you about those manifestations, ones that are sacred and are characterized by divine qualities. The lord of the universe sleeps for one thousand yugas. When one thousand yugas are over, the god of the gods manifests himself through his deeds. Brahma, Kapila, Parameshthi,[454] the gods, the saptarshis, the immensely illustrious Tryambaka,[455] the immensely great Sanatkumara and the great-souled Manu, the illustrious creator of subjects—all these ancient ones exist in that ancient god, who is like a blazing fire in his energy. When all mobile and immobile objects are destroyed, he exists in the midst of that ocean. At that time, the gods, the asuras and men are destroyed and so are the serpents and the rakshasas.

'At such a time, the danavas Madhu and Kaitabha were extremely difficult to assail and desired to fight. He killed them through his powers and granted them an infinite boon.[456] The one with the lotus in his navel slept on that ocean of waters and in ancient times, the gods, with the large numbers of rishis, were born from that lotus. That is the reason this cycle of creation is known as Poushkara.[457] The sacred texts of the Vedas speak about this ancient account.

'The great-souled one manifested himself in the form of a boar and this is pleasant to hear. This is when Vishnu, best among the gods, assumed the form of a boar. The Vedas were his feet. His tusks constituted the sacrificial altar. His teeth constituted the rites. His face was the place for the sacrificial fire. His tongues were the fire. His body hair was the *darbha* grass. Brahma was the immensely ascetic one's head. Day and night were his eyes. The sacred texts of

[453] Vaasudeva, Krishna.
[454] The supreme lord. It is not clear whom the text means by this.
[455] The three-eyed one, Shiva.
[456] Of emancipation.
[457] From *pushkara*, meaning lotus.

the Vedangas were his divine ornaments. His nose was the ghee. His snout constituted the sacrificial vessels. His great roar was the Sama hymns. He was full of dharma and the truth. He was handsome and his steps were revered because of their valour. His nails were the rites of atonement. The sacrificial animals were that patient and gigantic animal's thighs. His entrails were the udgatris. The oblations were his penis. The giant herbs were his testicles. The air was his inner atman. His curved trunk constituted the mantras. His blood was soma. The sacrificial altar was his shoulder. His smell constituted the oblations. His swift pace constituted havya and kavya. His body constituted the primary rituals. His radiance constituted the recital of vows of consecration. His heart constituted the dakshina. He was that great sacrifice. His lips constituted the attendant rituals. His ornaments were the procedures. His own shadow was the wife,[458] as he uplifted his bejewelled horn. Right up to the frontiers of the ocean, with its mountains, forests and groves, the earth was submerged in that single ocean of water.[459] The lord provided succour to the one who was dislodged into that single ocean of water. For the welfare of the worlds, he raised the earth up on his tusks. The one with the thousand heads, the origin of the gods, raised the earth again. Desiring the welfare of all creatures, in ancient times, having assumed the form of a sacrifice in the form of a boar, he raised up the goddess earth from the waters of the ocean. This cycle of creation is known as Varaha.[460]

'Now hear from me about Narasimha. He assumed the form of the king of animals[461] and killed Hiranyakashipu. O king! In an ancient krita yuga, an enemy of the gods was insolent because of his strength. This ancestor of the daityas performed supreme austerities for eleven thousand and five hundred years. He fasted and subsisted only on water. He was immobile, observed a vow of silence and was firm in his vows. O unblemished one! Brahma was delighted at his

---

[458] A sacrifice has to be performed with the wife.

[459] Having been taken down to the nether regions by the demon Hiranyaksha.

[460] Actually, Vaaraaha, after varaha (boar).

[461] A lion.

austerities, self-control, observances, discipline and brahmacharya. O lord of the earth! The illustrious Svayambhu himself appeared before him, on a radiant and celestial vehicle that had the complexion of the sun and was drawn by swans. The Adityas, the Vasus, the Sadhyas, the Maruts, the other gods, the Rudras who aid the universe, the rivers, the oceans, the nakshatras, the muhurtas, those who travel in the air, the giant planets, the devarshis, aged in their asceticism, the Siddhas, the saptarshis, the sacred rajarshis, the gandharvas and large numbers of apsaras were with him. The handsome one, the preceptor of everything mobile and immobile, was surrounded by all the gods. Brahma, supreme among those who know about the brahman, spoke these words to the daitya. "I am pleased with your devotion, austerities and excellent vows. O fortunate one! Ask for the boon you wish for, so that you may obtain what you desire." Hiranyakashipu replied, "O supreme among gods! May gods, asuras, gandharvas, humans and pishachas be unable to kill me. O grandfather of the worlds! May rishis not be able to curse me in rage, even when their austerities enable them to curse me in this fashion. This is the boon that I wish for. Let my death not come from any weapon, anything used to strike,[462] a mountain, a tree, anything dry, anything wet, or any other object. Let me be the lord of the sun, the moon, wind, fire, the water, the firmament, the nakshatras, the ten directions, ego, anger, desire, Varuna, Vasava, Yama, the granter of riches, the supervisor of riches,[463] yakshas and *kimpurusha*s."[464] Brahma said, "O son![465] This is a divine and extraordinary boon and I am conferring it on you. O son! There is no doubt that you will obtain everything that you desire." Having said this, the illustrious one departed through the sky. Worshipped by large numbers of brahmana rishis, he went to Vairaja, Brahma's

---

[462] The text uses both *astra* and *shastra*. These are both weapons and the words are often used synonymously. However, an astra is a weapon that is hurled or released, while a shastra is held in the hand.

[463] The granter of riches and the protector of riches are both usually Kubera. However, here, the two are mentioned separately.

[464] A *kinnara* or *kimpurusha* belongs to a semi-divine species, companions of Kubera.

[465] The word used is tata.

abode. On hearing about the boon that had been granted by the
grandfather, the gods, the serpents, the gandharvas and the sages
presented themselves before him. The gods said, "O illustrious one!
Because that boon has been granted and because he has pleased you,
the asura cannot be killed. O illustrious one! We should certainly
think of a means to bring about his death. O illustrious one! O
Svayambhu! O lord who has created all the creatures! O creator
of havya, kavya and the unmanifest *prakriti*!"[466] The god Prajapati
heard these words, which were for the benefit of the worlds. At that
time, the illustrious one spoke these words to all the large numbers
of gods. "O residents of heaven! He will certainly obtain the fruits
of his austerities. However, when the fruits of these austerities are
over, the illustrious Vishnu will bring about his death." Hearing
these words, spoken by the one who had been born from a lotus,
all the gods were delighted and returned to their respective celestial
regions. As soon as he had obtained the boon, he began to oppress
all the subjects. The daitya Hiranyakashipu was insolent because
he had obtained the boon. The immensely fortunate and virtuous
sages were in their hermitages, self-controlled and engaged in the
dharma of the truth. He oppressed them. The great asura defeated
the gods in the three worlds. The danava brought the three worlds
under his subjugation and started to reside in heaven. The danava
was intoxicated because he had obtained the boon. When he resided
on earth, he made sure that the shares in sacrifices were given to
daityas and that the gods obtained no shares in sacrifices. The
Adityas, the Sadhyas, the Vishvadevas and the Vasus approached
and sought refuge with the immensely strong Vishnu, the ultimate
refuge. Narayana is the god who is full of the brahman. He is the
sacrifice and its brahmana. He is the eternal god. He is the lord of
the past, the present and the future. He is worshipped by the worlds.
The gods sought refuge with the lord and god who is the ultimate
refuge. "O lord of the gods! Save us now, so that Hiranyakashipu
does not kill us. You are the supreme god. You are the supreme
preceptor. O supreme god! You are the supreme protector and
Brahma's origin. O one with eyes like a blooming lotus! O one who

---

[466] Nature.

is a terror to the side of the enemy! We have sought refuge with you,
for the sake of the destruction of Diti's lineage." Vishnu replied,
"O immortal ones! Abandon fear. I am granting you freedom from
fear. O gods! I will soon return heaven to you. I will slay the daitya
who is insolent because of the grant of the boon, together with his
companions. The Indra among the danavas cannot be slayed by the
immortals, Indra and the others. But I will kill him." Having said
this, the illustrious one took his leave of the residents of heaven. O
king! Hari went to Hiranyakashipu's assembly. He adopted a form
that was half that of a man and half that of a lion. In this form of
Narasimha, he rubbed his palms against each other. He looked like
a dense cloud. He roared like a dense cloud. His blazing energy was
like that of a dense cloud. He was as forceful as a cloud. The daitya
was extremely strong and proud. He was like an insolent tiger in
his valour. He was protected by a large number of proud daityas.
However, with one slap of his palm, he[467] killed them all. I have told
you about Narasimha.

'I will next tell you about vamana.[468] For the destruction of the
daityas, Vishnu adopted the form of a vamana. In ancient times, Bali,
powerful and strong, undertook a sacrifice.[469] Vishnu caused great
agitation through the valour of his three steps and disturbed the
great asuras—Viprachitti, Shibi, Shankuraya, Shanku, Ayahshira,
Ashvashira, the valiant Hayagriva, the swift Ketumat, Ugra, the
giant asura Ugravyagra, Pushkara, Pushkala, Ashvapati on his
horse, Prahlada, Ashvashira,[470] Kumbha, Samhlada, Gaganapriya,
Anuhlada, Harihara, Varaha, Samhara, Ruja, Sharabha, Shalabha,
Kupana, Kopana, Kratha, Brihatkirti, Mahajihva, Shankukarna,
Mahasvana, Dirghajihva, Arkanayana, Mridupada, Mridupriya,
Vayu, Gavishtha, Namuchi, Shambara, the great Vikshara,
Chandrahanta, Krodhahanta, Krodhavardhana, Kalaka, Kalakeya,

---

[467] Narasimha.
[468] The dwarf incarnation.
[469] Bali was generous. Vishnu asked for as much of land as could be
covered in three of his steps. When Bali agreed, Vishnu covered the three
worlds in his three steps and Bali had to be banished to the nether regions.
[470] Ashvashira is mentioned twice.

Vritra, Krodha, Virochana, Garishtha, Varishtha, Pralamba, Naraka, Indrapatana, Vatapi, Ketumat,[471] Baladarpita, Asiloma, Puloma, Bashkala, Pramada, Mada, Khasrima, Kalavadana, Karala, Keshi, Ekaksha, Chandraha, Rahu, Samhlada,[472] Srimara and Svana. They fought with *shataghnis*[473] and chakras in their hands, clubs in their hands, machines that hurled stones and javelins as weapons. They had mortars and pestles in their hands. They wielded battleaxes. Some held nooses and hammers in their hands, others held cudgels. Some danavas had tridents in their hands. Others used giant mountains as weapons. With diverse weapons and with varied attires, they were speedy and extremely terrible. Some had faces like tortoises or cocks, others had faces like rabbits or owls. Some had faces like mules or camels, others had faces like boars. There were fierce ones, with faces like *makaras*.[474] Other danavas had faces like jackals. Some had faces like mice or turtles. Others were terrible, with faces like wolves. Some had faces like cats or foxes. Others had gigantic faces. Some had faces like rams and ewes. Other fierce ones had faces like cows, goats and buffaloes. There were those with faces like lizards and porcupines, others with faces like herons. Some had faces like eagles, others with faces like rhinos and still others with faces like peacocks. Some were attired in elephant hides, others wore garments of black antelope skin. There were others who were attired in tattered rags and the barks of trees. Some asuras had headdresses, crowns and earrings. Some had diadems and long tufts of hairs. Others were extremely radiant, with necks like conch shells. The daityas were attired in many kinds of garments, wearing diverse garlands and unguents. Blazing in energy, they seized different kinds of weapons. Progressively, from every side, they surrounded Hrishikesha. He crushed all the daityas with his feet and the palms of his hands. Assuming a gigantic and

---

[471] Ketumat is mentioned twice.

[472] Samhlada is mentioned twice.

[473] A shataghni was a weapon that could kill one hundred at the same time and could have been a giant catapult.

[474] A *makara* is a mythical aquatic animal, but can be interpreted as a crocodile or a shark.

terrible form, he swiftly placed his first stride on earth. The earth was overwhelmed by his valour and the moon and the sun seemed to be strung between his breasts. As he encompassed the firmament with his second stride, the moon and the sun slid to his navel. When the valour of his third stride overwhelmed everything, they slid to his knees. The brahmanas have therefore spoken about Vishnu's infinite valour. Vishnu, supreme among strong ones, crushed the earth and slew all the bulls among the asuras. He then handed over the earth to Shakra. This is the way the great-souled one manifested himself in the form of a vamana. Brahmanas who know about the Vedas speak about this Vaishnava fame.

'The great-souled Vishnu, who is in the souls of all creatures, manifested himself yet again. He was born as Dattatreya, famous for his great compassion. The Vedas and the rites of the sacrifices had been destroyed. The dharma of the four varnas had become confused and decadent. Adharma started to flourish. Truth was destroyed and everything was based on falsehood. With dharma lacking a foundation, the subjects were afflicted. The great-souled one again established the dharma of the four varnas. He brought back the Vedas, with their sacrifices and rites. The intelligent Dattatreya also conferred a boon on the intelligent Kartavirya, the king of Haihaya. "O king! Because of what you have done for me with these two arms, there is no doubt that you will have one thousand arms. O lord of the earth! You will rule the entire earth. When you are present in a battle, large numbers of the enemy will find it impossible to look at you." This is the extraordinary and auspicious account of his prosperous Vaishnava manifestation. After this, Jamadagni's great-souled son[475] manifested himself. With his one thousand arms, Arjuna[476] was extremely difficult to defeat in a battle. Everyone was amazed to see the lord Rama slay such a king and his army. Rama brought down King Arjuna from his chariot on to the ground. Roaring like a cloud, he struck him as he willed. With a blazing battleaxe, the descendant of the Bhrigu lineage severed all the one thousand arms and all his kin. There were crores

[475] Parashurama.
[476] Kartavirya Arjuna.

of kshatriyas who inhabited the mountains Meru and Mandara. He destroyed them twenty-one times and removed all kshatriyas from earth. Bhargava, the extremely great ascetic, destroyed all the kshatriyas. He then sought to perform a horse sacrifice, so that all his sins might be extinguished. At that sacrifice, the descendant of the Bhrigu lineage was extremely generous with dakshina. Delighted, he gave the entire sun to Marichi's son, Kashyapa. At that great horse sacrifice, the immensely illustrious one, supreme among charioteers and greatly intelligent, gave away Varuna's horses, a sparkling chariot, an infinite quantity of gold, cattle and gigantic kings of elephants. Even now, for the welfare of the worlds, Jamadagni's resplendent son, the descendant of the Bhrigu lineage, repeatedly performs supreme austerities. The handsome one still resides on Mount Mahendra, supreme among mountains. The eternal Vishnu, lord of the gods, is without decay. This manifestation of the great-souled one is known as Jamadagnya.

'In the twenty-fourth yuga, when Vishvamitra was at the forefront, Dasharatha had a son and his eyes were like the petals of a lotus. The mighty-armed lord and god divided himself into four parts.[477] Rama was like the sun and his energy was famous in the worlds. To please the worlds, destroy rakshasas and make dharma prosper, the immensely illustrious one was born there. The lord of all creatures is established in all bodies. However, he came to be known as an Indra among men. The intelligent Vishvamitra gave him weapons, so that he might slay the enemies of the gods, who were unslayable, even by the gods. They created obstacles when sages, cleansed in their souls, performed sacrifices. Maricha and Subahu were supreme among strong ones. However, using his own strength, the great-souled one[478] baffled and killed them. In ancient times, as if sporting and playing, at the great-souled Janaka's sacrifice, he broke Maheshvara's[479] bow. He knew about all forms of dharma and resided in the forest for fourteen years, with Lakshmana as a follower. Rama was engaged in the welfare

[477] Rama, Lakshmana, Bharata and Shatrughna.
[478] Rama.
[479] Shiva's.

of all creatures. The beautiful Sita, famous among men, was by his
side. She always followed him, like Lakshmi follows her husband.
For fourteen years in the forest, Raghava tormented himself through
austerities. While he dwelt in Janasthana, he accomplished the task
of the residents of heaven. Following the footsteps of Sita,[480] the
great-minded one killed two terrible and valiant rakshasas named
Viradha and Kabandha. Those tigers among men were actually
gandharvas, who had been dislodged because of a curse. They were
killed, their bodies mangled by arrows released with great strength.
These arrows were like the rays of the fire and blazed like lightning.
They had colourful tufts and the shafts were made out of molten
gold. In their essence, they were like the vajra wielded by Indra of
the gods. For Sugriva's sake, in an encounter, he killed Vali, the
immensely strong Indra of the apes, and instated Sugriva in the
kingdom. Ravana, Indra among the rakshasas, was difficult to beat
and impossible to kill in a battle, even by large numbers of gods,
asuras, yakshas, rakshasas and birds. He was protected by a crore
of rakshasas and was like a thick and dark cloud. Ravana, lord of
the rakshasas, was a cruel rakshasa who had conquered the three
worlds. He was without decay and was impossible to withstand.
He was like a tiger in his valour. He was insolent because of his
boon and the large number of gods could not even look at him. In
the battle, he[481] killed Ravana, with his advisers and his soldiers.
Poulastya Ravana was cruel and immensely strong. He was gigantic
in form and his complexion was like that of a great cloud. In
ancient times, Rama, lord of creatures and tiger among men, swiftly
killed him. Madhu's son was a proud danava named Lavana. The
terrible and great asura had also obtained a boon. But he killed
him and other rakshasas, who were indomitable in any battle, in an
encounter in Madhuvana. These were the deeds of Rama, supreme
among those who uphold dharma. He performed ten praiseworthy
horse sacrifices. No inauspicious words were heard during his reign.
No contrary winds blew. There was no theft of riches. Rama's reign
was praised. Widows did not suffer difficulties because of lack of

---

[480] Who had been abducted by Ravana.
[481] Rama.

riches. The entire universe was peaceful. Rama's reign was praised. No creature suffered from fear. There were no natural catastrophes on account of water or fire. The aged did not have to perform funeral rites for the young.[482] Kshatriyas tended to brahmanas and vaishyas were devoted to kshatriyas. Without any sense of pride, shudras served the other three varnas. Wives did not oppress their husbands and husbands did not oppress their wives. The entire universe was peaceful and the earth was devoid of bandits. Rama alone was the lord. Rama was the protector. People lived for one thousand years and had one thousand sons. No creature suffered from disease. Rama's reign was praised. The gods, the rishis and all men lived together on earth. Rama's reign was praised. In this connection, those who know about the ancient accounts recite a chant. "The intelligent Rama imbibed the true purport of greatness. He was dark and young, with red eyes. His face was radiant and he was mild in speech. His arms extended to his thighs. His face was excellent and his shoulders were like that of a lion. He was mighty-armed."[483] Rama ruled for eleven thousand years and was the lord of Ayodhya. As long as the great-souled one reigned, there was the sound of hymns from the Rig, Sama and Yajur Vedas. Throughout the kingdom, there were the sounds of "Donate. Enjoy." He possessed the qualities of sattva. He blazed in his own energy. Rama, Dasharatha's son, surpassed even the sun and the moon. He completed hundreds of great sacrifices and gave away lots of dakshina. After this, the immensely strong Raghava left Ayodhya and went to heaven. Such was the mighty-armed descendant of the Ikshvaku lineage. After slaying Ravana and his companions, the lord went to heaven.

'After this, the great-souled Keshava manifested himself. This was for the welfare of all the worlds and was in the kalpa famous as Mathura.[484] The valiant one killed Salva,[485] Kamsa, Mainda,

---

[482] That is, the young did not die before the old.

[483] Though the text does not explicitly indicate this, the chant seems to end here.

[484] Maathura.

[485] Alternatively, Shalva.

Dvividha, Arishta, Vrishabha, Keshi, Putana, the servant maid of the daityas, the elephant Kuvalayapida, Chanura, Mushtika and other daityas who had assumed human bodies. The performer of extraordinary deeds severed Bana's[486] one thousand arms. In a battle, he slew Naraka and the immensely strong Yavana.[487] Displaying his energy on earth, the one who was evil in conduct[488] had seized all the riches of the kings and had slain many kings. In this way, for the welfare of the worlds, the great-souled one manifested himself.

'The lord will again appear as Kalki, in the house of Vishnuyasha. There are these and many other divine manifestations, with celestial qualities. The ones who know about the brahman have chanted about these in the ancient accounts. On hearing recitals of these manifestations, even the gods are confounded. They are described in the Puranas and are immersed in the sacred texts of the Vedas. I have only recited some of the indications. The lord is the preceptor of all the worlds and his deeds should be recited. When they are recited, the ancestors are pleased. The infinitely energetic Vishnu is the lord of yoga and his yoga is full of maya. If a man listens to this with hands joined in salutation, he is freed from all sins. Through the favours of the illustrious one, he swiftly obtains great prosperity and riches and all the objects of pleasure.'

Chapter 32

Vaishampayana said, 'Hear about Vishnu Hari, who pervaded the universe in krita yuga. His Vaikuntha nature is for the gods and his Krishna nature is for humans. His characteristics as a lord are evident in the depth of his mysterious deeds. O king! Listen accurately to the characteristics he has recently exhibited. The illustrious lord is unmanifest, but his signs are manifest. Narayana's soul is infinite and his powers are without decay. It is this eternal

---

[486] Banasura.
[487] Kalayavana.
[488] Meaning Naraka.

Narayana Hari who manifested himself through Brahma, Shakra, Soma, Dharma, Shukra and Brihaspati. This descendant of the Yadava lineage became Aditi's son and was famous as Vishnu, who was younger to Indra.[489] For the sake of slaying the enemies of the gods, the daityas, danavas and rakshasas, it was through his own favours that he was born as Aditi's son. In ancient times, the great soul of this lord created Brahma. In an ancient kalpa, it is he who created the grand ancestors, the Prajapatis. Their bodies were created from his body and led to Brahma's supreme lineage. It is this eternal and great-souled one who flowed in many forms through Brahma. Vishnu's extraordinary deeds have therefore been recited. Those deeds should be recited and are recited. Listen to me. O son![490] In the current krita yuga, after Vritra had been killed, there was a battle that was famous in the three worlds and this is known as tarakamaya. All the terrible danavas were insolent in that battle and killed the gods, with the gandharvas, the yakshas, the serpents and the charanas. They were slain and retreated. They lost their weapons in that battle. Searching for a saviour in their minds, they went to the god and lord Narayana.

'At this time, the radiant clouds started to shower down burning coal. In the firmament, this shrouded the sun, the moon and all the planets. Creatures were struck by terrible lightning and were distressed. The seven winds[491] started to blow with great force. Blazing rain showered down. There was thunder mixed with fire and wind, with the force of the vajra. There were terrible portents and the sky seemed to blaze. Thousands of meteors showered down. Anything that travelled in the sky fell down. The vimanas could no longer be controlled and were hurled up and flung down. It was like the fear that creatures confront at the end of the four yugas. When these evil portents manifested themselves, everything with form turned deformed. Everything was dimmed by the darkness and nothing could be seen. The ten directions were agitated by

---

[489] Aditi's sons were the Adityas. As an Aditya, Vishnu was Indra's younger brother.

[490] The word used is tata.

[491] The seven Maruts.

waves of darkness and could not be discerned. It was as if the naked darkness was only shrouded by dark clouds. The sky and the sun were enveloped in that terrible darkness. With his hands, the lord flung away those waves of darkness. Hari displayed his own divine form and that form was also dark. His complexion was as dark as the clouds and his hair was also as dark as the clouds. Krishna's energetic form was as dark as a mountain. He was attired in radiant yellow garments and his ornaments were made out of molten gold. His form was as dark as the smoke that is created by the fire that arrives at the time of the destruction of a yuga. There was a crown on his head and he had eight thick arms. Each of these hands held a glistening weapon. He looked like the rising summit of a mountain, flooded by the rays of the sun and the moon. He held the Nandaka sword in one hand, a sword that he loves to hold. In another hand, he held arrows that were like venomous serpents. Yet another hand held a fierce plough, marked with the signs of javelins. Three other hands held a conch shell, the chakra and a mace.[492] Another hand held the Sharnga bow, made out of horn. Vishnu was like a mountain, with forgiveness as its foundation. He was like a tree that brings prosperity. He was on a chariot yoked to tawny horses. The standard was adorned with Garuda. The sun and the moon were the wheels and Mount Mandara was the axle. The serpent Ananta was the reins and Mount Meru was the seat. It[493] was decorated with stars as flowers and the yoke was decorated with planets and nakshatras. The terrified gods, defeated by the daityas, saw him in the firmament, indicating freedom from fear. They saw the god stationed on that divine chariot and all the worlds seemed to be inside it. All the gods, with Shakra at the forefront, joined their hands in salutation. They honoured him with sounds of "victory" and sought refuge with the one whom one turns to for succour. Vishnu heard the words of the beloved gods. He made up his mind that he would destroy the danavas in a great battle. Vishnu was stationed in the

---

[492] The conch shell is named Panchajanya, the chakra is named Sudarshana and the mace is named Koumadaki. The last hand was free, in a sign of benediction, signifying assurance and freedom from fear.

[493] The chariot.

sky, assuming that supreme form. He spoke to all the gods, in words that amounted to a pledge. "O fortunate ones! Depart in peace. O large numbers of Maruts! Do not be afraid. As soon as I have defeated all the danavas, I will take back the three worlds." Since he always spoke the truth, they were content with Vishnu's words. The gods departed in great delight, as if they had obtained the supreme amrita. The clouds withdrew and were dispelled. Auspicious winds started to blow and the directions turned peaceful. The stellar bodies regained their radiance and started to circle the moon. There was no longer any dissension among the planets. The oceans became calm. The three roads that lead to heaven became free of dust.[494] The rivers assumed their natural state and the oceans were no longer agitated. With the impure senses under control, the inner souls of men became calm. The maharshis became devoid of sorrow and uttered hymns from the Vedas. The oblations offered at sacrifices became pure and succulent and the fire accepted them. Cheerful in their minds, all the worlds engaged in pursuits of dharma. Everyone had heard the pledge that Vishnu had uttered in his words.'

Chapter 33

Vaishampayana said, 'The daityas and danavas heard about the fear that would arise for them on Vishnu's account. Hearing about this terror, indomitable in battle, they started to make extensive arrangements for the battle. Maya was on an undecaying and golden chariot that was extremely handsome and had four wheels. It was three *nalva*s long.[495] It was stocked with gigantic weapons that had been prepared well. It was decorated with the skins of leopards and jingled with nets of bells. It was adorned with nets of gems and festooned with nets of gold. It was populated by

---

[494] These three roads are *devayana* (the path of the gods), *pitriyana* (the path of the ancestors) and the path of emancipation.

[495] A nalva is a measure of distance, usually taken to be 400 cubits. Maya's chariot was therefore 1,200 cubits long.

wolves and birds were seated on it. It roared like a cloud and there
were divine weapons in the quivers. This best of chariots moved on
its wheels, like a mountain. Stocked with maces and clubs, it looked
like an ocean. The ends of the wheels were encrusted with gold and
the yoke was also golden. With the best of flags and penants hoisted,
it looked like Mandara, with the sun shining down on it. While its
body was like that of a huge elephant or a cloud, in its radiance, it
sometimes looked like a lion. It was yoked to one thousand bears,
which roared like one thousand clouds. This blazing and divine
chariot, which could crush the chariots of the enemy, moved along
the sky. It was like Mount Meru, made radiant by the rays of the
sun. The one who wished to be victorious in battle was seated atop
it. Tara was borne along on an iron chariot that was one *krosha*
long.[496] This looked like a reddish mountain, tinged with a mass of
collyrium. The wheels were made of black iron and the yoke was
also made out of iron. It roared like a cloud and emitted flashes
from inside the darkness. There were giant nets of iron, with
windows carved out in them. It was stocked full with iron clubs and
bludgeons that could be flung. There were spears, and maces and
mallets were strewn around. With the javelins and battleaxes, it was
beautiful, but also generated fear. It was as if a second Mandara
had arisen, to strike at the enemy. That supreme chariot was yoked
to one thousand donkeys and borne along by them. The angry
Virochana was stationed in front of his soldiers, with a club in his
hand. He looked like a mountain with a resplendent peak. A chariot
yoked to one thousand horses bore the danava Hayagriva, ready to
crush the enemy. Varaha was in front of his army, like a mountain
with slopes. He stretched a giant bow that was many thousands[497]
long. The insolent Kshara shed tears of anger from his eyes. Desiring
to fight, he gnashed his teeth and his lips and face quivered. The
danava Tvashta was on a vehicle drawn by eighteen horses. The
valiant one designed the battle formations for the danavas. Shveta,
Viprachitti's son, was adorned with white earrings. He was stationed
ready for battle, like a white mountain. Arishta, Bali's son, fought

[496] A krosha is a measure of distance, equal to one-fourth of a yojana.
With a yojana taken as eight miles, a krosha is two miles.
[497] The text doesn't specific many thousands of what, probably cubits.

with excellent boulders. He looked like a mountain and stationed himself for battle. Kishora was delighted and looked like a young[498] horse that had been goaded. In the midst of the daitya soldiers, he looked like the rising sun. Lamba looked like a long cloud.[499] His garments and ornaments were long. In the battle formation of the daityas, he looked like the solar disc. Svarbhanu[500] fought with his teeth, lips and eyes as weapons. This planet, with a pleasant face, stood in front of the daityas and laughed. Some were resplendent on horses. Others were on the shoulders of elephants. There were some who rode on lions and tigers. There were others who rode on boars and bears. Some were borne by asses and camels. Others rode on clouds. Some rode on birds and others rode on the wind. Some fierce daityas, with malformed visages, were on foot. Some had a single foot, others were bipeds. Desiring to fight, they danced. Many danavas roared and shouted, roaring like proud tigers. All those bulls among the danavas roared. Those danavas wielded maces, clubs and fierce bows. They were used to physical exercise and their arms were like bludgeons. The best among the daityas sported and inspired their army with lances, nooses, swords, darts, goads, battleaxes, sharp shataghnis, boulders, mountains, bludgeons and other supreme weapons and chakras. Thus, all those danava soldiers were excited at the prospect of battle. They advanced towards the gods, as if the army was made out of clouds. With a depth of thousands, the daityas were extraordinary. That army was like a wave of wind, fire, water and mountains, advancing towards the battle. Intoxicated and desiring to fight, as they advanced, they seemed to shatter the firmament.'

Chapter 34

Vaishampayana said, 'O son! You have heard in detail about how the daitya soldiers readied for battle. Now hear in

---

[498] Kishora means young.

[499] Lamba means long.

[500] Rahu.

detail about all the Vaishnava soldiers of the gods. In due order, the Adityas, the Vasus, the Rudras and the immensely strong Ashvins arrayed themselves, with their soldiers and their followers. Puruhuta, the one with the one thousand eyes and the guardian of the worlds, was at the forefront of all the other gods, astride the divine elephant.[501] The chariot was along his left flank[502] and so was the forceful and supreme bird.[503] The chariot's wheels were beautiful and were decorated with gold and diamonds. Thousands of gods, gandharvas and yakshas followed. The radiant brahmana rishis and the assistant priests pronounced benedictions. Lightning flashed from the vajra, Indra's weapon. He was protected by large numbers of clouds, which looked like mountains and could move at will. As the illustrious Maghavan advanced on his elephant, stationed in the forefront of the battle, brahmanas offered oblations and chanted his praise. In heaven, Shakra's followers sounded celestial trumpets. Thousands of apsaras danced in front of Indra. His standard was made out of excellent bamboo and was as radiant as the sun. His supreme chariot was yoked to one thousand horses and could move as swiftly as thoughts or the wind. The dazzling chariot was driven by Matali and because of its energy, looked like Meru, surrounded on every side by the rays of the sun. Yama held aloft his mace, which signified destiny. It assured the arrays of the gods and terrified those of the daityas. On four sides, Varuna was protected by the oceans and serpents with flickering tongues. His handsome form was decorated with conch shells, pearls and bracelets and was made out of water. He held the noose of destiny. His horses had the hue of moonbeams and they sported with the thousands of waves that had been raised by the wind. His garments were white and his bracelets were beautifully decorated with coral. His excellent form was decorated with necklaces of dark jewels that were so heavy that they hung down up to his stomach. Wielding the noose, Varuna was stationed amidst the army of the gods, which, as it sought battle, was like an ocean that was ready to breach the

[501] Airavata, Indra's elephant.
[502] Though Indra rode on the elephant, his chariot was kept ready.
[503] Garuda.

shoreline. The lord and guardian of riches[504] was accompanied by yaksha and *raksha* soldiers and large numbers of guhyakas. He was decorated with conch shells and lotuses. The handsome king of the yakshas could be seen holding a club in his hand. The lord of riches fought from a vimana and he was stationed on that Pushpaka vimana. Naravahana,[505] king of the yakshas, looked beautiful and desired to do battle. Shiva's friend[506] looked as if Shiva himself was stationed there. Proud in their valour, the four guardians of the four quarters were stationed there—the one with the thousand eyes in the eastern direction, the lord of the ancestors in the southern direction, Varuna in the western direction and Naravahana in the northern direction. They protected their own respective directions and the army of the gods. Surya was on a chariot that travelled through the sky, yoked to seven horses. He blazed in his prosperity and dazzled with his rays. From sunrise to sunset, the circle of his travels takes him all the way up to Meru. The undecaying one scorches the worlds and travels up to the colourful gates of heaven. Blazing in his energy, he radiated one thousand rays. Stationed amidst the gods, the lord of days has twelve parts to his soul.[507] Soma was radiant on a chariot with white horses and white reins. He is the one who is full of cold and water and he is the one who floods the world. The lord of brahmanas possesses cool rays and his followers glanced towards him. His body is marked with the shadow of a hare and he is the one who destroys the darkness of the night. He is the lord of all stellar bodies in the sky and of all the succulent juices. He is the one who saves the herbs and he is the store of amrita. The amiable one is the primary source of food for the universe, cool and succulent juices. The danavas saw that Soma was stationed, with chill as a weapon. Vayu is the breath of life in all creatures and divides himself into five in humans. On the seven shoulders,[508] he roams around the three worlds. He is the lord with universal powers

---

[504] Kubera.
[505] Literally, one who is borne by men, a name used for Kubera.
[506] Kubera.
[507] The twelve months.
[508] The seven Maruts.

and is said to be the controller of fire. The seven musical notes are said to originate with him. He is said to be the supreme element. He is said to be in embodied beings. He is said to travel in the sky. He is swift and is the origin of sound. Because of his energy, Vayu is said to be in all elements. He began to flow in perverse directions, so that the daityas might be troubled. The Maruts, the gods, the gandharvas and large numbers of *vidyadharas*[509] began to sport with their swords, which were like snakes that had cast off their skins. From their arrows, the best among the gods created armies of fierce serpents that were full of rage and venom. With gaping mouths, these enveloped the firmament. To aid the large numbers of gods, the mountains presented themselves with mountain peaks and hundreds of trees, using these to strike the danava army.

'The god Hrishikesha has a lotus in his navel. He conquered the earth in three strides. He is the lord of the world and the universe. He arose like the fire at the end of a yuga, with black trails. He is the slayer of Madhu. He is the one who arose from the waters. He is the one who enjoys the havya and is revered in sacrifices. He is the earth, water and the firmament. He is the dark. He is the one who establishes peace and is the destroyer of the enemy. Like the sun and the fire, he arose, infinite in his energy. The wielder of the chakra and the mace was ready to slay the enemy, the army of the asuras. He arose, like the sun blazing amidst his solar disc. In his left hand, he wielded the giant club, the destroyer of all the asuras. It was dark in form and ensured death to the enemy. In his other hands, the immensely illustrious lord wielded other blazing weapons, including the Sharnga bow. The enemy of the serpents[510] was on the standard. That bird was Kashyapa's offspring and survived on serpents. The bird's speed was greater than that of the wind and he agitated the sky. An Indra among the serpents could be seen, trapped in his beak. He looked like Mandara, freed after the amrita had been churned.[511] He had exhibited his valour

---

[509] A vidyadhara is a supernatural and semi-divine being.

[510] Garuda.

[511] Amrita was obtained from the churning of the ocean and Mount Mandara was used as the churning rod.

in hundreds of conflicts between the gods and the asuras. There were the signs of the vajra on his body, inflicted by the great Indra, when he had tried to seize the amrita.[512] With his crested peak, he looked like a mountain that exuded minerals. His garment was made out of colourful feathers and his ornaments were fashioned out of molten gold. He was like the moon in his energy. Because he had eaten serpents, the radiant gems and jewels from those serpents stuck to the feathers on his broad chest. In sport, he spread his beautiful wings and shrouded the sky. These looked like clouds full of rain at the end of a yuga, tinged with Indra's bows.[513] He was adorned with blue, red and yellow penants. With these penants, he assumed the form of a gigantic standard. In the battle, Hari climbed on to this beautiful bird, Aruna's brother, as a mount. His own form was radiant, like that of Suparna, the supreme bird. The large number of gods and the self-controlled sages followed him. In praise of Gadadhara,[514] they chanted supreme mantras. Vaivasvata[515] was in the front, accompanied by Vaishravana.[516] They were urged by the unvanquished king of the gods, the lord of rains. When the battle presented itself, there were sparkling moonbeams everywhere. The wind began to roar and the fire started to blaze. Vishnu was surrounded by his traits of Jishnu, Sahishnu and Bhrajishnu.[517] The strong army advanced to do battle. The son of Angiras[518] proclaimed, "Let the gods have good fortune." Ushanas[519] proclaimed, "Let the daityas have good fortune."'

[512] When Garuda tried to seize the amrita, Indra struck him with the vajra.

[513] The wings looked like clouds. Indra's bow is the rainbow.

[514] The wielder of the club, Vishnu.

[515] Yama.

[516] Kubera.

[517] Jishnu means the victorious one, Sahishnu is the one who is patient and Bhrajishnu is the one who is radiant.

[518] Brihaspati, the preceptor of the gods.

[519] Shukracharya, the preceptor of the demons.

Chapter 35

Vaishampayana said, 'Then, there was a tumultuous battle between the two armies. The gods and the asuras sought to defeat each other. Brandishing many kinds of weapons, the danavas and the gods rushed towards each other. They fought with each other, like mountains against other mountains. As the gods and the asuras engaged, there was a marvellous battle. Dharma clashed against adharma and insolence against humility. As the mounts were goaded, blazing chariots advanced. In every direction, as they dashed forward with swords, the sky was agitated. Clubs were flung, arrows were shot. Bows were twanged and cudgels descended. As the gods and the danavas clashed, it was wonderful and terrible. The universe was terrified, as if the fire of destruction at the end of a yuga had been unleashed. In that battle, the danavas swiftly released clubs and flung mountains from their hands, striking the gods, with Indra at the forefront. They were slaughtered by the powerful danavas, who hoped for victory. In that great battle, the gods were distressed and overcome by grief. They were crushed by those nets of weapons. Their heads were shattered with clubs. When their chests were mangled by Diti's sons, copious quantities of blood began to flow from their wounds. Some were bound in nets of nooses. Others were afflicted by the arrows. The maya of the danavas penetrated them and they were incapable of regaining their senses. Their radiance vanished and they seemed to have lost their lives. Struck by the asuras, the army of the gods was soon incapable of raising weapons.

'The many-eyed Shakra penetrated the fierce army of the daityas. He shattered the nooses of maya and repulsed their arrows with his vajra. He killed the foremost among the daityas and rendered their great army weak. Through his net of weapons, he plunged their army into darkness. They could no longer discern each other, nor the gods or the mounts. Because of Puruhuta's energy, they were immersed in a terrible darkness. The best among the gods sought to free themselves from the noose of maya. While the bodies of that army of daityas were immersed in darkness, they brought them down. They fell down, bereft of their senses. Because of the darkness, they turned blue in complexion. Large numbers of danavas fell down, like mountains with their wings severed.[520] The Indras among the daityas seemed to be amidst a dense ocean of darkness. Overwhelmed by the darkness, the danavas were despatched to their death.

'At this, to burn down the darkness, Maya created a grand maya. He created a fire known as Ourva, the fire that is the origin of the fire that arrives at the end of a yuga. This maya created by Maya destroyed all the darkness. The daityas instantly regained their original forms and were ready to battle again. Resorting to the Ourvi maya, they burnt down the residents of heaven. They[521] thought about the moon, whose heart is made out of water and whose rays are cool. Burnt by the Ourva energy, their own energy was destroyed. The wielder of the vajra asked the gods what had happened.[522] They told him how they had been scorched by the arrows and burnt down by the maya of the danava soldiers.

'Thus urged, the king of the gods asked Varuna and he replied in these words. "O Shakra! In earlier times, a brahmana rishi had tormented himself through extremely terrible austerities. With qualities like those of Brahma, that energetic one's name was Urva. The undecaying universe, the sun included, was scorched by the fierceness of his austerities. With the gods and the devarshis, large numbers of sages presented themselves before him. In those ancient times, knowing of the rishi's supreme energy, the danava Hiranyakashipu, the lord of the danavas, also went there. The brahmana rishis spoke these words, which were full of dharma. 'O illustrious one! The foundation of this lineage and family of rishis has been severed. You are alone and without offspring. Without offspring, the gotra cannot continue. You have resorted to a vow of celibacy and are undergoing these hardships. O brahmana! There are many gotras of sages with cleansed souls. Since they were detached and without offspring, those remained in their bodies

---

[520] It is believed that mountains had once possessed wings.
[521] The gods.
[522] They weren't fighting and had sought refuge with the moon.

alone. There is no reason for you not to have offspring and have descendants. You are supreme in austerities and are like Prajapati in your radiance. By perpetuating your lineage, you will only extend yourself through them. Use the energy that you have accumulated and create a second body.' On being thus addressed by the sages, that sage's mind was disturbed. However, he did not accept the words of that large number of rishis and said this in reply. 'This is the eternal dharma of sages, laid down from ancient times. They should follow the noble path of surviving on wild roots and fruits alone.[523] If one has been born as a brahmana, one must follow the state of being a brahmana. If one conducts oneself well and resorts to the path of brahmacharya, one is following the path of the brahman. Three kinds of means of subsistence are indicated for brahmanas who dwell in the state of garhasthya.[524] However, we reside in forest hermitages and the life of the forest is decreed for us. We should not eat, or should only subsist on air. Or we can be *dantaulukhalinas*[525] or *ashmakuttas*.[526] We should practise ten austerities, five austerities, or seven austerities.[527] These are the extremely difficult austerities and vows we must be engaged in. We must honour brahmacharya and hope for the ultimate objective. A brahmana's attribute of being a brahmana is gauged from his practice of brahmacharya. Those who reside in the supreme regions and know about brahmacharya have said this. Patience is based on brahmacharya. Austerities are based on brahmacharya. Brahmanas who base themselves on brahmacharya find a state in heaven. There is no success without yoga. There is no fame without success. There are no worlds without fame. Brahmacharya is the foundation and is the supreme austerity. If one controls the senses and this collection of the five elements[528] and if one practises brahmacharya,

[523] For those who resort to vanaprastha or sannyasa.

[524] Teaching, performing sacrifices and receiving gifts.

[525] Those who use their teeth as mortars, that is, they eat raw grain that has not been ground.

[526] Those who eat raw grain after it has been ground on stone.

[527] This is a reference to the kinds and number of fires one uses in practising austerities.

[528] The body.

what other supreme austerity does that person need? Without yoga, what is the point of tending to the hair? Without resolution, what is the point of observing rites and vows? Without observing brahmacharya, these three are merely signs of vanity.[529] Who is a wife? What is intercourse? What does this distraction of the sentiment mean? Brahma created subjects through his mind, with mental resolution alone. Following Prajapati's deeds, if you possess austerities and energy in your infinite souls, create mental sons. An ascetic worships a vagina that has been created through the mind. There is no need for intercourse with a wife to sow the seed. That is not said to be an ascetic's vow. Without any fear, you have spoken to me about destroying dharma and artha. It is my view that is not virtuous and is against what is right. I can create a blazing and beautiful body from my own. Without intercourse with a wife, I can create a son who is just like myself. I will thus give birth to a second one from my own self. This is the decreed way for those who reside in the forest and he will burn down the subjects.' Urva resorted to austerities. He used some darbha grass and kneaded it against his thigh. Using his powers, he used these two as kindling and generated a fire. Even without any kindling, suddenly, a garland of flames emerged, breaking through his thigh. Desiring to burn down the universe, a son was generated from the fire. Since he emerged by penetrating Urva's thigh, this was known as the Ourva fire. This was an extremely angry fire that was capable of burning down the three worlds. As soon as he emerged, he addressed his father in blazing words. 'O father! This hunger is constricting me and it will only abandon me if I burn up the universe.' The flames rose up to heaven and he belched in the ten directions. He burnt down all the creatures and the flames spread, like the fire of destruction."

'Varuna continued, "At this time, Brahma appeared before the sage Urva. 'Show compassion for the worlds. Control the son you have created through your energy. O brahmana! If you act in this way towards your son, you will do what is beneficial. I will give him a place to dwell in and food that is like amrita. O supreme among eloquent ones! There is truth in my words and you should listen to

[529] Shaving the hair, rites and vows.

them.' Urva replied, 'I am blessed that you have shown me your favours. O illustrious one! You have now given me this benediction. It is my view that you have shown me a great favour by granting me this. It is now morning and my desires have been met by your arrival. O illustrious one! What oblations will my son be satisfied by? How will he find happiness? Where will he reside? What kind of food will he survive on? He is extremely energetic and these will have to be commensurate with his valour. Please lay these down.' Brahma responded, 'There is a region known as Vadavamukha[530] in the ocean and he will reside there. O brahmana! I have been born from water and water also constitutes my mouth. Let him always dwell there and drink oblations of water. Let that be your son's resting place and residence. O one who is excellent in his vows! When the end of the yuga arrives, with me, he will roam around, destroying all creatures and rendering them lifeless. I have made this fire of destruction reside in the waters. At the time of destruction, he will burn down all creatures, including the gods, the asuras and the rakshasas.' Having been flung there by the power of the grandfather, the fire agreed to this and, surrounded by an orb of flames, entered Vadavamukha. Realizing the power of the fire known as Ourva, Brahma and all the other maharshis followed their respective paths and returned to their destinations. On seeing this, Hiranyakashipu prostrated himself flat before Urva,[531] worshipped him and spoke these words. 'O illustrious one! The worlds have witnessed this. Retreat now. O best among the sages! The grandfather has been satisfied with your austerities. O one who is great in vows! I am your son and that of your son[532] too. If I can pride myself on my deeds and if I am engaged in worshipping you, know me as your servant. When you see that I have sought refuge with you, please arrive here. O best among sages! My defeat will be nothing but your defeat.' Urva replied, 'I am honoured that you have shown me your favours and that you consider me to be your preceptor. O one who

[530] Literally, mare's head. The subterranean fire is thus named.
[531] The text says Ourva (the fire), but presumably means Urva (the sage). But the difference between the two is blurred in the text.
[532] Ourva.

is excellent in vows! You no longer have anything to fear on account
of my austerities. Accept this maya, fashioned by my son. This has
no weaknesses and is incapable of being touched even by the real
fire. Whenever your lineage faces a hardship, this will remain under
your control. Use it to protect your own side and burn down that
of the enemy.' He bowed down before the bull among sages and
assented to this. Successful, the lord of the danavas cheerfully went
to heaven. This is a maya that is impossible to withstand and is
difficult for even the gods to repulse. This is a fire that was earlier
created by Ourva and is a fire that is due to Urva's son. There is
no doubt that even with that daitya[533] gone, the fire has not been
rendered powerless. Through his own energy, in ancient times, the
creator has created this curse for us. O Shakra! O illustrious one! If
you wish to be happy and to counter this, then give me your friend,
the moon, who originates from the water. Through your favours,
there is no doubt that I will then be able to destroy this maya."'

Chapter 36

Vaishampayana said, 'Shakra, who extended the prosperity
of the residents of heaven, was delighted at this and agreed.
Using dew as a weapon, he instructed Soma to fight. "O Soma!
Go and help the wielder of the noose[534] destroy the asuras, for
the sake of the victory of the residents of heaven. Your energy
is unmatched. You are the lord of all the lords among the stellar
bodies. Those who know about juices say that all the juices in the
worlds are based on you. Your waxing and waning is evident in the
ocean and in your circling in the sky. You circle through night and
day and this is used as a standard to measure time in the universe.
There is the mark of a hare on your lap and this is nothing but
a shadow of the worlds. A person who doesn't know about the
god Soma cannot be a person who knows about the nakshatras.

[533] Hiranyakashipu.
[534] Varuna.

Your path is above that of the sun and you are stationed above the stellar bodies. You dispel darkness with your body and illuminate the entire universe. You are like a white sun that is cool in body. O moon! You are the lord of the stellar bodies. You are the soul behind the measurement of time and you are the creator of the year. You are the one who is worshipped. You are the undecaying essence of the sacrifice.[535] You are the lord of herbs. You are the source of all sacrifices. You are the source of water. You are the one who quenches heat. You are cool in your rays. You are the store of amrita. You are fickle. You are the one who is drawn by white horses." Soma replied, "O king of the gods! O granter of boons! For the sake of the battle, you have spoken to me. I will shower down dew and dispel the maya of the daityas. I will quench the heat with my coldness. Behold them, encircled by ice. In this great battle, the large number of daityas will be left without maya and without insolence." The creator of ice then showered down ice, mixed with rain. The daityas were encircled by this terror, as if by a large number of clouds. In that great battle, Varuna and Soma struck them with the noose and with white beams. The danavas were slain by that shower of ice and by being struck with the noose. In the encounter, those two lords of the water fought with the noose and with ice. It was as if two mighty oceans, stores of water, were agitating the battleground. The danava soldiers were seen to be flooded by this. The entire world was enveloped and whirled around by this storm. The moon and Varuna used their beams and the noose to pacify the divine maya that had been fashioned by the daityas. In the battle, they were scorched by the cool beams and the water and slain by the noose. The daityas were like mountains without summits and were no longer capable of moving. The daityas were afflicted by the ice and fell down, slain by the cool beams. All their limbs were covered in the ice, like a fire that no longer possesses any heat. Fortune turned perverse for the daityas. Their colourful vimanas tottered and lurched. Their hands were bound down by the noose. They were enveloped by the cool beams.

[535] As soma.

'On seeing this, the danava Maya unleashed another divine and danava maya. He created a net of mountains and these boulders and mountains seemed to laugh out aloud. These were covered with ugly trees fierce at the tips and had forests that were thick with caves. They were populated by lions, tigers and elephants and gigantic elephants trumpeted. There were large numbers of wolves and there were trees that were whirled around by the wind. He created and unleashed this famous maya of mountains in every direction. Meanwhile his son, Krouncha, travelled in the sky, as he willed, showering down and slaying large numbers of gods with falling trees, torrents of boulders and thunderous rocks. This injected a new life into the danavas. That traveller in the night made Varuna's maya vanish. In the battle, large numbers of gods were struck with rocks and clouds of iron. There was a terrible shower of boulders, interspersed with trees and mountains. Strewn with mountains, the earth was so terrible that it was impossible to cross. In the encounter, several of the gods were seen to be struck by rocks, some others were afflicted by the boulders. Others were obstructed by the large number of trees. They were distracted and their weapons were shattered. The bows slipped from their hands. With the exception of Gadadhara,[536] the army of gods abandoned the battle.

'Advancing in the battle, the prosperous lord did not tremble. Gadadhara, the lord of the universe, is patient and he was not enraged. The one who knows about destiny was like a dark cloud. He wished to see the progress of destiny in the battle. Janardana wished to see the gods and the asuras crush each other.[537] Instructed by the illustrious one, the fire god and the wind god joined the battle. Goaded by Vishnu's words, they dispelled the maya. When they joined that great battle, all the clouds were flung aside. The mountains of maya were burnt, reduced to ashes and destroyed. The wind united with the fire and the fire was fanned by the wind. It was like the end of a yuga. The daitya soldiers were incinerated and lost their senses. The wind chased them and the fire followed

[536] The wielder of the club, Vishnu's name.
[537] He was biding his time.

behind the wind. The fire and the wind roamed around amidst
the army of the danavas, as if they were playing. The limbs of
some of the danavas were burnt. Others tried to rise, but fell down.
Vimanas dashed against other vimanas. With the wind bearing
him on his shoulders, the fire was successful in accomplishing his
task. When they returned after destroying that maya, everyone
praised Gadadhara. The daityas lost all enterprise and the three
worlds were freed from their bonds. All the gods were delighted
and exclaimed, "Wonderful. Wonderful." When the one with the
one thousand eyes was victorious and Maya was defeated, all the
directions became auspicious and the rites of dharma started. The
path of the moon was cleaned and the sun was reinstated along his
path. The worlds regained their natural states. Good conduct was
seen amidst men. Death was restricted to his limits.[538] Oblations
were offered to the fire. For the sake of heaven, it was seen that
sacrifices started to be performed for the gods. All the guardians of
the world were in control of their respective directions. Since there
were no longer any evil deeds, ascetics could adhere to virtuous
characteristics. The side of the gods was delighted and the side
of the daityas was distressed. In that battle, dharma possessed
three feet and adharma possessed only one.[539] The great gate of
remaining established on a virtuous path was opened up. People
adhered to their own dharma, as befitted their varnas and their
ashramas. The kings were radiant in protecting their subjects. The
world was peaceful and without any taints. The terrible darkness
was pacified. Having accomplished their task, the fire and the
wind retreated from the battle. The world sparkled and rites were
performed, praising their victory.

'On hearing about the great fear caused to the elder brothers of
the gods,[540] a famous danava named Kalanemi showed himself. His

---

[538] Meaning, there were no untimely death.

[539] Dharma possesses four feet. This probably means that though
dharma proved to be superior to adharma, there was still adharma left.
Dharma possesses three feet in treta yuga. But a reference to treta yuga isn't
indicated.

[540] The demons and the gods are cousins, the demons being older.

crown was like the sun and his ornaments and bracelets jingled. He
seemed to surpass Mandara and his gigantic body was encrusted
in silver. He possessed one hundred arms, with one hundred fierce
weapons held in them. He possessed one hundred faces and one
hundred heads. The handsome one was stationed there, like a
mountain with one hundred peaks. His gigantic frame seemed to
stretch forward, like a fire during the summer. His hair had a smoky
complexion. His beard was tawny. His teeth, lips and face jutted
out. His gigantic frame was so large that it seemed to encompass the
three worlds. His arms were as expansive as the sky and the stride
of his steps was like that of mountains. When he exhaled from his
mouth, that breath was like clouds raining down. His eyes were
red and he was cross-eyed. His broad chest was like Mandara. He
was ready to confront all the large number of gods in the battle,
from whichever direction they might advance. He enveloped the ten
directions and roared at the large number of gods. He was thirsty
and insolent, like Death that arises at the time of final destruction.
He stretched out his gigantic palm in assurance, with large finger
joints. Those fingers were long and adorned with ornaments and
the finger guards moved when he did this. The handsome one raised
his right hand in a sign of assurance. He addressed the danavas
and uttered these words, "Arise and strike the gods." In the battle,
all the gods glanced towards their enemy Kalanemi, who was
like destiny, and their eyes became full of fright and terror. All
the creatures looked at Kalanemi's stride. They thought this was
another Narayana, with his valiant three strides.[541] As he stepped
forward with his first stride, whirling winds were generated in the
sky. The asura advanced into the battle and terrified all the gods.
With Maya, that Indra among the asuras gradually advanced into
the battle and it seemed as if Kalanemi and that daitya[542] were like
Vishnu with Mandara. With Shakra at the forefront, all the gods
were distressed. They looked towards the terrible Kalanemi, who
was advancing like destiny.'

[541] A reference to the vamana incarnation.
[542] Maya.

Chapter 37

Vaishampayana said, 'The danava Kalanemi delighted the danavas. His great energy increased, like a cloud at the end of the summer. The lords of the danavas saw him increase his size, until it covered the three worlds. They forgot their exhaustion and arose, as if they had obtained supreme amrita. With Maya and Tara at the forefront, they abandoned their fear and terror. Desiring to fight, the danavas picked up their weapons again. They consulted amongst themselves, arranged themselves in battle formations and prepared to attack. Delighted, the danavas looked towards Kalanemi. With Maya at the forefront, they advanced towards the encounter. All of them abandoned their fear and happily presented themselves for the battle. The great asuras were Maya, Tara, Varaha, the valiant Hayagriva, Viprachitti's son Shveta, Khara, Lamba, Arishta, Bali's son Kishora, Ushtra and Svarbhanu, foremost among immortals and one who fought in a crooked way. All of them were accomplished in the use of weapons. All of them had resorted to austerities. All these accomplished danavas advanced behind the supreme Kalanemi. They used heavy clubs, chakras, battleaxes, maces that were like death, bludgeons that could be flung, boulders, summits of mountains, rocks that were plated, spears, catapults, supreme cudgels made of iron, heavy weapons that could kill, shataghnis, machines that were released from yokes to batter down gates, nooses, pointed and sharp darts, spikes, bonds, clubs that were like snakes with flickering tongues, arrows that were like serpents, vajras, other blazing weapons, javelins, unsheathed and sharp swords and white and sparkling tridents. Inspired in their minds, they seized these weapons. With Kalanemi at the forefront, they stood in the field of battle. With the best of these radiant weapons, the army of the daityas was resplendent. It looked like the sky, when a thick and blue cloud has arrived and has shut out the nakshatras.

'Protected by Shakra, the army of the gods was also resplendent. It blazed with the hot energy of the sun and with the cool energy of the moon. Though it possessed the force of the wind, it was peaceful. The flags were bedecked with a large number of stars. The clouds were like garments and planets and stellar bodies seemed to smile in it. It was protected by Yama, Indra, Varuna and the intelligent lord of riches.[543] Devoted to Narayana, the fire god and the wind god also blazed. That divine and large army of the gods was like a turbulent ocean. With yakshas and gandharvas, it was shining and fierce, giving rise to fear.

'The two armies clashed, like the friction between heaven and earth when the end of a yuga arrives. There was a terrible encounter between the gods and the danavas, with forgiveness versus valour and insolence versus humility. The gods and the asuras fiercely penetrated each other's armies. The vanguards and the rearguards wrathfully engaged, like two oceans full of water. The armies of the gods and the danavas cheerfully advanced against each other, like two elephants emerging from blossoming forests in mountains. Many drums, kettledrums and conch shells were sounded and this roar enveloped the directions, shrouding heaven, the firmament and earth. There was the twang of bowstrings, the slapping of palms and the swishing of bows. The roar of the daityas was dampened by the roar of the drums. They attacked each other and brought each other down. Desiring to fight, they attacked each other with their hands and wrestled with their arms. The gods attacked with terrible vajras and iron clubs. The danavas attacked with sharp swords and heavy bludgeons. They were brought down, their limbs battered with clubs and mangled with arrows. Some fell down. Others were dreadfully hurt. Still others lay down. Wrathfully and angrily, they attacked each other in that battle, using chariots, horses and swift vimanas. Some whirled around in that battle, others retreated. Chariots obstructed chariots and foot soldiers obstructed foot soldiers. The tumultuous clatter of chariots was borne along on the sounds that were already there, like the thunder of clouds carried in the sky by the rumblings of existing clouds. Some chariots were used to fight. Other chariots were used to obstruct. Because of the melee that was created, there were other chariots that were not in a position to move. They attacked each other in that battle. Some proud ones flung down the enemy. As they attacked each other

[543] Kubera.

with sword and shield, the ornaments jangled. In the battle, they attacked and mangled each other with weapons and vomited blood. It was like a sharp downpour when clouds assemble. Astra clashed against shastra. The agitated attacked the agitated with clubs. As that tumultuous battle raged, both the gods and the danavas were agitated. The danavas were like a giant cloud and the gods attacked them with radiant weapons. As they showered arrows on each other, the day of the battle turned catastrophic.

'While this was going on, the danava Kalanemi became angry. He was like a turbulent ocean that overflowed because of rain from a cloud. Showers of blazing vajras sought to afflict his head and body, which was like a mountain. But like a cloud that has discharged its lightning, these were fruitless. He sighed in rage. He frowned and perspired profusely. His breath seemed to be tinged with fire and flames seemed to issue from his mouth. His arms seemed to diagonally extend up into the sky and were like dark-hued serpents with five hoods and flickering tongues.[544] The arms held many kinds of weapons, like bows and clubs. The sky and the firmament seemed to be enveloped by them, as if by mountains. In the forefront of the battle, his garments fluttered in the wind. He was like Mount Meru itself, with its summit touched by the evening sun. The force of his thighs flung aside mountains, large summits, trees and brought down large numbers of gods, like a giant mountain shattered by the vajra. In that battle, the gods were incapable of standing before Kalanemi. He used many weapons and swords to mangle their heads and chests. Some were slain by the blows of his fists. Others were dismembered. The yakshas, gandharvas and birds were brought down, together with the large serpents. In the battle, the gods were terrorized by Kalanemi. Though they tried, they were bereft of their senses and were incapable of making efforts. In the battle, he used arrows to bind down Shakra, the thousand-eyed one, while he was astride Airavata[545] and he was incapable of moving. In the encounter, he deprived Varuna of his noose and repulsed him in every way, so that he looked like a cloud without any water

[544] The five fingers are being compared to the five hoods of serpents.
[545] Indra's elephant.

or an ocean without any water. Vaishravana[546] could assume any form at will and fought with clubs. However, the lord of riches was defeated, prevented from acting and lost his guardianship of the worlds. Yama is the one who takes everything away and uses death as a weapon. However, that immortal was deprived of all of Yama's powers and fled to his own direction. He appropriated the tasks of the guardians of the worlds and dividing his body into four parts, took over the four directions.[547] With Svarbhanu[548] indicating the way, he went to the the divine path followed by the nakshatras. He seized Lakshmi[549] from Soma and deprived him of his great kingdom. The sun, the one with the blazing rays, moves along the gate of heaven. However, he[550] seized his kingdom, the solar paths and the task of determining times of the day. Agni is the mouth of the gods.[551] On seeing him, he replaced Agni's mouth with his own. He swiftly defeated Vayu and brought him under his own subjugation. He forcibly brought the ocean and all the rivers under his control. Through his energy, he controlled all the bodies of water and made them part of his own body. He conquered all the waters, whether they were on heaven or on earth, including those that were protected well by the mountains. It was as if he established his own universe. Controlling all the great elements, he was as resplendent as Svayambhu himself. The daitya pervaded all the worlds and terrified all the worlds. He appropriated the sun, the moon and the planets and made the guardians of the worlds become parts of his own body. In the battle, having vanquished fire and the wind, the danava blazed. Because of his powers, in the worlds, he assumed the status of Parameshthi.[552] The large number of daityas praised him, as gods praised the grandfather.'

[546] Kubera.
[547] The four guardians of the worlds, in the four directions, are Indra, Varuna, Kubera and Yama. All four were defeated.
[548] Rahu.
[549] The goddess of prosperity.
[550] Kalanemi.
[551] Because Agni conveys oblations to the gods.
[552] In this context, this means Brahma.

Chapter 38

Vaishampayana said, 'There are five traits that are vested
with Narayana—the Vedas, dharma, forgiveness, truth and
prosperity. However, because of his perverse deeds, he did not
obtain any of these. The lord of the danavas desired this Vaishnava
status. Having not obtained it, he angrily rushed to Narayana. He
saw him there, astride Suparna,[553] holding the conch shell, chakra
and mace. For the destruction of the danavas, that sparkling mace
was being whirled around. He was astride that crested bird with
golden feathers, Kashyapa's offspring. He looked like a cloud that
was full of water and lightning seemed to issue from his garments.
In the battle, for the destruction of the daityas, he serenely waited
in his place. On seeing that Vishnu was not agitated, distressed in
his mind, the danava spoke these words. "From ancient times, right
from our noble danava ancestors, this one has been our enemy,
from the time of Madhu and Kaitabha, who resided in the waters. It
has indeed been said that our clashes with him have never brought
us peace. In encounters, this is the one who has slain many danavas.
In encounters, this is the one who has brought misery to women and
children.[554] He is the one who accomplished the task of ensuring
that danava women were no longer *simantinis*.[555] This is Vishnu
of the gods, who resides in Vaikuntha in heaven. He sleeps on
the serpent Ananta and on the waters. He is the self-creating one
who created Svayambhu.[556] He is the one who protects the gods
and he is the one who causes us injury. Hiranyakashipu was slain
because he confronted his rage. The gods hide in his shadow and
station themselves in the forefront of sacrifices. They thus enjoy the
oblations that are offered by maharshis at the three kinds of rites.[557]

---

[553] Garuda.

[554] By killing husbands and fathers.

[555] A simantini is a woman who is married (not widowed), denoted by
a parting of the hair.

[556] Brahma.

[557] This probably means nitya karma (daily rites), naimittika karma
(occasional rites) and kamya karma (rites performed for a specific objective).

He is the cause of the destruction of all those who hate the gods. In a battle, it is his chakra that penetrates our lineage. For the sake of the gods, it is indeed he who is prepared to give up his life in battles. He hurls the chakra towards the enemy and it is like the sun in its energy. He represents death for the daityas and he is stationed as if he is my death too. However, this evil-minded one has exceeded his earmarked timespan and will reap the consequences. It is through good fortune that this Vishnu has appeared before me now. Unless he bows down before me, he will be crushed by my arrows now. It is through good fortune that I have confronted the one who has earlier caused us injury in battles. It is this Narayana who slew danavas and inspired fear in them. In this encounter, I will use my arrows to swiftly kill Narayana. Though he is part of our kin,[558] he obstructs danavas in battles. In ancient times, this is the one who was known as Padmanabha.[559] In a terrible battle fought in the waters, he killed Madhu and Kaitabha. In earlier times, he divided his body into two, half man and half lion, and killed my father, Hiranyakashipu. As if she was celestial arani,[560] this is the one whom Aditi had borne in her womb earlier. In three strides, he conquered the three worlds.[561] Such is the one who has again appeared before me in the tarakamaya battle. Having faced me, he will be destroyed, with all the gods." In the encounter, he attacked Narayana with these and many other words. He was eloquent and used other similar disagreeable words in the battle. However, though he was thus attacked by that Indra among the asuras, Gadadhara was not enraged. With the strength of forgiveness in his mind, he smiled and spoke these words. "O daitya! Enough of this strength of insolence. Be steady against my strength of lack of anger. You will now be slain because of your sins of insolence. Your words have transgressed my threshold of forgiveness. It is my view that you are wicked. Shame on the strength of your words. Those who shout like women are

[558] Since they share a common father (Kashyapa), the gods and demons are cousins.

[559] Literally, the one with a lotus in his navel.

[560] Two pieces of wood used to generate fire through friction.

[561] A reference to the vamana incarnation.

not men. O daitya! I can see that you will venture along the path
trodden by your ancestors earlier. Having crossed the boundaries
that Prajapati decreed, how can one walk in comfort? You are one
who causes hardships to the gods and I will slay you. I will then re-
establish the gods in their respective places." The one who sports
the srivatsa mark spoke such words in the battle.

'But the danava laughed. He angrily seized chakras and other
weapons. In the battle, he seized all kinds of weapons in his one
hundred arms. His eyes red with anger, he struck Vishnu in the
chest with these. In the battle, with Maya and Tara at the forefront,
all the danavas rushed towards Vishnu, holding swords and other
weapons in their upraised arms. The extremely strong daityas struck
him with all kinds of upraised weapons. However, Hari did not
tremble in the battle, like an immobile mountain. The great asura,
Kalanemi, engaged with Suparna. He used all his strength, raised
a mighty club in his arms and angrily released this terrible and
flaming weapon at Garuda. Vishnu was astounded at the daitya's
deed. The club descended on Suparna's head. On seeing that
Suparna was wounded and hurt, he[562] felt as if his own body had
been hurt. His eyes red with rage, he seized the Vaikuntha chakra.
The lord's force increased and became like that of Suparna's.
His arms increased in size and enveloped the ten directions. The
directions, the sub-directions, the sky and the earth were permeated
by these. With this energy, he increased his size and again wished
to overcome the worlds. For the victory of the foremost gods, he
increased his size in the firmament. The rishis and the gandharvas
praised Madhusudana. His crown seemed to write in the sky and
his garments touched the clouds. His feet were on earth and his
arms covered the directions. Sudarshana was terrible and a sight
to be seen. It blazed like the fire. Its complexion was like that of
the sun's rays. It had one thousand blades and was the destroyer
of enemies. It was terrible, with a handle made out of diamonds.
Its inner parts were also made out of gold. It was smeared with the
fat, bones, marrow and blood of danavas who had been destroyed.
It was a weapon without a second. It was circular, right up to the

[562] Vishnu.

razor-sharp edges. It assumed whatever form it willed and could go wherever it wished. It was like an unthreaded garland. It had been created by Svayambhu himself and was a cause of fear to all those who were enemies. Since it was full of the rage of maharshis, it was always proud in a battle. When it was hurled in a great battle, all the mobile and immobile objects in the worlds were confounded. It was only predatory and similar beasts who were satisfied.[563] It was unmatched in its deeds and was like the rays of the sun. Blazing with rage, Gadadhara raised this chakra in the battle. With his own energy, Shridhara[564] dried up the danava's energy in the battle. With the chakra, he severed Kalanemi's arms. The daitya possessed one hundred curved and terrible heads that seemed to spit fire and laugh out aloud. Using his force and strength, Hari severed these with his chakra. Though his arms and heads were severed, the danava did not waver. The headless torso remained in the battle, like a tree bereft of its branches. Garuda stretched out his giant wings and his speed was like that of a storm. He struck Kalanemi with his chest and brought him down. Deprived of a head, the body whirled around in the sky and fell down. Dislodged from the firmament, it fell down and agitated the surface of the ground. When the daitya fell down, the gods and large numbers of rishis pronounced words of praise and collectively worshipped Vaikuntha.[565] There were other daityas who wished to exhibit their valour in the battle. In the encounter, he[566] grasped all of them with his arms and they were incapable of moving. He seized some of them by the hair. He afflicted the throats of others. When their heads were severed, some were brought down. Others were seized by the waist. Consumed by the mace and the chakra, they lost their spirits and lost their lives. All their limbs were dislodged from the sky and fell down on the ground. Purushottama slew all the daityas. Gadadhara thus accomplished a task that was dear to Shakra.

[563] Because they could feed on the dead.
[564] Vishnu's name, one who holds Shri.
[565] This probably means Sudarshana chakra.
[566] Vishnu.

'When they were crushed, the tarakamaya battle came to an
end. Brahma, the grandfather of the worlds, quickly arrived at the
spot, accompanied by all the brahmana rishis, gandharvas and large
numbers of apsaras. He worshipped the god Hari, the god of the
gods, and spoke these words. "O god! You have performed a great
deed and have uprooted the thorn of the gods. We are delighted
that the daityas have been slain. O Vishnu! You have slain the
great asura, Kalanemi, who was full of insolence. There is no one
other than you who could have killed him in a battle. He is the one
who defeated the gods and all the worlds, with their mobile and
immobile objects. He created hardships for the sages and roared
back at me too. His fierce oppressions have been terminated by you
and I am pleased at your deeds. You have brought down Kalanemi,
who was like death himself. O fortunate one! Come with me. Let
us go to the supreme celestial regions. The brahmana rishis have
assembled there and are waiting for you. You are supreme among
those who grant boons. What boon can I possibly grant you? For
the gods and the daityas, you are the supreme granter of boons. O
Vishnu! In this great battle, the three worlds have now emerged and
are bereft of thorns. Let them be returned to the extremely great-
souled Shakra." The illustrious Brahma spoke in this way to Lord
Hari. Addressing all the gods through Shakra, he[567] spoke these
auspicious words. "O residents of heaven who have assembled
here! Listen. With Purandara at the forefront, hear with bodies
that are now hale. In this battle, all the danavas, whose valour
was greater than that of Shakra and who followed Kalanemi, have
been slain. He has also been killed. However, there are two who
have emerged unscathed from this clash—Virochana's son,[568] Indra
among the daityas, and Svarbhanu, the great planet. Let Shakra and
Varuna head for whatever direction they desire. Let Yama protect
the southern quarters and let the lord of riches protect the north.
Let the moon roam around and at the right time, have conjunctions
with the nakshatras. With the seasons at the forefront, let the
years worship and follow the course of the sun. Let the brahmanas

567 Vishnu.
568 Meaning Bali.

perform the decreed rites and offer oblations into the fire. With
assistant priests, let them worship and offer the prescribed shares at
sacrifices. Let maharshis study and offer sacrifices and oblations to
the gods. Let the ancestors be cheerful and satisfied through funeral
ceremonies. Let the wind move along its paths. Let the three fires
blaze.[569] Let the three varnas[570] and the three worlds be satisfied
through their own natural qualities. Let sacrifices continue and
let brahmanas initiate themselves into these. As has been ordained
for sacrifices, let appropriate dakshina be distributed. Let the sun
satisfy the earth. Let Soma provide juices. Let Vayu provide the
breath of life in all living beings. Let everyone be content through
auspicious and peaceful deeds. O great Indra! As used to be the case
earlier, let all the waters in the rivers, the mothers of the worlds,
arise and flow down to the ocean. Let the gods abandon their fear
of daityas and depart in peace. Let everyone be fortunate. I will go
to Brahma's eternal world. In your own houses, in the world of
heaven and especially in battles, you should not remain content.
The danavas are always inferior. It is certain that they will strike,
whenever they find a weakness. Therefore, your sentiments must
be upright and peaceful and your intelligence must be virtuous."
Vishnu, whose valour is the truth, spoke in this way to the large
number of gods. With Brahma, the immensely illustrious one
then went to Brahma's world. This is how the wonderful battle of
tarakamaya was conducted between the danavas and Vishnu. This
is what you had asked me about.'

Chapter 39

Janamejaya asked, 'O brahmana! The god of the gods, the one
who was created from the water, went with Brahma to Brahma's
world. What did he do there and what did he do in Vaikuntha?
After Vishnu had been honoured by the gods because of his deed

---

[569] Ahavaniya, garhapatya and dakshinatya.
[570] The first three varnas.

of slaying the daityas, why did the original god[571] take the one who was created from the waters with him? What was his status in Brahma's world and what kind of yoga did he practise? What were the rituals that were followed by the lord who is the origin of all creatures there? While he was there, what happened to this great world and universe? How did it obtain the great prosperity that is desired by the gods and the asuras? At the end of the summer, how did he sleep on that undecaying ocean and how did he wake up? While he was in Brahma's world, how did he hold up the burden of the worlds? O supreme among brahmanas! I wish to hear about the celestial conduct of the illustrious one in heaven. Tell me the truth in detail. I wish to know about everything.'

Vaishampayana replied, 'Hear in detail about Narayana's conduct, about how he found delight with Brahma in Brahma's world. His wishes and his movements are subtle and even the gods find it difficult to follow them. I will tell you what I am capable of. Listen to me with single-minded attention. That god is nothing but the worlds and the three worlds are nothing but him. All this is full of that god and heaven is nothing but that god's consciousness. Know that everything that makes the gods prosper flows from Janardana. Know that everything that the gods undertake flows from Madhusudana. Learned and knowledgeable people know that the world is full of Agni and Soma. The learned know that the world, full of Soma and Agni, is nothing but Vishnu and the grandfather. Curds are made from milk and butter is created from curd. In that fashion, Janardana churns creatures out of this world. The paramatman is known to exist in senses and in creatures. In a similar way, Hari is known through the Vedas, the gods and the worlds. The embodied bodies of creatures on earth are pervaded by the senses. Similarly, the gods in heaven are pervaded by the lord's Vaishnava powers. The sacred paramatman distributes the fruits of sacrifices to the performers of sacrifices. He is the one who holds the strands of the worlds and mantras are used to honour him through those mantras. There are many who possess ultimate knowledge about these strands. But even they cannot see his limits.

[571] Brahma.

Know that Madhava is supreme in the worlds and that he is the ultimate destination. When the gods are immersed in darkness, he is the one who displays the divine path. Listen to the ancient account of what transpired in Brahma's world. He went to Brahma's world and saw the grandfather's abode. All the rishis worshipped Vishnu, whose deeds are noble. He saw that the maharshis had kindled a fire and were offering oblations into this. Following the ordinances that are laid down for such auspicious occasions, the immensely energetic one honoured them. He accepted his share at the sacrifice, which was established on his body alone. The rishis honoured the immensely radiant one and were honoured back in turn. The one who cannot be thought of roamed around Brahma's eternal world. He saw the auspicious sacrificial altars, which were bedecked with the best of sacrifices. He saw signs of the brahmana rishis performing hundreds of sacrifices. He inhaled the smoke that arose from these and heard the brahmanas chanting from the Vedas. He saw the sacrifices, which were nothing but manifestations of his own self. All the rishis, gods, priests and assistant priests raised their hands to revere him. They lowered their faces and told the auspicious one, "O best among the gods! O Padmanabha! O immensely radiant one! Welcome. Accept the hospitality of this sacrifice, performed with mantras. You are the auspicious sacrifice, the vessel and sacred padya in the vessel. You are the guest that the mantras have spoken about and it is evident that the guest has now manifested himself. O Vishnu! Ever since you left for the battle, our rites had ceased. It is not recommended that any rites should be performed in Vishnu's absence. This sacrifice, performed with dakshina, will lead to fruits. However, may we immediately obtain these, since we have been able to see you." The illustrious one agreed to this and honoured them back in return. With Brahma, the grandfather, he rejoiced in Brahma's world.'

Chapter 40

Vaishampayana said, 'Worshipped by the rishis, the lord Hari entered Brahma's ancient and divine abode, which was nothing but Narayana's hermitage. Cheerful in his mind, he took his leave from those who had come for the sacrifice.[572] He bowed down before the original god, Brahma, who had been born out of the lotus. He entered Narayana's hermitage, which was named after his own name. However, before entering, the illustrious one laid aside his weapons. He saw his own abode there, which was like the ocean. The large number of elements and the eternal maharshis resided there. The lords of the *samvartaka* clouds[573] were there and it was also a place inhabited by the nakshatras. It was enveloped in shrouds of darkness and even the gods and the asuras could not penetrate it. This wasn't the dominion of Vayu, the moon or the sun. That region was pervaded by Padmanabha's energy and form. The one with the thousand heads entered there, bearing an extremely great burden of matted hair, and prepared to lie down and sleep. Kali[574] knows about the time for the end of the worlds. She bears the form of destiny and her abode is in the eyes. That sleep presented herself before the great-souled one. He lay down on that divine bed, made cool by the waters of the ocean. Hari is supreme among those who follow vows and he followed the vow that is known as that of the single ocean.[575] For the creation of the universe, the great-souled lord lay down there. The gods and the large number of rishis continued to worship Vishnu. While he was asleep, a beautiful lotus manifested itself from his navel. This possessed the complexion of the sun and it was Brahma's original abode. While the great sage[576] slept, Brahma was like an original strand created from his upraised hand. This is how he whirls around all the worlds in the cycle of time. The breath is exhaled from his open mouth and the different categories of beings are created from his breath and merge into it again. Following this inviolate

[572] The sages.

[573] Clouds that are seen at the time of destruction.

[574] Kaali, the dark one, being used in the sense of a personified form of sleep.

[575] At the time of destruction, the universe is reduced to a single ocean and Narayana sleeps on the waters, following the vow of yoga.

[576] Vishnu.

principle, the four categories of beings[577] are created by Brahma himself and depending on their respective deeds, head towards their own destruction. Brahma himself, nor the undecaying brahmana rishis, know the nature of Vishnu's sleep and yoga, enveloped as he is in austerities. All the brahmana rishis, with Brahma at the forefront, do not know when he sleeps and when he awakes and is seated on his seat. Who is awake? Who sleeps? Who breathes? Who does not move? Who is the one who enjoys? Who is radiant and fair? Who is dark?[578] They are incapable of comprehending the god's divine origin. They are incapable of understanding his deeds and his birth. The rishis who know about what has been instructed in the ancient texts speak about his ancient character. The gods hear about his ancient conduct, described in the great Puranas and other texts. However, no one knows about his end. They know that the Vedas are themselves a manifestation of his own power and character. The Vedas and the popular texts are pervaded by these and one hears about them. When it is time for the creation of the worlds and for the destruction of the danavas, Madhusudana, the creator of beings, awakes. When Achyuta sleeps, the gods are incapable of looking at him. When it is the end of the summer and the end of the monsoon, he awakes from his sleep. When he sleeps, sacrifices and rites, accompanied by auspicious mantras, are not performed. Sacrifices are performed when Madhusudana wakes in the autumn. While Vishnu sleeps, Purandara, the lord of rain, peforms the Vaishnava tasks that must be performed as part of the yearly cycle. It is this deep maya that is present in the world in the form of sleep. Sometimes it suddenly assumes a hateful and terrible form and appears before kings as the night of destruction. Night is the destroyer of the day. On earth, it assumes this form, envelopes the bodies of all embodied creatures in terrible darkness and takes away half of their lives.[579] Sometimes, it penetrates them and makes

---

[577] Those born from eggs, those born from wombs, those born from sweat (worms and insects) and trees and plants. It might also mean the four varnas.

[578] These are rhetorical questions, the purport being that they do not know the answers to these.

[579] Because creatures sleep during the night.

them yawn repeatedly. They are incapable of withstanding its force, as if they have been immersed in the great ocean. Sleep pervades every creature in the world—because of eating, exertion, or when it is night. Sometimes, creatures on earth are destroyed while they are asleep. When it is time for creatures to die, it confronts them with terrible destruction. Even among the gods, with the exception of Narayana, no one is capable of withstanding it. The maya which emerges from Vishnu's body is a friend to the one who destroys everything. It can be seen in Narayana's face and in his lotus eyes. In a short while, all creatures in the world serve it and are confounded. Like a wife who is devoted to her husband, for a short while, for the sake of their own welfare, creatures should serve and bear the one with the black trails.[580] For the sake of confounding the worlds, the undecaying Vishnu slept and was immersed in sleep in Narayana's hermitage. The great-souled one slept for one thousand years. Krita yuga passed and so did treta yuga, supreme among yugas. At the end of dvapara yuga, the maharshis saw that the worlds were extremely miserable and praised the immensely energetic one, seeking to wake him.

'The rishis said, "Abandon this natural sleep, like garlands that have been enjoyed and have become old. With Brahma, all the gods are here, desiring to see you. They know about the brahman and chant hymns towards the brahman.[581] O Hrishikesha! The rishis, rigid in their vows, are praising you. O one who thinks of the creation of subjects! These elements, earth, space, fire, wind and water, and creatures are part of your own soul. O Vishnu! Listen to these auspicious words. The seven sages and other circles of sages are with them. O god! They are chanting your praise in divine and sweet words. O lotus-eyed one! Arise. O Padmanabha! O immensely radiant one! A task that will bring glory to the gods has presented itself."'

Vaishampayana continued, 'Hrishikesha arose in his supreme and blazing form, dispelling the waves of darkness that the entire

---

[580] A reference to sleep.

[581] This means the sages. Though the sages are speaking, they are referring to themselves in the third person.

universe had been immersed in. He saw all the assembled gods, together with the grandfather. They had assembled and wished to say something, because they were agitated because of the universe. With his eyes rested from the sleep, Hari spoke to the gods in words that were full of dharma, meaning and artha and wishing to ascertain the truth. "O gods! Whom is your conflict with? From where has fear arisen? What is the task and for whom? What has devolved on me? What has been caused by the danavas so that all is not well with the worlds? What has caused difficulties for men? I wish to quickly ascertain this. All of you know about the brahman. In your midst, I have abandoned my supreme bed and am stationed here, to do what is good for you. What can I do for you?"'

Chapter 41

Vaishampayana said, 'On hearing Vishnu's words, for the sake of the welfare of all the residents of heaven, Brahma, grandfather of the worlds, spoke these supreme words. "O Vishnu! From one battle to another battle, it is you who does the steering. O destroyer of asuras! As long as you are there, the gods have no fear. O lord of the gods! O slayer of enemies! Shakra's victory is based on you. How can men who endeavour to follow dharma suffer from fear? Men who are always devoted to truth and dharma are free from anxiety. Before their appointed times, Death is incapable of glancing towards them. Men, and their lords, the kings, do not falsely bear dissension towards each other and enjoy the one-sixth share.[582] They behave well towards their subjects and do not impose unwarranted taxes. They accumulate their treasures without these unwarranted taxes. They are forgiving and protect their respective dominions and prosperous habitations. They impose mild forms of punishment and sustain the four varnas. The advisers are virtuous and worshipped, without causing resentment among creatures. One-sixth the share

---

[582] Kings are entitled to one-sixth of all produce as a share, in the form of tribute or taxes.

is enjoyed and the army has the four kinds of forces.[583] Everyone is accomplished in dhanurveda.[584] Everyone is devoted to the Vedas. At the right time, they perform sacrifices and give copious quantities of dakshina at these sacrifices. They study the Vedas and maharshis initiate themselves into brahmacharya. Through funeral rites and offerings, they satisfy hundreds of ancestors. Of the three kinds of injunctions on earth, in the Vedas, in customary practice and as stated in the *Dharmashastras*,[585] there is nothing that is unknown to them. In terms of searching out what is best for others, those kings are equal to the maharshis. They are interested in tasks that will bring krita yuga back. Because of their powers, Vasava showers down auspicious rain at the right time and winds devoid of dust blow in the ten directions. There are no calamities on earth and the planets pursue their paths properly. The moon has amiable conjunctions with the nakshatras. In the right way, the sun moves along its two paths.[586] The fire is satisfied with many kinds of oblations that have auspicious fragrances. When everything is conducted properly in this way, the entire earth is satisfied and there is no fear of death among men. However, there are some kings who are more powerful than the others and they are afflicting the earth. In their blazing prosperity, they have followed each other. Because of the burden of oppression of these kings, the earth is exhausted and has appeared before us, like a boat that is about to sink. Freed of their bonds, the mountains seem to move, as if the end of the yuga has arrived. The waters are repeatedly agitated, as if releasing her sweat. The bodies and extensive dominions of these kshatriya men are full of energy and strength and are agitating the earth. In city after city, there are kings who are surrounded by crores of soldiers. This is also happening in many kingdoms and in hundreds and thousands of villages. Thousands of landlords have become powerful and strong.

[583] Infantry, cavalry, elephants and chariots.

[584] The art of fighting.

[585] Generally, sacred texts about dharma. Specifically, a class of texts.

[586] *Uttarayana*, the movement of the sun to the north of the equator, the period from the winter to the summer solstice and *dakshinayana*, the movement of the sun to the south of the equator, the period from the summer to the winter solstice.

Tens of thousands are sprouting in villages and in kingdoms, as if rendering the earth full of holes. She has been rendered powerless. With Time leading the way, she has come to my abode. O Vishnu! You are her supreme refuge. This earth is the arena of action and this earth is now pained. You should act so that the eternal universe does not suffer from further affliction. O Madhusudana! Her oppression is a great sin. If rites disappear from the worlds, the universe will be tainted. Oppressed by this wave of kings, it is evident that she is tired. She has abandoned her natural forgiveness. Though capable of moving, she has been rendered immobile. We have heard what she has said and you have also heard her. We wish to have a consultation with you, so that her burden can be reduced. When all kings are established on the virtuous path and kingdoms prosper, the three varnas of men[587] follow the brahmanas. All the varnas then speak truthful words and the varnas are devoted to dharma. All brahmanas are devoted to the Vedas and all men are devoted to brahmanas. When men pursue dharma, this is how the universe progresses. Therefore, we must consult so that dharma is not destroyed. There is no other virtuous path and dharma is the excellent cure. For relieving the burden of the earth, it is appropriate that the kings be slain. O immensely fortunate one! Come. Let us therefore have a consultation. With the earth at the forefront, let us go to the summit of Meru."'

Chapter 42

Vaishampayana said, 'In a voice that was like the thundering of the clouds, he[588] agreed to this. The one who dispels bad days and brings good days left, like a mountain tinged with lightning. He was adorned in pearls and jewels. His radiance was like that of the moon and clouds. With dark and matted hair, Hari was radiant in his dark complexion. There was dazzling hair on his

---

[587] Kshatriyas, vaishyas and shudras.
[588] Vishnu.

broad chest. The beautiful srivatsa mark was stretched between his
two nipples. The undecaying preceptor of the worlds was clad in
yellow garments. Hari was seen to be like a mountain, tinged by
the evening light. Following the words of the one born from the
lotus,[589] he departed on Suparna. Not taking their eyes off him, all
the gods followed him. In a short while, they reached the bejewelled
mountain. In the sky there, the gods saw the assembly hall, which
could assume any form at will. It was stretched out and attached
to the peak of Meru and was like the sun in its radiance. The
foundations were made out of golden pillars and the doors were
encrusted with diamonds. It was garlanded with a large number
of vimanas and was colourful, fashioned through the powers of
the mind. There were nets made out of gems. It was decorated
with jewels and could go wherever it wished. There were many
adornments fashioned out of gems. Everywhere, flowers blossomed.
It was divine and had been constructed by Vishvakarma.[590] It was
full of celestial maya. In cheerful frames of mind, following the
prescribed order, the gods entered the auspicious assembly hall and
sat down on their respective seats. As instructed, some of them sat
on seats, others seated themselves on vimanas. Some sat on thrones,
others on cushions and spreads.

'Urged by Brahma, the wind god Vayu asked everyone to be
quiet and this sound echoed throughout the auspicious assembly
hall. At this, there was silence throughout that conclave of the
residents of heaven. The earth spoke these words, which were full
of regret and self-pity. "In ancient times, when I was protected by
the one born from the lotus, two great asuras made out of earth
bound me down. When the great-souled Vishnu was sleeping on the
great ocean, like a log of wood, they emerged from the wax in his
ears. Goaded by Brahma's words, Vayu himself penetrated them.[591]
Those two great asuras grew and covered the sky. Having been
touched by Brahma, they obtained their breaths of life from Vayu.
One was soft and the other one was known to be hard. The soft

[589] Brahma.
[590] The architect of the gods.
[591] Thus giving them life.

one was named Madhu and the hard one was named Kaitabha.[592] Having obtained these names, those two daityas became powerful and insolent. There was nothing to fear and the entire universe was a single ocean of water. However, they desired to fight. On seeing them in front of him, Brahma, the grandfather of the worlds, sought refuge in that ocean of water and vanished. He had arisen from the lotus on Padmanabha's navel. Brahma, the one with the four faces, thought it desirable that he should hide inside the lotus. Narayana and the grandfather were both inside the water. Without any movement, they slept there for many years. After a long period of time, Madhu and Kaitabha came to the spot where Brahma was. The immensely radiant Padmanabha saw that the two terrible and great asuras, indomitable in battle, were swiftly advancing. There was a fierce encounter between them,[593] while the universe and the three worlds were immersed in that single ocean of water. That tumultuous encounter lasted for thousands of years. However, in that battle, the asuras were not exhausted at all. After a long period of time, the daityas, indomitable in battle, cheerfully spoke to the god, Narayana Hari. 'O supreme among gods! We are happy at this encounter with you and we are proud that in this battle, our death will be at your hands. However, slay us in a place that is not flooded with water. Once we have been slain, let us be reborn as your sons. If a person defeats us in battle, let it be such that we become his sons.' In the encounter, he seized the daityas with his arms and crushed them there.[594] Thus, Madhu and Kaitabha were slain. He flung the bodies into the water. Once flung into the waves in the water, the bodies of the daityas were fused into one and churned, releasing fat. That fat covered the water and the bodies disappeared. The illustrious Narayana again started to create subjects. It was because I was created with the fat of the daityas that I have come to be known as Medini.[595] For the sake of men, Padmanabha

---

[592] *Madhu* means soft and gentle. But the derivation of Kaitabha is contrived, since *kitaka* means hard.

[593] Narayana and the asuras.

[594] This being a place that was free of water.

[595] Medini is a name for the earth and meda is fat.

accomplished this through his eternal powers. While Markandeya looked on, he again assumed the form of a boar and raised me from the waters on a single tusk.[596] Later, in front of you, I was again struck by the daitya Bali and saved by Vishnu, through Vishnu's powers.[597] I am afflicted again and have come before Gadadhara. I am without a protector and he is the protector of the universe. I have sought refuge with the one who is the refuge. Agni is the preceptor of gold. The sun is said to be the preceptor of cows. Soma is the preceptor of nakshatras and Narayana is my preceptor. I alone hold up the world and its mobile and immobile objects. Though I hold them up, everything is actually held up by Gadadhara. When I was oppressed, Rama,[598] Jamadagni's son, became angry. To reduce my burden, he eliminated kshatriyas twenty-one times. Bhargava used me as a sacrificial altar and seemed to perform a funeral rite for his ancestors, the descendants of Kashyapa, offering the blood of kings. I was drenched with evil-smelling flesh, fat, bones and the blood of kshatriyas. It was as if a young maiden in her season stood before Kashyapa. The brahmana rishi told me, 'Why is your face downcast? You have taken the vow of being a wife to brave ones. Follow that vow of being the wife of a hero.' I told Kashyapa, the creator of the worlds, 'O brahmana! My husbands have been slain by the great-souled Bhargava. I am without brave kshatriyas, who earn a living through weapons. I am a widow and am not interested in sustaining cities that are empty. O illustrious one! Therefore, grant me a husband, who is a king and is like you. He should he able to protect the villages and the cities and me, extending up to the frontiers of the ocean.' On hearing this, the illustrious lord replied in words of assent and gave me Manu, an Indra among men. It is through Manu's auspicious powers, that the great lineage of Ikshvaku was generated. Over a long period of time, kings have come and kings have gone. This is what Manu, the intelligent Indra among men, gave me. I have been enjoyed by royal lineages that

[596] In the form of the varaha incarnation, the earth having been dragged down into the waters by the demon Hiranyaksha.

[597] The vamana incarnation.

[598] Parashurama.

were revered by the dynasties of maharshis. Many brave kshatriyas have conquered me and subsequently departed for heaven. Despite having obtained me, they came under the subjugation of time and met their destruction. It is for my sake that there have been conflicts in this world. Powerful kshatriyas, who did not withdraw from the field of battle, have fought. Their conduct has been determined by destiny. For the welfare of the universe, act so that these kings are destroyed in the field of battle. I am suffering from a heavy burden. Do this out of compassion for me. Let the handsome one who wields the chakra grant me freedom from fear. I am tormented and afflicted by the burden. I have come before you, seeking refuge. I am suffering from this great burden. Let Vishnu speak to me."'

Chapter 43

Vaishampayana said, 'On hearing the earth's words, all the residents of heaven thought about what might be done for her and spoke to the grandfather. "O illustrious one! Act so that the earth's burden may be reduced. You are the one who created the bodies in this world. You are the lord of the worlds. O lord of the gods! There are tasks that have to be performed by the great Indra, Yama, Varuna, the lord of riches, Narayana himself, the moon, the sun, the wind god, the Adityas, the Vasus, the Rudras who are the creators of the worlds, the Ashvins who are foremost among the gods, the Sadhyas who reside in heaven, Brihaspati, Ushanas, Time, Kali, Maheshvara, Brahma, Vishakha Guha,[599] the yakshas, the rakshasas, the gandharvas, the charanas, the giant serpents, the mountains that are best among mountains, the oceans, the giant waves, the divine rivers like Ganga and the others and other celestial rivers. O lord! Quickly instruct them about the portions they should resort to.[600] This is to accomplish the earth's task and to accomplish conflict among the kings. O grandfather! Among all of us, who

[599] Kartikeya.
[600] Their portions will be born on earth in different forms.

are the ones who should act so as to be born in different portions?
Who are the ones who will remain in heaven? Who are the ones
who will be born on earth as kings? Who will be assistant priests
among the brahmanas? Who will be born in lineages of kings? On
earth, who are the ones who will create bodies that are not born
from wombs?" The grandfather of the worlds was surrounded by
the gods and heard about the great resolution the gods had adopted
in accomplishing their tasks.

'He spoke these words. "O best among the gods! Your
resolution is agreeable to me. Use your energy to create your own
respective portions, which are equal to you, on earth. Let all the
best among gods use their energy to be thus incarnated. Think of the
goddess earth and obtain the prosperity of the three worlds. Know
that on earth, I have already done something in the Bharata lineage.
Knowing about what might happen to the earth, I have already
done this. O gods! In earlier times, I was seated on the western
shores of the ocean, with the great-souled Kashyapa, born from me.
We were conversing about what had transpired in the worlds earlier
and about what is in conformity with the Vedas. There were many
such earlier accounts, full of the qualities of power. While we were
conversing, Ganga and the ocean quickly came to me, with winds
stirring their waters. The beach was turbulent because of the force
of the wind and there were swift currents in the river. The ocean
was clad in colourful garments of water. His body was bedecked
with sparkling conch shells and pearls. There were ornaments made
out of coral and gems. Full because of the waxing of the moon,
the voice of the ocean rumbled. He transgressed his shoreline and
sought to overcome me. He drenched me with moving and saline
waters that drenched my seat. Because of the waves that arose, the
ocean disturbed that spot. I angrily spoke to him, asking him to be
peaceful. When I asked him to do this, the ocean became peaceful.
He withdrew the torrent of waves and stood there, blazing in his
regal prosperity. I then cursed the ocean and Ganga. There was a
reason behind this decision. It was done for the sake of your welfare.
'O ocean! You have presented myself before me in a form that is like
that of a king. Go. You will become a king and a lord of the earth.
Despite this, you will be able to sport in your natural form and

will be energetic. You will become a lord of men and an extender
of the lineage of the Bharatas. Since I asked you to be peaceful and
you adopted such a form, you will bear an excellent form in the
world and obtain fame. You will be Shantanu.[601] Ganga's limbs are
curved. This best of rivers will assume a form that is beautiful in all
her limbs and unite with you there.' When I spoke in this way, the
ocean was angry and replied. 'O lord! O lord of the gods! Why are
you cursing me? I have been created by you and have always been
devoted to doing what you have asked me to. I am like your son. I
should not be cursed. Why have you addressed me in such words? O
illustrious one! It is because of your favours that my force increases,
in accordance with the waxing of the moon. O Brahma! If I am
stirred because of that, how is it my fault? O illustrious one! I am
stirred by the wind. I am touched by the waxing of the moon. How
am I responsible for that and how can that be a reason to curse me?
I become turbulent because of strong winds, am strengthened by
the clouds and there is the waxing of the moons. These are the three
reasons behind my agitation. If I am guilty because of this, those
reasons have been created by you. O Brahma! You should pardon
me and take back your curse. Now that I have been disturbed by
this curse, I am without any support. O lord of the gods! Even if
you perceive some reason for guilt, you should exhibit compassion.
O god! Following your orders, this Ganga will now have to go to
earth. Even if I am guilty, she is guiltless and you should show her
your favours.' I then spoke to the great ocean in these gentle words.
He did not know about the cause of the gods and he was stirred by
the wind and terrified by the curse. 'O immensely intelligent one!
Depart in peace. Do not be frightened. I am pleased with you. O
lord of the rivers! Listen to the reason behind this curse. Go. Using
your own energy, adopt a body in the lineage of the Bharatas. O
lord of the rivers! Abandon and give up this form as an ocean. O
great ocean! Become a lord of the earth who is surrounded by royal
prosperity. O lord of the waters! In that portion, generated from
you, protect the four varnas. This best among rivers will adopt a

---

[601] *Shanta* means peaceful and *tanu* means body. Shantanu is hence
derived from these two words.

beautiful female form. At that time, in that beautiful form, Ganga will serve you. Following my instructions, this Jahnavi will find pleasure with you. O ocean! You will forget about the hardships this watery form brought you. On the instructions of the gods, you should swiftly act in this way. O ocean! Following the *prajapatya* rites, Ganga will marry you.[602] The eight Vasus have been dislodged from heaven and have gone to *rasatala*.[603] I am engaging you so that they may be born. I am giving those eight to you, to be born as your sons through Jahnavi's womb. They are like the sun in their qualities and bring pleasure to the gods. Quickly have these Vasus as your sons and make the lineage of the Kurus great. O ocean! You will then give up the human body and regain the form of an ocean.' O supreme among the gods! To ensure your welfare, this is what I have done in earlier times. I had foreseen the burden the earth would have to bear because of those kings. That is the reason I sowed the seeds of Shantanu's lineage on earth. O residents of heaven! The Vasus have been born as Ganga's sons. The eighth Vasu, Gangeya,[604] is still on earth. Seven Vasus have returned.[605] One still remains. Through a second wife, a second son will be born from Shantanu's body. This is the radiant and powerful King Vichitravirya. Vichitravirya will have two kings as sons. These will be the famous bulls among men, Pandu and Dhritarashtra. Pandu will have two young and beautiful wives. They will be the auspicious Kunti and Madri and they will be like goddesses on earth. King Dhritarashtra will have a single wife and she will be like him in conduct. She will be famous as Gandhari on earth and she will always be engaged in vows similar to those of her husband. That lineage will be divided into two parts, one on this side and one on the other. There will be a great conflict between the sons of the two kings. Because of that conflict between the sons, there will be a destruction of kings. There will be great fear, like the

---

[602] Prajapatya is one of the eight forms of marriage, one performed by the bride and groom taking seven steps around the sacred fire.

[603] Generally, the nether regions. There are actually seven nether regions—*atala, vitala, sutala,* rasatala, *talatala, mahatala* and *patala.*

[604] Meaning Bhishma.

[605] To heaven.

one that comes at the end of a yuga. The kings and their armies will bring down each other. The cities and the kingdoms will become devoid of inhabitants and the earth will be without enterprise. In ancient times, I had foreseen the end of dvapara yuga. At that time, using weapons, the kings and their mounts will be destroyed. When men are asleep and unconscious in the night, the one who will be born as Shankara's portion[606] will use the energetic agneya weapon and destroy the ones who remain. He will be like Death. When this performer of cruel deeds withdraws, the third dvapara yuga, which I have spoken about, will come to an end. When the portion of the great lord returns,[607] the fourth yuga, known as Maheshvara, will manifest itself[608] and this will be a yuga that is terrible and subhuman. Men will generally follow adharma and observe only a little bit of dharma. The propensity towards truth will be destroyed and the store of falsehood will increase. Men will only worship two gods, Maheshvara and Kumara. All men will have diminished lifespans. For the sake of the earth, this is the best decision—to bring about the destruction of kings. O gods! Without any delay, you should incarnate yourselves in your own portions. Kunti will bear the portions of Dharma and the others and so will Madri. As the foundation for conflict, Kali's portion will be born in Gandhari's womb. Goaded by destiny, kings will adopt either of the two sides. For the sake of the earth, all of them will be wrathful and will desire to fight. Let the earth, the sustainer of the world, go and bear them in her womb. This is the proper method for eliminating those kings, who will be famous in the worlds.'" On hearing the grandfather's words, the earth went away to wherever she had come from, biding her time for the destruction of the kings.

'To destroy the ones who hated the gods, Brahma urged the gods—the ancient rishi Nara, the serpent Shesha who holds up the earth, Sanatkumara, the Sadhyas, Agni, foremost among the gods, Varuna, Yama, the sun god, the moon god, the gandharvas, the apsaras, the Rudras, the Adityas and the Ashvins. The portions of

---

[606] A reference to Ashvatthama.
[607] That is, when Krishna dies.
[608] Kali yuga, described here as *maaheshvara* yuga.

all these gods should be incarnated on earth. This is what I have
spoken to you earlier about,[609] the incarnations of these portions.
On earth, some gods were born through wombs, others without
wombs. To slay daityas and danavas, these lords among men were
born. Some were as dense as *kshirika* trees.[610] Some could withstand
vajras. Some possessed the strength of ten thousand elephants.
Some were inferior in strength. They wielded clubs, maces and
spears. Their arms were like bludgeons. Some struck with summits
of mountains, others fought with clubs. There were hundreds and
thousands who were born in the Vrishni lineage. Gods were born
as kings in the Kuru and Panchala lineages. Some were prosperous
officiating priests, born in the families of brahmanas. There were
great archers who were skilled in the use of all weapons. There were
those who were devoted to the vows of the Vedas. When angry,
they were capable of shattering the earth, making mountains move,
rising up into the sky and agitating the great ocean. Brahma, the
lord of the past, the present and the future, instructed them in this
way, when they assembled before Narayana to ensure peace in the
world. Listen again to the account of Vishnu's descent on earth.
The lord, the lord of the richness of life, did this for the welfare of
the subjects. The intelligent Vasudeva was born in Yayati's lineage.
Born in that lineage, the lord Narayana performed deeds that were
revered and brought fame.'

Chapter 44

Vaishampayana said, 'Having been reassured about her well-
being, the earth left. In the Bharata lineage, the gods then

---

[609] In the Mahabharata.

[610] Since different kinds of trees are referred to as kshirika, the sense
has to be deduced. At a simple level, there is a sense of solidity. At a deeper
level, some kinds of kshirika (such as banyan trees) strike deep roots
and destroy the foundations of houses. Thus, these kings destroyed the
foundations of their lineages.

started to be incarnated in different portions. They were born in the portions of Dharma, Shakra, Pavana, the Ashvins, the physicians of the gods, and in Surya's portion.[611] The eighth of the Vasus, foremost among the gods, had already been born in his portion and had descended on earth. Death's portion descended on earth and so did Kali's portion. Soma's portion, Agni's portion and Varuna's portion descended on earth. Shankara's portion was incarnated and so were the portions of the Vishvadevas, residents of heaven. The portions of the gandharvas, serpents and yakshas also descended there. Narada was stationed in the sky and was coming down, towards the earth. Stationed there, he saw them descend and also saw that Narayana's portion was missing. He[612] was like a blazing fire, with eyes that were like the rising sun. A very large spread of matted hair hung down his left side. He was attired in garments that were as white as the moon. His ornaments were made out of gold. He held a giant veena, which clung to him like a beloved friend. His upper garment was made out of black antelope skin. His sacred thread was golden. He held a staff and a water pot and looked like Shakra himself. He secretly causes dissension in the world and is like a planet that engenders conflict. The maharshi is learned and knows about the knowledge of the gandharvas.[613] However, he is also attached to causing dissension. The brahmana finds pleasure in causing enmity. Indeed, he is like Kali in this. He is the one who chants the four Vedas. He is the foremost udgatri and officiating priest. Narada, the undecaying maharshi, roams around in Brahma's world.

'He stood in the assembly of the gods and angrily addressed Vishnu. "O Vishnu! The residents of heaven have incarnated themselves in their own portions. All of them have done this for the sake of the destruction of the kings. However, the destiny of the kshatriya kings is vested in you. It seems to me that, to accomplish this task, Nara and Narayana should also be engaged. O god! The

---

[611] Respectively, Yudhishthira, Arjuna, Bhima, Nakula, Sahadeva and Karna.

[612] What follows is Narada's description.

[613] That is, singing and dancing.

sight of the truth is determined by you and you know that they have not been engaged. O god of the gods! For the sake of the gods, they should also be employed in such a task. You are sight for the ones who possess sight. O lord! It is your power that is praised. You are foremost among the yogis who are engaged in yoga. You are the supreme objective among all kinds of objectives. O lord! You are supreme among all. You have seen that the portions of the gods have left. To aid the earth, why has your own portion not been engaged? With you, those divine portions will have a protector. That is the reason I am urging you. To rescue the earth, they have left on different kinds of tasks. O Vishnu! I have swiftly come here, to this assembly of the gods. I desired to urge you. Listen to the reason why I wished to do this. There are daityas who were killed by you in the tarakamaya battle. O Vishnu! Hear about the ones who have left for earth because of that. There is a city named Mathura on earth. It is on the banks of the Yamuna. It is prosperous, with many habitations. There was a great danava named Madhu and he was indomitable in battle.[614] He had a terrible forest named Madhuvana and he used to reside there. That extremely large spot is covered by gigantic trees. He had a great son and that danava's name was Lavana. He resided there and terrified everyone because of his strength. That danava sported there for many years. He was insolent and dislodged large numbers of gods from the worlds. Rama, Dasharatha's son, resided in Ayodhya, a place that was impossible to assail.[615] The one who knew about dharma ruled his kingdom and caused fright to the rakshasas. The terrible danava was proud of his strength and dwelt in the forest. He despatched a messenger who spoke harsh words to Rama. 'O Rama! I dwell inside your kingdom and I am your enemy. No king who is proud of his strength ever wishes to be a vassal. A king who desires the welfare of his subjects should devote himself to the vows of kings. He should desire to vanquish all his enemies and make the kingdom prosper. A king who desires to cause delight should not be content

---

[614] Not to be confused with the Madhu of Madhu–Kaitabha.

[615] There is a pun that a translation cannot capture. Ayodhya is the name of the place and also means something that cannot be assailed.

with wetting his hair at a consecration.[616] When one conquers the various senses, this is when one obtains a firm victory. In particular, a king must always desire that everything is proceeding properly. To convey instructions, in this world, there is no one who is equal to a preceptor. If an intelligent person is immersed in unwarranted pleasures, he cannot be said to be in the midst of dharma. A king who is superior in strength does not entertain fear of a king who is near his frontiers. All the senses are naturally prone to flourish. If a king acts agreeably towards his enemies, he robs himself of his prosperity. Confused because of a woman, you killed Ravana and his soldiers. I do not think this was desirable. This wasn't a great deed. It was a wicked one. Because of your vow, you resorted to residing in the forest. You killed inferior rakshasas there. This is not seen to be something recommended for the virtuous.[617] Dharma results from lack of rage. This auspicious trait conveys one to a virtuous end. Because of your confusion, you tainted the forest and killed many of its residents. Though you seemingly followed vows, that Ravana is blessed. He was slain in a battle over a woman, like one who follows the dharma of carnal pleasures. That evil-minded one could not control his senses and was slain in a battle. However, if you are truly valorous in battle, fight with me now.' Hearing the messenger's words, the one who spoke the truth said the following. Raghava did not lose his patience. Nor was he frightened. He smiled and said, 'O messenger! What you have said about a praiseworthy act is false. You have flung abuse at him. But I know the truth and am not disturbed. O stupid one! As long as I am established on the virtuous path, why should I now lament over Ravana being slain or about my wife being abducted? Righteous ones, based on the path of virtue, do not abuse through words. Destiny is always awake and distinguishes between the virtuous and the wicked. O messenger! You have accomplished your task of being an emissary. Now leave quickly. A person like me does not strike at inferior ones who

[616] The hair is sprinkled when a king is consecrated through an act of coronation. The word for king is derived from the word for causing delight and there is a pun in the Sanskrit text.

[617] Because there should be no violence in forest hermitages.

indulge in self-praise. This is my younger brother, Shatrughna, the
scorcher of enemies. He will counter the evil-minded daitya in a
battle.' Thus addressed, the messenger left with Sumitra's son,[618]
after taking the permission of the great-souled Raghava, Indra
among men. On a swift chariot, Sumitra's son reached the great
Madhuvana. Desiring to fight, he set up his camp on the outskirts
of the forest. Hearing the messenger's words, the daitya became
senseless with rage. He entered the forest and stationed himself,
ready to fight. A terrible encounter ensued between Sumitra's son
and the danava. Both of them were brave and persevering in the
field of battle. They struck each other with sharp and excellent
arrows. Neither of them was exhausted from the battle. Nor did
they retreat. Eventually, in the encounter, the danava was afflicted
by the arrows of Sumitra's son. The danava did not possess his
trident and suffered on that account. Shatrughna, the scorcher of
enemies, picked up a sword that had a golden handle and used that
to sever Lavana's head in the great battle. In the encounter, the
danava was thus killed by Sumitra's son, the one who delighted his
friends. Using his weapon, the intelligent one also cut down the
daitya's forest. Having cut down the forest, Sumitra's son created a
habitation there. The one who knew about supreme dharma
constructed a city at that spot. That city of Mathura is in the region
that was known as Madhuvana. In earlier times, after having killed
the danava in the battle, Shatrughna constructed it. The city is
extremely large and has mansions, walls and gates. It is full of rich
houses and is surrounded by prosperous kingdoms. Boundaries
have been laid down for well-planned gardens and groves. There
are high walls and moats encircle it. The tall mansions are like
headdresses, the palaces are like armlets. There are excellent gates
on all sides and the crossroads seem to be smiling. There are healthy
and brave men and it is populated by elephants, horses and chariots.
The city adorns the banks of the Yamuna and is like a crescent in
shape. It is sacred and protected. There are shops and the city is
proud because of its store of jewels. Since the god[619] showers down

[618] Meaning Shatrughna.
[619] Indra.

at the right time, the fields yield succulent produce. In that city, the men and women are seen to be cheerful. This city is nested in the dominion of the immensely valiant king, Shurasena, the extender of the Bhoja lineage. He was brave, with a large army, and is famous by the name of Ugrasena.[620] O Vishnu! In the tarakamaya battle, you killed the great daitya Kalanemi. He has been born as Ugrasena's son. His name is Kamsa and the large-eyed one is the extender of the Bhoja lineage. This king is brave and famous on earth. His tread is like that of a lion. He is terrible and causes fear to kings. So all the kings are scared of him. Since he has veered off the virtuous path, all creatures are frightened of him. Since his inner soul is terrible, he has immersed himself in terror. That has got united with insolence and the body hairs of the subjects stand up. He does not follow the dharma of kings, nor does he cause delight to his own side. He does not do what is agreeable for himself or his kingdom. He is fierce and always prone to excessive taxation. Having been defeated by you in the battle, he has been reborn there as Kamsa. With an asura in his inner soul, he behaves like a predatory beast and constrains people. In the water, there resided the brave Haya, famous by the name of Hayagriva.[621] That wicked Haya has been reborn as Keshi. That wicked one is skilled in neighing, but also sports a mane. He resides in Vrindavana, devouring the flesh of men. Bali's son was Arishta. That great asura can assume any form at will. He sports a hump and has assumed the form of a bull, bearing enmity towards cows. Diti's son, Rishta, was a superior danava. That daitya has assumed the form of an elephant and has become Kamsa's mount. There was an insolent daitya, famous by the name of Lamba. He has been reborn as Pralamba and dwells in a banyan tree in the Bhandira forest. The daitya known as Khara, supreme among asuras, has been reborn as Dhenuka. That terrible one dwells in a forest of palm trees and exterminates all the people who come there. There were two supreme danavas known as Varaha and Kishora. They have been reborn as the wrestlers Chanura and Mushtika and they are found in the arena. There were the danavas Maya and Tara,

---

[620] Shurasena and Ugrasena are the same person.
[621] Hayagriva was a demon killed by Vishnu.

who were like Death among danavas. They are in the city of
Pragyotisha, with Bhoumya Naraka.[622] O Vishnu! These are daityas
you killed and destroyed. However, on earth, they have assumed
the form of humans and are constricting men. It is through your
favours that the destruction of these danavas took place. They are
frightened of you in heaven. They are frightened of you in the ocean.
They are frightened of you on earth. However, there is no one else
they are scared of. O Shridhara![623] There is no one other than you
who can slay these wicked ones. Having been dislodged from
heaven, these daityas have left for the earth. O Keshava! As long as
you are awake, even if they are slain and uprooted on earth in their
human bodies, it will be extremely difficult for them to reach
heaven. O Vishnu! Therefore, you should yourself go to earth. For
the sake of the destruction of the danavas, you should create yourself
from your own self. When your unmanifest form becomes manifest,
it is sometimes seen and can sometimes not be seen, by the best of
the gods. You created the gods and they are being reborn on earth.
O Vishnu! Kamsa will be destroyed through your incarnation. It is
only then that the task the earth arrived for will be accomplished.
Your eyes are devoted to the land of Bharata and you undertake
important tasks there. O Hrishikesha! Therefore, go to earth and
slay the danavas."'

Chapter 45

Vaishampayana said, 'On hearing Narada's words, Madhusudana
smiled. The lord and the god, the one who is worshipped,
replied in these auspicious words. "O Narada! You have said this
for the welfare of the worlds. They are for well-being. Hear my
words of reply. It is known to me that the danavas have assumed
bodies and have been born on earth. I know which daitya has
assumed which body and I know about their forms. I know that

---

[622] Narakasura was the son of the earth (*bhumi*) and is known as
Bhoumya.
[623] Vishnu's name.

Kamsa has been born as Ugrasena's son on earth. I know about
the daitya Keshi having adopted the form of a horse. I know
about the elephant Utapalapida[624] and I know about the wrestlers
Chanura and Mushtika. I know about the daitya Arishta, who has
adopted the form of a bull. I know about the great asuras, Khara
and Pralamba. O brahmana! I know about Bali's daughter, Putana.
I know about Kaliya, who can be seen inside a pool in Yamuna.
O brahmana! Frightened of Vinata's son,[625] he resides there in the
form of a serpent. I know that Jarasandha is stationed at the head
of all the kings. I know about Naraka oppressing the virtuous in
Pragjyotishapura. I know that the earth, who loves me, is afflicted
by a great burden. I know everything about where these kings are. I
can see that when they are destroyed on earth in their human bodies,
they will not be able to enter Shakra's world and prevent virtuous
conduct there. I will now enter and immerse my atman in supreme
yoga. I will then be born on earth in a mortal and human form. I
will slay Kamsa and all the other great asuras. I will do whatever
is necessary to ensure peace. To proceed to that destination, I will
now enter yoga. I will slay the enemy, those who hate the excellent
immortals, in battle. It is for the sake of the world that the great-
souled ones have been born in their own portions. The gods, the
divine rishis, the gandharvas and the others have done this with my
consent. All this has been determined by me earlier." Having spoken
to Narada, he turned to Brahma, the grandfather, and said, "O
Brahma! Remain with me. O grandfather! Tell me whom I have to
slay in battle. Where will I be born? Where will I reside and what will
I wear?" Brahma replied, "O Narayana! O lord! Listen to me about
the means and about how you will obtain success. Hear about the
mother who will give birth to you on earth. O mighty-armed one!
You will be born in an excellent lineage on earth. The great lineage
of the Yadavas will sustain you. You will create yourself in that great
lineage and uproot the asuras. You will then establish wholesome
agreements among men. O Vishnu! In earlier times, the great-souled

---

[624] Kamsa's mount. The elephant is referred to as both Utapalapida and
Kuvalayapida. *Utpala* and *kuvalaya* both mean lotus and the elephant's
name literally means one who uproots lotuses.
[625] Garuda.

Varuna performed a sacrifice. However, Kashyapa seized the cows
that were to yield milk for that great sacrifice. Aditi and Surabhi
were two of Kashyapa's wives. Despite Varuna entreating them, they
did not return the cows. At this, Varuna approached me and bowed
his head down before me. He said, 'O illustrious one! My senior[626]
has appropriated my cows. Though my senior has accomplished
the objective of seizing the cows, he doesn't listen to my entreaties
of returning them, having been influenced by his wives, Aditi and
Surabhi. O lord! Those cows are divine and yield an eternal supply
of milk, as desired. Protected by their own energy, they graze right up
to the frontiers of the ocean. With the exception of Kashyapa, who
is capable of oppressing my cows? Their milk is like divine amrita
and there is an unlimited supply of this. You are the supreme refuge
and you must control anyone who had deviated, whether it is a lord,
a brahmana, a preceptor, or someone else who is superior. If the
powerful are not chastised, whether they perform an act knowingly
or unknowingly, there will be no preceptors in this world. Nor will
there be agreements among men. O illustrious one! You are capable
of taking action, as the case warrants. Return my cows to me and
I will return to the ocean. These cows are undecaying and they are
like goddesses to me. It is said that there is one conduct that must
be followed by the worlds, that of protecting cows and brahmanas.
Cows are the ones who must be protected first, because they are the
ones who save brahmanas.[627] If cows and brahmanas are saved, the
entire universe is saved.' O Achyuta! This is what Varuna, the lord
of the waters, told me. O one who knows about the truth! For the
sake of the cows, I cursed Kashyapa. 'The great-souled Kashyapa
has seized cattle. Therefore, following that trend, he will be born
as a cowherd on earth. His wives are the ones named Surabhi and
Aditi, who like an arani, gave birth to the gods. They will follow him
and become his wives there.' The one known as Vasudeva has been
born from Kashyapa's portion. He is like Kashyapa in his energy
and he dwells amidst cattle on earth. There is a mountain known
as Govardhana, not far from Mathura. He dwells amidst cattle

---

[626] Kashyapa is the father of the gods too. The Adityas, which includes
Varuna, are the sons of Aditi.

[627] By providing milk and other objects for sacrifices.

there and pays taxes to Kamsa. The intelligent Vasudeva has two wives—Devaki and Rohini, who are actually Aditi and Surabhi. O Madhusudana! For the sake of the worlds, you will incarnate yourself there. While you grow up, the residents of heaven will pronounce benedictions of victory over you. Creating yourself from your own self, descend there. Satisfy the wombs of Devaki and Rohini.[628] O mighty-armed one! With all the characteristics of a cowherd, you will be reared as a child there and become as strong as you once were, with your three strides. There are thousands of *gopa* daughters on earth.[629] You will overwhelm them and delight them with your own maya and forms of yoga. O Vishnu! Roam around in the woods and protect the cows, who will be blessed on seeing your form, adorned with garlands of wild flowers. O Vishnu! O lotus-eyed one! While you dwell as a child amidst those cowherds, everyone else will also behave like children. O Pundarikaksha! They will be devoted to you. Their minds will follow you. Whether you roam around in the woods, grazing cattle, and tend to them in their pens, or immerse yourself in the Yamuna, they will love you. Vasudeva will also dwell happily there, delighted that he can address you as 'son'. Who else but Kashyapa can address you as a son and is there anyone else whose son you can be? O Vishnu! With the exception of Aditi, who else is capable of delivering you? You will then use yoga to arise and advance towards victory. O Madhusudana! Let all of us now return to your respective abodes." Vishnu gave the gods permission to return to heaven. He went to his own region, the one to the north of the Kshiroda ocean.[630] There, on Mount Meru, there is a cave named Parvati that is extremely difficult to penetrate. The footprints of the one with three strides are there and are always worshipped on auspicious occasions. In that ancient place, Hari laid his body to rest. The lord harnessed his atman in yoga, so that he might be born in Vasudeva's house.'

This ends Harivamsha Parva.

---

[628] Krishna was born as Devaki's son and reared by Rohini.
[629] Gopas are cowherds.
[630] Literally, the ocean that yields milk.

Vishnu Parva

Chapter 46

Vaishampayana said, 'Knowing that Vishnu and parts of the gods would be born on earth, Narada went to Mathura to inform Kamsa that his destruction was imminent. He descended from heaven and stationing himself in a grove in Mathura, sent a message to Kamsa, Ugrasena's son. The lotus-eyed asura, Kamsa, was swift and valorous. On hearing about Narada's arrival, he emerged from his own city. He saw the praiseworthy guest, the divine rishi who was devoid of all sins. With a form that was like the sun's rays, he blazed in his energy. Following the prescribed rites, he honoured the rishi and worshipped him. He offered him a seat that was like the fire in its complexion. The sage who was Shakra's friend seated himself on that seat and addressed Ugrasena's son, who was extremely prone to anger. "O brave one! Following the prescribed rites, I have been worshipped by you. Once that is over, listen to my words and act in accordance with them. O son![631] I traversed the divine worlds, with Brahma's city as the foremost. I went to the gigantic Mount Meru, which is the sun's friend. I saw the grove of Nandana and the grove of Chaitraratha. With the gods, I bathed in all the excellent *tirtha*s. I saw the sacred river, with its three divine flows and the three courses that it follows.[632] In due order, I bathed in the celestial tirthas. I saw Brahma's abode, frequented by the brahmana rishis. It resounded

---

[631] The word used is tata.
[632] Ganga flows in heaven, on earth and in the nether regions.

with the sounds of gods and gandharvas and the sounds of the apsaras. On one occasion, I went to an assembly of the gods on Mount Meru. Grasping the veena, which I love, I went to Brahma's assembly there. With Brahma, I saw many gods seated there, on celestial seats, wearing white headdresses and adorned with diverse gems. I heard an extremely terrible consultation among the gods there and it was about the means to kill you and your followers. O Kamsa! Your father's sister, Devaki, is in Mathura. Your death will result through her eighth child. He will be everything to the gods. He will be the refuge of heaven. It is a supreme secret of the gods that he will be the reason for your death. He is supreme among the supreme. He is the self-creating one, from whom Svayambhu was created. This great and divine one will be born and I am incapable of even speaking about it. He prides himself that he has already been the cause of your death in the past.[633] O Kamsa! Remember that. If you can, endeavour to act, so that you can prevent the birth from taking place. I am pleased with you and that is the reason I have come here. Enjoy all the objects of pleasure. May you be fortunate. Let me leave now." Having said this, Narada departed.

'Having thought about this for a short while, Kamsa laughed loudly, showing his teeth. He smiled and spoke to the servants who stood in front of him. "It is indeed true that Narada has no spirit. Nor is he skilled. Whether I am fighting, lying down, distracted or intoxicated, the gods, along with Vasava, are incapable of frightening me. I am capable of agitating the earth with my two large arms. Who in this world of men is interested in trying to disturb me? From today, I will create great carnage among all creatures who follow the gods, whether they are men, birds, or large numbers of animals. Instruct the horse Keshi, Pralamba, Dhenuka, the bull Arishta, Putana and Kaliya that they can roam around the entire earth, assuming whichever form they wish to adopt. Let them strike all those who abuse our side. Find out about the progress of all those who are expecting on earth. Narada has said that we will suffer a great fear on account of conception. Be devoid of anxiety and enjoy yourself, in whatever form you desire. As long as you resort to me

[633] In the earlier life, as Kalanemi.

as a protector, there is nothing to fear from anything the gods might do. The brahmana Narada is addicted to creating dissensions and finds sport in doing this. He derives pleasure from causing conflict between people who reside in harmony. He is mobile and always travels around, trying to make people dance to his tune. He creates conflicts among kings, as if they are puppets on his string." Using words alone, he spoke in this way. After this, Kamsa entered his own residence, with his senses burning.'

Chapter 47

Vaishampayana said, 'Angrily, he[634] instructed all the advisers who were interested in his welfare. "All of you must make efforts to ensure that Devaki's embryo is destroyed. Let us destroy all the conceptions, starting with the first. When there is suspicion that injury may be caused, one must destroy the foundation. Let Devaki be protected in her house and guarded surreptitiously. Though she is protected by my soldiers, let her roam around freely, so that she is not scared. My women will keep count of the months, from when her menstrual flow starts. We will do the rest when we come to know that there has been a conception. Let Vasudeva be guarded, day and night, whether he lies down on the ground, or whether he is with women. Let those who are engaged in my welfare, women and eunuchs, do this, without being distracted. However, the reason for this should not be divulged. Men can only make those efforts that are humanly possible. However, hear how a person like me can counter destiny. By using a large number of appropriate mantras and by employing herbs well, it is possible to make efforts so that destiny turns favourable." These are the efforts Kamsa made to destroy Devaki's conception. Having heard about it from Narada, scared, he engaged in consultations.

'Having got to know about the possibility of injury, Kamsa made these efforts. Having heard about these, the valiant Vishnu,

[634] Kamsa.

who had disappeared, started to think. "The son of Bhoja will slay seven of Devaki's conceptions. I think my task should be to manifest myself in the eighth conception." Thinking in this way, he went to patala in his mind. The danavas known as Shadgarbhas were lying down there, waiting to be born. They were bright and valiant in form, like those who survive on amrita. They were the sons of Kalanemi and were like the immortals in battle. In ancient times, these daityas had worshipped the grandfather of the worlds. They had tormented themselves through fierce austerities and had sported matted hair. Pleased with them, Brahma had granted the Shadgarbhas a boon. "Tell me what you desire. What boon shall I bestow on you?" All those daityas had wanted the same thing and had told Brahma, "O illustrious one! If you are pleased with us, grant us this best of boons. O illustrious one! Let us not be killed by gods or serpents, or through the weapons of curses used by the self-controlled and supreme rishis. May we not be killed by lords among the yakshas, gandharvas, siddhas, charanas and humans. O illustrious one! If you wish to grant us a boon, let it be this." Having been thus addressed by them, Brahma had been extremely pleased in his mind. He had told them that it would be exactly as they had desired. Granting the Shadgarbhas the boon, Svayambhu had returned to heaven. At this, Hiranyakashipu[635] had been enraged and had spoken these words. "You abandoned me and sought a boon from the one who was born from a lotus. I am discarding my affection for you. You have become my enemies and I am casting you aside. Your father reared you and called you by the name of Shadgarbha. When all of you are conceived, it is this father who will kill you. You great asuras, the Shadgarbhas, will be conceived in Devaki's womb six times.[636] When you are conceived in this way, Kamsa will kill you." Vishnu went to patala, where those asuras were. Self-controlled, the Shadgarbhas were lying down in the water there, waiting to be conceived. He saw the Shadgarbhas lying down in the water there, treating the water like a womb. They were under the subjugation of sleep, the one who

[635] Their grandfather. Hiranyakashipu was Kalanemi's father.
[636] *Shadgarbha* means six conceptions.

has the form of the destroyer and makes everything disappear. In
the form of a dream, Vishnu entered their bodies. He took away
their breath of life and handed it over to Nidra.[637] Vishnu, with
truth as his valour, spoke to Nidra. "O Nidra! You have been
created by me. Go to Devaki's residence. Take the breaths of life
of these creatures known as the Shadgarbhas. In progressive order,
implant them in Devaki's womb. When these conceptions are
born and are conveyed to Yama's abode, Kamsa's efforts will be
fruitless and Devaki's efforts will be successful. I will show you my
favours. Because of my favours, you will be like me on earth. That
is the reason you will become a goddess who is worshipped by all
the worlds. Devaki's seventh conception will be my elder brother,
born from Soma's portion. In the seventh month, you will transfer
him to Rohini's womb. Since the conception will be transferred by
you, he will be known as Samkarshana.[638] He will become my elder
brother and will be as handsome as the moon. Kamsa will think
that out of fear from him, Devaki's seventh conception resulted
in a miscarriage and will try to kill me, the eighth conception.
Nandagopa is Kamsa's cowherd and his beloved and fortunate
wife is Yashoda, the extender of the Gopa lineage.[639] In our
lineage, you will be born through her, as the ninth conception.
You will be born on the ninth *tithi* of *krishnapaksha*.[640] When
it is just past midnight, I will use yoga as I please to free you
from that conception. Both of us will be born at the same time,
in the eighth month of pregnancy and so that Kamsa's reign is
over, the births will be interchanged. O goddess! I will go to
Yashoda and you will go to Devaki. This interchange, through
the use of yoga, will confuse Kamsa. He will grab you by the legs
and fling you against a stone. However, you will rise up into the
sky and obtain an eternal position. Like me, you will possess a
dark complexion, but your face will be like Samkarshana's. On

[637] The goddess of sleep, the personified form of sleep.
[638] *Samkarshana* means someone who has been dragged along or
pulled.
[639] The gopas are cowherds and look after cattle.
[640] Krishnapaksha is the dark lunar fortnight, tithi is a lunar day.

earth, your extensive arms will spread everywhere, just as my arms do.[641] You will wield a trident and a sword with a golden handle. You will hold a vessel full of honey and a sparkling lotus. You will wear a garment made of blue silk and your upper garment will be yellow. A necklace as radiant as moonbeams will grace your breasts. Divine and long earrings will adorn your ears. The radiance of the moon will manifest itself on your face. A diadem with three peaks will adorn your braided hair. Your arms will be as thick as clubs and like hissing serpents. Your standard will be adorned with the feathers of peacocks. Your radiant armlets will also be adorned with the feathers of peacocks. You will always be surrounded by large numbers of terrible bhutas[642] and they will follow your instructions. You will follow a vow of celibacy and go to heaven. There, the thousand-eyed one will perform the task I have entrusted him with. He will perform a celestial consecration for you and confer you with divinity. There, Vasava will accept you as his sister. Because you have the gotra of Kushika, you will become Koushiki.[643] He will grant you an eternal spot on Vindhya, best among mountains. From that spot, you will beautify the earth in one thousand different ways. In your mind, you will follow me and destroy the danavas Sumbha and Nisumbha, who dwell in the mountains.[644] You will roam around in the three worlds and be desired by the virtuous on earth. You will be immensely fortunate. You will be the granter of boons. You will assume whatever form you desire. You will be followed by ghosts and spirits. You will always love flesh and sacrifices. You will be worshipped on the ninth lunar day, with rites that involve sacrifices of animals. If a man knows about my power and bows down before you, there is nothing that he will find difficult to obtain, be it sons or riches.

[641] Probably implying that sleep overpowers everything.

[642] Spirits, ghosts.

[643] Since Indra has the gotra of Kushika, this must be because of becoming Indra's sister. There is a separate story about how Koushiki was formed when Parvati shed her dark complexion.

[644] This is in the form of the goddess Vindhyavasini, identified with Kali. The names of the demons should really be spelt as Shumbha and Nishumbha.

For men who are trapped in desolate regions, for those whose
boats have been shattered in the great ocean and for those who
have been waylaid by bandits, you will be the supreme salvation.
You will be success. You will be prosperity. You will be fortitude.
You will be fame. You will be modesty. You will be learning.
You will be good intentions. You will be intelligence. You will
be the evening. You will be the night. You will be radiance. You
will be sleep. You will be the night of destruction. When you
are worshipped, you will pacify difficulties faced by men from
bondage, slaying, terror, destruction of sons, destruction of riches,
disease, death and fear. By confounding Kamsa, you will alone
save the universe. When I come of age, I will myself kill Kamsa."
After instructing her in this way, the lord vanished. She assented.
Bowing down before him, she too departed.'

Chapter 48

Vaishampayana said, 'As had been told, Devaki, who was like
a goddess, conceived seven times. As soon as they were born,
Kamsa killed six of them by smashing them against stone. She[645]
transferred the seventh conception to Rohini. She[646] was then in
her season and was sleeping. When Nidra suddenly entered her in
the middle of the night, she fell down on the ground. In her sleep,
she saw that the conception had left her. When, in an instant,
she could no longer see the conception, she was distressed. In the
darkness of the night, Nidra spoke to the anxious Rohini, the
Rohini who was Vasudeva's wife, appearing as if she was Soma's
Rohini.[647] "O fortunate one! For your welfare, a conception has
been transferred from another womb to your womb. Thus, you will
have a son named Samkarshana." On realizing that she was going
to have a son, Rohini was somewhat ashamed. She entered her own

[645] Nidra, also referred to as Yogamaya.
[646] Devaki.
[647] The nakshatra Rohini, married to the moon god Soma.

house, like the extremely resplendent Rohini.[648] However, Devaki followed the path of conceiving and was pregnant again, with the birth for which Kamsa had destroyed seven conceptions. Through his own wishes, Hari was in her womb and the guards carefully protected that conception. On the same day, Yashoda conceived and this was nothing but Nidra, who had emerged from Vishnu's body and was following Vishnu's instructions. In the eighth month, before the full period of pregnancy was over, both women, Devaki and Yashoda, delivered at the same time. In the night, the lord Krishna was born in the Vrishni lineage and at the same time of the same night, Yashoda, who was the wife of Nandagopa, Kamsa's respected cowherd, gave birth to a girl. Yashoda and Devaki became pregnant at the same time. Devaki gave birth to Vishnu and Yashoda to a daughter at the same time. This was exactly at midnight when Abhijit nakshatra was in the ascendant. When Janardana was born, the oceans trembled, mountains moved and flames of the fire turned peaceful. Auspicious winds blew and the dust settled down. When Janardana was born, the stellar bodies were shining. Without being struck, the drums of the gods sounded in heaven. The lord of the gods[649] showered down flowers from the sky. Maharshis, gandharvas and apsaras presented themselves and praised Madhusudana with auspicious chants. Though Vasudeva loved his son, he was terrified. He swiftly grabbed the infant and entered Yashoda's house. Without Yashoda realizing, he left the infant son there. He picked up the infant daughter and laid her down next to Devaki, while she was asleep. Stupefied because of his fear, he interchanged the two infants. Successful in his intentions, Vasudeva entered his own house.

'Anakadundubhi[650] informed Kamsa, Ugrasena's son, about a beautiful daughter being born to him. On hearing this, with a force of guards, Kamsa swiftly came to the door of the valiant Vasudeva's house. The eloquent one censured the guard and quickly asked, "What has been born? Give it to me fast." With

---

[648] The nakshatra Rohini.
[649] Indra.
[650] Vasudeva.

Devaki leading the way, all the women lamented. Devaki said, "O Kamsa! A daughter has been born. O lord! Seven of my handsome and infant sons have been slain by you. This daughter is almost dead. If you want, take a look." On seeing that it was a daughter, Kamsa was happy. However, the one with the foolish intelligence said, "Since she has been born, the daughter must be killed." She was still lying down in a dishevelled state in the bed for delivery. Her hair was still wet with fluids from the womb. Like the earth in patience, she was laid down on the ground, in front of Kamsa. The man seized her by her feet and raised her. He violently raised her, whirled her around and flung her against stone. However, she wasn't crushed against the flat surface of the stone. Instead, she rose up into the sky. She suddenly gave up the body of the infant. With freely flowing hair, she rose upwards into the sky, adorned with divine garlands and unguents. The divine one always remained a maiden and was worshipped by the gods. She was attired in blue and yellow garments. Her breasts were like an elephant's hump. Her thighs were as extensive as a chariot. Her face was like the moon and she possessed four arms. Her complexion was like radiant lightning. Her eyes were like the rising sun. She had excellent breasts and her voice was like that of the evening clouds. She was like the night shrouded in greater darkness, surrounded by a large number of bhutas. She was radiant and she alternately danced and laughed. The terrible one rose up into the sky and drank the best of drinks. She laughed out loudly and angrily addressed Kamsa. "O Kamsa! You tried to kill me. O Kamsa! You raised me and violently flung me against a rock. Therefore, when it is time for your death and you are afflicted by your enemy, I will tear apart your body with my hands and drink your warm blood." Having spoken these terrible words, just as she wished, the goddess roamed around in the abode of the gods, together with her followers.

'When she had left, Kamsa thought that she was his death. Ashamed, he met Devaki in private and addressed her. "O aunt! To avoid my death, I destroyed your babies. O queen! But it seems that my death will come from some other source. I made such efforts because of my despair. I killed my relatives. Through my

manliness, I have not been able to overcome destiny. Give up all
thoughts about your children, though that is a reason for grief.
They have been destroyed because of destiny and I am only an
instrument. Destiny is the enemy of men and measures out time.
Time conveys everything and those like me are only instruments.
Do not worry about your sons. Abandon sorrow and lamentations.
This is generally the way of human birth. There is nothing that
can bypass destiny. O Devaki! Like a son, I am prostrating myself
and touching your feet with my head. Give up all anger that you
have for me. I myself know the injury that I have caused." She was
distressed and eyes overflowing with tears, she looked towards her
husband. She replied like a mother. "O Kamsa! O son! Arise. In
front of me, you killed my infant children. O son! However, you
were not the reason. The Destroyer, in the form of time, was the
reason. I have got over what you did by killing my infant sons.
You prostrated yourself and touched my feet with your head and
condemned your own deeds as abhorrent. At the time of delivery,
or in childhood, death cannot be avoided. The young also come
under the control of death. The old are almost dead. When he
is not born, an infant cannot be seen. He is like one who does
not exist. Those who are born, and those who are not born, go
wherever the ordainer conveys them. O son! Leave. There is no
reason for anger on my part. The death has been predetermined,
a cause only implements it. In truth, the creation of beings occurs
because of what destiny has determined earlier. Through the deeds
of the mother and the father, that deed is only implemented."
Hearing Devaki's words, Kamsa went to his own house. He was
miserable because his attempt had been countered. He was severely
distressed.'

Chapter 49

Vaishampayana said, 'Earlier, Vasudeva had heard that in
Vraja, Rohini had given birth to a son with a face that was
lovelier than the moon. He quickly went to Nandagopa and spoke

these auspicious words. "Go to Vraja with Yashoda. Perform the
birth rites and other rituals for the two infant boys there. O son![651]
Once you are in Vraja, rear them cheerfully. Protect Rohini's son
and my son in Vraja.[652] Everyone is prone to playing around in
childhood. Men are foolish in childhood. Everyone tends to be
fierce in childhood. Therefore, take care. During *pitripaksha*,[653] I
will become an object of discussion among those who have sons.[654]
Though I have a son, I won't be able to see the child's face. Truly,
though I possess wisdom, it is as if my wisdom has forcibly been
taken away from me. Our fear is that the hateful Kamsa may kill
the children. O Nandagopa! O son! Therefore, search for a means
whereby you can hide Rohini's son and mine. In this world, there
are many kinds of things that frighten children and hurt them. My
son is older and your son is younger.[655] Cheerfully, look towards
both with equal affection. They are equal in age and will grow
up together. O Nandagopa! Therefore, act so that everything is
well in Vraja. Do not ever arrange for the cows to be herded in
Vrindavana. Because Keshi, evil in sight, is there, there is reason to
fear a residence there. Protect the two infants from reptiles, insects,
birds and cows and calves in herds. O Nandagopa! The night is
over. Use a swift vehicle to quickly go to Vraja. Both to the left and
to the right, the birds here are urging you to make haste." Having
taken the permission of the great-souled Vasudeva in private, he[656]
cheerfully ascended the vehicle with Yashoda. The intelligent one
carefully carried the infant on his shoulders and laid him down on
a bed inside the palanquin. They left in secret along the beautiful

[651] The word used is tata. But it is by no means obvious who was older
in age, Nandagopa or Vasudeva.
[652] By Rohini's son, Vasudeva means Balarama. And by his son,
Vasudeva means Krishna.
[653] The period when funeral rites are performed in honour of the
ancestors.
[654] Because people will not realize that he has a son. Rites for the
ancestors are performed by a son.
[655] This causes confusion. By my son, Vasudeva means Balarama. And
by your son, he means Krishna.
[656] Nandagopa.

banks of the Yamuna, fanned by cool winds that were sprinkled
with water.

'On the banks of the Yamuna, in a place where cool winds
blew, he saw an auspicious region near Mount Govardhana. It was
a beautiful place, not frequented by any predatory beasts. There
were creepers, climbing plants and giant trees. There were carts near
the river and cows grazed on the grass. The cows grazed on the flat
ground and the level terrain was full of waterbodies. It was a spot
where the trees were marked by scars from the horns and shoulders
of bulls. However, it was a place frequented by wild crows, hawks
and flesh-eating vultures. There were foxes, lions and other wild
animals that lived off fat, marrow and flesh. There were the roars of
tigers and the place was populated by many kinds of birds. It was a
lovely place, with flowers and succulent fruit. There was sufficient
grass to graze on. Cows roamed around there. There were the
auspicious sounds made by cows. Gopa women lived there. In every
direction, one could hear the sounds of calves calling. There were a
large number of circles of carts. There were also plenty of trees with
thorns. Though wild, it was adequately covered by a large number
of trees that had fallen down.[657] It was decorated with pegs and
ropes for tying up the calves. The huts were covered with mats and
the ground was covered with heaps of dry cow dung. There were
many flat spots where healthy and well-fed people were walking
around. There were plenty of ropes and sounds of the churning of
milk could be heard. Copious quantities of buttermilk flowed. The
ground was wet with heaps of curds. As the gopa women churned
the milk, sounds arose from their bangles. Young gopa boys played
there, sporting feathers from crows. In the midst of the cattle
pounds, there were cattle pens with gates. The breeze was fragrant
with the smell of butter being made. Maidens attired in blue and
yellow garments were everywhere. These maidens were adorned
with wild flowers. On their heads, they bore pots of ghee, covered
with fine cloth. There were those who carried water along paths
that led from the banks of the Yamuna. He happily entered the

[657] These and the trees with thorns provided protection against
predatory beasts.

place where cattle wandered around, to the sound of cows mooing. Aged gopa men and women greeted him. The place appealed to him and he decided that this was a happy place to reside in. The goddess Rohini, who brought happiness to Vasudeva, was there. He entered and hid Krishna, who was like the rising sun.'

Chapter 50

Vaishampayana said, 'In Govraja,[658] Nandagopa lived and worked as a cowherd and a long period of time elapsed. The two infant boys grew up in happiness. The elder was named Samkarshana and the younger was named Krishna. Hari had entered inside Krishna's body and he was as dark as a cloud. He grew up amidst the cattle, like a cloud in the ocean. On one occasion, he was asleep under a cart. Yashoda, who loved her son, left him there and left for the river Yamuna. Playing around in his infancy, he flung his arms and legs around. Krishna cried in a sweet voice and stretched his legs up into the air. He cried because he wanted some milk. Bending over, he overturned the cart with one leg. Meanwhile, Yashoda bathed and returned quickly. Here breast was overflowing with milk, like Surabhi[659] when her calf has been tethered. She saw that despite there being no wind, the cart had been overturned. She lamented and swiftly picked up the infant. She did not understand the truth about how the cart had been overturned. She was frightened, but was also delighted that the infant was safe. She said, "O son! Your father[660] will be extremely angry. Who knows what he will tell me? You were sleeping under the cart and suddenly the cart was overturned. My bath would have been a miserable bath.[661] What was the need for me to go to the river? O son! With the cart overturned, I find you lying down in the open." Meanwhile, after grazing the cows

[658] Another name for Vraja.
[659] The celestial cow, or the mother of all cows.
[660] Meaning Nandagopa.
[661] Had you been crushed by the cart.

in the forest and clad in a brown garment, Nandagopa returned to Vraja. He saw the shattered vessels, pots and pitchers strewn around. The cart had been overturned. Its axle was broken and its wheels faced upwards. He was frightened. With tears in his eyes, he advanced quickly. He spoke words in anguish. "Is my son safe?" He then saw that his son was well and was drinking milk at the breast. He again asked, "Without a fight taking place between bulls, how did the cart overturn?" Yashoda was scared. She spoke in a voice that choked, "I do not know how the cart was overturned on the ground. O noble one! I had gone to the river, desiring to wash the clothes. On returning, I saw this calamity, of the cart being overturned on the ground." While they were conversing in this way, some other children said, "This child overturned the cart with his foot. We were wandering around, as we wished. We turned up here and saw this happen." On hearing this, all of them were astounded and their eyes widened in wonder. They placed the cart in its proper place and fastened the wheels again.

'Bhoja Kamsa's nursemaid was known by the name of Putana. She was seen in the middle of the night, in the form of a bird. She roared repeatedly, in a voice that was like that of a tiger. Her breasts flowing with milk, she stood on the axle of the cart. While people slept in the night, she offered her breasts to Krishna. Krishna sucked on her breast and sucked out her life too. With her breast torn out, she screamed. The bird suddenly fell down on the ground. At that sound, people were scared and awoke. Nandagopa, the gopas and Yashoda were worried. They saw the slain bird lying down on the ground, as if she had been shattered by the vajra. She had fallen down senseless, her breast severed. With Nandagopa at the forefront, they surrounded her and asked in terror, "What is this? Who has performed this act?" Astounded, the gopas returned to their own respective houses. In fear, Nandagopa asked Yashoda, "What kind of destiny is this? I do not know. I am greatly surprised. O timid one! I fear for my son. I am overcome by fear." Yashoda replied, "O noble one! I do not know what this is. I was asleep with the child and woke up because of the sound." When Yashoda said that she did not know, Nandagopa and his relatives were surprised. On account of Kamsa, they suffered from great fear.'

Chapter 51

Vaishampayana said, 'As time passed, those two amiable infants, named Samkarshana and Krishna, started to crawl. From infancy, the two of them seemed to be one. The infants were attached to each other. They seemed to be strung on the same thread. They were handsome and were as radiant as the young moon and the sun. They seemed to have been created from the same mould. They slept on the same bed. They shared the same food and seat. They wore the same kind of clothing. They followed the same childish tendencies. They undertook the same task. It was as if a single body had been divided into two parts. They behaved in the same way. Though they were still children, they exhibited the same kind of great valour. Among people, they seemed to be of the same size. They were born as humans to undertake the tasks of the gods. The protectors of the entire universe were surrounded by gopas, in the form of gopa infants. They were affectionate towards each other and dazzled when they played. They were like the sun and the moon in the eye, casting their powerful rays on each other. With arms that were like snakes, they moved around everywhere. With dust smearing all their limbs, they looked like proud baby elephants. Their limbs were sometimes covered with ashes and sometimes, they were smeared with cowdung. They ran around, like Kumara, the son of Pavaka.[662] Sometimes, as they crawled around on their knees, they were radiant. They played in the pens meant for calves and their limbs and heads became covered with cowdung. They blazed in their beauty and brought joy to their mother and father. There were occasions when they acted mischievously and laughed. They played like children and the curly hair descended over their eyes. The delicate infants possessed faces that were as bright as the moon. They were seen to be extremely addicted to roaming around all over Vraja. They were so indomitable that Nandagopa was incapable of controlling them.

[662] Kartikeya, the son of Agni (Pavaka).

'Once, Yashoda was angry with the lotus-eyed Krishna. She tied
a rope around his stomach and tied him to a mortar. "If you can,
free yourself and move around." Saying this, she concentrated on
her tasks. While Yashoda was thus engaged, he left the courtyard.
Krishna continued to engage in infantile pursuits and amazed Vraja.
When Krishna emerged, he continued to drag the mortar behind
him. There were a pair of *arjuna* trees in the forest. The child went
there and dragging the mortar behind him, passed between the
trees. As he tugged, the mortar was stuck horizontally between the
trees. He tugged. The two arjuna trees were uprooted, got stuck to
the mortar and were dragged along behind him. In sport, the child
dragged along the two Arjuna trees. The trees were uprooted and
shattered. He stood between them and laughed. He wished to show
the gopas his own divine strength. Because of the child's powers, the
rope also held firm. Gopa women were headed along a path that led
to the banks of the Yamuna river. They saw the child and cried out in
wonder. They rushed to Yashoda. With fear written on their faces,
the women told Yashoda, "O Yashoda! Come. Are you delaying
because of fear? The two arjuna trees in Vraja used to cater to our
needs. Those two large trees have fallen down on your son. Your
child is there, with the rope firmly tied to his stomach. Your son, a
mere child, is standing between the trees and laughing. O one with
evil intelligence! O stupid one! O one who is proud of her learning!
Arise and go there. Your son is alive, as if freed from the jaws of
death." Frightened, she arose violently, lamenting. She rushed to
the spot where the two large trees had fallen down. She saw her
infant child there, in between the two trees. With the rope tied to
his stomach, he was dragging the mortar. The gopa women went to
the aged and young gopas in Vraja and they assembled to see this
great wonder in the land of the gopas. The gopas who wandered
around in the forest conversed among themselves, as they willed.
"How did these trees fall down? They were the best of trees in the
land of the cowherds. There was no wind. There was no rain. There
was no lightning. There was no harm caused by elephants. How did
the trees fall down? Alas! Without their roots, the arjuna trees are
no longer beautiful. They have fallen down on the ground and are
like clouds without water. O Nandagopa! The trees that have come

to such a pass are pleased with you. Though they were uprooted, your infant son has escaped and is without injury. This is the third evil portent that has been seen in the land of the gopas. Putana was killed and the cart overturned. The trees are next. It is not proper that the gopas should continue to reside here. Evil portents are seen here and this is not desirable." Quickly, Nandagopa freed Krishna from the mortar and swiftly placed him on his lap, as if he had returned from the dead. Nandagopa scolded Yashoda severely and returned to his home. All the other gopa people also returned to their houses in the land of the gopas. Since Krishna had been tied with a rope around his stomach, all the gopa women in the land of the gopas chanted his name of Damodara.[663] O foremost among the Bharata lineage! While Krishna resided in the land of the gopas, as a child, these were his extraordinary exploits.'

Chapter 52

Vaishampayana said, 'Krishna and Samkarshana thus passed through the period of childhood. They spent seven years in the land of Vraja. They were dressed in blue and yellow[664] and respectively anointed with white and yellow sandalwood paste. They tended to calves and sported sidelocks.[665] They had handsome faces. They played on whistles made out of leaves[666] and these were extremely pleasant to hear. When they went to the forest, they were as beautiful as three-headed serpents. Their armlets were made out of peacock feathers and their crowns were made out leaves. Their breasts were adorned with garlands of wild flowers and they thus looked like blossoming trees. Their headdresses were made out

[663] From *dama* (rope) and *udara* (stomach).
[664] Samkarshana wore blue and Krishna wore yellow.
[665] The text says that they had *kakapaksha*. Literally, this means crow's wing. It is an expression used when the head is shaved and sidelocks are left.
[666] Probably palm leaves.

of lotuses and their sacred threads were made out of ropes. They
carried poles with pots slung at both ends. They played flutes among
the gopas. They sometimes laughed at each other. Sometimes, they
played. They lay down on beds made of leaves and sometimes, they
slept. In this way, they protected the calves and were radiant in
the great forest. They found delight in roaming around. They were
young and restless.

'Then, the handsome Damodara spoke to Samkarshana. "O
noble one! We cannot play with these cowherds any more. We know
everything about this place and have enjoyed everything that is to
be enjoyed. Since the gopas have destroyed the trees, the grass and
wood have also been exhausted. These groves and forests used to be
dense. But since those have been destroyed, as one wills, one can see
the sky. The doors to the cow pens used to be surrounded by trees.
However, all those radiant trees have been consumed as firewood
by the gopas. What used to be inexhaustible is now exhausted.
Firewood and grass used to be available nearby. However, we now
have to look for these in places that are far away. This forest only
has a little bit of water and kindling left. Its foundation has been
destroyed. Since trees are rare, we have to search for a place to rest.
This is terrible. Now that the birds which rested on them have left,
the trees have no more work to do. No happiness can be found here.
There is nothing left that is succulent. The wind no longer serves
any purpose. Like food without condiments, without birds, the
forest is deserted. The wood and vegetables produced by the forest
have been sold. Without the treasure of grass, this land of the gopas
is like a city. The ornament for hills is pasture. The ornament for
pasture is forests. Therefore, we should go to another forest where
the best of kindling can be found. As they wish, the cows will then
be able to graze on grass. Let us therefore go to a more prosperous
land of Vraja, where the forest is full of new grass. That will not
be a place where doors will have to be closed and houses and fields
fenced. In this world, Vraja is famous as a place where one can
roam around at will. Because of urine and excrement, caustic flows
have been generated. The cows do not enjoy the grass and this is
not good for the milk. The beautiful and new forests have generally
become flat terrain. Let us quickly leave with the cows and create

a Vraja somewhere else. It has been heard that there is a beautiful
forest strewn with abundant pasture. It is named Vrindavana and
there are succulent trees, fruits and water there. The forest there
possesses all the qualities and the forest has no crickets and thorns.
This is on the banks of the Yamuna and there are many *kadamba*
trees there. A pleasant and cool breeze blows through the forest
and the wind is auspicious in every direction. The gopa women will
wander around happily. The interiors of the forest are colourful
and wonderful. Not very far, there is a giant mountain named
Govardhana. Its summit is tall and it is as radiant as Mandara in
Nandana. In the midst of the forest, there is a *nyagrodha* tree[667]
with giant branches and it is one yojana tall. It is named Bhandira
and it is as beautiful as a blue cloud in the sky. The river Kalindi
runs through the middle,[668] like the parting of hair on the head of a
married woman. It flows like the supreme river Nalini in Nandana.
We will roam around cheerfully there and see Govardhana, the tree
Bhandira and the beautiful river Kalindi. Let us abandon this forest,
which is devoid of qualities, and dwell in the pastureland there. All
will be well if we go there. Let us think of an appropriate reason."
While the intelligent Vasudeva was speaking, hundreds of wolves
appeared. They fed on flesh, blood and marrow. When he thought
of them, those terrible ones appeared from his own body. Having
thus manifested themselves, hundreds of them spread in every
direction. On seeing the wolves appear and spread as they willed,
there was great fright in Vraja, among the cows, the calves, the men
and the gopa women. Some wolves were in packs of five, others
in packs of ten. Some were in packs of twenty, others in packs of
thirty. Still others were in packs of one hundred. They appeared
from Krishna's body, with the srivatsa mark on their bodies. They
were black in visage. They increased the terror of the gopas. They
devoured the calves and frightened the cows in Vraja. In the night,
they seized young children. The wolves destroyed Vraja. They were
unable to go to the forest, or protect the cows. They were unable
to collect anything from the forest, or cross the river. The wolves

---

[667] The Indian fig tree.
[668] Of the forest.

were like tigers in their valour. In this fashion, they rendered Vraja immobile and everyone was forced to gather together in one place.'

Chapter 53

Vaishampayana said, 'On seeing the invincible wolves spread thus, all the gopa men and women consulted each other and said, "We should no longer dwell here. We should leave for another great forest that is auspicious and pleasant, so that we can reside happily there, with our cows. Why should we tarry? Let us leave, with our treasure of cattle. Otherwise, the terrible wolves will kill all of us. We should leave for another Vraja. These wolves are fanged and have limbs that are smokey red. They drag us away with their mouths. Their faces are black. They cause terror by howling in the night. Because of the calamity brought about by the wolves, in every house, there are lamentations of, 'My son. My brother. My calf. My cow.'" Concerned by the sounds of weeping and the mooing of the cows, the gopa elders gathered together and decided to move Vraja. Nandagopa was like Brihaspati.[669] He ascertained that they had decided to leave for Vrindavana and establish another Vraja there, for the happiness of the cattle. He found out that they had decided to reside in Vrindavana. Therefore, he spoke these great words. "Since we have made up our minds, let us leave now. Without any delay, let everyone in gopa be instructed to make the arrangements." The ordinary men in gopa were accordingly informed. "Swiftly prepare the cows and yoke the wagons. Tether the calves and pack the vessels. Make arrangements to leave and reside in Vrindavana." They heard Nandagopa's words, which were spoken well. Everyone in Vraja arose, desiring to leave quickly. When everyone in Vraja arose, there was a great uproar among the gopas. People awoke and the carts were readied. The noise heard among the gopas was like the great roar of tigers, or like the sound of the ocean roaring. There were arrays of gopa women, with

[669] In his wisdom.

pots of milk and buttermilk carried on their heads and it seemed as if a row of stars had fallen down on Vraja. They were attired in garments that were blue, yellow and red. As the gopa women advanced in rows, they resembled Indra's bow.[670] The gopa men advanced along the road, with ropes and bundles of ropes tied to their bodies and they were as beautiful as trees with roots.[671] As that caravan of carts advanced, Vraja was radiant. These[672] looked like turbulent waves on the ocean, tossed around by the wind. In a short while, Vraja became empty. Throngs of crows circled around, amidst the discarded objects that were strewn everywhere.

'In due course, the group of gopas reached the forest of Vrindavana. For the benefit of the cows, they spread out their habitations over a large area. The carts were stretched along the boundary, in the shape of a half-moon. The area was one yojana in the middle and two yojanas in length. In every direction, it was protected by tall branches of trees and bushes and trees covered with thorns. The churning rods[673] were erected and tied down with ropes. The vessels for storing milk were cleaned with water. Pegs were driven into the ground and ropes and nooses were fastened to these. In every direction, poles were erected and the carts were tied to these. The vessels for storing milk were tied to the tops of these poles with ropes. Grass was gathered and mats of grass were used to cover these up. Branches were gathered from the trees. Spots were cleaned and the mortars set up. The eastern direction was sprinkled with water and fires were ignited. Beds covered with the hides of calves were unloaded. Some gopa women gathered the excellent water, others gazed at the forest. Others pulled down branches. The young and aged gopa employed their hands skilfully. Some used axes to collect firewood from the trees. Consequently, surrounded by groves, this new Vraja seemed even more beautiful. This new residence in the forest was blessed with rain that was like amrita. The forest had pasture in every season and the cows yielded

---

[670] The rainbow.
[671] The comparison is with banyan trees, with the roots hanging down.
[672] The carts.
[673] For churning milk.

milk, as one desired. They reached Vrindavana, which was like the pleasure garden of Nandana. Krishna, who roamed around in the forest, always sought to ensure what was good for the cattle. In his mind, he had earlier thought of this auspicious forest. This was the second fortnight in a hot summer month. Even then, because the god[674] showered down rain that was like amrita, grass grew there. The calves did not suffer there, nor did the cows, or the other men. Where Madhusudana is present, people prosper there. Having reached a place that was approved of by Krishna, the cows, the gopas and the young Samkarshana happily resided there.'

Chapter 54

Vaishampayana said, 'Thus, both of Vasudeva's sons reached Vrindavana. They wandered around, tending to the herds of calves. They spent their time happily in the forest, until summer was over. They played with the cowherds and bathed in the Yamuna. The monsoon season, which ignites desire in the mind, arrived. There was the great roar of clouds, adorned with Shakra's bow on their stomachs. They showered down. The sun could no longer be seen, nor the earth and the grass. Torrents of new water showered down from stormy clouds. This force made it seem as if the earth had obtained a new youth. Large numbers of shakragopas[675] were drenched with these new showers. Forest conflagarations and the resultant smoke were extinguished. The forest looked radiant. It was the time for peacocks with feathers to dance. The sounds of their engaging in intercourse could be heard. With the new rain, the trunks of young kadamba trees, which provided food for bees,[676] looked beautiful and it was as if these had assumed new bodies.

---

[674] Indra.

[675] A reddish insect, sometimes identified with a firefly. Also known as *indragopa*.

[676] The term used is six-legged, so in general, it could also apply to other insects.

Blossoming *kutaja*[677] flowers laughed. The fragrances of kadambas wafted through the forest. The earth was satisfied with the water and the heat was frightened by the clouds. The mountains had been scorched by the rays of the sun and forest conflagarations. The rain released from the clouds made them breathe again. Giant storms were created. There were masses of gigantic clouds. The earth, covered by the sky, looked like a great royal city.[678] In some places, kadamba flowers blossomed. In others, mushrooms sprouted. With the blossoming *nipa* flowers,[679] the forest seemed to be on fire. Sprinkled by Indra's water and spread by the wind, there was a new scent on earth. On inhaling this, the minds of people were agitated. Deer called proudly, frogs croaked. The earth seemed to be coloured with the new feathers on peacocks. Since copious quantities of water resulted from the rain, there were powerful whirlpools. The rivers broadened, uprooted trees from their banks and flowed downwards. The feathers of the birds got wet in the rain and they couldn't move them. Exhausted, they didn't wish to leave the tops of the trees. The clouds were dense with water. They showered and roared. The sun seemed to be submerged in the bellies of these new clouds. The earth's body was covered with green grass and it was beautiful, garlanded with moss and lichen. However, because of that torrent of water, it was difficult to discern paths. The mountains were adorned with trees. But because of the flood, those trees seemed to be severed by the vajra and fell down, as did the summits. The rain from the clouds flowed along the low ground and there were floods there, spreading through the forests. Following the roar of the clouds and drenched by the rain, wild elephants raised their faces and their trunks and it seemed as if the clouds had themselves descended on earth.

'On seeing that the monsoon had arrived and that there were dense clouds in the sky, Rohini's son[680] addressed Krishna in words that were appropriate for the occasion. "O Krishna! Behold these

[677] A kind of flower, the Wrightia.
[678] The clouds were like palaces and the winds were like flags.
[679] Another name for the kadamba.
[680] Balarama.

dark clouds, which seem to be adorned with cranes. They are the stealers of complexions. They have stolen your complexion and are in the sky. It is the time for you to sleep.[681] The sky has assumed your hue. Just as you cannot be discerned during the monsoon season, neither can the moon. The blue lotus is dark and the sky has assumed the shining complexion of a blue lotus, as if it is a bad day in a bad season. O Krishna! Behold. Mount Govardhana, which makes cows prosper, is beautiful. It is covered densely with clouds. In every direction, because water has descended from the rains, the dark antelopes are intoxicated and are happily roaming around in the forests. O one with eyes like a lotus! Delighted by the water, soft grass is covering the earth with new blades. Water is flowing through the mountains. There is water in the forests. The fields are covered with crops. Prosperity can be seen everywhere. O Damodara! The clouds are eloquent with their loud rumbling and swift winds have arisen, making those who are absent from home anxious.[682] O Hari! O Trivikrama![683] Your middle foot was placed in the sky. Though it possessed no arrows and no bowstring, it seemed to be decorated by the three colours of Indra's bow. The sun, the eye of the sky, roams in the sky, but does not shine.[684] The clouds have robbed it of its heat. The one with rays is bereft of rays. The clouds are pouring down incessantly and the roar of the clouds is like the roar of the oceans. The line that joins the sky with the earth seems to have been severed by these clouds. Thanks to the rain, the fragrance of nipa, arjuna and kadamba trees is spreading through the earth. As this wind roars, it ignites desire. It has been raining heavily and the large clouds are hanging over the ground. Because of these clouds, it seems as if the oceans have merged into the sky. The sky seems to have prepared for a battle. The sparkling lightning is like armour. The shining rain is like arrows and the rainbows are like bows. O one

[681] During the four monsoon months, Vishnu is believed to sleep.

[682] Customarily, those who were away from home returned home at the time of the monsoon.

[683] Vishnu's name, a reference to the valorous three strides in the vamana incarnation.

[684] Because of the rains.

with the beautiful face! The mountains, the forests, the trees and the summits are covered by dense clouds and are beautiful. They have the colour of the ocean. As the clouds shower down rain, they look like a herd of elephants scattering water from their trunks. The cool wind has arisen from the ocean and is mixed with drops of water. As this harsh wind blows, it makes the creepers tremble. Because of the water released by the clouds, the moon has disappeared in the night. The sun is submerged in the sky and the ten directions cannot be seen. Everything is adorned by water from the clouds and the ill effects of the summer have been abandoned. O Krishna! Look at Vrindavana. It looks like the Chaitraratha forest." In this way, Krishna's prosperous elder brother praised all the qualities of the monsoon. Having spoken in this way, the powerful one returned to Vraja.[685] At that time, with all the kin, Krishna and Samkarshana sported in that great forest, enjoying themselves.'

Chapter 55

Vaishampayana said, 'Krishna, the one with the beautiful face, could assume any form at will. On one occasion, he was wandering around in that supreme forest, without his senior, Samkarshana. He had sidelocks of hair. He was handsome and dark. His eyes were like the petals of lotuses. He had the srivatsa mark on his chest and looked like the moon with its mark.[686] There were anklets on his feet[687] and he was as radiant as a lotus. His delicate form was coppery in complexion and his tread was valorous. His yellow garments were like the filaments of lotuses and caused pleasure to men. In these thin garments, he looked like a cloud in the evening sky. His arms, worshipped by the residents of heaven, were anxiously engaged in virtuous tasks associated with forest pursuits and thus carried poles and ropes. In his childhood,

[685] The new Vraja, in Vrindavana.
[686] Of the hare.
[687] Some non-Critical versions say bracelets on the arms.

Pundarikaksha's beautiful lips and face were like a lotus in their fragrance. His beautiful face, with its flowing tresses and crest, was like a lotus. It looked as if a lotus flower had been circled by a throng of bees. There was a garland made out of arjuna, kadamba and nipa flowers on his beautiful head and these looked like stars in the sky. The brave one was radiant with another such garland[688] made out of all possible flowers. He looked like the sky personified, dark with clouds during the monsoon. The sacred thread around his beautiful throat was adorned with a single sparkling peacock feather and this was gently tossed around by the wind. Sometimes, he sang. Sometimes, he played. Sometimes, he roamed around. Sometimes, in that forest, he whistled on a whistle that was made out of leaves and this was pleasant to hear. Sometimes, when he so wished, he played on a flute used by gopas and this was extremely pleasant to hear. Sometimes, to bring delight to the cows, the handsome one went to the forest. The radiant lord, dark as a cloud, roamed around in Gokula.[689] He roamed around there, finding delight in the colourful forests. The sounds of the large number of peacocks ignited desire. In every direction, clouds rumbled and echoed. The paths were covered with green grass and the mushrooms were like ornaments. Water dripped from the new shoots, as if from the tusks of elephants. On every side, the forest inhaled the fragrance of the new blossoms, which was like the breath of a young woman at the time of desire. Krishna derived pleasure from that peaceful forest. He inhaled the new scents that were created by trees rubbing against each other.

'On one occasion, while roaming around with the cows, he saw a tree that was tall and huge and was supreme among trees. Though it stood on the ground, its thick store of leaves was like a cloud dense with water. It was populated by a large number of birds that had blue and colourful feathers. Covered with red fruit, the tree looked like a cloud tinged with the rainbow. The branches looked like houses and there were creepers and flowers. The large roots

[688] This garland was around his neck.
[689] Literally, a place where herds of cows are kept, being used for Vrindavana.

spread out and it rose up, holding up the wind and the clouds. It was like a lord of all the trees that were in that region. It performed the auspicious task of offering eternal protection against the rain. This nyagrodha tree, which was like a mountain, had the name of Bhandira. On seeing its beautiful form, the divine lord decided to reside there. For several days, with his friends, the cowherds, the unblemished Krishna sported himself there, as he used to do in heaven in earlier times. Krishna, residing in Bhandira, played with the cowherds. Some of them caused him pleasure by fashioning forest toys. Cheerful in their minds, other gopas sang. Taking pleasure in sporting, Krishna and the other cowherds sang to each other. While they sang, the brave one played on a whistle made of leaves, or on a flute or a lute.

'His eyes were like that of a cow or a bull. On one occasion, while tending to the cows, he went to the banks of the Yamuna, adorned with creepers and trees. A pleasant breeze was blowing, touching the water. Because of the waves, the river seemed curved. He saw the river Yamuna, covered with lotuses and lilies. There were excellent steps that led down to the water. The water was tasty. There were ponds and the water had a great force. Because of the force of the water and the wind, the trees in that forest bent down. There were the sounds of swans, ducks and cranes. Those addicted to intercourse were engaged in unions with each other. The water possessed all the qualities and all kinds of aquatic creatures lived there. There were colourful aquatic plants and because of these, the water assumed a greenish tinge. The flowing water was her feet.[690] The banks were her hips. The whirlpools were her deep navel. She was decorated with body hair made out of lotuses. The pools were like ripples on her stomach, with the waves marking three lines along it. The chakravaka birds were her breasts. The banks were like her lowered face. The foam was like her smiling teeth. When she was pleased, the swans were like her laughter. The beautiful red lotuses were like her eyelashes, when the one with the watery eyes lowered her eyebrows. The lakes constituted her extensive forehead. The beautiful one possessed moss for her hair. The currents were

[690] Yamuna is being compared to a woman.

like her long arms. The bends were like her long ears. Ducks were
her earrings. Beautiful lotuses were her eyes. Her garments were
made out of the clear water, with swans as the auspicious signs on
those garments. The banks were like ornaments and the shoals of
fish were like sparkling girdles. The boats were like linen garments.
The sound of cranes was like the tinkling of anklets. Crocodiles
and alligators were like marks on her limbs. She was adorned with
the auspicious mark of turtles. Predatory beasts and men drank her
water, as if they were feeding at her breasts. Since many predatory
beasts had drunk, the water was tainted. However, there were many
hermitages. Krishna wandered around in every direction, looking at
the beauty of the Yamuna, the queen of the ocean.

'As he wandered along that excellent river, he saw a supreme
pond. It was one yojana long and was difficult for even the gods to
cross. The water was deep and without any agitation, as quiet as the
ocean. The predatory beasts avoided this water. The shores were
empty of any aquatic birds. Full of fathomless water, it looked like
a sky that was full of clouds. The banks were difficult to climb and
along these, there were the large holes of serpents. The place was full
of poisonous smoke and fire that emanated from these serpents. The
water was shunned by animals. Those who desired water, could not
drink it. Virtuous ones, who bathed thrice a day, avoided the water.
Birds who flew in the sky were incapable of flying above it. Even if
a blade of grass fell into the water, it was consumed by the energy
of the fire. From a distance of one yojana all around, the terrible
banks were impossible to approach. The terrible bank blazed and
flamed because of that poisonous fire. It was only one krosha, to the
north of Vraja, which was unaffected. On seeing that gigantic lake,
Krishna began to think. "Whom does this great and radiant lake
belong to? This belongs to the one named Kaliya, who is like a mass
of collyrium. That lord of serpents himself resides in this terrible
lake. In ancient times, deprived by me of his residence in the ocean,
he has started to live here. He is afraid of Suparna, the king of the
birds who feeds on serpents. It is he who has poisoned everything
in the Yamuna, the one who unites with the ocean. Because of their
fear of the lord of the serpents, no one resides in this region. That
is the reason the forest has assumed such a terrible shape here and

is only covered by tall grass. This terrible spot is covered with the best of trees and has many other creepers and trees. All these are protected by the king of the serpents and by his advisers, who reside in the forest. That is the reason the forest has nothing in it. Like poison, it is impossible to touch. It has always been protected by them in every way. That is the reason the place is covered with moss, bushes, creepers and trees. It is my task to construct paths along both banks of the lake. It is therefore my duty to destroy the king of the serpents. The water of this river will then become clean and become an auspicious store of water. If I crush the serpent, the auspicious water will be enjoyed by Vraja. Everyone will then be able to roam around happily. This will become a tirtha and offer happiness in every way. That is the reason I was born as a gopa and started to dwell in Vraja, so as to uproot the deceitful and punish the evil-souled. Playing like a child, I will climb this kadamba tree. I will plunge into the terrible lake and chastise Kaliya."'

Chapter 56

Vaishampayana said, 'Having reached the banks of the river, Krishna firmly tied up his waistband. The young and quick one climbed the top of the kadamba. His form was like that of a cloud and his eyes were like lotuses. Krishna hung from a branch of the kadamba and then jumped into the middle of the lake, creating a noise. When Krishna jumped, the giant lake was agitated and overflowed. It was as if the ocean had been shattered with the force. The large residence of the serpent was agitated by that sound. Eyes dilated with rage, the serpent arose from the water. The lord of the serpents was angry and his complexion was like that of a mass of clouds. The ends of his eyes were as red as blood. Kaliya showed himself. He possessed five faces and flames issued with his breath. His tongues flickered and there were flames in his faces. There were five terrible hoods on all sides and these were large. The serpent was like the fire in his radiance and he covered the entire lake. He trembled in rage and blazed in energy. Because of his anger, all the water seemed to be boiling. Terrified, the river Yamuna seemed to flow backwards. The breath that issued from his faces was full of rage and fire. He saw Krishna playing like a child in the lake. At this, flames of fire and smoke issued from the mouths of the Indra among serpents. His anger created such a fire that the trees that were near the banks were instantly reduced to ashes, as if they had been conveyed at the end of a yuga. The Indra among serpents was infinitely energetic. His sons, wives, servants and other great serpents spouted terrible flames and poison emerged from their mouths, mixed with smoke. Those serpents coiled their bodies around Krishna and sought to crush him. His legs and arms could not move and he was like an immobile mountain. They bit him with their sharp fangs and water mixed with poison flowed. However, though the serpents descended on him, the valiant Krishna did not die.

'At this time, all the cowherds were terrified. Weeping, they rushed to Vraja. In voices choking with tears, they said, "Krishna has been submerged in the Kaliya lake and is unconscious. The king of serpents will devour him. Let us quickly go there." Hurrying, they told the cowherd Nandagopa, "The serpent is dragging your son into the great lake." Nandagopa heard these words. These words were as if the vajra had descended on him. He was distressed and distraught. Scared, he rushed towards the supreme lake. The young and the aged, maidens, the young Samkarshana and other people also went to the spot where the Indra among serpents was playing. With Nandagopa at the forefront, all the gopas had tears in their eyes. They lamented on the banks of that lake. They were ashamed and astounded. Stricken by grief, they repeatedly said, "Alas! Where is Krishna? Shame on us." Others wept in great sorrow and said, "We have been destroyed." The women looked towards Yashoda and shrieked, "You have been destroyed. Behold your beloved son. He is under the subjugation of the king of the serpents. He is being dragged in the coils of the snake, as if he is a deer. It is evident that your heart has an essence that is made out of stone. O Yashoda! On seeing your son in this state, how is it that it has not been shattered? We can see the miserable Nandagopa near the lake. His sight is fixed on his son's face and he seems to be unconscious. O Yashoda! We will follow you to the serpent's residence in this lake. All of us will submerge ourselves and not return without Damodara. What is day without the sun? What is night without the moon? What is a cow without a bull? What is Vraja without Krishna? Like cows without calves, we will not return without Krishna." Samkarshana was nothing but one body divided into two and knew that they[691] were two parts of the same body. On hearing the lamentations of the women and the residents of Vraja, he was enraged and addressed the undecaying Krishna. "O Krishna! O mighty-armed one! O Krishna! O extender of delight of the gopas! Swiftly destroy the king of the serpents, who has poison as his weapon. O son![692] O lord! These relatives are of the view that you are an ordinary human. Human in their intelligence, all of them are grieving piteously." On hearing the words of Rohini's son, his consciousness was aroused. He moved and stretched his hands and destroyed the coils of the serpents. He used his feet to crush the serpents that had arisen from the water. Krishna caught the hood with his own hand and lowered it. He then violently ascended the hood that was in the middle. Wearing beautiful armlets, Krishna stationed himself on that hood and started to dance. Crushed by Krishna, the serpent was exhausted. Blood emerged from its mouths. It lowered its heads and uttered these piteous words. "O Krishna! O one with the beautiful face! I was ignorant and exhibited my rage. I have been crushed. My poison has been destroyed. I have been subjugated. With my wives, sons and relatives, command me about what I should do. Whose subjugation should I accept? Please grant me my life." On seeing that the serpent had lowered his five hoods, the illustrious one, with the enemy of snakes on his banner,[693] lost his anger and replied to the lord of the serpents. "I will not grant you a place in these waters of the Yamuna. O snake! With your wives and relatives, go to the waters of the ocean. If I again see a snake on this ground or in these waters, I will slay him, even if he is your

---

[691] He and Krishna.

[692] The word used is tata.

[693] Garuda is the enemy of the snakes and is stationed on Vishnu's banner.

servant or son. Let these waters be auspicious. Leave for the great ocean. There is a sin in your residing here and it will bring about your great destruction. O snake! In the ocean, my footmark will be seen on your hood. Garuda, the enemy of serpents, will not strike you." The bull among the serpents accepted the mark of Krishna's footprints on his hood. While the gopas looked on, he vanished from the lake. When the snake had been vanquished and departed, Krishna arose and stood there. The astounded gopas praised him and circumambulated him. All of them, those who roamed around in the woods, were extremely delighted and told Nandagopa, "You are blessed. Since you possess such a son, you have been favoured. O unblemished one! From today, the gopas, the cows, the pasture and the water will be protected by Krishna, the lord with the long eyes. All the waters of the Yamuna, frequented by the sages, have become auspicious. Every place has become as agreeable as a tirtha and our cows will cheerfully roam here. It is evident that we gopas in the forest did not recognize what a great being Krishna is. In Vraja, he was like a hidden fire." Astounded, all of them praised the undecaying Krishna in this way. The large number of gopas then returned to Vraja, like the gods from Chaitraratha.'

Chapter 57

Vaishampayana said, 'When the king of the serpents was subdued in the lake in Yamuna, Rama[694] and Keshava roamed around in that region. One day, with cows that they were attached to, the two sons of Vasudeva went to the beautiful Mount Govardhana. To the north of Govardhana and on the banks of the Yamuna, the two brave ones saw a large and beautiful forest of palm trees. The beautiful forest of palm trees was covered by palm leaves. Extremely delighted, they wandered around there, like two young bulls. That region was plain and pleasant, without stones and rocks. Most of the extremely large ground was covered with darbha grass and

---

[694] Balarama.

dark earth. The palm trees possessed large trunks and their dark joints rose up. Because of the shining fruit that was at the top, they looked like elephants with their trunks raised up. There, Damodara, supreme among eloquent ones, spoke these words. "Wonderful. This forest region is full of ripe palm fruit. O noble one! They are tasty, fragrant, dark and juicy. With a little bit of effort, we should be able to bring down some ripe palm fruit. Since there is such a pleasant fragrance and such a sweet scent, it is my view that the juice will be like amrita." On hearing Damodara's words, Rohini's son laughed. Resolving to bring down the ripe palm fruit, they began to shake the trees.

'That forest of palm trees was not frequented by men and it was impossible to enter. The desolate plain was as if it had been constructed by ghosts. It was like an abode of maneaters. There was a terrible daitya named Dhenuka, assuming the form of an ass. Surrounded by a large herd of asses, it resided there. That terrible forest of palm trees was protected by the ass. That evil-minded one was a source of terror to men, birds and large numbers of predatory beasts. It heard the sound of the palm trees being shaken and the palm fruit falling. It was like an enraged elephant and could not tolerate this sound of the palm fruit. It angrily followed the sound and its face was suffused with insolence. Its eyes did not blink. It was skilled in neighing and it tore the earth with its hooves. It raised its tail and neighed. Its gaping mouth was like that of Death. On descending there, it saw that Rohini's son was stationed there. The evil ass saw Rohini's undecaying son amidst the palm fruit, erect like a standard. Using its teeth as a weapon, it bit him. Rohini's son was unarmed. The daitya turned its back. Facing the west, it struck him on the chest with its hind feet. Thereupon, he[695] caught the hindlegs of the ass who was a daitya. He whirled it and struck its face and shoulders on the top of the palm trees. Its waist and neck was broken. Its back was shattered. With its body deformed, the ass fell down on the ground, with the palm fruit. The ass was bereft of life and lost all its enterprise. He then flung its relatives also among the palm trees. The bodies of those asses fell down on the ground,

[695] Balarama.

with the palm fruit. It was as if the clouds had been dispersed from
the autumn sky. The daitya who was an ass and its relatives were
killed. The beautiful forest of palm trees seemed to become even
more beautiful. Freed from all danger, it became auspicious and
the desolate regions could now be seen. Cattle cheerfully started
to graze in that supreme forest of palm trees. All the gopas who
resided in the forest also went there. They were without sorrow and
all of them began to happily roam around in the forest. The cows
grazed happily. Those two,[696] who were like kings of elephants in
their valour, seated themselves on comfortable seats made out of
the leaves of trees.'

Chapter 58

Vaishampayana said, 'The two sons of Vasudeva were delighted.
They left that forest of palm trees and went to Bhandira again.
The ones with handsome faces tended to the herds of cattle and
made them prosper. They looked at the forest, which was full
of crops and trees. They challenged each other and sang. They
gathered trees. Those scorchers of enemies addressed the calves
and the cows by name. The ones with the auspicious marks bore
the tethering ropes on their shoulders. They wore garlands made
of wild flowers on their chests. They looked like two young and
horned bulls. One had the complexion of gold, the other of black
pigment. They wore clothes that resembled each other.[697] They
looked like white and black clouds, decorated with the great
Indra's weapon. Their ears were beautifully adorned with the tips
of kusha grass and flowers. Wearing forest garb, they wandered
along forest paths. With their followers, they roamed around in the
forest that was near Govardhana. Accomplished in many ordinary
games, they remained undefeated in these games. Though they

[696] Krishna and Balarama.
[697] Balarama was fair (like gold) and Krishna was dark (like black
pigment). But Balarama wore blue garments and Krishna wore yellow.

were worshipped by the gods, they had consecrated themselves to be born as men. Following that vow, they indulged in pastimes that were appropriate to those qualities.[698] On one occasion, while playing, they approached Bhandira. They approached that supreme nyagrodha tree, which was the best among trees. Accomplished in fighting, they stood together and swung from the branches. They flung stones and indulged in other forms of exercise. With the cowherds, they exhibited diverse techniques of fighting. Delighted, and as valiant as lions, they roamed around as they wished.

'Pralamba was supreme among asuras. While they were amusing themselves there, he arrived there, desiring to find a weakness in them. He donned the attire of a cowherd and adorned himself with wild flowers. He laughed and played and challenged the two brave ones. Pralamba, supreme among danavas, adopted the form of a human. Therefore, without any hesitation, he immersed himself in the midst of these men. All of them played with this enemy of the immortals. Since he was in the form of a cowherd, the gopas took him to be one of their relatives. Searching for a weakness, Pralamba had assumed the form of a gopa. He cast his terrible eye towards Krishna and Rohini's son. He was of the view that Krishna was extraordinary in valour and impossible to withstand. Therefore, the supreme among danavas made efforts to kill Rohini's son. There is a children's game known as *harinakridana*.[699] In pairs, all of them indulged in this game. Krishna jumped with Shridama, the son of a cowherd. The unblemished Samkarshana jumped with Pralamba. Some cowherds challenged other cowherds to a duel. With the least bit of effort, they jumped over each other. Krishna defeated Shridama and Rohini's son defeated Pralamba. The cowherds who were on Krishna's side defeated the ones who were on the other side. Cheerfully and quickly, they bore each other. Following the agreement, they ran up to the trunk of Bhandira and returned. The danava swiftly raised Samkarshana on his shoulder. However,

[698] Human qualities.

[699] Literally, playing like deer. This is like leapfrog, where one person jumps over another person's back. The defeated child has to carry the victorious child.

he quickly advanced in the reverse direction, like the moon being borne by a cloud. But he was unable to bear the weight of Rohini's intelligent son. Therefore, he expanded his body into a gigantic size, like the moon being invaded by clouds. Pralamba, supreme among danavas, exhibited his own form, which was like the banyan tree Bhandira, or like a black mountain that had been burnt down by fire. He wore a crown that was as fiery as the sun, with five tassels. The daitya's face was as radiant as a cloud when it has been lit up by the sun. He possessed a gigantic face and a large beak. He was as large as Death personified. He was terrible and his eyes were like the wheels of a wagon. The earth suffered from his footsteps. Pralamba was naked.[700] As adornment, he sported a long garland of flowers. Pralamba advanced gradually, like a cloud that is long and heavy with rain. The great asura seized Rohini's son with great force. He was like Death, when all the worlds are submerged in the great flood of the ocean. The young Samkarshana was abducted by Pralamba and looked like the moon, being carried away by a single cloud of destruction.

'Samkarshana realized that he was in danger. Perched on the shoulders of the daitya, the handsome one spoke to Krishna. "O Krishna! I am being carried away by this daitya, who is like a mountain peak in his radiance. He has exhibited great maya and assumed the form of a human. What should I do to chastise the one who is evil in his intelligence? In his insolence, the radiant Pralamba has doubled his size." Krishna knew about the conduct and strength of Rohini's son. Therefore, he smiled. Amused, he replied in words of assurance. "I see. It is evident that you have adopted the traits of a man and have kept it a secret that you pervade the universe. You are the supreme mystery among all mysteries. Remember the self that you adopt at the time of the destruction of the worlds, when they immerse themselves in the ocean. Submerge yourself in your own self. Remember your own conduct and behaviour as the ancient god in the water. Remember the form from which Brahma

[700] The word *ambara* has many meanings. We have taken it in the sense of the sky, in which case, Pralamba was naked. However, depending on the meaning of ambara, he could also have been attired in cotton, or in saffron.

resulted. The sky is your head. The water is your body. The earth
is your forgiveness. The fire is your mouth. Your breath is the life
force in all the worlds. It is you who created Manu through your
mind. You have a thousand faces. You have a thousand limbs.
You have a thousand feet and eyes. You have a navel with a lotus
in it. You are the one with a thousand rays. You are the slayer
of enemies. The residents of heaven see what you display to the
worlds. Who deserves to know what has not been uttered by you
earlier? In the worlds, everything that deserves to be known has
been instructed by you earlier. Even the gods do not know what
is known to you alone. The residents of heaven do not see that
space has been generated from your body and that they have also
been created by you. They only worship your artificial form. The
gods have not seen your limits. Therefore, it has been said that
you are infinite. You are subtle. You are great. You are one. You
are subtle and difficult to comprehend. You are the eternal pillar
and support on which the universe is established. You are the one
who holds up the entire universe, with its immobile and mobile
objects. The four seas are your extension. The four varnas are your
division. You are the lord of the four yugas in the worlds. You
are the one who enjoys the fruits of the four kinds of sacrifice. It
is my view that what I am to the worlds, you are also that. Both
of us belong to the same body. For the welfare of the universe, we
have divided ourselves into two. I am the eternal god of the worlds.
You are the eternal Shesha. Our body, divided into two, holds up
the universe. I am what you are. You are the eternal one and so
am I. We come from a single body. We are immensely strong and
have decided to divide ourselves into two. Why are you behaving in
this foolish way? Strike the danava on his head. O god! Using your
fists, which are like the blow of the vajra, strike the enemy of the
gods on his head." Thus, Krishna reminded Rohini's son about his
ancient nature. The one who pervades the inside of the three worlds
became full of strength. Using his fists, which were like the blow of
the vajra, the mighty-armed and brave one struck the evil Pralamba
on the head with great force. His skull was crushed and penetrated
his body. Without a head and without life, he sunk down on his
knees and fell down on the ground. Pralamba's body was scattered

through the universe, dispelled, like clouds in the sky. The shattered head and body began to exude blood, like the red-complexioned current that flows down from the summit of a mountain. Having slain Pralamba, Rohini's powerful son controlled his own strength and embraced Krishna. Krishna, the gopas and the gods in heaven were satisfied at the daitya having been slain and pronounced benedictions of victory over the immensely strong one. The gods situated in heaven pronounced, "The daitya has been killed through strength. The child is undecaying in his deeds. He will be known as Baladeva."[701] Because of his strength, people on earth came to know him as Baladeva. A daitya who was unassailable even to the gods was slain through his deeds.'

Chapter 59

Vaishampayana said, 'In this way, Krishna and Bala[702] roamed around in the forest and spent the monsoon months. When they returned to Vraja, the brave ones heard that the gopas in Vraja desired to observe Shakra's festival. Curious, Krishna spoke these words. "What is this festival of Shakra that everyone is happy about?" An aged gopa replied in these words. "O son! Listen to the reason why we perform a festival in Shakra's honour. O destroyer of enemies! Shakra is the lord of the gods and of the clouds. O Krishna! He is the eternal guardian of the worlds and this festival is for him. The clouds are urged by him and are adorned with his weapon. The crops follow his command and are generated from the new clouds. He is Puruhuta Purandara,[703] the one who ensures water in the clouds. When the illustrious one is pleased, he satisfies the entire universe. When that god is worshipped, he ensures the crops and we and other men enjoy them and obtain subsistence from them. When that god showers

---

[701] There is a pun on *baala* (child) and *bala* (strength).
[702] Balarama.
[703] Both are Indra's names.

in the worlds, crops result. The earth is satisfied and the universe is seen to be like amrita. Even when the calves have fed, the cows yield an abundant supply of milk. Grass grows and the cows and the bulls are nourished. There is no lack of crops. There is no lack of grass. Cattle and people do not suffer from hunger. This is seen to be the case when the clouds yield forth rain. Shakra milks the sun and provides the divine water. This new supply of milk is held by the clouds and flows from the clouds. Stirred by the wind, the clouds create a loud noise. Because of the force they have accumulated, people think that they are roaring. In this way, the clouds are united with the wind. The thunder has a sound like that of the vajra and seems to shatter the inside of everything. The vajra crushes the clouds and releases water from the sky. The many kinds of clouds wander at will, but Shakra is the lord and they are his servants. Sometimes, the clouds are scattered, signifying a bad day. Sometimes, there is a pearly white drizzle. Sometimes, the sky is thick with clouds. In this way, rain is formed by the sun and milk is generated from cows. For the sake of all the worlds, Parjanya showers down rain on earth. Since he showers down, all the kings are delighted with Shakra. We and other men worship the great lord of the gods." Krishna heard the aged gopa's words about Shakra's dominion.

'Damodara knew about Shakra's powers. But he spoke these words. "O gopa! We are gopas who wander around in the forest. We earn our subsistence from the richness of cattle. Therefore, know that cows, mountains and forests are our gods. Agriculture is subsistence for farmers. Trading is subsistence for merchants. Cattle are supreme for us and these are said to be the three means of subsistence.[704] Supreme divinity is constituted by whatever form of knowledge one is united with. If a man obtains fruits from someone, but performs good deeds in the name of someone else, such a person obtains a double misfortune—in this world and in the world hereafter. There is a boundary at the end of the field. It has been heard that there is a forest at the end of the boundary. There is a mountain at the end of the forest. Therefore, our refuge

[704] Agriculture, trade and animal husbandry.

is determined.[705] It has been heard that, in the forest, mountains can assume whatever forms they wish. Assuming their own forms, they find delight in their own respective summits. They[706] assume the form of lions with manes and tigers, supreme among taloned ones. They protect their own respective forests and scare those who want to cut down trees. There are those who are evil in conduct and are performers of harsh deeds. Despite earning a living from the forest, when they act in a perverse way, they kill them.[707] Brahmanas perform sacrifices through mantras. Farmers perform sacrifices through ploughing. We gopas should perform a sacrifice to the mountain. We should worship the mountain and the forest. It seems desirable to me that gopas should perform a *giriyajna*[708] in the forest. We should perform this rite at a fortunate place, under a tree, or at the foothill of the mountain. There, let us measure out the ground and slay animals at the sacrifice. Let us milk all the cows in the herd. What is the need to reflect further? Let all the cows be decorated with autumn flowers and let us circumambulate this supreme mountain. Having done this, let us again go to the forest. It is the agreeable and beautiful season of autumn. Clouds, the stores of water, have departed. The cows have obtained plenty of tasty grass that is full of energetic qualities. The *priyakas*[709] have blossomed. The clumps of reeds are sometimes fair and sometimes dark. There is tough grass everywhere. The sound of peacocks cannot be heard in the forest.[710] The sky sparkles and no water can be seen there. There are no cranes and there is no lightning. The clouds that still exist are like elephants that are not in musth. The remaining clouds are not troubled by the wind of the monsoon. Having begun to shed their heavy covering of leaves, the trees seem content. The sky seems to be ready for a coronation.[711] The white-complexioned clouds are like a headdress. The swans are like whisks. The full moon

[705] The mountain is the refuge.
[706] Mountains.
[707] The mountains kill those wicked ones.
[708] Literally, a sacrifice performed for the mountain.
[709] Kind of tree.
[710] Because monsoon is over.
[711] A king's coronation.

is like a sparkling umbrella. The water has diminished in all the waterbodies. The swans seem to be laughing at them and the cranes have abandoned them. The river is advancing towards her lord.[712] The two chakravaka birds are like her breasts. The banks are like her hips. The swans are like her smile. When it is night, night lotuses bloom in the water. There are stars in the sky, competing with each other. There are flocks of intoxicated curlews. The paddy fields are ripe and pale. Having enjoyed this beauty, the mind finds pleasure in the forest. With blooming lotuses, ponds, lakes, wells, paddy fields,[713] rivers and pools are blazing in their beauty. *Pankajas*, *padmas*[714] and other white flowers and blue utpalas are increasing the beauty of the waterbodies. Peacocks have got over their desire. The wind is blowing gently. There are no clouds in the sky. The ocean is quiet. As the seasons have progressed, the peacocks are relaxed in conduct and have ceased their dancing. Because of the scattered peacock feathers, the earth seems to possess many eyes. Yamuna's banks used to be dirty with mud. But the banks are now covered with *kasha* flowers.[715] Swans and herons have made their nests there. Paddy has ripened in the fields and the forests. Birds are shrieking, eating crops and aquatic plants. At the time of the monsoon, with the onset of the rains, the grass was tender. It has turned hard now. The moon has discarded its garment made of clouds. Ignited by the qualities of autumn, it seems to dwell happily in the clear sky. The cows yield double the quantity of milk and the bulls possess double the stamina. The forests are doubly prosperous and the earth is covered with crops with qualities. The stellar bodies are free from clouds. There are lotuses in the water. The minds of people are content. In the autumn, since the sky is free of fierce clouds, the sun blazes with its sharp energy and its rays dry up the earth. Kings desire to obtain victory and conquer the earth. They advance towards other kingdoms, infusing vigour in their soldiers. The mind is attracted towards the colourful beauty of the forests,

---

[712] The ocean.
[713] Or fields covered with water.
[714] These are two names for lotuses, as is utpala.
[715] Tall grass with white flowers.

with the coppery-hue of *bandhujiva* flowers and many regions
covered with mud. Trees, adornments of the forest, are found in
the forest. There are blossoming asanas, *saptaparnas*, *kovidaras*,
ishusahvas, *nikumbhas*, priyakas, *svarnakas*, *srimaras*, *pichukas*
and *ketakis* in every direction.[716] In Vraja in particular, autumn
has manifested itself in the form of the beautiful women of Vraja,
with the sound in the vessels as its laughter. There is no doubt that
in the world of the gods, the residents of heaven are waking up
the god who has the bird on his standard,[717] having happily slept
during the monsoon. After the monsoon has withdrawn, excellent
crops are obtained during the autumn. We should worship the god
who is the mountain and especially the cows. Let us decorate their
horns with peacock feathers. Let there be bells on their necks and
autumn flowers. Let us start giriyajna and worship the cows for
our good fortune. Let the gods worship Shakra and let us worship
the mountain. There is no doubt that we should use our strength to
perform a sacrifice for the cows. Do this if you agree with me and
if you are my well-wisher. There is no doubt that cows must always
be worshipped in every way. If you have been assured by me, if
you are pleased with me and if you desire prosperity, then act in
accordance with my words. Do not think about it."'

Chapter 60

Vaishampayana said, 'Those who earned their living from
tending to cows heard Damodara's words, which were like
amrita. Without any uncertainty, they replied, "O child! Your great

[716] Asana is probably a typo, since there is no identifiable tree by that
name. Saptaparna is the Indian devil tree (*Alstonia scholaris*), kovidara
is a kind of orchid, ishusahva cannot be identified, nikumbha is the wild
croton plant, priyaka is a tree of the *tomentosa* variety, svarnaka is the
golden shower tree, pichuka is the myna tree and ketaki is the fragrant crew
pine. This leaves srimara. This is probably intended as an adjective (fast-
growing) qualifying pichuka and is not a proper name.
[717] Vishnu, the bird being Garuda.

words increase the delight of the gopas. All of us are pleased with
your intelligence, which leads to the prosperity of men. You are our
refuge. You are our delight. You are the one who knows. You are the
succour. You are the one who grants freedom from fear. There is no
well-wisher like you. You are the one who has created this peaceful
Vraja. We are happy in this Gokula. We dwell here in peace, with
all our enemies pacified. It is as if we have come to heaven. Since
your birth, you have performed valorous tasks on earth, those that
are extremely difficult for even the gods to accomplish. Knowing
this, and your pride, there is wonder in our minds. In strength,
excellence, fame and valour, you are supreme among mortals, like
Purandara among the gods. In beauty, prosperity, favours, face
and smiles, you are supreme among mortals, like the moon among
the gods. There is no other man who is your equal in attire, form,
childhood behaviour and strength. O lord! You have spoken words
about giriyajna. Like the ocean against the shoreline, who is capable
of transgressing them? O son! From today, we stop Shakra's
sacrifice and start a prosperous sacrifice to the mountain, which
you have ordained for the welfare of the gopas and the cows. Let us
arrange for food, altars and delicious milk. Let beautiful vessels be
arranged near the wells. Let large pots be prepared for *payasam* and
food that is licked.⁷¹⁸ Let all the kinds of food, eatables and *peya* be
brought. Let there be vessels for meat and amusement. Let us spend
three nights in collecting milk and every kind of milk product. Let
buffaloes and other animals that will be eaten be given grain. Let
all the gopas be involved in arranging for this sacrifice." There was
happiness in Vraja and great delight throughout Gokula. There was
the blaring of trumpets and bulls bellowed. Calves mooed, increasing
the joy of the gopas. There were lakes of curds and whirlpools of
ghee. There were rivers of milk. Heaps of meat were readied and
mountains of rice were prepared. When the sacrifice commenced,
the mountain overflowed with cattle. There were satisfied gopa men
and beautiful gopa women. The sacrifice commenced by placing

---

⁷¹⁸ Payasam is rice cooked with milk and sugar. The four types of food
are those that are chewed (*charvya*), sucked (*choshya* or *chushya*), licked
(*lehya*) and drunk (peya).

kindling on the fire. With brahmanas, the gopas performed the sacrifice near the mountain. When the sacrifice was over, Krishna used his maya to assume the form of the mountain and consumed the rice, the milk, the excellent curds and the meat. The best among brahmanas were satisfied by being fed well. When they stood up, they were delighted in their minds and cheerfully uttered words of benediction. After the bath at the end of the sacrifice, as he desired, Krishna drank the milk. Assuming his divine form, he laughed and said, "I am content." The gopas saw Krishna stationed at the forefront, astride the summit of the mountain and in the form of the mountain, wearing divine garlands and smeared with celestial unguents. The lord enveloped everything with his celestial form. He bowed down with the gopas and worshipped his own self.[719] The gopas were astounded at the sight of the divinity astride the supreme mountain. They said, "O illustrious one! We are your servants. What work should we servants undertake?" From the mountain, he addressed the gopas in a powerful voice. "From today, if you are compassionate, you should worship me in the form of cows. I am your foremost god. I am auspicious and will satisfy all your desires. Through my powers, you will possess ten thousand cows and will enjoy them. In every forest, I will be auspicious towards all those who are devoted to me. Just as I am stationed in heaven, I will remain present with you. These are famous gopas, Nandagopa and the others, who are stationed here. Pleased with them, I will grant these gopas great prosperity. Be satisfied. These cows will quickly have calves. There is no doubt that I am supremely delighted with them." As a token of worship, the innumerable herds of cows and thousands of bulls circumambulated the supreme mountain. Milk-yielding cows and calves were adorned with garlands and anklets. There were hundreds and thousands of cattle with garlands on their horns. They were followed by a thick crowd of cowherds, smeared with unguents on their limbs and attired in red, yellow and white garments. Their armlets were made out of peacock feathers and they

[719] Krishna was in his form of a human gopa. But simultaneously, he also assumed the form of the mountain. Hence, there were two Krishnas, though the other gopas did not realize it.

carried staffs in their hands. Their hair was arranged and bound, with peacock feathers fixed at the ends. In the assembly, the gopas looked even more radiant. Some rode on bulls, while others danced happily. Other cowherds quickly ran after the cows. When the circumambulation and worship by the cows was over, the form of the mountain instantly vanished.[720] With the gopas, Krishna entered Vraja. They were astounded at giriyajna having been undertaken.'

Chapter 61

Vaishampayana said, 'When his sacrifice was stopped, Shakra, lord of the gods, was extremely enraged. He ordered the clouds known as Samvartaka to shower down rain.[721] "O clouds! O elephants![722] Listen to my words. If you wish to do what brings me pleasure, place devotion to your king at the forefront. Devoted to Damodara, Nandagopa and the other gopas who have arrived in Vrindavana, have shown disrespect towards my sacrifice. It is said that the livelihood of gopas is based on cows. Therefore, use wind and rain to oppress the cows for seven days. With the terrible rain, I will myself go there, astride Airavata. I will release rain and storm that are like the vajra. With that torrential rain, you will ride on the wind. Vraja and the cows will be destroyed and their lives on earth will be over." In this way, the lord instructed all the clouds. The chastiser of Paka wished to counter Krishna's instruction. In every direction, dark and terrible clouds enveloped the sky. They were like mountains and their rumbling was fearsome. They were adorned with Shakra's bow and gave rise to lightning. The clouds ensured that the sky was covered in darkness. Some clouds were like an array of elephants. Others were as radiant as crocodiles.[723]

---

[720] Not the real mountain, but the deity in the form of the mountain.

[721] These are clouds that appear at the time of the dissolution of the universe.

[722] Clouds are often compared to elephants.

[723] Makaras.

Other large clouds looked like mountains in the sky. Like a herd of supreme elephants, their bodies seemed to be bound to each other. They covered the entire sky, signifying the beginning of extremely bad times. The clouds began to shower down rain that was in the form of human hands, the trunks of elephants and bamboo poles. In the eyes of men, it was as if the fathomless and infinite ocean had taken over the sky. Extremely terrible times commenced. The birds stopped flying and diverse types of animals started to flee. In every direction, mountainous clouds rumbled in the sky. Those terrible clouds were in the sky and it was as if the sun and the moon were asleep. Because of that excessive rain, the earth became deformed. Because of the thickness of the clouds, the radiance of the planets and stars disappeared. Without the rays of the sun and the moon, everything was dark. Water was repeatedly released from the clouds. Everywhere, the earth overflowed with water. The peacocks called, but the other birds were silent. The rivers swelled and flowed downwards. The frogs were swept away in the flood. The clouds thundered and the rain roared. Because of that sound, the grass and trees trembled. The large number of gopas was afflicted by fear. They exclaimed, "The end of the worlds has arrived and the earth has become an ocean." The cows were immobile and petrified, weeping in their moos. Their ears did not move. They could not move their hooves and faces. The hair on their bodies was wet and stood erect. Their flanks and breasts were emaciated. Some were exhausted and gave up their lives. Some were afflicted and fell down. Other cows suffered from the cold and the rain and fell down with their calves. Some mother cows tried to give shelter to their calves under their bodies. Others were exhausted and gave up. Deprived of food, their stomachs were thin. Vanquished by the rain, some cows quivered and shrieked in their misery. Young calves raised their faces towards Damodara. In agony, with afflicted faces, they seemed to tell Krishna, "Save us." There was carnage among the cows. These were terrible times and there was fear for the gopas. On seeing this, Krishna was filled with anger.

'In wrath, he looked towards the cows and thought. The one who was pleasant in speech spoke these words to himself. "I will now uproot the mountain, with its groves and forests. The rain is

impossible to withstand and I will find a shelter for the cattle. I will
hold up the mountain and it will be like a shelter made out of earth for
them. This is under my control and I will save Vraja and the cows."
Vishnu, for whom truth is valour, thought in this way. He exhibited
the strength of his arms. He approached the mountain and held it up.
When he uprooted the mountain with his arms, Krishna looked like
another mountain. The mountain, surrounded by clouds, was held
up in his left hand. It was like a radiant house and would perform
the role of a shelter. The earth was dislodged from the summit of
the mountain. As he raised it up, rocks and boulders were dislodged
and trees uprooted. The summit was whirled around and staggered
in every way. The summit was raised up into the sky, like a bird.
The streams that flowed down its flanks became one. The mountain
moved, as if it had been struck by the vajra. Under it, people could
no longer feel the roar of the wind. Rain from the clouds did not
penetrate. There was no shower of rocks and boulders. There were
clouds around the summit, mixed with flows of water. Therefore,
the mountain looked as resplendent as a peacock spreading its
feathers. The vidyadharas,[724] serpents, gandharvas and rishis spoke
in melodious words and said that the mountain, flooded with
water, looked like a bird. It was severed from its foundation and
separated from the ground. It rested on Krishna's hand. The base
revealed iron, gold, antimony and silver. Some of these minerals
were separated, others cracked. The mountain penetrated the clouds
and looked like their summit. Because the mountain trembled, so
did the branches of trees. Flowers were loosened and scattered on
the ground everywhere. The offspring of birds became angry. They
emerged, thick in the middle and with *svastika* marks on their upper
bodies.[725] These travellers in the sky took to the sky. Numerous
birds were terrified and afflicted by the rain. They rose up into the
sky, but fell down again, distressed. Lions roared in rage, like clouds

[724] A vidyadhara is a supernatural being.
[725] The word *dvija*, used in the text, means oviparous. A bird is a
natural translation. However, a svastika mark has nothing to do with a
bird. Nagas (serpents) are identified with svastika marks on their hoods.
Therefore, serpents may have been meant.

thundering. The best of tigers roared, like the noise of rods inside churning pots. When the mountain was raised, its form became beautiful. Uneven spots, even those that were difficult of access, became flat. Showered by rain, the mountain seemed immobile. It looked like Tripura, stupefied by Rudra.[726] Using his hand like a staff, Krishna held up the giant mountain. Covered by blue and pink clouds, it looked like an umbrella. Covered by clouds, the caverns in the mountain seemed to be asleep. Indeed, the mountain seemed to be asleep, using Krishna's arm as a pillow. The sounds of birds in the trees ceased. Peacocks did not call in the forests. Without its summit, the mountain seemed to be without a support. As they were whirled around and moved, the mountain's peaks and forests seemed to be suffering from fever. Goaded by the great Indra and borne along by the wind, the clouds continued to incessantly shower down on the summit. Resting on the tip of Krishna's hand and encircled by clouds, the mountain seemed to be riding astride a chakra. It looked like a country invaded by a king. The large number of clouds continued to surround the mountain. It was like a large and prosperous kingdom, surrounding the capital city.

'With the mountain nestling on his hand, Krishna smiled. Stationed like Prajapati, the protector of the gopas spoke. "This is incapable of being performed by the gods. I have ordained this, using my divinity. O gopas! I have created a house out of this mountain. The cattle will find a refuge here, beyond the scope of the storm. Quickly bring the herds here, so that the cattle can find some peace. Let them happily reside in a spot where there is no wind. Vraja is where the herds are, where happiness can be found. I have repulsed the rain. Divide up this region among yourselves. Raising up the mountain, I have created a great expanse. I am capable of devouring the three worlds. Why leave this spot?" There was a great uproar. The cows mooed. The gopas entered, while the tumultuous roar of the clouds went on outside. The gopas divided the cows into herds and they entered. The recess under the stomach

[726] Shiva destroyed a city of the demons, named Tripura. Actually, this city consisted of three different cities. It floated in the sky. Shiva destroyed all three with a single arrow.

of the mountain was extensive. Krishna stood under the mountain, like a pillar, and raising up the mountain. He carried the mountain on his hand, as if it were a beloved guest. All Vraja's vessels, yokes and carts entered and found shelter there. In that house, carved out of the mountain, there was no fear from the rain. The wielder of the vajra saw that Krishna had performed a feat that was beyond the gods. His attempt having failed, the lord stopped the showers. Seven nights passed. Yet, his festival was not performed on earth. With the clouds, Vritra's slayer returned to supreme heaven. Seven nights passed and Shatakratu was dislodged from his attempt. The clouds departed. The sky was clear. The blazing sun shone during the day. Freed from exhaustion, the cows returned to their respective places, following the appointed paths. Vraja returned to its earlier spot. Krishna restored the best among mountains to its rightful place. The lord who is certainly the granter of boons was pleased.'

Chapter 62

Vaishampayana said, 'Govardhana was raised and Gokula was saved. On seeing this, Shakra was astounded and wished to meet Krishna. He ascended the elephant named Airavata, which was like a cloud without water, but intoxicated and wet with musth, and arrived on earth. Puruhuta Purandara saw that Krishna, unsullied in his deeds, was seated on a rock near Govardhana. He saw the child, blazing in great energy and undecaying in his radiance. Purandara recognized Vishnu, attired in the garb of a gopa. He was as dark as a palm tree and was marked with the srivatsa sign. Shakra, with eyes everywhere,[727] looked him up and down. He saw that he was united with prosperity and was like an immortal in the world of the mortals. On seeing him seated on the rock, Shakra was ashamed. He was cheerfully seated there. The excellent bird, who feeds on serpents,[728] was invisible, but used his

---

[727] Indra possesses one thousand eyes.
[728] Garuda.

wings to cast a shadow over him. Krishna, who knew about the progress of the worlds, was seated alone, near the mountain. The slayer of Bala[729] abandoned his elephant and approached. With the vajra in his hand, the lord who was the king of the gods was radiant. He was decorated with divine garlands and unguents. His crown had the complexion of the sun and sparkled like lightning. He approached and spoke in a delicate and celestial voice. "O Krishna! O mighty-armed one! O one who enhances the delight of kin! O Krishna! The task you accomplished to please the cows is one that is beyond the gods. I created clouds that were like the clouds that arrive at the end of a yuga. Nevertheless, you protected the cows. I am satisfied at this. With yoga you created yourself, you raised this supreme mountain up into the sky, like a house. Who will not be astounded at this? I was angry when my sacrifice was stopped. O Krishna! For seven nights, I showered down excessively on the cattle. The rain generated from the clouds is based on me. It is certain and is difficult for even the gods and the danavas to withstand. But you countered it. O Krishna! When you are enraged, the Vaishnava energy emerges. But I am extremely happy that you are able to conceal all of it in your human body. I think that the undecaying task of the gods has been accomplished. Though you have become a man, you are united with your own energy. O brave one! You are the leader of the gods. In all the tasks, you are at the forefront. Therefore, all the objectives will be accomplished and no one will be able to laugh at them. In the world of the gods, you alone are eternal. I do not see a second one who can hold up this burden. When there is a heavy burden, the best bulls are yoked. O one who has a bird as a mount! In that way, the gods seek refuge with you. O Krishna! The universe is in your body and you are its weapon. When he said that you are like gold among minerals, Brahma spoke well. The illustrious Svayambhu[730] himself, despite his intelligence and his age, is unable to follow you. He is like a lame person, running after someone who is fleet of foot. Himalaya is the best among mountains and Varuna's

[729] Indra killed a demon named Bala.
[730] Brahma.

abode[731] the best among waterbodies. Garuda is the best among
birds and you are supreme among gods. In the world, water is at
the bottom and the mountains are above it. The earth is above
mountains and men are above the earth. It is said that the path of
the birds is above the world of men. The sun is above the sky and
the sun is the gate to heaven. The world of the gods is beyond this
and this great and secret region can be accessed through celestial
vehicles. O Krishna! I am instated there, as Indra among the gods.
Brahma's world, served by large numbers of brahmana rishis, is
above heaven. The moon and the great-souled stellar bodies travel
there. Goloka, protected by the Sadhyas, is above that. O Krishna!
This great region is beyond everything and beyond the great sky.
Your world of austerities is progressively above that too. Though
all of us asked the grandfather, we are unable to comprehend
that. The terrible world of the nagas, meant for the performers
of evil deeds, is below all the worlds. The earth is a field for
action. It is a field for all action. The sky is a restless region. Its
conduct is like that of the wind. Heaven is the destination for
the performers of virtuous deeds, those who are upright and self-
controlled. The world of Brahma is the supreme destination for
those who follow Brahma in austerities. Cows go to Goloka and it
is extremely difficult to reach that destination. O Krishna! When
that world was afflicted,[732] you acted on your own. O patient one!
O brave one! You resorted to your perseverance and destroyed
the calamity the cows confronted. Urged by the cows and by the
immensely fortunate Brahma, I have come here, to honour you. O
Krishna! I am the lord of all creatures. I am Purandara, the king
of the gods. In earlier times, I was born in Aditi's womb, as your
elder brother. In the form of the clouds, I tried to show that my
energy was superior to your energy. O lord! You should pardon
me. O Krishna! Because of your own amiable energy, you should
pardon me. O one who is like an elephant in valour! Listen to
the words of Brahma and the cows. The illustrious Brahma and
the cows who are in the firmament and heaven have addressed

[731] The ocean.
[732] Because of Indra's rain.

you. They are pleased at your divine act of protecting the cows. "You have protected the cows. You have protected Goloka. Therefore, with the bulls, we will also prosper and grow. Farmers are pleased when there are bulls in the fields. The gods are pleased through oblations at sacrifices. Shri, who goes where she wants, becomes content through sacred cow dung. O immensely strong one! Therefore, since you have granted us our lives, you are our preceptor. Henceforth, you will be the king. You will be Indra."[733] Therefore, in my hands, I have brought his golden and celestial pot that is full of milk. Consecrate yourself with this. I will be Indra for the gods. You become Indra for the cows. In the worlds, and on earth, you will eternally be praised as Govinda.[734] The cows have established you as Indra and have placed you above me. O Krishna! In heaven, the gods will sing of you as Upendra.[735] In the year, four months have been earmarked for my worship.[736] I grant you the second half of these, to be known as autumn. From now on, men will know that two of these months are mine. My standard will always be worshipped in mid-year. At that time, because of the power of my water, peacocks will cast aside their pride. At other times, clouds will not roar and will possess little energy and pride. Depending on the rains and the season, all will be calm. In the months when Trishanku and Agastya wander, the one with the thousand rays will not scorch with his energy.[737] When it is autumn, the peacocks will become silent. They will only

[733] The text doesn't clearly indicate where the quote ascribed to Brahma and the cows should end. This seems the most likely.

[734] Basing the derivation on 'Go' plus 'Indra'. The straightforward meaning of Govinda is someone who causes delight to cows.

[735] Meaning, Indra's younger brother.

[736] The monsoon months.

[737] This is probably an astronomical reference and has little to do with the standard stories concerning Trishanku and Agastya. Astronomically, Trishanku is identified as the Southern Cross. Depending on the location in India, this can usually be seen on the southern horizon between April and June. Agastya is identified with the star Canopus, also seen on the southern horizon, though more clearly. Precession of the equinoxes makes it difficult to pinpoint astronomical references. The one with the thousand rays is the sun.

be happy as long as the water floods everything. Curlews will be excited and will sing and bulls will also be excited.[738] The cows will be happy and will yield a lot of milk. When the clouds retreat, the water will leave the earth. Resembling weapons, swans will fly around in the sky. Lotuses will grow in the water in ponds and rivers. Paddy will ripen in the fields and their tips will bend down. When rivers get swollen only in the middle, crops grow within the boundaries of their fields and the minds of sages are enchanted. When monsoon is over, it will be beautiful and there will be prosperous kingdoms on earth. The roads will be radiant and there will be fruit on the trees. The land will be full of sugar cane and sacrifices will be initiated. When auspicious autumn manifests itself, you will awake. O Krishna! Everything on this earth will be exactly as it is in heaven. On earth, men will worship you and me, Mahendra and Upendra, in the form of standards and poles. Men who know Mahendra and Upendra, base their conduct on us and bow down before us, will never face hardships." Shakra then grasped the pot, filled with divine milk, and consecrated Govinda, the one who knew yoga.

'On seeing that he was thus consecrated, with their herds, the cows sprinkled the undecaying Krishna with milk from their breasts. In every direction, from the sky, clouds showered down pearls and amrita, sprinkling the undecaying one with showers of water and consecrating him. All the trees exuded sap that was as white as milk. From the sky, flowers were showered down and trumpets were sounded. All the sages, eloquent and skilled in mantras, praised him. Freed from the form of a single ocean, the earth assumed its own form. The oceans were pacified. The winds blew such that the welfare of the universe could be ensured. The sun was on its path and the moon followed the conjunctions. Speckled shoots, flowers and fruit appeared on the trees. The elephants exuded musth. Animals in the forest were satisfied. The mountains were resplendent, decorated with minerals flowing from their bodies. The entire world was satisfied, as if satisfied with amrita, and became like the world of the gods. When Krishna was consecrated, it was as

---

[738] In the autumn.

if divine juices flowed from heaven. The undecaying Govinda, clad
in celestial and white garments, was consecrated by the cows.

'Shakra, the king of the gods, spoke to him. "O Krishna!
This was my first task, having been appointed by the cows. Now
hear the second reason behind my arrival. Act so as to establish
your dominion. Let Kamsa, Keshi, worst among horses, and
the intoxicated Arishta be killed quickly. Through your father's
sister, my portion has been born.[739] He is like me. Protect him,
respect him and make him your friend. Favoured by you, he
will follow your instructions. Remaining under your control, he
will obtain great fame. He will be the best archer in the Bharata
lineage. He will be like you and will not find delight in anyone
other than you. O Purushottama! Bharata[740] will be attached to
you and you will be attached to him. When both of you unite
together, the kings will confront their destruction. O Krishna! In
the midst of the rishis and the gods, I pledged this. My son will
be born to Kunti and he will be named Arjuna. He will be an
extender of the Kuru lineage. He will be accomplished in the use
of weapons and will be the best among archers. All the kings who
fight with weapons will be vanquished by him. He will follow
the dharma of kings and in the battle, fight the armies of brave
kings who love fighting. He will send them to their death. O lord!
With your exception, in the techniques he follows in wielding
weapons and in dexterity with the bow, no kings and gods will
be able to advance against him. He will be your friend and aide
in battles. O Govinda! For my sake, instruct him about yoga.
Regard him as my own self and always show him respect. You
always know everything about the worlds and about Arjuna. In
great battles, he will always be protected by you. Protected by
you, death will not be able to exert its influence over him. O
Krishna! Know me to be Arjuna and me to be your own self. Just
as I am to you, let Arjuna eternally be like that to you. Earlier, for
the sake of the gods, in three strides, you conquered and wrested
the worlds out of Bali's hands. However, because I was elder,

[739] Arjuna.
[740] Arjuna.

you made me the king. You are known to be full of truth. You are worshipped as truth. Truth is your valour. Resorting to truth, the gods invoke you for the destruction of their enemies. My son is named Arjuna. He is the son of your father's sister. In earlier times, he was your companion. Let there be friendship between you. O Krishna! Whether he is fighting, in his own place, in his own home, or in the field of battle, like a bull, always bear his burden. O Krishna! You can see into the future. When Kamsa is killed, there will be a great battle among the kings. There, brave men will perform superhuman deeds. Arjuna will enjoy victory and you will also obtain fame. O Krishna! You should act exactly in accordance with what I have said. O Achyuta! You should do this if you love me, the gods and truth." Krishna, who had become Govinda, heard Shakra's words. Pleased in his mind, he spoke these affectionate words. "O god! O Shakra! O Shachi's lord! I am pleased at having met you. In everything that you have said, there is nothing to be slighted. I know your sentiments. I know about Arjuna's birth. I know that my father's sister has been bestowed on Pandu, the lord of the earth. I know about Yudhishthira, the son obtained through Dharma. I know about Bhimasena, the son born from Vayu's body. I know that the virtuous Ashvins have had two righteous sons named Nakula and Sahadeva, born through Madri's womb. I know that my father's sister had a son named Karna, born through Surya while she was still a virgin, and that he has been sent to a suta household. I know about all the sons of Dhritarashtra, who desire to fight. I know that Pandu died because of a curse, as if he had been struck by thunder. O Shakra! Therefore, for the pleasure of the residents of heaven, return to heaven. In front of me, not a single one of Arjuna's enemies will be able to show his prowess. For Arjuna's sake, all the Pandavas will remain unharmed in battle. When the Bharata battle is over, I will return them to Kunti. O Shakra! Like a servant, I will do whatever your son, Arjuna, asks me to do. I am tied to you by affection." Krishna was always fixed to the truth. On hearing these agreeable words, spoken in a pleasant voice, and after meeting him, the lord of the gods returned to heaven.'

Chapter 63

Vaishampayana said, 'When Shakra left, the residents of Vraja honoured Krishna, who had held up Govardhana. The handsome one then entered Vraja. The aged and the kin were delighted and honoured him. They said, "We are blessed that you held up the mountain. The cows overcame their fear of the rain. We have been able to tide over a great fear. O Govinda! O immensely radiant one! You are like a god. O lord of the cows! We have witnessed your superhuman deed. O Krishna! O undecaying one! We have seen how you held up the mountain. O immensely strong one! Who are you, a Rudra, a Marut, or a Vasu? Why did Vasudeva become your father? You have censured us through your childhood actions in the forest and your birth.[741] O Krishna! Your deeds are divine. There is a doubt in our minds. Why are you censuring us by finding delight in the attire of a gopa? You are like a guardian of the world. Why are you protecting cows? Whether you are a god, a danava, a yaksha or a gandharva, you have been born as our relative. You are who you are. We bow down before you. For some reason, depending on your wishes, you have decided to reside with us. All of us are devoted to you. We seek refuge in you." On hearing the words of the gopas, the lotus-eyed Krishna smiled and replied to all the kin who had assembled. "All of you think that I am terrible in valour. That is not how you should think of me. I am your kin and relative. However, if you really wish to hear the truth, wait for an appropriate time. It is then that you will be able to hear about, and see, my true nature. If you now take pride in your relative being like a god in his radiance, you have shown me your favours. What is the need to know anything more?" When they were addressed by Vasudeva's son in this fashion, the gopas were silent. They covered their faces and went away, in different directions.

'In the night, Krishna saw the new and young moon. It was an autumn night and his mind turned towards enjoying himself. The roads of Vraja were tinged with dust from dried cow dung. The

---

[741] Because they did not recognize his divinity.

valiant one desired to organize a duel among the bulls. The valiant
one also organized a contest among the cowherds to see who was
the strongest. The brave lord proposed that cows should be seized
from the forest.[742] The one who knew about time was in his youth.
In the night, having regard to the time and showing proper respect,
he invited the young gopa maidens and enjoyed himself with them.
His face was beautiful, as if the moon had descended on earth. In
the night, the gopa women drank in the beauty of his face with
their eyes. Krishna was attired in excellent yellow silk garments and
this made him even more beautiful. He looked like a wet *haritala*
bird.[743] He was adorned in armlets and a colourful garland made of
wild flowers. Govinda was handsome and enhanced Vraja's beauty.
The gopa maidens said, "We bow down before Damodara." They
had witnessed his wonderful deeds in Vraja and knew about his
glorious truth. They crushed him against their thick breasts. The
beautiful women rolled their eyes and looked at his face. Though
they were restrained by their fathers, brothers and mothers, the
gopa women were driven by desire and searched Krishna out in
the night. All of them stood in lines and sported. The gopa maidens
organized contests, in which they sang about Krishna's character.
With their eyes fixed on Krishna, they mimicked Krishna. The young
maidens imitated Krishna's gait. With palm leaves in their hands,
some playfully struck each other. The women of Vraja talked about
Krishna's character. They danced, sang, sported and looked at him.
Delighted, the women of Vraja played in this way. Overcome by
their sentiments, the beautiful women sang in sweet voices. Devoted
to Damodara, they were delighted at having come to Vraja. With
dried cow dung smeared on their limbs, they surrounded Krishna.
They gave him pleasure, like she-elephants do to a male elephant.
They were completely immersed in him, their eyes showing their
attachment and their faces smiling. With eyes like black antelopes,
the women drank in Krishna with their eyes, but were not satisfied.
Thirsting with desire, the gopa maidens glanced at his face. In
the night, even when intercourse was over, driven by desire, they

[742] The contest of strength was in seizing these cows in the forest.
[743] A green pigeon with yellow feet.

continued to drink him in. The women laughed in delight. They were content when Damodara spoke some words. While thinking about intercourse, the partings in their hair were disturbed. The hair came loose and hung over the breasts of the gopa women. In this way, Krishna was like an ornament for the multitude of gopa women. In the moonlit night of autumn, he sported happily.'

Chapter 64

Vaishampayana said, 'One morning, when Krishna was engaged in pleasure, there was terror in Vraja, because Arishta showed himself. He was as dark as coal that has been burnt, or a cloud. His horns were sharp and his eyes were like the sun. He was black and his hooves were sharp at the tips. He was like the personified form of Death. He repeatedly licked his lips and gnashed his teeth. He insolently raised his tail. His hump was large and hard. His hump was extremely large. He was impossible to measure. His limbs were covered with urine and excrement and he severely terrified the cows. His waist was thick and his face was large. His knees were firm and his stomach was huge. As he walked, he shook his horns. The skin hung down from his neck. He was eager to mount the cows. There were marks on his face.[744] The tips of his horns were ready, poised for fighting. He was the slayer of enemy bulls. His name was Arishta. To the cows, Arishta seemed to be terrible in form. This was a daitya in the form of a bull and he dashed around Vraja. He caused miscarriages from the wombs of cows. He had intercourse with sick cows. He was so eager to mate that he attacked young cows. He was fearsome and used his horns as weapons. His weapons were impossible for the cattle to withstand. That bull found no pleasure unless he could fight with the cows in Vraja. On this occasion, this cow arrived before Krishna. The evil-souled one sought to terrify everyone, but he was on the path to Vaivasvata's[745] abode. The great bull roared, like Indra's vajra, or

---

[744] From striking trees, or from fighting with other bulls.
[745] Yama's.

like a cloud. He wished to destroy all the bulls in Vraja, including young calves that would become bulls. Krishna clapped his hands and confused him by roaring like a lion. In the form of a bull, the daitya then rushed towards Govinda. Raising his tail, the bull looked at Krishna with his eyes. He was enraged at the clapping of the hands. Desiring to fight, he bellowed. Krishna saw that the danava, in the form of a bull, was rushing towards him. But he remained immobile, like an immoveable mountain. The bull fixed his glance on his flanks and raised his head. It attacked quickly, desiring to slay Krishna. Krishna's complexion was like that of collyrium. He was like a bull against another bull. When the invincible bull advanced, he seized him. Krishna, who was himself like a bull, engaged with the great bull. As he[746] made a great noise, froth issued from his curved mouth. In the encounter, Krishna and the bull sought to counter each other. It was as if two quivering clouds had clashed against each other. He[747] destroyed the insolence of his strength. He kicked him between the horns with his feet. He squeezed Arishta's throat, as if it was a wet cloth. He uprooted the left horn, which was like Yama's staff. He then struck him on the face. Severely struck, he died. His horns were shattered and his bones were broken. The danava's shoulder buckled. Vomiting blood, he fell down, like a cloud releasing water. Govinda killed the insolent danava, who was in the form of a bull. On seeing this, everyone was extremely satisfied and uttered words of praise. Upendra, the one with a beautiful face, killed the bull at the end of the night. With eyes like a lotus, he again glittered in his radiance. All the gopas cheerfully worshipped the lotus-eyed Krishna, like the immortals worshipping Shakra in heaven.'

Chapter 65

Vaishampayana said, 'On hearing that Krishna was in Vraja and that he was growing like a fire, Kamsa became anxious. He

[746] Arishta.
[747] Krishna.

was worried and afraid. Putana had been killed and Kaliya had
been defeated. Dhenuka had been destroyed and Pralamba had
been brought down. Govardhana had been raised and Shakra's
instructions had been countered. Through praiseworthy deeds, the
cows had been protected. Arishta, the humped bull, had been killed
and the gopas were delighted. He could foresee his destruction and
suffered from great fear. The child had performed an unchildlike
deed and had dragged the trees down. He heard about these
unthinkable deeds and the prosperity of his enemy. The lord of
Mathura thought that his own harm was close. He lost his
consciousness, senses and mind and became like a lifeless image. In
the night, when all was quiet and still in Mathura, the lord of men
summoned his kin and his father, Ugrasena. He called Vasudeva,[748]
who was like a god, the Yadava Kamhvya, Satyaka, Daruka,
Kamhvya's younger brother, Bhoja, Vaitarana, the immensely
strong Vikadru, Bhayesakha, King Viprithu, Prithushriya, Babhru,
Danapati,[749] Kritavarma, Bhuriteja, who was never agitated, and
Bhurishrava. The lord of Mathura, the king who was Ugrasena's
son, summoned all these Yadavas and said, "Listen. All of you
know about every course of action. You are accomplished in all the
sacred texts. You are skilled in matters connected with policy. You
know about pursuing the three objectives.[750] In this world, in
determining action and in acting, you are like the gods. In observing
great conduct, you are as immobile as mountains. You show no
insolence in conduct. You are always ready to perform the tasks of
your seniors. All of you are skilled in counselling the king. All of
you are accomplished archers. Your fame is a light to the worlds.
You are conversant with the meanings of the Vedas. You know
about the creation of the ashramas and the due order of the varnas.
You are the ones who enunciate good policy. You are the leaders
who show the paths towards good policy. You are the ones who
shatter other kingdoms. You are the ones who save those who seek
refuge. In this way, your characters are faultless. You are prosperous

[748] Krishna's father.
[749] Literally, the generous one, Akrura's name.
[750] Dharma, artha and kama.

and at the forefront. Your favours can take care of heaven, not to
speak of this mere earth. Your conduct is like that of the rishis.
Your power is like that of the Maruts. Your anger is like that of the
Rudras. You blaze like Angiras. Extremely great ones like you,
famous in deeds, have upheld the Yadu lineage. On earth, your
bravery is like that of mountains. You possess such qualities and
have followed my inclination. Despite you being here, my misfortune
is increasing. How can you ignore that? This son of Nandagopa, is
famous as Krishna in Vraja. He is prospering like a cloud and is
destroying my foundations. I have been deserted by advisers. In the
absence of spies, I am blind. Because of this, Nandagopa's son is
protected in his house. He is like a disease that has been neglected.
He is like a full cloud. He is like a thundering cloud at the end of
summer. That evil-souled one is prospering. A performer of
extraordinary deeds has been born in Nandagopa's house. I do not
know what will come of him, nor about his yoga and his intentions.
I do not know how he has been generated. Is he the son of a god?
His deeds surpass those of gods and men. The bird, Putana, fed the
infant child milk at her breasts. In the course of drinking the
invincible one's milk, he sucked out her life. In the lake in Yamuna,
he crushed the serpent Kaliya. In an instant, he vanished from the
lake and was conveyed to rasatala. Nandagopa's son performed this
yoga and arose again.[751] Dhenuka was flung on the tops of palm
trees and killed. In an encounter, even the gods were incapable of
looking at Pralamba. However, the child struck him with a blow of
his fists and killed him, like an ordinary person. He destroyed
Vasava's festival. When Vasava showered down in anger, he held
up Mount Govardhana and removed the water from Gokula. In
Vraja, he uprooted the powerful Arishta's horns and killed him. He
sports like a child. But though he assumes the form of a child, these
are not the feats of a child. These are the deeds of the one who lives
in Vraja with the cows. It is certain that misfortune confronts me
and Keshi. I am certain that in earlier lives and bodies, he was the
cause of my death. It is as if he is standing in front of me, desiring
to fight. Who is this inauspicious one, in the form of a gopa, in the

[751] From the lake.

form of a man who is weakened by death? Who is the one with the powers of a god, playing in my Vraja? He is hiding his own form in an inferior body. Like a fire in a cremation ground, this is a god who is sporting. I have heard that in ancient times, to accomplish the tasks of the gods, Vishnu had conquered the entire earth in the form of a vamana. Vishnu displayed Vishnu's powers in a maned form.[752] He killed Hiranyakashipu, the grandfather of the danavas. In ancient times, he assumed the unthinkable form of Bhava[753] atop the white mountain and destroyed Tripura of the daityas. Bhargava Angiras gave refuge to his preceptor's son, using the maya of asuras to create a drought.[754] That god is infinite and eternal. He is undecaying and possesses one thousand faces. He assumed the form of a boar and raised the earth from the ocean. Earlier, for the sake of amrita, Vishnu assumed the form of a woman and ensured an extremely terrible battle between the gods and the asuras.[755] In ancient times, the gods and the daityas had gathered together for the sake of amrita. It has been heard that Vishnu adopted the form of a tortoise and bore Mandara. In Dasharatha's house, he divided his energy into four parts. Rama was born in this way and destroyed Ravana. Thus, he assumed different forms and deceived. He accomplished his own tasks and was successful in accomplishing the tasks of the gods. Therefore, it is certain that Vishnu, Shakra or a supreme Marut has arrived to destroy me. This is what Narada had told me earlier. O lords! Therefore, my mind is suspicious about Vasudeva[756] now. In particular, it is because of his intelligence that we face this difficulty. Narada met me in the forest of Khatvanga. For the second time, the brahmana again told me these words. "O Kamsa! You made great efforts to destroy the embryo. However, in the night, Vasudeva rendered all your efforts unsuccessful. O Kamsa! In the night, you flung a daughter against the rocks. Know

---

[752] As narasimha.

[753] Shiva.

[754] This hangs loose and does not belong. Bhargava Angiras is Shukracharya, the preceptor of the demons. The preceptor's son is Kacha, Brihaspati's son, Brihaspati being the preceptor of the gods.

[755] At the time of the churning of the ocean.

[756] Krishna's father.

that she was Yashoda's daughter. Krishna is Vasudeva's son.
Vasudeva is an enemy in the form of a friend. For the sake of your
death, in the night, he exchanged the two infants. Yashoda's
daughter is in the Vindhyas, supreme among mountains. She roams
around in the mountains and will kill the two danavas, Shumbha
and Nishumbha. Her consecration has been done and her attendants
are large numbers of spirits.[757] She loves great sacrifices of animals
and she is worshipped by the bandits. She is adorned with two pots,
one full of liquor and the other full of meat. She has colourful
armlets made out of peacock feathers and she is decorated with the
feathers of peacocks. That forest resounds with the noise of proud
cocks and crows. It is full of herds of goats and the birds do not
fight amongst themselves. The roars of lions, tigers and boars echo.
On every side, the forests are covered by thick trees. Celestial bees
are her whisks and there are divine mirrors there. There is the noise
of hundreds of divine trumpets. Using her own energy, she has
created that spot in Mount Vindhya. Causing terror to her enemies,
the beautiful mother always resides there. She lives there in great
delight, worshipped by the gods. This leaves Nandagopa's son, the
one who is spoken of as Krishna. In this connection, Narada told
me about an extremely important reason. 'Vasudeva's second son
will be known as Vaasudeva.[758] He will be your relative, but will be
the natural reason for your death. This Vaasudeva will be Vasudeva's
powerful son.' Under dharma, he is my relative. However, inside
his heart, he is my enemy. He is like a crow that plants its feet on
your head and desiring flesh, pecks out your eyes with its beak.
Vasudeva, with his sons and relatives, is like that. He enjoys being
at my side, but severs my foundations. One may be freed from the
sins of killing a foetus, a cow or a woman. But in this world, there
is no salvation for someone who is ungrateful, especially if he is a
relative. Such a person follows a path that leads downwards. An
ungrateful person is attached to a path that leads to a terrible end.
He treads the terrible path that leads to hell. Such a person has evil

[757] Bhutas.
[758] We have written it in this way so that there is no confusion with
Vasudeva.

in his heart and acts in a wicked way towards those who have
caused no injury. Should my relatives praise me more, or should
they praise his son more? I have sought the welfare of my relatives
and have followed the rules laid down by the seniors. When
elephants desire to fight a terrible duel, they ensure the destruction
of the herbs. After the duel is over, they eat together, in the great
forest. In the same way, when there is conflict among kin, injury is
caused to relatives. Those who are caught in the middle are killed.
O Vasudeva! Ignorantly, I nurtured you, ensuring this evil
destruction. You have caused this terrible harm to the lineage. You
are intolerant and like enmity. You are always evil in intelligence
and deceitful. O foolish one! You have made the lineage of the
Yadus miserable. O Vasudeva! Because of your age, I have fruitlessly
revered you. One does not become aged because one has grey hair
on the head, or because one lives for one hundred years. When the
intelligence matures, that is when one becomes the most aged among
men. Your intelligence is addicted to harshness. You are not
extremely learned. You are only aged in age, like a cloud during
autumn.[759] O Vasudeva! The virtuous know that your intelligence is
futile. You think that once Kamsa has been killed, your son will rule
over Mathura. Your hopes will be belied. Your age is futile. Your
intentions will be rendered false. No one who stands before me will
live. You use your intelligence to remain as a trusted person and
strike me. While you look on, I will act against both your sons. I
have never killed an aged person, a brahmana or a woman. In
particular, I have never killed a relative. You have been born and
reared here, nurtured by my father.[760] You are the husband of my
father's sister. You are the most senior among the Yadus. You
belong to this great and famous lineage of emperors. The virtuous
revere you as a senior. So do the Yadus, because your intelligence is
presumed to be based on dharma. What can we virtuous people do,
except to point out that this conduct is not appropriate for someone
who is foremost among the Yadu clan. Because of Vasudeva's evil
action, I may be killed or defeated. The virtuous men among the

---

[759] An autumn cloud only roars, but is powerless to rain down.
[760] Ugrasena.

Yadus now go around with their faces covered. In discussions, you are thinking of a means to kill me in an encounter. The Yadavas speak about the untrustworthy acts that you have committed. Conflict and enmity has arisen between me and Krishna. The Yadavas desire peace and an end to this conflict. Let Danapati quickly go to Vraja. Let him bring Nandagopa and the other gopas who will offer me tribute here. Let him tell Nandagopa that the annual taxes should be paid to me. Let him quickly go and bring all the gopas to this city. Let him say that Kamsa wishes to see Krishna and Samkarshana, Vasudeva's two sons, together with their servants and priests. They are accomplished in fighting in the arena and can fight according to the needs of the occasion. I have heard that they are firm in disposition and are great in their enterprise. We have two wrestlers who are ready, spirited and victorious. Let those two, who are accomplished in fighting, engage with them. I must see those two children, who are like the immortals. They are the foremost sons of my father's sister, though they roam around in the forest and dwell in Vraja. Go to Vraja and tell the residents of Vraja, "The cheerful king wishes to organize a sacrifice with a bow." Let them come here from Vraja and reside nearby, wherever they wish. Everything will be properly organized for all those who are invited. Let payasam, ghee, curds and other milk products be given. As is desired, let all kinds of food be offered. O Akrura! Follow my instructions. Go swiftly and bring them here. I am curious to see Samkarshana and Krishna. If they come, I will be supremely delighted. After I see those extremely valorous ones, I will do whatever is best. If they do not come, after hearing the words that I have spoken, I will crush them at the appropriate time. With children, it is good policy to use conciliation first. Quickly bring them here, after speaking sweet and gentle words. O Akrura! Do this and ensure my pleasure, which is extremely difficult to obtain. O one excellent in vows! Unless Vasudeva has instigated them to the contrary, ensure this." Vasudeva was like the earth in his patience. His soul was like the ocean. Despite being abused in this way, he did not lose his patience. Kamsa, lacking in foresight, struck him with words that were like stakes. However, fixing his mind on forgiveness, he did not reply. There were several there, who saw him abused in this fashion. They softly uttered words of "shame" and lowered their faces. Akrura was immensely energetic and possessed the knowledge of divine sight. Like a thirsty person who sees water, he was delighted at having been sent in this way. He instantly left Mathura. Danapati was happy that he would himself get to see Pundarikaksha.'

Chapter 66

Vaishampayana said, 'On seeing that the foremost among the Yadus[761] was thus abused, all the bulls among the Yadus covered their ears with their hands and thought that his[762] days were numbered. Andhaka, the foremost among eloquent ones, was not perturbed at these words. Full of energy, he replied in words that were driven by patience. "O son![763] It is my view that you have tired yourself out with words that should not be praised. These are inappropriate and reprehensible, especially when applied to relatives. A person who is not a Yadava should never hear the kind of words you have spoken. O brave one! Unlike you, Yadavas do not use force on other Yadavas. O son! Those of the Vrishni lineage will not find your words praiseworthy. A king of the Ikshvaku lineage disinherited his own sons.[764] You may be a Bhoja, a Yadava, or Kamsa himself. O son! But your head happens to be yours, irrespective of whether it is matted or shaven. One should grieve over Ugrasena. He is the destroyer of our lineage, since he has given birth to an evil-minded son like you. O son! The learned do not speak about their own qualities. Qualities become important when others speak of them. This is in conformity with the sayings of the Vedas. On earth, the lineage of the Yadus is censured by kings. After all, it

[761] Vasudeva.

[762] Kamsa's.

[763] The word used is tata.

[764] This is a reference to Yayati, who disinherited his son, Yadu, and Yadu's descendants.

is ruled by a foolish person who brings an end to his own lineage by
killing children. You have spoken these apparently righteous words,
as if they are full of virtue. However, those words only reveal the
intentions in your mind and you will not be successful. A senior,
especially a great one, should be respected and not reviled. Who
will regard abusing such a person as desirable? That is like killing a
brahmana. O son! Like the fire, those who are aged should always
be respected. Their anger can consume the worlds, even those that
are hidden. O son! Like a fish that finds its own way, those who
are learned and self-controlled, and always desire what is good for
themselves, must seek out the path of dharma. Because of your
insolence alone, you are striking those who are aged and like the
fire. Through your wicked words, you are striking at their inner
spots, like offering oblations without mantras. You have censured
Vasudeva because of his sons. This is false talk. I condemn your
inferior words. Even if a father is cruel, a son must not act cruelly
towards him. For the sake of a son, a father is always ready to
undertake hardships. If Vasudeva hid his own infant son, I think
he did what he should have done. Ask your own father about this.
By censuring Vasudeva and criticizing the lineage of the Yadus, you
have only injected poison and created enmity between the sons of
the Yadavas. Had Vasudeva performed an undesirable act vis-à-
vis his son, why did Ugrasena not destroy you when you were an
infant? A son always saves his father from the hell known as put.
Hence, people who know about dharma call a son putra.[765] The
young Krishna and Samkarshana have been born as Yadavas. You
have hated them since birth. Enmity has arisen in your mind. By
censuring Vasudeva, you have agitated the hearts of all the Yadus
and enraged Vaasudeva. By censuring Vasudeva, you have ensured
enmity in Krishna. It is because of this censure that these fearsome
portents have manifested themselves. At the end of the night, a
nightmare where one sees the fierce sting of serpents is evil. We
imagine that this means that the city will be without a protector.[766]

---

[765] Putra means son, derived from put (the hell named put) and trayate
(saves).
[766] Literally, the city will be a widow.

The terrible planet[767] is engulfing the rays of the nakshatra Svati. The planet Mars seems to be devouring the birds in the sky. A jackal has left the cremation ground and burning coals are emerging from its mouth. It is circling the city in the morning and in the evening, uttering terrible howls. There is the roar of meteors showering down on the earth. There is an earthquake and the summits of mountains are moving. At dawn and dusk, the mark of a club is seen on the solar disc. Birds and animals are moving in contrary directions. Svarbhanu[768] has devoured the sun and it is dark during the day. Smoke has descended and enveloped the directions. Though the sky is dry, there is lightning. Mixed with thunder and lightning, blood is showering down from the clouds. The gods have been dislodged from their temples. The birds have abandoned the trees. Those who know about portents say that this signifies the destruction of a king. We have witnessed all these inauspicious portents. You hate your relatives and have turned away from royal dharma. You are enraged without reason. You confront the fear of misfortune. Vasudeva is aged and firm in his vows. He is like a god. O evil-minded one! Because of your confusion, you have reviled him. How will you find peace in your heart? Henceforth, we will discard the affection we feel towards you. You ensure misfortune for your own lineage. We will not serve you any more. Danapati, who has left for the forest, is blessed. He will see Krishna, the one with eyes like lotus petals, the one who is the performer of unsullied deeds. Because of what you have done, this lineage of the Yadus has been severed at the foundations. Krishna will bring the kin together and assemble the clan. The intelligent Vasudeva has forgiven you. You have been cooked by time and are ignorant. Therefore, you speak as you will. O Kamsa! I think it is desirable that you should become Vasudeva's aide. If it so pleases you, go to Krishna's abode and be friendly with him." On hearing Andhaka's words, Kamsa's eyes became red with anger. Without saying anything, he went to his own residence. All the Yadavas, extensive in their learning, went to their own houses.

---

[767] Mars. Svati is in Virgo (Kanya) and Mars in Virgo is believed to be inauspicious.
[768] Rahu.

Condemned unfairly by Kamsa, they departed, unsuccessful in their intentions.'

Chapter 67

Vaishampayana said, 'Akrura was keen to see Krishna. As instructed, he left on the best of chariots, which could travel at the speed of thought. Krishna saw some auspicious omens, suggesting that a relative who was his father's equal was due to arrive. Earlier, the king of Mathura, Ugrasena's son,[769] had sent a messenger to Keshi, so as to bring about Upendra's[770] death. Keshi was one who caused difficulties among men. Hearing the words of the messenger, that invincible one went to Vrindavana and started to trouble the gopas. He was angry and wicked in his valour. He ate human flesh. In the form of a horse, the daitya caused great carnage. He killed the cows and cowherds and ate their flesh. He was impossible to control. With nothing to restrain him, the maned one wandered around at will. Wherever the evil-souled Keshi, the danava in the form of a horse, resided, that part of the forest became like a cremation ground. It was covered with the bones of men. He dug up the earth with his hooves. With great power, he brought down the trees. He neighed and challenged the wind. He leapt up into the sky. Intoxicated with extreme insolence, the wicked one roamed around in the forest. The terrible one who was Kamsa's follower was not troubled. The flesh-eater destroyed all the deer in the forest. In the form of a horse, the daitya sought to destroy all the gopas. The forest was greatly tainted because of his wicked conduct and men and cattle no longer tried to obtain subsistence from the forest. All shelters were removed from that region and all those paths became deserted. His conduct was insolent and he was terrible, eating human flesh. He angrily followed the sounds of humans. Having

---

[769] Kamsa.
[770] Vishnu, Krishna.

arrived at that forest, urged by destiny, on one occasion, he went to the place where the gopas dwelt.

'On seeing him, with the women and the children, the gopas ran away. Screaming, they sought refuge with Krishna, the protector of the universe. Hearing the sounds of crying and lamentation among the gopas, Krishna granted them freedom from fear and advanced against Keshi. Keshi raised his neck, baring his teeth and dilating his eyes. Neighing, he swiftly rushed against Govinda. Seeing that Keshi, the danava in the form of a horse, was charging, Govinda advanced, like a cloud against the moon. Krishna was right next to Keshi. Desiring Krishna's welfare and taking him to be human, the gopas said, "O Krishna! O son! Do not rashly advance against this evil horse. He is formidable and wicked and you are only a child. Let him be. O son! Though he is externally Kamsa's companion, internally, he is like Kamsa himself. This supreme and excellent horse is a danava and is unmatched in battle. This immensely strong horse frightens the soldiers of the enemy. He is foremost among all the performers of wicked deeds. There is no creature that can kill him." Hearing the words of the gopas and listening to them, Madhusudana, the destroyer of enemies, made up his mind to fight with Keshi. The horse moved in a circle, to the left and to the right. Angrily, he kicked the trees with his hind legs and brought them down. The hair on his face was long, while the hair that covered his shoulders was thick. Perspiration, signifying rage, started to exude from the curved parts of his forehead. Froth emerged from his mouth, laced with a shower of dust and he looked like the moon in the sky, covered with dew during the winter. As he neighed, froth emerged from his mouth and covered the lotus-eyed Govinda with saliva all over. When the horse struck the ground with his hooves, dust that was like pale *madhuraksha*[771] was raised and Krishna's hair was covered with red dust. Striking the ground with his hooves, Keshi leapt up. He bared his teeth and attacked Krishna. Keshi, supreme among horses, engaged with Krishna. Using his front legs, he struck Krishna on the chest. Using

---

[771] This can have multiple meanings: red sugar cane, fennel, a certain variety of asparagus.

his hooves, the powerful one repeatedly struck him on the sides. Using the terrible and sharp teeth in his mouth as a weapon, the angry horse bit Krishna's arm and left a mark there. The one with the long mane engaged with Krishna. Keshi was as radiant as a cloud that had engaged with the sun. The powerful horse struck Vasudeva on the chest with his chest. As his rage increased, his force and valour were doubled. As they engaged, the powerful and infinitely valorous Krishna also became angry. Using his hand, he struck him in the mouth. He was incapable of biting the hand, or withstanding the blow. His teeth were broken and torn from their foundations and he started to vomit frothy blood. His teeth were uprooted, his lips mangled and his throat choked. The eyeballs were deformed and came out of their sockets. His jaws were broken and blood flowed from his eyes. Though he raised his ears and made efforts, Keshi losts his consciousness. He used his legs to try and leap up again. He released urine and excrement. His body hair was wet. Eventually exhausted, his legs stopped moving. Krishna's hand dazzled inside Keshi's mouth. It looked like a cloud at the end of the summer, surrounded by the beams of a half-moon. Keshi's tired and immobile body still rested against Krishna. He looked like the moon in the morning, exhausted and resting against Mount Meru. Having been struck by Krishna's hand, Keshi's teeth fell down from his mouth. They looked like the white clouds of autumn, powerless without water. Having used his hand to destroy Keshi's body, Krishna's form looked extremely terrible, like that of the wielder of the pinaka[772] when an animal has been slain. Keshi's body was divided into two parts and lay down in the dust on the ground, each half possessing two legs, half a back and tail, one ear, one eye and one nose. Because of the injury suffered from Keshi's teeth, Krishna's hand looked radiant, like an aged *tala* tree in the forest, gored by the tusk marks of a king of elephants. Having brought about the destruction of Keshi and divided his body into two in the encounter, the lotus-eyed Krishna stood there, smiling.

'On seeing that Keshi had been killed, all the gopas and the gopa women were delighted, since their obstruction and impediment

---

[772] Shiva.

had been removed. According to their station and their age, they congratulated the handsome Damodara in affectionate words and repeatedly honoured him. "O son![773] You have accomplished the task of slaying a thorn of the worlds. O Krishna! This was a daitya who was wandering around on earth in will the form of a horse. You have brought peace to Vrindavana and it will be enjoyed by all the men and birds. O son! In the encounter, you have slain the wicked horse, Keshi. The evil-minded one killed many cowherds, cows, calves that were loved, and others, and destroyed this habitation. This performer of wicked deeds was about to become the ultimate destroyer. The deceitful one desired to make this world of men empty of men, so that he could reside here happily. Among those who desired to live, there was no one who was capable of standing before him, even among large numbers of gods, not to speak of those on earth." The brahmana sage, Narada, was travelling through the sky at that moment. Though he remained invisible, he honoured Krishna. "O Vishnu! O lord of the gods! O Krishna! I am pleased. By killing Keshi, you have accomplished a difficult task. Among the gods, with the possible exception of Tryambaka,[774] no one other than you could have done this. O son! I am always anxious to witness fights. Tormented by curiousity inside me, I have arrived here from heaven, wishing to see this encounter between a man and a horse. I have witnessed your other deeds, like killing Putana. O Govinda! I am satisfied with your deeds. The great Indra, the slayer of Bala, was also scared of Keshi, the evil-minded one who assumed the terrible form of a horse. You used your long arms to tear him into two. This is the kind of death that has been ordained by the creator of the universe.[775] Now that you have killed Keshi, listen to my instructions. You will become famous in the world by the name of Keshava. May you be fortunate in this world and may you swiftly accomplish whatever tasks are left. I have to quickly leave. In the midst of these tasks, while you sport as a man, the residents of heaven will enjoy them, since they have sought refuge

---

[773] The word used is tata.
[774] Shiva.
[775] Brahma.

in your strength. The time for the Bharata battle[776] is approaching. Heading for heaven, the kings are readying weapons for fighting. In the firmament, the paths are being cleansed for them to ascend to heaven on celestial vehicles. For these kings, places are being earmarked in Shakra's world. O Keshava! After Ugrasena's son has been pacified by you, there will be a great battle among the kings. Depending on the past deeds of those kings, at the time of the conflict, those kings will take sides. O lord! Yours is the royal seat and royal prosperity flows from you. There is no doubt that kings who ignore your power will lose their prosperity. O Krishna! O lord of the universe! This is my message to you, the one whose fame is spoken about in the sacred texts and the one on whom this universe and the divinity of the gods are established. O lord! I have witnessed your deeds and I have seen you. I will return again after you have chastised Kamsa. Let me leave now." Narada was accomplished in celestial songs and having heard his words, with the gopas, Krishna entered Vraja again.'

Chapter 68

Vaishampayana said, 'At that time, the rays of the sun had become mild and it was setting. The sky was tinged with the red of evening and the lunar disc was pale. The birds were in their nests and virtuous people were offering oblations into the fire. Everywhere, all the directions were enveloped in darkness. Everyone slept in the residences of the gopas. Jackals howled. Delighted at the prospect of eating flesh, night travellers wandered around. Once it was evening and the sun entered the cavern of evening, the shakragopa insects were delighted. For those who performed sacrifices in their houses,[777] it was the time to offer oblations. For those who had retired to the forest and for hermits,[778] it was the

[776] The battle in Kurukshetra.
[777] Those who were in a householder stage (garhasthya).
[778] Those who were respectively in vanaprastha and sannyasa.

time to recite mantras and offer oblations into the fire. The cows returned to Vraja and were milked. When the calves were tied up, the cows regarded this as inappropriate treatment and mooed. The cows were summoned, with heaps of ropes lying around. They cows were summoned through sounds, tied up and herded into their pens. In every diection, dried cow dung was piled up and ignited. The gopas returned, carrying firewood on their shoulders. The moon rose a bit, spreading its gentle beams. With the day gone, night had just started to arrive. The day was over and night was about to arrive, the radiance of the sun had departed and the energy of the moon had presented itself, it was the time to offer oblations into the fire and the cool moonbeams had arrived, it was evening and the entire universe was offering oblations into the fire, the west blazed, as if it was on fire, and the east and the north were dark, with only a few stars, the sky looked like a mountain that had been reduced to ashes, the birds returned, indicating a time for relatives to meet—this was the time when Danapati swiftly reached Vraja on his chariot.

'Having entered, Akrura respectively asked about the residence of Keshava, Rohini's son and Nandagopa. The immensely strong one was the equal of the Vasus. He descended from his chariot and entered Nandagopa's house, wishing to dwell there. As he entered through the gate, he saw Krishna stationed amidst the calves, milking the cows. He looked like a bull among the calves. The one who knew about dharma called out in a voice that choked with emotion. "O Keshava! O son! Come here." He had seen him lying down on his back, when youth had not manifested itself.[779] He now saw him again, surrounded by prosperity. Akrura praised Krishna. "This is Pundarikaksha. He is like a lion or a tiger in valour. His complexion is like a cloud that is full of water. His form is like that of an excellent mountain. He cannot be assailed in a battle. His chest bears the srivatsa mark. His virtuous and excellent arms are capable of slaying enemies. Though his soul is mysterious, he has manifested himself. In the universe, he is the foremost one to be worshipped. He is Vishnu in the attire of a gopa, his body

[779] When Krishna was an infant.

hair erect.[780] He seems to wear a diadem and his head seems to be covered by a blazing umbrella. His ears are adorned and deserve to be decorated with earrings. His extremely broad chest deserves to be decorated with garlands. He possesses two long, thick and round arms. Stirred by Manmatha's[781] flames, thousands of women worship his body. He is the eternal Vishnu, attired in yellow garments. For the sake of creatures, the destroyer of enemies has graced the earth with his feet. These feet traversed the three worlds. For the sake of creatures, they have now resorted to earth. The beautiful hand in front[782] is appropriate for wielding the chakra. The second, which is uplifted,[783] wishes to be united with the mace. He is the foremost bearer of burdens. He is the best among the gods. He has incarnated himself on earth and is resplendent now. Those who are accomplished and learned in their foresight about the future have foreseen this incarnation. This cowherd will extend the Yadava lineage, which has weakened. Because of his energy, hundreds and thousands will extend the Yadava lineage, like rivers filling up the great ocean. Everything in the universe is based on his eternal rule. He will slay the enemy kings and bring about a prosperity which is like that in krita yuga. He will be based on earth and will place the entire universe under his subjugation. He will be above all the kings, but will not be a king himself. In earlier times, it is indeed true that he conquered the worlds in three strides and made Purandara the king of the gods in heaven. Just as he conquered earlier in three strides, he will vanquish the earth. There is no doubt that he will instate Ugrasena as the king. He has wiped away a lot of enmity. The sacred texts have asked questions about him in many ways. In ancient accounts, brahmanas who know about the brahman have sung about him. He is the Keshava whom the worlds desire. He has now arisen and has used his intelligence to manifest himself in human form. Following the prescribed rites, I will now worship his residence here. As if I am using mantras, I will worship

---

[780] The body hair stands up when Vishnu/Krishna confronts a devotee.
[781] Manmatha is the god of love.
[782] The right hand.
[783] The left hand.

Vishnu in my mind. Though I know that he has been born as a
man, I know that he is superhuman and others who possess divine
sight also know this. In the night, I will consult with Krishna, who
himself knows everything. If he so agrees, I will go with him."[784]
On seeing Krishna, he cited these and many other reasons. With
Krishna and the others, he entered Nandagopa's house.'

Chapter 69

Vaishampayana said, 'The infinitely generous one[785] entered
Nandagopa's house with Keshava and summoning all the gopa
elders, spoke to them. Delighted to have met Krishna and Rohini's
son, he spoke to them too. "O son! For the sake of welfare, let us
go to the city of Mathura tomorrow. Let all those in Vraja and all
the cowherds also go. Kamsa has instructed that the appropriate
yearly taxes must be paid. There is a great and grand bow sacrifice
that Kamsa is organizing. You can see that grand sacrifice and meet
your relatives. You will meet your father Vasudeva, who has always
suffered and is incessantly miserable because his sons were killed.
He has always been oppressed by the wicked-minded Kamsa. This
oppression has tired him out. He is miserable and is suffering from
old age too. Separated from you, he is terrified and scared of Kamsa.
Day and night, he is consumed by anxiety in his heart. O Govinda!
You will also see Devaki, who has not held sons at her breasts. She
is like a goddess, but is suffering, bereft of all her radiance. Because
of grief on account of hers sons, she has dried up. She wishes to see
you. Because of the separation, she is tormented by grief. She is like
Surabhi,[786] without her calf. Her eyes are always overflowing with
tears. She is always dressed in old garments. She is like the moon's
radiance, when it has been eclipsed by Svarbhanu.[787] Desiring your

---

[784] To Mathura.
[785] Akrura.
[786] The celestial cow.
[787] Rahu.

arrival, she always wishes to see you. Because of grief on account of
you, that ascetic lady is suffering. Since she has been separated from
you, she has not heard your childhood conversation. O lord! She is
unaware of your beauty and the radiance of your moon-like face.
O Krishna! Though Devaki gave birth to you, she suffers. What
is the point of having given birth? It would have been better for
her to be childless. It is said that women who have no children
only suffer from one kind of grief. But one who has a son, and
does not obtain fruits through that son, is tormented by the birth.
In qualities and granting others freedom from fear, you are a son
who is Shakra's equal. Such a mother should not suffer. Your aged
mother and father are the servants of others. Because of you, Kamsa,
who doesn't possess foresight, abuses them. Having delivered you,
Devaki should be revered, like the earth. However, she is immersed
in an ocean of grief and should be saved. O Krishna! Vasudeva is
immensely strong. He is aged and loves his son. If you unite him
with his son, you will act in accordance with dharma. In the lake
in Yamuna, you crushed the extremely evil-minded serpent. You
raised up a large mountain[788] from the ground. You brought down
the powerful and insolent Arishta. You killed the evil-souled Keshi,
who robbed the lives of others. You must make efforts to save those
aged and miserable ones. O Krishna! You should think about the
means of following dharma. O Krishna! Your father was abused in
the assembly and all those who witnessed it were extremely miserable
and shed tears from their eyes. O Krishna! Your mother, Devaki,
is incapacitated. She has suffered from many miseries on account
of Kamsa destroying her conceptions. As has been indicated, it is
said that everyone who is born must quietly repay the debt to the
mother and the father. O Krishna! If you do this, you will show
favours to your mother and your father. Unmatched dharma will
be done and they will abandon their grief." Krishna knew what
the infinitely generous one was saying. The energetic Keshava was
not enraged, but restrained him. With Nandagopa at the forefront,
the assembled gopas heard Akrura's words and prepared to follow
Kamsa's instructions. All the residents of Vraja made arrangements

---

[788] Govardhana.

for departure. The aged gopas readied everything. As could be afforded, taxes were arranged—bulls, ghee, buffaloes, other gifts, milk and curds. All these components of tribute to Kamsa were arranged. All the leaders among the gopas made these arrangements for departure. Akrura remained awake, conversing with Krishna. Rohini's son was the third one present and the night passed in this way.'

Chapter 70

Vaishampayana said, 'The morning sparkled and the birds began to make a noise. When night was over, the moon withdrew its beams. The sky turned red and all the stellar bodies vanished. It was dawn and the surface of the earth became wet with dew. The stars dimmed, as if they were about to go to sleep. As the night disappeared, the form of the sun made its appearance. The beams of the moon lost their lustre and melted away. There were many cows in the grounds that had been readied for departure. There were the sounds of milk being churned in the pots. The young calves were tied up with ropes. All the roads in Vraja were filled with gopas. There were many heavy vessels that were loaded on the carts. The chariots and mounts left quickly, leaving everything else behind. Krishna, Rohini's son and the infinitely generous one—these three departed on a chariot, like lords of the three worlds. When they reached the banks of the Yamuna, Akrura told Krishna, "O son! Let us stop the chariot here. Tend to the horses. Give fodder to the horses. The vessel for the horses is on the chariot. O son! Make these efforts and wait for me for a short while. I will worship the lord of the serpents and the lord of all the worlds[789] in this pool in the Yamuna, using the divine Bhagavat mantra. I will bow down before the handsome serpent who bears the svastika mark on his hood. He is the divine and thousand-headed Ananta, attired in blue garments. I will consume all the poison that flows out from that god of dharma, like

---

[789] Shesha and Vishnu respectively.

the immortals partaking of amrita. He bears the svastika mark and his tongue is forked. He is the one who is adorned with prosperity. For the sake of peace, he is surrounded by all the snakes. Until I return from the pool and from that Indra among serpents, both of you be seated here and wait for me." Happily, Krishna replied, "O one who follows dharma! Go, without any delay. Without you, we are incapable of being well." The infinitely generous one immersed himself in the pool in the Yamuna.

'He saw rasatala, the world of the snakes, as it indeed was. He saw him[790] with his one thousand faces, a standard with a golden palm tree held aloft his head. A plough was held in one hand and there was a club near his stomach. He was attired in dark garments. He was fair, with a pale face. He was adorned in a single earring. He was intoxicated and his eyes were like the petals of a lotus that was asleep. The serpent was seated on a white seat, made out of the coils of his own body. He was seated with the svastika mark and looked like the best of mountains. His head, decorated in gold, was inclined towards the left. His chest was adorned with a garland of lotus flowers that were made out of gold. The scorcher of enemies was mighty-armed and his limbs were smeared with red sandalwood paste. He was fair in complexion and there was a lotus on his navel. The powerful one blazed in energy. He saw the lord of the serpents, the lord who was there when everything was a single ocean. The lord, the Indra among those who forked tongues, was being worshipped by Vasuki and other serpents. The serpents Kambala and Ashvatara fanned him with whisks. The divine lord, who has no origin, was seated on a throne of dharma. Vasuki, the lord of serpents, was stationed near him. He was surrounded by snakes who were advisers, Karkotaka being the foremost. They bathed him and consecrated him as the king, with waters from the single ocean, poured from divine and golden pots that were strewn with lotus flowers. He saw Vishnu seated on his[791] lap, attired in yellow garments and with an extremely dark complexion, with the srivatsa mark on

[790] Shesha.
[791] Shesha's.

his chest.⁷⁹² He saw another lord, Samkarshana, who was seated, with a complexion that was like that of the moon. However, he wasn't seated on a divine seat. At this, he suddenly tried to speak to Krishna.⁷⁹³ But Krishna used his own energy to stop him from speaking. He saw the undecaying and illustrious lord amidst all those serpents. Astounded, the infinitely generous one surfaced again. He saw Bala and Keshava, extraordinary in forms, seated on the chariot and glancing at each other. Filled with curiosity, Akrura immersed himself again and saw the eternal god, attired in blue garments, being worshipped. He saw him seated on the lap of the one with the one thousand hoods. Akrura saw Krishna being worshipped according to the proper rites. Having surfaced again, the infinitely generous one chanted the mantra in his mind and returned to the chariot along the same route. When Akrura returned, Keshava cheerfully asked him, "What happened in the Bhagavat pool? How was the world of the serpents? You took a long time. Is your delay because of some distraction? I think you must have seen something extraordinary and did not wish to leave." He replied to Krishna, "There are no marvels without you. There is nothing in the mobile or immobile worlds that occurs otherwise. O Krishna! There, I saw a marvel that is extremely rare on earth. Here, it is exactly as it was there, and I am delighted. O Krishna! I saw a form that is extraordinary in the worlds. After this, there is no other wonder that I wish to see. O lord! Therefore, let us proceed to Kamsa's royal city. We should leave so as to reach before the sun signals the end of the day."'

Chapter 71

Vaishampayana said, 'All those infinitely energetic ones yoked that supreme chariot and entered that foremost city when the

---

⁷⁹² The Critical Edition has a typo that we have corrected. It says udara (stomach), though it should be *urasa* (chest).
⁷⁹³ As Vishnu.

sun was turning red. The intelligent Akrura, who was like the sun
in his energy, took the brave Krishna and Samkarshana to his own
house. Danapati was scared. He told the two, who were excellent
in complexion, "O sons! You should abandon all desire of going
to Vasudeva's house. Because of you, Kamsa abuses the aged one.
Day and night, he censures him, asking him to leave the place."
Krishna replied, "O one who follows dharma! We will not debate
this with you. O brave one! We will go and see the royal roads
of Mathura." Having obtained permission, those two brave ones
left, desiring to see. They were like two elephants that had been
tied up, but were now released, desiring to fight. Along the road,
they saw a washerman who had dyed some clothes. They asked him
to give them bright clothes. The washerman said, "Who are you?
You are foolish residents of the forest who are asking for royal
garments. You don't seem to have any fear. I ensure that Kamsa
obtains clothes from many different countries. I dye hundreds of
garments with many colours that one wants. Who are you? Which
forest were you born in? You have been reared with animals. On
seeing these many red garments, you seem to be attracted to them.
Alas! You have abandoned your lives. You are foolish, ordinary
and ignorant people. Having come here, you are asking for
inappropriate clothes." Krishna became angry with the washerman
who was limited in intelligence. He was stupid and desired his own
harm. That is the reason he spoke words that were like poison. He[794]
struck the washerman on the head with a palm that was like the
vajra and he fell down, having lost his life. His head was shattered.
On seeing that he was dead, his wives started to lament and shriek.
With dishevelled hair, they swiftly went to Kamsa's house. Those
two chose some excellent garments. Seeking garlands, they went
to the road along which there were shops that sold garlands. They
were attracted to the fragrances, like elephants. There was a man
named Gunaka. He earned his living from selling garlands and he
was pleasant in speech. Though he earned his living from selling
garlands, he was wealthy. There were many garlands in the shop.
Gently, Krishna spoke these words to him. "Give us some garlands."

[794] Krishna.

At that time, without any hesitation, the garland maker told them that he would give them some. The person who earned his living from selling garlands was happy and gave them many garlands. The handsome one replied, "Everything that I have is yours." Delighted in his mind, Krishna granted Gunaka a boon. "O amiable one! Because you have sought refuge with me, you will obtain riches and prosperity." The garland maker was happy at having received this boon. He lowered his face. He prostrated his head before Krishna and received the boon. The one who earned his living from selling garlands thought that they might be yakshas. Therefore, he was also scared and anxious and did not reply. Vasudeva's two sons continued to proceed along the royal road. They saw Kubja,[795] who was carrying a plate laden with pastes. Krishna told Kubja, "O one with eyes like lotus petals! Who are these pastes for? You should quickly tell us." She used to walk in a crooked way, like lightning. She stood and looked at him. She then replied to the lotus-eyed Krishna, whose voice was like the rumbling of a cloud. "I am carrying these pastes to the king's bathing chamber. O fortunate ones! Come and spend some time with me. There is love in my heart for you. O amiable ones! Since you do not know me, where have you come from? I am loved by the great king and an employed for the purpose of pastes." As Kubja stood there, smiling, Krishna told her, "Give us pastes that are appropriate for our bodies. O one with the beautiful face! We are wrestlers and have come to this country as guests. We have come to see this great and prosperous kingdom and this divine and grand bow sacrifice." She replied to Krishna, "Now that I have seen you, you have become my beloved. Accept this excellent paste, which is fit to be given to the king." They smeared the pastes on their limbs and started to dazzle. They looked like two bulls in a tirtha in the Yamuna, limbs covered with mud. As if playing, Krishna gently pressed the hump with two fingers of his hand. When Krishna pressed, the crooked body straightened and the one with the beautiful smiles stood upright. The one with the large breasts was as straight as a creeper around a pole and laughed out aloud. Intoxicated and in love with Krishna, she said,

[795] Kubja means someone who is crooked or hump backed.

"O beloved one! Where are you going? I will detain you. Remain here and accept me." They clapped their hands and smiled at each other. On seeing this and hearing about it, the onlookers laughed a great deal at Kubja. Krishna smiled and took his leave of Kubja, who was overcome by desire.

'Having taken their leave of Kubja, they entered the king's assembly. They had been reared in Vraja and were adorned and attired like cowherds. They entered the king's abode, their faces hiding their intentions. Without being suspected, those two children entered the chamber where the bows were kept. Proud of their strength, they were like two lions who had been born in the forests in the Himalayas. They wished to see the giant bow, which had been appropriately decorated. Those two brave ones asked the person who was in charge of the weapons. "O one who guards Kamsa's bow! Hear our words. O amiable one! Where is Kamsa's great and decorated bow kept? If you so desire, show it to us." He showed them the bow, which was like a pillar. No man was capable of wielding it, not to speak of the gods, along with Vasava. The valiant Krishna seized it and raised it. Cheerful in his mind, the lotus-eyed one grasped it in his hands. He raised the bow, worshipped by the daityas, as he wished. The strong one tried to bend the bow, but he was unsuccessful in bending it. It was like a serpent and though Krishna tried to bend it, he couldn't. Instead, that decorated bow snapped in the middle. Krishna, who was swift in his valour, broke that excellent bow. With Samkarshana, the youth then departed at great speed. The sound of the bow shattering resounded in the air. This filled all the directions and made the inner quarters tremble. The man who was in charge of the weapons was terrified by this speed and valour. Trembling like a crow, he went to the king and said, "Listen to what I have to say. An extraordinary event has occurred in the chamber where the bow was kept. It has just happened and it deserves the respect of the universe. There were two men who came together, wearing locks of hair. They were dressed in blue and yellow garments. They were smeared with yellow and white paste. They were as brave as sons of the gods. Those children were like fires. Those two amiable ones stood in the chamber meant for the bow, as if they had suddenly arrived from the firmament. I saw that they were attired in beautiful garments and garlands. One among them possessed eyes like a lotus. He was dark and was attired in yellow garments and garlands. He seized that jewel among bows, which is impossible for even the gods to grasp. With great strength, the child picked up the giant bow, as if it was the entrails of a crow. As if he was playing, he applied force to the bow, but could not bend it. Using the strength of his hands, he tried to bend it, though there was no arrow attached. As he grasped it in his hand, it made a great sound and broke into two parts. That jewel among bows shattered, as if it had been struck by an elephant. Having broken it, the infinitely valorous one departed with the speed of the wind. O king! Having broken it, he has left. I do not know who he is." Hearing about how the bow had been broken, Kamsa was anxious in his mind. He allowed the guard of the weapons to leave and entered his excellent house.'

Chapter 72

Vaishampayana said, 'The extender of the Bhoja lineage thought about the bow being shattered. He quickly went to the arena to see the viewing gallery. The supreme among kings saw that everything had been arranged in the arena. Arrays of firm platforms had been fixed, without any gaps. There were excellent walls, decorated with galleries. There were extensive shades, all supported on a single pillar. Everything had been arranged properly and the arena was superb. There were fountains of water and excellent steps for climbing on to the galleries. Seats had been spread around for the king and there were paths to walk along. The galleries were so spread out that they could accommodate large numbers of people. On seeing that the arena had been decorated, the intelligent one said, "Let colourful garlands and flags be used tomorrow. Let there be beautiful covers and fragrances. Let the canopy and the arena be strewn with flowers. Let the arena be wiped clean with cow dung. Let the gallery be decorated with beautiful curtains. In due order, let there be pots filled with drinking water. Everywhere, let there be excellent and golden pots filled with water. Let us think of offerings and pots filled with drinks. Let wrestlers be invited and let them be seated ahead of all the arrays. Accordingly, instruct the wrestlers and the spectators. Let the arena and the gallery be decorated properly." The king thus instructed that excellent arrangements should be made. Having left the arena, he entered his own house.

'There, he summoned the two invincible wrestlers, Chanura and Mushtika. Those two wrestlers were extremely brave and strong, skilful in fighting. Heeding Kamsa's instructions, they cheerfully entered. He saw that those two wrestlers, famous in the world, had arrived. Kamsa addressed them in words that explained what he meant. "You are my famous wrestlers. You hold aloft the standard of valour. As is proper, you are therefore worshipped and, in particular, shown respect. Remember the good deeds I have done and the honour I have shown you. Using your own energy, you must now perform a great task for me. There are two cowherds who have been reared in Vraja—Samkarshana and Krishna. Though they are children, they have conquered all exhaustion. Those two roam around in the forest. They have come here, to this arena for fighting, desiring to fight. There is no doubt that you should bring them down quickly and kill them. You should not act towards them as if they are fickle children. You should not ignore them. You must make efforts. In the encounter that follows when they come to the arena, if you restrain those two gopas, you will ensure what is best for me, now and in the future." Chanura and Mushtika heard the affectionate words of the king and became cheerful in their minds. The wrestlers were revered for their fighting and said, "When those two, the worst among gopas, stand in front of us, they will head towards their death. Those two ascetics have already gone to the land of the dead. If they fight against us, they will face a great calamity. We will be full of anger at those two foremost ones, who dwell in the forest." In this way, those two bulls among wrestlers uttered words that were full of poison. Having taken the permission of the Indra among men, they returned to their own houses.'

Chapter 73

Vaishampayana said, 'Kamsa spoke to Mahamatra, who earned a living through elephants.[796] "Summon the elephant Kuvalayapida and station him at the gate. He is strong. His eyes are crazy with intoxication. He is fickle and angry with men. He becomes fierce and terrible when he sees a rival elephant. Urge him towards those two residents of the forest. Arrange it so that those two inferior sons of Vasudeva lose their lives. In the arena, I wish to see that you and that king among elephants are fierce and kill those two, who earn subsistence through cows. On seeing that those two have been brought down, the foundations of Vasudeva and his relatives will be severed. He will be without a support. With his wife, he will be destroyed. All the foolish Yadavas have sought refuge with Krishna. On seeing that Krishna has been brought down, all their hopes will be destroyed. They will be killed by that king of elephants, by the wrestlers, or by me. With the city bereft of Yadavas, I will roam around happily. My father is an extender of the Yadava lineage and I have abandoned him. I have abandoned the remaining Yadavas who have taken Krishna's side. Ugrasena desired to have a son. But Narada has told me that I have not been born through a man who is limited in valour. There is a mountain named Suyamuna. When my mother was in her season, because she was curious, she went to the forest with other women. There were beautiful and lovely trees on that summit. She roamed around on the summit of the mountain and in caverns and rivers. She heard the sweet songs of the kinnaras resounding. She heard words that were pleasant to hear and excited desire. Having heard the calls of the peacocks and the chirping of the birds and seen all this, she desired to follow the dharma of women. At this time, a breeze wafted through the forest. It carried the scent of flowers and ignited desire. Adorned with bees, the kadamba trees were stirred by the

---

[796] As a common noun, *mahamatra* means chief adviser or chief minister. Here, it is being used as a proper noun and Mahamatra is the name of Kamsa's mahout.

breeze. This increased their fragrances and it was enough to drive one senseless. *Kesara* trees[797] showered down flowers that ignited desire. Decorated with flowers and thorns, the nipa trees were like shining lamps. The earth was covered by new grass and seemed to be adorned with shakragopas. It assumed a form that looked like that of a young woman. The handsome lord of Soubha, the danava named Drumila, arrived there. Assuming Ugrasena's form, he raped my mother. Taking him to be her husband, she submitted to him. However, she subsequently suspected and thought that she had been dishonoured. When she arose, she was frightened and said, 'It is certain that you are not my husband. Who are you? Why did you violate me in this disguised form? I follow the vow of a single husband and have been tainted by you. O wicked one! You have assumed the form of my husband and perpetrated an inferior deed. O worst of your lineage! What will my relatives angrily tell me? I will have to live, derided by my husband's family. Since you have acted in this way, shame on you. You come from a wicked lineage. Your senses have made you deviate. You cannot be trusted. Driven by desire, you have violated another person's wife.' When she censured him in this way, the danava became angry. He wrathfully retorted, 'My name is Drumila and I am the energetic lord of Soubha. O foolish one! Taking yourself to be learned, why are you reprimanding me? You have taken a man as your husband and he is inferior in energy and valour. O one who prides herself on being a woman! Women are not tainted by adultery. The learned ones do not restrain women, especially those who are human, in this way. I have heard of many women who have transgressed by committing adultery. They have given birth to infinitely valourous sons who are like the gods. In this world, you take yourself to be the only one who follows the dharma of being excessively devoted to her husband. You take yourself to be pure, brandish your hair,[798] and speak whatever you wish. O one who wished to have intercourse! You asked me, who am I? I will tell you. You will have a son named Kamsa and he will destroy his enemies.' At this, she was again enraged and cursed this boon.

---

[797] *Mimusops elengi.*
[798] The parting in the hair, signifying the marital status.

Distressed, the queen spoke to the danava, who had spoken in this evil way. 'O extremely wicked one! Shame on your conduct. You have criticized all women. There are women who are wicked in conduct and there are women who follow the vow of being devoted to their husbands. O worst of your lineage! Those are the women who hold up all the worlds. You have granted me a son who will be the destroyer of good conduct. I do not approve of this. Listen to what I have to say. A man will be born in my husband's lineage. He will cause the death of the son you have bestowed on me.' Thus addressed, Drumila departed through the sky. Grieving, my mother returned to the city on the same day. O one who looks after the elephant! I am Ugrasena's *kshetraja* son.[799] Having been abandoned by my mother and my father, I have established myself through my own energy. Both of them hate me and my relatives especially do so. I will slay those two cowherds. Go. Ascend the elephant and equip it with a goad, a spear and a spike. O Mahamatra! Be steady and quickly station yourself at the gate."'

Chapter 74

Vaishampayana said, 'That day was over. When the second day presented itself, the great arena was filled with citizens who wished to see the encounter. The stage was supported on eight colourful pillars. There were walls and altars at the gates. There were windows in the shape of the half-moon and the excellent platform was decorated. The beautiful eastern gate was thrown open and adorned with garlands and ropes. It was ornamented and radiant, like a cloud in the autumn sky. The wrestling arena was prepared well and was equipped with everything required for fighting. The beautiful wrestling arena looked like a mass of clouds, or like the ocean. There were rows of people in the gallery, which was as resplendent as a mountain. Those from the inner quarters

---

[799] *Kshetra* means field, signifying the mother. Kshetraja means someone born from the mother, in the father's field.

were not very far from the spectators' gallery. Their gallery blazed in gold and was adorned with nets of jewels. Decorated by those jewels, they looked like the summits of mountains. With blazing curtains as covers, they looked like mountains with wings. There were whisks and the sounds of laughter and the tinkling of ornaments. There were many kinds of gems, colourful in their rays. There was a separate gallery for the courtesans, draped with clean covers. With the best of courtesans seated there, they were as resplendent as celestial vehicles. There were the best of seats and golden couches. Colourful cushions were strewn around and there were bouquets and trees. The place was decorated with golden pots filled with water for drinking. There were baskets filled with fruit and arrangements were made for drinks. There were many other galleries, bound down with piles of wood. There were many such sparkling galleries, strewn with covers. There were other excellent galleries, shrouded in fine nets through which one could see. These viewing galleries for women sparkled like swans in the sky. The beautiful eastern gate was as radiant as the summit of Meru. The colourful pillars were inlaid with gold leaves. Kamsa's viewing gallery blazed even more. It was decorated with garlands of flowers and bore all the signs of his residence. The entire arena was full of people and resounded with the noise of crowds of people. The wrestling arena bore the complexion of a turbulent ocean.

'It quietened down when the king arrived in his viewing gallery and instructed that the elephant Kuvalayapida should be stationed at the arena's gate. He was attired in white garments and was fanned with sparkling fans and whisks. With a white crown, he dazzled, like the moon surrounded by white clouds. The intelligent one happily seated himself on his throne. On seeing his unmatched beauty, the citizens pronounced benedictions for his victory. Brandishing their garments in the air, the wrestlers entered the arena. Having entered the arena, those powerful ones seated themselves in three rows. Trumpets were sounded. Slapping their chests, Vasudeva's two sons happily presented themselves at the gate of the arena. As those handsome ones quickly entered, they were halted by the crazy elephant, which had been severely goaded for this purpose. The evil-souled and maddened elephant curled its trunk. Carefully

goaded, it sought to kill Bala and Keshava. When the elephant tried
to scare him, Krishna laughed. He censured the evil-souled Kamsa's
intolerance. "Indeed, Kamsa will quickly go to Vaivasvata's
abode, since he desires to use this elephant to attack me." Having
approached, the elephant roared like a cloud. The lord Govinda
suddenly leapt up and clapped his hands. With the elephant in front
of him, he slapped his chest and created a noise. Shridhara[800] seized
the trunk and pressed it against his chest. He passed between the
elephant's tusks and between its legs. Krishna teased the elephant,
like the wind teasing the clouds. Krishna avoided the trunk and
passed through the tusker's tusks. Emerging from between the legs,
he seized it by the tail. Though it wished to kill Krishna, that gigantic
animal was incapable and stupefied. As its body was crushed, the
elephant began to trumpet. It sank down on to the ground on its
knees and its tusks struck the ground. It exuded musth in its rage,
like a cloud at the end of the summer. Like a child, Krishna played
with the elephant. Because of the hatred towards Kamsa, he then
made up his mind to kill it. Placing his right foot against its temple,
he uprooted both its tusks and struck it with those. The elephant
was struck by its own tusks, which were like the vajra. Thus struck,
it released urine and excrement and screamed in pain. Its limbs
mangled by Krishna, the elephant's senses were afflicted. Copious
streams of blood began to flow from its temples. Halayudha[801]
powerfully tugged at its tail, like Vinata's son[802] pulling at a serpent
that is hidden in the slope of a mountain. Krishna slew the elephant
with a tusk. With another stroke of that same tusk, he slew the one
who was astride the elephant.[803] Deprived of its tusks, the supreme
elephant emitted a mighty shriek. With Mahamatra, it fell down,
like a mountain shattered by the vajra. Having killed the supreme
elephant that roared, Pundarikaksha entered the arena, which was
like an ocean, with his elder brother.'

[800] Vishnu and Krishna's name.
[801] The one with a *hala* (plough) as *ayudha* (weapon), Balarama.
[802] Garuda.
[803] Mahamatra.

Chapter 75

Vaishampayana said, 'Placing his elder brother ahead of him, the lotus-eyed Krishna powerfully entered the arena, his garments waving around in the wind. Devaki's son carried the elephant's tusks in his excellent hands. The fat and the blood seemed to have created playful armlets on his arms. He leapt like a lion and was like a thundering cloud. He seemed to move the earth with the slapping of his hands. Ugrasena's son saw him, holding up the elephant's tusk as a weapon. Extremely pale in fear, he angrily looked towards Krishna. Keshava was resplendent, with the elephant's tusk in his hand. He looked like a mountain with a single peak, with the half-moon just above it. When Govinda leapt around, that entire arena, which was like an ocean, was filled with sounds made by that mass of people. As had been decided earlier, Kamsa commanded Chanura. "You should make efforts to fight with Krishna." Chanura's eyes became coppery red with rage. He advanced to fight, like a cloud that was full of water. The assembled people were instructed to be quiet. The assembled Yadavas collectively spoke these words. "There will be a wrestling match in this arena. Let no questions be raised. Let there be no cowardice. It was decided earlier that the strength of arms will be shown, without the use of weapons. Those who know about the progress of time have laid down the rules. What must be done has also been instructed. For exhaustion, there must always be water. Dried cow dung must always be kept ready for the wrestlers.[804] The judges have instructed that the duel must be one by one, stationed on the ground, or stationed in any other mode.[805] If a person is stationed in the arena, depending on whether he is a child, middle-aged, old, thin or strong, a rival must be found for him from within that same category. It has been decreed that a wrestling bout must be fought on the basis of strength or techniques. The learned

---

[804] So that they can smear their bodies with dried cow dung and drink water when they are tired.

[805] One person must fight against one person at a time. If the rival stands on the ground, one must also stand on the ground. If the rival stands somewhere other than on the ground, one must also stand there.

know that once a rival has been brought down, nothing further must be done to him. In the arena, the wrestling match between Krishna and the one from Andhra[806] is about to commence. Krishna is a child and the one from Andhra is massive. We should reflect about this." At this, an uproar arose among the assembled people.

'Govinda leapt around and spoke these words. "I am a child. The one from Andhra is massive, with a body that is like a mountain. I take delight at the prospect of wrestling with someone who has strength in his arms. So far as I am concerned, there will be no deviation from the rules set for wrestling. It is my view that one should not sully those who wrestle with bare arms. There is the dharma of dried cow dung and there is the dharma of water. One must attire oneself in ochre garments. These rules have been thought of for the arena. When one follows the vow of fighting in an arena, success comes from self-control, firmness, valour, exercise, good conduct and strength. However, if anyone brings a trace of enmity to this wrestling match here, it will be my task to suppress him and satisfy the universe. He has been born in Karusha and has the name of Chanura. Though he fights with the strength in his arms, one needs to think about the deeds he has done. Invincible in the duel, he has slain many wrestlers. By exhibiting that power in the arena, he has tainted the path followed by wrestlers. Warriors who are accomplished in the use of weapons must fight with weapons in the field of battle. However, for a wrestler who is accomplished in the arena, bringing down his rival represents success. A person who is victorious in a battle obtains eternal fame. Even if a person is slain by weapons in the field of battle, the vault of heaven has been earmarked for him. The slayer and the slain, both obtain success in a battle. That is a great journey that leads to the loss of one's life and it is one that is worshipped by the virtuous. But along this path, success comes from strength and techniques. If a person dies in an arena, where is the heaven for him? What love can the victor have for such a victory? Because of the sins of a king who prides himself on being learned, if a wrestler exhibits his power and kills another wrestler, he is nothing but a murderer." Having conversed

[806] Chanura.

in this way, an extremely terrible duel took place between them. It was as terrible as two elephants fighting in the forest. They used their arms to engage with each other and countered each other in wonderful ways. They raised the opponent and brought him down. They pushed and tugged. They struck each other with fists and made sounds like boars. They rained blows, which were like the vajra, on each other. They used their nails as spikes. They used terrible kicks. They struck with their thighs and butted with their hands, making sounds like stones striking against stones. There was a fierce duel, using the strength of arms and without resorting to weapons. In the midst of the assembly, those brave ones used their strength alone. Everyone present was delighted and roars of approval arose. Other people in the galleries uttered words of praise.

'Kamsa's face was full of sweat and he glanced towards Krishna. Using his left hand, he indicated that the trumpets should cease. He instructed that the trumpets and the drums should stop. The innumerable divine trumpets that were blaring in the sky also stopped. However, as Hrishikesha, the lotus-eyed one, continued to fight, all the trumpets began to sound of their own accord. The gods were in celestial vehicles that could travel as they wished, together with beautiful vidyadharas. Though remaining invisible, they assembled, desiring Krishna's victory. All the saptarshis who were in the sky exclaimed, "May Krishna defeat the danava Chanura who has assumed the form of a wrestler." Devaki's son played with Chanura for a long time. But on discerning Kamsa's sentiments, he summoned up all his strength. The earth trembled. The arena started to move around. The best of gems fell down from Kamsa's crown. Chanura had already lived his life. With his arms, Krishna bent him. He struck him on the head with his fist and on the chest with his knee. Tears and blood flowed from his eyes and his eyeballs emerged from their sockets, hanging like bells from a seat on an elephant. With his eyes gouged out, he fell down in the middle of the arena. Bereft of life and with his lifespan over, Chanura lay down on the ground. Bereft of life Chanura's body lay down in the arena. The large road was seen to be obstructed, as if by a mountain.'

Chapter 76

Vaishampayana said, 'Chanura was proud of his strength. On seeing that he had been killed, in that arena, Rohini's son seized Mushtika. Krishna seized Tosalaka.[807] At first, those two wrestlers[808] were senseless with rage. Having come under the subjugation of time, they engaged with Rama and Krishna. The powerful Krishna raised up Tosalaka, who was like the summit of a mountain. He whirled him around one hundred times and dashed him down on the ground. That powerful one was afflicted and oppressed by Krishna. Copious quantities of blood emerged from his mouth and he was about to die. The immensely strong Samkarshana fought for a long time. The wrestler from Andhra[809] was a great wrestler and exhibited various techniques. The energetic and brave one[810] struck him on the head with a blow of his fist and it was like the vajra. It was as if the vajra had shattered a huge mountain. His head was shattered. On his face, the eyes emerged from their sockets. Uttering a loud roar, he fell down there. After killing the wrestler from Andhra and Tosalaka, Krishna and Samkarshana leapt around in the middle of the arena, their eyes red with anger. They were terrible to behold. When the wrestler from Andhra[811] and the great wrestler, Mushtika, had been killed, no other wrestlers were left in the arena. On seeing this, all the gopas, with Nandagopa at the forefront, stood rooted at the spot. Their limbs trembled because of fear. Full of questions, Devaki also trembled and glanced towards Krishna. Tears of joy flowed from her eyes. On having seen Krishna, her eyes were filled with tears. Because of his affection, Vasudeva discarded his old age and became young. With their eyes, the best among courtesans drank in Krishna's face, like bees doing this to lotuses in the twinkling of an eye.

'There were beads of sweat on Kamsa's face and between his brows. Having seen Krishna, his inner hatred led to these

[807] Also written as Toshalaka.
[808] Mushtika and Tosalaka.
[809] Mushtika.
[810] Balarama.
[811] Now meaning Chanura.

manifestations. The fire in his inner heart and mind blazed and it was as if his breath was fanned by the wind of rage, emitting smoke towards Keshava. His lips trembled and he furrowed his eyebrows. Because of his rage, Kamsa's face assumed the form of the red sun. There were beads of sweat on a face that was red with rage. This looked like dew created by the rising sun. Angrily, he instructed many men, "These gopas roam around in the forest. Expel them from the assembly. They are wicked and deformed. I do not wish to see them. The gopas do not deserve to remain in my kingdom. Nandagopa is wicked in intelligence and regards me as someone who is evil in conduct. Bind him in iron chains and iron shackles. Vasudeva is wicked in conduct and has always acted deceitfully towards me. He deserves a punishment that is not meant for the aged. I will quickly kill him. These ordinary gopas are devoted to Damodara. Seize their cattle and any other riches that they possess." In harsh words, Kamsa issued these commands. Krishna, with truth as his valour, glanced towards his face. Keshava was angry at what had been said about his father and Nandagopa. He saw the distress of his relatives and that Devaki was senseless. The mighty-armed Achyuta climbed up, for Kamsa's destruction. He was as forceful as a maned lion, born with valour. From the middle of the arena, Krishna jumped up, to near Kamsa's throne. He was like a cloud tinged with lightning, fanned by the wind. All those who were in the middle of the arena didn't actually see him leap up.[812] The residents of the city only saw him standing next to Kamsa. Kamsa was under the subjugation of the dharma of time. He saw Govinda near him and thought that the lord had descended there from the sky. In the midst of that assembly in the arena, Krishna used his arms, which were like clubs, and seized Kamsa by the hair on his head. The crown, decorated with gold and diamonds, fell down. His head was seized by Krishna's hands. With the hair grasped by the hands, Kamsa was unable to make any efforts. He was senseless and didn't know what to do. Seized by the hair, he sighed gently. Kamsa was incapable of looking towards Krishna's face. The earrings were dislodged from his ears. The necklace was torn away

---

[812] It happened too fast.

from his chest. With his arms hanging down, the ornaments were dislodged from his body. His upper garment was dislodged. The throne moved violently. Thus grabbed by Krishna's energy, Kamsa trembled. Keshava dragged him down from the gallery on to the middle of that great arena. With his hair seized with great force, Kamsa confronted a great hardship. The immensely radiant king of Bhoja was thus dragged by Krishna along that arena. As his body was dragged along, potholes were created there. In that arena, Krishna played around and dragged him along. When he had lost his life, Krishna flung Kamsa's body a long distance away. A body that was used to happiness lay down on the ground. It was pale and covered with dust, the opposite of what used to happen earlier. He was without a crown and his face was dark. The eyes were closed. The radiance was destroyed. It was as if a lotus no longer had its petals. Kamsa wasn't slain in a battle, wounded by arrows. He died from being grasped by the neck. He thus deviated from the path meant for the brave. He had been violently dragged along. Marks could be seen on the body, wounds made in the flesh by Keshava's nails, while he was still alive. Having slain him, Pundarikaksha's joy doubled. With the thorn dead, he worshipped at Vasudeva's feet. The delight of the Yadu lineage lowered his head and kneaded his mother's feet. Krishna was sprinkled with the milk that flowed from this happiness. Krishna, blazing in his own energy, asked about the welfare of all the Yadavas, in due order and according to age. Kamsa's brother was named Sunama. Using his arms, Baladeva, with dharma in his soul, brought him down and defeated him. Those two brave and victorious ones had conquered their anger. They had been reared in Vraja for a long period of time. Cheerful in their minds, they went to the residence of their own father.'

Chapter 77

Vaishampayana said, 'On seeing that their husband had been killed, like a planet that had lost its splendour, all of Kamsa's wives surrounded the dead Kamsa from all sides. Having lost his

life, the lord of the earth was sleeping on a bed on the ground. The
wives saw this and grieved, like female deer when the male deer has
been slain. "O mighty-armed one! Alas! We have been killed. Our
hopes have been destroyed. Our relatives have been killed. We are
the brave wives of a brave person. We have been devoted to the
vows of the brave. O tiger among kings! Those who have seen how
you came about your end are grieving. With your relatives, we are
lamenting. O immensely strong one! We are without a foundation.
Abandoned by you, we beautiful ones are without subsistence.
Now that you have died, you have left us without a protector.
When we are pale in our limbs, desiring to have intercourse and
like creepers that cannot move, who will convey us to our beds?
O amiable one! Your breath has now merged with the air and
your beautiful face is being scorched by the sun, like a lotus that is
deprived of water. These ears are empty and are no longer adorned
by earrings. Your head has always loved earrings and is now lying
down on the ground. O brave one! Your crown was decorated
with all the jewels. Where is it now? It possessed the complexion
of the sun and brought prosperity to your head. We are the wives
and women who adorned your inner quarters. Now that you have
gone to another world, what will these miserable ones do? Wives
who are virtuous are never deprived from objects of pleasure and
are never abandoned by their husbands. If that is indeed the case,
where are you going? Time, which circles in its tasks, is immensely
powerful. Time is like an enemy who is swiftly taking you away
from us. We do not deserve unhappiness and have always enjoyed
happiness. O lord! We are overcome by distress. How will we live
as widows? For women of good character, the husband alone is the
supreme refuge. You have been our objective. Death has proved to
be stronger and has taken you away. We are now in the state of
widows. Our minds are full of sorrow and grief. It is certain that we
will be immersed in weeping. Where will we go without you? Time
has left with you and so has the time for playing on your lap. We
have been deprived in an instant. The fortune of men is transient. O
one who grants honours! Alas! We are distressed. We are miserable.
All of us must have committed the same crime. That is why we have
become widows at the same time. We found delight in intercourse

and you nurtured us. You have left for heaven. All of us desire you.
Abandoning us, where are you going? O lord! We are lamenting
like female ospreys. O protector of the universe! O one who grants
honours! You should reply to us. O great king! Your wives are
lamenting in this way and your relatives are sorrowing. To us, your
departure seems to be terrible. O handsome one! There is no doubt
that the beautiful women in the other world must be more beautiful
than us. O brave one! That is the reason you have abandoned the
people in your own household and have left. O brave one! O lord
of the earth! Your wives are piteously shrieking and weeping. Then,
why are you not waking up now? Alas! This last journey of men
is pitiable. They must neglect the wives and leave. It is better for
women to have no husband than for women to have a husband who
is brave. That is because the women in heaven love brave ones more
and are also loved by those brave ones. You loved to fight and you
have swiftly been rendered invisible. Death has struck all of us in our
inner organs. In battles, you have killed Jarasandha's soldiers and
have defeated the yakshas. O lord of the universe! How could you
have been slain by an ordinary human? In a battle, you have fought
with Indra, using arrows in that encounter. You have vanquished
the immortals in a battle? How could you have been slain by a
mortal? The ocean cannot be agitated and you agitated it with your
shower of arrows. You defeated the wielder of the noose[813] and
seized all his jewels. Vasava was deficient in showering down. For
the sake of the citizens, you penetrated the clouds with your arrows
and used your strength to cause rain. All the kings were forced to
submit to your powers. They sent excellent and expensive gems and
garments to you. Witnessing your valour, the enemies thought that
you were like a god. How could this terrible fear, which caused
loss of life, arrive? With our lord having been brought down, we
confront the prospect of being addressed as widows. We were not
distracted. But we have been deprived by death and have become
distracted. O lord! Even if you wanted to leave and forget us, it was
your duty to tell us that you were going and take our leave. O lord!
Show us your favours. We are scared. Our heads are lowered at

[813] Varuna, the lord of the ocean.

your feet. O lord of Mathura! There has been enough of residence
at a distant spot. Return. O brave one! Alas! How can you lie down
on a bed of grass and dust? Does your mind not suffer because of
lying down on the ground? Who struck us while we were asleep?
Who struck us suddenly? Who has struck all these women in this
extremely terrible way? As long as women are alive, they have to
weep and lament. We are weeping. Why should we not depart with
our husband?"

'At this time, Kamsa's mother also arrived there. She was
miserable and trembling. "Where is my child? Where is my son?"
She wept piteously. She saw her dead son, who was like a pale
moon. Her heart was shattered and she lamented repeatedly. She
glanced towards her son and exclaimed, "I have been killed. Alas!"
Afflicted and miserable, she lamented and wept with her daughters-
in-law. She loved her son. Miserably, she raised his head on her lap.
Having done this, she thought of her son and wept in piteous words.
"O son! You followed the vow of heroes. You brought delight to
your relatives. O son! Why do you want to leave so quickly? O son!
Without a bed, why are you sleeping in this way? O son! Those
with your kind of signs should not sleep in this way on the ground.
In ancient times, Ravana, who was superior in strength in all the
worlds, chanted a shloka in an assembly of rakshasas and this is
revered by virtuous men. 'Because of the energy I have obtained,
I am capable of slaying the gods. However, it is certain that I will
confront a terrible fear that will come through my relatives.' In that
way, though my intelligent son loves his relatives, a great fear will
arise on account of the relatives and lead to loss of life." Weeping
and senseless, she spoke these words to her husband and king,
the aged Ugrasena, who was also senseless. She was like Surabhi,
deprived of her calf. "O king! O one with dharma in his soul! Come
and see your son, the lord of men. He is lying down on a bed meant
for heroes, like a mountain that has been shattered by the vajra.
O great king! He has now died and gone to Yama's abode. We
should perform the funeral rites that befit his departure. Brave ones
enjoy kingdoms. We have been defeated. Go and instruct Krishna
about performing Kamsa's funeral rites. All enmity is pacified after
death. There is peace. The funeral rites must be performed. The

dead do not commit any crimes." She spoke these words to the lord
of the Bhojas. Then, miserable, she started to tear out her hair. She
glanced towards her son's face and lamented piteously. "O king!
Your wives deserved happiness. What will they do now? You were
their husband. Though they had an excellent husband, their hopes
have been belied. Can't you see your aged father? He is dried up,
like a pond without water and is under Krishna's subjugation. O
son! I am your mother. Why are you not speaking to me? You have
abandoned your beloved relatives and have left for a long journey.
O brave one! Alas! I am unfortunate and have been deprived by
death. O one who were accomplished in policy! You enveloped me.
But unfortunate as I am, you have been taken away from me. O
leader of the herd! Your herd of servants has received gifts from you
and has been satisfied by your qualities. They are weeping. O tiger
among men! O long-armed one! O immensely strong one! Arise.
Save all the people who are miserable, in the city and in the inner
quarters." Extremely stricken by grief, Kamsa's women wept a lot.
The sun was tinged by the hue of dusk and prepared to set.'

Chapter 78

Vaishampayana said, 'Miserable, Ugrasena approached Krishna.
Because he was tormented on account of his son, his sighs were
like that of a person who has drunk poison. He saw Krishna in the
house, surrounded by Yadavas, overcome by the prospect of Kamsa
having been killed and lamenting. Having heard many extremely
piteous lamentations by Kamsa's women, he was censuring himself
in that assembly of Yadavas. "Alas! Because of childishness, I have
succumbed to the human trait of rage. Because of my act, thousands
of Kamsa's wives have become widows. Indeed, even an ordinary
person will take pity on women. Because I have brought down
their husband, they are weeping piteously. It is indeed the case
that lamentations increase sorrow. Knowing this, compassion for
women will be generated even in the lord of death. Earlier, it was
my view that the slaying of Kamsa was the best. He created enmity

towards the virtuous and was full of wickedness. In this world, an
easy death is preferable for men who have deviated in conduct and
are limited in intelligence. That is better than being alive and hated.
Kamsa was addicted to evil and was not respected by the virtuous.
As long as he was alive, that deviant was cursed by everyone. Why
should there be compassion towards him? Those who perform
pure deeds and observe austerities obtain the fruits of being able
to reside in heaven. In that fashion, they also obtain fame in this
world. If people are engaged in the good, if the subjects are devoted
to dharma and if men conduct themselves according to dharma,
there is no reason for the king to be a deviant. Death reduces the
qualities of those who are evil in conduct by one-fourth. In this
world, the best dharma is one that ensures the world hereafter. The
gods excessively protect a man who is devoted to dharma. In this
world, it is extremely easy to find the performers of evil deeds. From
here, Kamsa wouldn't have obtained an end meant for the virtuous.
However, I have countered his evil deeds by severing them at the
roots. Therefore, comfort all the women who are overcome by grief.
Comfort the citizens and all the other ranks in the city." Govinda
was speaking in this way.

'Anxious because of his son's wicked acts and lowering his
face, Ugrasena entered the house of the Yadus. In that assembly of
the Yadus, he spoke to Pundarikaksha Krishna. He was distressed
and spoke in a faltering voice that choked with tears. "In your
rage, you have killed my son. You have despatched your enemy
towards Yama's direction. These deeds are in accordance with
your own dharma and your name will be remembered on earth.
For the sake of your well-wishers, you have established the proud
Yadava lineage. To all the vassal kings, your power has become
evident. Your friends will worship you. Those who seek riches will
search you out as a refuge. Ordinary people will follow you and
brahmanas will praise you. Advisers, who are foremost in deciding
on war and peace, will bow down before you. O Krishna! Accept
Kamsa's inexhaustible army, consisting of elephants, horses,
chariots and large numbers of foot soldiers, riches, grain, all the
other gems and spreads, women, gold, garments and everything
else that is in the nature of wealth. O Krishna! When an encounter

is over, this has been recommended. O slayer of enemies! You have established the Yadus on earth. O brave one! Hear these words, being spoken by a miserable person. He has been consumed by your rage. Kamsa was the performer of inauspicious deeds. O Govinda! Through your favours, let his funeral rites be performed. Distressed as I am, after performing funeral rites for the king, I, with my daughters-in-law and my wives, will roam around with animals.[814] O Krishna! I only desire to perform the funeral rites for a relative. Once I have done this, all my worldly debts will have been extinguished. Without following any other rites, I will only light his funeral pyre and offer him water. After that, I will be free from all debts to Kamsa. O Krishna! Show affection towards me and command only this much. Once this deed has been performed, that miserable person will obtain a desirable end." Hearing these words, Krishna was extremely delighted. He replied to Ugrasena in these assuring words. "O tiger among kings! Your words befit your conduct and your lineage. O king! What you have spoken about is history and couldn't have been avoided. After death, Kamsa will obtain a good destination. O father! Act in accordance with the words I speak. I have nothing to do with the kingdom. There is no desire for the kingdom in me. I did not bring down Kamsa because I desired the kingdom. Your son was a deformity in his lineage and I brought him, and his brother, down for the welfare of the worlds and for the sake of fame. I will roam around in the forest with the gopas, amidst cattle. I will happily roam around as I wish, like an elephant. I am saying this truthfully, one hundred times. Let it be known that I am not interested in the kingship. Act accordingly. You are respected and are the foremost lord among the Yadus. You be the king. O supreme among kings! For the sake of victory, be consecrated in your own kingdom. If you wish to do something that brings me pleasure and if you are not distressed, accept from me your own kingdom, one that you have been deprived of for a long time." At this, he[815] was ashamed. He lowered his face. In that assembly of the Yadus, Govinda, the one who knew about yoga,

---

[814] That is, retire to the forest.
[815] Ugrasena.

instated him as the king. The prosperous King Ugrasena wore a
crown. With Krishna, he performed Kamsa's funeral rites. On
Krishna's instructions, the foremost among the Yadavas followed
the king along the path that led to the city, like the gods following
Shatakratu.

'When night was over, the sun arose. The bulls among the
Yadus performed the final funeral rites for Kamsa. They placed
Kamsa's body on a palanquin. In due order, they performed the
virtuous and ordained rites. The king's son[816] was taken to the
northern banks of the Yamuna. As is proper, the funeral rites were
performed by applying fire to the pyre. His brother was the mighty-
armed Sunama. With the Yadavas, Krishna performed his final
rites too. The Vrishni and Andhaka maharathas offered them water
and said, "After death, may they obtain the eternal." Distressed in
their minds, the Yadavas offered them water. With Ugrasena at the
forefront, they then entered the city of Mathura.'

Chapter 79

Vaishampayana said, 'With Rohini's powerful son, Krishna
happily resided in the city of Mathura, inhabited by the Yadavas.
As he attained youth, his body blazed in royal prosperity. Adorned
with jewels, the brave one dwelt in Mathura. After some time, Rama
and Keshava went to the preceptor from Kashi, Sandipani, who
now resided in the city of Avanti.[817] They went there to learn about
dhanurveda. Rama and Janardana informed him about their gotra.
They studied, served him with humility and followed good conduct.
The one from Kashi imparted pure knowledge to them. Those two
brave ones could remember everything that they had heard. In
sixty-four days and nights, they studied and learnt all the Vedas and
the Vedangas. In a short period of time, the preceptor instructed
them about the weapons used in battle and the four elements of

---

[816] Kamsa's dead body.
[817] Today's Ujjain.

dhanurveda.[818] On noticing their superhuman intelligence, the preceptor thought the moon and sun gods had arrived there. On auspicious occasions, he saw that the great-souled ones worshipped the three-eyed Mahadeva himself. O descendant of the Bharata lineage! When they had become successful,[819] Krishna, together with Rama, asked Sandipani, "What will we give our preceptor?"[820] Knowing of their powers, the preceptor happily replied, "I desire that you should give me my son. He is dead and submerged in the salty ocean. Only one son was born to me and he was killed by a whale, while we were visiting places of pilgrimage in Prabhasa. Bring him back to me." Taking Rama's permission, Krishna agreed. The energetic Hari went to the ocean and entered the water. There, he saw the ocean standing before him, hands joined in salutation. He asked him, "Where does Sandipani's son live now?" The ocean replied, "O Madhava! There is a great daitya named Panchajana. He adopted the form of a whale and has devoured the child." Purushottama approached Panchajana and killed him. But Achyuta could not find his preceptor's infant son. Having slain Panchajana, Janardana obtained the conch shell that is famous among gods and men as Panchajanya. Purushottama then defeated the god Vaivasvata.[821] From Yama's eternal abode, he brought back his preceptor's son, who had been dead for a long time. Sandipani's son had been dead for a long time. However, through the infinitely energetic one's favours, he was again reunited with his body. All the creatures were astounded at witnessing this great wonder, something that was unthinkable. Having obtained his preceptor's son, Panchajanya and many expensive jewels, Madhava, the lord of

---

[818] The four elements are interpreted in different ways—elephants, horses, chariots and foot soldiers is one possibility. A more common interpretation is the four techniques of applying a weapon—invoking, applying, releasing and withdrawing. This interpretation is usually used for divine weapons. Yet another possible interpretation is initiation, comprehension, accomplishment and application, a template for all use of weapons.

[819] In their studies.

[820] When a student has completed studying, a fee (dakshina) must be paid to the *guru* (preceptor).

[821] Yama.

the universe, returned. Those many kinds of expensive jewels had
belonged to the rakshasas. Vasava's younger brother brought them
back and offered them to his preceptor. In a short period of time,
those two became best in the worlds in the use of the mace and
the club, all kinds of weapons and in wielding the bow.[822] Krishna
gave all those jewels. He also gave Sandipani's son the form and
the age that he had possessed.[823] O king! Sandipani from Kashi was
delighted at being united with his son, who had been dead for a long
time. He worshipped Rama and Keshava.

'Having become accomplished in the use of weapons,
Vasudeva's two brave sons, excellent in their vows, took their leave
of their preceptor and returned to Mathura. With Ugrasena at the
forefront, all the Yadavas, along with the children, were delighted
that the two descendants of the Yadu lineage had returned. The
arrays of ordinary people, the advisers, the priests and the young
and the aged of the city welcomed them back. They played on
trumpets and musical instruments and praised Janardana. In every
direction, the roads dazzled with flags and garlands. Everyone in
the inner quarters of the palace was happy. With Govinda's arrival,
it was as if a sacrifice to Indra was being observed. Along the royal
roads, singers sang happy songs. In agreeable tones, the Yadavas
chanted praises and benedictions. Govinda and Rama, the two
brothers famous in the worlds, arrived. Everyone in the city was
without fear and amused themselves with their relatives. There was
no distress there. No one was miserable or senseless. O king! This
is what happened when Govinda turned up in Mathura. The birds
sang sweet songs. The cows, horses and elephants were happy. All
the large numbers of men and women were happy in their minds.
Auspicious winds started to blow. The ten directions were emptied
of dust. The gods were happy in all the temples. All the signs in
the world were like those in an earlier krita yuga. When Janardana
reached the city, this is what was witnessed. At an auspicious and
sacred time, Govinda, the destroyer of enemies, entered the city of
Mathura on a chariot that was yoked to tawny horses. Upendra, the

---

[822] There is abruptness in this shloka being here.
[823] When he had died.

scorcher of enemies, entered beautiful Mathura. He was followed
by large numbers of Yadus, like Shakra by large numbers of gods.
With happy faces, those two descendants of the Yadu lineage entered
Vasudeva's house, like the moon and the sun atop a mountain.
They left their weapons in the house. Then, Vasudeva's two sons,
supreme among the Yadus, roamed around as they willed and
amused themselves. The two with the handsome faces were formed
out of a single entity. For some time, they followed Ugrasena and
amused themselves in Mathura.'

Chapter 80

Vaishampayana said, 'After some time, the lord of Rajagriha, the
powerful King Jarasandha, heard about Kamsa's death.[824] He
arrived, surrounding himself with a large army with six sections.[825]
Having heard about Kamsa's death through spies, he was angry
and wished to slay the Yadus. The king of Magadha had two
daughters named Asti and Prapti. These two fortunate ones were
Jarasandha's daughters. They were large-breasted and thin at the
waist. King Barhadratha[826] had bestowed them on Kamsa, as wives.
Having imprisoned his father, Ahuka,[827] the king[828] sported himself
with them. Finding support in Jarasandha, he slighted the Yadavas.
You have heard a lot about King Shurasena.[829] To accomplish the
objectives of his relatives, Vasudeva was always on Ugrasena's side.
Therefore, Kamsa could not tolerate him. Once the evil-souled
Kamsa had been killed, with the support of Rama and Krishna and
surrounded by the Bhojas, the Vrishnis and the Andhakas, Ugrasena
became the king. For the sake of his beloved daughters, who were the

---

[824] Jarasandha was the king of Magadha and his capital was in
Rajagriha (Rajgir).

[825] Elephants, horses, chariots, foot soldiers, stores of grain and shops.

[826] Jarasandha, Jarasandha's father was Brihadratha.

[827] Ugrasena.

[828] Kamsa.

[829] Vasudeva's father.

wives of a hero, the powerful King Jarasandha arrived in Mathura. Overcome with rage at the Yadus, he made every kind of effort. He was joined by the kings who were under his power and by his friends, relatives and well-wishers. Surrounded by their soldiers, all of them followed him. They were great archers and immensely valorous. They wished to do what was agreeable to Jarasandha. Dantavaktra of Karusha, the powerful king of Chedi, the lord of Kalinga, the supremely strong Poundra, the deceitful Kaishika, King Bhishmaka, Bhishmaka's son Rukmi, foremost among wielders of the bow and one who always wished to rival Vasudeva[830] and Arjuna in strength, Venudari, Shrutarva, Kratha, Amshuman, the powerful king of Anga, the lord of Vanga, Koushalya, the king of Kashi, the lord of Dasharna, the brave Suhveshvara, the lord of Videha, the powerful king of Madra, the lord of Trigarta, the king of Salva,[831] the brave and immensely strong Darada, the lord of the Yavanas, the valiant Bhagadatta, the king of Souvira, Shaibya, Pandya, supreme among the strong, Subala, the king of Gandhara, the immensely strong Nagnajit, these and other powerful maharatha kings followed Jarasandha, driven by their hatred for Janardana. Equipped with a lot of grain and firewood, they entered the kingdom of Shurasena. With their armies, they laid siege to Mathura.'

Chapter 81

Vaishampayana said, 'The kings were entrenched in the forests around Mathura. With Janardana at the forefront, all the Vrishnis saw this. Cheerfully, Krishna spoke these words to Rama. "There is no doubt that the task of the gods will be accomplished swiftly. King Jarasandha has been attracted to this place. The tips of the penants can be seen on his chariots, stirring in the wind. O noble one! The men desire victory and their white umbrellas are stretched out before us, blazing like the moon. The kings and the chariots are

---

[830] Vaasudeva, Krishna.
[831] Alternatively, Shalva.

in front of us, with sparkling white arrays of umbrellas. They are advancing towards us, like an array of swans in the sky. There is no doubt that King Jarasandha will confront his destiny. In this battle with us, he is the first guest we will welcome in this encounter. O noble one! When the kings advance, let us remain together. When the battle commences, we can test how strong they are." Krishna, who was assured and eager to fight, spoke in this way. He glanced at all the kings and the supreme and undecaying ones on the side of the Yadus. In his heart, the one who knew about all kinds of advice spoke these words to himself. "Because of what has been decreed in the sacred texts, kings who remain in the paths of other kings will face destruction. I think that all these bulls among kings have already been slain by Death. Their bodies can already be seen to be headed towards heaven. These foremost among kings oppressed the earth with their floods of soldiers and exhausted by that burden here, she went to heaven. Because of these armies and kingdoms, there is no space on earth. Indeed, in a short while, the surface of the ground will be emptied. Hundreds and large numbers of kings will be brought down." Jarasandha, the lord of all the kings, was enraged. The immensely radiant one was followed by thousands of kings. There were tall and excellent horses, well controlled through reins. In some places, chariots that could freely advance were ready for battle. There were supreme elephants that were like clouds, with golden harnesses and giant bells. Mahamatras accomplished in fighting were astride them. Others astride horses looked around, ready to leap. The cavalry was like a cloud. The foot soldiers were ready to strike. Wielding fierce swords and shields, that infantry seemed to stretch up to the sky. Those thousands of foot soldiers were like descending serpents. In this way, the four divisions of the army were as vibrant as clouds. The powerful King Jarasandha advanced, firm in his resolution. There was the clatter of chariots. There was the trumpeting of crazy elephants. The horses neighed and the foot soldiers roared. All the directions, the city and the forests were filled with this noise. The king was seen, with an army that was like the ocean. That army of the lord of the earth had many proud warriors. The roar the army made was like the thundering of a cloud. The chariots advanced like the wind. The elephants

were like clouds. The horses were swift. The foot soldiers were like
birds.[832] That army was a mixture of all these, crazy elephants and
chariots. It looked like a cloud extending up to the ocean, at the end
of the summer. With Jarasandha at the forefront, that army of all
the kings surrounded the city and set up camp there. The tents in
that encampment were beautiful. It looked like the great ocean on a
full moon night in *shuklapaksha*.

'When night was over, the kings arose. They were eager to fight
and break into the city. All the kings assembled near the Yamuna
to hold consultations and decide on a time to commence battle. The
tumultuous sound made by the kings could be heard. It was as if
the oceans were being splintered at the end of a yuga. There were
aged attendants with cloaks[833] and headdresses, with staffs made
of cane in their hands. On the instructions of the king, they asked
everyone to be quiet. The army was then seen to quieten down.
It was as silent as the great ocean, when fish and crocodiles were
quiet. Though ready, that large ocean was silent. Like Brihaspati,
Jarasandha spoke these extensive words. "This army of kings will
swiftly advance. Groups of men will surround the city from every
side. Arrange catapults for hurling boulders and iron clubs. Hold
up bows, spikes and javelins. Quickly break down the city with
large numbers of spades and shovels. Kings who are well versed
in techniques of fighting will be stationed a short distance away.
From today, the soldiers will lay siege to the city. Let storms of
arrows be showered down from the sky. Following my command,
let the kings be stationed on the ground around the city. Without
any delay, let them quickly climb up into the city. Madra, the lord
of Kalinga, Chekitana, Bahlika, Gonarda, the king of Kashmira,
the lord of Karusha, Druma, kimpurushas from the mountains
and Damana will swiftly attack the city's western gate. Pourava
Venudari, the king of Vidarbha, Somaka, Rukmi, the lord of
Bhoja, Suryaksha from Malava, Vinda and Anuvinda from Avanti,
the valiant Dantavaktra, Chhagali, Purumitra, King Virata, the
king of Koshambi, the king of Malava, Shatadhanva, Viduratha,

[832] As in, flocks of birds.
[833] *Kanchuka*, alternatively, jacket or armour.

Bhurishrava, Trigarta and Bana from the land of the five rivers are kings who are as powerful as the lord of the vajra.[834] They will attack the city's northern gate and its fortifications. Uluka, Kaitaveya, the brave son of Amshuman, Ekalavya, Brihatkshatra, Kshatradharma, Jayadratha, Uttamouja, Shalya, Kourava, the king of Kekaya, the king of Vidisha, Vamadeva and Saketa, the lord of Sini, will take their battle formations to the city's eastern gate. They will swiftly attack, like clouds aided by the wind. I, Darada and the king of Chedi will armour ourselves and take care of the city's southern gate. In this way, the city will quickly be attacked from all directions. It will be struck by great fear, as if it has been struck by a bolt of lightning. Those who hold clubs will use clubs. Those who use maces as weapons will use maces. The others will use many kinds of weapons and break down the city. Today, this city is uneven.[835] The task before all you kings is to level it down to the ground." Jarasandha arranged the four divisions of his army in battle formations. With all the kings, he angrily attacked. The Dasharhas also armed themselves. Arranging themselves in battle formations, they counter-attacked. A terrible battle commenced and it was like an encounter between the gods and the asuras. With chariots and elephants, the few engaged with the many.[836]

'Vasudeva's two sons were seen to emerge from the city. At this, the army of the best of men was agitated.[837] The mounts were terrified and stupefied. Armed on their chariots, the Yadavas[838] roamed around. It was as if two wrathful makaras were agitating the ocean. On seeing all the signs that a battle was about to commence, those two intelligent Yadavas thought of their ancient weapons. In that encounter, those blazing weapons fell down from the sky. Those divine weapons were gigantic and extremely firm. They seemed to lick their lips. As those gigantic weapons manifested themselves, they were followed by predatory creatures. Thirsty, those terrible

---

[834] Indra.
[835] Because of its buildings and fortifications.
[836] The Yadavas were fewer in number.
[837] Jarasandha's army.
[838] Krishna and Balarama.

ones wished to devour the flesh of the kings in the battle. Those divine weapons were garlanded and could terrify those who travelled in the sky. Blazing in their radiance, they illuminated the ten directions. They were the plough named Samvartaka, the club Soubhadra,[839] the supreme bow Sharnga and the mace Koumadaki. These are Vishnu's four energetic weapons. In that great battle, they arrived for the Yadavas. With his right hand, Rama picked up the plough, which was like a flagpole. It was adorned with celestial garlands. In the battle, it creeped along like a serpent. With his left hand, the best among the Satvatas[840] picked up the beautiful and supreme club Sounanda. It was one that caused misery to enemies. The valiant Vishnu picked up the famous bow, named Sharnga. It deserved to be seen by all the worlds and thundered like a cloud. To accomplish what the gods has asked him to, the lotus-eyed one picked up the mace in his other hand. It was named Koumadaki. Thus armed, those two brave ones assumed forms like that of Vishnu. In the battle, Rama and Govinda prepared to counter-attack the enemy. Seizing the weapons, those two brave ones were like each other. Rama and Govinda bore the signs of being the elder and the younger brother.

'Like two gods, those brave ones counter-attacked the enemy. Rama was enraged, like an Indra of serpents. The brave one raised the plough and roamed around in the battle, like Death amidst the enemy. He dragged down large numbers of chariots that belonged to the great-souled kshatriyas. He exhibited the fruits of his rage among the elephants and the horses. Rama roamed around and crushed in that battle. He flung elephants away with his plough. He struck them with the club. He was like a mountain. In the encounter, the bulls among kshatriyas were struck by Rama. Afflicted in the battle, those brave ones approached Jarasandha. Jarasandha, established in the dharma of kshatriyas, told them, "How can you suffer in a field of battle? Shame on your conduct as kshatriyas. The learned say that those who are deprived of their chariots and run away from the field of battle commit a sin equal to the killers

[839] Alternatively, Sounanda.
[840] Balarama.

of foetuses. How can you be terrified and retreat? Shame on your conduct as kshatriyas. Goaded by my words, swiftly return to the field of battle. In this encounter, I will dispatch the gopas to Yama's eternal abode." Thus, all the kshatriyas were urged by Jarasandha. Cheerfully, they stationed themselves in the battle and released nets of arrows. The horses possessed golden harnesses. The chariots roared like clouds. Urged by the mahamatras, the elephants were like clouds. Their bodies were covered in armour and they sported swords. They raised weapons, flags and penants aloft. The bows were strung and the quivers were full of arrows. They wielded javelins. On their chariots, the kings were radiant as they advanced in the battle. All of them had umbrellas above their heads and they were fanned with beautiful whisks. The charioteers who advanced into the battle were the best among warriors. They held heavy clubs and maces that could be flung.

'Krishna advanced on a supreme chariot, with Suparna on a standard above his head. He pierced Jarasandha with eight arrows and pierced his charioteer with five sharp arrows. Making efforts, the brave one killed his[841] horses. On seeing that he was in difficulties, maharatha Chitrasena, the commander of the army of Kaishika, pierced Krishna with arrows. Kaishika[842] also pierced Baladeva with three arrows. Using broad-headed arrows, Baladeva shattered his bow into two fragments. He swiftly showered down arrows and oppressed him. Chitrasena was angry and pierced him with nine arrows. Kaishika pierced him with five arrows and Jarasandha with seven. Janardana pierced each of them with three arrows. Baladeva pierced each of them with five sharp arrows. The valiant Baladeva used broad-headed arrows to shatter Chitrasena's chariot and shattered his bow into two fragments. He[843] was deprived of his chariot and his bow was shattered. The brave one seized a club and angrily attacked the one with a club,[844] desiring to slay him. Wishing to kill Chitrasena, Rama was shooting sharp arrows at

[841] Jarasandha's.
[842] That is, Chitrasena.
[843] Chitrasena.
[844] Balarama.

him. However, the immensely strong Jarasandha severed his bow.
The lord of Magadha then angrily attacked him with a club. To
fight with the advancing Jarasandha, Rama seized a mace. They
wished to kill each other and a duel commenced between them.
Jarasandha was surrounded by a mighty army and the immensely
strong one fought against Rama and Krishna and the Bhojas. There
was a tumultuous battle between the soldiers on the two sides and
there was a great roar, like that of a turbulent ocean. O king! A great
uproar arose in both the armies, as flutes, kettledrums, drums and
conch shells were sounded in their thousands. The soldiers slapped
their arms and chests and there was pandemonium everywhere.
Because of the hooves and axles of chariots, dust rose up. They
seized great weapons and bows and arrows. The brave ones who
were present roared at each other. There were charioteers, horse
riders and thousands of foot soldiers. Extremely strong elephants
attacked fearlessly. There was a fierce fight between the Vrishni
warriors and those on Jarasandha's side. Ready to give up their
lives, they did not retreat. They struck each other in terrible ways.

'Armoured, Shini, Anadhrishti, Babhru, Viprithu and Ahuka
attacked half the army, placing Baladeva at the forefront. O
descendant of the Bharata lineage! This was directed towards the
southern flank of the enemy soldiers, the part that was protected
by the king of Chedi and Jarasandha. The immensely valourous
Shalya, Salva and other kings were to the north. Ready to give up
their lives, they released showers of arrows. Armoured, Agavaha,
Prithu, Kahva and Viduratha attacked the other half of the army,
placing Hrishikesha at the forefront. This was the part that was
protected by Bhishmaka and the great-souled Rukmi. The east
and the south were protected by brave soldiers. A tumultuous and
great battle raged and they were ready to give up their lives in this.
Javelins, swords, spikes and a large number of arrows were released.
Satyaki, Chitraka, Shyama, the valiant Yuyudhana,[845] Rajadhideva,
Mridura, the immensely strong Shvaphalka, Satraji and Prasena
surrounded themselves with a large army. In the encounter, they
counter-attacked the battle formations that were on the left flank.

---

[845] Since Yuyudhana is Satyaki's name, this is inconsistent.

Mridura protected half of the battle arrays and fought with many
kings, Venudari being the foremost.'

Chapter 82

Vaishampayana said, 'There was an extremely great battle
between the Vrishnis and the great advisers, kings and other
followers of the Magadha side. Rukmi fought with Vasudeva,[846]
Bhishmaka with Ahuka, Kratha with Vasudeva, Kaishika with
Babhru, Gada with the king of Chedi and Dantavaktra with
Shambhu. Other brave Vrishnis fought with great-souled kings. O
bull among the Bharata lineage! There was a battle and soldiers
fought with soldiers. O king! Elephants fought with elephants,
horses with horses, foot soldiers with foot soldiers, chariots with
chariots and warriors with warriors, without getting mixed up.[847]
King Jarasandha attacked Rama and there was an encounter that
made the body hair stand up, like that between the great Indra and
Vritra. O king! They caused a great carnage in each other's army. In
both the armies, mud was created from the flesh and blood. A large
number of headless torsos were seen to rise up. There was a great
carnage of soldiers and it is impossible to count this.

'From a chariot, Rama struck Jarasandha with arrows that
were like venomous serpents. Though he was enveloped, the king
of Magadha counter-attacked. Their weapons were exhausted.
They were without their chariots. Their horses were slain. Their
charioteers were killed. Those brave ones seized clubs and dashed
towards each other. As those two brave ones raised their giant
clubs the earth trembled. Those two great-souled ones looked like
mountains with summits. Other encounters ceased, so that one
could see the duel between these two bulls among men. They were
famous for fighting with clubs and angrily attacked each other. Both

[846] Krishna.
[847] That is, equals fought with equals. One on a horse did not fight
with one on a chariot.

of them had had excellent teachers and these two immensely strong
ones were famous in the world. In the encounter, they attacked each
other like crazy elephants. In every direction, thousands of gods,
gandharvas, siddhas, supreme rishis and apsaras assembled.[848] O
king! Ornamented, the firmament glittered even more with these
yakshas, gandharvas and maharshis, as if by a large number of
stellar bodies. The immensely strong Jarasandha attacked Rama.
He circled around from the left, while Baladeva circled around
from the right. They were accomplished in fighting with clubs and
struck each other. They were like tusked elephants and the sound
filled the ten directions. As Rama brought down his club, the sound
of thunder was heard. The sound of Jarasandha's tread was like
the shattering of mountains. Rama was supreme among those who
fought with the club and the blows from the club in Jarasandha's
hand could not make him tremble. He was as unmoved as Mount
Vindhya. The brave lord of Magadha was also able to withstand
the force of Rama's club. He possessed great fortitude and resorted
to his training. At this time, an excellent voice was heard from the
firmament, spoken by one who was a witness to everything in the
world. "O Madhava! Do not be distressed. He will not be killed
by you. His death has been ordained by me. Therefore, it is best to
restrain yourself. In a short while, the lord of Magadha will give
up his life." On hearing this, Jarasandha was distracted. Thus, the
wielder of the plough did not strike him again. The Vrishnis and the
kings also stopped fighting. O great king! Those great-souled ones
had fought for a long time, killing each other.

'Jarasandha and the kings were defeated and retreated. The
sun had set and no one followed them in the night. The immensely
strong ones[849] were successful in accomplishing their objective.
Worshipping Keshava and summoning their own soldiers, they
happily entered the city. Though they had defeated Jarasandha,
the Vrishnis thought that they hadn't quite vanquished him. O
tiger among Kurus! That king was extremely strong. The Yadavas
fought with Jarasandha on eighteen occasions. However, those

[848] As spectators.
[849] The Yadavas.

maharathas weren't able to slay him in those battles. O bull among the Bharata lineage! He possessed twenty akshouhinis and these assembled for the sake of King Jarasandha. O bull among the Bharata lineage! O Indra among the kings! That of the Vrishnis was limited and was overwhelmed when attacked by Barhadratha and the kings. However, having defeated King Jarasandha of Magadha in the battle, the maharathas, the lions among the Vrishnis, roamed around happily.'

Chapter 83

Vaishampayana said, 'At this time, remembering the good deeds that the gopas had done, Rama took Krishna's permission and went to Vraja alone. He saw the extensive and beautiful forests and the fragrant ponds that they had enjoyed earlier. Swiftly entering Vraja, the lord who was Krishna's elder brother attired himself in beautiful forest garb. Following the ordained rites, as they used to do earlier, he asked about the welfare of all the gopas, in due order and proceeding according to age. He happily spoke to all of them. He told the gopa women delightful and sweet accounts. Rama was supreme among those who granted pleasure and had returned after residing elsewhere. Affectionately, the aged gopas addressed him in pleasant words. "O mighty-armed one! O one who gives delight to the lineage of the Yadus! Welcome. O son! Now that you have returned, we are happy to see that you have come back. O brave one! We are delighted that you have returned. Rama, who creates fear among the enemy, is famous in the three worlds. O descendant of the Yadava lineage! There is no doubt that we have been nurtured by you. O son! All the creatures who reside in the land of your birth are happy. O one with the unblemished face! O son! We wished that you should return, so that we could see you and it is certain that your decision will also be honoured by the thirty gods. It is through good fortune that you brought down and killed Kamsa's wrestlers. It is your younger brother's greatness that Ugrasena has been instated. We have heard about your encounter

with the whale in the ocean[850] and how weapons descended for you
in a battle.[851] Even the gods talk about your entry into Mathura.
You have established the earth, which was terrified because of all
the kings. As was the case earlier, we are fortunate to witness your
arrival. We, and our relatives, are satisfied and delighted at this."
Rama replied to all those who were stationed there. "Among all
the Yadavas, you are indeed my relatives. Our childhood was spent
with you. It is with you that we found pleasure in the forest. It is
you who have reared us. How can we act in a contrary way? We
ate in your homes. We protected your cattle. All of you are our
relatives. You are our well-wishers and we are bound to you." In
the midst of the gopas, the one whose weapon was the plough spoke
the truth in this way. The faces of the gopa women were seen to be
delighted.

'The immensely strong Rama went to the inside of the forest, to
find pleasure there. Knowing what was appropriate to the time and
the place, the cowherds offered Rama, the one who knew about his
soul, the liquor known as Varuni. At that time, surrounded by his
kin, the fair-complexioned Rama went to the interior of the forest
and drank this intoxicating drink. They presented to him diverse
kinds of forest produce—beautiful flowers and fruit, many kinds
of food that were fragrant and pleasing to the heart and many
blooming lotuses and water lilies that were freshly plucked. Some
of the beautiful hair on his head was tied in a braid. A dazzling
earring hung from one ear. He was smeared with sandalwood paste
and *agaru*.[852] A garland of wild flowers hung down. Rama's form
was resplendent, like Mandara in Kailasa. His blue garment bore
the complexion of a cloud. With his dazzling and sparkling form,
he looked like the moon amidst a garland of dense clouds. He held
the plough, which was like a serpent, in one hand. The radiant
mace adhered to his other hand. The best among strong ones was
intoxicated. With beads of sweat, his head swayed, like the moon
on a winter's night. Intoxicated, he told Yamuna, "O great river! I

---

[850] Panchajana.
[851] With Jarasandha.
[852] Paste from the agallochum tree.

desire to have a bath. O one who heads towards the ocean! Reveal your sparkling form and come here." She thought his speech was affected by intoxication. In addition, she was confounded by her own womanly nature. Therefore, ignoring him, she did not come to the spot. Overcome with intoxication, the powerful Rama became enraged. The powerful one raised the plough in his hand, with the tip lowered for tilling. As he dragged her,[853] the garland fell down and the pollen from the flowers reddened the water. With the tip of the plough, Rama dragged the great river Yamuna to the bank, as if he was chastising a wayward woman. The flow of water and the pools full of water were disturbed and the terrified river followed the path indicated by the plough. Attracted to the path indicated by the plough and terrified by the fear of Samkarshana, the force meandered from its course and followed him, like a distressed woman. As the flow of water reached, the banks were like lips and the gentle waters were agitated. Wearing strands of foam that were like a girdle, the water reached the banks and seemed to smile. There were turbulent waves. The chakravaka birds were like upturned breasts. The deep force followed that curved path and terrified fish and aquatic birds went with the flow. Her limbs were decorated with flocks of swans and her linen garments were made out of kasha.[854] The water deviated in this way, with the trees along the bank like her flowing tresses. The one who heads towards the ocean was agitated at her limbs thus being dragged by the plough. She was like a drunk and wanton woman advancing along a royal road. The speedy flow of water was dragged with great force and meandered. She was forced to follow a course that was different from her former course and made to flow through the forest of Vrindavana. The river Yamuna was brought right into the middle of Vrindavana and the birds that dwelt along the banks seemed to cry. The river was thus brought into the forest of Vrindavana. Assuming the form of a woman, Yamuna told Rama, "O Rama! Be pacified. Because of the perverse deed I performed, I am terrified. My watery form has turned contrary. O Rohini's son! Because of

[853] Dragged Yamuna with the plough.
[854] Kind of grass.

what you have done, among rivers, I have turned false. O mighty-
armed one! Thus attracted by you, I have deviated from my normal
course. My co-wives,[855] proud of their force, will certainly reach the
ocean earlier. Since my water has followed a contrary course, their
foam will laugh at me. O brave one! O Krishna's elder brother! I am
beseeching you. Show me your favours. I have been dragged by your
weapon. Restrain your rage. O one with the plough as a weapon! I
am lowering my head at your feet. O mighty-armed one! Instruct me
about the course I should follow. Where will I go?" The one with
the plough as his weapon saw that Yamuna was speaking in this
way. Having got over his exhaustion, the powerful one spoke these
words to the ocean's wife. "O beautiful one! Your course is the one
that has been indicated by the plough. Provide water at all the spots
that have been thus indicated. O one with the beautiful brows! O
one who heads towards the ocean! These are my instructions. O
immensely fortunate one! Go in peace and cheerfully, wherever you
wish. As long as the worlds remain, my fame will be established."
On seeing that Yamuna had been attracted all the residents of Vraja
praised Rama and bowed down before him.

'He then took his leave of the immensely speedy one and all the
residents of Vraja. Rohini's son thought about this in his mind and
made a resolution. He quickly returned to Mathura again. Having
gone to Mathura, Rama went to Madhusudana's house and saw the
undecaying essence of the revolving earth[856] there. Dressed in forest
attire and with a garland of wild flowers on his chest, he went and
saw Janardana, who was lying down. Govinda saw that Rama, the
wielder of the plough, had quickly returned. He arose and gave him
the best of garments. When Rama was seated, Janardana asked him
about Vraja's welfare, about all the relatives and about the cattle.
Rama spoke to his brother, who had uttered those pleasant words.
"O Krishna! All is well. Everyone that you have asked about is
fine." In front of Vasudeva,[857] Rama and Keshava then recounted
all the wonderful things that had happened in the past.'

[855] The other rivers, all rivers are the wives of the ocean.
[856] Krishna.
[857] Krishna's father.

Chapter 84

Vaishampayana said, 'After some time, in the assembly of the Yadus, Pundarikaksha spoke excellent words that were full of import. "This land of the Yadavas, around Mathura, has made our kingdom prosper. We have been born here and have been reared in Vraja. Our miseries are over and the enemies have been defeated. On account of the conflict with Jarasandha, there was an enmity among the kings. We possess mounts and an infinite number of foot soldiers. We have wonderful jewels and many friends. But this region around Mathura is small and our enemies can penetrate easily. Our prosperity over our enemies is due to our forces and our friends. We have crores of young ones and large numbers of infantry. Because of this, our residence here is seen to be difficult. O bulls among the Yadavas! Therefore, the idea of living here doesn't appeal to me. Pardon me, but I will set up another city. There is an intention behind my words and I have spoken with reason. At the right time, for your sake, I always speak agreeable words in the assembly of the Yadus." Cheerful in their minds, all of them told him, "For the welfare of the people, accomplish whatever it is that you wish." The Vrishnis held excellent consultations and discussed this. "He[858] cannot be killed by us. The enemy's army is extremely large. Because of those kings, there has been a great destruction of soldiers. Even in one hundred years, we will not be able to slay all of their soldiers who remain. Therefore, we agree with the decision." At this, the king[859] and Kalayavana attacked Mathura with a large army. Jarasandha's army was huge and impossible to withstand. They also heard about Kalayavana's arrival.

'Keshava, who always speaks the truth, again told the Yadavas, "Today is an auspicious day to leave, along with all those who follow us." On Keshava's instructions, all the Yadavas emerged. Because of the large number of soldiers and elephants, this looked like the waves in an ocean. With Vasudeva at the forefront, all the

---

[858] Jarasandha.
[859] Jarasandha.

wives were assembled. There were armed crazy elephants, chariots
and horses. All the drums were sounded. With their riches, kin and
relatives, all the Yadavas abandoned Mathura and left. There were
chariots decorated with gold, and crazy and supreme elephants. There
were speedy horses, lashed with whips by the riders. O bull among
the Bharata lineage! Cheerfully, the Vrishnis headed in a western
direction, resplendent as they drove along their respective forces.
The best among the Yadavas were ornaments in the field of battle.
With Vasudeva[860] leading the way, they were at the forefront of the
army. They arrived at a spot that was colourful with creepers, with
forests of coconut trees. There were groves of beautiful *nagakeshara*
and ketaki flowers. There were *pumnagas*[861] and many palm trees.
There were some vines of grapes too. The bulls among the Yadus
reached a marshy region that belonged to the king of Sindhu.[862] They
loved pleasure and this was an enchanting spot. All the Yadavas
were delighted, like the gods when they reach heaven. Krishna, the
slayer of enemy heroes, thought about constructing a city. He saw
that extensive region, adorned by marshes along the ocean. It was
good for the mounts and the ground was wet and red. It possessed all
the signs required for setting up a prosperous city. Breezes blew from
the ocean. There was water from the ocean. This beautiful dominion
of the king of Sindhu bore all the auspicious signs required for a city.
Not very far away, there was a mountain by the name of Raivataka.
It dazzled in every direction and was like Mount Mandara. This was
where Ekalavya resided and also the place where Drona lived for a
long time. There were many men and all kinds of jewels. An excellent
spot was created for the king's pleasure. This extensive place was
named Dvaravati.[863] It was like a board for an *ashtapada* game.[864]

---

[860] Vaasudeva, Krishna.

[861] Another name for the nagakeshara.

[862] *Sindhu* should be interpreted as water here. The king of Sindhu thus
means the king of the water, that is, the ocean.

[863] Dvaraka. Dvaravati means a place with gates (*dvara*). The text
suggests that the place already existed, but the Yadavas built a new city
there.

[864] Ashtapada is a precursor to modern chess and was played on a 8x8
square. The city was in the shape of such a square.

Keshava made up his mind to construct a city there. The Yadavas found the prospect of the soldiers residing there agreeable. While it was still day and the night was red, the bulls among the Yadavas and the commanders of the army made arrangements for camps to be set up. Keshava and the Yadavas were firm in their decision to live there. The lord, the foremost among the Yadus, resolved to build a city at the spot. Gada's elder brother,[865] best among men and supreme among the Yadavas, made up his mind to follow the instructions for construction and set up buildings that were named. O king! Having obtained the city of Dvaravati, with his relatives, he was delighted, like the large number of gods on reaching heaven, and decided to reside there. Knowing about Kalayavana and the fear that was caused by Jarasandha, Krishna, the slayer of Keshi, went to the city of Dvaravati.'

Chapter 85

Janamejaya said, 'O illustrious one! I wish to hear in detail about the conduct of the great-souled and intelligent Vasudeva, best among the Yadus. Why did Madusudana abandon Mathura? It was an important place in the middle of the country and the residence of Lakshmi. It was seen to be like a summit of the earth, with a lot of riches and grain. It was the best of places for noble people to reside in. O supreme among brahmanas! Why did Dasharha abandon it without fighting? How did Kalayavana react to Krishna? Having reached Dvaraka, fortified with water, what did the mighty-armed, great-minded and great yogi, Janardana, do? What bravery did Kalayavana possess? Whom was the valiant one born to? Why did Janardana consider him to be irresistible?'

Vaishampayana replied, 'The great ascetic, Gargya, was the preceptor of the Vrishnis and the Andhakas. He had earlier been a brahmachari and did not take a wife. Therefore, that undecaying one held up his seed. O lord of the earth! His brother-in-law accused

[865] Gada was Krishna's younger brother.

Gargya of not being a man. O king! The one who had conquered
everything was thus accused in that city. Desiring a son, he departed
and performed extremely difficult austerities. For twelve years, he
only survived on powdered iron. He thought of Mahadeva and
worshipped the wielder of the trident. Rudra granted him the boon
that he would obtain a son who would possess every kind of energy
and would be able to vanquish the Vrishnis and the Andhakas in
battle. The supreme lord of the Yavanas heard about this boon of
the birth of a son. Through ill fortune, he didn't have a son, but
desired a son. The king had the best among brahmanas[866] brought
to him and reassured him. The king of the Yavanas kept him
among the gopas and amidst gopa women. There was an apsara
named Gopali there, disguised in the attire of a gopa woman. The
undecaying Gargya's seed was difficult to sustain, but she bore it
in her womb. Through the desire of the wielder of the trident, a
brave and extremely strong son was born to Gargya, through a wife
who was in human form. His name was Kalayavana. This child was
reared in the inner quarters of the king who didn't have a son. When
that king died, Kalayavana became the king. Desiring to fight, this
king asked Narada, supreme among brahmanas, and was informed
about the lineage of the Vrishnis and the Andhakas. Through
Narada, Madhusudana got to know about the boon that had been
granted. Therefore, he ignored the Yavana's increasing energy. The
mlechchha[867] kings sought refuge with him and started to follow
him. There were Shakas, Tusharas, Daradas, Paradas, Tanganas,
Khashas, Pahlavas and other hundreds of mlecchas who were from
the Himalayas. The king was surrounded by these bandits, as if by
locusts. Attired in diverse garments and wielding fierce weapons,
they attacked Mathura. There were thousands and tens of thousands
of elephants, horses, mules and camels. Because of this large army,
the earth trembled. That king enveloped the sun's path with dust.
Because of the urine and excrement released by the soldiers, a river
was created. O lord of men! Since this river was created through

---

[866] Gargya.

[867] A mlechchha is a barbarian, meaning that mlechchhas do not speak
Sanskrit and are not aryas.

the urine and excrement released by horses and camels, it came to
have the name of Ashvashakrit.[868] On hearing that a large army
was advancing, Vasudeva, foremost among the Vrishnis and the
Andhakas, summoned his relatives and said, "A terrible and great
fear has arisen before the Vrishnis and the Andhakas. Because of the
boon that has been granted by the wielder of the trident, this enemy
cannot be killed by us. We have used all the recommended means of
conciliation with him. However, he is intoxicated by the insolence
of his strength and desires to fight. Narada has told me that our
residence here is over. King Jarasandha is always intolerant towards
us. There are other kings who cannot bear the power of the Vrishnis.
Some kings are dissatisfied with us on account of Kamsa's death.
Having sought refuge with Jarasandha, they desire to restrain us
too. Those kings have killed many relatives of the Yadus." Keshava
decided that they could no longer prosper in that city.

'Having decided to leave, he sent a messenger.[869] He placed a
large serpent in a pot and it had the hue of lampblack. It was dark and
fierce, with venomous poison. Krishna sent this. Govinda covered
up the pot and sent this through a messenger, intending it as a sign
that would frighten the king. The messenger showed Kalayavana
the pot. O bull among the Bharata lineage! He said, "Krishna is like
this black serpent." Understanding that the Yadavas were trying
to scare him, Kalayavana filled up the pot with fierce ants. That
serpent was bitten all over by these fierce ants. With all its limbs
bitten, it was reduced to nothing. Covering up the pot, the lord of
the Yavanas sent it back to Krishna, as a sign of his superiority.
Vasudeva saw the signs and understood. He decided to swiftly leave
Mathura and go to Dvaraka. O king! Thinking of a means to bring
an end to the enmity, the immensely illustrious Vasudeva made the
Vrishnis reside in Dvaraka. Madhusudana, the great yogi and tiger
among men, then went to Mathura on foot, taking only his arms as
weapons. On seeing him, Kalayavana was delighted. The immensely
strong one emerged and began to angrily follow Krishna, who was
in front. Wherever Govinda went, the lord of the Yavanas followed,

[868] Literally, the excrement of horses.
[869] To Kalayavana.

desiring to kill him. However, the king wasn't able to seize the one
whose dharma was yoga. The immensely illustrious Muchukunda
was Mandhata's son. In ancient times, the immensely strong one
was successful in the battle between the gods and the asuras. Since
he had been completely exhausted, he accepted a boon from the
gods that he would be able to sleep and said, "O gods! If anyone
wakes me up while I am asleep, let me be able to burn him down
through the flames of rage in my eyes." He repeatedly said this.
Shakra and the thirty gods agreed. With the permission of the gods,
he went to a place that was inaccessible to men. Exhausted and
tired, he entered a mountainous cave. He slept for a long time, until
he was seen by Krishna. All of this had been narrated to Vasudeva
by Narada, including the energetic boon that the gods had granted
the king. Followed by the mlechchha enemy, Krishna humbly
entered Muchukunda's cave. Keshava, supreme among intelligent
ones, stood near the royal sage's head, avoiding his path of vision.
The evil-minded Yavana entered and saw the sleeping king, who
was like Death. Like an insect that is destroyed by a flame, taking
him to be Vasudeva,[870] he kicked the king with his feet. Rajarshi
Muchukunda awoke at the touch of the feet. He was enraged at his
sleep having been disturbed by the kick with the feet. Remembering
the boon granted by Shakra, he looked at whoever was in front
of him. Through the rage in the sight, everything was instantly
consumed. In an instant, the fire generated from the energy in the
eyes burnt up Kalayavana, like a fire consumes a dry tree. Having
been successful, the intelligent and handsome Vasudeva spoke these
excellent words to the king who had been sleeping for a long time.
"O king! Narada told me that you have been sleeping for a long
time. You have performed an extremely great task for me. May you
be fortunate. I am leaving." The king saw the sign that Vasudeva
was short.[871] He realized that a long period of time had elapsed.

'The king asked Govinda, "Who are you and why have you come
here? How long have I been asleep? If you know, tell me." Vasudeva
replied, "In the solar dynasty, there was a king named Yayati and he

[870] It was dark inside the cave.
[871] Down the yugas, height decreases.

was the son of Nahusha. His eldest son was Yadu. He had four other brothers who were younger.[872] O lord! I am Vasudeva's son and have been born in Yadu's lineage. O king! I am known as Vasudeva and I am the one who has come here. I got to know from Narada that you were born in treta yuga. Know that it is kali yuga now.[873] What else can I do for you? O king! My enemy was granted a boon by the gods. Consequently, he could not be slain by me in battle, even if I tried for one hundred years. He has been burnt down by you." Having said this, Krishna emerged through the mouth of the cave and he was followed by the king. The intelligent Krishna was satisfied at his success. The king saw that the earth was full of short men. They were limited in enterprise, limited in strength and limited in bravery and valour. He saw that someone else was ruling in his kingdom. Taking his leave of Govinda, he entered a great forest. Having made up his mind to perform austerities, the king went to the Himalayas. Resorting to austerities, he freed himself from his body. Because of the auspicious deeds that he himself had done, the king ascended to heaven. The great-minded Vasudeva, with dharma in his soul, had thought of a means to destroy his enemy and returned to the soldiers.[874] Now that the lord of the soldiers had been killed, the intelligent one seized large numbers of chariots, elephants, horses, armour, weapons, armaments and standards. With a contented mind, Janardana went to the city of Dvaravati, filled it with these copious riches and told King Ugrasena everything.'

Chapter 86

Vaishampayana said, 'The sun arose and the morning sparkled. Hrishikesha seated himself near the boundary of the forest

[872] Yavana (Devayani's son, along with Yadu) and Druhyu, Anu and Puru (Sharmishtha's sons).
[873] Not quite, it was still the end of dvapara yuga, though kali yuga was imminent.
[874] Kalayavana's soldiers.

and performed the morning meditation. He roamed around in that region, searching for a place for the fort. The foremost among the Yadava lineage were also present with the descendant of the Yadu lineage. It was the best day, with the nakshatra Rohini in the ascendant. Supreme brahmanas pronounced benedictions. With a great deal of auspicious words, work commenced for building the fort. The lotus-eyed slayer of Keshi, supreme among eloquent ones, spoke these best of words to the Yadavas, like Vritra's enemy speaking to the gods. "Look at the spot that I have chosen. It is like a residence of the gods. I have also thought of a name that will make the city famous. This city constructed by me on earth will be known by the name of Dvaravati. This will be a beautiful city, like Shakra's Amaravati. I will have buildings constructed here, with signs and measurements.[875] There will be four royal roads and level grounds for the inner quarters. Devoid of anxiety and like the gods, all of you will enjoy yourselves. With Ugrasena at the forefront, you will be able to restrain the large numbers of enemies. Take the equipment used for construction and mark out three crossroads. Mark out the measurements for the royal roads and the walls. Let the best of artisans be summoned and employed in the construction of the houses. Let men be sent to different countries to fetch artisans." They were eager to begin the construction of the houses and Krishna instructed them in this way. Cheerfully, they started on their tasks. The best among Yadavas had measuring tapes in their hands. O great king! On this auspicious day, they worshipped the brahmanas. For the gods, Vasudeva had the ordained rites performed. The immensely intelligent Govinda spoke these words to the architects. "This is the spot where you must construct an excellent temple for us, where our gods can be worshipped. Mark out the crossroads and the roads." The architects agreed to what the mighty-armed one had said. They followed the prescribed instructions and brought the material required for building the fort. The gates and the buildings were measured out properly. In due order, places were laid out for Brahma and the other gods. Four altars were laid out for four divinities—water, fire, the lord of the

---

[875] To distinguish one kind of building from another.

gods[876] and millstone and mortar. There were four gates for the four gods—Grihakshetra, Aindra, Bhallata and Pushpadanta.[877] The great-souled Yadavas engaged themselves in constructing the houses.

'Madhava thought about how the city could be swiftly constructed. His intelligence was divine and he thought of a means for firm and swift construction. "This city will be agreeable and will enhance the prosperity of the Yadavas. The lord Vishvakarma is Prajapati's son and is foremost among the artisans of the gods. He will use his intelligence to construct this city." Krishna stood there alone, facing the gods. He thought of him[878] in his mind, so that he might arrive. At that instant, the immensely intelligent Vishvakarma, preceptor of artisans and best among the gods, stood in front of Krishna. Vishvakarma said, "O Vishnu! O one who is firm in his vows! I have been summoned here by your divine mind. I have come here as a servant. Instruct me about what I should do. O god! You are the lord of the gods. You are as undecaying as Tryambaka.[879] O god! O lord! I revere you and there is no difference between him and you. O one who knows about the three worlds! O mighty-armed one! All knowledge comes from your words. I can see the truth about this. Instruct me about what must be done." Keshava heard Vishvakarma's humble words. The best among the Yadus, Kamsa's enemy, spoke these unmatched words in reply. "You know about the meanings of the sacred texts, mysterious even to the gods. O best among the gods! We are going to reside here and it is certainly your task to build a residence for us. O one who is excellent in vows! You must construct a residence on earth. In every way, the houses must reflect my powers. It must be the best on earth, just as Amaravati is in heaven. O immensely intelligent one! You alone are capable of performing this task. It is your task to build me a place

---

[876] Indra.

[877] This is a reference to principles of *vastu* shastra. The gate to the north and the divinity there is known as Bhallata; to the east is Jayanta (Indra's son, hence Aindra); to the west is Varuna (or Pushpadanta); and to the south is Grihakshetra.

[878] Vishvakarma.

[879] Shiva.

that is like heaven. Let mortal people see my prosperity in this city of the Yadu lineage." Vishvakarma heard these words, spoken by the lord of intelligence, Krishna, whose deeds were unsullied and who was the destroyer of the enemies of the gods. He said, "O lord! I will do everything that you have asked me to. But this city will not be sufficient to house all your people. This beautiful city will extend in the future and become prosperous. However, the four oceans will also freely roam around here. O Purushottama! If the ocean, the lord of the waters, withdraws and leaves some space, this city will bear all the signs of being extensive." Krishna, the intelligent one, was addressed in this way and he had already thought about this. The supreme among eloquent ones spoke these words to the ocean, the lord of the rivers. "O ocean! O store of the waters! If you have any respect for me, withdraw on your own and leave a space of twelve yojanas. If you grant me this space, the city and the area will be sufficient to support and sustain all my soldiers." Hearing Krishna's words, the great ocean, the lord of the male and female rivers united with the wind and withdrew. Vishvakarma was delighted that a space sufficient for the city had been created. The ocean thus showed its respect towards Govinda. Vishvakarma spoke these words to Krishna, the descendant of the Yadu lineage. "O Govinda! Let everyone occupy the residences today. O lord! Without any delay, I have used the powers of my mind to construct this city. It is garlanded with houses and walls. It is a beautiful city, with excellent gates and the best of walls. There are multi-storeyed buildings that are like armlets, standing out like humps on the earth." There were extensive inner quarters that could cater to Krishna's needs. That city was constructed at a spot that was worshipped by the gods. This is how the beautiful city of Dvaravati was constructed at that time. Vishvakarma used his Vaishnavi mental powers.

'There were beautiful men and women there. Merchants were like adornments, with many kinds of wares. It was as if something travelling around in the sky[880] had come down to earth. There was clean water in the ponds. There were handsome gardens. It

[880] Meaning a celestial city.

was beautiful in all its limbs, like a woman with large eyes. There were prosperous squares and the best of houses looked like clouds. The beautiful palaces rose indistinctly up into the sky. The place resounded with the noise of large numbers of people who came from all the extensive kingdoms on earth. Cool breezes wafted in from the waves of the lord of the waters. There were beautiful groves and agreeable and pleasant people. Dvaraka was as radiant as the sky with its stars. The walls had the complexion of the sun and were decorated with molten gold. The grand houses were full of gold and their chambers echoed. The gates were like white clouds. Along the extensive roads, there were beautiful and excellent palaces in some places. Krishna, and all the descendants of the Yadava lineage, resided in that city. With people desiring to live there, it sparkled like the moon in the sky. Vishvakarma created the city and made it like Shakra's city. Having done this and worshipped by Govinda, that god left for heaven.

'Krishna, who knew his soul, again had a thought about how he could satisfy the large numbers of people with wealth. In the night, in his own house, the lord Upendra summoned Shankha, Vaishravana's possession and the supreme jewel among all treasures.[881] Knowing of Keshava's summons, Shankha, the king of the guhyakas,[882] himself approached the lord of Dvaravati. Shankha humbly joined his hands in salutation. He addressed Krishna, as if he was addressing Vaishravana himself. "O illustrious one! My task is to protect the riches of the gods. O mighty-armed one! O descendant of the Yadu lineage! Instruct me about what must be done." Hrishikesha instructed Shankha, supreme among the guhyakas. "The people here are suffering on account of limited riches. Fill them up with wealth. I do not wish to see people who are hungry, weak and distressed, or poor people in the city who keep saying, 'Give.'" The *nidhi* bowed his head down before Keshava and followed his instructions. He commanded all the other nidhis that all the houses in Dvaravati should be

---

[881] Vaishravana means Kubera. Kubera has nine treasures (nidhi) and Shankha (literally, conch shell) is one of these.
[882] The king of the guhyakas is technically Kubera, not Shankha.

showered with riches. All of them followed this command. There was no poor man there, nor one who suffered from misfortune. In every house in Dvaravati, there was no one who was emaciated or miserable.

'Purushottama again summoned Vayu. To do what was agreeable to the Yadavas, the illustrious one arrived there. The source of the breath of life in creatures presented himself before Gada's elder brother, when that lord and god, who holds up all the secrets, was seated alone. "O god! O one who swiftly goes everywhere! What is my task? O unblemished one! I am yours, just as I am a messenger of the gods." Purushottama Krishna told Maruta, the life breath of the universe who had presented himself before him, the secret. "O Maruta! Go to the lord of the gods and the immortals and persuade them. Bring the assembly hall Sudharma[883] from the gods. The Yadavas are valiant and devoted to dharma. There are thousands of them. They should be in that assembly and not in an artificial one. O Vayu! O one who can go wherever you want! O one who can assume any form you want! That eternal assembly hall is capable of holding up the Yadus, just as it holds up the gods." He accepted the words spoken by Krishna of the unsullied deeds. Adopting a speed that was appropriate to his own nature, Vayu went to heaven. He reported Krishna's words and entreated all the gods. Having obtained the assembly hall Sudharma, he again returned to earth. He gave Sudharma to Krishna of the unsullied deeds, the one who was excellent in the pursuit of dharma.[884] Having handed over the assembly hall of the gods to the divinity, Vayu vanished. For the foremost among the Yadavas, Keshava placed Sudharma in the centre of Dvaravati, just as it was used for the gods in heaven. Thus, the undecaying Hari adorned his own city with objects and ornaments from heaven, from earth and from the water, as if a woman was being beautified. He established rules for merchants and ordinary people to follow. He appointed supervisors to look after the soldiers and

[883] The name of the assembly hall of the gods.
[884] The translation cannot capture the pun. *Sudharma* means excellent in the pursuit of dharma and Krishna is referred to as Sudharma.

after the environment. Ugrasena was the king and Kashya[885] was the priest. Anadhrishti was the commander in chief and Vikradu was chief among the ministers. Ten aged Yadavas, ornaments of their families, were appointed by the intelligent one to ascertain that there were no gaps in any of the performed tasks. Daruka, the excellent charioteer, became Keshava's charioteer. Satyaki, for whom truth was his valour, became the foremost warrior among all the warriors. The unblemished Krishna thus established rules for the city to follow. With the Yadus, the creator of the worlds, found pleasure on earth. Revata's daughter, Revati, possessed good conduct. With Krishna's permission, Baladeva married her.'

Chapter 87

Vaishampayana said, 'At this time, the powerful Jarasandha wished to do what would be agreeable to the king of Chedi and urged all the kings that Rukmini, the daughter of Bhishmaka, should be bedecked in golden ornaments and be married to King Shishupala. O descendant of the Bharata lineage! Suvaktra, the infinitely energetic son of Dantavaktra, who was an equal of the thousand-eyed one in battle and accomplished in the use of maya; the immensely strong son of Vasudeva from Poundra;[886] the brave Sudeva, who alone was the lord of an entire akshouhini; the brave and powerful son of Ekalavya; the son of the king of Pandya; the lord of Kalinga; King Venudari, against whom Krishna had done disagreeable things; Amshumanta; Kratha; Shrutarvana; Kalinga, who destroyed his enemies; the lord of Gandhara; the mighty-armed Patusha; and the lord of Kashi.'[887]

---

[885] The one from Kashi, presumably Sandipani.

[886] This Vasudeva is not to be confused with Krishna.

[887] Because of the way shlokas have been excised out in the Critical Edition, this sentence is left dangling. These kings came for Rukmini's *svayamvara*. Rukmini was the daughter of King Bhishmaka and her brother was Rukmi.

Janamejaya asked, 'O supreme among brahmanas! In which country was King Rukmi, supreme among those who knew about the Vedas, born? Where did that radiant one take birth?'

Vaishampayana replied, 'There was a rajarshi named Yadava and a son named Vidarbha was born to him. He lived in Vidarbha, on the southern flank of the Vindhya mountains. He had immensely strong sons and Kratha and Kaishika were foremost among them. They were full of valour and were kings who established separate lineages. O king! The Vrishnis were born in the lineage of Bhima.[888] Amshuman was born in Kratha's lineage and Bhishmaka in Kaishika's. People refer to him[889] as Hiranyaloma and the lord of the southern regions. Protected by Agastya, this king resided in Kundina.[890] O lord of the earth! He had a son named Rukmi and a daughter named Rukmini. The immensely strong Rukmi obtained divine weapons from Druma. He also obtained the *brahmastra*[891] from Rama, Jamadagni's son. He always sought to rival Krishna, the performer of extraordinary deeds. O king! There was no one on earth who could rival Rukmini in beauty. On hearing about her, the immensely radiant Vasudeva desired her. In a similar way, on hearing about him, she desired Janardana. Because of his energy, valour and strength, she thought that he should be her husband. Krishna asked for her. However, because of his hatred and because of Kamsa's death, the immensely strong Rukmi did not bestow her on Krishna. King Jarasandha asked King Bhishmaka, who was terrible in his valour, that she should be given to the son of the king of Chedi, Sunitha.[892] Vasu, the king of Chedi,[893] had a son named Brihadratha. In earlier times, he was the one who built the city of Girivraja[894] in Magadha. The immensely strong Jarasandha was born as his son. The king of Chedi, Damaghosha, was also born in

---

[888] One of Vidarbha's sons.

[889] Bhishmaka.

[890] This has been identified as the region of Kaundinyapura in Amaravati division of Vidarbha (Maharashtra).

[891] Divine weapon named after Brahma.

[892] That is, Shishupala. Sunitha was one of Shishupala's names.

[893] This is Uparichara Vasu.

[894] Rajagriha or Rajgir.

Vasu's lineage. Through his wife Shrutashrava, Vasudeva's[895] sister, Damaghosha had five sons who were terrible in their valour— Shishupala, Dashagriva, Raibhya, Upadisha and Bali. All of them were powerful, brave and immensely strong, accomplished in the use of all weapons. Knowing that Jarasandha belonged to a similar lineage, Sunitha gave him his own son and he[896] protected him and brought him up as his own son. Placing Jarasandha at the forefront, the immensely strong enemy of the Vrishnis, Chedi,[897] sought to do many things that were disagreeable to the Vrishnis. When his son-in-law, Kamsa, was killed in the encounter, thanks to Krishna, Jarasandha bore enmity towards the Vrishnis. For the sake of Sunitha, he asked Bhishmaka for Rukmini. Bhishmaka bestowed Rukmini on the valiant Shishupala.[898] With the king of Chedi and Dantavaktra, King Jarasandha left for Vidarbha. The intelligent Vasudeva from Poundra followed him and so did the immensely strong kings of Anga, Vanga and Kalinga. Rukmi received and welcomed all the kings who had arrived. After having been supremely honoured, they were taken towards the city. To cause pleasure to their father's sister, Rama and Krishna, together with the other Vrishnis, also arrived, with chariots and forces. Following the prescribed rites, the lords of Kratha and Kaishika worshipped and honoured them, but made them reside outside.[899]

'The marriage was to take place the next day. When Jyeshtha nakshatra[900] was in the ascendance, the beautiful Rukmini went out to worship at a temple outside, on a chariot yoked to four horses. Her form blazed, decorated with the auspicious marks. She was surrounded by a large army and wished to worship Indrani. On seeing her there, Krishna thought that Lakshmi had manifested herself. She was near the temple, in that supremely

[895] Krishna's father.
[896] Jarasandha.
[897] Shishupala.
[898] That is, Bhishmaka gave word that he would bestow her on Shishupala.
[899] Outside the city.
[900] The text says Aindre. Since Jyeshtha nakshatra is associated with Indra, this means Jyeshtha.

beautiful form. She blazed like the flame of a fire and was like
an illusion that had come down to earth. It was as if the grave
earth goddess had herself arisen from the ground. It was as if the
pleasant beams of the moon had adopted the personified form
of a woman on earth. She was like Shri on a lotus, or like one of
Shri's future aides. Even the gods found it impossible to look at
her and Krishna saw her in his mind. She was almost dark.[901] She
wasn't plump and her eyes were large. Her lips were coppery red
and her eyes were beautiful. Her thighs were thick and her hips
and breasts were heavy. She was a grown-up but young maiden,
beautiful in all her limbs. Her face was like the moon. The tips of
her nails were coppery red. She possessed excellent eyebrows. Her
blue-black hair was curled. Her teeth were even, white and sharp.
Her radiance illuminated her. In beauty, fame and prosperity, this
was a woman who was unmatched on earth. Attired in a white
linen garment, Rukmini seemed to have the form of a goddess.
On seeing the one who was beautiful to behold, Krishna's desire
increased, like the flames of a fire increase when oblations are
poured into it. Having consulted with Rama and the Vrishnis, the
extremely strong Keshava made up his mind to abduct her. When
she had completed the worship of the gods and was emerging
from the temple of the gods, Krishna suddenly picked her up and
placed her on his supreme chariot.

'Balarama uprooted a tree, so that he might repel enemies who
would advance. He also instructed the Dasharhas to be ready in
every possible way. Many kinds of chariots, raising giant standards,
horses and elephants surrounded the one who used the plough
as a weapon. Having abducted Rukmini, Krishna swiftly headed
towards his own city. The valiant one left the burden for Rama
and Yuyudhana to bear. There were also Akrura, Viprithu, Gada,
Kritavarma, Chakradeva, Sunakshatra, the immensely strong
Sarana, Nivrittashatru, Vikranta, Bhangakara, Viduratha, Ugrasena,

[901] The text uses the word *shyama*. The natural meaning of this is dark.
However, shyama also means a woman who hasn't been married (or is a
virgin). Interpretations take this to mean sixteen years of age, but that isn't
warranted.

Kanka, Shatadyumna, Rajadhideva, Mridura,[902] Prasena, Chitraka, Atidanta, Brihaddurga, Shvaphalka, Chitraka[903] and Prithu. Keshava Madhusudana left the task to other foremost Vrishnis and Andhakas. Having imposed this heavy burden on them, he left for Dvaravati. Dantavaktra, Jarasandha and the valiant Shishupala became enraged. They armoured themselves and advanced, wishing to kill Janardana. The lords of Anga, Vanga and Kalinga, along with the valiant Poundra, also advanced. So did the king of Chedi[904] and his brothers, who were excellent maharathas. Wrathfully, the brave Vrishni maharathas countered them, placing Samkarshana at the forefront, just as the Maruts do with Vasava. In that great battle, the immensely strong Jarasandha descended. However, Yuyudhana pierced him with six iron arrows. Akrura pierced Dantavaktra with nine arrows and Karusha struck him back with ten swift arrows. Viprithu pierced Shishupala with seven arrows. However, the powerful Shishupala struck him back with eight arrows. Gaveshana pierced the king of Chedi with six arrows. Anirdanta shot eight arrows and Brihaddurga five. The king of Chedi pierced each of them with five arrows and using four arrows, slew four of Viprithu's horses. Using a broad-headed arrow, he severed the head of his enemy, Brihaddurga. He despatched Gaveshana's charioteer to Yama's abode. With his horses slain, the immensely strong Viprithu abandoned his own chariot and swiftly clambered on to the chariot of the valiant Brihaddurga. Since the horses were running wild, Viprithu's charioteer quickly climbed onto Gaveshana's chariot and controlled them. With a bow and arrows in his hand, Sunitha was prancing around along the path of the chariots. They angrily surrounded him and showered him with arrows. With a barbed arrow, Chakradeva shattered Dantavaktra's chest. In the encounter, he next pierced Patusha with twenty-five arrows. When he had been

[902] The text says Mridara. But this must be a typo and we have corrected it.

[903] The text mentions Chitraka twice. Since non-Critical versions say Satyaka, this must also be a typo and should read Satyaka.

[904] Since Shishupala has already been mentioned, it is not clear who this is.

pierced with ten sharp arrows that struck at his inner organs, Bali
shattered Chakradeva with ten arrows. Standing some distance
away, he pierced Viduratha with five arrows and Viduratha pierced
him back with six sharp arrows. He[905] pierced the immensely strong
Bali back with thirty arrows. Kritavarma shattered the prince with
three arrows.[906] He slew his charioteer and shattered the upraised
standard. Enraged, Poundra pierced him back with six arrows that
had stone arrowheads. With broad-headed arrows with drooping
tufts, he severed his bow. Nivrittashatru struck Kalinga wih sharp
arrows and the king of Kalinga struck him on the neck with a
javelin. Using an elephant, Kanka fought against the valiant Anga's
elephant. He struck Anga with a javelin and Anga pierced him
with arrows. Chitraka, Shvaphalka and maharatha Satyaka drove
Kalinga's army away with iron arrows. Rama became angry in his
duel with the king of Vanga. He uprooted a tree and used it to
kill the elephant of the king of Vanga. After killing it, the valiant
Samkarshana ascended a chariot and picked up a bow. Using iron
arrows, he killed many Kaishika soldiers. Using six arrows, he
killed the brave and great archer, Karusha. Angrily, the maharatha
slew one hundred soldiers from Magadha. Having killed them, the
mighty-armed one advanced against Jarasandha. As he attacked,
he was pierced by three iron arrows. The one who used his club
as his weapon angrily struck him back with eight iron arrows.
Using a broad-headed arrow, he severed his[907] standard, which was
studded with jewels. A fierce encounter ensued between them, like
that between the gods and the asuras. Trying to kill each other,
they showered down arrows. Thousands of elephants angrily
engaged with rival elephants. Chariots clashed against chariots and
horse riders against horse riders. Foot soldiers attacked rival foot
soldiers with spears and shields in their hands. They roamed around
separately, severing the heads from the torsos. With a great sound,
swords descended on armour. The sound made by descending
arrows was like the noise made by birds. Kettledrums, conch shells,

[905] This seems to be Chakradeva.
[906] From what follows, this seems to be Poundraka's son.
[907] Jarasandha's.

drums and flutes emitted sounds in the battle. However, the noise made by the weapons and by the great-souled ones twanging their bows was louder.'

Chapter 88

Vaishampayana said, 'Rukmi heard that Rukmini had been abducted by Krishna. In Bhishmaka's presence, he angrily took a vow. "If I do not kill Govinda in a battle and do not bring Rukmini back, I will not enter Kundina. I say this truthfully." The brave one ascended a chariot with a standard, stocked with all the best weapons. Surrounded by a large army, the angry one quickly left. He was followed by all the kings who resided along *dakshinapatha*[908]—Kratha, Amshuman, Shrutarva, the brave Venudari, Bhishmaka's sons on their chariots, supreme among charioteers, and the best from the land of Kratha and Kaishika. All of them were maharathas. Those angry ones travelled some distance and on the banks of the Narmada, saw Govinda with his beloved. Asking the soldiers to wait, Rukmi, who was insolent of his prowess, desired to have a duel on chariots and challenged Madhusudana. He pierced Govinda with sixty-four sharp arrows. In the encounter, Govinda pierced him back with seventy arrows. Making efforts, the immensely strong one severed his[909] standard and severed the head of the valiant one's charioteer from his body. On seeing that he[910] was in trouble, all the kings from the southern region surrounded Janardana, wishing to kill him. The mighty-armed Amshuman pierced him with ten arrows. Angrily, Shrutarva shot five arrows at him and Venudari shot seven. Govinda shattered the brave Amshuman's chest. The king was hurt and sank down

---

[908] Literally, the southern path. In course of time, this was the southern part of the trade route that led from Bihar, through Uttar Pradesh and Madhya Pradesh, to the ports in Gujarat.

[909] Rukmi's.

[910] Rukmi.

on the seat of his chariot. With four arrows, he slew Shrutarva's four horses. He severed Venudari's standard and pierced him in his right hand. In that way, he pierced Shrutarva with five arrows and he was so pained that he sat down and leaned against his standard, exhausted. The foremost among the Krathas and the Kaishikas attacked Vasudeva from every direction with an array of chariots and showered down arrows on him. Janardana fought against them in that battle, severing their arrows with his arrows. He used arrows to kill the angry ones who were making efforts. There were some brave ones who angrily attacked. The immensely strong one used sixty-four sharp arrows to kill some of them. On seeing that his own army was being driven away, Rukmi was filled with anger. He pierced Keshava in the chest with five sharp arrows. He pierced the charioteer with three sharp arrows and severed the standard with an arrow with a drooping tuft. Keshava angrily pierced him back with six arrows. As Rukmi was making efforts, he severed his bow. Desiring to kill Krishna, Rukmi picked up another bow. He released divine and blazing weapons towards the brave one. The immensely strong Krishna repelled all these weapons with his weapons. He again used three arrows to splinter his bow and shatter his chariot. With his bow severed and deprived of his chariot, the brave and valiant one seized a sword and a shield and, like Garuda, leapt down from his chariot. In that encounter, as he descended with the sword, Keshava cut down the sword and angrily shattered his chest with three iron arrows. The mighty-armed one made a loud noise and fell down on the ground. The king was senseless and unconscious, like a mountain shattered by the vajra. Keshava again pierced all the kings with arrows. On seeing that Rukmi had fallen down, those kings ran away.

'Rukmini saw that her brother was trembling on the ground. Desiring her brother's life, she fell down at her husband's feet. Keshava raised her, embraced her and comforted her. Granting Rukmi freedom from fear, he left for his own city. The Vrishnis defeated Jarasandha and the kings. Placing the one with the plough as his weapon at the front, they happily left for Dvaraka. Once Pundarikaksha had left the field of battle, Shrutarva came to the field of battle. He picked up Rukmi on his chariot and left for his own city. Rukmi was proud of his strength. Since he was unable to bring his sister back, he had failed in his pledge. Therefore, he did not wish to enter the city of Kundina. So as to reside in Vidarbha, be constructed another great city and that became famous on earth as Bhojakatam. Dwelling there, the powerful and immensely strong one protected the southern direction. The great-minded King Bhishmaka lived in Kundina.

'Having reached Dvaraka with the Vrishni army, the lord Rama followed the prescribed rites and had Keshava and Rukmini married. With his beloved wife, he obtained supreme delight, like in earlier times, Rama with Sita and Poulami with Purandara.[911] This beautiful one was Krishna's eldest wife. She had the trait of being devoted to her husband and possessed the qualities of beauty and good conduct. Through her, he had ten maharatha sons—Charudeshna, Sudeshna, the immensely strong Pradyumna, Sushena, Charugupta, the brave Charubahu, Charuvinda, Sucharu, Bhadracharu and Charu, supreme among strong ones. There was also a daughter named Charumati. They were accomplished in dharma and artha. They were skilled in the use of weapons and were indomitable in battle. Madhusudana had seven other fortunate wives. The mighty-armed one married those who were born in noble lineages and possessed qualities—Kalindi, Mitravinda, Satya, the daughter of Nagnajit, the daughter of Jambavat, Rohini, who was beautiful in form, the daughter of the king of Madra, who possessed good conduct and auspicious eyes, the daughter of Satrajit, Satyabhama, Lakshmana, whose smiles were beautiful, and Sudatta, the daughter of Shaibya, who was like an apsara in her beauty.[912] The infinitely valorous one also had another sixteen

[911] This is Rama of the Ramayana. Poulami is Puloma's daughter, Shachi, Indra's wife.

[912] There is an inconsistency in the numbers. The number (and names) of Krishna's wives varies from text to text. If one sticks to the *Harivamsha*, Rukmini is not mentioned in a list of wives. She was too important and was equated with Shri or Lakshmi. The seven wives were Kalindi (Surya's daughter), Mitravinda (the daughter of the king of Avanti), Satya (the daughter of Nagnajit), Jambavati (the daughter of Jambavat), Rohini (Shrutakirti's daughter), Satyabhama (Satrajit's daughter) and Lakshmana

thousand wives. Hrishikesha married all of these at the same
time. All of them possessed supreme garments and ornaments and
deserved to enjoy pleasure. Through them, thousands of brave sons
were born. All of them were powerful maharathas, accomplished in
the use of all weapons. These immensely fortunate and immensely
strong ones performed sacrifices and other sacred tasks.'

Chapter 89

Vaishampayana said, 'After some time had passed, the valiant
Rukmi, the scorcher of enemies, arranged for his daughter's
svayamvara. The kings and the princes were summoned there by
Rukmi. From many directions, those prosperous and immensely
valorous ones assembled there. Surrounded by princes, Pradyumna
went there. The maiden desired him and he desired the one with
the auspicious eyes. This lady from Vidarbha possessed beauty
and radiance and her name was Shubhangi. At that time, Rukmi's
daughter was famous on earth. All the great-souled kings seated
themselves. The maiden from Vidarbha chose Pradyumna, the
slayer of enemies. That youth was accomplished in the use of all
weapons and was capable of withstanding a lion. Keshava's son was
unmatched in the world in his beauty. The princess also possessed
the qualities of age and beauty and desired him, just as Narayani
Chandrasena desired her husband.[913] When the svayamvara was
over, the kings left for their own cities. With the maiden from
Vidarbha, Pradyumna left for Dvaraka. There, he had a son who
was like an offspring of the gods. He was famous as Aniruddha
and his deeds were unmatched on earth. He was accomplished in

---

(daughter of the king of Madra). Rohini was also known as Bhadra and
Shaibya was not one of the main wives.

[913] There are different stories about Mudgala. He was both a king and
a sage. In some accounts, Mudgala's wife was Indrasena, referred to as
Chandrasena here. In other accounts, Indrasena was his daughter-in-law.
Indrasena was Narayana's daughter.

dhanurveda, the Vedas and the sacred texts of policy. O king! When Aniruddha came of age, he chose Rukmi's granddaughter, named Rukmavati, as his wife. She was like Rukmini and possessed the complexion of gold.[914] The king was of the view that Aniruddha possessed the qualities. Hence, Rukmi was affectionately disposed towards the alliance with Rukmini's descendant.[915] He forgot about his rivalry and enmity with Krishna. O Janamejaya! He happily said that he would bestow her.

'With their forces, Keshava, Rukmini's son and his son,[916] Samkarshana and the other Vrishnis went to Vidarbha. All Rukmi's relatives and well-wishers were also invited by Rukmi and those kings also went there. O great king! When an auspicious nakshatra was in ascendance in the sky, that grand festival of Aniruddha's marriage was concluded honourably. O descendant of the Bharata lineage! Aniruddha accepted the hand of the maiden from Vidarbha. The Vrishnis were honoured like the immortals and enjoyed themselves there.

'The intelligent king of Ashmaka, Venudari, Aksha, Shrutarva, Chanura, Kratha, Amshuman, Jayatsena, the immensely strong king of Kalinga, the king of Pandya and the prosperous king of Rishika—all these great kings from the southern region assembled. All of them secretly approached the lord Rukmi and told him, "You are skilled in playing with the dice and we also wish to play. Despite not being that skilled, Rama loves to play with the dice. With you at the forefront, we wish to defeat him." Thus addressed, the idea of playing with the dice appealed to maharatha Rukmi. There was an auspicious assembly hall with golden pillars. It was decorated with flowers and had been sprinkled with sandalwood water. All of them happily entered that place, smearing themselves with fragrant pastes. Desiring victory, all of them seated themselves on golden seats. The deceitful ones, who were accomplished in playing with the dice, challenged Baladeva, who cheerfully said, "Let us play. What is your stake?" The kings from the southern regions

[914] *Rukma* is gold, which explains her name.
[915] Aniruddha.
[916] Pradyumna and Aniruddha.

wished to win through deceit and brought thousands of pearls, jewels and gold. The game of dice, which would destroy all their delight, commenced. It always leads to terrible conflict and brings destruction to those who are evil-minded. In the match with Rukmi, Baladeva offered ten thousand golden coins as stake. Though the maharatha tried, Rukmi defeated him. With a similar stake, he again defeated Baladeva. Rukmi defeated Keshava's great-souled elder brother several times and won the stakes of one crore of gold coins. Cheerfully, the deceitful one said, "I have won." He prided himself and laughed at the one who has the plough as a weapon. "Today, in the game with the dice, I have defeated the prosperous Baladeva and have won an unlimited quantity of gold. He is invincible, but is weak and ignorant." On hearing this, the king of Kalinga laughed a lot, exhibiting his teeth. The one with the plough as his weapon was enraged. He heard the words spoken by Rukmi about his defeat, the sharp words of insult uttered by Bhishmaka's son. However, though he was angry, the one who knew about dharma conquered his rage. That censure made him wrathful. But Rohini's immensely strong son mentally resorted to patience. Controlling himself, he spoke these words. "My next stake is of ten thousand crores.[917] O lord of men! Accept this stake and throw the black dice and the red dice in this place that is full of dust."[918] Speaking these words, Rohini's son challenged Rukmi, who didn't say anything, but offered a stake again. King Rukmi cheerfully threw the dice and when the four-sided dice had stopped rolling, the king had been defeated.[919] However, he told Bala, "Baladeva has not followed dharma in defeating me." Baladeva resorted to the patience in his mind and controlling himself, did not say anything. Rukmi smiled and told Baladeva, "I have really won." Baladeva heard the words spoken by the king, about him having resorted to deceit. Though he was again overwhelmed by rage, he did not say anything in reply. At this time, a deep and invisible voice that spoke the truth was heard from

[917] Of gold coins.

[918] Alternatively, in this place that is full of the rajas quality.

[919] The text uses the word *chaturaksha*. This means a die with four spots. Therefore, it was a four-sided, not six-sided, one.

the sky and this increased the great-souled Baladeva's rage. "The prosperous Bala has won through the use of dharma. Even though he has not said anything, he has obtained success through his deeds.[920] It should indeed be considered that he mentally accepted it." On hearing the words thus spoken from the sky, the powerful Samkarshana arose and grabbed the gold-red board. Using this, he beat Rukmini's elder brother[921] down on the earth. Rama, bull among the Yadu lineage, was enraged at the cruel words spoken by the one who abused him and laughed at him. He slew him with the ashtapada board. Withdrawing a bit, he angrily uprooted the teeth of the king of Kalinga and in his rage, roared like a lion. Raising his sword, he terrified the kings. The supreme among strong ones uprooted a golden pillar. Dragging it like a giant elephant, he went out through the gates of the assembly hall, frightening the Krathas and the Kaishikas. The bull among the Yadava lineage killed Rukmi, who was skilled in deceit. Like a lion amidst small animals, he frightened all the enemies. Surrounded by his own relatives, Rama went to his camp and told Krishna everything that had happened. The immensely radiant Krishna did not tell Rama anything at the time. He controlled himself and shed tears of rage.[922] Vasudeva, the slayer of enemy heroes, had not killed him earlier. However, that powerful king, who was like the wielder of the vajra, was slain by the ashtapada in Rama's hands, in that gathering over gambling with the dice. That great king, Bhishmaka's son, had studied under Druma and Bhargava[923] and was equal to Druma and Bhargava. He was accomplished in battle and always performed sacrifices. When he was brought down, all the Vrishnis and Andhakas were distressed in their minds. O bull among the Bharata lineage! I have thus told you everything about Rukmi's death and about how his

[920] This needs explanation. Rukmi had flung the dice, without waiting for Balarama to offer a stake, or accept the challenge. Balarama had not said anything. Hence, the formalities of the challenge being accepted had not been completed.

[921] That is, Rukmi.

[922] After all, Rukmi was his relative and matrimonial ally and the historical enmity had ended.

[923] Parashurama.

enmity with the Vrishnis arose. O great king! The Vrishnis gathered
together all the different kinds of riches. Seeking refuge with Rama
and Krishna, they left for the city of Dvaravati.'

Chapter 90

Janamejaya said, 'O brahmana rishi! I wish to again hear about
the greatness of the intelligent Baladeva, who is Shesha who holds
up the earth. He was extremely strong and a mass of energy.
He couldn't be vanquished. People who know about the ancient
accounts speak about the great-souled one. O brahmana! I wish
to hear the truth about his deeds. He is known as the immensely
energetic and original god, the serpent Ananta.'

Vaishampayana replied, 'In the Puranas, one reads about him
as the king of the serpents, the one who holds up the earth. He is the
handsome Shesha, the store of energy. He is the Purushottama who
does not tremble. He is the preceptor of yoga. He is great in valour.
He is immensely strong. He is supremely strong among the strong.
He defeated Jarasandha in a duel with the clubs, but did not kill him.
O lord of the earth! There were many kings and lords of the earth
who followed Magadha in the battle, but all of them were defeated
in the encounter. Bhima was terrible in his valour and possessed
the strength of ten thousand elephants. However, he was defeated
by Baladeva in a wrestling bout. When Samba, Jambavati's son,
abducted Duryodhana's daughter, he was imprisoned in the city of
Nagasahvya.[924] Hearing this, the one with the plough as his weapon
angrily went there. Rama went there to free him, but did not get
him.[925] The powerful one was overcome by great rage. The powerful
one raised his plough, which was invincible, impenetrable, divine,
unmatched and like Brahma's staff. He invoked it with mantras.
The immensely strong one fixed the plough against the wall of the

---

[924] Nagasahvya is another name for Hastinapura. Samba was
imprisoned.
[925] When he peacefully asked for Samba.

Kourava city and pushed it towards the Ganga river. On seeing that
the city was being whirled around, the intelligent King Duryodhana
released Samba and his wife. The extremely great-souled Rama
offered himself to the king of the Kurus and accepting him as a
disciple in fighting with the clubs. O Indra among kings! O king!
Since that time, when the city had been whirled around, it became
tilted towards the Ganga. This extraordinary deed of Rama's is
famous on earth. O king! In earlier times, what Shouri[926] did in
Bhandira has already been recounted. With a single blow of his fist,
the one with the plough as his weapon killed Pralamba. He flung
the gigantic Dhenuka on the top of a tree. The great river Yamuna
is Yama's sister, with a forceful flow of water and a garland of
waves. She is the one who flows towards the store of saline water.
Dragged by the plough, she was brought towards the city. I have
spoken about all these aspects of Baladeva's greatness. He is the
immeasurable Ananta. He is the extremely great-souled Shesha.
This is the supreme among men, the wielder of the plough, who
performed many other such supreme deeds. I have spoken about
these deeds and they can be gleaned in detail from the Puranas.'

Chapter 91

Janamejaya said, 'O great sage! When Rukmi was killed, the
mighty-armed and valiant Vishnu returned to Dvaraka. Tell me
what he did thereafter.'

Vaishampayana replied, 'Surrounded by all of them, the
illustrious and valiant Vishnu, the descendant of the Yadava
lineage, returned to the city of Dvaraka. Pundarikaksha returned
with jewels and many kinds of riches and in the proper way, made
arrangements for the Nairittas[927] to be repulsed. The daityas and
danavas caused many hurdles. The mighty-armed one slew these
great asuras, who were the recipients of boons. The danava named

---

[926] Shura's descendant, Balarama.
[927] Demons, rakshasas.

Naraka created an obstacle at the time. He was a great enemy of
the king of the gods and terrified large numbers of gods. He dwelt
in Murtilinga and obstructed all the gods, acting against sages and
men.[928] Tvashta's daughter, Kasheru, was beautiful in her limbs.
When she was fourteen years old, Bhouma assumed the form of
an elephant and had intercourse with her. Having violated that
beautiful one, Naraka, the lord of Pragjyotisha, confounded and
lacking any fear about his own destruction, spoke these words.
"There are many kinds of riches amidst gods and men and there is
the radiant wealth on earth and in the oceans. From today, all the
Nairittas, accompanied by the daityas and the danavas, will seize
those for me." In this way, Bhouma accumulated supreme jewels
and many kinds of garments. But he did not use them. The powerful
Naraka also abducted gandharva maidens, those from gods and
men, and seven categories of apsaras. There were fourteen thousand
and twenty-one hundred of these. All of them wore a single braid
and followed the vows of the virtuous. Not distressed in his soul,
on the mountain known as Mani, Bhouma built a supreme city
for them.[929] This was in Alaka, in the kingdom of Mura. Ten of
Mura's sons and the best among the Nairittas worshipped the lord
of Pragjyotisha and protected this city. Having obtained a boon,
the great asura lived beyond the city.[930] For the sake of her earrings,
the great asura oppressed Aditi.[931] With all those large numbers of
asuras, the great asura perpetrated terrible deeds, the likes of which
had not been done earlier. He was born from the goddess earth
and owned the city of Pragjyotisha. He had four guards who were
invincible in battle—Hayagriva, Nisunda, Vira and Panchajana.

[928] Naraka was the son of the earth (bhumi) and lived in
Pragjyotishapura. Murtilinga is identified as Pragjyotishapura. As a son of
the earth, he was known as Bhouma. Murtilinga can also be interpreted as
his having adopted an earthy form.

[929] Alternatively, the city was known as Maniparvata.

[930] The text uses the word *tamasa*. This primarily means darkness, but
a secondary meaning is a city. It is possible that there is a typo and this
should read *tapasa*. That makes better sense. Having performed austerities,
the great asura obtained a boon.

[931] Aditi was the mother of the gods and Naraka stole her earrings.

The great asura, Mura, and his one thousand sons, had obtained boons. With malformed rakshasas, they thus obstructed the path of the gods and terrified the performers of good deeds. It was to kill them that the mighty-armed Janardana, the wielder of the conch shell, chakra, mace and sword, was born in the lineage of the Vrishnis through Devaki and Vasudeva. To think of a means to accomplish the objective of the gods, the Indra among men, famous in the world for his energy, resided in Dvaraka.

'The city of Dvaraka was more beautiful than Vasava's eternal abode. It was protected by the giant ocean and adorned by five mountains. There was an assembly hall with golden gates there and it possessed the complexion of a city of the gods. It was known by the name of Sudasharha. It was extensive and one yojana wide. With Rama and Krishna at the forefront, all the Vrishnis and Andhakas resided there, protecting the entire progress of the worlds. O bull among the Bharata lineage! On one occasion, all of them were seated there. A breeze with divine fragrances began to blow and flowers showered down. In the midst of a net of radiance, a joyous sound arose in the firmament. In an instant, this settled down on the ground. Vasava was seen in the centre of this energy, astride a white elephant and surrounded by a large number of gods. Rama, Krishna, the king[932] and the Vrishnis and Andhakas arose and worshipped the great-souled lord of the gods. He swiftly descended from the elephant and embraced Janardana, then embracing Baladeva and King Ahuka. Paying regard to their ages, he embraced the other Vrishnis, seated in their respective places. Worshipped by Rama and Krishna, he entered the auspicious assembly hall. The lord of the gods seated himself there, akin to an ornament in that assembly hall. As is proper, he accepted the rituals of arghya. Touching his auspicious face with a hand of assurance, the immensely energetic Vasava then spoke to Vasava's younger brother. "O Devaki's son! O Madhusudana! Listen to the words I speak. O afflicter of enemies! Listen to the reason why I have come here now. There is a Nairitta named Naraka. Having obtained a boon from Brahma, he has become insolent. In his confusion,

[932] Ugrasena.

that son of Diti has seized Aditi's earrings. He always engages
in tasks that are disagreeable to the gods and the rishis. Finding
an opportunity, slay that wicked and harsh person. This Garuda
can go wherever he wants and will take you there. Vinata's son is
extremely energetic and travels in the sky. He possesses the valour
of being able to go wherever he wants. Bhouma, the asura Naraka,
cannot be killed by any creature.[933] Having slain that wicked one,
you should swiftly return." Pundarikaksha Keshava was addressed
by the king of the gods in this way. The mighty-armed one took
a pledge that he would destroy Naraka. Assisted by Satyabhama
and with Shakra, the wielder of the conch shell, chakra, mace and
sword, the lord of Garuda, made arrangements for departure. As
the lions among the Yadus looked on, with Vasava, the powerful
one rose up, on the shoulders of the seven winds. Indra was astride
the supreme of elephants, Janardana was astride Garuda. From a
distance, they were as radiant as the sun and the moon. Praised by
the gandharvas and the apsaras, Madhava and Shakra gradually
disappeared in the sky. Having decided on what needed to be done,
Vasava, the lord of the gods, returned to his own residence and
Krishna left for Pragjyotisha.

'He slew the large numbers of rakshasas who were at the
forefront of Naraka's large army. He then saw six thousand of
Mura's followers, armed with nooses. Destroying all those nooses,
he killed Mura and his aides with razor-sharp arrows. He crossed
the mass of rocks and uprooted Nisunda. He uprooted the one
who had single-handedly fought against the gods for one thousand
years. O bull among the Bharata lineage! A terrible encounter,
using many kinds of weapons, ensued, like that between the gods
and the asuras. Basing himself on Garuda, the mighty-armed one
shot multicoloured and large arrows and killed the great asuras.
Clashing against Janardana, the shrieking danavas were brought
down by arrows and the sword and mangled by the plough. Burnt
down by the fire, some danavas fell down from the sky. Some
were dragged close and, malformed in face, gave up their lives.
He killed the extremely terrible and great asura, Hayagriva. The

[933] This was Brahma's boon.

descendant of the Yadava lineage was infinite in his energy and invincible before everyone. In the middle of Lohitaganga,[934] in Alaka, the illustrious Purushottama, Devaki's son, killed the evil-souled Virupaksha. The tiger among men, the scorcher of enemies, killed eight hundred thousand danavas and attacked Pragjyotisha. He killed Naraka's terrible and great asura, Panchajana. He next approached the city of Pragjyotisha, blazing in its prosperity, and a battle resulted. There was an extremely terrible encounter with Naraka. I will briefly tell you about it. Listen attentively. Naraka, who terrified large numbers of gods, fought with Purushottama, as if he was the energetic Madhu[935] fighting with Madhusudana. Madhusudana fought with Naraka for some time. After this, using his blazing and fierce chakara, he severed him into two. Divided into two parts by the chakra, his body fell down on the ground. Like the summit of a mountain, it was severed into two parts by the chakra. On seeing that her son had fallen down, the earth picked up the earrings. She gave them to Govinda and said, "O Govinda! He was given by you and he has been taken away by you. O god! These are the earrings. Please protect his subjects."'

Chapter 92

Vaishampayana said, 'After Bhouma Naraka, who was like Vasava in his valour, was killed, Vishnu, Vasava's younger brother, saw Naraka's residence. Entering Naraka's treasure house, Janardana saw an infinite quantity of riches and many kinds of jewels. There were gems, pearls, corals and a store of lapis lazuli. There were large heaps of silver and a store of diamonds. There was molten gold and pots full of refined gold. These blazed like the fire and were also as cool as the moon's beams. There were extremely expensive couches and thrones. He saw the large and beautiful royal umbrella, golden in complexion. It was as cool as the moon's beams

[934] This is clearly the Brahmaputra river.
[935] Demon killed by Vishnu.

and looked like a cloud that was about to shower down. There were hundreds and thousands of streams of pure and sparkling gold. We have heard that all this was seized by Naraka from Varuna earlier. The many kinds of riches that he saw in Naraka's residence are not matched by what exists with King Kubera, Shakra or Yama. That kind of store of riches has not been seen before, nor heard of. When Bhouma, Nisunda and danava Hayagriva were killed, the danavas who were left and those who were entrusted with the task of guarding the treasure troves, brought all these riches and everything in the inner quarters to Keshava. It was Janardana who deserved these extremely expensive objects. The danavas said, "There are many kinds of gems, jewels and riches. There are fierce elephants, their goads decorated with coral. Bows and spears are tied to their giant flanks with golden ropes. They are decorated with beautiful flags and many kinds of cushions and seats. There are twenty thousand male elephants and forty thousand female elephants. There are eight hundred thousand horses that have come from the best of regions. O Janardana! There are as many cattle as you wish for. All of these will be taken to the residences of the Vrishnis and the Andhakas. There are beds and seats, covered with the fine hide of goats. There are birds who are pleasant to look at and they can chirp agreeably. There is sandalwood and agaru. There is also turmeric.[936] By following dharma, there are riches that you can obtain in the three worlds. All of these will be available in the residences of the Vrishnis and the Andhakas." All the jewels of the gods and the gandharvas and all the riches of the serpents were available in Naraka's residence. Examining them, Hrishikesha accepted all these. He made the danavas deliver all these to the city of Dvaraka. Madhava himself held aloft Varuna's umbrella, which seemed to shower down gold, and mounted the bird Garuda, supreme among birds.

'Looking like an embodied cloud, he went to Maniparvata, best among mountains. An auspicious breeze started to blow there and a golden-hued and pure radiance sparkled, emanating from the gems and surpassing that of the sun. Madhusudana saw

---

[936] *Kaliyaka*. It is possible that this should actually be *kaleyaka*, a kind of fragrant wood.

lapis lazuli there and walls, flags, gates and couches. Maniparvata
possessed the radiance of a cloud tinged with lightning. There were
colourful and decorated celestial vehicles and beautiful palaces.
There, Madhusudana saw the best of women and their complexion
was like that of gold. They were the wives and daughters of the
best of gandharvas and gods. He saw the wide-hipped ones. They
had been imprisoned in a cave in the mountain. They had been
brought there by Naraka and guarded in every possible way. Those
unvanquished ones resided in a region that was like that of the
gods. They happily lived there like goddesses, abandoning desire.
The mighty-armed one was surrounded by women who possessed
a single braid of hair. All of their garments were ochre and all of
them had controlled their senses. Because of vows and fasting, their
limbs were emaciated. They were waiting, desiring to seek Krishna.
All those women joined their hands in salutation and assembled
around the lion of the Yadu lineage. Knowing that Naraka, the
great asura Mura, Hayagriva and Nisunda had been killed, they
surrounded Krishna. All the aged danava guards also joined their
hands in salutation before the descendant of the Yadu lineage and
he honoured those who were senior in age. Those supreme women
looked at the one with the eyes of a bull. All of them resolved
that he would be their husband. His face was like the moon. The
ones who had controlled their senses glanced at him. They happily
spoke these words to the mighty-armed one. "In earlier times, the
wind that speaks the truth has spoken to us in these words. So has
devarshi Narada, who knows about the nature of all creatures. 'The
god, Vishnu Narayana, holds the conch shell, the chakra, a mace
and a sword. Having slain Bhouma Naraka, he will become your
husband.' O scorcher of enemies! We have heard about you for
a long time and we are able to see our beloved now. Today, we
are satisfied at having been able to see the great soul." Vasava's
younger brother comforted all those women. All of them possessed
eyes like lotus petals. Madhava looked towards them and spoke to
them. As is proper, Keshava comforted them and addressed them.
Madhusudana instructed the servants that they[937] should be seated

937 The women.

on vehicles. There were thousands of rakshasa servants, with the
speed of the wind. As they raised the palanquins, a great sound arose.
The foremost summit of the mountain was extremely revered. It had
gates adorned with jewels and gold and it sparkled like the sun and
the moon. There were large numbers of birds and elephants there
and predatory beasts, deer and serpents. There were extensive stony
slopes, inhabited by large numbers of monkeys. Ranku and ruru
deer and boar inhabited the place. The giant summit was adorned
by the tops of many kinds of trees. It was extremely wonderful and
unthinkable and full of many kinds of animals. It echoed with the
noise made by herons, pheasants and peacocks. With his two hands,
the extremely strong Vishnu uprooted the shining peak and placed
it on Garuda, supreme among birds. The bird Garuda, supreme
among birds, carried Maniparvata, Janardana and his wife,[938]
as if it was mere sport. The king of birds was like the summit of
a huge mountain and used the strength of his wings and a great
noise erupted in all the directions. He broke down the peaks of
mountains and flung away trees, scattering and dispelling some of
the clouds. He passed the regions of the two gods, the sun and the
moon. Obeying Janardana's instructions, the bird's speed was like
that of the wind.

'Madhusudana reached Mount Meru, inhabited by the gods
and the gandharvas. O lord of men! He saw all the residences of
the gods, of the Vishvadevas, the Maruts and the Sadhyas. The
scorcher of enemies passed over these and the radiant residences
of the Ashvins. The scorcher of enemies reached the world
of the gods, attained by the performers of auspicious deeds.
Janardana reached Shakra's abode and entered. On seeing the
lord of the gods, he got down from Tarkshya.[939] Shatakratu,
the king of the gods, was delighted to see him and welcomed
him. Achyuta Janardana, best among men, gave him the divine
earrings and, with his wife, worshipped the best among the
gods. Thus worshipped, the king of the gods worshipped him
back with jewels. Satyabhama was appropriately greeted by

[938] Satyabhama.
[939] Garuda.

Puloma's daughter.[940] Together, Vasava and Vasudeva went to the sacred and prosperous abode of Aditi, the mother of the gods. There, Aditi was being worshipped in every direction by the apsaras. The two great-souled and immensely fortunate ones saw the ascetic one. Placing Janardana ahead of him, Shachi's consort worshipped her and gave her the earrings, telling her what had happened. Delighted, Aditi embraced and greeted her two sons. She uttered identical words of benediction over both of them. Puloma's daughter and Satyabhama were filled with great joy. They touched the sacred feet of the goddess who deserves to be revered. Affectionately, the illustrious mother of the gods addressed them and spoke these words to Janardana. "No creature will be able to assail you. No one will be able to slay you. Like the king of the gods, you will be worshipped in the worlds. Satyabhama, supreme among women, is extremely fortunate. O Krishna! As long as you remain in human form, this wife of yours will always be young and old age will not touch her." The immensely strong Krishna was thus honoured by the mother of the gods.

'Honoured with jewels, he then took his leave of the king of the gods. With Satyabhama, he climbed onto Vinata's son. Praised by the divine rishis, he circled around the pleasure garden of the gods. The mighty-armed one saw Vasava's pleasure garden. Worshipped by the gods, the great Parijata tree was there. This celestial tree blossoms with flowers all the time, with sacred and supreme fragrances. Men who approach it remember the incidents of their earlier lives. It was protected by the gods. However, the infinitely valourous Vishnu uprooted the giant tree.[941] As they left for Dvaravati with the speed of the wind, Satyabhama and Hari saw divine apsaras. The king of the gods heard about what Krishna had done, but said, "What the mighty-armed one has done meets with my approval." Worshipped by the gods and praised by large numbers of maharshis, Krishna, the scorcher of enemies, left the world of the gods for Dvaraka. In a short while, the mighty-armed one covered that great distance.

[940] Shachi.
[941] To take it with him.

Worshipped by the king of the gods, he saw the city of the Yadavas. Thus, Vasava's illustrious younger brother performed a great task. Astride Garuda, the prosperous Vishnu reached Dvaraka.'

Chapter 93

Vaishampayana said, 'Astride Garuda, Krishna saw the city of Dvaraka. It was like a residence of the gods and echoed in all directions.[942] After the visit to Maniparvata was over, Devaki's son proceeded there. The king of the gods summoned Vishvakarma and told him, "O supreme among artisans! If you wish to do what brings me pleasure and also for Krishna's pleasure, make the city of Dvaraka beautiful, like heaven, with gardens and groves. O best among the gods! Make it like my city. Whatever stores of riches you can see in the three worlds, swiftly assemble those in the city of Dvaravati. Krishna is always ready to undertake the tasks of the gods. The immensely strong one immerses himself in terrible battles." Accepting Indra's words, Vishvakarma went to the city and in every direction, sought to make it like Indra's Amaravati. Following divine instructions, Vishvarkarma ornamented it and, astride the bird, the lord of Dasharha saw this. The lord Narayana Hari saw the city of Dvaraka and was about to enter. He was delighted to see that it had become full of riches. As he headed towards Dvarka, Dasharha saw the trunks of trees that were beautiful to behold, colourfully created by Vishvakarma. There were blossoming lotuses along the banks and swans on the water, which dazzled like the water of the Ganga. The city was surrounded by moats. The walls had the complexion of the sun. Embellished with gold and silver, the tops looked like a garland of clouds against the sky. The groves were like Nandana and Chaitraratha. Beautiful Dvaraka was as resplendent as the clouds against the sky. The beautiful peaks and caverns of Mount Raivataka shone. In the eastern direction, there was a handsome gate, constructed out

[942] As a result of the ocean.

of jewels and gold. The southern gate was entwined with creepers
of five colours. The undecaying western gate looked like Indra's
standard. O bull among kings! The gate towards the northern
direction was adorned by Mount Venuman, as resplendent and
white as Mount Mandara. Towards Raivataka, there was the large
forest of Panchajanya, with a hue that was speckled and grey. In
every direction, there were other colourful forests too. There was
the great forest of Meruprabha, covered throughout with creepers.
The forest of Bharga dazzled, while that of Pushpaka was large.
The forests known as Shatavarta and Karavirakarambhi were
adorned with trees like *akshaka, bijaka* and *mandara*.[943] In every
direction, Mount Venuman was rendered beautiful by large forests
that were as shining as Chaitraratha and Nandana. O descendant
of the Bharata lineage! In the eastern direction, there was a
beautiful and sparkling lake that was filled with aquatic plants with
petals like lapis lazuli, and so was the river Mandakini. Urged by
Vishvakarma and to ensure Keshava's pleasure, many gods and
gandharvas were seated on the summits. The river Mandakini in
Dvaravati had fifty different outlets. With auspicious waters, it
entered the city and dazzled every direction. The city was large and
immeasurable and was surrounded by a fathomless moat. There
were the best of palaces and these were painted as white as milk.
The city of Dvaraka was protected by fierce shataghnis and adorned
with machines of war. There were large and iron chakras. The city
possessed eight thousand chariots that were decorated with bells.
Standards arose aloft them, as in the city of the gods. The city was
like a mountain, eight yojanas wide and twelve yojanas long. The
habitations in the city of Dvaraka could be seen to occupy double
that area. There were eight main roads and sixteen large squares.
There was a single highway and it seemed to have been constructed
by Ushanas[944] himself. The women could also fight, not to speak of
the Vrishni maharathas. Along seven major roads, there were paths
that led to the battle formations. These had been laid out by the

[943] Akshaka is a creeping plant (*Dalbergia oujeinensis*), bijaka is the
citron tree and mandara is the tree of paradise.
[944] Shukracharya.

divine Vishvakarma himself. This was the best and supreme city of the illustrious Dasharhas.

'Delighted, Devaki's son saw the houses. The steps were decorated with gold and jewels, causing pleasure to men. There were palaces and squares that echoed loudly. There were fluttering flags and swimming pools. The white tops of the white buildings were decorated with refined gold. The beautiful tops of the buildings looked like the colourful summits of mountains. Decorated with five colours, it seemed as if flowers had showered down on them. They looked like many different kinds of mountains and resounded like thunder. They blazed like a forest conflagaration and had been created by Vishvakarma. Because of the paint, they rose up into the sky like mountains and were like the sun and the moon. Vasudeva[945] was the immensely fortunate Dasharha and his house, surrounded by clouds, was like the house of Indra Parjanya. The illustrious one's beautiful house had been constructed by Vishvakarma himself and could be seen in Dvaraka, surrounded by the clouds. Vasudeva's residence could be seen and it extended for four yojanas. It was large and immeasurable and was filled with great quantities of wealth. Instructed by Vasava, the immensely fortunate Tvashtri had constructed this city on earth and it was full of the best of palaces and mountains. The palaces had the complexion of gold and all creatures found them to be delightful. Rukmini's supreme house had been constructed by Vishvakarma. It was large and golden and it rose up, like the summit of Mount Meru. Yet again, Satyabhama's house was white and was filled with all the objects of pleasure. It had colourful steps decorated with jewels and sparkled, with the complexion of the sun. It was adorned with flags. The best of adorned palaces was for Jambavati. There were flags on four sides and the residence was located on even terrain. Like the sun, this residence surpassed all the other residences in its brilliance. Like the rising sun in complexion, this was located between the other two.[946] This divine building had been created by Vishvakarma and was like the peak of Mount Kailasa. There was

[945] Krishna.
[946] The other two houses, of Rukmini and Satyabhama.

a house that blazed like molten gold and was like the flames of a fire. It was as large as the ocean and was famous by the name of Meru. O best among the Bharata lineage! Gandhari, born in a noble lineage as the daughter of the king of Gandhara, resided there and served Keshava.[947] There was a house known as Padmakuta. It was immensely radiant and possessed the complexion of a lotus. This large residence was supremely revered and was Bhima's abode.[948] There was a palace that possessed the complexion of the sun and had all the objects and qualities to satisfy desire. O best among the Kuru lineage! The wielder of the Sharnga bow earmarked this for Lakshmana.[949] O descendant of the Bharata lineage! There was a palace that was green in colour, with the complexion of lapis lazuli. All creatures knew this as a supreme building. This abode, worshipped by the gods and the rishis, was where Mitravinda[950] resided. She was Vasudeva's queen and her residence was like an ornament. Vishvakarma constructed a foremost palace. This was extremely peaceful and was like an immobile mountain. This was praised by all the gods and was famous as Ketuman. This was where Vasudeva's queen Sudatta resided.[951] Tvashtri had himself constructed this best of palaces. It was auspicious and full of all the jewels, extending for one yojana. There was also an extremely handsome and resplendent resting house for the great-souled Keshava. Flags with golden poles indicated the way towards this. Flags fluttered along the way towards Vasudeva's house. Here and there, nets of jewels were laid out.

'The lion of the Yadu lineage had brought the giant mountain of Vaijayanta. Its peak was known as Hamsakuta and this was

[947] The wife known as Satya, daughter of Nagnajit, the king of Gandhara.

[948] Bhima probably means Kalindi, Surya's daughter. But later, there is a reference to Subhima, who seems to be equated with Madri. However, Madri should be Lakshmana.

[949] The daughter of the king of Madra.

[950] The daughter of the king of Avanti.

[951] Sudatta's name has not featured earlier. Since Rohini's house has not been mentioned so far, Sudatta could be one of Rohini's names. But later, there is a suggestion that Sudatta was Shaibya's name.

placed in the lake known as Indradyumna. It[952] was as tall as
sixty palm trees taken together and its expanse was half a yojana.
There were kinnaras and infinitely energetic giant serpents as its
inhabitants. It was famous in the worlds and while all the beings
looked on, he had brought it there. The supreme summit of Mount
Meru obstructs the path of the sun. It is encrusted with celestial
gold and is famous in the three worlds. For Krishna's sake,
Vishvakarma had uprooted it and brought it there. The summit
was extremely radiant and was decorated with all the herbs. To
accomplish the intention behind Indra's words, Tvashtri had
brought it there. Keshava had himself brought Parijata there. This
was a supreme tree, protected by the gods. Krishna, the performer
of extraordinary deeds, had brought it there, along with hundreds
of lotus flowers and golden and celestial vehicles. For Vasudeva's
sake, a place known as Brahmasthala had been laid out, with giant
trees. There were gems, water lilies and fragrant lotuses there. There
were ponds and lakes, with jewels, gold and boats. The excellent
banks were decorated with the best of trees, with hundreds of
branches—sala, palm trees, kadambas and sandalwood. There
were trees that could be found in the Himalayas and Meru. For
the sake of the lion among the Yadus, Vishvakarma had them
brought and laid out there. The groves had trees with red, yellow,
pink and white flowers and these yielded every kind of seasonal
fruit. In that supreme of cities, there were rivers and pools with
sparkling water. Yellow sand and gravel lined the banks. There
were other rivers with golden gravel and sand along the banks,
with blossoming aquatic plants and many kinds of trees and
creepers. The supreme trees were filled with happy and excited
groups of peacocks and cuckoos. In the city, abodes were created
for herds of elephants, cattle, buffaloes, boars, animals and birds.
With golden walls, the city was beautiful. Hundreds of buildings
could be seen there and these were one hundred cubits tall. All
these were created by Vishvakarma. Bhouma[953] laid out these
large mountains, rivers, pools, forests and groves there.'

[952] The peak.
[953] Vishvakarma's name.

Chapter 94

Vaishampayana said, 'The one with eyes like a bull looked at such a Dvaraka. Krishna saw his own residence, adorned with one hundred palaces. There were thousands and tens of thousands of white pillars, encrusted with gems. There were blazing and excellent gates and resplendent trees decorated with jewels. Here and there, dazzling and colourful sacrificial altars could be seen, made out of gold. There were extensive and large pillars made out of crystal, decorated with gold everywhere. The pools had water lilies and red and fragrant lotuses. The steps were adorned with jewels and were colourful because of the gems and the gold. There were happy and excited groups of peacocks and cuckoos. There were excellent ponds with blooming lotuses. Vishvakarma arranged for the mountains, ramparts and buildings. These were one hundred cubits tall and the city was surrounded by a moat. That house for the lion among the Vrishnis was also constructed by Vishvakarma. In every direction, it extended for half a yojana and it was like the great Indra's house. Astride Garuda's shoulder, Shouri[954] reached it and happily blew on his white conch shell, one that made the body hair of the enemies stand up. On hearing the sound of the conch shell, the ocean was greatly agitated. The entire sky was stupefied and was immobile, like a painting. The Kukuras and Andhakas heard Panchajanya's[955] roar. On seeing Garuda, all their sorrows were dispelled. The one with the conch shell, chakra and mace in his hand was seated astride Garuda. On seeing the one who was like the sun in his energy, the entire earth rejoiced. All the residents of the city sounded trumpets. The drums made a loud noise. All of them roared like lions. All the Dasharhas and all the Kukuras and Andhakas were delighted. They assembled to see Madhusudana. Placing Vasudeva[956] at the forefront and with the sound of drums and conch shells, King Ugrasena went to Vasudeva's[957] house. Devaki happily welcomed them and tended

[954] Krishna.
[955] Krishna's conch shell.
[956] Krishna's father.
[957] Krishna's, Vaasudeva's.

to them, as did Rohini and all of Ahuka's women who were present
there. Astride Suparna, Krishna went to his own residence. As if
he was followed by the gods, Hari roamed around in that spot.
Krishna, the descendant of the Yadu lineage, got down at the gate of
his house. As is proper, the bull among the Yadavas worshipped the
Yadavas. Honoured by Rama, Ahuka, Gada, Akrura, Pradyumna
and the others, Shouri accepted Maniparvata and entered.
Pradyumna, Rukmini's son brought the large tree, Parijata, loved
by Shakra, and entered the house. Because of Parijata's powers,
all the people could see the superhuman properties of each other's
bodies and were delighted. The lords among the Yadavas cheerfully
praised Govinda. The prosperous one entered the house that had
been prepared by Vishvakarma. With the Vrishnis, Achyuta, the
one whose soul is immeasurable placed the peak of Maniparvata in
the inner quarters. The one who triumphs over enemies worshipped
the divine Parijata, supreme among trees, in an excellent place that
he liked. Keshava, the destroyer of enemy heroes, then took leave
of his kin. He honoured the women with what had been taken
away by Naraka—garments, ornaments, objects of pleasure, female
servants, stores of wealth, necklaces that had the splendour of the
moon's beams and extremely radiant jewels that were like the sun.
Vasudeva honoured the women with these. So did Devaki, Rohini,
Revati and Ahuka. Satyabhama, supreme among women, brought
good fortune. Rukmini, Bhishmaka's daughter, became the mistress
of the household. Depending on what they deserved, Krishna
instructed that they should be given mansions, tall buildings, houses
and everything else that was needed.'

Chapter 95

Vaishampayana said, 'Then, Vasudeva honoured Garuda and
treating him like a friend, gave him permission to return home.
Having obtained permission, Garuda honoured and bowed down
before Janardana. The bird who roams around in the sky rose up
and then went wherever he desired. Because of the wind raised

by his wings, the ocean, the abode of the makaras, was agitated. With great speed, he reached the eastern ocean. Before departing, Garuda said that he would return whenever he was needed for some task. Then, Krishna met his father, the aged Anakadundubhi. Madhava also met King Ugrasena, Baladeva, Sandipani from Kashi and the brahmana, Gargya. In a similar way, he met the other aged Vrishnis, Bhojas and Andhakas and honoured each of those Dasharhas by giving them jewels obtained through his own valour. "The Andhakas and Vrishnis have become victorious and all those who hate brahmanas have been killed. Madhusudana has returned unscathed from the battle. A man who was adorned with earrings and who was extremely respected all over Dvaravati made this announcement at all the crossroads.[958] Janardana approached Sandipani first. Then he humbly worshipped Ahuka, the king of the Vrishnis. After this, with Rama, Vasava's younger brother worshipped his father, whose eyes were overflowing with tears and who was senseless with joy. He then approached all those who remained and honoured them, depending on what they deserved. Adhokshaja[959] addressed all the Dasharhas by name. With Upendra at the forefront, all of them sat down on the best of divine seats, adorned with all kinds of jewels. On Krishna's instruction, men brought the infinite store of riches that had been accumulated by the servants to the assembly hall.[960] To the sound of drums being beaten, Janardana honoured and worshipped all the best of Dasharhas and Yadus. On Krishna's instructions, the best of Dasharhas entered the beautiful assembly hall, decorated with jewels, trees and gates, and seated themselves on excellent seats. Surrounded in all directions by lions among men and by the Yadus, he dazzled and sparkled even more, like a lion in a mountain cavern. With Rama, and placing the Vrishnis ahead of him, Govinda worshipped Ugrasena, who was seated on a large and golden seat. All those brave ones were happily seated there,

[958] This was clearly on royal instructions.

[959] Vishnu's and Krishna's name.

[960] The men are servants of the Yadavas, while the servants in the text refer to Narakasura's servants.

according to age. Madhusudana addressed the best among Yadus who were in that assembly hall.'

Chapter 96

'Vasudeva said, "The evil-souled Bhouma Naraka has been slain because of your good deeds, the strength of your austerities and meditation and because of the intentions you bore against him. The maidens who were imprisoned and protected in that great city have been freed. The summit of Maniparvata has been uprooted and brought here. The servants collected an extremely great store of riches and I have brought it here. That belongs to you."'

Vaishampayana said, 'Having said this, he stopped. On hearing Vasudeva's words, the Bhojas, Vrishnis and Andhakas were filled with joy and their body hair stood up. They worshipped Janardana. The best among men joined their hands in salutation and said, "O mighty-armed one! O Devaki's son! It is not extraordinary that you should accomplish this extremely difficult task, which even the gods would have found most difficult. You have yourself obtained objects of pleasure and jewels and are nurturing your relatives with these." All the women among the Dasharhas and all of Ahuka's wives joyously came to the assembly hall, desiring to see Vasudeva. With Devaki as the seventh, the seven daughters of Devaka were there,[961] and so was Rohini, beautiful in face. They saw Krishna and the mighty-armed Rama, seated. Ignoring the precedence of age, Rama and Keshava first greeted Rohini and then, Devaki, Devaka's daughter. Because of these two sons, she[962] looked even more radiant, like Aditi, the mother of the gods, with

[961] This requires interpretation. Devaka had seven daughters—Sahadeva, Shantideva, Shrideva, Devarakshita, Vrikadevi, Upadevi and Devaki. Devaki was the youngest. All of them were married to Vasudeva, Krishna's father.
[962] Devaki.

Mitra and Varuna. At that time, her[963] daughter approached those two best among men. Men knew her as Ekamsha, the one who could assume any form at will. She was born at the same instant as the lord[964] and it was because of her acts that Purushottama was able to slay Kamsa and his soldiers. This maiden was brought up among the Vrishnis, worshipped by them. Because of Vasudeva's[965] instructions, she had been reared as a son. She was born at the same instant and men knew her as Ekamsha. This maiden, Yogamaya, was invincible and was born for Keshava's protection. Cheerful in their minds, all the Yadavas worshipped her. Divine in form, she was born so that she could protect the god, Krishna. Madhava saw that his beloved friend had come, and like a friend, held her with his right hand. In that way, the extremely strong Rama also embraced the beautiful one. He inhaled the fragrance of her head and held her with his left hand. Between Rama and Krishna, everyone saw their beloved sister. Her hands held a golden lotus and she was like Shri, whose abode is the lotus. All the women who had assembled showered down a great shower of parched grain and many kinds of auspicious flowers. They then departed to wherever they had come from. All the Yadavas worshipped Janardana. They happily sat down and praised his extraordinary deeds. The mighty-armed one, who enhanced the affection of the citizens, was worshipped. Because of his great deeds, he amused himself among them, like a god.

'When all of the Yadavas were seated around Janardana, on the instructions of Indra of the gods, Narada came to that assembly hall. He deserved worship and was worshipped by all the descendants of Shura, the bulls among the Yadus. Govinda was seated on a grand seat and he touched him with his hand. After he was happily seated, he spoke to the Vrishnis, who were also seated. "O bulls among men! Know that I have come here because of Shakra's words. O tigers among kings! Hear about Krishna's valour.

---

[963] Devaki's, and because of what has been mentioned earlier, Yashoda's. Her daughter is Yogamaya.

[964] Krishna.

[965] Krishna's.

Since his childhood, Keshava has performed these deeds. Kamsa, Ugrasena's son, crushed all his relatives. The evil-minded one seized the kingdom and bound his father, Ahuka. The worst of the lineage sought refuge with Jarasandha, his father-in-law. The evil-minded one showed disrespect to all the Bhojas, Vrishnis and Andhakas. The powerful Vasudeva[966] wished to accomplish the task of his kin. To protect Ugrasena, he protected his own son. Madhusudana, the one with dharma in his soul, resided in the groves of Mathura, with the gopas and performed extremely extraordinary deeds. All the Shurasenas saw these extremely wonderful deeds. Hear about them. When he was lying down, he flung up his legs and destroyed a cart. There was a fierce demoness who had assumed the form of a bird. She was terrible and her name was Putana. She was extremely large and extremely strong. She was killed. Her breast was tinged with poison and she offered it to the great-souled one. Those who roam around in the forest saw that this demoness was killed. Since he was born again, he came to be known as Adhokshaja.[967] As a child, Purushottama was extremely extraordinary. While playing, he overturned the cart with his toe. He was tied to a mortar with rope and did something that was quite unlike a child. Therefore, Vasudeva came to be known as Damodara.[968] The great serpent, Kaliya, was impossible to withstand and extremely strong. In the pool in the Yamuna, Vasudeva playfully vanquished him. Akrura saw the lord go to the abode of the nagas. He assumed a divine form and was worshipped by the serpents there. The intelligent Krishna saw the cattle were afflicted by the cold and the wind. For seven nights, the great-souled one held up Mount Govardhana. That is because Vasudeva wanted to save the cows and the calves. Arishtaka[969] was extremely wicked and extremely strong. He was giant in form and killed men. Vasudeva, the lord of cattle, killed

---

[966] Krishna's father.

[967] Despite being under the cart, Krishna wasn't killed. In that sense, he was born again. *Adha* means under and *aksha* means wheel. Adhokshaja is one who is born under the wheels.

[968] Someone with rope (dama) around his stomach (udara).

[969] The same as Arishta.

him and flung him down on the ground. The danava Dhenuka was giant in form and extremely strong. To save cattle, Vasudeva killed the evil-minded one. Sunama had come, at the head of an army of soldiers, to sieze him. But the slayer of enemies used wolves to drive him away. He then again roamed around in the forest, in the company of Rohini's son, causing fear to Kamsa. The king of Bhoja sent a horse, which was capable of fighting, to the forest. However, Shouri Purushottama killed it. Kamsa's aide was the danava Pralamba, giant in form. Rohini's intelligent son brought him down with a blow of the fist. Vasudeva's two sons are like sons of the gods. Those two great-souled ones grew up and were taught good conduct by the brahmana Gargya. Since their birth, the supreme rishi Gargya, who knew about the truth, performed their *samskaras* at the appropriate time.[970] When these best among men attained youth, they were like crazy lion cubs on the slope of the Himalayas. These two immensely strong ones stole the hearts of the gopa women. Those two brave ones were as radiant as the gods and roamed around in Vraja. Nandagopa's cowherds were incapable of looking at them.[971] Their chests were broad and their arms were large. They were like the trunks of sala trees. On hearing about them, Kamsa and his advisers were distressed. When Kamsa was unable to seize Bala and Keshava, he became angry and imprisoned Vasudeva[972] and his relatives. Like a thief, along with Ugrasena, Anakadundubhi suffered that severe imprisonment and hardship for a long period of time. With the support of Jarasandha, Ahvriti and Bhishmaka, Kamsa imprisoned his father and ruled over the kingdom of Shurasena. After some

[970] There are thirteen samskaras or sacraments. The list varies a bit. But one list is *vivaha* (marriage), *garbhalambhana* (conception), *pumshavana* (engendering a male child), *simantonnayana* (parting the hair, performed in the fourth month of pregnancy), *jatakarma* (birth rites), *namakarana* (naming), *chudakarma* (tonsure), *annaprashana* (first solid food), *keshanta* (first shaving of the head), *upanayana* (sacred thread), *vidyarambha* (commencement of studies), *samavartana* (graduation) and *antyeshti* (funeral rites).

[971] In the sense of glancing towards them with eyes of rivalry.

[972] Krishna's father.

time, King Kamsa decided to hold a great festival in Mathura in
honour of Pinaki[973] and issued instructions. O lord of the earth!
Wrestlers, dancers, singers and those accomplished in singing and
dancing assembled there from many countries. Following proper
rites, the greatly energetic Kamsa made skilled artisans construct
an extremely expensive arena. There were thousands of galleries
there, for the residents of the city and the countryside. These were
filled with spectators, like stellar bodies in the sky. Kamsa, the
prosperous king of Bhoja, ascended the extremely expensive royal
gallery, like a person of virtuous deeds climbing on to a celestial
vehicle. Kamsa stationed a brave and crazy elephant at the gate to
the arena, stocked with a large supply of weapons and attended by
valiant and brave guards. The great Bhoja had heard that Rama
and Krishna, tigers among men, had arrived, like the sun and the
moon. To ensure his protection, the king made every kind of effort.
Thinking of Rama and Krishna, he could not sleep happily at
night. Having heard about that supreme assembly, the brave Rama
and Krishna entered there, like tigers entering a pen of cows. The
guards prevented the bulls among men from entering. However,
those slayers of enemies killed Kuvalayapida and its rider. Those
invisible ones then entered the arena. Keshava and Bala crushed
Chanura and Andhra. They brought down Ugrasena's evil-souled
son[974] and his younger brother. The tasks accomplished by the lion
among the Yadus are extremely difficult, even for the gods. Where
is the other man who is capable of undertaking the other tasks
that Keshava has done? Shouri has brought a wealth of riches here
for you and, earlier, even the likes of Prahlada, Bali and Shambara
could not accumulate anything like this. He is the one who attacked
the daityas Mura and Panchajana. He crossed over a range of
mountains and slew Nisunda and his followers. He killed Bhouma
Naraka, who had seized the auspicious earrings. Amidst the gods
in heaven, Keshava earned great fame. Resorting to the strength of
Krishna's arms, you are devoid of sorrow, fear and obstructions.
O Yadavas! Without any anger, perform many kinds of sacrifices.

[973] The wielder of pinaka, Shiva.
[974] Kamsa.

The intelligent Krishna has performed a great task for the gods. I have told you what is beneficial and do this quickly. May you be fortunate. O best among the Yadus! I will attentively do whatever you desire. I am established in you and you are established in me. These are the words conveyed by the chastiser of Paka to Krishna. Pleased, the best among the gods has sent me and I am also content. Wherever there is humility, prosperity exists there. Wherever there is prosperity, good behaviour exists there. Wherever the great-souled Krishna exists, good behaviour, humility and prosperity are always present."'

Chapter 97

'Narada said, "He destroyed Mura's noose and killed Nisunda and Naraka. He again made the route towards the city of Pragjyotisha peaceful. Through the twang of his bow and the roar of Panchajanya, Shouri terrified kings who challenged him in battle. Keshava, bull among the Vrishnis, swiftly abducted Rukmini, who was protected by those from the southern regions, with battle formations that were as large as the clouds. The wielder of the conch shell, chakra and mace, who was on a chariot that was as radiant as the sun and roared like clouds, obtained the daughter of Bhoja[975] as his queen. He vanquished Ahvriti[976] in Jaruthi, Kratha and Shishupala. In his rage, he killed Indradyumna and the yavana Kasheruman. The one who wields a firm bow destroyed Salva, the lord of Soubha, and Soubha. With his chakra, Purushottama shattered thousands of mountains. Pundarikaksha brought down Dyumatsena. In the twinkling of an eye, the tiger among men went to the summit of Mount Mahendra and slew Ravana's followers, who roamed around fearlessly there. On the banks of the Iravati, the great Bhoja, the wielder of the Sharnga bow, killed Gopati and Talaketu, who were like the fire and the sun in battle. In

[975] Meaning Bhishmaka.
[976] The Mahabharata refers to him as Ahuti.

Akshaprapatana, Krishna brought down the danavas Nimi[977] and
Hamsa and destroyed their kingdoms. The great-souled Keshava
burnt down Varanasi. He slew the king of Kashi and his relatives
and destroyed his kingdom. Krishna, the performer of extraordinary
deeds, used arrows with drooping tufts to defeat Yama in a battle
and brought back Indrasena's son. Having reached the summit of
Lohita, Krishna defeated Varuna, the immensely strong lord of the
ocean, along with all the aquatic creatures. He went to the great
Indra's abode and performed an unthinkable task. He seized the
Parijata tree, protected by the great-souled gods, from Indra of the
gods. Janardana killed all the kings from Pandya, Poundra, Matsya,
Kalinga and Vanga. Having slain one hundred and one great-
souled kings in battle, the intelligent one obtained the beautiful
Gandhari[978] as his queen. In that way, in Kunti's presence, the lord
Madhusudana played with the wielder of the Gandiva[979] and defeated
him. Purushottama defeated Drona, Drona's son, Kripa, Karna,
Bhimasena,[980] Suyodhana and all their assembled followers. Desiring
to accomplish what was agreeable to Babhru,[981] the lord, the wielder
of the conch shell, chakra and sword abducted the daughter of the
king of Souvira. For the sake of Venudari, Purushottama conquered
the entire earth, with all its horses, chariots and elephants. In an
earlier body, Bhoja Hari Madhava obtained energy and strength
through austerities and won the three worlds from Bali. Along
the road towards the city of Pragjyotisha, the danavas attacked
him with thunder, lightning, clubs and summits of mountains
and tried to terrify him with the threat of death. The immensely
strong Krishna defeated Bana, the immensely brave and supremely
prosperous son of Bali, along with his followers. The mighty-armed
and immensely strong Janardana killed Kamsa's advisers—Pitha,

[977] In non-Critical versions, this name is written as Dimbha.
[978] Not to be confused with Dhritarashtra's wife.
[979] Arjuna. This is the straight translation, with some contest between
Krishna and Arjuna. In a convoluted translation, one can interpret this to
mean that Krishna ensured that Arjuna was victorious.
[980] This is incongruous. Non-Critical versions say Bhishma, which fits
better.
[981] Another name for Akrura.

Paithika and Asiloma. The tiger among men, the slayer of enemies, killed the immensely illustrious Jambha, Airavata and Virupa. In the water, Pundarikaksha vanquished the greatly energetic Kaliya, lord of the serpents, and despatched him to the ocean. Hari, tiger among men, defeated Vaivasvata Yama and brought Sandipani's dead son back to life. In this way, the mighty-armed one chastised all the evil-souled ones. He slew Bhouma Naraka and seized the bejewelled earrings. To bring pleasure to the one with the vajra in his hand, he gave these to the mother of the gods. In this fashion, the lord Krishna, the immensely illustrious lord of all the worlds, caused terror among the daityas, who tried to create fear among the gods. After establishing dharma in the mortal world, performing an infinite number of tasks for the gods and observing sacrifices and rites with copious quantities of dakshina, he will return to his own abode. The immensely illustrious Krishna will bring about the end of the beautiful and prosperous Dvaraka through some reeds, make it merge into his own self and submerge in the ocean. Dvaraka is full of many jewels and is marked with hundreds of sanctuaries[982] and sacrificial altars. With all its groves, it will be sent to Varuna's abode. Those who know take it to be like the sun god's abode. However, abandoned by Vasudeva, the wielder of the Sharnga bow, it will be flooded by the ocean. Among gods, asuras and men, there has not been, nor will there ever be, a resident of the city who is Madhusudana's equal. Vishnu Narayana is himself the moon and the sun. In this way, he will bring about what has been ordained for the Dasharhas. He is immeasurable. He is uncontrollable. He is under his own control and goes wherever he wishes. Like a child playing with toys, he always amuses himself with creatures. We are incapable of gauging the mighty-armed Madhusudana. He is supreme among the supreme and there is nothing other than his universal form. He should be praised in hundreds of ways and in hundreds and thousands of ways. No one has ever been able to see an end to his deeds. With Samkarshana as an aide, in childhood and middle age, Pundarikaksha has performed such deeds. The great

[982] *Chaityas*. The word chaitya has several meanings—sacrificial shed, temple, altar, sanctuary and a tree that grows along the road.

yogi, Vyasa, is immensely intelligent and can see everything directly. Because of his foresight, he possesses foresight and he spoke about all this long ago.'"

Vaishampayana continued, 'Using the great Indra's words, the rishi praised Govinda in this way. Worshipped by all the Yadus, Narada then returned to heaven. As they deserved and following the proper rites, Pundarikaksha Govinda Madhusudana then gave away his riches to the Vrishnis and the Andhakas. Having obtained these riches, the great-souled Yadavas resided in the city of Dvaraka. Following the rituals, they performed rites and sacrifices and gave away copious amounts of dakshina.'

Chapter 98

Janamejaya said, 'O illustrious one! Among the thousands of his wives, eight are spoken about. Tell me about the offspring that he had through these eight.'

Vaishampayana replied, 'It is generally said that all the eight queens had children. All these offspring were brave. I will tell you about his sons. Listen. Rukmini, Satyabhama, the queen who was Nagnajit's daughter, Sudatta Shaibya, Lakshmana of the beautiful smiles, Mitravinda, Kalindi, Pouravi Jambavati and Subhima Madri.[983] Hear about Rukmini's children. Pradyumna was born first and he was the son who killed Shambara. The second was Charudeshna, who was a maharatha and a lion among the Vrishnis. There were also Charubhadra, Bhadracharu, Sudamshtra, Druma, Sushena, Charugupta, Charuvinda and Charuman. The youngest was Charubahu and there was a daughter named Charumati. Satyabhama gave birth to sons named Bhanu, Bhimaratha, Kshupa, Rohita, Diptiman, Tamrajaksha and Jalantaka. Through the one who has

[983] These are the names of the eight wives and the sentence is left incomplete. This list causes more problems, with nine names rather than eight. More importantly, Sudatta seems to be equated with Shaibya, Subhima with Madri and Jambavati's name seems to be Pouravi. None of this fits.

Garuda on his standard, four sisters were born to these. Jambavati
gave birth to a son named Samba and he was an ornament in the
field of battle. She also had sons named Mitravan and Mitravinda[984]
and a daughter named Mitravati. Know that Mitravaha and Sunitha
were the sons of Nagnajit's daughter. There were also sons named
Bhadrakara and Bhadravinda and a daughter named Bhadravati.
Samgramjit was born to Sudatta Shaibya and so were Satyajit,
Senajit and the brave Sapatnajit. The sons of Subhima Madri were
Vrikashva, Vrikanivritti and the prince Vrikadipti. Now hear about
Lakshmana's offspring. She gave birth to Gatravan, Gatragupta and
the valiant Gatravinda, along with a younger sister named Gatravati.
Kalindi had sons named Ashruta and Shrutasattama. Madhusudana
gave Ashruta to Shrutasena.[985] Hrishikesha gave his wife this son
and happily said, "For an eternity, he will be the heir to both of
you."[986] The son born through Brihati was known as Gada.[987] The
son through Shaibya was known as Angada and she also gave birth
to Kumuda and Shveta and a daughter named Shveta.[988] Chitrasena's
sons were Agavaha, Sumitra, Shuchi, Chitraratha and Chitrasena[989]
and her daughters were Chitra and Chitravati. Vanastamba gave
birth to Stamba and Stambavana. Upasanga had sons named Vajra
and Sukshipra. Koushiki's son was Sutasoma.[990] Youdhishthiri had
sons named Yudhishthira,[991] Kapali and Garuda and they were
colourful in fighting.

'O supreme among kings![992] Through the princess of Vidarbha,
Pradyumna had a son named Aniruddha. In battles, this warrior

[984] Not to be confused with Krishna's wife Mitravindaa.

[985] This is another wife, Shrutasenaa, whose name has not been
mentioned earlier.

[986] That is, Kalindi and Shrutasena.

[987] Not to be confused with Krishna's younger brother.

[988] That is, Shvetaa.

[989] The mother was Chitrasenaa and the son was Chitrasena.

[990] This wife's name is stated as Somaa.

[991] Obviously not to be confused with the Pandava Yudhishthira.

[992] This is addressed to Janamejaya and we have corrected the text
a bit. As stated, the text describes Pradyumna as supreme among kings,
which can't be right.

had a deer on his standard. Through Revati, Baladeva had the sons Nishatha and Ulmuka. These brothers were supreme among men and were like the gods. Shouri[993] had two other wives—Sutanu and Narachi. Poundra and Kapila were Vasudeva's sons. Narachi gave birth to Kapila and Sutanu's son was Poundra. Between the two, Poundra became a king and Kapila left for the forest. The immensely strong Vasudeva[994] had a brave son through Turya. His name was Jara and he was best among archers, becoming the lord of the nishadas. Through Samba, Kashya obtained a spirited son named Suparshva. Aniruddha had a son named Sanu and Sanu's son was Vajra. Vajra's son was Prativaha and Sucharu was Prativaha's son. The youngest of the descendants of Vrishni, Anamitra, had a son named Shini. Shini's son was Satyavak and Satyavak's son was the maharatha Satyaka. Satyaka had the brave son known as Yuyudhana.[995] Yuyudhana's son was Asanga and Asanga's son was Bhumi. Bhumi's son was Yugandhara. Thus ends the description of the lineage.'

Chapter 99

Janamejaya said, 'You have earlier spoken about Pradyumna, the slayer of Shambara. How was he born and how did he kill Shambara? Please tell me.'

Vaishampayana replied, 'Through Rukmini, Vasudeva had a son named Pradyumna. He was firm in his vows and prosperous and desirable. He was as handsome as the god of love.[996] Before seven nights were over, in the night, Kalashambara stole Krishna's infant child from the chamber where he had been delivered. Krishna knew about this. However, he followed the maya practised by the gods and did not restrain the danava, who was invincible in battle. The great asura was under the subjugation of death and following

---

[993] Krishna.
[994] Krishna's father.
[995] Also known as Satyaki.
[996] Kama.

his own maya, seized him in both his hands and went away to his own city. He had a wife named Mayavati. Because of her own maya, she was pretty and possessed beauty and the qualities. However, she was without a child. Goaded by destiny, the danava gave Vasudeva's son to his beloved queen, as if he was her own son. The danava lady was overcome with affection for him. The lotus-eyed one reared Krishna's son and imparted all her knowledge of maya to him. When he became a youth, Pradyumna looked like the god of love. He became accomplished in the use of all weapons and also in what brought pleasure to women. The beautiful Mayavati desired the handsome one. She glanced at him and smiled at him. She sought to tempt him through signs. When the queen desired him, he addressed the one with the beautiful smiles. "Why are you abandoning your maternal instincts and acting in a perverse way? Alas! You possess the fickleness of women and are wicked in conduct. You have abandoned your feelings towards a son and have taken to a path of desire. O amiable one! Why have you deviated from good conduct? I am certainly not your son. O queen! Why are you behaving in this way? I wish to know the truth. It is indeed the case that the nature of women is as fickle as lightning. They desire men, just as clouds desire the summits of mountains. O amiable one! O beautiful one! Tell me whether I am your son or not. I wish to know the truth. Why are you attracted to me?" The timid one was addressed in this way and her senses were afflicted by passion. In private, she spoke these words to her beloved, Keshava's son. "O amiable one! You are not my son, nor is Shambara your father. You are handsome and brave and have been born as a descendant of the Vrishni lineage. You are Vasudeva's son. You are the one who enhances Rukmini's delight. While you were an infant, as soon as you were born, you were abducted on the seventh day, while you lay down on your back as an infant, in the chamber where you were delivered. O brave one! My husband, who possesses strength and valour, abducted you. He trespassed into the great house of Vasudeva, your father, who is like the chastiser of Paka. Shambara abducted you. Your mother is miserable and has been grieving about you since your childhood. O brave one! She is greatly distressed, like Surabhi over her calf. Your father, the one with Garuda on his banner, is greater than Shakra.

He does not know that you have been abducted as an infant and
are here. O handsome one! You are a Vrishni youth. You are not
Shambara's son. O brave one! The danavas do not give birth to sons
like this. Since I have not given birth to you, I desire you. O amiable
one! On beholding your beauty, my heart suffers and is weak. O
handsome one! O Varshneya! You are in my mind and you should
satisfy the desire that is there in my heart. O amiable one! I have
told you about my sentiments. You are not my son. Nor are you
Shambara's son." He heard everything that Mayavati had spoken.

'The son of the wielder of the chakra became angry and called
out to Shambara. Kalashambara was brave and knew about all
kinds of maya. The maya he knew was undecaying in any battle.
However, though he used all this maya, he was slain on the eighth
day of the encounter. The supreme among asuras was killed in
the city of Rikshavanta. Taking the queen Mayavati, he[997] then
went to his father's city. He was swift in his valour and resorted
to maya, travelling through the sky. He reached the beautiful city,
protected by his father's energy. From the sky, the child descended
into Keshava's inner quarters. He was with Mayavati and looked as
handsome as the god of love. When he descended like that, Keshava's
queens were astounded. Some were happy, but others were scared.
He was like Kama and had arrived with his beloved. With happy
faces, they drank him in with their eyes. They saw him walk one
step at a time, face lowered in modesty. All of Krishna's wives were
delighted and overcome with affection. Rukmini loved her son and
had been afflicted by grief. Surrounded by a hundred co-wives, she
saw him and spoke these words, her voice choking with tears. "This
is indeed the son of a blessed woman. He is handsome to behold
and has a long life. In the first bloom of youth, he is like the god
of love. O son! Who is the lady who has been blessed by fortune,
with a living son like you? You are as dark as a cloud. Why have
you come here with your wife? It is evident that my son Pradyumna
would also have been of your age, had he not forcefully been taken
away by Death. Or is it the case that my speculation is not in vain
and you are a son of the Vrishni lineage? I have recognized you

[997] Pradyumna.

through the signs. You are like Janardana without his chakra. Your face, your hair and the ends of your hair are like Narayana's. Your head, chest and arms are like those of the wielder of the plough, my elder brother-in-law. Who are you, standing here? Your body is as radiant as all those of the Vrishni lineage. Behold. Your body is as supreme as that of the divine Narayana." At this time, Krishna suddenly entered. He had heard Narada's words about Shambara's killing. He saw his eldest son, who had been successful and had all the signs of the god of love. Happily, Janardana also saw his daughter-in-law, Mayavati. He swiftly spoke to the queen Rukmini, who was like a goddess. "O queen! This lord who has come here, holding a bow, is your son. He is accomplished in fighting with maya and has killed Shambara. He has destroyed the maya of all those who obstruct the gods. This auspicious and virtuous lady is your son's wife. She has been reared in Shambara's house and is famous by the name of Mayavati. Taking her to be Shambara's wife, you should not be distressed. In ancient times, Manmatha was destroyed and became Ananga.[998] This maiden is Kama's wife. She is the auspicious Rati, desired by Kama. Assuming a form through maya, this auspicious one confounded the daitya. In her youth, this beautiful lady was never under his subjugation. Using her own maya, she assumed a form and engaged with Shambara. This beautiful one is my son's wife and your daughter-in-law. This pretty one will help the one who is loved by the worlds.[999] Let my daughter-in-law enter the house and let her be worshipped. For a long time, your son had remained perished. Now that he has returned, love him.'"

Chapter 100

Vaishampayana said, 'In the same month when Shambara, who wished to destroy himself, abducted Pradyumna, Jambavati

---

[998] Manmatha or Kama is the god of love. He was burnt down by Shiva's rage and became Ananga, the one without a body.

[999] Pradyumna.

gave birth to Samba. Since childhood, Rama taught him to show respect and all the Vrishnis respected him, just after Rama. All the enemies who lived in the border regions had been killed. As soon as he was born, Krishna entered that auspicious city, like an immortal entering Shakra's garden. On witnessing the prosperity of the Yadavas, Vasava disliked the prosperity he himself had obtained. Because of their fear of Janardana, the kings[1000] did not find any peace either. After some time, all the kings assembled for Duryodhana's sacrifice in the city of Varanasahvya.[1001] They heard about the prosperity of Madhava Janardana and his sons and about the city of Dvaravati, nestled along the shores of the ocean. All the kings on earth sent messengers and made peace with him. Wishing to see Hrishikesha's prosperity, they went to Krishna's house. There were all those who followed Dhritrarashtra, with Duryodhana at the forefront. There were Dhrishtadyumna and the other kings, with the Pandavas at the forefront. There were Pandyas, Cholas, lords from Kalinga, Bahlikas, Dravidas, Shakas and kings who were protected by eighteen akshouhinis. They arrived at the city of the Yadavas, protected by Govinda's arms. Those lords entered their own camps, which surrounded Mount Raivataka on all sides for a stretch of one yojana. With the bulls among the Yadavas, the prosperous and lotus-eyed Hrishikesha emerged and approached those lords among men. Amidst all those lords among men, the slayer of Madhu, best among the Yadus, stood out, like the moon in the autumn sky. Krishna welcomed them according to status and according to age and seated himself on a golden throne. The kings also sat down in diverse places. Those lords among men seated themselves on colourful thrones and seats. That assemblage of the Yadavas and the lords among men dazzled, like an assembly of the gods and the asuras in Brahma's abode. While Krishna looked on, in that meeting of the Yadus and the kings, wonderful stories were recounted.

'At this time, with a roar like that of the clouds, the wind began to blow. Lightning flashed and it was as if a tumultuous and terrible

---

[1000] Enemy kings.
[1001] Hastinapura.

day had arrived. Shattering the clouds that were like a bad day,
Narada appeared. There was a veena in his hand and his hair was
matted. As resplendent as a fire, he descended in the middle of the
kings. Narada was like the flames of a fire. The handsome sage was
Shakra's friend. When Narada, bull among sages, descended on
the ground, the giant clouds that were like the signs of a bad day
disappeared. It is as if he submerged himself into the midst of an
ocean that was made out of the kings. The undecaying sage spoke to
the best of the Yadus,[1002] who was seated. "O Purushottama! Among
all the gods, you alone are extraordinary. O mighty-armed one! You
are blessed. There is no one like you in the worlds." Hearing this,
the lord smiled and replied to the sage. "I am extraordinary and
blessed because of the dakshina I receive." Thus addressed in the
middle of the kings, the best among sages said, "O Krishna! You
have said enough. I am going wherever I came from." The kings
saw him start to leave. They had not understood the secret mantra
spoken by the lord of the world or Narada's words. They said, "O
Madhava! Narada said that you were extraordinary and blessed and
you told him that this was because of the dakshina. We have not
understood the great and divine words of the mantra. O Krishna! If
we deserve to hear this, we desire to know the truth about this." At
this, Krishna told all those bulls among kings, "This can be heard
and the brahmana Narada will tell you about it. O Narada! Tell the
kings about what they desire to hear. Tell them the truth about your
question and the meaning in my words of reply." He[1003] sat down on
a sparkling seat decortated with gold and spoke about his powers.
"O best among men who have assembled here! Listen. This question
is about the greatness of someone who has enabled me to cross over
to the other side. On one occasion, I was on the banks of the Ganga,
the guest of a person who bathes thrice a day. The night was over and
the sun could be seen. I was roaming around, alone. I saw a tortoise
whose body was made out of two shells. It possessed the complexion
of a mountain peak. In every direction, the radius of its circumstance
was one yojana. It possessed four legs. It was wet and smeared with

[1002] Krishna.
[1003] Narada.

mud. The tortoise was shaped like my veena and its shell was as tough as an elephant's hide. I touched the one who roams around in the water with my hand and said, 'O tortoise! It is my view that you possess a wonderful body and are blessed. Throughout, your body is covered with a shell that cannot be penetrated. Without any fear and without any kinds of thoughts, you roam around in the water.' The tortoise that roams around in the water spoke to me, as if it was a man. 'O sage! What is extraordinary about me? O lord! Why should I be blessed? The river Ganga is blessed. What can be more amazing than that? There are ten thousand creatures like me roaming around in the water.' Curious, I presented myself before the river Ganga and said, 'O best among rivers! You are blessed. You are always wonderful to behold. Inside you, there are many predatory aquatic creatures with gigantic bodies. You possess pools and head towards the ocean. You protect the abodes of ascetics.'"'

Vaishampayana continued, 'The brahmana Narada was loved by the gods, the gandharvas and Shakra. On hearing this, Ganga assumed a bodily form and replied to him. "O best among brahmanas! I am not blessed. Nor is my form extraordinary in any way. You are established in the truth. You have vexed me with your words. In this world, the most extraordinary object is the ocean. O brahmana! It is blessed. Like me, hundreds of wide rivers go there."

'Narada continued, "Hearing the words of the one with the three courses,[1004] I presented myself before the ocean and said, 'O great ocean! You are indeed extraordinary in the worlds. You are blessed. O lord of the waters! You are the origin of all aquatic creatures. The rivers that nurture the worlds convey their water to you. These wives,[1005] revered by the worlds, come here.' Stirred by the wind, the waves rose up from the surface of the water. Thus addressed, the ocean replied to me in these words. 'O supreme among brahmanas! The gods and the gandharvas do not regard me as wonderful. O sage! The earth provides me a foundation and it is blessed. With the exception of the earth, what is supremely wonderful in this world?' The ocean indeed possessed the earth as a foundation. On hearing

---

[1004] Ganga, flowing in heaven, on earth and in the nether regions.
[1005] Of the ocean.

the ocean's words, I was overcome with curiousity. I spoke to the earth, the refuge of the universe. 'O earth! O beautiful one! You are the origin of all creatures. You are blessed. With your immense forgiveness, you are extraordinary among creatures. You truly sustain the worlds and are the origin of humans. Forgiveness was born from you. Those who head to heaven commit their acts on you.' At these words of praise spoken by me, she was ashamed. Discarding her natural patience, she replied to me. 'O one who likes fights and dissension! The gods and the gandharvas do not regard me in this way. I am not blessed. Nor am I wonderful. My fortitude is like that of others. O best among brahmanas! These mountains, which hold me up, are blessed. Since they act like bridges for the worlds, they are seen to be blessed.' Because of the earth's words, I presented myself before the mountains and said, 'O those who hold up the earth! You are seen to be blessed and extremely wonderful. All of you are the stores of jewels—gold, the best among gems and minerals. You will remain eternally on earth.' Hearing my words, the best among mountains, decorated with forests, spoke these words of assurance. 'O brahmana rishi! We are not blessed. Nor are we wonderful. Brahma Prajapati is blessed. He is wonderful, even among the gods.' Therefore, I presented myself before the four-faced Svayambhu, the god who is the creator of the worlds. I lowered my face and progressively bowed down before him.[1006] When I finished speaking to the preceptor of the world and the one who had created himself, I said, 'O illustrious one! You are extraordinary and blessed. I do not see any other creature who is your equal. Everything, mobile and immobile, has been generated from you. O lord of the gods! The gods, the danavas, the mortals in the worlds, every other kind of creature with senses and a body, and everything else has originated from you. The gods have indeed resulted from you. You are the eternal god of the gods. That is the reason you are the creator and the origin of the worlds.' The illustrious Brahma, the grandfather of the worlds, replied, 'O Narada! Why are you speaking to me in these words, addressing me

---

[1006] The progressively suggests that Narada bowed down before each of the four faces in turn.

as blessed and extraordinary? The Vedas are supremely wonderful. The Vedas are blessed. The truth and vision of the Vedas sustain the worlds. My view is that the truth exists in the Rig Veda, the Sama Veda, the Yajur Veda and the Atharva Veda. O brahmana! Know that I am pervaded by them and that I am sustained by them.' Hearing Parameshthi's words and urged by Svayambhu, my mind turned towards a detailed exposition of the Vedas. Because of Svayambhu's words, I presented myself before the four Vedas. Honouring them with mantras and words, I said, 'You are blessed. You are auspicious. You are always wonderful and famous. Prajapati said that you are the foundation for all the brahmanas. Svayambhu has settled the question about who is supreme in this world. In learning or in austerities, there is nothing that is superior to you.' The Vedas stood before me and replied in these words. 'The sacrifices performed by those who are devoted to the atman are extraordinary and blessed. O Narada! We have been created by the creator for sacrifices. Therefore, sacrifices are superior to us and we are not under our own control. The Vedas are superior to Svayambhu, but that supreme objective is superior to them too.' At this, I spoke to the sacrifices, with the fire that burn in households as the foremost. 'O sacrifices! Your energy is indeed seen to be supreme. Those are the words of Brahma, repeated to me by the Vedas. In this world, I cannot think of anything more extraordinary than you. You are blessed, because you keep the brahmanas under your control. You are the ones who satisfy the fire and it is through you that all the gods obtain their shares and are satisified, just as the maharshis are with mantras.' After I had spoken these words, *agnishtoma* and the other sacrifices, with all the sacrificial altars and stakes, spoke these excellent words to me. 'O sage! The expressions extraordinary and blessed are not appropriate for us. The supreme wonder is Vishnu and he is our supreme destination. Everything that is offered as oblations into the sacred fire and is consumed by us is given to Pundarikaksha, who is an embodiment of the worlds.' My destination is also Vishnu and I descended on earth to see him. I have seen Vishnu, surrounded by all of you. O kings! In the midst of all of you, I told him, 'O Janardana! You are extraordinary. You are blessed.' With dakshina, he gave an appropriate response to my words and thus my words were rendered complete. All the sacrifices, with dakshina, have Vishnu as a destination. With the dakshina, my question was answered. What was initially stated by the tortoise thus progressively came to this. With the dakshina, all the words terminated in that being. This is the decisive answer to what you asked me. I have told you everything. I will now return to wherever I have come from.'''

Vaishampayana continued, 'When Narada had departed for heaven, all the lords of the earth were astounded. With their soldiers and their mounts, they returned to their own kingdoms. With the Yadus, who were like the fire, the brave Janardana, bull among the Yadus, entered his own residence.'

Chapter 101

Janamejaya said, 'O supreme among brahmanas! I wish to again hear about the supreme greatness of the mighty-armed Krishna, the lord of the universe. I am not yet satisfied with hearing about the great-souled and intelligent one's deeds, as can be ascertained from the Puranas.'

Vaishampayana replied, 'Even if I speak for one hundred years, I am incapable of describing all his powers. O great king! However, hear about the supreme Govinda. When Bhishma was lying down on his bed of arrows, he urged Bibhatsu,[1007] the wielder of Gandiva, to describe Keshava's greatness. O great king! O Kourava! In the midst of the kings, he spoke to his elder brother Yudhishthira, who had vanquished his enemies. Listen to this.

'Arjuna said, "On an earlier occasion, with my soldiers, I had gone to Dvaraka to visit my allies.[1008] Worshipped by the best of Bhojas, Vrishnis and Andhakas, I lived there. During that time, on one occasion, the mighty-armed Madhusudana, with dharma in his soul, followed the rites mentioned in the sacred texts and initiated

---

[1007] Arjuna's name.
[1008] In the sense of matrimonial allies.

himself in a vow that lasted for a day. While he was thus initiated in that vow and seated, a supreme brahmana came to Krishna and exclaimed, 'Save me.' The brahmana said, 'O lord! You have the right to protect me. Protect me. One-fourth of the fruits that come from following the dharma of protection go to the protector.' Vasudeva replied, 'O best among brahmanas! Do not be frightened. O unblemished one! What will I save you from? O fortunate one! Tell me the truth and I will act, even if it is extremely difficult to do so.' The brahmana said, 'O mighty-armed one! O lord! My sons die the instant they are born. O Krishna! Three have already died and you must save the fourth. My brahmana wife is in the delivery chamber now and protection must be ensured there. O Janardana! Act so that my offspring does not die.' At this, Govinda told me, 'I have initiated myself in a vow. However, it is one's task to protect a brahmana in every possible situation.' O supreme among men! On hearing Krishna's words, I replied, 'O Govinda! Engage me. I will protect the brahmana from fear.' O lord of men! Hearing this, Janardana smiled and replied, 'Who will protect you?' I was ashamed. Knowing that I was ashamed, Janardana again said, 'O best among Kouravas! If you are capable of protecting, go. The maharatha Vrishnis and Andhakas will advance in front of you, with the exception of the mighty-armed Rama and the immensely strong Pradyumna.' I was surrounded by a great army of Vrishni soldiers. Placing the brahmana in front, I left with these soldiers."'

Chapter 102

'Arjuna said, "O descendant of the Bharata lineage! At an auspicious moment, we reached that village. All the mounts were exhausted and arrangements were made for staying. O descendant of the Kuru lineage![1009] I dwelt in the middle of the village, with the Vrishni soldiers spread out on every side of the habitation. The directions were ablaze and flaming birds and

[1009] Yudhishthira.

animals that shrieked in harsh tones scared and distressed me by the noise they made. The sun had turned pale and the twilight assumed the complexion of a red hibiscus. Large meteors showered down and made the earth tremble. I saw that large and terrible meteors were showering down, making the body hair stand up. The people were anxious and I commanded that all the arrangements should be made. Yuyudhana was at the forefront of the Vrishni and Andhaka maharathas. All of them yoked and readied their chariots and so did I. When midnight had passed, the brahmana was weak with fear. Scared, he came to me and spoke these words. 'The time has come for my brahmana wife to deliver. Remain steady and attentive, so that we are not deceived.' In a short while, I heard a piteous and distressed lamentation from the brahmana's house. 'Being taken away. Being taken away.' Then, I heard the child's cry from the sky, 'Alas!' Though he was being taken away, I did not see the rakshasa. O father![1010] We showered arrows in all the directions and blocked all the directions. Nevertheless, that child was taken away. When the infant child was abducted, the brahmana cried piteously. He spoke to me in harsh and terrible words. The Vrishnis were bereft of their senses and did not know what to do. The brahmana specially addressed me. 'You told me that you would protect. Nevertheless, you did not protect my son. O evil-minded one! Hear the other words that I have to say and you deserve them. Krishna is infinite in his intelligence and you always seek to rival him. Had Govinda been here, this unfortunate incident wouldn't have happened. O foolish one! A protector obtains one-fourth of the fruits of dharma that result from the act of protection. But a person who fails to protect obtains a share of the sin. You pledged that you would protect. However, you were incapable of protecting. This Gandiva of yours is not invincible. Your prowess and fame are also not inviolate.' I departed without saying anything to the brahmana. With the sons of the Vrishnis and the Andhakas, I went to the immensely radiant Krishna. Having gone to Dvaravati, I saw the slayer of Madhu. Govinda noticed that I was ashamed and tormented by grief. On seeing that I was ashamed, Madhava comforted me. He reassured

---

[1010] The word used is tata.

the brahmana and spoke these words. He told Daruka, 'Yoke the horses, Sugriva, Shaibya, Meghapushpa and Balahaka.'[1011] Krishna Shouri made Daruka descend and asked me to be the charioteer, asking the brahmana to climb on to the chariot. O bull among the Kourava lineage! Krishna, the brahmana and I left for the northern direction, the one that belongs to Soma.""

Chapter 103

'Arjuna said, "We crossed over clusters of mountains, rivers and lakes and I saw the ocean, the abode of makaras. The ocean himself arose and welcomed Janardana, hands joined in salutation. Offering arghya, he asked, 'What can I do for you?' Accepting the worship, Janardana replied, 'O lord of the male and female rivers! I desire a path for my chariot.' The ocean joined his hands in salutation and spoke to the one who has Garuda on his standard. 'O illustrious one! Be pacified. If I give you a path, others will also proceed along that same route. O Janardana! Earlier, I have been established by you as someone who is fathomless. If you make me shallow, it will be a path that can be travelled on. Others will also proceed, including kings who are intoxicated because of their insolence. O Govinda! Bearing this in mind, do whatever is beneficial.' Vasudeva replied, 'O ocean! For the sake of the brahmana and for my sake, act in accordance with my words. With my exception, no other man will ever be able to transgress you.' Should he continue to be an obstruction, the ocean was scared of being cursed. Therefore, the ocean again spoke to Janardana and agreed. 'O father![1012] O Keshava! I am drying up and providing a path for you to traverse on. Proceed along that, with your chariot, your charioteer and your standard.' Vasudeva replied, 'Earlier, I have given you the boon that you will never dry up. Men will never know about the many kinds of riches that are stored inside you. O

[1011] The names of Krishna's horses. Daruka was Krishna's charioteer.
[1012] The word used is tata.

virtuous one! Stupefy the waters, so that I can pass on my chariot. A man will never be able to discern any sign of your jewels.' The ocean agreed and the stupefied waters retreated. We proceeded along a ground that was radiant with the hue of jewels.

'"Having crossed over the ocean, we crossed over Uttara Kuru. In a short while, we passed over Gandhamadana too. Seven mountains presented themselves before Keshava—they were named Jayanta, Vaijayanta, Nila, Mount Rajata, the giant Meru, Kailasa and Indrakuta. They were many-complexioned and radiant and were wonderful in many other ways. They presented themselves before Govinda and asked, 'What shall we do?' Madhusudana welcomed them back in the prescribed way. They prostrated themselves before Hrishikesha, who spoke to them. 'Grant me a passage now, so that my chariot can proceed along that.' O bull among the Bharata lineage! On hearing Krishna's words, the mountains agreed. They gave him the desired path. They then vanished and this seemed even more extraordinary to me. Without any obstructions, the chariot proceeded, like the sun through a net of clouds. O unblemished one! However, the horses dragged the chariot along with difficulty. There was a darkness that was like mud and one could only feel one's way through touch. The darkness that arose was like a mountain. O king! On confronting this, the horses stood stationary, unable to move. At this, Govinda shattered the darkness with his chakra. The sky could again be seen and so could the supreme path for the chariot. Having emerged from that darkness, I could see the sky again. I regained my consciousness and my fear was dispelled. O supreme among eloquent ones! I next saw a blazing energy. It pervaded all the worlds and stationed itself, in the form of an embodied being. Hrishikesha entered that blazing mass of energy. I, and the excellent brahmana, remained on the chariot. In an instant, the supreme lord, Krishna, emerged, carrying with him the four sons of the brahmana. Janardana gave all these sons to the brahmana, the three who had been abducted earlier and the newborn son. O father! O lord! O king! On seeing the sons again, the brahmana was delighted. I was also supremely delighted and astounded. O bull among the Bharata lineage! After this, all of us, including the brahmana's sons, returned the way we had gone.

O supreme among kings! In a short while, we reached Dvaraka again. It was surprising that we returned before half a day was over. The immensely illustrious Krishna fed the brahmana and his sons. He satisfied them with riches and sent them home.'"

Chapter 104

' Arjuna said, "Having been successful, Krishna fed many hundreds of brahmanas who were like rishis. With them, I, and all the Vrishnis and Bhojas, also ate. O descendant of the Bharata lineage! We conversed about divine and wonderful accounts. When these tales were over, I approached Janardana. I asked Krishna about what had happened and about what I had seen. 'O lotus-eyed one! How did you manage to stupefy the ocean? O Achyuta! How could you create a path through the mountains? How could you shatter the terrible darkness of the clouds with your chakra? You then entered a supreme energy. Where did that come from? O lord! Why were the children taken away? After that, how did you make the long journey brief? How did we manage to go and return in such a short while? O Keshava! Please tell me everything about what happened.'

"'Vasudeva replied, 'That great-souled one[1013] stole the children so that he could see me. He knew that Krishna would do this for the sake of a brahmana and not otherwise. O best among the Bharata lineage! You saw a mass of extraordinary brahman energy. That was I and that was my eternal energy. O descendant of the Bharata lineage! That is my supreme nature, manifest and unmanifest. O supreme among the Bharata lineage! In this world, those who enter that are emancipated. O Partha! That is the supreme destination of those who practise sankhya, of yogis and ascetics. That is the state of the supreme brahman and that divides up everything in the universe. O descendant of the Bharata lineage! You should know that the mass of energy is me. I am the stupefied water of the ocean.

[1013] The mass of energy.

I am the one who stupefied the water. I am the seven mountains that
were progressively seen by you. I am the dense mass of darkness and
I am the one who shattered them. I am the destiny for all creatures. I
am spoken of as dharma. The four varnas have originated from me
and so have the four ashramas. All the four directions are nothing
but four different aspects of my soul. O descendant of the Bharata
lineage! Know that I am the one who created the four Vedas.'"

'Arjuna said, "O illustrious one! O lord of all the creatures.
O lord! I wish to comprehend you. O Purushottama! I am seeking
refuge with you and am asking you. I bow down before you."

'"Vasudeva replied, 'O descendant of the Bharata lineage! O
Pandava! Know that Brahma, brahmanas, austerities, truth, *ukthyas*
and *brihadrathas*[1014] have originated in me. O mighty-armed one! O
Dhananjaya! I love you and you love me. O unblemished one! You
should know the truth about me and that is the reason I am telling
you this. I am the Yajur, Sama, Rig and Atharva Vedas. O bull
among the Bharata lineage! The rishis, the gods and sacrifices come
from my energy. So do the earth, the wind, space, water, energy
as the fifth, the moon, the sun, days, nights, fortnights, months,
kshapas,[1015] muhurtas, kalas and years. O Partha! The different
kinds of mantras, all the sacred texts and the different kinds of
knowledge that are to be known—all these have originated in me. O
Kounteya! O descendant of the Bharata lineage! Know that creation
and destruction are immersed in me. Existence, non-existence, and
the state that is neither existence nor non-existence—all these are
aspects of my soul.'"

'Arjuna said,[1016] "Pleased with me, Krishna told me all this.
Since then, my mind has always been submerged in Janardana. This
is how I heard about, and witnessed, Keshava's greatness. O Indra

---

[1014] Ukthyas are verses (usually from the Yajur and Sama Vedas) that
are recited, while brihadrathas are verses that are sung.

[1015] Kshapa means night and also means a day of twenty-four hours.
Kshana is a measurement of time, with differing interpretations. A second
or an instant is accurate enough. Muhurta is forty-eight minutes. Kala is a
small unit of time, roughly one minute, though interpretations vary.

[1016] Arjuna is now speaking to Yudhishthira.

among kings! Everything else that you have asked me about is also immersed in Janardana.'"

Vaishampayana continued, 'The best among the Kurus, Dharmaraja Yudhishthira, heard this. In his mind, he worshipped Purushottama Govinda. The king, and all his brothers, were astounded. So were the kings who had assembled there.'

Chapter 105

Janamejaya said, 'O best among brahmanas! I wish to again hear the truth about the immeasurable deeds of the intelligent lion among the Yadus. I have heard that the immensely radiant one performed many deeds, innumerable that were divine and several that were also ordinary. O great sage! I am delighted at hearing about these diverse deeds. O father![1017] You should tell me everything about them.'

Vaishampayana replied, 'I have told you about many wonderful deeds of the great-souled Keshava. O king! Hear about them again. O virtuous one! There is no end to his deeds and I am incapable of recounting them. O tiger among the Bharata lineage! I cannot describe the great-souled one's deeds in detail. O descendant of the Bharata lineage! My words will certainly touch only a bit of them. Vishnu is infinite in his valour and is famous for his generous deeds. O king! I will describe them progressively. Listen with single-minded attention. The intelligent lion among the Yadus resided in Dvaravati. He agitated kings, the foremost among the kings and their kingdoms.[1018] He killed the danava Vichakra, who sought to create dissension among the Yadus. The great-souled one then went to the city of Pragjyotisha. In the midst of the ocean, he slew the evil-souled danava, Naraka. He vanquished Vasava in an encounter and forcefully seized Parijata. In a pool in Lohita, the illustrious one defeated Varuna. Along the southern path, he killed

---

[1017] The word used is tata.
[1018] Kings who were enemies.

Karusha Dantavaktra. When Shishupala completed one hundred
sins, he killed him.[1019] He went to the city of Shonita, protected by
Shankara. Bali's son, Bana, was immensely valorous and possessed
one thousand arms. O great king! He defeated him in a great battle,
but allowed him to remain alive. In the midst of the mountains,
the great-souled one vanquished the fire god. He defeated Salva
in an encounter and brought down Soubha.[1020] He agitated all the
oceans and obtained Panchajanya. He killed Hayagriva and other
immensely strong kings. After Jarasandha was killed, he freed all
the kings. On a chariot, he defeated the king of Gandhara and
abducted his daughter. Deprived of their kingdom, the Pandavas
were afflicted by grief and he protected them. He burnt down
Puruhuta's terrible forest, known as Khandava.[1021] He arranged
for Agni to give Gandiva to Arjuna. O Janamejaya! At the time
of the terrible conflict,[1022] he acted as a messenger. This foremost
among the Yadus made the lineage of the Yadus prosper. In front
of Kunti, he took a pledge about the Pandavas. "When the Bharata
war is over, I will return your sons to you." He freed the immensely
energetic Nriga from a terrible curse.[1023] In a battle, he killed the
one who was famous as Kalayavana. There were two immensely
valourous apes, Mainda and Dvivida. He defeated them in a battle
and also vanquished Jambavat, who was unassailable. O king!
Sandipani's son and your father[1024] had come under Vaivasvata's
subjugation, but he used his energy to bring them back to life. He
fought many terrible battles, leading to the destruction of the best of
men. He slew all those kings and performed extraordinary deeds in
battles. O Janamejaya! I have told you about this earlier.'[1025]

[1019] Described in the Mahabharata.

[1020] Described in the Mahabharata.

[1021] Described in the Mahabharata, Puruhuta is Indra's name.

[1022] The battle of Kurukshetra.

[1023] King Nriga inadvertently donated the same cow to two brahmanas.
He was cursed and became a lizard that lived in a well. Krishna rescued him
from this curse.

[1024] Parikshit.

[1025] A reference to the Mahabharata.

Chapter 106

Janamejaya said, 'O supreme among brahmanas! I have heard the truth about the excellent accounts of the immeasurable deeds performed by the intelligent Vasudeva. You have earlier mentioned the great asura, Bana. O one rich in austerities! I wish to hear about this in detail. How did Vasudeva defeat Bana in a battle? The angry one wished to challenge him[1026] in a duel. How did he escape with his life?'

Vaishampayana replied, 'O king! Hear attentively to the account of the great battle that took place in this world of men between the infinitely energetic Krishna and Bana. Bali's son was insolent in battles and was aided by Rudra and Skanda. However, he was vanquished and allowed to escape with his life. The great-souled Shankara granted him[1027] a boon that he would always be near him and bestowed on him eternal lordship over the ganas.[1028] He went to Rudra, bowed down before him and greeted him. Bali's son asked the following question to the one who has the bull on his standard. "With your support and with my insolent pride and soldiers, I have defeated the gods, the Sadhyas and large numbers of Maruts. They are terrified at their defeat and have lost all hope of vanquishing me. They now dwell happily in the vault of heaven. Therefore, I despair of being able to fight again and do not desire to remain alive any more. If I cannot fight, my possession of these arms[1029] is pointless. Hence, tell me if there is going to a battle again. O god! Without an encounter, I can find no delight. Show me your favours." At this, the illustrious one, with the bull on his standard, laughed. He said, "O Bana! O danava! There will be a battle. Hear about it. O son![1030] Your standard is fixed in its appropriate place. When it is broken, there will be a battle." Having been thus addressed, Bana laughed and was extremely delighted. With a happy face, he fell down at

---

[1026] Krishna.
[1027] Bana.
[1028] Ganas are companions of Shiva.
[1029] The one thousand arms.
[1030] The word used is tata.

his feet and said, "It is good fortune that my possession of one thousand arms will not be in vain. It is through good fortune that, in a battle, I will again defeat the one with one thousand eyes." The eyes of the scorcher of enemies filled with tears of joy. He joined five hundred pairs of hands in salutation and prostrating himself on the ground, worshipped the god.

'Maheshvara said, "Arise! Arise! O brave one! You will obtain an unmatched encounter in a battle, one that befits your arms, your own self and your lineage."'

Vaishampayana continued, 'Bana was thus addressed by the great-souled Tryambaka. He arose with great delight and quickly bowed down before the one with the bull on his banner. Bana, the destroyer of enemy cities, took Shitikantha's[1031] leave and went to his own residence and to the chamber where his giant standard was kept. Seated there, he laughed and spoke to Kumbhanda. "I will tell you what has brought this delight to my mind." He[1032] laughed and spoke to Bana, who was unmatched in battle. "O king! What will you tell me? What will I find agreeable? O excellent one! Your eyes are dilated with wonder and you seem to be overjoyed. What have you got through Shitikantha's favours and Skanda's protection? Has the wielder of the trident instructed that you will obtain the kingdom of the three worlds? Scared of you, will Indra find refuge in the nether regions? Will Diti's sons overcome their fear of Vishnu? Scared of the chakra, they have to reside in abodes in the water. When the one with the Sharnga bow, chakra and mace in his hands is stationed in a supreme battle, will the asuras no longer be scared and terrified of Vishnu? Resorting to your strength, will they be able to give up the nether regions and go somewhere else? Will the great asuras reside where the gods now dwell? O king! Your father, Bali, has been bound down because of Vishnu's strength. Abandoning that bondage in the water, will he get his kingdom back again? O father![1033] Will we see your father, Virochana's son, adorned in divine garlands and garments and smeared with celestial

---

[1031] Shiva's name.
[1032] Kumbhanda.
[1033] The word used is tata.

paste? O lord! Earlier, the three worlds were taken away in three strides. Having defeated all the residents of heaven, will we again get them back? The god Narayana possesses a gentle and deep voice and the blare of the conch shell precedes him. He is the conqueror of armies. Will we vanquish him? O father! Is the one with the excellent face, the one with the bull on his banner, pleased with you? Your heart is beating and I notice tears of joy. By satisfying the lord[1034] and through Kartikeya's favours, have you got back all our status on earth?" The bull among men was thus urged by Kumbhanda's words. Bana, supreme among eloquent ones, loved to speak and said the following. "O Kumbhanda! For a long time, I have not had the opportunity to fight. That is what I cheerfully asked the powerful Shitikantha for. 'O extremely great god! I desire a fight. How can I obtain an encounter that will please my mind?' At this, Hara, the god of the gods and the slayer of enemies, laughed for an extremely long time. He then spoke these agreeable words. 'O Bana! You will obtain an extremely great and unmatched encounter. O asura! When your standard, with the peacock on it, breaks, there will be a great battle.' I was extremely delighted with what the illustrious one, the one with the bull on his standard, had said. I bowed my head down before the god and came to you." Having been thus addressed, Kumbhanda spoke to the king. "Alas! O king! I do not find what the god has said to be auspicious." While they were conversing with each other in this way, the upraised standard fell down with great force, struck by Shakra's vajra. The asura saw that the supreme standard had fallen down. Thinking that the battle was at hand, he was greatly delighted.

'Struck by Shakra's vajra, the earth trembled. From the interiors of the earth, rats began to howl. Vasava, the god of the gods, started to shower down. The city of Shonita was filled with blood everywhere.[1035] Shattering the sun, giant meteors fell down on the surface of the ground. Since its own path was obstructed, the sun oppressed the earth. Hundreds and thousands of terrible

---

[1034] Shiva.

[1035] Shonita was the name of Bana's city. Since *shonita* also means blood, there is a pun.

streams of blood descended on sanctuaries and trees and the stars fell down. O lord of the earth! Though it wasn't the right time, the sun was eclipsed by Rahu. Signifying a time for the destruction of the worlds, huge storms manifested themselves. A comet remained stationary in the southern direction. Extremely terrible winds began to blow incessantly. In the evening sky, the sun was covered by clubs with three colours—white and red at the ends and black-necked and tinged with lightning in the centre. Bana's nakshatra at birth was Krittika. A retrograde Angaraka[1036] entered it and seemed to censure it in every possible way. There was a chaitya tree with many branches, worshipped by all the daughters of the great-souled danavas. This fell down on the ground. In this fashion, there were many portents and ill omens. However, Bana, intoxicated with pride and insolence, did not understand the nature of these. Bana's adviser, Kumbhanda, possessed foresight and was conscious of what was likely to happen. He described these many portents.

'Happy, Bana had an excellent drink. Intoxicated with valour, he amused himself with the daitya and danava women. Overcome by thoughts, Kumbhanda went to the king's residence. Having seen these unthinkable omens, he reflected on what they might mean. "The king is evil in his intelligence and intoxicated. The great asura hopes to be victorious. He desires a battle and because of his intoxication, does not see any of these omens. These great portents cannot be false. Will all these portents that have been seen be rendered false? The one with the three eyes[1037] and the valiant Kartikeya are here. Will they help to overcome these taints and will we be able to avoid defeat? Because of the power of these portents, there can be a great destruction. It is my view that these portents will not be rendered false. There is no doubt that these omens will come to pass. Because of the oppression caused by the king, the danavas have been tainted. Bhava, the lord and creator of the universe and of large numbers of gods and danavas, and Kartikeya reside in our city. Bhava always loves Guha[1038] more than his own life. That apart, Bana has always

---

[1036] Mars.
[1037] Shiva.
[1038] Bhava is Shiva and Guha is Kartikeya.

been specially loved by Bhava. Bana is aided by both Bhava and
Kumara. That being the case, who is capable of approaching Bana
in an encounter?" Kumbhanda, who knew about the truth, thought
in this way. The great asura's intelligence was always devoted to
what would ensure benefit. Even if they perform auspicious deeds,
those who obstruct the gods will confront destruction in a battle,
just as Bali was bound up.'

Chapter 107

Vaishampayana said, 'With the goddess,[1039] once Bhava went to
the beautiful banks of a river. The lord sported there with the
beautiful one. In every direction, hundreds of apsaras played. The
lords of the gandharvas were there, in a forest that had flowers
from all the seasons. There were blossoming Parijata and *santanaka*
flowers. In every direction, this fragrance wafted along the banks
of the river. Thousands of flutes, veenas, drums and trumpets were
played and the songs of the apsaras could be heard. Bards, minstrels
and large numbers of apsaras praised the god of the gods, the one
with an excellent garlanded body, attired in red garments. Adopting
the form of the goddess,[1040] Chitralekha, supreme among apsaras,
pleased Bhava and the goddess laughed at this. With beautiful faces
and adopting the form of the goddess, all the apsaras sported with
him and the goddess laughed out loudly at this. In every direction,
there were sounds of amusement and great joy and Bhava was
delighted.

'Bana's beautiful daughter, named Usha, was present there and
on the banks of the river, she saw the god sporting with the goddess.
In Parvati's presence, Usha articulated her desire. "A woman who
sports with her husband is fortunate." Discerning Usha's wish,
the goddess, the daughter of the mountain, gently spoke these
words to Usha, causing her joy. "O Usha! Soon, you will also

[1039] Parvati.
[1040] Parvati.

amuse yourself with your husband, just as Shankara, the slayer of
enemies, is finding pleasure with me, the goddess." When she was
addressed by the goddess in these words, Usha's heart was filled
with thoughts. "When will I amuse myself with my husband?" At
this, the daughter of the Himalayas smiled and spoke these words.
"O Usha! O fortunate one! Listen. This is how the union will come
about. In the palace, in the month of Vaishakha, in the evening of
the twelfth lunar day, the person who will have intercourse with
you in your dreams will become your husband." Surrounded by
maidens, the daughter of the daitya was addressed in this way. She
joyfully retreated and roamed around happily. When day was over,
having played and sported with Uma, all those women went away.
Some left on horses, others on elephants and chariots. Some of them
travelled through the sky. All of them happily returned to their own
cities.

'It became the month of Vaishakha. On the twelfth day of
shuklapaksha, surrounded by large numbers of her friends, the
beautiful one was lying down in the palace. A man arrived in Usha's
dreams and had intercourse with her. Though she wept, because
of the words of the goddess, she was violated. She was violated in
her sleep and became a woman. Covered with blood, she suddenly
woke up in the night and started to weep. On seeing her crying
in this way, Chitralekha,[1041] her friend, was scared. However, in
gentle words, she comforted her about this wonderful incident. "O
Usha! Do not be frightened. Why are you weeping and lamenting?
You are Bali's son's daughter and are also famous. O one with the
beautiful brows! Why should you be frightened? For someone like
you, there is no fear in the worlds. O one with the beautiful thighs!
Since your father destroys the gods in battle, you are the one who
should generate fear. Arise! O fortunate one! Arise! O beautiful
one! Your sorrow is pointless. O one with the beautiful face! In this
residence, there is nothing for you to fear. With all the gods, the
lord of the gods, Shachi's consort, was unsuccessful in invading this
city and and was driven away by your father in an encounter. All
these large numbers of gods are scared of your father in a battle."

[1041] The same as the apsara mentioned earlier.

Usha replied, "I am a virtuous lady and have been violated in this
way. How can I be interested in remaining alive? What will I tell
my father, the enemy of the gods and the slayer of enemies! My
lineage is extremely energetic and I have polluted it in this way.
I think it is better for me to die. It is not desirable that I should
remain alive. I am known as a maiden. Having done this, how can
I be interested in remaining alive? I have been known as a woman
who was the best among the virtuous. However, I have polluted
my lineage and brought disgrace to my family. I have no refuge
now. How can I be interested in remaining alive?" Surrounded by
large numbers of her friends, Usha, the lotus-eyed one, lamented
for a long period of time in this way, her eyes full of tears. With all
her friends, bereft of her senses, she wept like someone who was
without a protector. All of them surrounded Usha, their eyes also
full of tears, and said, "O queen! O one with the beautiful brows! If
something is done with a wicked mind, there may be an auspicious
or inauspicious consequence. However, in your mind, you did not
do anything evil. O fortunate one! Since this intercourse occurred in
your dream, there has been no deviation from your vows. O queen!
There has been no transgression because of this act of intercourse.
It is said on earth that a woman is tainted through a sin that occurs
in one of three ways: the mind, words, and specially through deeds.
O timid one! Your mind is always upright and has not been tainted.
You have always followed brahmacharya. How can you be tainted
by this sin? You were asleep. You are virtuous, pure in sentiments
and spirited. If you have been brought about to this state, there
is no destruction of dharma in that. When a wicked mind first
instigates a person to evil action, it is only then that a person is
wicked. O beautiful one! You are virtuous. You have been born in
a noble lineage. You are beautiful. You are controlled and follow
brahmacharya. Yet, you have been brought about to this state.
Destiny cannot be overcome." Eyes filled with tears, Kumbhanda's
daughter[1042] spoke the following supreme words to the one who
was weeping. "O Usha! While you were thinking about your
husband, the goddess spoke to you, in the presence of the god of

[1042] Chitralekha.

the gods. O beautiful one! Remember those words. In the month of Vaishakha, in the night, on the twelfth day of shuklapaksha, while you are lying down in the palace and weeping, you will be made a woman. That brave person, the slayer of enemies, will become your husband. Recognizing your wish, the goddess had cheerfully told you this. The words spoken by Parvati cannot be false. O one with a face like the moon! That being the case, why are you weeping?" Bana's daughter, the one with the auspicious eyes, was addressed in this way and remembered the words spoken by the goddess. She overcame her sorrow. Usha replied, "O beautiful one! When the goddess was sporting with Bhava, I now remember the words that she spoke. Everything that she said has come true in the grounds of this palace. The wife of the protector of the worlds told me about my husband. The task is to now decide how we find out who he is." Kumbhanda's daughter was skilled in discerning the truth and determining good policy. Having been addressed in this way, she again spoke these words. "O queen! With the exception of you, no one knows the truth about his lineage, his deeds or his manliness. O unblemished one! With the exception of what you saw in your sleep, no one has seen him or heard of him. O timid one! How will we know about the one who gave you that blazing pleasure? O friend! O dark-eyed one! O one who desired intercourse! While you wept, he used his valour to enter the inner quarters and enjoyed you. He cannot be an ordinary person. Otherwise, he would not have been able to single-handedly enter our city. He must be a slayer of enemies. The Adityas, the Vasus, the Rudras and the Ashvins, greatly energetic and terrible in valour, are incapable of entering the city of Shonita. This slayer of enemies has stepped over Bana's head and entered the city of Shonita. He is a hundred times better than they are. O one with the auspicious eyes! Why should a woman who has a husband like that, who is accomplished in fighting, not be interested in remaining alive or enjoying herself? A woman with a husband like this is favoured and blessed. O one who wishes to satisfy her desires! You have obtained this through the favours of Parvati, the goddess. Without any fear, listen to what must be done. One must find out whose son he is, his name and his lineage." Usha, consumed by desire, was addressed in these words.

She affectionately replied to Kumbhanda's daughter, Chitralekha, the apsara, "O friend! O friend! How will we find out?" Immersed in her thoughts, she spoke words that are extremely difficult to utter. "O friend! O beautiful one! Listen to my final words. O lotus-eyed one! If you do not bring my beloved husband here today, I will give up my beloved life. He is beautiful, with eyes like lotus petals. His valour is like that of a crazy elephant." Chitralekha smiled and gently spoke these words to Usha. "O Usha! O beautiful one! O one who is excellent in her vows! I do not understand. How will we know? O friend! However, using my intelligence, this is what we are capable of doing. Listen to my words. That is the way you will obtain what you desire. O friend! O timid one! In the next seven days, I will draw pictures of all the gods, danavas, yakshas, the distinguished ones in powers, beauty and birth, the foremost beings among all those who exist everywhere and the best and famous people in the world of men. I will show them to you through my drawings and you will be able to identify your husband." Having said this, in the next seven days, she drew all their pictures. The beautiful one drew pictures of these best of people.

'Chitralekha spread out the pictures that she had herself drawn and showed them to her friends, especially to Usha. "These are the gods. These are the best among those of the danava lineage. These are the kinnaras, serpents and yakshas. These are all the rakshasas. These are special men among all those who are men. Glance at all of them, in the pictures that I have drawn of them. O friend! I have drawn them. Which is the form of your husband? Recognize the one you saw in your dream." Progressively, the one who was overcome by desire looked at all of them. Having passed over all the Yadus, she saw the descendant of the Yadu lineage. On seeing Aniruddha, her eyes dilated with wonder. She told Chitralekha, "O friend! This is the one who has perpetrated that theft on me. Earlier, when I was lying down in the palace and dreaming, he is the one who violated me. O auspicious one! I know him by his form. Where has this thief come from? O Chitralekha! O beautiful one! Tell me the truth about him. What are his qualities and conduct? O beautiful one! What is his lineage and what is his name?" Chitralekha replied, "This is the grandson of the intelligent Krishna, the protector of the three worlds. O large-eyed one! He is terrible in his valour. He is your husband and he is Pradyumna's son. In valour, there is no one in the three worlds who is his equal. He uproots mountains and uses them to shatter other mountains. Since he is a bull among the Yadus, you are blessed and favoured. The wife of the one with the three eyes has decided well. You have obtained a virtuous husband who is your equal." Usha said, "O large-eyed one! O beautiful one! If this is my husband, an equal of the immortals, swiftly bring him here and save my life." Hearing Usha's words, Chitralekha spoke these words. "O fortunate one! O one with the beautiful smiles! You should listen to my words. O queen! Bana's city is protected in every direction. O timid one! In that way, Dvaraka is especially difficult to penetrate. It is impossible to enter the city of Dvaraka undetected. Protect me and your own self, especially from your father." Usha said, "O friend! Aniruddha's face is like the full moon. If I do not see it today, I will go to Yama's abode. If you know me and if you are affectionate towards me as a friend, listen to what I say. Swiftly go and bring my beloved. Grant me my beloved and grant me my life." Chitralekha replied, "O timid one! I will leave now and enter the city of Dvaraka. I will bring your husband, the extender of the Vrishni lineage, here today." Her words were inauspicious and would signify fear for the danavas. However, having said this, Chitralekha, who possessed the speed of thought, vanished. In a short instant, in three muhurtas, he left the city of Bana and reached Dvaraka, protected by Krishna. It was like the summit of Kailasa, adorned with beautiful palaces. She saw Dvaraka, which was like a star in the firmament.'

Chapter 108

Vaishampayana said, 'In the middle of Dvaraka, adorned with palaces, she saw the house where Pradyumna's son dwelt happily. She swiftly entered that large residence. She saw him amidst the women, like a moon that has just arisen. He was playing and amusing himself with the women, served by them. He was supremely

handsome and was drinking the liquor madhvika. He was seated on
an excellent seat, like Ailavila.[1043] The spirited Chitralekha began
to think. "How will I accomplish my task? How will I remain safe
and perform my duty?" Hidden, the illustrious Chitralekha thought
in this way. The one with the auspicious eyes was invisible because
she shrouded herself, using the knowledge of darkness.[1044] Despite
remaining amidst the women in the palace, she rendered herself
invisible. She seized Pradyumna's son, who was invincible in battle,
and leapt up into the sky. She made him vanish from there. Using
the path frequented by the siddhas and the *charanas*, with the speed
of thought, she suddenly entered the city of Shonita. Surrounded by
her friends in the palace, Usha was astounded to see him. Now that
he had reached, she made him enter her own house. On seeing her
beloved and on her intention having been accomplished, her eyes
dilated with joy. However, the accomplished and beautiful one was
also overcome by fear. She quickly told Chitralekha, "O friend! O
one who is accomplished in all tasks! How will we manage to keep
this act a secret? As long as it is a secret, we are safe. If it comes
out, there will be a threat to our lives." The ornamented one was
in a secret place and quickly spoke these words. She was with her
beloved, but was also frightened and scared. Undetected by anyone,
they united with each other and she found pleasure with Aniruddha.

'The bull among the Yadus was adorned in divine garlands and
garments and smeared with celestial unguents and paste. He united
with Usha. However, at one particular time, he was detected by
Bana's guards. Those spies and men told Bana everything, without
leaving anything out, about how his daughter had been violated.
Bali's son, Bana, the slayer of brave enemies and the performer of
terrible deeds, commanded an army of servants. "All of you go
together and slay the evil-minded one. He has polluted our lineage
and character. He is tainted and wicked in his soul. By raping Usha,

[1043] Meaning Kubera. According to some accounts, Vishrava was the
son of Pulastya and Vishrava's wife was Ilavida or Ilavila. The son of this
union was Ailavila or Ailabila. Ailavila performed austerities and became
Kubera, the lord of riches.
[1044] Tamasa, alternatively, illusion (maya) known to the demons.

it is as if he has molested our great lineage. She was not bestowed on him by us. He seized her himself and violated her. What kind of valour is this? What kind of fortitude is this? What kind of impertinence is this? He is evil-minded. Like an extremely foolish child, he has entered the city and the residence." Those angry danavas raised many kinds of weapons and assumed many kinds of forms. They attacked, wishing to kill Pradyumna's son. He heard their voices and all their roars. The brave one suddenly arose, like an elephant that has been struck. The mighty-armed one bit his lips. On seeing him climb on to the palace, all of them were afflicted by fear and fled. The one who was accomplished in fighting in many kinds of ways picked up a gigantic club that was kept at the gate of the inner quarters. To kill them, he flung this at them. All of them showered down arrows, clubs, javelins, swords, spears and tridents, trying to kill him in that field of battle. The one who was in the soul of all beings[1045] was not agitated. He roared like a cloud at the end of summer. In every direction, he slew them with iron arrows and clubs. He was like the sun in the sky, surrounded in every direction by clouds. Standing amidst them, he struck them with a terrible club. The infinitely energetic one slew them with that fierce club. Terrified, all of them ran away, like clouds driven away by the wind. Aniruddha cheerfully roared. He roared like a lion and roamed around. He was like a cloud in the sky at the end of summer, thundering loudly. He roared at the danavas who were indomitable in battle, "Stay." Pradyumna's son, the slayer of enemies, slaughtered all of them.

'In the battle, all of them were killed by the great-souled one. They retreated from the encounter. They were scared and went to Bana. Blood flowing from their limbs, they reached Bana and sighed. The daityas could not find any peace. They were immobile and their eyes were terrified. The king urged them, "Do not be frightened. Do not be scared. Abandon your fear. O bulls among the danavas! Remain together and fight. Why have you run away, abandoning the fame that is known in the worlds. You have been overcome by lassitude. You are unconscious, like eunuchs. Whom

---

[1045] Because he was part of Vishnu.

are you frightened of, that you are running away collectively? You are accomplished in fighting in many kinds of ways. Yet, all of you are the worst of your lineages. I will fight without you. There is no need for you to aid me. May you cease to exist. Go away from me and be destroyed." This is what he told them. The powerful one, fierce and eloquent, spoke in different ways to urge and goad the terrified ones. He again despatched ten thousand brave ones to fight. Large numbers of demons were instructed to seize him.[1046] There was an extremely large army there, raising many kinds of weapons. Bana's army covered everything, their eyes blazing. It was as if the firmament was covered with many kinds of clouds tinged with lightning. In every direction, some of them were stationed on the ground, like trumpeting elephants. Others were in the sky, like clouds at the end of the summer. An extremely terrible encounter raged again. Everywhere, the words "stay", "wait" were heard. In that encounter, it was a great wonder, since a single person fought against many extremely brave danavas who attacked him. The immensely strong one seized their clubs and spears and used these to kill them in the great battle. In the forefront of the battle, he again seized a terrible club. In the encounter, he used this to slay large numbers of immensely strong daityas. The slayer of enemies grasped a sword and a shield in the encounter. In the forefront of the battle, he roamed around in many modes of fighting—circling around, leaping up, descending, leaping up and jumping down, traversing diagonally. He exhibited such thirty-two modes of fighting.[1047] In the forefront of the battle, a single person seemed to appear in thousands of forms. In the encounter, he sported in many ways, like Death with a gaping jaw. They sought to torment him. However, their bodies covered with blood, they were again routed and fled to where Bana was stationed in the battle. On their elephants, horses and chariots, they fled in the different directions. Those fierce ones uttered terrible shrieks of desperation. They were afflicted by fear and climbed over each other. They vomited blood. Overcome by

---

[1046] Aniruddha.
[1047] Dhanurveda texts mention thirty-two techniques of fighting with a sword and a shield. Their names aren't always listed.

depression, they retreated from the fight. Earlier, when they had fought in a battle, the danavas had never suffered from the kind of terror they faced in their encounter with Aniruddha. Some of them vomited blood. Others fell down on the surface of the ground. With clubs, spears and swords in their hands, the danavas looked like the summits of mountains. Overcome by fear in the battle, they abandoned Bana and fled. The danavas were defeated and fled into the extensive sky.

'On seeing that the large army had been routed and that he was alone, Bana blazed in rage, like a fire that has been fed with kindling. The valiant one ascended a chariot that was driven by Kumbhanda. He raised a fierce sword and went to where Aniruddha was. In his one thousand arms, he also held aloft javelins, swords, clubs, spears and battleaxes and they looked like hundreds of standards raised for Shakra. The mighty-armed one's hands were protected with finger guards made out of lizard skin. With diverse weapons, the supreme among danavas was radiant. He angrily roared like a lion and twanged his giant bow. Eyes red with rage, he shouted, "Stay. Wait." Pradyumna's unvanquished son heard the words Bana had spoken in the battle. He glanced at him and laughed. The giant chariot[1048] was adorned with hundreds of bells and roared. It possessed red flags and penants. It was covered with bear-skin and was ten nalvas in size.[1049] The great-souled one's chariot was yoked to one thousand horses. Wielding the sword and the shield, he[1050] saw it descend on him. Bana saw him standing on the ground, wielding the sword and the shield. He was extremely delighted at the prospect of being able to kill Pradyumna's son. Yadava held a sword in his hand and was bereft of armour. Though he was stationed in the battle, he was of the view that his adversary could not be defeated. Desiring to slay Aniruddha in the battle, from every direction, Bana shot a net of small arrows towards his head. He repulsed these thousands of arrows with his shield and remained stationed there, like a rising

---

[1048] Bana's.
[1049] A nalva is a measure of distance, equal to 400 hastas or cubits.
[1050] Aniruddha.

sun. The descendant of the Yadu lineage countered Bana in the encounter and was seen to be like a solitary elephant in the forest, standing in front of a lion. Bana used thousands of sharp and swift arrows that could pierce the inner organs to strike Pradyumna's unvanquished son. The mighty-armed one was severely struck by Bana's arrows with drooping tufts. He blazed in anger and desired to perform an extremely difficult feat. Having been struck by the showers of Bana's arrows, blood flowed from his limbs. However, extremely enraged, he dashed towards Bana's chariot. Pradyumna's son was severely struck with swords, clubs, spears, battleaxes, javelins and torrents of arrows. But he did not waver. In the forefront of the battle, he violently leapt up and using his sword, killed Bana's horses and sliced through his chariot. But Bana was accomplished in different modes of fighting. He again enveloped him with showers of arrows, spears and javelins and rendered him invisible. The large numbers of *nairittas* thought that he had been killed and roared. However, he suddenly leapt up and stationed himself on the flank of the chariot. Enraged, Bana seized a javelin in the battle. It was fierce in form and terrible. It was adorned with bells and blazed and flamed. It sparkled like Yama's staff and was as radiant as the sun. It blazed like a giant meteor and he hurled it towards his enemy's head. The supreme among men saw that the javelin was descending, about to rob him of his life. He leapt up and seized it. The immensely strong one used Bana's own javelin to strike him. Thus pierced in the body, he fell down on the surface of the ground.

'While he was unconscious, Kumbhanda spoke these words to him. "O Indra among danavas! How can you ignore the enemy who has presented himself before you? O brave one! You seem to be indifferent. Regain your purpose. Resort to maya and fight. Otherwise, he cannot be killed. Abandon this distraction and protect yourself and me. If you do not kill him now, all of us will be destroyed." The Indra among danavas was goaded by Kumbhanda's words. The supreme among eloquent ones was angered and spoke these harsh words. "In this battle, I will rob him of his life and dispatch him to death. I will seize him, like Garuda does the serpents." As soon as he said this, he, his chariot,

his horses, his standard and his charioteer vanished,[1051] like a city
of the gandharvas. Pradyumna's unvanquished son realized that
Bana had disappeared. Full of manliness, he searched in the ten
directions. Bali's angry son thus resorted to the knowledge of
tamasa. He was powerful because of his knowledge of maya. While
remaining hidden, he released sharp arrows. From every side, these
arrows became snakes and bound up Pradyumna's son. In many
ways, his body was bound up in the coils of these serpents. Bound
up in all of his limbs, Pradyumna's son was captured in the battle.
Though he was unharmed, he was rendered as immobile as Mount
Mainaka. He was rendered immobile in the coils of these snakes
and serpents, flames spitting from their mouths. However, like a
mountain, Pradyumna's son was not scared in the battle. He was
rendered stationary by the arrows that had become snakes and
serpents. But though they coiled all around him, the one who is
the soul of all creatures was not distressed. Bana, who was fierce
with words, clung to his flagpole and angrily censured him with
these harsh words. "O Kumbhanda! Quickly kill this defiler of the
lineage. He is tainted in his soul and his conduct has tainted me
in this world." Addressed in these words, Kumbhanda spoke these
words. "O king! I will say something. If you so desire, listen to my
words. We should find out whose son he is and where he has come
from. He is like Shakra in his valour. Who has brought him here?
O king! In this great battle, I have seen him fight in many kinds of
ways. He was seen to sport in the battle, like a son of the gods. He
is full of strength and spirit. He is accomplished in all the sacred
texts.[1052] O supreme among daityas! He has not committed any
sin that warrants his being killed. Having ascertained, slay him, or
show him honours. There is a great sin from killing him and there
are great qualities in protecting him. He is best among men and
should be respected in every way. O king! Behold this best among
men. He is full of valour and is suffering because the serpents have
bound him up in every part of his body. However, even though this

[1051] This must have been a new chariot and horses.

[1052] This should probably read shastra (weapon) and not shaastra
(sacred text).

powerful one has come to this state, he doesn't pay the slightest bit
of attention to it. Coiled by the serpents, blood is flowing from his
body. There are three furrows on his forehead and he is stationed
there, not thinking of us at all. O king! This is despite his having
been reduced to this state. He has resorted to the strength of his own
arms and does not think of you at all. He is brave and youthful. Who
is he? In the battle, you have one thousand arms, while he possesses
only two. He has strength and valour. O king! If it pleases you, find
out who he is." On hearing Kumbhanda's words, Bana relaxed the
severe coils of the serpents.[1053] Having fought with Aniruddha, he
entered his own house.'

Chapter 109

Vaishampayana said, 'Unable to see their beloved husband, all
the women in Aniruddha's household, who were like kinnara
ladies, wept. "Alas! Though Krishna is still here as our protector,
shame on this world. We are overcome by fear and terrified. We
are weeping like those without protectors. The foremost among
the gods, the Adityas, the large numbers of Maruts and all the
gods who reside in heaven depend on the shelter provided by his
arms and have originated from him. However, a great fear has
arisen in this world. His grandson, the brave Aniruddha, has
been taken away from us by someone. Alas! It is certain that evil-
minded person doesn't face any fear in this world. He has ignited
Vasudeva's anger, which is extremely difficult to withstand. He
is being whirled around inside the jaws of Death and is poised on
the tips of Death's teeth. Because of his confusion, in a battle, he
will face Vasudeva as an enemy. That person, even if he happens
to be Shatakratu himself, has acted in this way and has caused
displeasure to the bull among the Yadus. How will he escape with
his life? We are grieving because of what he has done. We have
been deprived by him. Deprived of our beloved, we face death

[1053] As will become clear later, Aniruddha was still bound.

ourselves." They spoke repeatedly in this way and wept. Those supreme women shed inauspicious tears from their eyes. Their eyes were full of tears and looked like lotuses immersed in water at the advent of the rainy season. Their radiant and auspicious eyes were like the feathers of swans, tinged with blood. As they lamented like thousands of female curlews in the sky, a great noise arose from their palaces. This terrible uproar signified the arrival of some fear. On hearing this, all the bulls among men quickly rushed there, leaving their own houses. "What is this evil? Why is this loud uproar being heard from Aniruddha's house? While we are protected by Krishna, what is this fear that has arisen?" They were confused and affectionately spoke to each other in this way. They emerged like suffering lions from their caves.

'With the use of maya, Krishna's drum was sounded. At this sound, all of them assembled and stood there. The Yadavas asked each other, "What is this?" All of them spoke to each other and conversed with each other. The Yadavas, unassailable in battle, stood there, sighing. Their eyes were full of tears and their eyes were red with anger. When all of them were silent, Viprithu spoke these words to Krishna, supreme among strikers, who was sighing repeatedly. "O Indra among men! Why are you standing here, overcome by thoughts? All the Yadavas find life by resorting to the strength of your arms. O Krishna! Depending on you, we have been divided into various groups. Shakra's victory and defeat depends on your strength and that is the reason he sleeps happily. Why are you overcome by thoughts? All of your kin are agitated in this ocean of grief. O mighty-armed one! You are the only one who can save them from this submergence. Why are you immersed in thoughts and why are you not saying anything? O god! O Madhava! You do not deserve to be immersed in futile thoughts." Thus addressed, Krishna again sighed for a long time. The one who had a way with words then spoke these words, like Brihaspati himself. "O Viprithu! I am immersed in thoughts because I have been thinking about what needs to be done. I have thought about what you said, but am unable to find a clear answer. Standing in the midst of this large number of Dasharhas, I am now speaking these words, which are full of reason. O Yadavas! All of you listen to me, about why

I am overcome by thoughts. Since the brave Aniruddha has been
abducted, all the kings on earth think that we and all our relatives
are incapable. In earlier times, our king, Ahuka, was abducted by
Salva. We fought an extremely terrible battle and brought him
back. When he was a child, Pradyumna was abducted by Shambara.
Having slain him in a battle, Rukmini's son returned. This is indeed
a great hardship. Where has Pradyumna's son gone? O bulls among
men! I cannot think of a sin like this. Who is the one whose ash-
smeared feet have descended on my head? In a battle, I will rob
him and his relatives of their lives." Thus addressed by Krishna,
Satyaki spoke these words. "O Krishna! Let spies be employed to
seek out Aniruddha's path." Krishna smiled and spoke these words
to Ahuka. "O king! Please instruct spies to be employed inside the
kingdom and outside it." The illustrious king instructed that spies
should be employed in every direction and along every path, inside
the kingdom and outside it. "Search the mountains Venumanta
and Raivataka, covered with creepers. Use swift horses to search
the paths on Mount Rikshavanta. Search each and every garden
and the paths in every direction. In every direction, go to all the
gardens, even if they are deserted. Mount thousands of horses and
large numbers of chariots. Swiftly search for the descendant of the
Yadu lineage along all the paths." The commander, Anadhrishti,
seemed to be scared and terrified and spoke these words to Krishna
Achyuta, the perfomer of unsullied deeds. "O Krishna! O lord! If
it pleases you, listen to my words. For a long time, my mind has
turned towards telling you something. Asiloma, Puloma, Nisunda
and Naraka have been slain. Soubha, Salva, Mainda and Dvivida
have also been killed. You have killed the extremely great Hayagriva
and his followers. For the sake of the gods, you have engaged in
such extremely terrible encounters. Through your deeds, in battle
after battle, you have destroyed them. O Govinda! You have done
all this and you have no one to act as your *parshni*.[1054] O Krishna!
With your followers, you have accomplished these deeds in battles.

[1054] Parshni has different meanings. When four horses are attached to a
chariot, it means one of the outside horses. It can also mean one of the two
charioteers who drive the outside horses, as opposed to the main charioteer

You performed the extremely difficult task of seizing the Parijata tree. O Krishna! At that time, Shakra, accomplished in fighting, was himself astride Airavata's head. However, using the valour of your arms, you vanquished him. There is no doubt that he has taken it upon himself to bear enmity towards you. Because of that, he has thought his task is to be hostile towards you. Therefore, Maghavan has himself abducted Aniruddha. There is no one else who is capable of bearing this great enmity towards you." Addressed in these words, Krishna sighed like a serpent. The intelligent one spoke these words to the immensely strong Anadhrishti. "O commander! O son![1055] It cannot be like that. The gods are not the perpetrators of inferior deeds. They are not ungrateful. Nor are they impotent. They are not insolent or foolish. My efforts are for the gods and for the great destruction of the danavas. It is to bring them pleasure that I have killed the insolent and extremely great asuras in battle. I am devoted to them and my mind is immersed in them. I am engaged in doing what they find agreeable. Knowing this, how can they commit this crime against me? They are truthful and are never inferior. They are devoted to those who follow them. Know that this transgression isn't theirs. You have spoken foolishly." Having heard Krishna's words, Akrura, who was skilled in speaking words that were full of reason, spoke these words. His speech was sweet and gentle. "O lord! It is certain that our tasks are for Shakra. The tasks that we perform are the same as the tasks required by Shachi's consort. We are protected by the gods and we also protect the gods. We have assumed human forms to accomplish the tasks of the gods." Purushottama was thus urged by Akrura's words. Krishna again spoke in a tone that was gentle and deep. "This abduction of Pradyumna's son hasn't been done by the gods, the gandharvas, the yakshas or the rakshasas. This abduction has been done by a lady who is a courtesan. The daitya and danava women are courtesans and accomplished in the use of maya. There is no doubt that such a person has abducted him. There cannot be fear from anyone else."

(*sarathi*), or someone who guards the axles. In this context, it simply means that Krishna has no aide.
[1055] The word used is tata.

When these words were spoken, sweet sounds of praise were heard
in Madhava's house, uttered by the bards and the minstrels.

'All the spies also returned and assembled at the gate. In soft
tones, they spoke these words. "O king! We searched each one of
hundreds of gardens, mountains, caverns, rivers and ponds, but
could not trace his footprints. O descendant of the Yadu lineage!
You should think of some other means and instruct us. Command
us so that we can quickly seek out Aniruddha's tracks." All of them
were distressed in their minds and their eyes were full of tears. They
asked each other, "What shall we do next?" There were some who
bit their lips. There were others whose eyes were full of tears. There
were some brave men whose foreheads were furrowed in thought.

'A sparkling morning dawned and the sun arose. To the great
sound of trumpets and conch shells, the mighty-armed Krishna was
awoken in his house. Narada entered the assembly hall alone. He
seemed to be smiling. The lord Krishna, impossible for even armies
to defeat, was distracted. However, he arose and offered Narada
madhuparka[1056] and a cow. He[1057] seated himself on a sparkling
spread that was covered with cushions. Seated upright, he spoke
these words that were full of import. "Why are you overcome by
thoughts, as if you are enveloped in darkness and alone? All your
enterprise seems to have been destroyed and you are as insensible as
eunuchs." The great-souled Narada addressed them in these words.
Vasudeva replied, "O illustrious one! You should hear what I am
about to say. O brahmana! O one who is excellent in his vows!
Someone has abducted Aniruddha in the night. It is because of this
that all of us seem to be insensible and are immersed in thoughts."
Narada was thus addressed by the great-souled Keshava. He laughed
and retorted, "O Madhusudana! You should listen to me. There
was an extremely great battle between two great men and it is now
over. In that great battle, Aniruddha single-handedly fought against
Bana. Bana, unmatched in his energy, has a daughter named Usha.
For her sake, the apsara Chitralekha swiftly abducted him. There
was an extremely fierce and great battle between Pradyumna's son

[1056] A mixture of honey offered to a guest.
[1057] Narada.

and Bana, like the encounter between Bali and Vasava. Aniruddha
did not retreat from that battle. Out of fear for him, the immensely
strong Bana resorted to maya and bound him up in the coils of
serpents. For the sake of fame and victory, arise quickly. O son![1058]
For the sake of victory, this is not the time to protect one's life."
Addressed in these words, the powerful and valorous Vasudeva
gave instructions that arrangements should be made for his
departure. Sandalwood powder and parched rice were sprinkled in
every direction. The mighty-armed Janardana made arrangements
for departure. Narada said, "O Krishna! You should remember
Vinata's son.[1059] O mighty-armed one! There is no one else who
is capable of going there. O Janardana! Pradyumna's son has been
taken to the city of Shonita and it is eleven thousand yojanas away.
Vinata's powerful son is immensely brave and possesses the speed of
thought. In an instant, he alone can show you Bana." Having heard
his words, Hari thought of Garuda and he arrived at Krishna's side
and stood there cheerfully.

'Jishnu wore bracelets and was dark in complexion. His hair
was dark. He possessed four teeth and four arms. He knew the four
Vedas and six Vedangas. He bore the srivatsa mark and his eyes
were like lotuses. His body hair stood up and his speech was gentle.
His fingers were even. His nails were even. His fingers and the tips
of his nails were red. His voice was gentle and deep. He was mighty-
armed and his arms were round. His arms stretched down to his
knees. His face was like that of a lion. He was young and was capable
of standing up before a lion. He blazed like a thousand suns shining
together. This resplendent lord is in the souls of all creatures. He is
the lord who thought of the creation of beings. Delighted, Prajapati
had granted him the eight qualities and powers.[1060] Among all the

[1058] The word used is tata.

[1059] Garuda.

[1060] Yoga leads to eight major siddhis or powers. These are *anima*
(becoming as small as one desires), *mahima* (as large as one desires),
laghima (as light as one wants), *garima* (as heavy as one wants), *prapti*
(obtaining what one wants), *prakamya* (travelling where one wants),
vashitvam (powers to control creatures) and *ishitvam* (obtaining divine
powers). These are the eight qualities mentioned.

lords of creatures, sadhyas and gods, he is eternal. He is praised in
the chants of bards, minstrels and raconteurs and is honoured by
the immensely fortunate rishis who are accomplished in the Vedas
and the Vedangas. Having made up his mind to leave, the mighty-
armed and powerful Vasudeva conveyed instructions for Dvaraka.
The god ascended Garuda, with the wielder of the plough behind
him. Pradyumna, the afflicter of enemies, was behind Bala.[1061] "O
mighty-armed one! Defeat Bana and his followers in the battle. In
a great encounter, no one is capable of standing before you. There
is no doubt that Lakshmi will show you her favours and that there
is victory in your valour. Vanquish the enemy, the Indra among the
daityas, and his soldiders, in the battle." From the sky, the siddhas,
charanas and large numbers of maharshis pronounced these words
in every direction. Keshava departed for the battle.'

Chapter 110

Vaishampayana said, 'There was the sound of trumpets and the
loud blare of conch shells. Thousands of bards, minstrels and
panegyrics chanted his praise. Men who were anxious for victory
praised him with words of benediction. Hari assumed a blazing form
that was like that of the moon, the sun and Venus.[1062] The form of
Vinata's son rising up was extremely dazzled and that radiance was
enchanced by Hari's energy. With eight hands, Krishna assumed a
form that was like that of a mountain. Desiring Bana's destruction,
Pundarikaksha dazzled. The hands on the right held a sword, the
chakra, a mace and an arrow. The hands on the left held a shield,
the Sharnga bow and a conch shell. The wielder of the Sharnga
bow assumed one thousand heads. Samkarshana also assumed
one thousand forms. Astride Garuda, Rama was like the rising

[1061] Balarama.

[1062] The text says Shakra, which is almost certainly a typo, though it
does make sense. Non-Critical versions say Shukra (Venus) and we have
changed Shakra to Shukra.

moon. The unassailable one wielded white weapons and looked like the summited Kailasa. Wishing to display his valour in the battle, the great-souled and mighty-armed Pradyumna manifested Sanatkumara's form. With the force of his wings, the powerful one[1063] flung away and shattered many mountains, obstructing the path of the wind. Garuda adopted a speed that was greater than that of the wind. He followed the auspicious path adopted by large numbers of siddhas and charanas. Rama spoke these words to Krishna, who was unmatched in battle. "O Krishna! We have been robbed of our own splendour. This is something that has never happened before. How did it occur? It is clear that all of us have assumed a golden complexion. Tell me the truth about what has happened. Is this because we have reached the slopes of Meru?" The illustrious one replied, "O wielder of the plough! We have been struck by the radiance of the ahavaniya fire.[1064] Our reddish hue is the result of that." Rama said, "If we are near and if our resplendence has been lost because of that, use your intelligence to determine what is beneficial and what must be done next." The illustrious one replied, "O Vinata's son! Do what must be done next. After you have decided what must be done, I will determine our next course of action." Hearing these words of the great-souled Keshava, Vinata's powerful son quickly went to the Ganga. He picked up water from there and sprinkled the fire with it. The ahavaniya fire was thus pacified. "It is my view that the three, Krishna, Samkarshana and the immensely strong Pradyumna, are capable of taking on the three worlds."[1065] When the fire was pacified, the king of birds continued to advance. He created a terrible and loud noise from the strength with which he was flapping his wings.

'On seeing this, the fires, followers of Rudra, began to think. "Who are these, astride Garuda? They have many forms and signify fear. Who are these three men and why have they come here?" The fires that travel in the mountains could not arrive at any conclusion. A battle commenced between them and the three Yadavas. An

---

[1063] Garuda.
[1064] Which emerged to protect Bana's city.
[1065] These are words spoken by Garuda.

uproar arose. Anxious to know what was going on, Bana sent a man,
who possessed the speed of thought, to go and witness everything.
He agreed and went to see the battle that was going on, the great
encounter as the fires clashed against Vasudeva. All the fires were
there. There were the five fires which are famous as being associated
with the utterance of "svadha"—Kalmasha, Khasrima, Dahana,
Shoshana and the immensely strong Tapana. There were other
immensely fortunate ones, accompanied by their own soldiers. The
five fires associated with the utterance of "svaha" also fought—
Patara, Pataga, Svarna, Agadha and Bhraja. The two great-souled
and immensely radiant conflagrations associated with the divisions
of *jyotishtoma* and vashatkara also fought.[1066] In between these two
was the lord, the maharshi Angiras.[1067] On seeing Angiras stationed
on his chariot, Purushottama Krishna smiled repeatedly and spoke
these words. "O fires! Remain here. I will generate a fear among
you. You will be consumed by my energy and devastated, will flee
in different directions." At this, Angiras attacked him with a blazing
spear. In that great battle, he was enraged and wished to take away
Krishna's life. However, he[1068] fought with supreme arrows that
were supreme and sharp, with tips in the form of the crescent moon
and like the Destroyer, Yama. Using these, he severed that blazing
trident. The extremely illustrious one used a blazing arrow with a
broad shaft. It was like Yama. Using this, he struck him[1069] in the
chest and roared. With blood flowing all over his body, the fire
became senseless. With his body numb, he violently fell down on
the ground. At this, the remaining four fires, the sons of Brahma,[1070]
quickly fled towards Bana's city.

'The lotus-eyed one held the conch shell up to his mouth and
it looked as if the moon was poised amidst clouds. With the force
of the wind, he blew into it. The valiant one blew on the conch

[1066] There was a class of soma sacrifices known as jyotishtoma.
[1067] Angiras is often portrayed as a personification of Agni and as
Vishnu's enemy.
[1068] Krishna.
[1069] Angiras.
[1070] It isn't possible to deduce which four are being singled out.

shell and generated fear. Krishna, the performer of extraordinary deeds, entered Bana's city. Bana's soldiers suddenly emerged from all sides, blowing on conch shells and creating a loud noise through drums. That army of servants was sent into the great battle. There were many crore of these and they wielded blazing weapons. In that encounter, they united together, looking like a giant mass of clouds adhering to each other. It seemed to be immeasurable and indestructible and was like a mass of collyrium. Those daityas, danavas and rakshasas wielded blazing weapons. There were the best of demons and they assembled and fought with Krishna. All of them had blazing mouths, like flames of fires into which oblations are fed. In that battle, they drank the blood of those four.[1071] The mighty-armed Rama spoke these words to Keshava. "O Krishna! O mighty-armed one! O Krishna! Create a great fear in them." Krishna was thus urged by the intelligent Balabhadra.[1072] Purushottama was the best among those accomplished in astras and shastras. To slay them, he picked up the agneya weapon, as resplendent as the Destroyer, Yama. The large number of carnivorous asuras was driven away by this weapon's energy. However, he swiftly went to the spot where that army could be seen. He glanced at that army of demons, wielding spikes, spears, javelins, swords, tridents, clubs and other weapons. Adopting many kinds of fearful forms, they looked like mountains or clouds. All the warriors were stationed there, with large numbers of mounts. They looked like clouds scattered away by the wind and clinging to mountains. Astride Vinata's son, Rama saw this army and told Krishna, "O Krishna! O mighty-armed one! O Krishna! This army can be seen. O Purushottama! I wish to fight against them in this battle." Krishna replied, "The same kind of intention has also been generated in me. I also wish to advance against these ones, who are indomitable in battle. I will fight on the east and let Suparna[1073] be ahead of me. Let Pradyumna be to my left and you can be to my right. In this fierce and great battle, we will protect each other." Astride that supreme bird, they thus spoke

[1071] Krishna, Balarama, Pradyumna and Garuda.
[1072] Balarama.
[1073] Garuda.

to each other. Rohini's son assumed a terrible form and fought, using the summits of mountains, clubs, bludgeons and ploughs. He was like Time, which burns down all creatures at the end of a yuga. He dragged them with the tip of his plough and uprooted them with his club. Extremely strong and accomplished in all the modes of fighting, he roamed around in that encounter. Pradyumna, tiger among men, fought in every direction and repulsed thousands of danavas with showers of arrows. Janardana blew on his conch shell several times. He was like a gentle mass of collyrium and wielded the conch shell, the chakra and the mace. In that battle, Vinata's powerful son attacked the enemy and struck them with the force of his wings, mangling them with the tip of his beak and his talons. The army of daityas was terrible in valour, but was slaughtered. In that encounter, it was routed with a shower of arrows. When the army was routed, Jvara[1074] desired to save it and attacked. He possessed three feet and three heads and was indomitable in encounters. He was like Yama. He was fierce and used ashes as his weapon. He roared like a storm, or like thousands of clouds. He angrily faced the wielder of the plough and said, "What kind of strength do you possess? In this battle, why are you not looking at me? Wait. In the forefront of this encounter, you will not be able to escape with your life." Saying this, he laughed and attacked the wielder of the plough. He generated great fear with his terrible fists, which looked like the fire that comes at the time of the destruction of a yuga. Adopting thousands of different forms, he whirled around in that battle and in a short instant, Rohini's son was no longer able to see where he was stationed. Unmatched in his energy, Jvara flung ashes and these descended on the target, the body that was like a mountain.[1075] From his chest, those blazing ashes fell on the summit of Meru and shattered the peak of the mountain. Krishna's elder brother was struck by the blazing ashes, hurled with anger. He sighed and yawned repeatedly and fell asleep. His eyes were filled with weakness and he was incessantly distracted. His body hair stood up and his sight faded. He sighed as if he was crazy.

[1074] The personified form of fever.
[1075] Balarama's body.

Maddened and unconscious, the wielder of the plough spoke to Krishna, "O Krishna! O mighty-armed one! O Krishna! This is a terrifying blaze. O son![1076] I am burning all over my body. How can I obtain peace?" Addressed in this way, he embraced the wielder of the plough. When Krishna embraced him with great affection, he was freed from the burning. Extremely wrathful, Vasudeva spoke to Jvara. "Come. O Jvara! In this great battle, fight against me with all your strength. O one who is accomplished in fighting! In this encounter, show me what you possess." Using two of his right hands, Jvara then flung ashes at him. These blazed and were greatly powerful. In an instant, Krishna, supreme among strikers, assumed a blazing form and that fire was pacified. With three of his hands, which were like snakes, Jvara struck Krishna on the neck and beat him on the chest with his fists. There was a tumultuous battle between those two lions among men, the great Jvara and the great-souled Krishna. There was a roar like that of thunder descending on mountains. There was an extremely terrible battle, with Krishna and Jvara striking each other with their hands. There were loud noises, "You should not strike like this." For a short instant, those two extremely great-souled ones fought with each other. Jvara was adorned in golden and colourful ornaments and roamed around in the sky. In that battle, he was crushed by the strength of arms[1077] and the lord of the universe seemed to be like Yama, the destroyer.'

Chapter 111

Vaishampayana said, 'Krishna, the afflicter of enemies, thought that Jvara was dead. With the strength of his arms, he flung him down on the ground. However, as soon as he was released from the arms, he entered Krishna's body. Krishna, infinite in his energy, could not free his body from his grasp. The infinitely energetic one was pervaded by Jvara. Krishna seemed to totter and repeatedly

[1076] The word used is tata.
[1077] The strength of Krishna's arms.

circled around on the ground. Krishna yawned. Yet again, he suffered severely. The body hair stood up on his body and he was overcome by sleep. Purushottama realized that Jvara had overcome him. He created another Jvara, so as to destroy the older Jvara. The infinitely energetic one struck Jvara in this way. At that time, an invisible voice was heard from the sky. "O Krishna! O mighty-armed one! O Krishna! O extender of the delight of the Yadu lineage! O unblemished one! You should not kill this Jvara. Instead, you should protect him." Addressed in these words, Hari himself released him. Jvara said, "Let me be the only Jvara on this earth. O ornament of assemblies! Through your favours, let there be no other Jvara." The illustrious one replied, "May you be happy. May you be the single Jvara in this world. The Jvara that was created by me will merge into me." Jvara said, "I am blessed that you have shown me your favours. You have done something that is agreeable to me. O one who wields the chakra as a weapon! Command me. What will I do to ensure your pleasure?" The illustrious one replied, "In this great battle, both you and I only used the strength and valour of our arms as weapons. O Jvara! If a man bows down single-mindedly before me and reads this, he will be cured of all fever." The great-souled Krishna himself addressed Jvara in this way. He bowed his head down before Krishna and left the field of battle.'

Chapter 112

Vaishampayana said, 'Then those three, who were like fires, united and started to fight again.[1078] They fought, stationed in that battle astride Vinata's son. Those extremely strong ones showered down arrows and mangled all the armies. Extremely strong, Vinata's son roared in that battle. The large army of the great-souled danavas was afflicted by the chakra, the plough and the shower of arrows and was enraged. Krishna's arrows emitted fire and the blaze increased, like dead wood on fire is fanned by

[1078] Krishna, Balarama and Pradyumna.

the wind and the feeding of kindling.[1079] In the forefront of that battle, there were thousands of danavas. They were illuminated as they were burnt down by the rays, like the fire of destruction that comes at the end of a yuga. That large army of soldiers wielded many kinds of weapons and was routed. Bana restrained them and spoke these words. "Why have you become faint-hearted and overcome by fear? You have been born in the lineage of the daityas, yet you are running away from this great battle. You are capable of roaming around in the sky. Why are you fleeing, abandoning your armour, swords, clubs, spears, blades,[1080] shields and battleaxes? You should show respect to your own kin and your residence in Hara's company. You should not be distressed and flee. I am stationed here." However, despite being addressed in these words, all the danavas were afflicted by fear. They did not listen, or even think about it. They ran away. However, there was some numbers of demons who were still left at the forefront of the army. These remnants again made up their mind to fight.

'The valiant Kumbhanda was Bana's friend and aide. On seeing that the army was shattered, he spoke these words. "Bana is stationed in the battle and so are Shankara and Guha.[1081] Why are you overcome by fear and abandoning this battle?" The valiant Nandishvara[1082] was stationed on his chariot. Rudra bit his lips and advanced towards where Hari was. His chariot was yoked to lions. It made a loud clatter and seemed to swallow up the sky. It looked like the moon on a full moon light, freed from the clouds. Hari was in the front, astride Vinata's son. Angrily, Hara[1083] pierced him with one hundred iron arrows. Hara, the slayer of enemies, afflicted him with these arrows. Angrily, Hari grasped the supreme *parjanya* weapon. Hundreds of thousands of arrows with drooping tufts were released and from all directions, they descended on Hara's body. Rudra, supreme among those who are skilled in all weapons, became angry. He released the

---

[1079] The anger of the demons enchanced the power of Krishna's arrows.
[1080] Two different words are used for swords, *asi* and *khadga*.
[1081] Kartikeya.
[1082] Lord of Nandi, Shiva's name.
[1083] Shiva.

extremely terrible agneya weapon. It was extraordinary. From all
directions, those four[1084] were enveloped by these arrows and couldn't
be seen. Their bodies were mangled and they were burnt by the fire.
The supreme among asuras roared like lions. Since Hari had been
rendered invisible by the agneya weapon, they thought that he had
been killed. However, the powerful Vasudeva, supreme among those
who were accomplished in the use of all weapons, wished to destroy
the enemy and picked up the *varuna* weapon. When the intelligent
Vasudeva raised the varuna weapon, the agneya weapon was pacified
by varuna's energy. However, Bhava released four weapons that were
like the fire that arrives at the time of the destruction of a yuga—
paishacha, rakshasa, *roudra* and *angiras*. To counter these weapons,
Vasudeva released *vayavya, savitra, vasava* and *mohana*. Keshava
countered the four weapons with four of his. He then picked up
the *vaishnava* weapon, which was like Death with a gaping mouth.
When the vaishnava weapon was released, all the supreme ones
among the asuras fled in different directions, their eyes confounded
with terror. The world was immersed in darkness and Tryambaka
seemed to blaze. Nandi and Rudra, on his chariot, could no longer be
seen. The one with four faces[1085] seized the arrow that had brought
an end to Tripura. Because of his rage and strength, his form doubled
in radiance. Desiring to unleash it, the three-eyed one affixed it to his
bow. However, the great-souled Vasudeva, who knew the intention
behind everything, discerned this. Therefore, Purushottama picked
up the weapon known as *jrimbhana*. The immensely strong one acted
swiftly and made Hara yawn.[1086] He blew on his conch shell and
extended the Sharnga bow. All the creatures who were present saw
the god[1087] yawn.

'Guha was on a chariot and Kumbhanda steered the horses that
were yoked to it.[1088] He attacked Krishna, Bala and Pradyumna.

[1084] Krishna, Balarama, Pradyumna and Garuda.
[1085] Shiva.
[1086] Jrimbhana means yawning.
[1087] Shiva.
[1088] There is abruptness because the Critical Edition excises shlokas.
Shiva withdrew from the battle.

With arrows marking their bodies, those three looked like fires.
Though blood flowed from their limbs, they fought back against
Guha. Those three were conversant with modes of fighting. They
shot three supreme arrows that blazed in their energy—vayavya,
agneya and parjanya. The great-souled one[1089] wielded a radiant
bow and his torrent of arrows blazed. He devoured that storm of
arrows with the maya of his weapons. In the battle, Guha bit his
lips. He picked up the weapon known as brahmashiras. It was like
Death and was impossible to withstand. The brahmashiras was
invoked and it was as resplendent as the one with one thousand
rays.[1090] It was fierce and supremely unassailable. It would ensure
the destruction of the worlds. All the great beings fled in different
directions. The valiant Keshava picked up the chakra that destroyed
Keshi. It was capable of countering and destroying the energy
of all weapons. The great-souled one's chakra is famous in the
worlds and cannot be countered. Through its energy, it made the
brahmashiras weapon lose its lustre. It was like the giant solar disc
losing its radiance because of clouds during the rainy season. The
immensely energetic brahmashiras lost its valour and its radiance.
At this, Guha was enraged. He seized a golden javelin that was
like a giant meteor. It was as radiant as the fire that comes at the
time of the destruction of a yuga. It was decorated with bells and
garlands and he hurled this javelin. With a blazing mouth, that
giant javelin seemed to yawn in the sky and descended, desiring
to slay Krishna. All the immortals, with Indra at the forefront,
were greatly distressed. They saw that blazing javelin and said that
Krishna would be consumed. In the great battle, as the giant javelin
approached, Krishna censured it with words of humkara and it
fell down on the ground.[1091] When the great javelin fell down on
the ground, all the gods, with Vasava, uttered words of praise and
roared like lions. When the gods roared, the powerful Vasudeva,
the destroyer of all creatures, again picked up the chakra. As the

[1089] Guha.
[1090] The sun.
[1091] Humkara means to utter the sound hum, a sound believed to
possess special powers.

infinitely energetic Krishna whirled the chakra around, the goddess Koutavi saw this.[1092] She exclaimed, "Shame! Shame! Retreat! Retreat!" She stood in front of him.

'At that time, there was the blaring of trumpets and the great beating of drums. As the daityas roared like lions, Bana attacked Krishna. In the battle, the bull among the Yadus saw that he was advancing. Accordingly, the infinitely energetic Krishna mounted Vinata's son. Bana said, "Wait. Hold on. Before me, you will not escape with your life today. You will not be able to see Dvaraka and your well-wishers who reside in Dvaraka. O Madhava! You will not be able to see the trees with golden complexions at the tips. Urged by destiny, you will face me in this encounter. You will be overcome by me and die. In this battle, what will an eight-handed person do againt one with one thousand arms? O one with Garuda on his banner! Approach me and fight. In this battle today, I will vanquish you and your relatives. Slain in the city of Shonita, you will remember Dvaraka. Today, you will think my one thousand arms actually number one crore. They wield many kinds of weapons and are adorned in diverse kinds of armlets." The torrent of his words roared, like the waters of the ocean. He roamed around, like the terrible waters when they are agitated by the wind. His eyes were full of anger. He was like a giant sun that had arisen for the destruction of the universe. The illustrious one replied, "O Bana! Why are you roaring? When brave ones are stationed in battle, they do not roar. Come and fight in this battle. Why are you roaring in this pointless way? O Diti's descendant! Had encounters been won through words, you would have always triumphed. You have ranted a lot. O Bana! Come. Defeat me, or be vanquished and lie down on the ground, covering your face. O asura! Be miserable and lie down for a last time."

'Having spoken these words, in that battle, Krishna pierced him with a torrent of swift arrows that struck at his inner organs. They were invincible and blazed in their energy. However, Bana

---

[1092] Koutavi is an eighth part of the goddess Parvati. She interceded, to prevent Krishna and Kumara from fighting against each other. Accordingly, Kumara retreated.

smiled and countered Krishna with a blazing shower of arrows. The extremely terrible encounter commenced. As the battle continued, the energetic one shrouded the revered Keshava with arrows, swords, maces, clubs, spears, javelins and spikes. The eight-armed one fought with the thousand-armed one. The wielder of the conch shell, chakra and mace fought with Bana. There was a supreme and divine weapon that had been created through great austerities. In any battle, it was impossible to withstand and could destroy all enemies. This had been created earlier by Brahma, and Bali's son released this. All the directions were enveloped and the discs of all the luminous bodies lost their radiance. A terrible dust arose and nothing could be seen. The danavas honoured Bana and uttered words of praise. As the gods roamed around, they exclaimed, "Alas! Shame!" From the strength and force of that weapon, an extremely terrible shower of arrows rained down, resplendent and fierce in form and extremely swift. The wind stopped blowing. The clouds ceased to move. When that arrow was released, Keshava was consumed. However, Madhusudana picked up an extremely swift weapon, which was named parjanya. In the encounter, the illustrious one was like the Destroyer, Yama. Having invoked the parjanya weapon with a mantra, he pacified the danava's weapon. All the large number of gods were delighted and cheered. O great king! When that weapon was destroyed, Diti's son became senseless with rage. Keshava was on Garuda and he again enveloped him with clubs, javelins and spears. Keshava, the slayer of enemies, again swiftly repulsed all these showers of arrows. The mounts of the two, the god and the daitya, also fought with each other. In the encounter, Garuda fought with the peacock.[1093] The peacock and Garuda angrily struck at each other with blows from wings and beaks, feet, nails and talons. The peacock blazed in energy. But Vinata's son angrily seized him by the head and struck him with his beak. The immensely strong one struck him on his right wing. He repeatedly dealt fierce blows on his flanks with his feet. The immensely strong one quickly seized him and dragged him along. He

---

[1093] The peacock is actually Kumara's mount. So this probably belongs in an earlier section.

became unconscious and fell down from the sky, like a mountain. When the peacock was brought down by the bird Garuda, Bana was without a protector. He became extremely anxious and began to think about what he should do.

'Rudra got to know that Bana was distressed in his mind and extremely miserable in the battle. Anxious and miserable, the illustrious one thought about what he could do to offer protection. In a rumbling voice, Mahadeva spoke to Nandi. "O Nandikeshvara! Take this chariot and go where Bana is stationed in the battle. Take these large number of demons with you. My mind is awhirl. O son![1094] Go and use your powers to save Bana." Nandi, supreme among charioteers, agreed and left on that chariot. He went to where Bana was and spoke these soft words to Bana. "O daitya! O immensely strong one! Swiftly ascend this chariot." Thus addressed, he climbed onto Mahadeva's chariot. The infinitely energetic one was astride Bhava's chariot. He was supreme among those who were accomplished in the use of weapons and invoked the terrible and blazing weapon, brahmashiras. The extremely valiant Bana was angry and used this weapon. Brahmashiras blazed and the worlds were agitated. It had actually been created by the one who was born from a lotus[1095] for the protection of the worlds. However, the powerful Krishna destroyed this weapon with his chakra and told Bana, who was unmatched in battle and famous and illustrious in the worlds, "O Bana! What did you boast about? Wasn't that in vain? I am stationed before you in this battle. Be a man and fight with me. Earlier, there used to be an extremely strong person by the name of Kartavirya Arjuna. He possessed one thousand arms. However, in an encounter, he was defeated by the two-armed Rama.[1096] Your arms were created because of your valour and you were insolent about them. In this field of battle, I will pacify your insolence with my chakra. Remain until I have destroyed the insolence that has been generated by your arms. In this field of battle, you will not escape from me today." The tiger

[1094] The word used is tata.
[1095] Brahma.
[1096] Parashurama.

among men roared like a cloud at the end of the summer and seized
the thousand-sided chakra, so as to pacify Bana's arms, who was
like an insect drawn to the flames. The chakra had been created by
Prajapati and its energy blazed, like the moon. It was full of energy
and extremely radiant, like the sun. His own body enveloped in
energy, he stood in front of Bana. On seeing that the illustrious
one was stationed in the field of battle, raising the chakra, Koutavi
stationed herself in front of Vasudeva. Invisible to others, she shed
her garments and stood before him again, naked. To save Bana,
Vijaya[1097] stationed herself there. The noble one, eyes coppery red
and naked, again stationed herself in the battle. Intent on saving
Bana, she spoke these words. "O god! Bana is unmatched in battle
and you should not kill him." The mighty-armed Krishna, supreme
among strikers, became enraged. In the battle, he whirled around
the supreme chakra and spoke to Bana. "On each occasion when
you fight in this encounter, Koutavi is stationed in front of you.
You seem to be incapable of fighting. Shame on your manliness."
Krishna was immensely strong and knew about supreme weapons.
Saying this, he closed his eyes and hurled the chakra towards Bana.
Vishnu's weapon possessed an excellent nave. In the field of battle,
it whirled around like a circle of fire and was so swift that it could
not be seen. One by one, in the field of battle, the chakra sliced off
Bana's one thousand arms.[1098] Torrents of blood started to flow
from his body. With his arms severed, the giant asura looked like a
mountain.

'To slay Bana, Achyuta again wished to hurl the chakra.
However, with Kumara, Mahadeva arrived before him and said,
"O Krishna! O great god! O Purushottama! O Krishna! I know
you. You are the one who killed Madhu and Kaitabha. You are
the eternal god of the gods. O god! You are the destination of
the worlds. The universe has been generated from you. The three
worlds, with the gods, the asuras and humans, cannot vanquish
you. Therefore, withdraw the divine chakra that you have raised.
It is terrible towards enemies and will certainly destroy everything

[1097] Parvati's form, being equated with Koutavi.
[1098] Bana was thus left with only two arms.

in this battle. O slayer of Keshi! I have granted Bana freedom from fear. You should pardon me. Otherwise, my words will be rendered false." The illustrious one replied, "O god! Let Bana remain alive. I will withdraw the chakra. O god! You are always revered by the gods and the asuras. O Maheshvara! I bow down before you. I will depart, not having accomplished the task I set out to do.[1099] Grant me permission." Speaking to Mahadeva in this way, Krishna quickly mounted Garuda and went to where Pradyumna's son was, bound down by the arrows.

'When Krishna had left, Nandi addressed Bana in these auspicious words. "O Bana! For your welfare, you should go and dance before him." Blood flowed from his body and he was urged by Nandi's words. For the sake of his life, Bana arrived before Shankara. The danava was senseless and because of his fear, started to dance. He was in a distressed state and his eyes were numb with fear. Maheshvara said, "O Bana! Ask for whatever boon there is in your mind. O one with the excellent face! I am pleased with you and the time has come to grant you a boon." Bana replied, "O lord! May I never suffer from old age and may I always be immortal. O god! If it so pleases you, this is the first boon I ask for." Maheshvara said, "O Bana! You will be like the gods and you will never face death. Now ask for another boon. I am always kindly disposed towards you." Bana replied, "O Bhava! Blood is flowing from my body and I am suffering from wounds. In such a state, if devotees dance before you, may they have sons." Maheshvara said, "If devotees fast, are full of forgiveness, truthfulness and uprightness and dance before me in this way, that shall indeed happen." Bana replied, "I am suffering from severe pain because of the terrible strike of the chakra. O Bhava! As the third boon, may I find peace." Maheshvara said, "It shall be that way and you will be fortunate. Pain will not be able to affect you. The wounds will be removed from your body and you will be rendered hale. O asura! Ask for a desired fourth boon and I will grant it to you. O son![1100] I will not refuse you. O one with the excellent face! I always show you my favours."

[1099] Killing Bana.
[1100] The word used is tata.

Bana replied, "O lord! May I be the first among the large number of *pramathas*.[1101] O lord! May I be famous and renowned by the name of Mahakala." Maheshavara said, "O one who is famous for his strength and manliness! Ask for another boon and I will grant it to you. O great asura! Ask what you wish for. What will make you happy?" Bana replied, "O supreme among gods! May my body never suffer from any deformities. O Bhava! Though I only have two arms now, may I never be deformed." Bana was stationed near him and Mahadeva told him, "O Bana! It shall be exactly as you have said." The illustrious one with the three eyes said this. As all the creatures looked on, surrounded by his followers, he vanished from there.'

Chapter 113

Vaishampayana said, 'The arrows, in the form of giant serpents, had coiled themselves around Aniruddha's body. On seeing Garuda, all these serpents quickly let go of his body. Assuming their natural form, all those arrows embedded themselves in the ground. On seeing Krishna and touched by him, the great-souled Aniruddha was delighted. He joined his hands in salutation and said, "O god of the gods! You are always triumphant in battle. Who is capable of standing before you? Not even Shatakratu himself." The illustrious one replied, "Let us swiftly mount Garuda and leave for the city of Dvaraka." Having vanquished the great asura, Bana, all those bulls among men climbed astride Garuda and left on their long journey.

'They travelled through the sky in Varuna's direction.[1102] They saw thousands of multi-hued ones roaming around in the forests along the ocean.[1103] The undecaying god, the origin of all the worlds, was astride Garuda. On seeing Bana's cows, he decided to

---

[1101] Attendants of Shiva and Kumara.

[1102] Varuna's direction is the west.

[1103] Inexplicably, the Critical Edition excises a shloka, so that we do not know what these things were. They were Varuna's cows. Non-Critical

seize them. "Satyabhama told me to bring Bana's cows. The great asuras drink their milk and do not suffer from any decay. As long as it does not interfere with any other task, she asked me to bring them. However, if it interferes with any other task, she told me not to bother about it. Having seen Varuna's abode, I can now see the cows. Let all of us enter there and do what needs to be done." Thus addressed, Garuda agreed. He agitated the ocean by the force of his wings and suddenly submerged, reaching Varuna's abode. Varuna's extremely terrible army saw that Vasudeva was in front of them and attacked, wielding many kinds of weapons. In that encounter, thousands of Varuna's soldiers violently attacked. However, they were routed and he entered Varuna's abode. Varuna's soldiers used blazing weapons in the encounter, with sixty-six thousand chariots. But in every direction, that army was scorched by the storm of Krishna's arrows. They were routed and distressed. Unable to remain there, they sought refuge with Varuna.

'Varuna was there, praised in many ways by large numbers of rishis, gods, gandharvas and apsaras. A white umbrella was held aloft the radiant one's body. Water flowed from his body and he held aloft his supreme bow. The lord of the waters was enraged. With his sons, grandsons and forces, he stretched his giant bow and challenged Krishna in the battle. Varuna blew on his conch shell. Like Hara in his anger, he enveloped Hari with his net of arrows. At this, the immensely strong one blew on Panchajanya, which had emerged out of the waters. In every direction, Janardana caused anxiety through his shower of arrows. In that encounter, Varuna was afflicted by many storms of arrows. However, he smiled and continued to fight back against Krishna. Stationed in the battle, Vasudeva invoked the terrible vaishnava weapon with a mantra and spoke to the one who was stationed in front of him. "This vaishnava weapon is extremely terrible and crushes enemies. Be steady, because I have raised it to kill you now." The god raised the vaishnava weapon. However, the immensely strong Varuna invoked the varuna weapon and roared. O one who is victorious

---

editions explain this and also say that these were actually Bana's cows, seized by Varuna.

in assemblies! From the mouth of the varuna weapon, jets of water streamed out and the vaishnava weapon pacified them. All the water was scorched and seemed to be set on fire by the great valour of the vaishnava weapon. Terrified, everyone fled in different directions.

'On seeing the blaze, Varuna spoke these words. "Remember your former unmanifest nature. You are overwhelmed by your manifest[1104] attributes. O immensely fortunate one! Vanquish the tamas quality. Why are you confounded by the rajas quality? O lord of yoga! O immensely intelligent one! You are always based on the quality of sattva. Abandon ego and the taints that come by resorting to the five elements.[1105] In your Vaishnava form, I am your elder.[1106] Because of the attributes of being an elder, I should be revered. Why do you desire to burn me down? O supreme among fighters! Fire cannot be overcome with fire. Discard your rage. You are the origin of the universe and I cannot exert my powers over you. You created nature earlier and all its transformations originate in your soul. Dharma has been thought of as the first seed. One must first resort to dharma. The qualities of hot and cold are known to be the original attributes of nature. You are the original creator of this universe. That being the case, what do you expect me to think? You cannot be vanquished. You are always eternal. You are the self-creating one and are the one who thought of creating all beings. O immensely radiant one! You are without destruction and without decay. O unblemished one! Protect me. I am one who should be protected. I am bowing down before you. You are the original doer in the worlds. You are the one who has extended them in many ways. O great god! Why are you playing like a child with a puppet? I am not one who has injured nature. Nor am I one who abuses nature. O Purushottama! When there are transformations in nature, you are the one who acts in the proper way so as to correct these transformations. You are the one who always acts against the ones who are wicked and know about adharma. These taints

[1104] That is, human.

[1105] Ignorance, ego, passion, hatred and addiction.

[1106] This is a reference to Vishnu's ten incarnations. The *matsya* (fish) incarnation was in the ocean and came before the Krishna incarnation.

of nature are always associated with the quality of tamas. They are also tainted by the quality of rajas and confusion results from that. You know about what is supreme and best. You know about everything. The proper kinds of prosperity are based on you. You are yourself Prajapati. Why are you confusing all of us?" Addressed in this way, Krishna laughed and spoke these words. "O god! O one who is terrible in valour! To pacify me, give me the cows." Varuna replied, "O god! In earlier times, I had an agreement with Bana. Having concluded such an agreement, how can I act so as to render it false? O one with eyes like a bull! As long as I am alive, I cannot give the cows away. That was the agreement. Kill me and take the cows away." Having said this, Varuna released those extremely illustrious cows. Madhava laughed and honoured the god Varuna's words.[1107] Like Shakra surrounded by the immortals, he left for Dvaraka.

'O ornament of assemblies! The gods, the Maruts, the Sadhyas, the Adityas, the Vasus and the immensely strong Ashvins followed the undecaying lord of the universe, the origin of all beings. They arrived and followed his trail of fame and victory. The wielder of the chakra and the mace saw Dvaraka, garlanded with gates, from a long distance away and blew on Panchajanya. All those in Dvaravati heard the roar of the gods arriving and the blare of Panchajanya. They were supremely delighted. The Yadavas worshipped Krishna, seated astride Vinata's son in his great prosperity. He looked like a mass of blue collyrium. In every direction, rishis, gods, gandharvas and charanas stationed themselves above Dvaraka and chanted Govinda's praise. The supreme among the Dasharhas witnessed this extraordinary sight of Purushottama returning after vanquishing Bana and Mahadeva. With the immensely fortunate Krishna, the maharatha among the Satvatas, having returned, the residents of Dvaraka spoke about this in many ways. "We are blessed. We have been favoured by the lord of the universe. He is the protector and the preserver. He is the long-armed Janardana. Mounted on Vinata's son, he defeated Bana, who was extremely difficult to vanquish. Pundarikaksha has returned and our minds are delighted." The

[1107] He left without the cows.

residents of Dvaraka conversed in this way. The maharatha gods
entered Vasudeva's house. Their celestial vehicles roamed around in
the sky above. In every direction, they could be seen stationed there,
in many different kinds of forms. Thousands of radiant and celestial
vehicles were seen, with lions, bulls, deer, serpents, horses, cranes
and peacocks inside them. "These are the Rudras, the Adityas,
the Vasus, the Ashvins, the Sadhyas and the other gods. Worship
them in the proper order."[1108] "This is an extraordinary wonder.
We have obtained this good fortune because we have sought refuge
with Vasudeva." Such words were heard everywhere. From every
direction, the citizens showered down sandalwood powder and
showers of flowers and worshipped the residents of heaven. All the
residents of Dvaraka bowed down before the gods and worshipped
them with parched grain and incense, using controlled words and
intelligence.

'Ahuka, Vasudeva,[1109] Samba, the descendant of the Yadu
lineage, Satyaki, Ulmuka and the immensely strong Viprithu were
embraced by the valiant one.[1110] He inhaled the fragrances of their
heads. Vasava spoke these words to Andhaka, Shubhaksha and all
the Satvatas. "This descendant of the Yadu lineage[1111] displayed his
fame and manliness in the battle. While Mahadeva and Guha looked
on, he defeated Bana in an encounter and returned to Dvaraka. Hari
caused supreme destruction to the arms of the thousand-handed
one. He left him with two arms and returned to his own city. There
is a reason why the great-souled Krishna was born among men.
He has accomplished all that was required and has dispelled our
sorrows. We are full of delight and will drink the tasty madhu and
madhvika.[1112] For a long period of time, we will now enjoy our
dominions. All of us depend on the arms of this great-souled one.
All our grief has been destroyed. All of us rejoice and will enjoy
the happiness meant for immortals." Having said this, Purandara

---

[1108] Krishna said this.
[1109] Krishna's father.
[1110] Krishna.
[1111] Krishna.
[1112] Different types of liquor.

embraced the lotus-eyed Krishna and left for heaven, surrounded by large numbers of immortals.

'Surrounded by large numbers of Yadus, Krishna reached Dvaraka and rejoiced. O lord of the earth! This is the reason Vishnu, best among the lineage of the Yadus, took an incarnation on earth. He was famous by the name of Vasudeva. This is the reason why the prosperous lord was born in the lineage of Vasudeva.[1113] That is the reason he was born among the Vrishnis, as Devaki's son. This is what you had asked me about. O Janamejaya! Earlier, in connection with Narada's question, I had told you about this briefly. I have now recounted everything in detail. You had a grave doubt about Vishnu's residence in Mathura and about why he became Vasudeva. I have explained this to you. There is nothing else that is wonderful. Krishna is the store of everything extraordinary. Among everything wonderful that has been created, there is nothing more wonderful than Vishnu.[1114] He is most blessed among those who are blessed. He ensures blessings. He creates blessings. Among gods and daityas, there is nothing more blessed than Achyuta. He is the Adityas, the Vasus, the Rudras, the Ashvins, the Maruts, the sky, the earth, the directions, water, light, the creator, the preserver, the destroyer, destiny, truth, dharma, austerities, the eternal brahman and the entire universe. O descendant of the Bharata lineage! Bow down before the lord of the gods. I have thus spoken about the battle with Bana and Keshava's greatness. If one hears about this, one can ensure the establishment of an unmatched lineage. If a person nurtures this account of the supreme battle with Bana and Keshava's greatness, one never serves the cause of adharma. I have thus recounted everything about Vishnu's conduct. O son![1115] O Janamejaya! When the sacrifice was over, this is what you had asked me about. O king! If a person nurtures all of this extraordinary account in his heart, he never obtains anything inauspicious and enjoys a long life.'

[1113] Krishna's father.
[1114] Meaning Krishna.
[1115] The word used is tata.

Suta[1116] said, 'The king who was Parikshit's son was told this by Vaishampayana. With the bulls among the brahmanas, he heard all about *Harivamsha*. O Shounaka! I have told you everything, in brief and in detail. What do you want me to talk about next?'

This ends Vishnu Parva.

[1116] Lomaharshana.

Bhavishya Parva

Chapter 114

Shounaka asked, 'O Lomaharshana! Which of Janamejaya's sons does one read about? Who established the lineage of the great-souled Pandavas?'

Suta replied, 'Parikshit's son had two sons through the princess of Kashi. They were king Chandrapida and Suryapida, who knew about *moksha*. Chandrapida had one hundred sons who were excellent archers. As descendants of Janamejaya, these kshatriyas were famous on earth. The eldest of these was Satyakarna, who was a king in Varanasahvya.[1117] The mighty-armed one performed sacrifices, with copious quantities of dakshina. Satyakarna's heir was the powerful Shvetakarna. The one with dharma in his soul didn't have any sons and retreated to a hermitage in the forest. While he was in the forest, he had a son through a Yadava lady, who was Sucharu's daughter. Her name was Malini and she possessed excellent eyebrows. She was like a garland to her brothers. Once she had given birth, Shvetakarna,

[1117] Hastinapura.

425

the lord of subjects, left for the undecaying and great journey
that his ancestors had earlier followed.[1118] On seeing that he was
leaving, Malini followed him at the rear. It was on this path that
the one with the excellent brows gave birth to a lotus-eyed son.
In earlier times, the immensely fortunate Droupadi, had followed
her husbands. In that way, having given birth, she followed the
king. The delicate infant wept on that mountainous path. Out
of compassion for the great-souled one, the clouds offered him
cover. Shravishtha's sons were two brahmanas named Pippaladas.
Out of compassion for him, they brought him home and bathed
him in water. While he was playing in the mountains, his flanks
became covered with blood. Those flanks became as dark as the
complexion of a goat. When he grew up, that is the reason he
came to be known as Ajaparshva.[1119] The name that was given to
him thus came to be Ajaparshva. Those two[1120] reared him in the
household of Vemaka. To obtain a son, Vemaka's son got him
married off. He, and the two brahmanas who were his advisers,
were known as Vemaki's sons.[1121] Their sons and grandsons lived
for a time that was appropriate for the yuga.[1122] In this way, the
Pourava lineage was established by the Pandavas. In this connect,
Yayati, Nahusha's son chanted a shloka. This was at the time when
the intelligent one was delighted at having been able to transfer his
former old age.[1123] "There is no doubt that there may be a time
when the earth doesn't have a moon, a sun, or the planets. But
it shall never be the case that the earth is without the Pourava
lineage."'

[1118] A reference to the Pandavas leaving on their final and great journey.
[1119] Literally, the flank of a goat.
[1120] The two brahmanas.
[1121] Vemaki was Vemaka's wife.
[1122] As one moves from satya yuga to kali yuga, the lifespan progressively
declines.
[1123] To enjoy the pleasures of life, Yayati had wanted to temporarily
transfer his old age to one of his sons. The only son who agreed to accept
the old age was Puru. The other sons refused and were disinherited.

Chapter 115

Shounaka said, 'Vyasa's intelligent disciple[1124] had earlier recounted all of *Harivamsha*, with all of its parvas. I have told you about this. This immortal tales are full of *itihasa*.[1125] It pleases and is like amrita to all of us. It frees us from all sins. King Janamejaya heard about this supreme account. O Souti! After the snake sacrifice was over, what did he do?'

Suta[1126] replied, 'King Janamejaya heard this supreme account. I will tell you about what happened after the snake sacrifice was over. When the snake sacrifice was over, the king who was Parikshit's son began to collect the material required for a horse sacrifice. He summoned the officiating priests, priests and preceptors and said, "I wish to perform a horse sacrifice. Release the horse." Hearing what he desired to do, the great-souled Krishna Dvaipayana, undistressed in his spirit and one who knew everything about the past, the present and the future, quickly came to see Parikshit's son. The king who was Parikshit's son saw that the rishi had arrived. Following the sacred texts, he gave him arghya, padya and a seat and worshipped him. O Shounaka! When he was seated, and so were the assistant priests, many kinds of stories that were in conformity with the Vedas were told.

'When those accounts were over, the king urged the sage who was the grandfather and great-grandfather of the Pandavas and of himself. "There are many kinds of stories in the Mahabharata and they cover a huge expanse. When I hear about them, in an instant, I am transported to delight. These detailed accounts lead to prosperity and fame for everyone. O brahmana! You composed it, like milk stored in a conch shell. Comparable satisfaction cannot be found in amrita, or in the happiness in heaven. The satisfaction obtained from listening to the Mahabharata account is superior. O one who knows everything! O illustrious one! I imagine that

---

[1124] Vaishampayana.

[1125] Literally, itihasa means, this is indeed what happened. It is thus history.

[1126] The same as Souti.

the reason for the destruction of the Kurus was the royal sacrifice.
That is my view. Like a flood, there was a great destruction of kings
and it was impossible to withstand. I think that the royal sacrifice
was engineered so as to bring about the battle. I have heard that
Soma thought of the royal sacrifice earlier. After that, there was an
extremely great battle known as the tarakamaya encounter. When
that was over, Varuna performed an extremely great sacrifice and
this led to a battle between the gods and the asuras which led to
the destruction of all creatures. The royal sage, Harishchandra,
performed a sacrifice. There was a battle known as Adibaka
there and it led to the destruction of kshatriyas. Later, the noble
Pandava[1127] performed an extremely difficult sacrifice that was like
the fire and this sowed the seeds of the Mahabharata destruction.
That was the foundation of the battle that led to the destruction
of the worlds. Why was that great royal sacrifice not stopped?
The different limbs of a royal sacrifice are extremely difficult to
satisfactorily complete. If those limbs are not performed properly,
a destruction of the subjects is certain. You are the grandfather of
all the ancestors who have come earlier. You know about the past
and the future. You are the protector and the origin of our lineage.
O illustrious one! You are the leader and you are intelligent. Why
did you make us deviate from good policy? Why were those men
like those with a bad leader? Why were they without a protector?
Why did they commit crimes?" Vyasa replied, "O child! Your
grandfathers were driven by destiny. They did not ask me about
the future. When I am not asked, I do not speak. I do not see any
means of countering the future that has been determined. I do not
see any means of saving oneself from the destiny that has been
ordained. However, since you have asked me, I will tell you about
what is going to transpire. But destiny is extremely powerful. Even
if you hear about it, you will not act accordingly. Your manliness
will make you exert yourself and try. But what has been written by
destiny is extremely difficult to transgress, like the shoreline. It has
been said that the horse sacrifice is the best sacrifice for kshatriyas.
However, because of its superiority, Vasava will obstruct your

[1127] Yudhishthira.

sacrifice. O king! If you are capable, never perform this sacrifice. If manliness can be made subservient to destiny, do not perform this sacrifice. Then no crime will be committed against Shakra by you, by your preceptors, or by your officiating priests. However, destiny is the supreme lord. Listen to me. Its arrangement and its function, indeed every mobile and immobile object in the three worlds, is under the subjugation of destiny. When there is a destruction of the yuga, all kings who perform sacrifices go to heaven. So do brahmanas who sell the fruits of sacrifices."[1128] Janamejaya asked, "What will be the consequences if I refrain from the horse sacrifice? O illustrious one! On hearing this, if I am capable, I will refrain from it." Vyasa replied, "O lord! The consequence will be that the brahmanas will be enraged. Make efforts to refrain from it. You will then be fortunate. O scorcher of enemies! If you perform this horse sacrifice, as long as the earth sustains itself, there will not be any kshatriyas there." Janamejaya said, "If I refrain from the horse sacrifice, there will be energy and blazing curse of the brahmanas. I will become the instrument for that. That is the reason why a terrible fear is generated in me. How will a person like me, who is the performer of good deeds, be associated with this ill fame? A bird that was once bound no longer wants to take to the skies when it is released. Like that, I will not be interested in facing people. You have foreseen the future destruction that will come from undertaking this sacrifice. Like that, assure me if there is any way to prevent its recurrence." Vyasa replied, "If one refrains from this sacrifice, the gods will reside in brahmanas. That is because, when energy is withdrawn, energy resides only in energy. When the land is tilled, there will be a brahmana of the Kashyapa lineage, by the name of Senani. In kali yuga, he will again perform a horse sacrifice. O Indra among kings! After that, in that lineage, there will be a person who will perform a royal sacrifice. He will be like a white planet[1129] that is the harbinger of destruction. The fruits that men obtain from sacrifices depend on their strength. That is the

---

[1128] The sense is that though brahmanas and kings have a vested interest in performing sacrifices, these are futile.

[1129] *Shvetagraha*, probably signifying a comet.

reason, at the end of a yuga, the rishis roam around at the gates.[1130] That is when the lives of men depend on their earlier deeds. When one life is over, they roam around in the worlds, depending on the deeds they have performed. At that time, the dharma that is based on the four ashramas becomes weak. At that time, great fruits are obtained from the subtle dharma that is based on giving donations, though it is difficult to observe. At that time, men obtain success through limited austerities. O Janamejaya! When the end of a yuga arrives, men who immerse themselves in dharma are blessed."'

Chapter 116

'Janamejaya said, "O brahmana! I do not know about what is imminent, nor about what the future will bring.[1131] Therefore, I wish to know about what will happen after the end of dvapara yuga. Driven by our thirst for dharma, we desire an era when, through a little bit of deeds, one can obtain happiness and achieve dharma. The end of the yuga[1132] has arrived, causing anxiety among subjects. O one who knows about dharma! You should tell me about the signs of dharma being destroyed."'

Suta replied, 'The illustrious one[1133] thinks about the true nature of future destinations and was thus asked about the signs that come at the end of the yuga. Earlier, he had replied.

'Vyasa said, "At the end of the yuga, there will be kings who will use their powers to only protect their own shares. The shares of sacrifices will no longer be protected, because they will seize these for themselves. Those who aren't kshatriyas will become kings. Brahmanas will obtain a livelihood through modes meant for shudras.

[1130] This is unclear, presumably to bar entry. This is generally a description of kali yuga.

[1131] This is interpreted as Janamejaya not knowing whether he will die soon, or will live for a long time.

[1132] Of dvapara yuga.

[1133] Vyasa. Janamejaya had asked Vyasa and Lomaharshana is repeating this to Shounaka.

When the yuga is destroyed, shudras will follow the conduct meant for brahmanas. O bull among the Bharata lineage! O Janamejaya! When it is the end of a yuga, *kandaprishthas* and learned brahmanas will be seated in the same row and eat the sacrificial food together.[1134] O Janamejaya! When it is the end of a yuga, there will be men who are artisans, those who are devoted to falsehood, those who are addicted to liquor and flesh and those who regard their wives as enemies. Thieves will follow the conduct of kings and kings will follow the conduct of thieves. When it is the end of a yuga, servants will enjoy what they have not been instructed to enjoy. Riches will be praised and the conduct of the virtuous will not be revered. When it is the end of a yuga, those who are outcasts will not be condemned. Mortals will be devoid of their senses. They will sport dishevelled hair, or shave their heads. Without attaining the age of sixteen years, men will have children. When it is the end of a yuga, inhabitants will sell food, auspicious objects will be sold at the crossroads and women will sell their hair. Everyone will speak about the brahman.[1135] Everyone will be accomplished in the Vedas.[1136] When it is the end of a yuga, shudras will say *bho*.[1137] The brahmanas will sell austerities, sacrifices and the truth of the Vedas. When it is the end of a yuga, the seasons will behave in contrary fashion. Shudras will observe dharma, following the livelihood indicated by Shakya Buddha. They will display their white teeth and not lower their eyes. They will shave their heads and dress themselves in ochre garments. There will be a large number of predatory beasts and the number of cattle will decline. When it is the end of a yuga, tasty food will be difficult to come by and learning will

---

[1134] Literally, kandaprishtha means the back of an arrow. These are brahmanas who earn a living by selling arrows and other weapons and are brahmanas who have deviated. They should not be seated in the same rank as learned, *shrotriya* brahmanas.

[1135] Even those who are not entitled to.

[1136] The text uses the word *vajasaneya* to signify this. Everyone will project themselves as an expert on the Vedas, whether they are accomplished or not.

[1137] It is impossible to translate 'bho'. A loose translation would be 'Hello'. Shudras should display respect towards others. Instead of this, they will use such familiar terms of address.

decline. Outcasts will reside in the centre and those who should be in the centre will reside where outcasts should be. When it is the end of a yuga, inferior subjects will be allowed to go everywhere. When the yuga is destroyed, two-year-old bulls will be used to plough and till and the rain will shower down in extraordinary ways. When the yuga withdraws itself, men will no longer follow dharma. The land will become a desert and highways will traverse through the interiors of cities. When it is kali yuga, everyone will become a trader. Sons will no longer render offerings to their ancestors. Driven by avarice and falsehood, they will act against each other and steal each other's shares. When it is the end of a yuga, women who have lost their beauty, form and riches, will still decorate their hair. When it is the end of a yuga, householders will no longer possess a refuge and will be terrified. They will believe that no one should be loved as much as a wife. There will be many who are wicked in conduct and ignoble. Nevertheless, they will be handsome. When it is the end of a yuga, one of the signs is that there will be few men and many women. There will be many beggars in this world and they will give to each other.[1138] The kings will punish and afflict those who are not thieves and people will face destruction. Seeds sown will not lead to crops. The young will follow the conduct of the old. When the yuga is over, people will be happy with whatever they obtain in this world. Harsh winds will blow during the rainy season, inferior and laced with showers of stones. When it is the end of a yuga, there will be suspicion about the world hereafter. Kings will follow the conduct of vaishyas and earn a living from riches and grain. When the yuga is over, brahmanas will also follow this kind of conduct. There will be violations of agreements and contracts. As the yuga starts to decay, debts will not be repaid. When the yuga is destroyed, pursuit of future fruits will be unsuccessful.[1139] Instead, joy and anger will be successful among men. For the sake of milk, even goats will be milked. Those who do not know the sacred texts will behave as if they are wise. When it is the end of a yuga, they will nevertheless become expounders of the sacred texts. Without consulting the elders, everyone will be presumed to

[1138] Without judging the merits of the recipient.
[1139] Meaning fruits in the next world.

know everything. When the end of the yuga presents itself, there will be no one who deserves the appellation of being wise. When kshatriyas engage in contrary deeds, brahmanas will not restrain them. When the end of the yuga presents itself, kings will generally be thieves. O Janamejaya! When there is an end of the yuga, *kundas*,[1140] shudras,[1141] deceitful people and drunkards become expounders of the brahman and perform horse sacrifices. When the end of the yuga presents itself, brahmanas become greedy for riches and perform sacrifices for those for whom sacrifices should not be performed and eat that which should not be eaten. They desire objects of pleasure and do not study anything. Women adorn themselves with a single conch shell and bind themselves up with *gavedhuka*.[1142] There are no nakshatras and the directions reverse themselves. When that next yuga[1143]appears, the red hue of evening burns in all the directions. Sons engage fathers in tasks and daughters-in-law employ mothers-in-law. Men will intercourse with women who are not from their own varnas. Men who observe agnihotra sacrifices will eat without having performed the required rites earlier. With offering shares of sacrifices as alms, men will themselves eat them first. While husbands are asleep, wives will cheat and go to someone else. While wives are asleep, men will go to the wives of others. Everyone will have some disease and some kind of mental suffering. Everyone will envy others. When the era ends, people will harm others, without having been injured earlier."'

Chapter 117

'Janamejaya asked, "When the world is agitated like this, who will protect men? Where will they reside? What will be their

---

[1140] Sons born to a married woman through adultery, while the husband is still alive.

[1141] The text uses the word *vrisha*s, which is synonymous.

[1142] It is not clear what this is, probably some kind of grass.

[1143] Kali yuga.

conduct? What will they eat? Where will they roam around? What will be their deeds? How will they die? What will be their size? What will be their lifespan? After how many measures of time, will krita yuga arrive again?"'

'Vyasa replied, "Dharma falls down from its elevated status and people are devoid of qualities. They give up good conduct for evil conduct and their lifespans diminish. As the lifespans diminish, their strength also suffers. As the strength suffers, they become pale. As they become pale, they suffer from diseases and ill health. Because of diseases and ill health, they lose their learning. From this state of lack of knowledge, awareness about the atman will arise. Once this awakening occurs, they will become attached to the conduct of dharma. In this fashion, after several measures of time are over, krita yuga will be obtained again. Some will be instructed about the conduct of dharma.[1144] Some will follow the middle path.[1145] Some will be prone to debating. Others will be curious about the cause behind everything. Some will be determined to follow what can be witnessed and proved. Others will pride themselves on their learning and not believe in proofs, arguing that nothing exists. Other people will see that what has been spoken about in the Vedas has not been proved. Some will be non-believers. Some will bring about the destruction of dharma. Men will be foolish and wicked, priding themselves on their learning. Unconscious about the knowledge of the sacred texts, they will be disrespectful and only believe in the present. They will be insolent and addicted to arguing. Dharma will be dislodged in this way. But there will be a few remaining ones who will follow what is auspicious, full of generosity and the truth. However, most will follow the senses and eat everything. They will be devoid of qualities and without any shame. These will be the filthy signs of the decline of the worlds then. People from the inferior varnas will adopt the eternal conduct prescribed for brahmanas. When the world is flooded by these astringent signs, knowledge and learning will be destroyed. But then, those who are detached obtain success in a short period of time. When there are

[1144] This is still in the state of kali yuga.
[1145] Dharma mixed with adharma.

those astringent signs, the yuga decays. There are great wars, loud
roars, giant showers and immense fear. Rakshasas appear in the
form of brahmanas. Kings listen to hearsay. When the end of the
yuga presents itself, the earth will be agitated. Proud sages will not
utter svadha and vashatkara. Predatory beasts appear in the form of
brahmanas who eat everything and fail in their vows. They become
stupid, selfish, greedy, inferior and evil in attire. They follow
deviant conduct and are dislodged from eternal dharma. They steal
the jewels of others and rape the wives of others. They follow desire
and are evil-souled. They are untruthful and love to be rash. Men
who are similar in power and conduct are seen to be everywhere.
There are sages who appear in many different forms and claim that
it does not exist.[1146] However, depending on the best of men, krita
yuga will arise again. All of them will recite the accounts[1147] and be
worshipped by men. But people will steal crops and steal garments.
They will steal food and drinks and even the vessels in which these
are kept. Thieves will steal from thieves. Those who kill others will
in turn be killed by others. Because thieves ensure the destruction
of other thieves, there will be peace. Without any essence, the earth
will be agitated and no rites will take place in it. Oppressed by
the burden of taxes, men will resort to the forest. When the rites
of sacrifices are no longer observed, rakshasas, carnivorous beasts,
insects, rats and snakes will make men suffer. O best among men!
When the yuga is destroyed, peace, alms, health, objects, relatives
and instructions are destroyed. They will protect themselves and
steal from themselves, accumulating whatever is appropriate for
the yuga. In groups, they will roam around in different countries.
With their relatives, they will be dispossessed and dislodged from
their own countries. They will flee in fear, carrying their young
ones on their shoulders. Afflicted by fear and hunger, men will
find refuge along the river Koushiki. Men will find refuge in Anga,
Vanga, Kalinga, Kashmira, Mekala, Rishikanta and the valleys of
mountains. With bands of mlechchhas, men will reside everywhere
in the Himalayas, the shores of the salty ocean and forests. The

[1146] Probably a reference to the atman.
[1147] Of dharma.

earth will not be empty, but it will not be full either. Those who should protect will not be able to act as protectors and rule, because they won't possess the power. Men will survive on deer, fish, birds, carnivorous beasts, all kinds of insects, honey, vegetables, fruits and roots. Like hermits, they will attire themselves in many kinds of rags, leaves, bark and hides that they make themselves. Those who live in the upper regions will desire the seeds, wood and grain that grow in the plains and make efforts to rear goats, sheep, donkeys and camels. For the sake of water, those who live along banks will dam and obstruct the flows of rivers. They will buy and sell cooked food among themselves.[1148] Sons will be born to them without the interval of a year between the two births. They will have many wives, but no sons. They will be cruel and devoid of qualities. Driven by time, men will be like this. The subjects will follow the worst among all inferior kinds of dharma. The maximum lifespan of mortals will be thirty years. They will be weak, without possessions and overcome by the rajas quality. Disease will lead to the destruction of their senses. The lifespan will be reduced further because of the violence that they cause to each other. Though they will love the sight of virtuous people, they will themselves need to be tended to. However, because of uncertainty about the nature of conduct, they will praise the truth. When no gains are obtained from the sins of desire, they will follow dharma. Afflicted by the decay of their own side, they will restrain their wicked behaviour. Dharma possesses the four feet of serving, donations, truthfulness and the protection of life, and in this, men will come to follow it. But because they are insolent about dharma, those qualities will also be transformed. Having savoured the good taste of dharma, they will assume they know it and speak about it. Just as there is decay in progression, there is also expansion in progression. Hence, when dharma is duly accepted, there will be krita yuga again. The good deeds of krita yuga are said to subsequently decay. This is just like the moon becoming pale in complexion, as a result of the progression of time. In kali yuga, the moon is shrouded in darkness.

[1148] According to the injunctions, cooked food should not be bought and sold.

But it is also in kali yuga that the full moon destroys the darkness. The learned know that the supreme meaning of dharma is in the essence of the Vedas. Something that is indeterminate and unknown is regarded as something to be given away.[1149] Rites, donations, austerities and brahmacharya are known to be extremely revered. Qualities are obtained by refraining from deeds, but qualities are also obtained by resorting to true deeds. From one yuga to another yuga, on seeing men who follow the dictates of the time and the place, rishis have pronounced benedictions over them. From one yuga to another yuga, sacred and auspicious benedictions are obtained in this world by those who follow dharma, artha and kama and the rites of the Vedas. The yugas circle around for a long time, depending on their nature and conduct, as determined by the creator. In this world of mortals, creation and destruction also circle around, neither remaining for more than an instant."'

Chapter 118

Suta said, 'King Janamejaya was assured in this way and the advisers also heard the words spoken by the rishi about the past and the future. Like the taste of amrita provided by the moon, the ears were satisfied by the sweet words spoken by the maharshi. They were full of dharma, artha, kama and compassion and delighted the brave ones. The entire assembly heard this beautiful account. Some listened and shed tears. Others heard and meditated. The itihasa was composed by the rishi who was Parashara's son.[1150] The illustrious rishi took his leave of the assistant priests and circumambulated. He said that he would see them again and departed. In the world, he is spoken of as the best of speakers. All the virtuous ones, stores of austerities, followed the supreme among rishis as he departed.

[1149] That is, regarded as valueless. Unless comprehended, the true value of dharma is also not realized.

[1150] This is a reference not only to *Harivamsha*, but also to the Mahabharata.

When the illustrious Vyasa had left, the brahmanas, the maharshis, the officiating priests and the kings also returned to wherever they had come from. Having extinguished his enmity towards the extremely terrible serpents, the king[1151] also relinquished his anger, like a serpent that has released its poison. Astika, the great sage who was the hotri, saved the serpent Takshaka, whose head blazed from the fire, and returned to his own hermitage. Surrounded by men, the king also returned to Hastinapura. He ruled happily and the subjects were delighted.

'After some time had elapsed, King Janamejaya consecrated himself for a horse sacrifice, at which, copious quantities of dakshina would be offered, as is proper. Following the prescribed rites, when the horse had been slain, Queen Vapushtama, the princess of Kashi, went and slept with the horse.[1152] On seeing her beautiful limbs, Vasava entered the body of the dead horse and had intercourse with her. When this transgression occurred, realizing the truth, the king told the adhvaryu, "The horse isn't dead." The adhvaryu replied, "This revival has happened because of Indra." Thus addressed, the royal sage cursed Purandara. Janamejaya said, "If I have obtained the fruits of sacrifices, if I have performed austerities and protected the subjects, then, through the fruits of all these, let everyone hear what I have to say. O Shounaka![1153] Indra of the gods is fickle and has not been able to conquer his senses. Therefore, from today, no kshatriya will perform a horse sacrifice." Angrily, King Janamejaya told the officiating priests, "Because of your weakness, this sacrifice has been tainted. You will not dwell in my dominion. With your relatives, you will be banished." Thus addressed, the officiating brahmanas became angry and abandoned the king. Because of his

[1151] Janamejaya.

[1152] Vapushtama, the princess of Kashi, was Janamejaya's queen. In a horse sacrifice, a horse was left free to wander around in different kingdoms. If other kings did not seize it, they accepted the sovereignty of the one conducting the sacrifice. If they seized it, there would be a battle. A horse sacrifice established a king as an emperor. Once the horse returned after its travels, it was killed, often by the queen. In ritual, the queen would sleep with the dead horse. The horse's entrails would also be burnt.

[1153] Since Janamejaya is speaking, this is a typo and does not belong.

rage, the king also instructed the women who were in his wife's quarters. "Vapushtama has been unfaithful. Expel her from my house. She has placed her feet, covered with ashes, on my head.[1154] She has destroyed my greatness. She has polluted my fame and respect. She is like a faded garland and I do not wish to see her. If a man's beloved wife has been crushed by someone else, he will not be able to eat any tasty food, or sleep happily at night." Enraged, the king who was Parikshit's son spoke in this way. However, Vishvavasu, the king of the gandharvas, spoke to him. "You may have performed three hundred sacrifices, but Vasava does not tolerate you. He made Vapushtama your wife and she is not to be blamed. O king! This queen is the apsara Rambha, born as the daughter of the king of Kashi. She is the best among women. She should be recognized as a jewel. To create an obstruction to the sacrifice, Indra was looking for a weakness. O best among the Kuru lineage! Had you accomplished the sacrifice, you would have rivalled Vasava in prosperity. O king! Shakra was scared of the fruits you would reap from the sacrifice. O lord! That is the reason Indra destroyed the sacrifice. Desiring to obstruct the sacrifice, Vasava resorted to the use of maya. He found a weakness in the sacrifice and the dead horse seemed to come alive. Indra desired to have intercourse with Rambha, who is the same as Vapushtama. You have cursed your preceptors, though they performed three hundred sacrifices for you. Indra has managed to make you and the brahmanas waver from receiving the fruits. One who has performed three hundred sacrifices should face this unpalatable truth. In truth, Vasava was always frightened of the brahmanas. With a single act of maya, Shakra managed to overcome both his fears.[1155] Purandara is extremely energetic and always desires victory. Will he ever commit the wicked conduct of violating his grandson's wife?[1156] His intelligence is supreme. His dharma is supreme. His self-control is

[1154] Figuratively speaking.

[1155] Of Janamejaya and of the brahmanas.

[1156] Grandson in an extended sense, Indra's son was Arjuna, Arjuna's son was Abhimanyu, Abhimanyu's son was Parikshit and Parikshit's son was Janamejaya. Indra did this because the queen was actually Rambha.

supreme. His prosperity is supreme. Such are the deeds of the one with the tawny horses.[1157] O performer of three hundred sacrifices! You are as invincible as him. You should not find fault with Vasava, your preceptors, Vapushtama, or with your own self. Destiny is always impossible to cross. Because of your prosperity, Indra of the gods became angry and entered the horse. Those who desire happiness should seek the favours of the gods. When there is a strong flow of water, it is impossible to fight against it. She is a jewel among women and has not been tainted. Free yourself from your anxiety and enjoy her. O king! If a woman who has not sinned is discarded, you will be cursed. Women cannot be tainted, especially those who are divine. Even if the radiance of the sun, the flames of the fire and the oblations offered into the fire attempt to pollute women, they remain untainted. The learned always accept, nurture and worship them. Women of good conduct must be revered and worshipped. They are like Shri."[1158] Thus entreated by Vishvavasu, he was pleased with Vapushtama. Discarding his false suspicions and following the rites of dharma, he obtained supreme peace.

'He gave up all the exhaustion that was in his mind. Janamejaya sought to obtain fame for himself. He ruled over the kingdom with dharma and intelligence. Delighted in his mind, he found pleasure with Vapushtama. He did not cease worshipping brahmanas, nor did he retreat from conducting sacrifices. He did not deviate from protecting his kingdom, nor did he censure Vapushtama. It is impossible to act against what destiny has ordained. This is what the ascetic[1159] had instructed him about earlier. As the king reflected on that conversation, he overcame all his anger.

'A man who reads this great poem[1160] composed by the great-souled rishi is worshipped. He obtains an excellent lifespan, which is extremely difficult to obtain. He attains emancipation and the fruits of knowing everything. Just as Shatakratu was released from his sins, a man who reads this is freed from his sins. In that way,

[1157] Indra.
[1158] Lakshmi, the goddess of wealth and prosperity.
[1159] Vyasa.
[1160] *Mahakavya*.

he also obtains all the diverse objects of desire. Once all desire has been satisfied, he enjoys bliss for a long period of time. A tree yields auspicious fruit and from that fruit, trees are again generated. In that way, these words were composed by the rishi and also enhance the maharshi's power. Those who are without sons obtain extremely radiant sons. Those who have dislodged regain their own status again. There is no disease and there is freedom from bondage. One obtains the fruits of auspicious rites and all the qualities. If a maiden listens to the auspicious words of the sage, she obtains a virtuous husband. She gives birth to handsome sons who possess all the qualities, are full of valour and delight people. Those who follow the conduct of kshatriyas conquer the earth. They obtain unmatched riches and victory over enemies. Vaishyas obtain large quantities of wealth. Shudras who listen to this obtain a desirable end. This is the ancient account of the conduct of great-souled ones. A person who studies it obtains auspicious intelligence. He abandons misery and becomes free from attachment. Detached, he roams around the earth. You must remember that this account was recited in an assembly of brahmanas. If you remember this, patience will again be generated in you and will roam around the world, happy. The great-souled rishi composed this account about the conduct of those who were brave in their deeds. I have recounted it, briefly and in detail. What else do you desire that I should speak about?'

This ends Bhavishya Parva.
This also ends Harivamsha.

About the Translator

Bibek Debroy is a renowned economist, scholar and translator. He has worked in universities, research institutes, industry and for the government. He has widely published books, papers and articles on economics. As a translator, he is best known for his magnificent rendition of the Mahabharata in ten volumes, published to wide acclaim by Penguin Books India. He is also the author of *Sarama and Her Children*, which splices his interest in Hinduism with his love for dogs.